Robert Louis Stevenson (1850–94), was born and educated in Edinburgh. He was a sickly child, and most of his adult years were to be spent travelling in search of a climate which would do least damage to his lungs. Following the family tradition in civil engineering, he went to Edinburgh University in 1867. More interested in literature and the bohemian life, he changed to law and qualified as an advocate in 1875. Thereafter he gave himself to his creative ambitions, with frequent visits to London and to France, where he met Fanny Osbourne, a married American woman who was to become his future wife.

Stevenson began with essays, short stories and travel writing, most notably *Travels with a Donkey in the Cevennes* (1879). He went to California to marry Fanny in 1880. The journey nearly killed him, but he wrote of his experiences in *Across the Plains* (1892), *The Amateur Emigrant* (1895) and *The Silverado Squatters* (1883). He is, perhaps, best remembered for his first novel *Treasure Island* (1883), and his early reputation was made with this and other examples of adventure fiction, not least *Dr Jekyll and Mr Hyde* which appeared as a paperback thriller in 1886. The great Scottish novels followed, with *Kidnapped* (1886), *The Master of Ballantrae* (1889), and *Weir of Hermiston* (1896), which was left unfinished at his death. *Catriona* (1893), was always planned as the immediate sequel to *Kidnapped*, but had been delayed in the writing.

Stevenson spent seven years in the South Seas, settling for the last five on the island of Upolu in Samoa, where he died suddenly from a cerebral stroke at the age of forty-four.

Robert Louis Stevenson

THE SCOTTISH NOVELS

Kidnapped · Catriona

The Master of Ballantrae

Weir of Hermiston

CANONGATE

CLASSICS

58

First published as a Canongate Classic in 1995 by
Canongate Books Ltd, 14 High Street Edinburgh
EHI ITE. Introductions copyright © Jenni Calder
1989, Roderick Watson 1992 and 1995.

The publishers gratefully acknowledge general sub-
sidy from the Scottish Arts Council towards the
Canongate Classics series and a specific grant towards
the publication of this volume.
Printed in Finland by W.S.O.Y.

British Library Cataloguing in Publication Data
A catalogue record for this book is available on
request from the British Library

ISBN 0 86241 533 0

KIDNAPPED

BEING MEMOIRS OF THE ADVENTURES
OF DAVID BALFOUR IN THE YEAR 1751.
HOW HE WAS KIDNAPPED AND CAST AWAY;
HIS SUFFERINGS IN A DESERT ISLE;
HIS JOURNEY IN THE WILD HIGHLANDS;
HIS ACQUAINTANCE WITH ALAN BRECK STEWART
AND OTHER NOTORIOUS HIGHLAND JACOBITES;
WITH ALL THAT HE SUFFERED AT THE HANDS OF HIS UNCLE
EBENEZER BALFOUR OF SHAWS, FALSELY SO-CALLED:

WRITTEN BY HIMSELF, AND NOW SET FORTH BY
ROBERT LOUIS STEVENSON

——

Introduced by Jenni Calder

Contents

Introduction

Kidnapped is an adventure story. But it is also a study of character, and that character relates to a particular time and place. The time is a few years after the Jacobite Rising of 1745, a time of painful disruption but also of reconstruction. The place is Scotland: the Lowlands, where life seems ordered and stable, and the Highlands, apparently anarchic and hostile.

Stevenson wrote *Kidnapped* in Bournemouth, confined to the south of England by his precarious state of health. Its publication in 1886 confirmed his reputation as a novelist. His *Strange Case of Dr Jekyll and Mr Hyde*, published earlier the same year, 1886, brought him popularity; *Kidnapped* brought critical respect. It is a delicately balanced book, expertly controlled, sharply focused, and written with an affectionate irony. It is perhaps the finest of Stevenson's novels.

This adventure story has at its centre a young man who is not by nature adventurous. David Balfour is cautious and canny, his values shaped by a decent and limited upbringing. As the tale unfolds he experiences abduction, assault, shipwreck, destitution, and on several occasions is brought near to death. He is tricked, exploited and pursued as an outlaw. Yet he is not changed by these adventures. For him the 'real' world remains the secure territory of his belief in class and property, where authority banishes extremes and decency and hard work are rewarded. His encounter with a world of fierce loyalties and aggression, of treachery and violence, of raw emotion and idealism, does not reshape his views or values.

David's adventure is framed by two symbols of authority and stability. It begins when he leaves his home, sped on his way by Mr Campbell, the local minister. It ends with David 'at the very doors of the British Linen Bank', ready to claim his inheritance. In between he encounters aspects of Scotland he had never imagined, and discovers that survival requires more than pragmatism and a belief in rational behaviour. He confronts people who behave in a way quite outside his own experience. He is drawn into a network of feelings and actions in which conventional morality is ineffective, or seen to be shallow.

It is like a nightmare. The innocent but shrewd David is almost killed by his Uncle Ebeneezer. He is rudely snatched away with the intention of removing him to the Colonies. He finds himself helping to defend the life of a Highlander with a price on his head. He nearly drowns, and then struggles for survival in an environment that he finds totally hostile. He is implicated in a murder. The Highlands that Stevenson describes are not romantically picturesque or heroically challenging. They are grim and merciless. Their inhabitants speak a language and behave in a manner that David does not understand. It is a country of savage mountains, of moors 'lying as waste as the sea', a fearful landscape 'broken up with bogs and hags and peaty pools; some had been burnt black in a heath fire; and in another place there was quite a forest of dead firs, standing like skeletons'. Stevenson wrote this at a time when his contemporaries were increasingly admiring the scenic magnificence of the Highlands, but Stevenson clearly wrote his own experience into *Kidnapped*:

> 'the rain driving sharp in my face or running down my back in icy trickles; the mist enfolding us like as in a gloomy chamber—or perhaps, if the wind blew, falling suddenly apart and showing us the gulf of some dark valley where the streams were crying aloud'.

The terrain itself is a major character in the drama and underlines the division between Lowland assumptions and aspirations and Highland experience. Bridging the gulf is the other dominant character in David's adventure, Alan Breck Stewart. The friendship between David and Alan Breck is at the heart of the narrative. Alan Breck is generous and charming, childish and conceited. David finds him both attractive and exasperating, and the reader shares this response. The man who after the fight in the round-house boasts of his own prowess, forgetful of the fact that David has in effect saved his life, reveals a damaging self-pride. Yet there is something appealing about his frank self-congratulation, more appealing, as David himself almost realizes, than David's own priggish superiority.

The richness of the friendship is developed through the counterpoise of character traits and behaviour. Alan is colourfully heroic, but David is courageous too, and has already displayed an ability to get himself out of trouble, before he meets Alan. As Cluny Macpherson says of David, he is 'too nice and convenanting', but he also has 'the spirit of a very pretty gentleman'. And the boastful Alan, who considers himself a very much prettier gentleman, concedes defeat with grace and admiration when Robin Oig outdoes him in the piping contest. As Alan and David flee through the heather, the one to return to the safety of the burgh of Queensferry, the other to escape from Scotland altogether, the balance of their relationship constantly shifts. The climax of both the adventure and the relationship comes in Cluny's hideout on Ben Alder. As David subsides into a fever of exhaustion, 'a . . . black, abiding horror—a horror of the place I was in, and the bed I lay in, and the plaids on the wall, and the voices, and the fire, and myself', Alan and Cluny gamble with greasy playing cards. When he recovers it is to find that Alan has lost all his money, and David's too, to Cluny.

The quarrel that follows, each wrapped in his own pride, both polarizes them and highlights the reality of their friendship. Their reconciliation marks the beginning of the end of the story. The highest mountains and wildest moors are behind them. When they reach the Braes of Balquidder they are on the edge of a country that is more benign, and the presence of the landscape is less insistently felt. There are dangers still to be faced; the wild country has helped to protect them from the redcoats who are increasingly numerous as David and Alan make their way south. And even when David at last regains 'the long street of Queensferry' he is not yet safe, for he has to prove his identity as a loyal subject of King George. David Balfour has yet to 'come to life again'. Happy as he is when the transformation is accomplished, it means also the inevitable parting with the outlaw and outcast who befriended and rescued him. Yet Mr Balfour is not quite the Whig and Hanoverian he once was. He and Alan part on Corstorphine Hill: 'Neither one of us looked the other in the face. . . . But as I went on my way to the city, I felt so lost and

lonesome, that I could have felt it in my heart to sit down by
the dyke, and cry and weep like any baby.' For Alan there is a
ship that will take him into exile. For David the busy streets
of Edinburgh, 'a cold gnawing in my inside like a remorse for
something wrong', and the British Linen Bank.

The topography of David Balfour's journey, from the
Borders village of his birth to the House of Shaws, from
Queensferry to the island of Erraid, from Appin to Ben
Alder, from Rannoch Moor to the shores of the Forth, is
much more than the configuration of place. It is a political
and social map of Scotland in 1751. Through David's res-
ponses Stevenson guides the reader's attention to the divisions and contrasts that characterized the country and, in
Stevenson's view, continued to lie at the root of the Scottish
character. The contrasts lie partly in the landscape itself.
David leaves a pleasant village where 'the blackbirds are
whistling in the garden lilacs'. He approaches Edinburgh: 'I
saw all the country fall away before me down to the sea; and
in the midst of this descent, on a long ridge, the city of
Edinburgh smoking like a kiln.' Around the House of Shaws
are wooded hills and 'wonderfully good' crops. But in the
Highlands the landscape is harsh and threatening, and the
imprint of humankind much more fragile.

The wildness of the Highlands is not just in the mountains
and the moors or the character of the people. It is perhaps
even more forcefully in the lack of cultivation and the meagre
dwellings, both of which suggest an altogether less substantial and ordered existence than David is used to. The inn
at Kinlochaline is 'the most beggarly vile place that ever pigs
were styed in, full of smoke, vermin, and silent Highlanders'. The missionary Mr Henderland lives in a house of
turf and can only offer porridge for supper. Cluny Macpherson lives in a hillside shack of wattle and moss. In such
circumstances David finds Highland pride, at once courteous
and fiery, both comic and irritating. He judges from appearances, and has to learn that they can be misleading. He
encounters sullenness, aggression and distrust, but also
generosity, warmth, loyalty and courage of a kind which are
equally beyond his narrow view of human behaviour.

The ironic counterpart to David's Highland adventures
are those that belong to the Lowlands. In the Highlands
family loyalty is intense; in the Lowlands David's own uncle

tries to get rid of him. In the Highlands it is behaviour that denotes a gentleman, not dress. When David returns to his own country his first thought is to get out of his 'unseemly tatters'. At the beginning of *Catriona*, the sequel to *Kidnapped*, David's first action is to acquire decent clothes, with the aim of looking 'comely and responsible, so that servants should respect me'.

The irony of these contrasts centres on David himself, for he, so acute and self-possessed, so observant of the comportment of others, has certain blindspots when he looks at himself. Stevenson's gentle exposure of these is one of the triumphs of the book. David is keenly aware of the childlike sensitivities of Alan Breck, quick to take offence and retreat into sulks, but does not recognize parallel inclinations in his own nature. The Highlander and the Lowlander remain irreconcilable, however strong the affection and the mutual debts that bind them. Alan Breck is as ill at ease in the environment that sustains David as David is in Alan's native territory. Each in his way is an innocent, and neither has any wish to adapt.

These are themes that are explored further in *Catriona*, which, though written several years later and many thousands of miles from Scotland, begins exactly where *Kidnapped* ends, in Edinburgh's High Street. And indeed Stevenson ends *Kidnapped* with a beginning, the beginning of a new life which fits David's own idea of himself. Early in the novel he challenges his uncle with the words, 'I was brought up to have a good conceit of myself'. This 'good conceit' carries him through his adventures if not with the panache of Alan Breck at least with confidence and courage. His adventures weaken him physically, and make him dependent, but they do not dent his confidence or undermine his very real courage.

Kidnapped has been criticized for not sustaining the narrative of adventure. But the adventure lies in the contrasts and confrontations, and the tensions that arise from these. In a sense the adventure lies in Scotland itself, in the physical and psychic divisions that, in the interpretation of Stevenson and others, delineate the country's character. The difficulty David Balfour has in accepting a code which condones murder (as Alan Breck and his fellow clansmen accept the murder of the Red Fox), his problems with the tribal, rather than class, values of the Highlands, are not just inherent in David's character: they are part of Scotland's heritage.

Thus a novel of character and action has psychological and moral currents of some depth, though they are developed with a light touch. They are all part of the territory that fascinated Stevenson throughout his writing life. In later years he would write about other times and other places, but his mind and imagination never left Scotland. *Kidnapped* was part of his attempt to explain the country to himself. In the process he wrote with energy, conviction and clarity, to produce a tale that remains fresh and vivid, no matter how often one goes back to it.

                                                    Jenni Calder

Dedication

TO CHARLES BAXTER, WRITER TO THE SIGNET.

My dear Charles Baxter,

If you ever read this tale, you will likely ask yourself more questions than I should care to answer: as for instance how the Appin murder has come to fall in the year 1751, how the Torran rocks have crept so near to Earraid, or why the printed trial is silent as to all that touches David Balfour. These are nuts beyond my ability to crack. But if you tried me on the point of Alan's guilt or innocence, I think I could defend the reading of the text. To this day you will find the tradition of Appin clear in Alan's favour. If you inquire, you may even hear that the descendants of 'the other man' who fired the shot are in the country to this day. But that other man's name, inquire as you please, you shall not hear; for the Highlander values a secret for itself and for the congenial exercise of keeping it. I might go on for long to justify one point and own another indefensible; it is more honest to confess at once how little I am touched by the desire of accuracy. This is no furniture for the scholar's library, but a book for the winter evening school-room when the tasks are over and the hour for bed draws near; and honest Alan, who was a grim old fire-eater in his day, has in this new avatar no more desperate purpose than to steal some young gentleman's attention from his Ovid, carry him awhile into the Highlands and the last century, and pack him to bed with some engaging images to mingle with his dreams.

As for you, my dear Charles, I do not even ask you to like the tale. But perhaps when he is older, your son will; he may then be pleased to find his father's name on the fly-leaf; and in the meanwhile it pleases me to set it there, in memory of many days that were happy and some (now perhaps as pleasant to remember) that were sad. If it is strange for me to look back from a distance both in time and space on these bygone adventures of our youth, it must be stranger for you who tread the same streets—who may to-morrow open the door of the old Speculative, where we begin to rank with Scott and Robert Emmet and the beloved and inglorious Macbean—or may pass the corner of the close where that great society, the L. J. R., held its meetings and drank its beer, sitting in the seats of Burns and his companions. I think I see you, moving there by plain daylight, beholding with your natural eyes those places that have now become for your companion a part of the scenery of dreams. How, in the intervals of present business, the past must echo in your memory! Let it not echo often without some kind thoughts of your friend

R.L.S.

SKERRYVORE,
  BOURNEMOUTH.

I. I SET OFF UPON MY JOURNEY TO THE HOUSE OF SHAWS

I WILL BEGIN the story of my adventures with a certain morning early in the month of June, the year of grace 1751, when I took the key for the last time out of the door of my father's house. The sun began to shine upon the summit of the hills as I went down the road; and by the time I had come as far as the manse, the blackbirds were whistling in the garden lilacs, and the mist that hung around the valley in the time of the dawn was beginning to arise and die away.

Mr Campbell, the minister of Essendean, was waiting for me by the garden gate, good man! He asked me if I had breakfasted; and hearing that I lacked for nothing, he took my hand in both of his and clapped it kindly under his arm.

'Well, Davie, lad,' said he, 'I will go with you as far as the ford, to set you on the way.'

And we began to walk forward in silence.

'Are ye sorry to leave Essendean?' said he, after a while.

'Why, sir,' said I, 'if I knew where I was going, or what was likely to become of me, I would tell you candidly. Essendean is a good place indeed, and I have been very happy there; but then I have never been anywhere else. My father and mother, since they are both dead, I shall be no nearer to in Essendean than in the Kingdom of Hungary; and to speak truth, if I thought I had a chance to better myself where I was going, I would go with a good will.'

'Ay?' said Mr Campbell. 'Very well, Davie. Then it behoves me to tell your fortune; or so far as I may. When your mother was gone, and your father (the worthy, Christian man) began to sicken for his end, he gave me in charge a certain letter, which he said was your inheritance. "So soon," says he, "as I am gone, and the house is redd up and the gear disposed of" (all which, Davie, hath been done) "give my boy this letter into his hand, and start him off to the house of Shaws, not far from Cramond.

That is the place I came from," he said, "and it's where it befits that my boy should return. He is a steady lad," your father said, "and a canny goer; and I doubt not he will come safe, and be well liked where he goes." '

'The house of Shaws!' I cried. 'What had my poor father to do with the house of Shaws?'

'Nay,' said Mr Campbell, 'who can tell that for a surety? But the name of that family, Davie boy, is the name you bear—Balfours of Shaws: an ancient, honest, reputable house, peradventure in these latter days decayed. Your father, too, was a man of learning as befitted his position; no man more plausibly conducted school; nor had he the manner or the speech of a common dominie; but (as ye will yourself remember) I took aye a pleasure to have him to the manse to meet the gentry; and those of my own house, Campbell of Kilrennet, Campbell of Dunswire, Campbell of Minch, and others, all well-kenned gentlemen, had pleasure in his society. Lastly, to put all the elements of this affair before you, here is the testamentary letter itself, superscrived by the own hand of our departed brother.'

He gave me the letter, which was addressed in these words: 'To the hands of Ebenezer Balfour, Esquire, of Shaws, in his house of Shaws, these will be delivered by my son, David Balfour.' My heart was beating hard at this great prospect now suddenly opening before a lad of sixteen years of age, the son of a poor country dominie in the Forest of Ettrick.

'Mr Campbell,' I stammered, 'and if you were in my shoes, would you go?'

'Of a surety,' said the minister, 'that would I, and without pause. A pretty lad like you should get to Cramond (which is near in by Edinburgh) in two days of walk. If the worst came to the worst, and your high relations (as I cannot but suppose them to be somewhat of your blood) should put you to the door, ye can but walk the two days back again and risp at the manse door. But I would rather hope that ye shall be well received, as your poor father forecast for you, and for anything that I ken, come to be a great man in time. And here, Davie, laddie,' he resumed, 'it lies near upon my conscience to improve this parting, and set you on the right guard against the dangers of the world.'

Here he cast about for a comfortable seat, lighted on

a big boulder under a birch by the trackside, sate down upon it with a very long, serious upper lip, and the sun now shining in upon us between two peaks, put his pocket-handkerchief over his cocked hat to shelter him. There, then, with uplifted forefinger, he first put me on my guard against a considerable number of heresies, to which I had no temptation, and urged upon me to be instant in my prayers and reading of the Bible. That done, he drew a picture of the great house that I was bound to, and how I should conduct myself with its inhabitants.

'Be soople, Davie, in things immaterial,' said he. 'Bear ye this in mind, that, though gentle born, ye have had a country rearing. Dinnae shame us, Davie, dinnae shame us! In yon great, muckle house, with all these domestics, upper and under, show yourself as nice, as circumspect, as quick at the conception, and as slow of speech as any. As for the laird—remember he's the laird; I say no more: honour to whom honour. It's a pleasure to obey a laird; or should be, to the young.'

'Well, sir,' said I, 'it may be; and I'll promise you I'll try to make it so.'

'Why, very well said,' replied Mr Campbell, heartily. 'And now to come to the material, or (to make a quibble) to the immaterial. I have here a little packet which contains four things.' He tugged it, as he spoke, and with some difficulty, from the skirt pocket of his coat. 'Of these four things, the first is your legal due: the little pickle money for your father's books and plenishing, which I have bought (as I have explained from the first) in the design of re-selling at a profit to the incoming dominie. The other three are gifties that Mrs Campbell and myself would be blithe of your acceptance. The first, which is round, will likely please ye best at the first off-go; but, O Davie, laddie, it's but a drop of water in the sea; it'll help you but a step, and vanish like the morning. The second, which is flat and square and written upon, will stand by you through life, like a good staff for the road, and a good pillow to your head in sickness. And as for the last, which is cubical, that'll see you, it's my prayerful wish, into a better land.'

With that he got upon his feet, took off his hat, and prayed a little while aloud, and in affecting terms, for a young man setting out into the world; then suddenly took me in his arms and embraced me very hard; then held me at arm's length, looking at me with his face all working with sorrow; and then whipped about, and crying good-bye to me, set off backward by the way that we had come at a sort of jogging run. It might have been laughable to another; but I was in no mind to laugh. I watched him as long as he was in sight; and he never stopped hurrying, nor once looked back. Then it came in upon my mind that this was all his sorrow at my departure; and my conscience smote me hard and fast, because I, for my part, was overjoyed to get away out of that quiet country-side, and go to a great, busy house, among rich and respected gentlefolk of my own name and blood.

'Davie, Davie,' I thought, 'was ever seen such black ingratitude? Can you forget old favours and old friends at the mere whistle of a name? Fie, fie; think shame!'

And I sat down on the boulder the good man had just left, and opened the parcel to see the nature of my gifts. That which he had called cubical, I had never had much doubt of; sure enough it was a little Bible, to carry in a plaid-neuk. That which he had called round, I found to be a shilling piece; and the third, which was to help me so wonderfully both in health and sickness all the days of my life, was a little piece of coarse yellow paper, written upon thus in red ink:

TO MAKE LILLY OF THE VALLEY WATER

Take the flowers of lilly of the valley and distil
them in sack, and drink a spooneful or two as there
is occasion. It restores speech to those that have
the dumb palsey. It is good against the Gout;
it comforts the heart and strengthens the memory;
and the flowers, put into a Glasse, close stopt,
and set into ane hill of ants for a month, then take it
out, and you will find a liquor which comes from the
flowers, which keep in a vial; it is good, ill or
well, and whether man or woman.

And then, in the minister's own hand, was added:
Likewise for sprains, rub it in; and for the cholic,
a great spooneful in the hour.

To be sure, I laughed over this; but it was rather tremulous laughter; and I was glad to get my bundle on my staff's end and set out over the ford and up the hill upon the farther side; till, just as I came on the green drove-road running wide through the heather, I took my last look of Kirk Essendean, the trees about the manse, and the big rowans in the kirkyard where my father and my mother lay.

ON THE FORENOON of the second day, coming to
the top of a hill, I saw all the country fall awayy before me
down to the sea; and in the midst of this descent, on a long
ridge, the city of Edinburgh smoking like a kiln. There was
a flag upon the castle, and ships moving or lying anchored
in the firth; both of which, for as far away as they were,
I could distinguish clearly; and both brought my country
heart into my mouth.

Presently after, I came by a house where a shepherd
lived, and got a rough direction for the neighbourhood of
Cramond; and so, from one to another, worked my way
to the westward of the capital by Colinton, till I came out
upon the Glasgow road. And there, to my great pleasure
and wonder, I beheld a regiment marching to the fifes, every
foot in time; an old red-faced general on a grey horse at
the one end, and at the other the company of Grenadiers,
with their Pope's-hats. The pride of life seemed to mount
into my brain at the sight of the redcoats and the hearing
of that merry music.

A little farther on, and I was told I was in Cramond
parish, and began to substitute in my inquiries the name of
the house of Shaws. It was a word that seemed to surprise
those of whom I sought my way. At first I thought the
plainness of my appearance, in my country habit, and that
all dusty from the road, consorted ill with the greatness of
the place to which I was bound. But after two, or maybe
three, had given me the same look and the same answer,
I began to take it in my head there was something strange
about the Shaws itself.

The better to set this fear at rest, I changed the form of
my inquiries; and spying an honest fellow coming along
a lane on the shaft of his cart, I asked him if he had ever
heard tell of a house they called the house of Shaws.

6

He stopped his cart and looked at me, like the others.

'Ay,' said he. 'What for?'

'It's a great house?' I asked.

'Doubtless,' says he. 'The house is a big, muckle house.'

'Ay,' said I, 'but the folk that are in it?'

'Folk?' cried he. 'Are ye daft? There's nae folk there—to call folk.'

'What?' says I; 'not Mr Ebenezer?'

'Oh, ay,' says the man, 'there's the laird, to be sure, if it's him you're wanting. What'll like be your business, mannie?'

'I was led to think that I would get a situation,' I said, looking as modest as I could.

'What?' cries the carter, in so sharp a note that his very horse started; and then, 'Well, mannie,' he added, 'it's nane of my affairs; but ye seem a decent-spoken lad; and if ye'll take a word from me, ye'll keep clear of the Shaws.'

The next person I came across was a dapper little man in a beautiful white wig, whom I saw to be a barber on his rounds; and knowing well that barbers were great gossips, I asked him plainly what sort of a man was Mr Balfour of the Shaws.

'Hoot, hoot, hoot,' said the barber, 'nae kind of a man, nae kind of a man at all'; and began to ask me very shrewdly what my business was; but I was more than a match for him at that, and he went on to his next customer no wiser than he came.

I cannot well describe the blow this dealt to my illusions. The more indistinct the accusations were, the less I liked them, for they left the wider field to fancy. What kind of a great house was this, that all the parish should start and stare to be asked the way to it? or what sort of a gentleman, that his ill-fame should be thus current on the wayside? If an hour's walking would have brought me back to Essendean, I had left my adventure then and there, and returned to Mr Campbell's. But when I had come so far a way already, mere shame would not suffer me to desist till I had put the matter to the touch of proof; I was bound, out of mere self-respect, to carry it through; and little as I liked the sound of what I heard, and slow as I began to travel, I still kept asking my way and still kept advancing.

It was drawing on to sundown when I met a stout, dark, sour-looking woman coming trudging down a hill; and she, when I had put my usual question, turned sharp about, accompanied me back to the summit she had just left, and pointed to a great bulk of building standing very bare upon a green in the bottom of the next valley. The country was pleasant round about, running in low hills, pleasantly watered and wooded, and the crops, to my eyes, wonderfully good; but the house itself appeared to be a kind of ruin; no road led up to it; no smoke arose from any of the chimneys; nor was there any semblance of a garden. My heart sank. 'That!' I cried.

The woman's face lit up with a malignant anger. 'That is the house of Shaws!' she cried. 'Blood built it; blood stopped the building of it; blood shall bring it down. See here!' she cried again—'I spit upon the ground, and crack my thumb at it! Black be its fall! If ye see the laird, tell him what ye hear; tell him this makes the twelve hunner and nineteen time that Jennet Clouston has called down the curse on him and his house, byre and stable, man, guest, and master, wife, miss, or bairn—black, black be their fall!'

And the woman, whose voice had risen to a kind of eldritch sing-song, turned with a skip, and was gone. I stood where she left me, with my hair on end. In these days folk still believed in witches and trembled at a curse; and this one, falling so pat, like a wayside omen, to arrest me ere I carried out my purpose, took the pith out of my legs.

I sat me down and stared at the house of Shaws. The more I looked, the pleasanter that country-side appeared; being all set with hawthorn bushes full of flowers; the fields dotted with sheep; a fine flight of rooks in the sky; and every sign of a kind soil and climate; and yet the barrack in the midst of it went sore against my fancy.

Country folk went by from the fields as I sat there on the side of the ditch, but I lacked the spirit to give them a good-e'en. At last the sun went down, and then, right up against the yellow sky, I saw a scroll of smoke go mounting, not much thicker, as it seemed to me, than the smoke of a candle; but still there it was, and meant a fire, and warmth, and cookery, and some living inhabitant that must have lit it; and this comforted my heart wonderfully—more, I feel sure, than a whole flask of the lily of the valley water that Mrs Campbell set so great a store by.

So I set forward by a little faint track in the grass that led in my direction. It was very faint indeed to be the only way to a place of habitation; yet I saw no other. Presently it brought me to stone uprights, with an unroofed lodge beside them, and coats of arms upon the top. A main entrance, it was plainly meant to be, but never finished; instead of gates of wrought iron, a pair of hurdles were tied across with a straw rope; and as there were no park walls, nor any sign of avenue, the track that I was following passed on the right hand of the pillars, and went wandering on toward the house.

The nearer I got to that, the drearier it appeared. It seemed like the one wing of a house that had never been finished. What should have been the inner end stood open on the upper floors, and showed against the sky with steps and stairs of uncompleted masonry. Many of the windows were unglazed, and bats flew in and out like doves out of a dovecote.

The night had begun to fall as I got close; and in three of the lower windows, which were very high up, and narrow, and well barred, the changing light of a little fire began to glimmer.

Was this the palace I had been coming to? Was it within these walls that I was to seek new friends and begin great fortunes? Why, in my father's house on Essen-Waterside, the fire and the bright lights would show a mile away, and the door open to a beggar's knock.

I came forward cautiously, and giving ear as I came, heard some one rattling with dishes, and a little dry, eager cough that came in fits; but there was no sound of speech, and not a dog barked.

The door, as well as I could see it in the dim light, was a great piece of wood all studded with nails; and I lifted my hand with a faint heart under my jacket, and knocked once. Then I stood and waited. The house had fallen into a dead silence; a whole minute passed away, and nothing stirred but the bats overhead. I knocked again, and hearkened again. By this time my ears had grown so accustomed to the quiet, that I could hear the ticking of the clock inside as it slowly counted out the seconds; but whoever was in that house kept deadly still, and must have held his breath.

I was in two minds whether to run away; but anger got the upper hand, and I began instead to rain kicks and buffets on the door, and to shout out aloud for Mr Balfour. I was in full career, when I heard the cough right overhead, and jumping back and looking up, beheld a man's head in a tall nightcap, and the bell mouth of a blunderbuss, at one of the first storey windows.

'It's loaded,' said a voice.

'I have come here with a letter,' I said, 'to Mr Ebenezer Balfour of Shaws. Is he here?'

'From whom is it?' asked the man with the blunderbuss.

'That is neither here nor there,' said I, for I was growing very wroth.

'Well,' was the reply, 'ye can put it down upon the doorstep, and be off with ye.'

'I will do no such thing,' I cried. 'I will deliver it into Mr Balfour's hands, as it was meant I should. It is a letter of introduction.'

'A what?' cried the voice, sharply.

I repeated what I had said.

'Who are ye, yourself?' was the next question, after a considerable pause.

'I am not ashamed of my name,' said I. 'They call me David Balfour.'

At that, I made sure the man started, for I heard the blunderbuss rattle on the window-sill; and it was after quite a long pause, and with a curious change of voice, that the next question followed:

'Is your father dead?'

I was so much surprised at this, that I could find no voice to answer, but stood staring.

'Ay,' the man resumed, 'he'll be dead, no doubt; and that'll be what brings ye chapping to my door.' Another pause, and then, defiantly, 'Well, man,' he said, 'I'll let ye in'; and he disappeared from the window.

3. I MAKE ACQUAINTANCE OF MY UNCLE

PRESENTLY THERE CAME a great rattling of chains and bolts, and the door was cautiously opened, and shut to again behind me as soon as I had passed.

'Go into the kitchen and touch naething,' said the voice; and while the person of the house set himself to replacing the defences of the door, I groped my way forward and entered the kitchen.

The fire had burned up fairly bright, and showed me the barest room I think I ever put my eyes on. Half-a-dozen dishes stood upon the shelves; the table was laid for supper with a bowl of porridge, a horn spoon, and a cup of small beer. Besides what I have named, there was not another thing in that great, stone-vaulted, empty chamber, but lockfast chests arranged along the wall and a corner cupboard with a padlock.

As soon as the last chain was up, the man rejoined me. He was a mean, stooping, narrow-shouldered, clay-faced creature; and his age might have been anything between fifty and seventy. His nightcap was of flannel, and so was the nightgown that he wore, instead of coat and waistcoat, over his ragged shirt. He was long unshaved; but what most distressed and even daunted me, he would neither take his eyes away from me nor look me fairly in the face. What he was, whether by trade or birth, was more than I could fathom; but he seemed most like an old, unprofitable serving-man, who should have been left in charge of that big house upon board wages.

'Are ye sharp-set?' he asked, glancing at about the level of my knee. 'Ye can eat that drop parritch.'

I said I feared it was his own supper.

'Oh,' said he, 'I can do fine wanting it. I'll take the ale, though, for it slockens my cough.' He drank the cup about half out, still keeping an eye upon me as he drank; and then suddenly held out his hand. 'Let's see the letter,' said he.

I told him the letter was for Mr Balfour; not for him.

'And who do ye think I am?' says he. 'Give me Alexander's letter!'

'You know my father's name?'

'It would be strange if I didnae,' he returned, 'for he was my born brother; and little as ye seem to like either me or my house, or my good parritch, I'm your born uncle, Davie, my man, and you my born nephew. So give us the letter, and sit down and fill your kyte.'

If I had been some years younger, what with shame, weariness, and disappointment, I believe I had burst into tears. As it was, I could find no words, neither black nor white, but handed him the letter, and sat down to the porridge with as little appetite for meat as ever a young man had.

Meanwhile, my uncle, stooping over the fire, turned the letter over and over in his hands.

'Do ye ken what's in it?' he asked, suddenly.

'You see for yourself, sir,' said I, 'that the seal has not been broken.'

'Ay,' said he, 'but what brought you here?'

'To give the letter,' said I.

'No,' says he, cunningly, 'but ye'll have had some hopes, nae doubt?'

'I confess, sir,' said I, 'when I was told that I had kinsfolk well-to-do, I did indeed indulge the hope that they might help me in my life. But I am no beggar; I look for no favours at your hands, and I want none that are not freely given. For as poor as I appear, I have friends of my own that will be blithe to help me.'

'Hoot-toot!' said Uncle Ebenezer, 'dinnae fly up in the snuff at me. We'll agree fine yet. And, Davie, my man, if you're done with that bit parritch, I could just take a sup of it myself. Ay,' he continued, as soon as he had ousted me from the stool and spoon, 'they're fine, halesome food—they're grand food, parritch.' He murmured a little grace to himself and fell to. 'Your father was very fond of his meat, I mind; he was a hearty, if not a great eater; but as for me, I could never do mair than pyke at food.' He took a pull at the small beer, which probably reminded him of hospitable duties; for his next speech ran thus: 'If ye're dry, ye'll find water behind the door.'

To this I returned no answer, standing stiffly on my two feet, and looking down upon my uncle with a mighty angry heart. He, on his part, continued to eat like a man under some pressure of time, and to throw out little darting glances now at my shoes and now at my home-spun stockings. Once only, when he had ventured to look a little higher, our eyes met; and no thief taken with a hand in a man's pocket could have shown more lively signals of distress. This set me in a muse, whether his timidity arose from too long a disuse of any human company; and whether perhaps, upon a little trial, it might pass off, and my uncle change into an altogether different man. From this I was awakened by his sharp voice.

'Your father's been long dead?' he asked.

'Three weeks, sir,' said I.

'He was a secret man, Alexander—a secret, silent man,' he continued. 'He never said muckle when he was young. He'll never have spoken muckle of me?'

'I never knew, sir, till you told it me yourself, that he had any brother.'

'Dear me, dear me!' said Ebenezer. 'Nor yet of Shaws, I daresay?'

'Not so much as the name, sir,' said I.

'To think o' that!' said he. 'A strange nature of a man!' For all that, he seemed singularly satisfied, but whether with himself, or me, or with this conduct of my father's, was more than I could read. Certainly, however, he seemed to be outgrowing that distaste, or ill-will, that he had conceived at first against my person; for presently he jumped up, came across the room behind me, and hit me a smack upon the shoulder. 'We'll agree fine yet!' he cried. 'I'm just as glad I let you in. And now come awa' to your bed.'

To my surprise, he lit no lamp or candle, but set forth into the dark passage, groped his way, breathing deeply, up a flight of steps, and paused before a door, which he unlocked. I was close upon his heels, having stumbled after him as best I might; and he bade me go in, for that was my chamber. I did as he bid, but paused after a few steps, and begged a light to go to bed with.

'Hoot-toot!' said Uncle Ebenezer, 'there's a fine moon.'

'Neither moon nor star, sir, and pit-mirk,' said I. 'I cannae see the bed.'

'Hoot-toot, hoot-toot!' said he. 'Lights in a house is a thing I dinnae agree with. I'm unco feared of fires. Good night to ye, Davie, my man.' And before I had time to add a further protest, he pulled the door to, and I heard him lock me in from the outside.

I did not know whether to laugh or cry. The room was as cold as a well, and the bed, when I had found my way to it, as damp as a peat-hag; but by good fortune I had caught up my bundle and my plaid, and rolling myself in the latter, I lay down upon the floor under lee of the big bedstead, and fell speedily asleep.

With the first peep of day I opened my eyes, to find myself in a great chamber, hung with stamped leather, furnished with fine embroidered furniture, and lit by three fair windows. Ten years ago, or perhaps twenty, it must have been as pleasant a room to lie down or to awake in, as a man could wish; but damp, dirt, disuse, and the mice and spiders had done their worst since then. Many of the window-panes, besides, were broken; and indeed this was so common a feature in that house, that I believe my uncle must at some time have stood a siege from his indignant neighbours—perhaps with Jennet Clouston at their head.

Meanwhile the sun was shining outside; and being very cold in that miserable room, I knocked and shouted till my gaoler came and let me out. He carried me to the back of the house, where was a draw-well, and told me to 'wash my face there, if I wanted'; and when that was done, I made the best of my own way back to the kitchen, where he had lit the fire and was making the porridge. The table was laid with two bowls and two horn spoons, but the same single measure of small beer. Perhaps my eye rested on this particular with some surprise, and perhaps my uncle observed it; for he spoke up as if in answer to my thought, asking me if I would like to drink ale—for so he called it.

I told him such was my habit, but not to put himself about.

'Na, na,' said he; 'I'll deny you nothing in reason.'

He fetched another cup from the shelf; and then, to my

great surprise, instead of drawing more beer, he poured an accurate half from one cup to the other. There was a kind of nobleness in this that took my breath away; if my uncle was certainly a miser, he was one of that thorough breed that goes near to make the vice respectable.

When we had made an end of our meal, my uncle Ebenezer unlocked a drawer, and drew out of it a clay pipe and a lump of tobacco, from which he cut one fill before he locked it up again. Then he sat down in the sun at one of the windows and silently smoked. From time to time his eyes came coasting round to me, and he shot out one of his questions. Once it was, 'And your mother?' and when I had told him that she, too, was dead, 'Ay, she was a bonnie lassie!' Then, after another long pause, 'Whae were these friends o' yours?'

I told him they were different gentlemen of the name of Campbell; though, indeed, there was only one, and that the minister, that had ever taken the least note of me; but I began to think my uncle made too light of my position, and finding myself all alone with him, I did not wish him to suppose me helpless.

He seemed to turn this over in his mind; and then, 'Davie, my man,' said he, 'ye've come to the right bit when ye came to your Uncle Ebenezer. I've a great notion of the family, and I mean to do the right by you; but while I'm taking a bit think to mysel' of what's the best thing to put you to—whether the law, or the meenistry, or maybe the army, whilk is what boys are fondest of—I wouldnae like the Balfours to be humbled before a wheen Hieland Campbells, and I'll ask you to keep your tongue within your teeth. Nae letters; nae messages; no kind of word to onybody; or else—there's my door.'

'Uncle Ebenezer,' said I, 'I've no manner of reason to suppose you mean anything but well by me. For all that, I would have you to know that I have a pride of my own. It was by no will of mine that I came seeking you; and if you show me your door again, I'll take you at the word.'

He seemed grievously put out. 'Hoots-toots,' said he, 'ca' cannie, man—ca' cannie! Bide a day or two. I'm nae warlock, to find a fortune for you in the bottom of a parritch bowl; but just you give me a day or two, and say naething to naebody, and as sure as sure, I'll do the right by you.'

'Very well,' said I, 'enough said. If you want to help me, there's no doubt but I'll be glad of it, and none but I'll be grateful.'

It seemed to me (too soon, I daresay) that I was getting the upper hand of my uncle; and I began next to say that I must have the bed and bedclothes aired and put to sun-dry; for nothing would make me sleep in such a pickle.

'Is this my house or yours?' said he, in his keen voice, and then all of a sudden broke off. 'Na, na,' said he, 'I didnae mean that. What's mine is yours, Davie, my man, and what's yours is mine. Blood's thicker than water; and there's naebody but you and me that ought the name.' And then on he rambled about the family, and its ancient greatness, and his father that began to enlarge the house, and himself that stopped the building as a sinful waste; and this put it in my head to give him Jennet Clouston's message.

'The limmer!' he cried. 'Twelve hunner and fifteen—that's every day since I had the limmer rowpit! Dod, David, I'll have her roasted on red peats before I'm by with it! A witch—a proclaimed witch! I'll aff and see the session clerk.'

And with that he opened a chest, and got out a very old and well-preserved blue coat and waistcoat, and a good enough beaver hat, both without lace. These he threw on anyway, and taking a staff from the cupboard, locked all up again, and was for setting out, when a thought arrested him.

'I cannae leave you by yoursel' in the house,' said he. 'I'll have to lock you out.'

The blood came into my face. 'If you lock me out,' I said, 'it'll be the last you see of me in friendship.'

He turned very pale, and sucked his mouth in. 'This is no the way,' he said, looking wickedly at a corner of the floor—'this is no the way to win my favour, David.'

'Sir,' says I, 'with a proper reverence for your age and our common blood, I do not value your favour at a boddle's purchase. I was brought up to have a good conceit of myself; and if you were all the uncle, and all the family, I had in the world ten times over, I wouldn't buy your liking at such prices.'

Uncle Ebenezer went and looked out of the window for a while. I could see him all trembling and twitching, like a man with palsy. But when he turned round, he had a smile upon his face.

'Well, well,' said he, 'we must bear and forbear. I'll no go; that's all that's to be said of it.'

'Uncle Ebenezer,' I said, 'I can make nothing out of this. You use me like a thief; you hate to have me in this house; you let me see it, every word and every minute; it's not possible that you can like me; and as for me, I've spoken to you as I never thought to speak to any man. Why do you seek to keep me, then? Let me gang back—let me gang back to the friends I have, and that like me!'

'Na, na; na, na,' he said, very earnestly. 'I like you fine; we'll agree fine yet; and for the honour of the house I couldnae let you leave the way ye came. Bide here quiet, there's a good lad; just you bide here quiet a bittie, and ye'll find that we agree.'

'Well, sir,' said I, after I had thought the matter out in silence, 'I'll stay a while. It's more just I should be helped by my own blood than strangers; and if we don't agree, I'll do my best it shall be through no fault of mine.'

FOR A DAY that was begun so ill, the day passed fairly well. We had the porridge cold again at noon, and hot porridge at night: porridge and small beer was my uncle's diet. He spoke but little, and that in the same way as before, shooting a question at me after a long silence; and when I sought to lead him in talk about my future, slipped out of it again. In a room next door to the kitchen, where he suffered me to go, I found a great number of books, both Latin and English, in which I took great pleasure all the afternoon. Indeed the time passed so lightly in this good company, that I began to be almost reconciled to my residence at Shaws; and nothing but the sight of my uncle, and his eyes playing hide and seek with mine, revived the force of my distrust.

One thing I discovered, which put me in some doubt. This was an entry on the fly-leaf of a chapbook (one of Patrick Walker's) plainly written by my father's hand and thus conceived: 'To my brother Ebenezer on his fifth birthday.' Now, what puzzled me was this: That as my father was of course the younger brother, he must either have made some strange error, or he must have written, before he was yet five, an excellent, clear, manly hand of writing.

I tried to get this out of my head; but though I took down many interesting authors, old and new, history, poetry, and story-book, this notion of my father's hand of writing stuck to me; and when at length I went back into the kitchen, and sat down once more to porridge and small beer, the first thing I said to Uncle Ebenezer was to ask him if my father had not been very quick at his book.

'Alexander? No him!' was the reply. 'I was far quicker mysel'; I was a clever chappie when I was young. Why, I could read as soon as he could.'

This puzzled me yet more; and a thought coming into my head, I asked if he and my father had been twins.

He jumped upon his stool, and the horn spoon fell out of his hand upon the floor. 'What gars ye ask that?' he said, and caught me by the breast of the jacket, and looked this time straight into my eyes: his own, which were little and light, and bright like a bird's, blinking and winking strangely.

'What do you mean?' I asked, very calmly, for I was far stronger than he, and not easily frightened. 'Take your hand from my jacket. This is no way to behave.'

My uncle seemed to make a great effort upon himself. 'Dod, man David,' he said, 'ye shouldnae speak to me about your father. That's where the mistake is.' He sat a while and shook, blinking in his plate. 'He was all the brother that ever I had,' he added, but with no heart in his voice; and then he caught up his spoon and fell to supper again, but still shaking.

Now this last passage, this laying of hands upon my person and sudden profession of love for my dead father, went so clean beyond my comprehension that it put me into both fear and hope. On the one hand, I began to think my uncle was perhaps insane and might be dangerous; on the other, there came up into my mind (quite unbidden by me and even discouraged) a story like some ballad I had heard folk singing, of a poor lad that was a rightful heir and a wicked kinsman that tried to keep him from his own. For why should my uncle play a part with a relative that came, almost a beggar, to his door, unless in his heart he had some cause to fear him?

With this notion, all unacknowledged, but nevertheless getting firmly settled in my head, I now began to imitate his covert looks; so that we sat at table like a cat and a mouse, each stealthily observing the other. Not another word had he to say to me, black or white, but was busy turning something secretly over in his mind; and the longer we sat and the more I looked at him, the more certain I became that the something was unfriendly to myself.

When he had cleared the platter, he got out a single pipeful of tobacco, just as in the morning, turned round a stool into the chimney corner, and sat a while smoking, with his back to me.

'Davie,' he said, at length, 'I've been thinking'; then he paused, and said it again. 'There's a wee bit siller that I half promised ye before ye were born,' he continued; 'promised it to your father. Oh, naething legal, ye understand; just gentlemen daffing at their wine. Well, I keepit that bit money separate—it was a great expense, but a promise is a promise—and it has grown by now to be a maitter of just precisely—just exactly'—and here he paused and stumbled—'of just exactly forty pounds!' This last he rapped out with a sidelong glance over his shoulder; and the next moment added, almost with a scream, 'Scots!'

The pound Scots being the same thing as an English shilling, the difference made by this second thought was considerable; I could see, besides, that the whole story was a lie, invented with some end which it puzzled me to guess; and I made no attempt to conceal the tone of raillery in which I answered—

'Oh, think again, sir! Pounds sterling, I believe!'

'That's what I said,' returned my uncle: 'pounds sterling! And if you'll step out-by to the door a minute, just to see what kind of a night it is, I'll get it out to ye and call ye in again.'

I did his will, smiling to myself in my contempt that he should think I was so easily to be deceived. It was a dark night, with a few stars low down; and as I stood just outside the door, I heard a hollow moaning of wind far off among the hills. I said to myself there was something thundery and changeful in the weather, and little knew of what a vast importance that should prove to me before the evening passed.

When I was called in again, my uncle counted out into my hand seven and thirty golden guinea pieces; the rest was in his hand, in small gold and silver; but his heart failed him there, and he crammed the change into his pocket.

'There,' said he, 'that'll show you! I'm a queer man, and strange wi' strangers; but my word is my bond, and there's the proof of it.'

Now, my uncle seemed so miserly that I was struck dumb by this sudden generosity, and could find no words in which to thank him.

'No a word!' said he. 'Nae thanks; I want nae thanks. I do my duty; I'm no saying that everybody would have done it; but for my part (though I'm a careful body, too) it's a pleasure to me to do the right by my brother's son; and it's a pleasure to me to think that now we'll agree as such near friends should.'

I spoke him in return as handsomely as I was able; but all the while I was wondering what would come next, and why he had parted with his precious guineas; for as to the reason he had given, a baby would have refused it.

Presently, he looked towards me sideways.

'And see here,' says he, 'tit for tat.'

I told him I was ready to prove my gratitude in any reasonable degree, and then waited, looking for some monstrous demand. And yet, when at last he plucked up courage to speak, it was only to tell me (very properly, as I thought) that he was growing old and a little broken, and that he would expect me to help him with the house and the bit garden.

I answered, and expressed my readiness to serve.

'Well,' he said, 'let's begin.' He pulled out of his pocket a rusty key. 'There,' says he, 'there's the key of the stair-tower at the far end of the house. Ye can only win into it from the outside, for that part of the house is no finished. Gang ye in there, and up the stairs, and bring me down the chest that's at the top. There's papers in't,' he added.

'Can I have a light, sir?' said I.

'Na,' said he, very cunningly. 'Nae lights in my house.'

'Very well, sir,' said I. 'Are the stairs good?'

'They're grand,' said he; and then as I was going, 'Keep to the wall,' he added; 'there's nae banisters. But the stairs are grand under foot.'

Out I went into the night. The wind was still moaning in the distance, though never a breath of it came near the house of Shaws. It had fallen blacker than ever; and I was glad to feel along the wall, till I came the length of the stair-tower door at the far end of the unfinished wing. I had got the key into the keyhole and had just turned it, when all upon a sudden, without sound of wind or thunder, the whole sky lighted up with wild fire and went black again. I had to put my hand over my eyes to get back to the colour of the darkness; and indeed I was already half blinded when I stepped into the tower.

It was so dark inside, it seemed a body could scarce

breathe; but I pushed out with foot and hand, and presently struck the wall with the one, and the lowermost round
of the stair with the other. The wall, by the touch, was of
fine hewn stone; the steps too, though somewhat steep and
narrow, were of polished mason-work, and regular and solid
under foot. Minding my uncle's word about the banisters, I
kept close to the tower side, and felt my way in the pitch
darkness with a beating heart.

The house of Shaws stood some five full storeys high,
not counting lofts. Well, as I advanced, it seemed to me
the stair grew airier and a thought more lightsome; and
I was wondering what might be the cause of this change,
when a second blink of the summer lightning came and
went. If I did not cry out, it was because fear had me by
the throat; and if I did not fall, it was more by Heaven's
mercy than my own strength. It was not only that the flash
shone in on every side through breaches in the wall, so that
I seemed to be clambering aloft upon an open scaffold, but
the same passing brightness showed me the steps were of
unequal length, and that one of my feet rested that moment
within two inches of the well.

This was the grand stair! I thought; and with the
thought, a gust of a kind of angry courage came into my
heart. My uncle had sent me here, certainly to run great
risks, perhaps to die. I swore I would settle that 'perhaps',
if I should break my neck for it; got me down upon my
hands and knees; and as slowly as a snail, feeling before
me every inch, and testing the solidity of every stone, I
continued to ascend the stair. The darkness, by contrast
with the flash, appeared to have redoubled; nor was that
all, for my ears were now troubled and my mind confounded
by a great stir of bats in the top part of the tower, and the
foul beasts, flying downwards, sometimes beat about my
face and body.

The tower, I should have said, was square; and in every
corner the step was made of a great stone of a different shape,
to join the flights. Well, I had come close to one of these
turns, when, feeling forward as usual, my hand slipped
upon an edge and found nothing but emptiness beyond it.
The stair had been carried no higher: to set a stranger
mounting it in the darkness was to send him straight to his
death; and (although, thanks to the lightning and my own

precautions, I was safe enough) the mere thought of the peril in which I might have stood, and the dreadful height I might have fallen from, brought out the sweat upon my body and relaxed my joints.

But I knew what I wanted now, and turned and groped my way down again, with a wonderful anger in my heart. About half-way down, the wind sprang up in a clap and shook the tower, and died again; the rain followed; and before I had reached the ground level it fell in buckets. I put out my head into the storm, and looked along towards the kitchen. The door, which I had shut behind me when I left, now stood open, and shed a little glimmer of light; and I thought I could see a figure standing in the rain, quite still, like a man hearkening. And then there came a blinding flash, which showed me my uncle plainly, just where I had fancied him to stand; and hard upon the heels of it, a great tow-row of thunder.

Now, whether my uncle thought the crash to be the sound of my fall, or whether he heard in it God's voice denouncing murder, I will leave you to guess. Certain it is, at least, that he was seized on by a kind of panic fear, and that he ran into the house and left the door open behind him. I followed as softly as I could, and, coming unheard into the kitchen, stood and watched him.

He had found time to open the corner cupboard and bring out a great case bottle of aqua vitæ, and now sat with his back towards me at the table. Ever and again he would be seized with a fit of deadly shuddering and groan aloud, and carrying the bottle to his lips, drink down the raw spirits by the mouthful.

I stepped forward, came close behind him where he sat, and suddenly clapping my two hands down upon his shoulders—'Ah!' cried I.

My uncle gave a kind of broken cry like a sheep's bleat, flung up his arms, and tumbled to the floor like a dead man. I was somewhat shocked at this; but I had myself to look to first of all, and did not hesitate to let him lie as he had fallen. The keys were hanging in the cupboard; and it was my design to furnish myself with arms before my uncle should come again to his senses and the power of devising evil. In the cupboard were a few bottles, some apparently of medicine; a great many bills and other papers, which

I should willingly enough have rummaged, had I had the time; and a few necessaries, that were nothing to my purpose. Thence I turned to the chests. The first was full of meal; the second of money-bags and papers tied into sheaves; in the third, with many other things (and these for the most part clothes) I found a rusty, ugly-looking Highland dirk without the scabbard. This, then, I concealed inside my waistcoat, and turned to my uncle.

He lay as he had fallen, all huddled, with one knee up and one arm sprawling abroad; his face had a strange colour of blue, and he seemed to have ceased breathing. Fear came on me that he was dead; then I got water and dashed it in his face; and with that he seemed to come a little to himself, working his mouth and fluttering his eyelids. At last he looked up and saw me, and there came into his eyes a terror that was not of this world.

'Come, come,' said I, 'sit up.'

'Are ye alive?' he sobbed. 'O man, are ye alive?'

'That am I,' said I. 'Small thanks to you!'

He had begun to seek for his breath with deep sighs. 'The blue phial,' said he—'in the aumry—the blue phial.' His breath came slower still.

I ran to the cupboard, and, sure enough, found there a blue phial of medicine, with the dose written on it on a paper, and this I administered to him with what speed I might.

'It's the trouble,' said he, reviving a little; 'I have a trouble, Davie. It's the heart.'

I set him on a chair and looked at him. It is true I felt some pity for a man that looked so sick, but I was full besides of righteous anger; and I numbered over before him the points on which I wanted explanation: why he lied to me at every word; why he feared that I should leave him; why he disliked it to be hinted that he and my father were twins—'Is that because it is true?' I asked; why he had given me money to which I was convinced I had no claim; and, last of all, why he had tried to kill me. He heard me all through in silence; and then, in a broken voice, begged me to let him go to bed.

'I'll tell ye the morn,' he said; 'as sure as death I will.'

And so weak was he that I could do nothing but consent.

I locked him into his room, however, and pocketed the key; and then returning to the kitchen, made up such a blaze as had not shone there for many a long year, and wrapping myself in my plaid, lay down upon the chests and fell asleep.

MUCH RAIN FELL in the night; and the next morning there blew a bitter wintry wind out of the north-west, driving scattered clouds. For all that, and before the sun began to peep or the last of the stars had vanished, I made my way to the side of the burn, and had a plunge in a deep whirling pool. All aglow from my bath, I sat down once more beside the fire, which I replenished, and began gravely to consider my position.

There was now no doubt about my uncle's enmity; there was no doubt I carried my life in my hand, and he would leave no stone unturned that he might compass my destruction. But I was young and spirited, and like most lads that have been country-bred, I had a great opinion of my shrewdness. I had come to his door no better than a beggar and little more than a child; he had met me with treachery and violence; it would be a fine consummation to take the upper hand, and drive him like a herd of sheep.

I sat there nursing my knee and smiling at the fire; and I saw myself in fancy smell out his secrets one after another, and grow to be that man's king and ruler. The warlock of Essendean, they say, had made a mirror in which men could read the future; it must have been of other stuff than burning coal; for in all the shapes and pictures that I sat and gazed at, there was never a ship, never a seaman with a hairy cap, never a big bludgeon for my silly head, or the least sign of all those tribulations that were ripe to fall on me.

Presently, all swollen with conceit, I went up-stairs and gave my prisoner his liberty. He gave me good morning civilly; and I gave the same to him, smiling down upon him from the heights of my sufficiency. Soon we were set to breakfast, as it might have been the day before.

'Well, sir,' said I, with a jeering tone, 'have you nothing

more to say to me?' And then, as he made no articulate reply, 'It will be time, I think, to understand each other,' I continued. 'You took me for a country Johnnie Raw, with no more mother-wit or courage than a porridge-stick. I took you for a good man, or no worse than others at the least. It seems we were both wrong. What cause you have to fear me, to cheat me, and to attempt my life—'

He murmured something about a jest, and that he liked a bit of fun; and then, seeing me smile, changed his tone, and assured me he would make all clear as soon as we had breakfasted. I saw by his face that he had no lie ready for me, though he was hard at work preparing one; and I think I was about to tell him so, when we were interrupted by a knocking at the door.

Bidding my uncle sit where he was, I went to open it, and found on the doorstep a half-grown boy in sea-clothes. He had no sooner seen me than he began to dance some steps of the sea-hornpipe (which I had never before heard of, far less seen) snapping his fingers in the air and footing it right cleverly. For all that, he was blue with the cold; and there was something in his face, a look between tears and laughter, that was highly pathetic and consisted ill with this gaiety of manner.

'What cheer, mate?' says he, with a cracked voice.

I asked him soberly to name his pleasure.

'Oh, pleasure!' says he; and then began to sing:

'For it's my delight, of a shiny night,
In the season of the year.'

'Well,' said I, 'if you have no business at all, I will even be so unmannerly as to shut you out.'

'Stay, brother!' he cried. 'Have you no fun about you? or do you want to get me thrashed? I've brought a letter from old Heasy-oasy to Mr Belflower.' He showed me a letter as he spoke. 'And I say, mate,' he added, 'I'm mortal hungry.'

'Well,' said I, 'come into the house, and you shall have a bite if I go empty for it.'

With that I brought him in and set him down to my own place, where he fell-to greedily on the remains of breakfast, winking to me between whiles, and making many faces, which I think the poor soul considered manly.

Meanwhile, my uncle had read the letter and sat thinking; then suddenly, he got to his feet with a great air of liveliness, and pulled me apart into the farthest corner of the room.

'Read that,' said he, and put the letter in my hand.

Here it is, lying before me as I write:

> The Hawes Inn, at the Queen's Ferry
> Sir,—I lie here with my hawser up and down,
> and send my cabin-boy to informe. If you have any
> further commands for over-seas, to-day will be
> the last occasion, as the wind will serve us well out
> of the firth. I will not seek to deny that I have had
> crosses with your doer, Mr Rankeillor; of which,
> if not speedily redd up, you may looke to see
> some losses follow. I have drawn a bill upon you,
> as per margin, and am, sir, your most obedt.,
> humble servant,
>
> Elias Hoseason

'You see, Davie,' resumed my uncle, as soon as he saw that I had done, 'I have a venture with this man Hoseason, the captain of a trading brig, the *Covenant*, of Dysart. Now, if you and me was to walk over with yon lad, I could see the captain at the Hawes, or maybe on board the *Covenant*, if there was papers to be signed; and so far from a loss of time, we can jog on to the lawyer, Mr Rankeillor's. After a' that's come and gone, ye would be swier to believe me upon my naked word; but ye'll believe Rankeillor. He's factor to half the gentry in these parts; an auld man, forby: highly respeckit; and he kenned your father.'

I stood awhile and thought. I was going to some place of shipping, which was doubtless populous, and where my uncle durst attempt no violence, and, indeed, even the society of the cabin-boy so far protected me. Once there, I believed I could force on the visit to the lawyer, even if my uncle were now insincere in proposing it; and perhaps, in the bottom of my heart, I wished a nearer view of the sea and ships. You are to remember I had lived all my life in the inland hills, and just two days before had my first sight of the firth lying like a blue floor, and the sailed ships moving on the face of it, no bigger than toys. One thing with another, I made up my mind.

'Very well,' says I, 'let us go to the Ferry.'

My uncle got into his hat and coat, and buckled an old rusty cutlass on; and then we trod the fire out, locked the door, and set forth upon our walk.

The wind, being in that cold quarter, the north-west, blew nearly in our faces as we went. It was the month of June; the grass was all white with daisies and the trees with blossom; but, to judge by our blue nails and aching wrists, the time might have been winter and the whiteness a December frost.

Uncle Ebenezer trudged in the ditch, jogging from side to side like an old ploughman coming home from work. He never said a word the whole way; and I was thrown for talk on the cabin-boy. He told me his name was Ransome, and that he had followed the sea since he was nine, but could not say how old he was, as he had lost his reckoning. He showed me tattoo marks, baring his breast in the teeth of the wind and in spite of my remonstrances, for I thought it was enough to kill him; he swore horribly whenever he remembered, but more like a silly schoolboy than a man; and boasted of many wild and bad things that he had done: stealthy thefts, false accusations, ay, and even murder; but all with such a dearth of likelihood in the details, and such a weak and crazy swagger in the delivery, as disposed me rather to pity than to believe him.

I asked him of the brig (which he declared was the finest ship that sailed) and of Captain Hoseason, in whose praise he was equally loud. Heasy-oasy (for so he still named the skipper) was a man, by his account, that minded for nothing either in heaven or earth; one that, as people said, would 'crack on all sail into the day of judgment'; rough, fierce, unscrupulous, and brutal; and all this my poor cabin-boy had taught himself to admire as something seamanlike and manly. He would only admit one flaw in his idol. 'He ain't no seaman,' he admitted. 'That's Mr Shuan that navigates the brig; he's the finest seaman in the trade, only for drink; and I tell you I believe it! Why, look 'ere'; and turning down his stocking, he showed me a great, raw, red wound that made my blood run cold. 'He done that—Mr Shuan done it,' he said, with an air of pride.

'What!' I cried, 'do you take such savage usage at his hands? Why, you are no slave, to be so handled!'

'No,' said the poor moon-calf, changing his tune at once, 'and so he'll find! See 'ere'; and he showed me a great case-knife, which he told me was stolen. 'Oh,' says he, 'let me see him try; I dare him to; I'll do for him! Oh, he ain't the first!' And he confirmed it with a poor, silly, ugly oath.

I have never felt such pity for any one in this wide world as I felt for that half-witted creature; and it began to come over me that the brig *Covenant* (for all her pious name) was little better than a hell upon the seas.

'Have you no friends?' said I.

He said he had a father in some English seaport, I forget which. 'He was a fine man, too,' he said; 'but he's dead.'

'In Heaven's name,' cried I, 'can you find no reputable life on shore?'

'Oh no!' says he, winking and looking very sly; 'they would put me to a trade. I know a trick worth two of that, I do!'

I asked him what trade could be so dreadful as the one he followed, where he ran the continual peril of his life, not alone from wind and sea, but by the horrid cruelty of those who were his masters. He said it was very true; and then began to praise the life, and tell what a pleasure it was to get on shore with money in his pocket, and spend it like a man, and buy apples, and swagger, and surprise what he called stick-in-the-mud boys. 'And then it's not all as bad as that,' says he; 'there's worse off than me: there's the twenty-pounders. Oh, laws! you should see them taking on. Why, I've seen a man as old as you, I dessay'—(to him I seemed old)—'ah, and he had a beard, too—well, and as soon as we cleared out of the river, and he had the drug out of his head—my! how he cried and carried on! I made a fine fool of him, I tell you! And then there's little uns, too: oh, little by me! I tell you, I keep them in order. When we carry little uns, I have a rope's end of my own to wollop 'em.' And so he ran on, until it came in on me that what he meant by twenty-pounders were those unhappy criminals who were sent over-seas to slavery in North America, or the still more unhappy innocents who were kidnapped or trepanned (as the word went) for private interest or vengeance.

Just then we came to the top of the hill, and looked

down on the Ferry and the Hope. The Firth of Forth (as is very well known) narrows at this point to the width of a good-sized river, which makes a convenient ferry going north, and turns the upper reach into a land-locked haven for all manner of ships. Right in the midst of the narrows lies an islet with some ruins; on the south shore they have built a pier for the service of the Ferry; and at the end of the pier, on the other side of the road, and backed against a pretty garden of holly-trees and hawthorns, I could see the building which they call the Hawes Inn.

The town of Queensferry lies farther west, and the neighbourhood of the inn looked pretty lonely at that time of day, for the boat had just gone north with passengers. A skiff, however, lay beside the pier, with some seamen sleeping on the thwarts; this, as Ransome told me, was the brig's boat waiting for the captain; and about half a mile off, and all alone in the anchorage, he showed me the *Covenant* herself. There was a sea-going bustle on board; yards were swinging into place; and as the wind blew from that quarter, I could hear the song of the sailors as they pulled upon the ropes. After all I had listened to upon the way, I looked at that ship with an extreme abhorrence; and from the bottom of my heart I pitied all poor souls that were condemned to sail in her.

We had all three pulled up on the brow of the hill; and now I marched across the road and addressed my uncle. 'I think it right to tell you, sir,' says I, 'there's nothing that will bring me on board that *Covenant*.'

He seemed to waken from a dream. 'Eh?' he said. 'What's that?'

I told him over again.

'Well, well,' he said, 'we'll have to please ye, I suppose. But what are we standing here for? It's perishing cold; and if I'm no mistaken, they're busking the *Covenant* for sea.'

AS SOON AS we came to the inn, Ransome led us up the
stair to a small room, with a bed in it, and heated like an
oven by a great fire of coal. At a table hard by the chimney,
a tall, dark, sober-looking man sat writing. In spite of the
heat of the room, he wore a thick sea-jacket, buttoned to
the neck, and a tall hairy cap drawn down over his ears;
yet I never saw any man, not even a judge upon the bench,
look cooler, or more studious and self-possessed, than this
ship-captain.

He got to his feet at once, and coming forward, offered
his large hand to Ebenezer. 'I am proud to see you, Mr
Balfour,' said he, in a fine deep voice, 'and glad that ye
are here in time. The wind's fair, and the tide upon the
turn: we'll see the old coal-bucket burning on the Isle of
May before to-night.'

'Captain Hoseason,' returned my uncle, 'you keep your
room unco hot.'

'It's a habit I have, Mr Balfour,' said the skipper. 'I'm
a cold-rife man by my nature; I have a cold blood, sir.
There's neither fur, nor flannel—no, sir, nor hot rum,
will warm up what they call the temperature. Sir, it's the
same with most men that have been carbonadoed, as they
call it, in the tropic seas.'

'Well, well, captain,' replied my uncle, 'we must all be
the way we're made.'

But it chanced that this fancy of the captain's had a great
share in my misfortunes. For though I had promised myself
not to let my kinsman out of sight, I was both so impatient
for a nearer look of the sea, and so sickened by the closeness
of the room, that when he told me to 'run down-stairs and
play myself awhile', I was fool enough to take him at his
word.

Away I went, therefore, leaving the two men sitting down

to a bottle and a great mass of papers; and crossing the road in front of the inn, walked down upon the beach. With the wind in that quarter, only little wavelets, not much bigger than I had seen upon a lake, beat upon the shore. But the weeds were new to me—some green, some brown and long, and some with little bladders that crackled between my fingers. Even so far up the firth, the smell of the sea water was exceedingly salt and stirring; the *Covenant*, besides, was beginning to shake out her sails, which hung upon the yards in clusters; and the spirit of all that I beheld put me in thoughts of far voyages and foreign places.

I looked, too, at the seamen with the skiff—big brown fellows, some in shirts, some with jackets, some with coloured handkerchiefs about their throats, one with a brace of pistols stuck into his pockets, two or three with knotty bludgeons, and all with their case-knives. I passed the time of day with one that looked less desperate than his fellows, and asked him of the sailing of the brig. He said they would get under way as soon as the ebb set, and expressed his gladness to be out of a port where there were no taverns and fiddlers; but all with such horrifying oaths, that I made haste to get away from him.

This threw me back on Ransome, who seemed the least wicked of that gang, and who soon came out of the inn and ran to me, crying for a bowl of punch. I told him I would give him no such thing, for neither he nor I was of an age for such indulgences. 'But a glass of ale you may have, and welcome,' said I. He mopped and mowed at me, and called me names; but he was glad to get the ale, for all that; and presently we were set down at a table in the front room of the inn, and both eating and drinking with a good appetite.

Here it occurred to me that, as the landlord was a man of that county, I might do well to make a friend of him. I offered him a share, as was much the custom in these days; but he was far too great a man to sit with such poor customers as Ransome and myself, and he was leaving the room, when I called him back to ask if he knew Mr Rankeillor.

'Hoot, ay,' says he, 'and a very honest man. And, oh, by-the-bye,' says he, 'was it you that came in with Ebenezer?' And when I had told him yes, 'Ye'll be no friend of his?' he asked, meaning, in the Scottish way, that I would be no relative.

I told him no, none.

'I thought not,' said he; 'and yet ye have a kind of gliff of Mr Alexander.'

I said it seemed that Ebenezer was ill-seen in the country.

'Nae doubt,' said the landlord. 'He's a wicked auld man, and there's many would like to see him girning in a tow: Jennet Clouston and mony mair that he has harried out of house and hame. And yet he was ance a fine young fellow, too. But that was before the sough gaed abroad about Mr Alexander; that was like the death of him.'

'And what was it?' I asked.

'Ou, just that he had killed him,' said the landlord. 'Did ye never hear that?'

'And what would he kill him for?' said I.

'And what for, but just to get the place,' said he.

'The place?' said I. 'The Shaws?'

'Nae other place that I ken,' said he.

'Ay, man?' said I. 'Is that so? Was my—was Alexander the eldest son?'

''Deed was he,' said the landlord. 'What else would he have killed him for?'

And with that he went away, as he had been impatient to do from the beginning.

Of course, I had guessed it a long while ago; but it is one thing to guess, another to know; and I sat stunned with my good fortune, and could scarce grow to believe that the same poor lad who had trudged in the dust from Ettrick Forest not two days ago, was now one of the rich of the earth, and had a house and broad lands, and if he but knew how to ride, might mount his horse to-morrow. All these pleasant things, and a thousand others, crowded into my mind, as I sat staring before me out of the inn window, and paying no heed to what I saw; only I remember that my eye lighted on Captain Hoseason down on the pier among his seamen, and speaking with some authority. And presently he came marching back towards the house, with no mark of a sailor's clumsiness, but carrying his fine, tall figure with a manly bearing, and still with the same sober, grave expression on his face. I wondered if it was possible that Ransome's stories could be true, and half disbelieved them; they fitted so ill with the man's looks. But indeed, he was neither so good as I supposed him, nor quite so bad as Ransome did; for, in fact, he was two men, and left the better one behind as soon as he set foot on board his vessel.

The next thing, I heard my uncle calling me, and found the pair in the road together. It was the captain who addressed me, and that with an air (very flattering to a young lad) of grave equality.

'Sir,' said he, 'Mr Balfour tells me great things of you; and for my own part, I like your looks. I wish I was for longer here, that we might make the better friends; but we'll make the most of what we have. Ye shall come on board my brig for half-an-hour, till the ebb sets, and drink a bowl with me.'

Now, I longed to see the inside of a ship more than words can tell; but I was not going to put myself in jeopardy, and I told him my uncle and I had an appointment with a lawyer.

'Ay, ay,' said he, 'he passed me word of that. But, ye see, the boat'll set ye ashore at the town pier, and that's but a penny stonecast from Rankeillor's house.' And here he suddenly leaned down and whispered in my ear: 'Take care of the old tod; he means mischief. Come aboard till I can get a word with ye.' And then, passing his arm through mine, he continued aloud, as he set off towards his boat: 'But come, what can I bring ye from the Carolinas? Any friend of Mr Balfour's can command. A roll of tobacco? Indian feather-work? a skin of a wild beast? a stone pipe? the mocking-bird that mews for all the world like a cat? the cardinal bird that is as red as blood?—take your pick and say your pleasure.'

By this time we were at the boat-side, and he was handing me in. I did not dream of hanging back; I thought (the poor fool!) that I had found a good friend and helper, and I was rejoiced to see the ship. As soon as we were all set in our places, the boat was thrust off from the pier and began to move over the waters; and what with my pleasure in this new movement and my surprise at our low position, and the appearance of the shores, and the growing bigness of the brig as we drew near to it, I could hardly understand what the captain said, and must have answered him at random.

As soon as we were alongside (where I sat fairly gaping at the ship's height, the strong humming of the tide against its sides, and the pleasant cries of the seamen at their work) Hoseason, declaring that he and I must be the first aboard, ordered a tackle to be sent down from the main-yard. In this I was whipped into the air and set down again on the deck, where the captain stood ready waiting for me, and instantly slipped back his arm under mine. There I stood some while, a little dizzy with the unsteadiness of all around me, perhaps a little afraid, and yet vastly pleased with these strange sights; the captain meanwhile pointing out the strangest, and telling me their names and uses.

'But where is my uncle?' said I, suddenly.

'Ay,' said Hoseason, with a sudden grimness, 'that's the point.'

I felt I was lost. With all my strength, I plucked myself clear of him and ran to the bulwarks. Sure enough, there was the boat pulling for the town, with my uncle sitting in the stern. I gave a piercing cry—'Help, help! Murder!'—so that both sides of the anchorage rang with it, and my uncle turned round where he was sitting, and showed me a face full of cruelty and terror.

It was the last I saw. Already strong hands had been plucking me back from the ship's side; and now a thunderbolt seemed to strike me; I saw a great flash of fire, and fell senseless.

I CAME TO myself in darkness, in great pain, bound hand and foot, and deafened by many unfamiliar noises. There sounded in my ears a roaring of water as of a huge mill-dam; the thrashing of heavy sprays, the thundering of the sails, and the shrill cries of seamen. The whole world now heaved giddily up, and now rushed giddily downward; and so sick and hurt was I in body, and my mind so much confounded, that it took me a long while, chasing my thoughts up and down, and ever stunned again by a fresh stab of pain, to realise that I must be lying somewhere bound in the belly of that unlucky ship, and that the wind must have strengthened to a gale. With the clear perception of my plight, there fell upon me a blackness of despair, a horror of remorse at my own folly, and a passion of anger at my uncle, that once more bereft me of my senses.

When I returned again to life, the same uproar, the same confused and violent movements, shook and deafened me; and presently, to my other pains and distresses, there was added the sickness of an unused landsman on the sea. In that time of my adventurous youth, I suffered many hardships; but none that was so crushing to my mind and body, or lit by so few hopes, as these first hours on board the brig.

I heard a gun fire, and supposed the storm had proved too strong for us, and we were firing signals of distress. The thought of deliverance, even by death in the deep sea, was welcome to me. Yet it was no such matter; but (as I was afterwards told) a common habit of the captain's, which I here set down to show that even the worst man may have his kindlier sides. We were then passing, it appeared, within some miles of Dysart, where the brig was built, and where old Mrs Hoseason, the captain's mother, had come some years before to live; and whether outward or inward bound, the *Covenant* was never suffered to go by that place by day, without a gun fired and colours shown.

I had no measure of time; day and night were alike in that ill-smelling cavern of the ship's bowels where I lay; and the misery of my situation drew out the hours to double. How long, therefore, I lay waiting to hear the ship split upon some rock, or to feel her reel head foremost into the depths of the sea, I have not the means of computation. But sleep at length stole from me the consciousness of sorrow.

I was wakened by the light of a hand-lantern shining in my face. A small man of about thirty, with green eyes and a tangle of fair hair, stood looking down at me.

'Well,' said he, 'how goes it?'

I answered by a sob; and my visitor then felt my pulse and temples, and set himself to wash and dress the wound upon my scalp.

'Ay,' said he, 'a sore dunt. What, man? Cheer up! The world's no done; you've made a bad start of it, but you'll make a better. Have you had any meat?'

I said I could not look at it; and thereupon he gave me some brandy and water in a tin pannikin, and left me once more to myself.

The next time he came to see me, I was lying betwixt sleep and waking, my eyes wide open in the darkness, the sickness quite departed, but succeeded by a horrid giddiness and swimming that was almost worse to bear. I ached, besides, in every limb, and the cords that bound me seemed to be of fire. The smell of the hole in which I lay seemed to have become a part of me; and during the long interval since his last visit I had suffered tortures of fear, now from the scurrying of the ship's rats, that sometimes pattered on my very face, and now from the dismal imaginings that haunt the bed of fever.

The glimmer of the lantern, as a trap opened, shone in like the heaven's sunlight; and though it only showed me the strong, dark beams of the ship that was my prison, I could have cried aloud for gladness. The man with the green eyes was the first to descend the ladder, and I noticed that he came somewhat unsteadily. He was followed by the captain. Neither said a word; but the first set to and examined me, and dressed my wound as before, while Hoseason looked me in my face with an odd, black look.

'Now, sir, you see for yourself,' said the first: 'a high fever, no appetite, no light, no meat: you see for yourself what that means.'

'I am no conjurer, Mr Riach,' said the captain.

'Give me leave, sir,' said Riach; 'you've a good head upon your shoulders, and a good Scotch tongue to ask with; but I will leave you no manner of excuse: I want that boy taken out of this hole and put in the forecastle.'

'What ye may want, sir, is a matter of concern to nobody but yoursel',' returned the captain; 'but I can tell ye that which is to be. Here he is; here he shall bide.'

'Admitting that you have been paid in a proportion,' said the other, 'I will crave leave humbly to say that I have not. Paid I am, and none too much, to be the second officer of this old tub; and you ken very well if I do my best to earn it. But I was paid for nothing more.'

'If ye could hold back your hand from the tin-pan, Mr Riach, I would have no complaint to make of ye,' returned the skipper; 'and instead of asking riddles, I make bold to say that ye would keep your breath to cool your porridge. We'll be required on deck,' he added, in a sharper note, and set one foot upon the ladder.

But Mr Riach caught him by the sleeve.

'Admitting that you have been paid to do a murder—' he began.

Hoseason turned upon him with a flash.

'What's that?' he cried. 'What kind of talk is that?'

'It seems it is the talk that you can understand,' said Mr Riach, looking him steadily in the face.

'Mr Riach, I have sailed with ye three cruises,' replied the captain. 'In all that time, sir, ye should have learned to know me: I'm a stiff man, and a dour man; but for what ye say the now—fie, fie!—it comes from a bad heart and a black conscience. If ye say the lad will die—'

'Ay, will he!' said Mr Riach.

'Well, sir, is not that enough?' said Hoseason. 'Flit him where ye please!'

Thereupon the captain ascended the ladder; and I, who had lain silent throughout this strange conversation, beheld Mr Riach turn after him and bow as low as to his knees in what was plainly a spirit of derision. Even in my then state of sickness, I perceived two things: that the mate was touched with liquor, as the captain hinted, and that (drunk or sober) he was like to prove a valuable friend.

Five minutes afterwards my bonds were cut, I was hoisted on a man's back, carried up to the forecastle, and laid in a bunk on some sea-blankets; where the first thing that I did was to lose my senses.

It was a blessed thing indeed to open my eyes again upon the daylight, and to find myself in the society of men. The forecastle was a roomy place enough, set all about with berths, in which the men of the watch below were seated smoking, or lying down asleep. The day being calm and the wind fair, the scuttle was open, and not only the good daylight, but from time to time (as the ship rolled) a dusty beam of sunlight shone in, and dazzled and delighted me. I had no sooner moved, moreover, than one of the men brought me a drink of something healing which Mr Riach had prepared, and bade me lie still and I should soon be well again. There were no bones broken, he explained: 'A clour on the head was naething. Man,' said he, 'it was me that gave it ye!'

Here I lay for the space of many days a close prisoner, and not only got my health again, but came to know my companions. They were a rough lot indeed, as sailors mostly are; being men rooted out of all the kindly parts of life, and condemned to toss together on the rough seas, with masters no less cruel. There were some among them that had sailed with the pirates and seen things it would be a shame even to speak of; some were men that had run from the king's ships, and went with a halter round their necks, of which they made no secret; and all, as the saying goes, were 'at a word and a blow' with their best friends. Yet I had not been many days shut up with them before I began to be ashamed of my first judgment, when I had drawn away from them at the Ferry pier, as though they had been unclean beasts. No class of man is altogether bad; but each has its own faults and virtues; and these shipmates of mine were no exception to the rule. Rough they were, sure enough; and bad, I suppose; but they had many virtues. They were kind when it occurred to them, simple even beyond the simplicity of a country lad like me, and had some glimmerings of honesty.

There was one man of maybe forty, that would sit on my

berthside for hours, and tell me of his wife and child. He was a fisher that had lost his boat, and thus been driven to the deep-sea voyaging. Well, it is years ago now; but I have never forgotten him. His wife (who was 'young by him', as he often told me) waited in vain to see her man return; he would never again make the fire for her in the morning, nor yet keep the bairn when she was sick. Indeed, many of these poor fellows (as the event proved) were upon their last cruise; the deep seas and cannibal fish received them; and it is a thankless business to speak ill of the dead.

Among other good deeds that they did, they returned my money, which had been shared among them; and though it was about a third short, I was very glad to get it, and hoped great good from it in the land I was going to. The ship was bound for the Carolinas; and you must not suppose that I was going to that place merely as an exile. The trade was even then much depressed; since that, and with the rebellion of the colonies and the formation of the United States, it has, of course, come to an end; but in these days of my youth, white men were still sold into slavery on the plantations, and that was the destiny to which my wicked uncle had condemned me.

The cabin-boy Ransome (from whom I had first heard of these atrocities) came in at times from the round-house, where he berthed and served, now nursing a bruised limb in silent agony, now raving against the cruelty of Mr Shuan. It made my heart bleed; but the men had a great respect for the chief mate, who was, as they said, 'the only seaman of the whole jing-bang, and none such a bad man when he was sober.' Indeed, I found there was a strange peculiarity about our two mates: that Mr Riach was sullen, unkind, and harsh when he was sober, and Mr Shuan would not hurt a fly except when he was drinking. I asked about the captain; but I was told drink made no difference upon that man of iron.

I did my best in the small time allowed me to make something like a man, or rather I should say something like a boy, of the poor creature, Ransome. But his mind was scarce truly human. He could remember nothing of the time before he came to sea; only that his father had made clocks, and had a starling in the parlour, which could whistle

'The North Countrie'; all else had been blotted out in these years of hardship and cruelties. He had a strange notion of the dry land, picked up from sailors' stories: that it was a place where lads were put to some kind of slavery called a trade, and where apprentices were continually lashed and clapped into foul prisons. In a town, he thought every second person a decoy, and every third house a place in which seamen would be drugged and murdered. To be sure, I could tell him how kindly I had myself been used upon that dry land he was so much afraid of, and how well fed and carefully taught both by my friends and my parents: and if he had been recently hurt, he would weep bitterly and swear to run away; but if he was in his usual crackbrain humour or (still more) if he had had a glass of spirits in the round-house, he would deride the notion.

It was Mr Riach (Heaven forgive him!) who gave the boy drink; and it was, doubtless, kindly meant; but besides that it was ruin to his health, it was the pitifullest thing in life to see this unhappy, unfriended creature staggering, and dancing, and talking he knew not what. Some of the men laughed, but not all; others would grow as black as thunder (thinking, perhaps, of their own childhood or their own children) and bid him stop that nonsense, and think what he was doing. As for me, I felt ashamed to look at him, and the poor child still comes about me in my dreams.

All this time, you should know, the *Covenant* was meeting continual head-winds and tumbling up and down against head-seas, so that the scuttle was almost constantly shut, and the forecastle lighted only by a swinging lantern on a beam. There was constant labour for all hands; the sails had to be made and shortened every hour; the strain told on the men's temper; there was a growl of quarrelling all day long from berth to berth; and as I was never allowed to set my foot on deck, you can picture to yourselves how weary of my life I grew to be, and how impatient for a change.

And a change I was to get, as you shall hear; but I must first tell of a conversation I had with Mr Riach, which put a little heart in me to bear my troubles. Getting him in a favourable stage of drink (for indeed he never looked near me when he was sober) I pledged him to secrecy, and told him my whole story.

He declared it was like a ballad; that he would do his best to help me; that I should have paper, pen, and ink, and write one line to Mr Campbell and another to Mr Rankeillor; and that if I had told the truth, ten to one he would be able (with their help) to pull me through and set me in my rights.

'And in the meantime,' says he, 'keep your heart up. You're not the only one, I'll tell you that. There's many a man hoeing tobacco over-seas that should be mounting his horse at his own door at home; many and many! And life is all a variorum, at the best. Look at me: I'm a laird's son and more than half a doctor, and here I am, man-Jack to Hoseason!'

I thought it would be civil to ask him for his story.

He whistled loud.

'Never had one,' said he. 'I liked fun, that's all.' And he skipped out of the forecastle.

ONE NIGHT, ABOUT twelve o'clock, a man of Mr
Riach's watch (which was on deck) came down for his
jacket; and instantly there began to go a whisper about
the forecastle that 'Shuan had done for him at last'. There
was no need of a name; we all knew who was meant; but
we had scarce time to get the idea rightly in our heads, far
less to speak of it, when the scuttle was again flung open,
and Captain Hoseason came down the ladder. He looked
sharply round the bunks in the tossing light of the lantern;
and then, walking straight up to me, he addressed me, to
my surprise, in tones of kindness.

'My man,' said he, 'we want ye to serve in the round-
house. You and Ransome are to change berths. Run away
aft with ye.'

Even as he spoke, two seamen appeared in the scuttle,
carrying Ransome in their arms; and the ship at that
moment giving a great sheer into the sea, and the lantern
swinging, the light fell direct on the boy's face. It was as
white as wax, and had a look upon it like a dreadful smile.
The blood in me ran cold, and I drew in my breath as if I
had been struck.

'Run away aft; run away aft with ye!' cried Hoseason.

And at that I brushed by the sailors and the boy (who
neither spoke nor moved), and ran up the ladder on deck.

The brig was sheering swiftly and giddily through a long,
cresting swell. She was on the starboard tack, and on the left
hand, under the arched foot of the fore-sail, I could see the
sunset still quite bright. This, at such an hour of the night,
surprised me greatly; but I was too ignorant to draw the
true conclusion—that we were going north-about round
Scotland, and were now on the high sea between the Orkney
and the Shetland Islands, having avoided the dangerous
currents of the Pentland Firth. For my part, who had been

so long shut in the dark and knew nothing of head-winds, I thought we might be half-way or more across the Atlantic. And indeed (beyond that I wondered a little at the lateness of the sunset light) I gave no heed to it, and pushed on across the decks, running between the seas, catching at ropes, and only saved from going over-board by one of the hands on deck, who had been always kind to me.

The round-house, for which I was bound, and where I was now to sleep and serve, stood some six feet above the decks, and considering the size of the brig, was of good dimensions. Inside were a fixed table and bench, and two berths, one for the captain and the other for the two mates, turn and turn about.

It was all fitted with lockers from top to bottom, so as to stow away the officers' belongings and a part of the ship's stores; there was a second store-room underneath, which you entered by a hatchway in the middle of the deck; indeed, all the best of the meat and drink and the whole of the powder were collected in this place; and all the firearms, except the two pieces of brass ordnance, were set in a rack in the aftermost wall of the round-house. The most of the cutlasses were in another place.

A small window with a shutter on each side, and a skylight in the roof, gave it light by day; and after dark, there was a lamp always burning. It was burning when I entered, not brightly, but enough to show Mr Shuan sitting at the table, with the brandy bottle and a tin pannikin in front of him. He was a tall man, strongly made and very black; and he stared before him on the table like one stupid.

He took no notice of my coming in; nor did he move when the captain followed and leant on the berth beside me, looking darkly at the mate. I stood in great fear of Hoseason, and had my reasons for it; but something told me I need not be afraid of him just then; and I whispered in his ear, 'How is he?' He shook his head like one that does not know and does not wish to think, and his face was very stern.

Presently Mr Riach came in. He gave the captain a glance that meant the boy was dead as plain as speaking, and took his place like the rest of us; so that we all three stood without a word, staring down at Mr Shuan, and Mr Shuan (on his side) sat without a word, looking hard upon the table.

All of a sudden he put out his hand to take the bottle; and at that Mr Riach started forward and caught it away from him, rather by surprise than violence, crying out, with an oath, that there had been too much of this work altogether, and that a judgment would fall upon the ship. And as he spoke (the weather sliding-doors standing open) he tossed the bottle into the sea.

Mr Shuan was on his feet in a trice; he still looked dazed, but he meant murder, ay, and would have done it, for the second time that night, had not the captain stepped in between him and his victim.

'Sit down!' roars the captain. 'Ye sot and swine, do ye know what ye've done? Ye've murdered the boy!'

Mr Shuan seemed to understand; for he sat down again and put up his hand to his brow.

'Well,' he said, 'he brought me a dirty pannikin!'

At that word, the captain and I and Mr Riach all looked at each other for a second with a kind of frightened look; and then Hoseason walked up to his chief officer, took him by the shoulder, led him across to his bunk, and bade him lie down and go to sleep, as you might speak to a bad child. The murderer cried a little, but he took off his sea-boots and obeyed.

'Ah!' cried Mr Riach, with a dreadful voice, 'ye should have interfered long syne. It's too late now.'

'Mr Riach,' said the captain, 'this night's work must never be kennt in Dysart. The boy went over-board, sir; that's what the story is; and I would give five pounds out of my pocket it was true!' He turned to the table. 'What made ye throw the good bottle away?' he added. 'There was nae sense in that, sir. Here, David, draw me another. They're in the bottom locker'; and he tossed me a key. 'Ye'll need a glass yourself, sir,' he added, to Riach. 'Yon was an ugly thing to see.'

So the pair sat down and hob-a-nobbed; and while they did so, the murderer, who had been lying and whimpering in his berth, raised himself upon his elbow and looked at them and at me.

That was the first night of my new duties; and in the course of the next day I had got well into the run of them. I had to serve at the meals, which the captain took at regular hours, sitting down with the officer who was off duty; all the day through I would be running with a dram to one or other of my three masters; and at night I slept on a blanket thrown on the deck boards at the aftermost end of the round-house, and right in the draught of the two doors. It was a hard and a cold bed; nor was I suffered to sleep without interruption; for some one would be always coming in from deck to get a dram, and when a fresh watch was to be set, two and sometimes all three would sit down and brew a bowl together. How they kept their health, I know not, any more than how I kept my own.

And yet in other ways it was an easy service. There was no cloth to lay; the meals were either of oatmeal porridge or salt junk, except twice a week, when there was duff: and though I was clumsy enough and (not being firm on my sea-legs) sometimes fell with what I was bringing them, both Mr Riach and the captain were singularly patient. I could not but fancy they were making up lee-way with their consciences, and that they would scarce have been so good with me if they had not been worse with Ransome.

As for Mr Shuan, the drink, or his crime, or the two together, had certainly troubled his mind. I cannot say I ever saw him in his proper wits. He never grew used to my being there, stared at me continually (sometimes, I could have thought, with terror) and more than once drew back from my hand when I was serving him. I was pretty sure from the first that he had no clear mind of what he had done, and on my second day in the round-house I had the proof of it. We were alone, and he had been staring at me a long time, when, all at once, up he got, as pale as death, and came close up to me, to my great terror. But I had no cause to be afraid of him.

'You were not here before?' he asked.

'No, sir,' said I.

'There was another boy?' he asked again; and when I had answered him, 'Ah!' says he, 'I thought that,' and went and sat down, without another word, except to call for brandy.

You may think it strange, but for all the horror I had, I was still sorry for him. He was a married man, with a wife in Leith; but whether or no he had a family, I have now forgotten; I hope not.

Altogether it was no very hard life for the time it lasted,

which (as you are to hear) was not long. I was as well fed as the best of them; even their pickles, which were the great dainty, I was allowed my share of; and had I liked, I might have been drunk from morning to night, like Mr Shuan. I had company, too, and good company of its sort. Mr Riach, who had been to the college, spoke to me like a friend when he was not sulking, and told me many curious things, and some that were informing; and even the captain, though he kept me at the stick's end the most part of the time, would sometimes unbuckle a bit, and tell me of the fine countries he had visited.

The shadow of poor Ransome, to be sure, lay on all four of us, and on me and Mr Shuan, in particular, most heavily. And then I had another trouble of my own. Here I was, doing dirty work for three men that I looked down upon, and one of whom, at least, should have hung upon a gallows; that was for the present; and as for the future, I could only see myself slaving alongside of negroes in the tobacco fields. Mr Riach, perhaps from caution, would never suffer me to say another word about my story; the captain, whom I tried to approach, rebuffed me like a dog and would not hear a word; and as the days came and went, my heart sank lower and lower, till I was even glad of the work which kept me from thinking.

MORE THAN A WEEK went by, in which the ill-luck
that had hitherto pursued the *Covenant* upon this voyage
grew yet more strongly marked. Some days she made a little
way; others, she was driven actually back. At last we were
beaten so far to the south that we tossed and tacked to and
fro the whole of the ninth day, within sight of Cape Wrath
and the wild, rocky coast on either hand of it. There followed
on that a council of the officers, and some decision which I
did not rightly understand, seeing only the result: that we
had made a fair wind of a foul one and were running south.

The tenth afternoon, there was a falling swell and a thick,
wet, white fog that hid one end of the brig from the other.
All afternoon, when I went on deck, I saw men and officers
listening hard over the bulwarks—'for breakers', they
said; and though I did not so much as understand the
word, I felt danger in the air, and was excited.

May-be about ten at night, I was serving Mr Riach and
the captain at their supper, when the ship struck something
with a great sound, and we heard voices singing out. My
two masters leaped to their feet.

'She's struck,' said Mr Riach.

'No, sir,' said the captain. 'We've only run a boat down.'
And they hurried out.

The captain was in the right of it. We had run down
a boat in the fog, and she had parted in the midst and
gone to the bottom with all her crew, but one. This man
(as I heard afterwards) had been sitting in the stern as a
passenger, while the rest were on the benches rowing. At
the moment of the blow, the stern had been thrown into
the air, and the man (having his hands free, and for all
he was encumbered with a frieze overcoat that came below
his knees) had leaped up and caught hold of the brig's
bowsprit. It showed he had luck and much agility and

unusual strength, that he should have thus saved himself
from such a pass. And yet, when the captain brought him
into the round-house, and I set eyes on him for the first
time, he looked as cool as I did.

He was smallish in stature, but well set and as nimble
as a goat; his face was of a good open expression, but
sunburnt very dark, and heavily freckled and pitted with
the small-pox; his eyes were unusually light and had a kind
of dancing madness in them, that was both engaging and
alarming; and when he took off his great-coat, he laid a pair
of fine, silver-mounted pistols on the table, and I saw that he
was belted with a great sword. His manners, besides, were
elegant, and he pledged the captain handsomely. Altogether
I thought of him, at the first sight, that here was a man I
would rather call my friend than my enemy.

The captain, too, was taking his observations, but rather
of the man's clothes than his person. And to be sure, as soon
as he had taken off the great-coat, he showed forth mighty
fine for the round-house of a merchant brig: having a hat
with feathers, a red waistcoat, breeches of black plush, and
a blue coat with silver buttons and handsome silver lace:
costly clothes, though somewhat spoiled with the fog and
being slept in.

'I'm vexed, sir, about the boat,' says the captain.

'There are some pretty men gone to the bottom,' said the
stranger, 'that I would rather see on the dry land again than
half a score of boats.'

'Friends of yours?' said Hoseason.

'You have none such friends in your country,' was the
reply. 'They would have have died for me like dogs.'

'Well, sir,' said the captain, still watching him, 'there are
more men in the world than boats to put them in.'

'And that's true too,' cried the other, 'and ye seem to be
a gentleman of great penetration.'

'I have been in France, sir,' says the captain, so that it
was plain he meant more by the words than showed upon
the face of them.

'Well, sir,' says the other, 'and so has many a pretty man,
for the matter of that.'

'No doubt, sir,' says the captain; 'and fine coats.'

'Oho!' says the stranger, 'is that how the wind sets?'
And he laid his hand quickly on his pistols.

'Don't be hasty,' said the captain. 'Don't do a mischief, before ye see the need for it. Ye've a French soldier's coat upon your back and a Scotch tongue in your head, to be sure; but so has many an honest fellow in these days, and I dare say none the worse of it.'

'So?' said the gentleman in the fine coat: 'are ye of the honest party?' (meaning, Was he a Jacobite? for each side, in these sort of civil broils, takes the name of honesty for its own).

'Why, sir,' replied the captain, 'I am a true-blue Protestant, and I thank God for it.' (It was the first word of any religion I had ever heard from him, but I learnt afterwards he was a great church-goer while on shore.) 'But, for all that,' says he, 'I can be sorry to see another man with his back to the wall.'

'Can ye so, indeed?' asks the Jacobite. 'Well, sir, to be quite plain with ye, I am one of those honest gentleman that were in trouble about the years forty-five and six; and (to be still quite plain with ye) if I got into the hands of any of the red-coated gentry, it's like it would go hard with me. Now, sir, I was for France; and there was a French ship cruising here to pick me up; but she gave us the go-by in the fog—as I wish from the heart that ye had done yoursel'! And the best that I can say is this: If ye can set me ashore where I was going, I have that upon me will reward you highly for your trouble.'

'In France?' says the captain. 'No, sir; that I cannot do. But where ye come from—we might talk of that.'

And then, unhappily, he observed me standing in my corner, and packed me off to the galley to get supper for the gentleman. I lost no time, I promise you; and when I came back into the round-house, I found the gentleman had taken a money-belt from about his waist, and poured out a guinea or two upon the table. The captain was looking at the guineas, and then at the belt, and then at the gentleman's face; and I thought he seemed excited.

'Half of it,' he cried, 'and I'm your man!'

The other swept back the guineas into the belt, and put it on again under his waistcoat. 'I have told ye, sir,' said he, 'that not one doit of it belongs to me. It belongs to my chieftain'—and here he touched his hat—'and while I would be but a silly messenger to grudge some of it that the rest might come safe, I should show myself a hound indeed if I bought my own carcase any too dear. Thirty guineas on the sea-side, or sixty if ye set me on the Linnhe loch. Take it, if ye will; if not, ye can do your worst.'

'Ay,' said Hoseason. 'And if I give ye over to the soldiers?'

'Ye would make a fool's bargain,' said the other. 'My chief, let me tell you, sir, is forfeited, like every honest man in Scotland. His estate is in the hands of the man they call King George; and it is his officers that collect the rents, or try to collect them. But for the honour of Scotland, the poor tenant bodies take a thought upon their chief lying in exile; and this money is a part of that very rent for which King George is looking. Now, sir, ye seem to me to be a man that understands things: bring this money within the reach of Government, and how much of it'll come to you?'

'Little enough, to be sure,' said Hoseason; and then, 'If they knew,' he added, dryly. 'But I think, if I was to try, that I could hold my tongue about it.'

'Ah, but I'll begowk ye there!' cried the gentleman. 'Play me false, and I'll play you cunning. If a hand's laid upon me, they shall ken what money it is.'

'Well,' returned the captain, 'what must be must. Sixty guineas, and done. Here's my hand upon it.'

'And here's mine,' said the other.

And thereupon the captain went out (rather hurriedly, I thought), and left me alone in the round-house with the stranger.

At that period (so soon after the forty-five) there were many exiled gentlemen coming back at the peril of their lives, either to see their friends or to collect a little money; and as for the Highland chiefs that had been forfeited, it was a common matter of talk how their tenants would stint themselves to send them money, and their clansmen outface the soldiery to get it in, and run the gauntlet of our great navy to carry it across. All this I had, of course, heard tell of; and now I had a man under my eyes whose life was forfeit on all these counts and upon one more; for he was not only a rebel and a smuggler of rents, but had taken service with King Louis of France. And as if all this were not enough, he had a belt full of golden guineas round his loins. Whatever my opinions, I could not look on such a man without a lively interest.

'And so you're a Jacobite?' said I, as I set meat before him.

'Ay,' said he, beginning to eat. 'And you, by your long face, should be a Whig?'

'Betwixt and between,' said I, not to annoy him; for indeed I was as good a Whig as Mr Campbell could make me.

'And that's naething,' said he. 'But I'm saying, Mr Betwixt-and-Between,' he added, 'this bottle of yours is dry; and it's hard if I'm to pay sixty guineas and be grudged a dram upon the back of it.'

'I'll go and ask for the key,' said I, and stepped on deck.

The fog was as close as ever, but the swell almost down. They had laid the brig to, not knowing precisely where they were, and the wind (what little there was of it) not serving well for their true course. Some of the hands were still hearkening for breakers; but the captain and the two officers were in the waist with their heads together. It struck me, I don't know why, that they were after no good; and the first word I heard, as I drew softly near, more than confirmed me.

It was Mr Riach, crying out as if upon a sudden thought:

'Couldn't we wile him out of the round-house?'

'He's better where he is,' returned Hoseason; 'he hasn't room to use his sword.'

'Well, that's true,' said Riach; 'but he's hard to come at.'

'Hut!' said Hoseason. 'We can get the man in talk, one upon each side, and pin him by the two arms; or if that'll not hold, sir, we can make a run by both the doors and get him under hand before he has the time to draw.'

At this hearing, I was seized with both fear and anger at these treacherous, greedy, bloody men that I sailed with. My first mind was to run away; my second was bolder.

'Captain,' said I, 'the gentleman is seeking a dram, and the bottle's out. Will you give me the key?'

They all started and turned about.

'Why, here's our chance to get the firearms!' Riach cried; and then to me: 'Hark ye, David,' he said, 'do ye ken where the pistols are?'

'Ay, ay,' put in Hoseason. 'David kens; David's a good lad. Ye see, David my man, yon wild Hielandman is a danger to the ship, besides being a rank foe to King George, God bless him!'

I had never been so be-Davided since I came on board; but I said yes, as if all I heard were quite natural.

'The trouble is,' resumed the captain, 'that all our fire-locks, great and little, are in the round-house under this man's nose; likewise the powder. Now, if I, or one of the officers, was to go in and take them, he would fall to thinking. But a lad like you, David, might snap up a horn and a pistol or two without remark. And if ye can do it cleverly, I'll bear it in mind when it'll be good for you to have friends; and that's when we come to Carolina.'

Here Mr Riach whispered him a little.

'Very right, sir,' said the captain; and then to myself: 'And see here, David, yon man has a beltful of gold, and I give you my word that you shall have your fingers in it.'

I told him I would do as he wished, though indeed I had scarce breath to speak with; and upon that he gave me the key of the spirit locker, and I began to go slowly back to the round-house. What was I to do? They were dogs and thieves; they had stolen me from my own country; they had killed poor Ransome; and was I to hold the candle to another murder? But then, upon the other hand, there was the fear of death very plain before me; for what could a boy and a man, if they were as brave as lions, against a whole ship's company?

I was still arguing it back and forth, and getting no great clearness, when I came into the round-house and saw the Jacobite eating his supper under the lamp; and at that my mind was made up all in a moment. I have no credit by it; it was by no choice of mine, but as if by compulsion, that I walked right up to the table and put my hand on his shoulder.

'Do ye want to be killed?' said I.

He sprang to his feet, and looked a question at me as clear as if he had spoken.

'Oh!' cried I, 'they're all murderers here; it's a ship full of them! They've murdered a boy already. Now it's you.'

'Ay, ay,' said he; 'but they haven't got me yet.' And then looking at me curiously, 'Will ye stand with me?'

'That will I!' said I. 'I am no thief, nor yet murderer. I'll stand by you.'

'Why, then,' said he, 'what's your name?'

'David Balfour,' said I; and then thinking that a man with so fine a coat must like fine people, I added for the first time 'of Shaws.'

It never occurred to him to doubt me, for a Highlander is used to see great gentlefolk in great poverty; but as he had no estate of his own, my words nettled a very childish vanity he had.

'My name is Stewart,' he said, drawing himself up. 'Alan Breck, they call me. A king's name is good enough for me, though I bear it plain and have the name of no farm-midden to clap to the hind-end of it.'

And having administered this rebuke, as though it were something of a chief importance, he turned to examine our defences.

The round-house was built very strong, to support the breaching of the seas. Of its five apertures, only the skylight and the two doors were large enough for the passage of a man. The doors, besides, could be drawn close: they were of stout oak, and ran in grooves, and were fitted with hooks to keep them either shut or open, as the need arose. The one that was already shut, I secured in this fashion; but when I was proceeding to slide to the other, Alan stopped me.

'David,' said he—'for I cannae bring to mind the name of your landed estate, and so will make so bold as call you David—that door, being open, is the best part of my defences.'

'It would be yet better shut,' says I.

'Not so, David,' says he. 'Ye see, I have but one face; but so long as that door is open and my face to it, the best part of my enemies will be in front of me, where I would aye wish to find them.'

Then he gave me from the rack a cutlass (of which there were a few besides the firearms), choosing it with great care, shaking his head and saying he had never in all his life seen poorer weapons; and next he set me down to the table with a powder-horn, a bag of bullets, and all the pistols, which he bade me charge.

'And that will be better work, let me tell you,' said he, 'for a gentleman of decent birth, than scraping plates and raxing drams to a wheen tarry sailors.'

Thereupon he stood up in the midst with his face to the

door, and drawing his great sword, made trial of the room he had to wield it in.

'I must stick to the point,' he said, shaking his head; 'and that's a pity, too. It doesn't set my genius, which is all for the upper guard. And now,' said he, 'do you keep on charging the pistols, and give heed to me.'

I told him I would listen closely. My chest was tight, my mouth dry, the light dark to my eyes; the thought of the numbers that were soon to leap in upon us kept my heart in a flutter; and the sea, which I heard washing round the brig, and where I thought my dead body would be cast ere morning, ran in my mind strangely.

'First of all,' said he, 'how many are against us?'

I reckoned them up; and such was the hurry of my mind, I had to cast the numbers twice. 'Fifteen,' said I.

Alan whistled. 'Well,' said he, 'that can't be cured. And now follow me. It is my part to keep this door, where I look for the main battle. In that, ye have no hand. And mind and dinnae fire to this side unless they get me down; for I would rather have ten foes in front of me than one friend like you cracking pistols at my back.'

I told him, indeed I was no great shot.

'And that's very bravely said,' he cried, in a great admiration of my candour. 'There's many a pretty gentleman that wouldnae dare to say it.'

'But then, sir,' said I, 'there is the door behind you, which they may perhaps break in.'

'Ay,' said he, 'and that is a part of your work. No sooner the pistols charged, than ye must climb up into yon bed where ye're handy at the window; and if they lift hand against the door, ye're to shoot. But that's not all. Let's make a bit of a soldier of ye, David. What else have ye to guard?'

'There's the skylight,' said I. 'But indeed, Mr Stewart, I would need to have eyes upon both sides to keep the two of them, for when my face is at the one, my back is to the other.'

'And that's very true,' said Alan. 'But have ye no ears to your head?'

'To be sure!' cried I. 'I must hear the bursting of the glass!'

'Ye have some rudiments of sense,' said Alan, grimly.

BUT NOW OUR TIME of truce was come to an end. Those on deck had waited for my coming till they grew impatient; and scarce had Alan spoken, when the captain showed face in the open door.

'Stand!' cried Alan, and pointed his sword at him.

The captain stood, indeed; but he neither winced nor drew back a foot.

'A naked sword?' says he. 'This is a strange return for hospitality.'

'Do ye see me?' said Alan. 'I am come of kings; I bear a king's name. My badge is the oak. Do ye see my sword? It has slashed the heads off mair Whigamores than you have toes upon your feet. Call up your vermin to your back, sir, and fall on! The sooner the clash begins, the sooner ye'll taste this steel throughout your vitals.'

The captain said nothing to Alan, but he looked over at me with an ugly look. 'David,' said he, 'I'll mind this'; and the sound of his voice went through me with a jar.

Next moment he was gone.

'And now,' said Alan, 'let your hand keep your head, for the grip is coming.'

Alan drew a dirk, which he held in his left hand in case they should run in under his sword. I, on my part, clambered up into the berth with an armful of pistols and something of a heavy heart, and set open the window where I was to watch. It was a small part of the deck that I could overlook, but enough for our purpose. The sea had gone down, and the wind was steady and kept the sails quiet; so that there was a great stillness in the ship, in which I made sure I heard the sound of muttering voices. A little after, and there came a clash of steel upon the deck, by which I knew they were dealing out the cutlasses and one had been let fall; and after that, silence again.

I do not know if I was what you call afraid; but my heart beat like a bird's, both quick and little; and there was a dimness came before my eyes which I continually rubbed away, and which continually returned. As for hope, I had none; but only a darkness of despair and a sort of anger against all the world that made me long to sell my life as dear as I was able. I tried to pray, I remember, but that same hurry of my mind, like a man running, would not suffer me to think upon the words; and my chief wish was to have the thing begin and be done with it.

It came all of a sudden when it did, with a rush of feet and a roar, and then a shout from Alan, and a sound of blows and some one crying out as if hurt. I looked back over my shoulder, and saw Mr Shuan in the doorway, crossing blades with Alan.

'That's him that killed the boy!' I cried.

'Look to your window!' said Alan; and as I turned back to my place, I saw him pass his sword through the mate's body.

It was none too soon for me to look to my own part; for my head was scarce back at the window, before five men carrying a spare yard for a battering-ram, ran past me and took post to drive the door in. I had never fired with a pistol in my life, and not often with a gun; far less against a fellow-creature. But it was now or never; and just as they swang the yard, I cried out, 'Take that!' and shot into their midst.

I must have hit one of them, for he sang out and gave back a step, and the rest stopped as if a little disconcerted. Before they had time to recover, I sent another ball over their heads; and at my third shot (which went as wide as the second) the whole party threw down the yard and ran for it.

Then I looked round again into the deck-house. The whole place was full of the smoke of my own firing, just as my ears seemed to be burst with the noise of the shots. But there was Alan, standing as before; only now his sword was running blood to the hilt, and himself so swelled with triumph and fallen into so fine an attitude, that he looked to be invincible. Right before him on the floor was Mr Shuan, on his hands and knees; the blood was pouring from his mouth, and he was sinking slowly lower, with a terrible, white face; and just as I looked, some of those from behind caught hold of him by the heels and dragged him bodily out of the round-house. I believe he died as they were doing it.

'There's one of your Whigs for ye!' cried Alan; and then turning to me, he asked if I had done much execution.

I told him I had winged one, and thought it was the captain.

'And I've settled two,' says he. 'No, there's not enough blood let; they'll be back again. To your watch, David. This was but a dram before meat.'

I settled back to my place, re-charging the three pistols I had fired, and keeping watch with both eye and ear.

Our enemies were disputing not far off upon the deck, and that so loudly that I could hear a word or two above the washing of the seas.

'It was Shuan bauchled it,' I heard one say.

And another answered him with a 'Wheesht, man! He's paid the piper.'

After that the voices fell again into the same muttering as before. Only now, one person spoke most of the time, as though laying down a plan, and first one and then another answered him briefly, like men taking orders. By this, I made sure they were coming on again, and told Alan.

'It's what we have to pray for,' said he. 'Unless we can give them a good distaste of us, and done with it, there'll be nae sleep for either you or me. But this time, mind, they'll be in earnest.'

By this, my pistols were ready, and there was nothing to do but listen and wait. While the brush lasted, I had not the time to think if I was frighted; but now, when all was still again, my mind ran upon nothing else. The thought of the sharp swords and the cold steel was strong in me; and presently, when I began to hear stealthy steps and a brushing of men's clothes against the round-house wall, and knew they were taking their places in the dark, I could have found it in my mind to cry out aloud.

All this was upon Alan's side; and I had begun to think my share of the fight was at an end, when I heard some one drop softly on the roof above me.

Then there came a single call on the sea-pipe, and that was the signal. A knot of them made one rush of it, cutlass in hand, against the door; and at the same moment, the glass of the skylight was dashed in a thousand pieces, and a man leaped through and landed on the floor. Before he got his feet, I had clapped a pistol to his back, and might have shot him, too; only at the touch of him (and him alive) my whole flesh misgave me, and I could no more pull the trigger than I could have flown.

He had dropped his cutlass as he jumped, and when he felt the pistol, whipped straight round and laid hold of me, roaring out an oath; and at that either my courage came again, or I grew so much afraid as came to the same thing; for I gave a shriek and shot him in the midst of the body. He gave the most horrible, ugly groan and fell to the floor. The foot of a second fellow, whose legs were dangling through the skylight, struck me at the same time upon the head; and at that I snatched another pistol and shot this one through the thigh, so that he slipped through and tumbled in a lump on his companion's body. There was no talk of missing, any more than there was time to aim; I clapped the muzzle to the very place and fired.

I might have stood and stared at them for long, but I heard Alan shout as if for help, and that brought me to my senses.

He had kept the door so long; but one of the seamen, while he was engaged with others, had run in under his guard and caught him about the body. Alan was dirking him with his left hand, but the fellow clung like a leech. Another had broken in and had his cutlass raised. The door was thronged with their faces. I thought we were lost, and catching up my cutlass, fell on them in flank.

But I had not time to be of help. The wrestler dropped at last; and Alan, leaping back to get his distance, ran upon the others like a bull, roaring as he went. They broke before him like water, turning, and running, and falling one against another in their haste. The sword in his hands flashed like quicksilver into the huddle of our fleeing enemies; and at every flash there came the scream of a man hurt. I was still thinking we were lost, when lo! they were all gone, and Alan was driving them along the deck as a sheepdog chases sheep.

Yet he was no sooner out than he was back again, being as cautious as he was brave; and meanwhile the seamen continued running and crying out as if he was still behind them; and we heard them tumble one upon another into the forecastle, and clap-to the hatch upon the top.

The round-house was like a shambles; three were dead inside, another lay in his death agony across the threshold; and there were Alan and I victorious and unhurt.

He came up to me with open arms. 'Come to my arms!' he cried, and embraced and kissed me hard upon both cheeks. 'David,' said he, 'I love you like a brother. And oh, man,' he cried in a kind of ecstasy, 'am I no a bonny fighter?'

Thereupon he turned to the four enemies, passed his sword clean through each of them, and tumbled them out of doors one after the other. As he did so, he kept humming and singing and whistling to himself, like a man trying to recall an air; only what *he* was trying, was to make one. All the while, the flush was in his face, and his eyes were as bright as a five-year-old child's with a new toy. And presently he sat down upon the table, sword in hand; the air that he was making all the time began to run a little clearer, and then clearer still; and then out he burst with a great voice into a Gaelic song.

I have translated it here, not in verse (of which I have no skill) but at least in the king's English. He sang it often afterwards, and the thing became popular; so that I have heard it, and had it explained to me, many's the time.

This is the song of the sword of Alan:
The smith made it,
The fire set it;
Now it shines in the hand of Alan Breck.

Their eyes were many and bright,
Swift were they to behold,
Many the hands they guided:
The sword was alone.

The dun deer troop over the hill,
They are many, the hill is one;
The dun deer vanish,
The hill remains.

Come to me from the hills of heather,
Come from the isles of the sea.
O far-beholding eagles,
Here is your meat.

Now this song which he made (both words and music)

in the hour of our victory, is something less than just to me, who stood beside him in the tussle. Mr Shuan and five more were either killed outright or thoroughly disabled; but of these, two fell by my hand, the two that came by the skylight. Four more were hurt, and of that number, one (and he not the least important) got his hurt from me. So that, altogether, I did my fair share both of the killing and the wounding, and might have claimed a place in Alan's verses. But poets (as a very wise man once told me) have to think upon their rhymes; and in good prose talk, Alan always did me more than justice.

In the meanwhile, I was innocent of any wrong being done me. For not only I knew no word of the Gaelic; but what with the long suspense of the waiting, and the scurry and strain of our two spirits of fighting, and, more than all, the horror I had of some of my own share in it, the thing was no sooner over than I was glad to stagger to a seat. There was that tightness on my chest that I could hardly breathe; the thought of the two men I had shot sat upon me like a nightmare; and all upon a sudden, and before I had a guess of what was coming, I began to sob and cry like any child.

Alan clapped my shoulder, and said I was a brave lad and wanted nothing but a sleep.

'I'll take the first watch,' said he. 'Ye've done well by me, David, first and last; and I wouldn't lose you for all Appin—no, nor for Breadalbane.'

So he made up my bed on the floor, and took the first spell, pistol in hand and sword on knee; three hours by the captain's watch upon the wall. Then he roused me up, and I took my turn of three hours; before the end of which it was broad day, and a very quiet morning, with a smooth, rolling sea that tossed the ship and made the blood run to and fro on the round-house floor, and a heavy rain that drummed upon the roof. All my watch there was nothing stirring; and by the banging of the helm, I knew they had even no one at the tiller. Indeed (as I learned afterwards) they were so many of them hurt or dead, and the rest in so ill a temper, that Mr Riach and the captain had to take turn and turn like Alan and me, or the brig might have gone ashore and nobody the wiser. It was a mercy the night had fallen so still, for the wind had gone down as soon as the rain began. Even as it was, I judged by the wailing of a great number of gulls that went crying and fishing round the ship, that she must have drifted pretty near the coast or one of the islands of the Hebrides; and at last, looking out of the door of the round-house, I saw the great stone hills of Skye on the right hand, and, a little more astern, the strange isle of Rum.

ALAN AND I SAT down to breakfast about six of the clock. The floor was covered with broken glass and in a horrid mess of blood, which took away my hunger. In all other ways we were in a situation not only agreeable but merry; having ousted the officers from their own cabin, and having at command all the drink in the ship—both wine and spirits—and all the dainty part of what was eatable, such as the pickles and the fine sort of biscuit. This, of itself, was enough to set us in good humour; but the richest part of it was this, that the two thirstiest men that ever came out of Scotland (Mr Shuan being dead) were now shut in the fore-part of the ship and condemned to what they hated most—cold water.

'And depend upon it,' Alan said, 'we shall hear more of them ere long. Ye may keep a man from the fighting but never from his bottle.'

We made good company for each other. Alan, indeed, expressed himself most lovingly; and taking a knife from the table, cut me off one of the silver buttons from his coat.

'I had them,' says he, 'from my father, Duncan Stewart; and now give ye one of them to be a keep-sake for last night's work. And wherever ye go and show that button, the friends of Alan Breck will come around you.'

He said this as if he had been Charlemagne, and commanded armies; and indeed, much as I admired his courage, I was always in danger of smiling at his vanity: in danger, I say, for had I not kept my countenance, I would be afraid to think what a quarrel might have followed.

As soon as we were through with our meal, he rummaged in the captain's locker till he found a clothes-brush; and then taking off his coat, began to visit his suit and brush away the stains, with such care and labour as I supposed to have been only usual with women. To be sure, he had

64

no other; and besides (as he said) it belonged to a King and so behoved to be royally looked after.

For all that, when I saw what care he took to pluck out the threads where the button had been cut away, I put a higher value on his gift.

He was still so engaged, when we were hailed by Mr Riach from the deck, asking for a parley; and I, climbing through the skylight and sitting on the edge of it, pistol in hand and with a bold front, though inwardly in fear of broken glass, hailed him back again and bade him speak out. He came to the edge of the round-house, and stood on a coil of rope, so that his chin was on a level with the roof; and we looked at each other a while in silence. Mr Riach, as I do not think he had been very forward in the battle, so he had got off with nothing worse than a blow upon the cheek: but he looked out of heart and very weary, having been all night afoot, either standing watch or doctoring the wounded.

'This is a bad job,' said he at last, shaking his head.

'It was none of our choosing,' said I.

'The captain,' says he, 'would like to speak with your friend. They might speak at the window.'

'And how do we know what treachery he means?' cried I.

'He means none, David,' returned Mr Riach; 'and if he did, I'll tell ye the honest truth, we couldnae get the men to follow.'

'Is that so?' said I.

'I'll tell ye more than that,' said he. 'It's not only the men; it's me. I'm frich'ened, Davie,' And he smiled across at me. 'No,' he continued, 'what we want is to be shut of him.'

Thereupon I consulted with Alan, and the parley was agreed to and parole given upon either side; but this was not the whole of Mr Riach's business, and he now begged me for a dram with such instancy and such reminders of his former kindness, that at last I handed him a pannikin with about a gill of brandy. He drank a part, and then carried the rest down upon the deck, to share it (I suppose) with his superior.

A little after, the captain came (as was agreed) to one of the windows, and stood there in the rain, with his arm in a sling, and looking stern and pale, and so old that my heart smote me for having fired upon him.

Alan at once held a pistol in his face.

'Put that thing up!' said the captain. 'Have I not passed my word, sir? or do ye seek to affront me?'

'Captain,' says Alan, 'I doubt your word is a breakable. Last night ye haggled and argle-bargled like an apple-wife; and then passed me your word, and gave me your hand to back it; and ye ken very well what was the upshot. Be damned to your word!' says he.

'Well, well, sir,' said the captain, 'ye'll get little good by swearing.' (And truly that was a fault of which the captain was quite free.) 'But we have other things to speak,' he continued, bitterly. 'Ye've made a sore hash of my brig; I haven't hands enough left to work her; and my first officer (whom I could ill spare) has got your sword throughout his vitals, and passed without speech. There is nothing left me, sir, but to put back into the port of Glasgow after hands; and there (by your leave) ye will find them that are better able to talk to you.'

'Ay?' said Alan; 'and faith, I'll have a talk with them mysel'! Unless there's naebody speaks English in that town, I have a bonny tale for them. Fifteen tarry sailors upon the one side, and a man and a halfling boy upon the other! Oh, man, it's peetiful!'

Hoseason flushed red.

'No,' continued Alan, 'that'll no do. Ye'll just have to set me ashore as we agreed.'

'Ay,' said Hoseason, 'but my first officer is dead—ye ken best how. There's none of the rest of us acquaint with this coast, sir; and it's one very dangerous to ships.'

'I give ye your choice,' says Alan. 'Set me on dry ground in Appin, or Ardgour, or in Morven, or Arisaig, or Morar; or, in brief where ye please, within thirty miles of my own country; except in a country of the Campbells'. That's a broad target. If ye miss that, ye must be as feckless at the sailoring as I have found ye at the fighting. Why, my poor country people in their bit cobles pass from island to island in all weathers, ay, and by night too, for the matter of that.'

'A coble's not a ship, sir,' said the captain. 'It has nae draught of water.'

'Well, then, to Glasgow if ye list!' says Alan. 'We'll have the laugh of ye at the least.'

'My mind runs little upon laughing,' said the captain. 'But all this will cost money, sir.'

'Well, sir,' says Alan, 'I am nae weathercock. Thirty guineas, if ye land me on the sea-side; and sixty, if ye put me in the Linnhe Loch.'

'But see, sir, where we lie, we are but a few hours' sail from Ardnamurchan,' said Hoseason. 'Give me sixty, and I'll set ye there.'

'And I'm to wear my brogues and run jeopardy of the redcoats to please you?' cries Alan. 'No, sir, if ye want sixty guineas, earn them, and set me in my own country.'

'It's to risk the brig, sir,' said the captain, 'and your own lives along with her.'

'Take it or want it,' says Alan.

'Could ye pilot us at all?' asked the captain, who was frowning to himself.

'Well, it's doubtful,' said Alan. 'I'm more of a fighting man (as ye have seen for yoursel') than a sailor-man. But I have been often enough picked up and set down upon this coast, and should ken something of the lie of it.'

The captain shook his head, still frowning.

'If I had lost less money on this unchancy cruise,' says he, 'I would see you in a rope's-end before I risked my brig, sir. But be it as ye will. As soon as I get a slant of wind (and there's some coming, or I'm the more mistaken) I'll put it in hand. But there's one thing more. We may meet in with a king's ship and she may lay us aboard, sir, with no blame of mine: they keep the cruisers thick upon this coast, ye ken who for. Now, sir, if that was to befall, ye might leave the money.'

'Captain,' says Alan, 'if ye see a pennant, it shall be your part to run away. And now, as I hear you're a little short of brandy in the forepart, I'll offer ye a change: a bottle of brandy against two buckets of water.'

That was the last clause of the treaty, and was duly executed on both sides; so that Alan and I could at last wash out the round-house and be quit of the memorials of those whom we had slain, and the captain and Mr Riach could be happy again in their own way, the name of which was drink.

BEFORE WE HAD done cleaning out the round-house, a breeze sprang up from a little to the east of north. This blew off the rain and brought out the sun.

And here I must explain; and the reader would do well to look at a map. On the day when the fog fell and we ran down Alan's boat, we had been running through the Little Minch. At dawn after the battle, we lay becalmed to the east of the Isle of Canna or between that and Isle Eriska in the chain of the Long Island. Now to get from there to the Linnhe Loch, the straight course was through the narrows of the Sound of Mull. But the captain had no chart; he was afraid to trust his brig so deep among the islands; and the wind serving well, he preferred to go by west of Tiree and come up under the southern coast of the great Isle of Mull.

All day the breeze held in the same point, and rather freshened than died down; and towards afternoon, a swell began to set in from round the outer Hebrides. Our course, to go round about the inner isles, was to the west of south, so that at first we had this swell upon our beam, and were much rolled about. But after nightfall, when we had turned the end of Tiree and began to head more to the east, the sea came right astern.

Meanwhile, the early part of the day, before the swell came up, was very pleasant; sailing, as we were, in a bright sunshine and with many mountainous islands upon different sides. Alan and I sat in the round-house with the doors open on each side (the wind being straight astern) and smoked a pipe or two of the captain's fine tobacco. It was at this time we heard each other's stories, which was the more important to me, as I gained some knowledge of that wild Highland country, on which I was so soon to land. In those days, so close on the back of the great rebellion, it was needful a man should know what he was doing when he went upon the heather.

It was I that showed the example, telling him all my misfortune; which he heard with great good nature. Only, when I came to mention that good friend of mine, Mr Campbell the minister, Alan fired up and cried out that he hated all that were of that name.

'Why,' said I, 'he is a man you should be proud to give your hand to.'

'I know nothing I would help a Campbell to,' says he, 'unless it was a leaden bullet. I would hunt all of that name like blackcocks. If I lay dying, I would crawl upon my knees to my chamber window for a shot at one.'

'Why, Alan,' I cried, 'what ails ye at the Campbells?'

'Well,' says he, 'ye ken very well that I am an Appin Stewart, and the Campbells have long harried and wasted those of my name; ay, and got lands of us by treach-ery—but never with the sword,' he cried loudly, and with the word brought down his fist upon the table. But I paid the less attention to this; for I knew it was usually said by those who have the underhand. 'There's more than that,' he continued, 'and all in the same story: lying words, lying papers, tricks fit for a peddler, and the show of what's legal over all, to make a man the more angry.'

'You that are so wasteful of your buttons,' said I, 'I can hardly think you would be a good judge of business.'

'Ah!' says he, falling again to smiling, 'I got my wastefulness from the same man I got the buttons from; and that was my poor father, Duncan Stewart, grace be to him! He was the prettiest man of his kindred; and the best swordsman in the Hielands, David, and that is the same as to say, in all the world. I should ken, for it was him that taught me. He was in the Black Watch, when first it was mustered; and like other gentleman privates, had a gillie at his back to carry his firelock for him on the march. Well, the king, it appears, was wishful to see Hieland swordmanship; and my father and three more were chosen out and sent to London town, to let him see it at the best. So they were had into the palace and showed the whole art of the sword for two hours at a stretch, before King George and Queen Carline, and the Butcher Cumberland, and many more of whom I havenae mind. And when they were through, the King (for all he was a rank usurper) spoke them fair and gave each man three guineas in his hand. Now, as they were going out of the palace, they had a porter's lodge to go by; and it came in on my father, as he was perhaps the first private Hieland gentleman that had ever gone by that door, it was right he should give the poor porter a proper notion of their quality. So he gives the King's three guineas into the man's hand, as if it was his common custom; the three others that came behind him did the same; and there they were on the street, never a penny the better for their pains. Some say it was one, that was the first to fee the King's porter; and some say it was another; but the truth of it is, that it was Duncan Stewart, as I am willing to prove with either sword or pistol. And that was the father that I had, God rest him!'

'I think he was not the man to leave you rich,' said I.

'And that's true,' said Alan. 'He left me my breeks to cover me, and little besides. And that was how I came to enlist, which was a black spot upon my character at the best of times, and would still be a sore job for me if I fell among the redcoats.'

'What,' cried I, 'were you in the English army?'

'That was I,' said Alan. 'But I deserted to the right side at Preston Pans—and that's some comfort.'

I could scarcely share this view: holding desertion under arms for an unpardonable fault in honour. But for all I was so young, I was wiser than say my thought. 'Dear, dear,' says I, 'the punishment is death.'

'Ay,' said he, 'if they got hands on me, it would be a short shrift and a lang tow for Alan! But I have the King of France's commission in my pocket, which would aye be some protection.'

'I misdoubt it much,' said I.

'I have doubts mysel',' said Alan, drily.

'And, good heaven, man,' cried I, 'you that are a condemned rebel, and a deserter, and a man of the French King's—what tempts ye back into this country? It's a braving of Providence.'

'Tut,' says Alan, 'I have been back every year since forty-six!'

'And what brings ye, man?' cried I.

'Well, ye see, I weary for my friends and country,' said

he. 'France is a braw place, nae doubt; but I weary for the heather and the deer. And then I have bit things that I attend to. Whiles I pick up a few lads to serve the King of France: recruits, ye see; and that's aye a little money. But the heart of the matter is the business of my chief, Ardshiel.'

'I thought they called your chief Appin,' said I.

'Ay, but Ardshiel is the captain of the clan,' said he, which scarcely cleared my mind. 'Ye see, David, he that was all his life so great a man, and come of the blood and bearing the name of kings, is now brought down to live in a French town like a poor and private person. He that had four hundred swords at his whistle, I have seen, with these eyes of mine, buying butter in the market-place, and taking it home in a kale-leaf. This is not only a pain but a disgrace to us of his family and clan. There are the bairns forby, the children and the hope of Appin, that must be learned their letters and how to hold a sword, in that far country. Now, the tenants of Appin have to pay a rent to King George; but their hearts are staunch, they are true to their chief; and what with love and a bit of pressure, and maybe a threat or two, the poor folk scrape up a second rent for Ardshiel. Well, David, I'm the hand that carries it.' And he struck the belt about his body, so that the guineas rang.

'Do they pay both?' cried I.

'Ay, David, both,' says he.

'What? two rents?' I repeated.

'Ay, David,' said he. 'I told a different tale to yon captain man; but this is the truth of it. And it's wonderful to me how little pressure is needed. But that's the handiwork of my good kinsman and my father's friend, James of the Glens; James Stewart, that is: Ardshiel's half-brother. He it is that gets the money in, and does the management.'

This was the first time I heard the name of that James Stewart, who was afterwards so famous at the time of his hanging. But I took little heed at the moment, for all my mind was occupied with the generosity of these poor Highlanders.

'I call it noble,' I cried. 'I'm a Whig, or little better; but I call it noble.'

'Ay,' said he, 'ye're a Whig, but ye're a gentleman; and that's what does it. Now, if ye were one of the cursed race of Campbell, ye would gnash your teeth to hear tell of it.

If ye were the Red Fox. . . .' And at that name, his teeth
shut together, and he ceased speaking. I have seen many a
grim face, but never a grimmer than Alan's when he had
named the Red Fox.

'And who is the Red Fox?' I asked, daunted, but still
curious.

'Who is he?' cried Alan. 'Well, and I'll tell you that.
When the men of the clans were broken at Culloden, and
the good cause went down, and the horses rode over the
fetlocks in the best blood of the north, Ardshiel had to flee
like a poor deer upon the mountains—he and his lady
and his bairns. A sair job we had of it before we got him
shipped; and while he still lay in the heather, the English
rogues, that couldnae come at his life, were striking at his
rights. They stripped him of his powers; they stripped him
of his lands; they plucked the weapons from the hands of
his clansmen, that had borne arms for thirty centuries; ay,
and the very clothes off their backs—so that it's now a sin
to wear a tartan plaid, and a man may be cast into a gaol if
he has but a kilt about his legs. One thing they couldnae
kill. That was the love the clansmen bore their chief. These
guineas are the proof of it. And now, in there steps a man,
a Campbell, red-headed Colin of Glenure—'

'Is that him you call the Red Fox?' said I.

'Will ye bring me his brush?' cries Alan, fiercely. 'Ay,
that's the man. In he steps, and gets papers from King
George, to be so-called King's factor on the lands of Appin.
And at first he sings small, and is hail-fellow-well-met
with Sheamus—that's James of the Glens, my chieftain's
agent. But by-and-bye, that came to his ears that I have just
told you; how the poor commons of Appin, the farmers and
the crofters and the boumen, were wringing their very plaids
to get a second rent, and send it over-seas for Ardshiel and
his poor bairns. What was it ye called it, when I told ye?'

'I called it noble, Alan,' said I.

'And you little better than a common Whig!' cries Alan.
'But when it came to Colin Roy, the black Campbell blood
in him ran wild. He sat gnashing his teeth at the wine table.
What! should a Stewart get a bite of bread, and him not be
able to prevent it? Ah! Red Fox, if ever I hold you at a
gun's end, the Lord have pity upon ye!' (Alan stopped
to swallow down his anger.) 'Well, David, what does he

do? He declares all the farms to let. And thinks he, in his black heart, I'll soon get other tenants that'll overbid these Stewarts, and Maccolls, and Macrobs (for these are all names in my clan, David) "and then," thinks he, "Ardshiel will have to hold his bonnet on a French roadside."'

'Well,' said I, 'what followed?'

Alan laid down his pipe, which he had long since suffered to go out, and set his two hands upon his knees.

'Ay,' said he, 'ye'll never guess that! For these same Stewarts, and Maccolls, and Macrobs (that had two rents to pay, one to King George by stark force, and one to Ardshiel by natural kindness), offered him a better price than any Campbell in all broad Scotland; and far he sent seeking them—as far as to the sides of Clyde and the cross of Edinburgh—seeking, and fleeching, and begging them to come, where there was a Stewart to be starved and a red-headed hound of a Campbell to be pleasured!'

'Well, Alan,' said I, 'that is a strange story, and a fine one too. And Whig as I may be, I am glad the man was beaten.'

'Him beaten?' echoed Alan. 'It's little ye ken of Campbells and less of the Red Fox. Him beaten? No: nor will be, till his blood's on the hillside! But if the day comes, David man, that I can find time and leisure for a bit of hunting, there grows not enough heather in all Scotland to hide him from my vengeance!'

'Man Alan,' said I, 'ye are neither very wise nor very Christian to blow off so many words of anger. They will do the man ye call the Fox no harm, and yourself no good. Tell me your tale plainly out. What did he next?'

'And that's a good observe, David,' said Alan. 'Troth and indeed, they will do him no harm; the more's the pity! And barring that about Christianity (of which my opinion is quite otherwise, or I would be nae Christian) I am much of your mind.'

'Opinion here or opinion there,' said I, 'it's a kent thing that Christianity forbids revenge.'

'Ay,' said he, 'it's well seen it was a Campbell taught ye! It would be a convenient world for them and their sort, if there was no such a thing as a lad and a gun behind a heather bush! But that's nothing to the point. This is what he did.'

'Ay,' said I, 'come to that.'

'Well, David,' said he, 'since he couldnae be rid of the loyal commons by fair means, he swore he would be rid of them by foul. Ardshiel was to starve: that was the thing he aimed at. And since them that fed him in his exile wouldnae be bought out—right or wrong, he would drive them out. Therefore he sent for lawyers, and papers, and redcoats to stand at his back. And the kindly folk of that country must all pack and tramp, every father's son out of his father's house, and out of the place where he was bred and fed, and played when he was a callant. And who are to succeed them? Bare-leggit beggars! King George is to whistle for his rents; he maun dow with less; he can spread his butter thinner: what cares Red Colin? If he can hurt Ardshiel, he has his wish; if he can pluck the meat from my chieftain's table, and the bit toys out of his children's hands, he will gang hame singing to Glenure!'

'Let me have a word,' said I. 'Be sure, if they take less rents, be sure Government has a finger in the pie. It's not this Campbell's fault, man—it's his orders. And if ye killed this Colin to-morrow, what better would ye be? There would be another factor in his shoes, as fast as spur can drive.'

'Ye're a good lad in a fight,' said Alan; 'but man! ye have Whig blood in ye!'

He spoke kindly enough, but there was so much anger under his contempt that I thought it was wise to change the conversation. I expressed my wonder how, with the Highlands covered with troops and guarded like a city in a siege, a man in his situation could come and go without arrest.

'It's easier than ye would think,' said Alan. 'A bare hillside (ye see) is like all one road; if there's a sentry at one place, ye just go by another. And then heather's a great help. And everywhere there are friends' houses and friends' byres and haystacks. And besides, when folk talk of a country covered with troops, it's but a kind of a byword at the best. A soldier covers nae mair of it than his boot-soles. I have fished a water with a sentry on the other side of the brae, and killed a fine trout; and I have sat in a heather bush within six feet of another, and learned a real bonny tune from his whistling. This was it,' said he, and whistled me the air.

'And then, besides,' he continued, 'it's no sae bad now as it was in forty-six. The Hielands are what they call pacified. Small wonder, with a never a gun or a sword left from Cantyre to Cape Wrath, but what tenty folk have hidden in their thatch! But what I would like to ken, David, is just how long? Not long, ye would think, with men like Ardshiel in exile and men like the Red Fox sitting birling the wine and oppressing the poor at home. But it's a kittle thing to decide what folk'll bear, and what they will not. Or why would Red Colin be riding his horse all over my poor country of Appin, and never a pretty lad to put a bullet in him?'

And with this Alan fell into a muse, and for a long time sate very sad and silent.

I will add the rest of what I have to say about my friend, that he was skilled in all kinds of music, but principally pipe-music; was a well-considered poet in his own tongue; had read several books both in French and English; was a dead shot, a good angler, and an excellent fencer with the small sword as well as with his own particular weapon. For his faults, they were on his face, and I now knew them all. But the worst of them, his childish propensity to take offence and to pick quarrels, he greatly laid aside in my case, out of regard for the battle of the round-house. But whether it was because I had done well myself, or because I had been a witness of his own much greater prowess, is more than I can tell. For though he had a great taste for courage in other men, yet he admired it most in Alan Breck.

IT WAS ALREADY late at night, and as dark as it ever would be at that season of the year (and that is to say, it was still pretty bright), when Hoseason clapped his head into the round-house door.

'Here,' said he, 'come out and see if ye can pilot.'

'Is this one of your tricks?' asked Alan.

'Do I look like tricks?' cries the captain. 'I have other things to think of—my brig's in danger!'

By the concerned look of his face, and, above all, by the sharp tones in which he spoke of his brig, it was plain to both of us he was in deadly earnest; and so Alan and I, with no great fear of treachery, stepped on deck.

The sky was clear; it blew hard, and was bitter cold; a great deal of daylight lingered; and the moon, which was nearly full, shone brightly. The brig was close hauled, so as to round the south-west corner of the Island of Mull; the hills of which (and Ben More above them all, with a wisp of mist upon the top of it) lay full upon the larboard bow. Though it was no good point of sailing for the *Covenant*, she tore through the seas at a great rate, pitching and straining, and pursued by the westerly swell.

Altogether it was no such ill night to keep the seas in; and I had begun to wonder what it was that sat so heavily upon the captain, when the brig rising suddenly on the top of a high swell, he pointed and cried to us to look. Away on the lee bow, a thing like a fountain rose out of the moonlit sea, and immediately after we heard a low sound of roaring.

'What do ye call that?' asked the captain, gloomily.

'The sea breaking on a reef,' said Alan. 'And now ye ken where it is; and what better would ye have?'

'Ay,' said Hoseason, 'if it was the only one.'

And sure enough just as he spoke there came a second fountain further to the south.

'There!' said Hoseason. 'Ye see for yourself. If I had kent of these reefs, if I had had a chart, or if Shuan had been spared, it's not sixty guineas, no, nor six hundred, would have made me risk my brig in sic a stoneyard! But you, sir, that was to pilot us, have ye never a word?'

'I'm thinking,' said Alan, 'these'll be what they call the Torran Rocks.'

'Are there many of them?' says the captain.

'Truly, sir, I am nae pilot,' said Alan; 'but it sticks in my mind there are ten miles of them.'

Mr Riach and the captain looked at each other.

'There's a way through them, I suppose?' said the captain.

'Doubtless,' said Alan; 'but where? But it somehow runs in my mind once more, that it is clearer under the land.'

'So?' said Hoseason. 'We'll have to haul our wind then, Mr Riach; we'll have to come as near in about the end of Mull as we can take her, sir; and even then we'll have the land to kep the wind off us, and that stoneyard on our lee. Well, we're in for it now, and may as well crack on.'

With that he gave an order to the steersman, and sent Riach to the foretop. There were only five men on deck, counting the officers; these were all that were fit (or, at least, both fit and willing) for their work; and two of these were hurt. So, as I say, it fell to Mr Riach to go aloft, and he sat there looking out and hailing the deck with news of all he saw.

'The sea to the south is thick,' he cried; and then, after a while, 'It does seem clearer in by the land.'

'Well, sir,' said Hoseason to Alan, 'we'll try your way of it. But I think I might as well trust to a blind fiddler. Pray God you're right.'

'Pray God I am!' says Alan to me. 'But where did I hear it? Well, well it will be as it must.'

As we got nearer to the turn of the land the reefs began to be sown here and there on our very path; and Mr Riach sometimes cried down to us to change the course. Sometimes, indeed, none too soon; for one reef was so close on the brig's weather board that when a sea burst upon it the lighter sprays fell upon her deck and wetted us like rain.

The brightness of the night showed us these perils as clearly as by day, which was, perhaps, the more alarming. It showed me, too, the face of the captain as he stood by the steersman, now on one foot, now on the other, and sometimes blowing in his hands, but still listening and looking and as steady as steel. Neither he nor Mr Riach had shown well in the fighting; but I saw they were brave in their own trade, and admired them all the more because I found Alan very white.

'Ochone, David,' says he, 'this is no the kind of death I fancy.'

'What, Alan!' I cried, 'you're not afraid?'

'No,' said he, wetting his lips, 'but you'll allow yourself, it's a cold ending.'

By this time, now and then sheering to one side or the other to avoid a reef, but still hugging the wind and the land, we had got round Iona and begun to come alongside Mull. The tide at the tail of the land ran very strong, and threw the brig about. Two hands were put to the helm, and Hoseason himself would sometimes lend a help; and it was strange to see three strong men throw their weight upon the tiller, and it (like a living thing) struggle against and drive them back. This would have been the greater danger, had not the sea been for some while free of obstacles. Mr Riach, besides, announced from the top that he saw clear water ahead.

'Ye were right,' said Hoseason to Alan. 'Ye have saved the brig, sir; I'll mind that when we come to clear accounts.' And I believe he not only meant what he said, but would have done it; so high a place did the *Covenant* hold in his affections.

But this is matter only for conjecture, things having gone otherwise than he forecast.

'Keep her away a point,' sings out Mr Riach. 'Reef to windward!'

And just at the same time the tide caught the brig, and threw the wind out of her sails. She came round into the wind like a top, and the next moment struck the reef with such a dunch as threw us all flat upon the deck, and came near to shake Mr Riach from his place upon the mast.

I was on my feet in a minute. The reef on which we had struck was close in under the south-west end of Mull, off a little isle they call Earraid, which lay low and black upon the larboard. Sometimes the swell broke clean over us; sometimes it only ground the poor brig upon the reef, so that we could hear her beat herself to pieces; and what with the great noise of the sails, and the singing of the wind, and the flying of the spray in the moonlight, and the sense of danger, I think my head must have been partly turned, for I could scarcely understand the things I saw.

Presently I observed Mr Riach and the seamen busy round the skiff; and still in the same blank, ran over to assist them; and as soon as I set my hand to work, my mind came clear again. It was no very easy task, for the skiff lay amidships and was full of hamper, and the breaking of the heavier seas continually forced us to give over and hold on; but we all wrought like horses while we could.

Meanwhile such of the wounded as could move came clambering out of the fore-scuttle and began to help; while the rest that lay helpless in their bunks harrowed me with screaming and begging to be saved.

The captain took no part. It seemed he was struck stupid. He stood holding by the shrouds, talking to himself and groaning out aloud whenever the ship hammered on the rock. His brig was like wife and child to him; he had looked on, day by day, at the mishandling of poor Ransome; but when it came to the brig, he seemed to suffer along with her.

All the time of our working at the boat, I remember only one other thing: that I asked Alan, looking across at the shore, what country it was; and he answered, it was the worst possible for him, for it was a land of the Campbells.

We had one of the wounded men told off to keep a watch upon the seas and cry us warning. Well, we had the boat about ready to be launched, when this man sang out pretty shrill: 'For God's sake, hold on!' We knew by his tone that it was something more than ordinary; and sure enough, there followed a sea so huge that it lifted the brig right up and canted her over on her beam. Whether the cry came too late or my hold was too weak, I know not; but at the sudden tilting of the ship I was cast clean over the bulwarks into the sea.

I went down, and drank my fill; and then came up, and got a blink of the moon; and then down again. They say a man sinks the third time for good. I cannot be made like other folk, then; for I would not like to write how often I went down or how often I came up again. All the while, I was being hurled along, and beaten upon and choked, and then swallowed whole; and the thing was so distracting to my wits, that I was neither sorry nor afraid.

Presently, I found I was holding to a spar, which helped me somewhat. And then all of a sudden I was in quiet water, and began to come to myself.

It was the spare yard I had got hold of, and I was amazed to see how far I had travelled from the brig. I hailed her, indeed; but it was plain she was already out of cry. She was still holding together; but whether or not they had yet launched the boat, I was too far off and too low down to see.

While I was hailing the brig, I spied a tract of water lying between us, where no great waves came, but which yet boiled white all over and bristled in the moon with rings and bubbles. Sometimes the whole tract swung to one side, like the tail of a live serpent; sometimes, for a glimpse, it all would disappear and then boil up again. What it was I had no guess, which for the time increased my fear of it; but I now know it must have been the roost or tide race, which had carried me away so fast and tumbled me about so cruelly, and at last, as if tired of that play, had flung out me and the spare yard upon its landward margin.

I now lay quite becalmed, and began to feel that a man can die of cold as well as of drowning. The shores of Erraid were close in; I could see in the moonlight the dots of heather and the sparkling of the mica in the rocks.

'Well,' thought I to myself, 'if I cannot get as far as that, it's strange!'

I had no skill of swimming, Essen water being small in our neighbourhood; but when I laid hold upon the yard with both arms, and kicked out with both feet, I soon begun to find that I was moving. Hard work it was, and mortally slow; but in about an hour of kicking and splashing, I had got well in between the points of a sandy bay surrounded by low hills.

The sea was here quite quiet; there was no sound of any surf; the moon shone clear; and I thought in my heart I had never seen a place so desert and desolate. But it was dry land; and when at last it grew so shallow that

I could leave the yard and wade ashore upon my feet, I cannot tell if I was more tired or more grateful. Both at least, I was: tired as I never was before that night; and grateful to God as I trust I have been often, though never with more cause.

WITH MY STEPPING ashore I began the most unhappy part of my adventures. It was half-past twelve in the morning, and though the wind was broken by the land, it was a cold night. I dared not sit down (for I thought I should have frozen), but took off my shoes and walked to and fro upon the sand, barefoot, and beating my breast, with infinite weariness. There was no sound of man or cattle; not a cock crew, though it was about the hour of their first waking; only the surf broke outside in the distance, which put me in mind of my perils and those of my friend. To walk by the sea at that hour of the morning, and in a place so desert-like and lonesome, struck me with a kind of fear.

As soon as the day began to break I put on my shoes and climbed a hill—the ruggedest scramble I ever undertook—falling, the whole way, between big blocks of granite or leaping from one to another. When I got to the top the dawn was come. There was no sign of the brig, which must have lifted from the reef and sunk. The boat, too, was nowhere to be seen. There was never a sail upon the ocean; and in what I could see of the land, was neither house nor man.

I was afraid to think what had befallen my shipmates, and afraid to look longer at so empty a scene. What with my wet clothes and weariness, and my belly that now began to ache with hunger, I had enough to trouble me without that. So I set off eastward along the south coast, hoping to find a house where I might warm myself, and perhaps get news of those I had lost. And at the worst, I considered the sun would soon rise and dry my clothes.

After a little, my way was stopped by a creek or inlet of the sea, which seemed to run pretty deep into the land; and as I had no means to get across, I must needs change my direction to go about the end of it. It was still the roughest kind of walking; indeed the whole, not only of Earraid, but of the neighbouring part of Mull (which they call the Ross) is nothing but a jumble of granite rocks with heather in among. At first the creek kept narrowing as I had looked to see; but presently to my surprise it began to widen out again. At this I scratched my head, but had still no notion of the truth; until at last I came to a rising ground, and it burst upon me all in a moment that I was cast upon a little, barren isle, and cut off on every side by the salt seas.

Instead of the sun rising to dry me, it came on to rain, with a thick mist; so that my case was lamentable.

I stood in the rain, and shivered, and wondered what to do, till it occurred to me that perhaps the creek was fordable. Back I went to the narrowest point and waded in. But not three yards from shore, I plumped in head over ears; and if ever I was heard of more it was rather by God's grace than my own prudence. I was no wetter (for that could hardly be) but I was all the colder for this mishap; and having lost another hope, was the more unhappy.

And now, all at once, the yard came in my head. What had carried me through the roost, would surely serve me to cross this little quiet creek in safety. With that I set off, undaunted, across the top of the isle, to fetch and carry it back. It was a weary tramp in all ways, and if hope had not buoyed me up, I must have cast myself down and given up. Whether with the sea salt, or because I was growing fevered, I was distressed with thirst, and had to stop, as I went, and drink the peaty water out of the hags.

I came to the bay at last, more dead than alive; and at the first glance, I thought the yard was something further out than when I left it. In I went, for the third time, into the sea. The sand was smooth and firm and shelved gradually down; so that I could wade out till the water was almost to my neck and the little waves splashed into my face. But at that depth my feet began to leave me and I durst venture in no further. As for the yard, I saw it bobbing very quietly some twenty feet in front of me.

I had borne up well until this last disappointment; but at that I came ashore, and flung myself down upon the sands and wept.

The time I spent upon the island is still so horrible a

thought to me, that I must pass it lightly over. In all the books I have read of people cast away, they had either their pockets full of tools, or a chest of things would be thrown upon the beach along with them, as if on purpose. My case was very different. I had nothing in my pockets but money and Alan's silver button; and being inland bred, I was as much short of knowledge as of means.

I knew indeed that shell-fish were counted good to eat; and among the rocks of the isle I found a great plenty of limpets, which at first I could scarcely strike from their places, not knowing quickness to be needful. There were, besides, some of the little shells that we call buckies; I think periwinkle is the English name. Of these two I made my whole diet, devouring them cold and raw as I found them; and so hungry was I, that at first they seemed to me delicious.

Perhaps they were out of season, or perhaps there was something wrong in the sea about my island. But at least I had no sooner eaten my first meal than I was seized with giddiness and retching, and lay for a long time no better than dead. A second trial of the same food (indeed I had no other) did better with me and revived my strength. But as long as I was on the island, I never knew what to expect when I had eaten; sometimes all was well, and sometimes I was thrown into a miserable sickness; nor could I ever distinguish what particular fish it was that hurt me.

All day it streamed rain; the island ran like a sop; there was no dry spot to be found; and when I lay down that night, between two boulders that made a kind of roof, my feet were in a bog.

The second day I crossed the island to all sides. There was no one part of it better than another; it was all desolate and rocky; nothing living on it but game birds which I lacked the means to kill, and the gulls which haunted the outlying rocks in a prodigious number. But the creek, or straits, that cut off the isle from the main land of the Ross, opened out on the north into a bay, and the bay again opened into the sound of Iona; and it was the neighbourhood of this place that I chose to be my home; though if I had thought upon the very name of home in such a spot, I must have burst out weeping.

I had good reasons for my choice. There was in this part

of the isle a little hut of a house like a pig's hut, where fishers used to sleep when they came there upon their business; but the turf roof of it had fallen entirely in; so that the hut was of no use to me, and gave me less shelter than my rocks. What was more important, the shell-fish on which I lived grew there in great plenty; when the tide was out I could gather a peck at a time: and this was doubtless a convenience. But the other reason went deeper. I had become in no way used to the horrid solitude of the isle, but still looked round me on all sides (like a man that was hunted) between fear and hope that I might see some human creature coming. Now, from a little up the hillside over the bay, I could catch a sight of the great, ancient church and the roofs of the people's houses in Iona. And on the other hand, over the low country of the Ross, I saw smoke go up, morning and evening, as if from a homestead in a hollow of the land.

I used to watch this smoke, when I was wet and cold, and had my head half turned with loneliness; and think of the fireside and the company, till my heart burned. It was the same with the roofs of Iona. Altogether, this sight I had of men's homes and comfortable lives, although it put a point on my own sufferings, yet it kept hope alive, and helped me to eat my raw shell-fish (which had soon grown to be a disgust) and saved me from the sense of horror I had whenever I was quite alone with dead rocks, and fowls, and the rain, and the cold sea.

I say it kept hope alive; and indeed it seemed impossible that I should be left to die on the shores of my own country, and within view of a church tower and the smoke of men's houses. But the second day passed; and though as long as the light lasted I kept a bright look-out for boats on the Sound or men passing on the Ross, no help came near me. It still rained; and I turned in to sleep, as wet as ever and with a cruel sore throat, but a little comforted, perhaps, by having said good night to my next neighbours, the people of Iona.

Charles the Second declared a man could stay out-doors more days in the year in the climate of England than in any other. This was very like a king with a palace at his back and changes of dry clothes. But he must have had better luck on his flight from Worcester than I had on that miserable isle. It was the height of the summer; yet it rained for more than twenty-four hours, and did not clear until the afternoon of the third day.

This was the day of incidents. In the morning I saw a red deer, a buck with a fine spread of antlers, standing in the rain on the top of the island; but he had scarce seen me rise from under my rock, before he trotted off upon the other side. I supposed he must have swum the straits; though what should bring any creature to Earraid, was more than I could fancy.

A little after, as I was jumping about after my limpets, I was startled by a guinea-piece, which fell upon a rock in front of me and glanced off into the sea. When the sailors gave me my money again, they kept back not only about a third of the whole sum, but my father's leather purse; so that from that day out, I carried my gold loose in a pocket with a button. I now saw there must be a hole, and clapped my hand to the place in a great hurry. But this was to lock the stable door after the steed was stolen. I had left the shore at Queensferry with near on fifty pounds; now I found no more than two guinea-pieces and a silver shilling.

It is true I picked up a third guinea a little after, where it lay shining on a piece of turf. That made a fortune of three pounds and four shillings, English money, for a lad, the rightful heir of an estate, and now starving on an isle at the extreme end of the wild Highlands.

This state of my affairs dashed me still further; and indeed my plight on that third morning was truly pitiful. My clothes were beginning to rot; my stockings in particular were quite worn through, so that my shanks went naked; my hands had grown quite soft with the continual soaking; my throat was very sore, my strength had much abated, and my heart so turned against the horrid stuff I was condemned to eat, that the very sight of it came near to sicken me.

And yet the worst was not yet come.

There is a pretty high rock on the north-west of Earraid, which (because it had a flat top and overlooked the Sound) I was much in the habit of frequenting; not that ever I stayed in one place, save when asleep, my misery giving me no rest. Indeed I wore myself down with continual and aimless goings and comings in the rain.

As soon, however, as the sun came out, I lay down on the top of that rock to dry myself. The comfort of the sunshine is a thing I cannot tell. It set me thinking hopefully of my deliverance, of which I had begun to despair; and I scanned the sea and the Ross with a fresh interest. On the south of my rock, a part of the island jutted out and hid the open ocean, so that a boat could thus come quite near me upon that side, and I be none the wiser.

Well, all of a sudden, a coble with a brown sail and a pair of fishers aboard of it, came flying round that corner of the isle, bound for Iona. I shouted out, and then fell on my knees on the rock and reached up my hands and prayed to them. They were near enough to hear—I could even see the colour of their hair; and there was no doubt but they observed me, for they cried out in the Gaelic tongue, and laughed. But the boat never turned aside, and flew on, right before my eyes, for Iona.

I could not believe such wickedness, and ran along the shore from rock to rock, crying on them piteously; even after they were out of reach of my voice, I still cried and waved to them; and when they were quite gone, I thought my heart would have burst. All the time of my troubles I wept only twice. Once, when I could not reach the yard; and now, the second time, when these fishers turned a deaf ear to my cries. But this time I wept and roared like a wicked child, tearing up the turf with my nails and grinding my face in the earth. If a wish would kill men, those two fishers would never have seen morning, and I should likely have died upon my island.

When I was a little over my anger, I must eat again, but with such loathing of the mess as I could now scarce control. Sure enough, I should have done as well to fast, for my fishes poisoned me again. I had all my first pains; my throat was so sore I could scarce swallow; I had a fit of strong shuddering, which clucked my teeth together; and there came on me that dreadful sense of illness, which we have no name for either in Scotch or English. I thought I should have died, and made my peace with God, forgiving all men, even my uncle and the fishers; and as soon as I had thus made up my mind to the worst, clearness came upon me: I observed the night was falling dry; my clothes were dried a good deal; truly, I was in a better case than ever before, since I had landed on the isle; and so I got to sleep at last, with a thought of gratitude.

The next day (which was the fourth of this horrible life of mine) I found my bodily strength run very low. But the sun shone, the air was sweet, and what I managed to eat of the shell-fish agreed well with me and revived my courage.

I was scarce back on my rock (where I went always the first thing after I had eaten) before I observed a boat coming down the Sound, and with her head, as I thought, in my direction.

I began at once to hope and fear exceedingly; for I thought these men might have thought better of their cruelty and be coming back to my assistance. But another disappointment, such as yesterday's, was more than I could bear. I turned my back, accordingly, upon the sea, and did not look again till I had counted many hundreds. The boat was still heading for the island. The next time I counted the full thousand, as slowly as I could, my heart beating so as to hurt me. And then it was out of all question. She was coming straight to Earraid!

I could no longer hold myself back, but ran to the sea side and out, from one rock to another, as far as I could go. It is a marvel I was not drowned; for when I was brought to a stand at last, my legs shook under me, and my mouth was so dry, I must wet it with the sea-water before I was able to shout.

All this time the boat was coming on; and now I was able to perceive it was the same boat and the same two men as yesterday. This I knew by their hair, which the one had of a bright yellow and the other black. But now there was a third man along with them, who looked to be of a better class.

As soon as they were come within easy speech, they let down their sail and lay quiet. In spite of my supplications, they drew no nearer in, and what frightened me most of all, the new man tee-hee'd with laughter as he talked and looked at me.

Then he stood up in the boat and addressed me a long while, speaking fast and with many wavings of his hand. I told him I had no Gaelic; and at this he became very angry, and I began to suspect he thought he was talking English. Listening very close, I caught the word 'whateffer' several times; but all the rest was Gaelic, and might have been Greek and Hebrew for me.

'Whatever,' said I, to show him I had caught a word.

'Yes, yes—yes, yes,' says he, and then he looked at the other men, as much as to say, 'I told you I spoke English,' and began again as hard as ever in the Gaelic.

This time I picked out another word, 'tide'. Then I had a flash of hope. I remembered he was always waving his hand towards the mainland of the Ross.

'Do you mean when the tide is out—?' I cried, and could not finish.

'Yes, yes,' said he. 'Tide.'

At that I turned tail upon their boat (where my adviser had once more begun to tee-hee with laughter) leaped back the way I had come, from one stone to another, and set off running across the isle as I had never run before. In about half an hour I came out upon the shores of the creek; and, sure enough, it was shrunk into a little trickle of water, through which I dashed, not above my knees, and landed with a shout on the main island.

A sea-bred boy would not have stayed a day on Earraid; which is only what they call a tidal islet, and except in the bottom of the neaps, can be entered and left twice in every twenty-four hours, either dry-shod, or at the most by wading. Even I, who had the tide going out and in before me in the bay, and even watched for the ebbs, the better to get my shell-fish—even I (I say) if I had sat down to think, instead of raging at my fate, must have soon guessed the secret, and got free. It was no wonder the fishers had not understood me. The wonder was rather that they had ever guessed my pitiful illusion, and taken the trouble to come back. I had starved with cold and hunger on that island for close upon one hundred hours. But for the fishers, I might have left my bones there, in pure folly. And even as it was, I had paid for it pretty dear, not only in past sufferings, but in my present case; being clothed like a beggarman, scarce able to walk, and in great pain of my sore throat.

I have seen wicked men and fools, a great many of both; and I believe they both get paid in the end; but the fools first.

15. THE LAD WITH THE SILVER BUTTON: THROUGH THE ISLE OF MULL

THE ROSS OF MULL, which I had now got upon, was rugged and trackless, like the isle I had just left; being all bog, and briar, and big stone. There may be roads for them that know that country well; but for my part I had no better guide than my own nose, and no other landmark than Ben More.

I aimed as well as I could for the smoke I had seen so often from the island; and with all my great weariness and the difficulty of the way, came upon the house in the bottom of a little hollow, about five or six at night. It was low and longish, roofed with turf and built of unmortared stones; and on a mound in front of it, an old gentleman sat smoking his pipe in the sun.

With what little English he had, he gave me to understand that my shipmates had got safe ashore, and had broken bread in that very house on the day after.

'Was there one,' I asked, 'dressed like a gentleman?'

He said they all wore rough great-coats; but to be sure, the first of them, the one that came alone, wore breeches and stockings, while the rest had sailors' trousers.

'Ah,' said I, 'and he would have a feathered hat?'

He told me, no, that he was bare-headed like myself.

At first I thought Alan might have lost his hat; and then the rain came in my mind, and I judged it more likely he had it out of harm's way under his great-coat. This set me smiling, partly because my friend was safe, partly to think of his vanity in dress.

And then the old gentleman clapped his hand to his brow, and cried out that I must be the lad with the silver button.

'Why, yes!' said I, in some wonder.

'Well, then,' said the old gentleman, 'I have a word for you that you are to follow your friend to his country, by Torosay.'

He then asked me how I had fared, and I told him my tale. A south-country man would certainly have laughed; but this old gentleman (I call him so because of his manners, for his clothes were dropping off his back) heard me all through with nothing but gravity and pity. When I had done, he took me by the hand, led me into his hut (it was no better) and presented me before his wife, as if she had been the Queen and I a duke.

The good woman set oat-bread before me and a cold grouse, patting my shoulder and smiling to me all the time, for she had no English; and the old gentleman (not to be behind) brewed me a strong punch out of their country spirit. All the while I was eating, and after that when I was drinking the punch, I could scarce come to believe in my good fortune; and the house, though it was thick with the peat-smoke and as full of holes as a colander, seemed like a palace.

The punch threw me in a strong sweat and a deep slumber; the good people let me lie; and it was near noon of the next day before I took the road, my throat already easier and my spirits quite restored by good fare and good news. The old gentleman, although I pressed him hard, would take no money, and gave me an old bonnet for my head; though I am free to own I was no sooner out of view of the house, than I very jealously washed this gift of his in a wayside fountain.

Thought I to myself: 'If these are the wild Highlanders, I could wish my own folk wilder.'

I not only started late, but I must have wandered nearly half the time. True, I met plenty of people, grubbing in little miserable fields that would not keep a cat, or herding little kine about the bigness of asses. The Highland dress being forbidden by law since the rebellion, and the people condemned to the lowland habit, which they much disliked, it was strange to see the variety of their array. Some went bare, only for a hanging cloak or great-coat, and carried their trousers on their backs like a useless burthen; some had made an imitation of the tartan with little parti-coloured stripes patched together like an old wife's quilt; others, again, still wore the highland philabeg, but by putting a few stitches between the legs, transformed it into a pair of trousers like a Dutchman's. All those makeshifts were condemned and punished, for the law was harshly applied, in hopes to break up the clan spirit; but in that out-of-the-way, sea-bound isle, there were few to make remarks and fewer to tell tales.

They seemed in great poverty; which was no doubt natural, now that rapine was put down, and the chiefs kept no longer an open house; and the roads (even such a wandering, country by-track as the one I followed) were infested with beggars. And here again I marked a difference from my own part of the country. For our lowland beggars—even the gownsmen themselves, who beg by patent—had a louting, flattering way with them, and if you gave them a plack and asked change, would very civilly return you a boddle. But these Highland beggars stood on their dignity, asked alms only to buy snuff (by their account) and would give no change.

To be sure, this was no concern of mine, except in so far as it entertained me by the way. What was much more to the purpose, few had any English, and these few (unless they were of the brotherhood of beggars) not very anxious to place it at my service. I knew Torosay to be my destination, and repeated the name to them and pointed; but instead of simply pointing in reply, they would give me a screed of the Gaelic that set me foolish; so it was small wonder if I went out of my road as often as I stayed in it.

At last, about eight at night, and already very weary, I came to a lone house, where I asked admittance, and was refused, until I bethought me of the power of money in so poor a country, and held up one of my guineas in my finger and thumb. Thereupon, the man of the house, who had hitherto pretended to have no English, and driven me from his door by signals, suddenly began to speak as clearly as was needful, and agreed for five shillings to give me a night's lodging and guide me the next day to Torosay.

I slept uneasily that night, fearing I should be robbed; but I might have spared myself the pain; for my host was no robber, only miserably poor and a great cheat. He was not alone in his poverty; for the next morning, we must go five miles about to the house of what he called a rich man to have one of my guineas changed. This was perhaps a rich man for Mull; he would have scarce been thought so in the south; for it took all he had, the whole house was turned upside

down, and a neighbour brought under contribution, before
he could scrape together twenty shillings in silver. The odd
shilling he kept for himself, protesting he could ill afford
to have so great a sum of money lying 'locked up'. For all
that he was very courteous and well spoken, made us both
sit down with his family to dinner, and brewed punch in a
fine china bowl, over which my rascal guide grew so merry
that he refused to start.

I was for getting angry, and appealed to the rich man
(Hector Maclean was his name) who had been a witness
to our bargain and to my payment of the five shillings. But
Maclean had taken his share of the punch, and vowed that
no gentleman should leave his table after the bowl was
brewed; so there was nothing for it but to sit and hear
Jacobite toasts and Gaelic songs, till all were tipsy and
staggered off to the bed or the barn for their night's rest.

Next day (the fourth of my travels) we were up before
five upon the clock; but my rascal guide got to the bottle
at once, and it was three hours before I had him clear of
the house, and then (as you shall hear) only for a worse
disappointment.

As long as we went down a heathery valley that lay before
Mr Maclean's house, all went well; only my guide looked
constantly over his shoulder, and when I asked him the
cause, only grinned at me. No sooner, however, had we
crossed the back of a hill, and got out of sight of the house
windows, than he told me Torosay lay right in front, and that
a hill-top (which he pointed out) was my best landmark.

'I care very little for that,' said I, 'since you are going
with me.'

The impudent cheat answered me in the Gaelic that he
had no English.

'My fine fellow,' I said, 'I know very well your English
comes and goes. Tell me what will bring it back? Is it
more money you wish?'

'Five shillings mair,' said he, 'and hersel' will bring ye
there.'

I reflected a while and then offered him two, which he
accepted greedily, and insisted on having in his hands at
once—'for luck', as he said, but I think it was rather
for my misfortune.

The two shillings carried him not quite as many miles;

at the end of which distance, he sat down upon the wayside and took off his brogues from his feet, like a man about to rest.

I was now red-hot. 'Ha!' said I, 'have you no more English?'

He said impudently, 'no'.

At that I boiled over and lifted my hand to strike him; and he, drawing a knife from his rags, squatted back and grinned at me like a wild-cat. At that, forgetting everything but my anger, I ran in upon him, put aside his knife with my left and struck him in the mouth with the right. I was a strong lad and very angry, and he but a little man; and he went down before me heavily. By good luck, his knife flew out of his hand as he fell.

I picked up both that and his brogues, wished him a good morning and set off upon my way, leaving him bare-foot and disarmed. I chuckled to myself as I went, being sure I was done with that rogue, for a variety of reasons. First, he knew he could have no more of my money; next, the brogues were worth in that country only a few pence; and lastly the knife, which was really a dagger, it was against the law for him to carry.

In about half-an-hour of walk, I overtook a great, ragged man, moving pretty fast but feeling before him with a staff. He was quite blind, and told me he was a catechist, which should have put me at my ease. But his face went against me; it seemed dark and dangerous and secret; and presently, as we began to go on alongside, I saw the steel butt of a pistol sticking from under the flap of his coat-pocket. To carry such a thing meant a fine of fifteen pounds sterling upon a first offence, and transportation to the colonies upon a second. Nor could I quite see why a religious teacher should go armed, or what a blind man could be doing with a pistol.

I told him about my guide, for I was proud of what I had done, and my vanity for once got the heels of my prudence. At the mention of the five shillings he cried out so loud that I made up my mind I should say nothing of the other two, and was glad he could not see my blushes.

'Was it too much?' I asked, a little faltering.

'Too much!' cries he. 'Why, I will guide you to Torosay myself for a dram of brandy. And give you the great pleasure of my company (me that is a man of some learning) in the bargain.'

I said I did not see how a blind man could be a guide; but at that he laughed aloud, and said his stick was eyes enough for an eagle.

'In the Isle of Mull, at least,' says he, 'where I knew every stone and heather-bush by mark of head. See, now,' he said, striking right and left, as if to make sure, 'down there a burn is running; and at the head of it there stands a bit of a small hill with a stone cocked upon the top of that; and it's hard at the foot of the hill, that the way runs by to Torosay; and the way here, being for droves, is plainly trodden, and will show grassy through the heather.'

I had to own he was right in every feature, and told my wonder.

'Ha!' says he, 'that's nothing. Would ye believe me now, that before the Act came out, and when there were weepons in this country, I could shoot? Ay, could I!' cries he, and then with a leer: 'If ye had such a thing as a pistol here to try with, I would show ye how it's done.'

I told him I had nothing of the sort, and gave him a wider berth. If he had known, his pistol stuck at that time quite plainly out of his pocket, and I could see the sun twinkle on the steel of the butt. But by the better luck for me, he knew nothing, thought all was covered, and lied on in the dark.

He then began to question me cunningly, where I came from, whether I was rich, whether I could change a five-shilling piece for him (which he declared he had that moment in his sporran) and all the time he kept edging up to me, and I avoiding him. We were now upon a sort of green cattle-track which crossed the hills towards Torosay, and we kept changing sides upon that like dancers in a reel. I had so plainly the upper-hand that my spirits rose, and indeed I took a pleasure in this game of blind-man's buff; but the catechist grew angrier and angrier, and at last began to swear in Gaelic and to strike for my legs with his staff.

Then I told him that, sure enough, I had a pistol in my pocket as well as he, and if he did not strike across the hill due south I would even blow his brains out.

He became at once very polite; and after trying to soften me for some time, but quite in vain, he cursed me once more in the Gaelic and took himself off. I watched him striding along, through bog and brier, tapping with his stick, until he turned the end of a hill and disappeared in the next hollow. Then I struck on again for Torosay, much better pleased to be alone than to travel with that man of learning. This was an unlucky day; and these two, of whom I had just rid myself one after the other, were the two worst men I met with in the Highlands.

At Torosay, on the sound of Mull and looking over to the mainland of Morvern, there was an inn with an innkeeper, who was a Maclean, it appeared, of a very high family; for to keep an inn is thought even more genteel in the Highlands than it is with us, perhaps as partaking of hospitality, or perhaps because the trade is idle and drunken. He spoke good English, and finding me to be something of a scholar, tried me first in French, where he easily beat me, and then in the Latin, in which I don't know which of us did best. This pleasant rivalry put us at once upon friendly terms; and I sat up and drank punch with him (or to be more correct, sat up and watched him drink it) until he was so tipsy that he wept upon my shoulder.

I tried him, as if by accident, with a sight of Alan's button; but it was plain he had never seen or heard of it. Indeed, he bore some grudge against the family and friends of Ardshiel, and before he was drunk he read me a lampoon, in very good Latin, but with a very ill meaning, which he had made in elegiac verses upon a person of that house.

When I told him of my catechist, he shook his head, and said I was lucky to have got clear off. 'That is a very dangerous man,' he said; 'Duncan Mackiegh is his name; he can shoot by the ear at several yards, and has been often accused of highway robberies, and once of murder.'

'The cream of it is,' says I, 'that he called himself a catechist.'

'And why should he not?' says he, 'when that is what he is? It was Maclean of Duart gave it to him because he was blind. But, perhaps, it was a peety,' says my host, 'for he is always on the road, going from one place to another to hear the young folk say their religion; and doubtless, that is a great temptation to the poor man.'

At last, when my landlord could drink no more, he

showed me to a bed, and I lay down in very good spirits; having travelled the greater part of that big and crooked Island of Mull, from Earraid to Torosay, fifty miles as the crow flies and (with my wanderings) much nearer a hundred, in four days and with little fatigue. Indeed I was by far in better heart and health of body at the end of that long tramp than I had been at the beginning.

THERE IS A regular ferry from Torosay to Kinlochaline on the mainland. Both shores of the Sound are in the country of the strong clan of the Macleans, and the people that passed the ferry with me were almost all of that clan. The skipper of the boat, on the other hand, was called Neil Roy Macrob; and since Macrob was one of the names of Alan's clansmen, and Alan himself had sent me to that ferry, I was eager to come to private speech of Neil Roy.

In the crowded boat this was of course impossible, and the passage was a very slow affair. There was no wind, and as the boat was wretchedly equipped, we could pull but two oars on one side, and one on the other. The men gave way, however, with a good will, the passengers taking spells to help them, and the whole company giving the time in Gaelic boat-songs. And what with the songs, and the sea air, and the good nature and spirit of all concerned, and the bright weather, the passage was a pretty thing to have seen.

But there was one melancholy part. In the mouth of Loch Aline we found a great sea-going ship at anchor; and this I supposed at first to be one of the King's cruisers which were kept along that coast, both summer and winter, to prevent communication with the French. As we got a little nearer, it became plain she was a ship of merchandise; and what still more puzzled me, not only her decks, but the sea-beach also, were quite black with people, and skiffs were continually plying to and fro between them. Yet nearer, and there began to come to our ears a great sound of mourning, the people on board and those on the shore crying and lamenting one to another so as to pierce the heart.

Then I understood this was an emigrant ship bound for the American colonies.

We put the ferry-boat alongside, and the exiles leaned over the bulwarks, weeping and reaching out their hands to my fellow-passengers, among whom they counted some near friends. How long this might have gone on I do not know, for they seemed to have no sense of time: but at last the captain of the ship, who seemed near beside himself (and no great wonder) in the midst of this crying and confusion, came to the side and begged us to depart.

Thereupon Neil sheered off; and the chief singer in our boat struck into a melancholy air, which was presently taken up both by the emigrants and their friends upon the beach, so that it sounded from all sides like a lament for the dying. I saw the tears run down the cheeks of the men and women in the boat, even as they bent at the oars; and the circumstances, and the music of the song (which is one called 'Lochaber no more') were highly affecting even to myself.

At Kinlochaline I got Neil Roy upon one side on the beach, and said I made sure he was one of Appin's men.

'And what for no?' said he.

'I am seeking somebody,' said I; 'and it comes in my mind that you will have news of him. Alan Breck Stewart is his name.' And very foolishly, instead of showing him the button, I sought to pass a shilling in his hand.

At this he drew back. 'I am very much affronted,' he said; 'and this is not the way that one shentleman should behave to another at all. The man you ask for is in France; but if he was in my sporran,' says he, 'and your belly full of shillings, I would not hurt a hair upon his body.'

I saw I had gone the wrong way to work, and without wasting time upon apologies, showed him the button lying in the hollow of my palm.

'Aweel, aweel,' said Neil; 'and I think ye might have begun with that end of the stick, whatever! But if ye are the lad with the silver button, all is well, and I have the word to see that ye come safe. But if ye will pardon me to speak plainly,' says he, 'there is a name that you should never take into your mouth, and that is the name of Alan Breck; and there is a thing that ye would never do, and that is to offer your dirty money to a Hieland shentleman.'

It was not very easy to apologise; for I could scarce tell him (what was the truth) that I had never dreamed he would set up to be a gentleman until he told me so. Neil on his part had no wish to prolong his dealings with me, only to fulfil his orders and be done with it; and he made haste to give me my route. This was to lie the night in Kinlochaline in the public inn; to cross Morvern the next day to Ardgour, and lie the night in the house of one John of the Claymore, who was warned that I might come; the third day, to be set across one loch at Corran and another at Balachulish, and then ask my way to the house of James of the Glens, at Aucharn in Duror of Appin. There was a good deal of ferrying, as you hear; the sea in all this part running deep into the mountains and winding about their roots. It makes the country strong to hold and difficult to travel, but full of prodigious wild and dreadful prospects.

I had some other advice from Neil; to speak with no one by the way, to avoid Whigs, Campbells, and the 'red-soldiers'; to leave the road and lie in a bush, if I saw any of the latter coming 'for it was never chancy to meet in with them'; and in brief, to conduct myself like a robber or a Jacobite agent, as perhaps Neil thought me.

The inn at Kinlochaline was the most beggarly vile place that ever pigs were styed in, full of smoke, vermin, and silent Highlanders. I was not only discontented with my lodging, but with myself for my mismanagement of Neil, and thought I could hardly be worse off. But very wrongly, as I was soon to see; for I had not been half an hour at the inn (standing in the door most of the time, to ease my eyes from the peat smoke) when a thunderstorm came close by, the springs broke in a little hill on which the inn stood, and one end of the house became a running water. Places of public entertainment were bad enough all over Scotland in those days; yet it was a wonder to myself, when I had to go from the fireside to the bed in which I slept, wading over the shoes.

Early in my next day's journey I overtook a little, stout, solemn man, walking very slowly with his toes turned out, sometimes reading in a book and sometimes marking the place with his finger, and dressed decently and plainly in something of a clerical style.

This I found to be another catechist, but of a different order from the blind man of Mull: being indeed one of those sent out by the Edinburgh Society for Propagating Christian Knowledge, to evangelise the more savage places of the Highlands. His name was Henderland; he spoke

with the broad south-country tongue, which I was beginning to weary for the sound of; and besides common
countryship, we soon found we had a more particular bond
of interest. For my good friend, the minister of Essendean,
had translated into the Gaelic in his by-time a number of
hymns and pious books, which Henderland used in his
work, and held in great esteem. Indeed it was one of these
he was carrying and reading when we met.

We fell in company at once, our ways lying together as
far as to Kingairloch. As we went, he stopped and spoke
with all the wayfarers and workers that we met or passed;
and though of course I could not tell what they discoursed
about, yet I judged Mr Henderland must be well liked in
the countryside, for I observed many of them to bring out
their mulls and share a pinch of snuff with him.

I told him as far in my affairs as I judged wise: as far,
that is, as they were none of Alan's; and gave Balachulish
as the place I was travelling to, to meet a friend; for I
thought Aucharn, or even Duror, would be too particular
and might put him on the scent.

On his part, he told me much of his work and the people
he worked among, the hiding priests and Jacobites, the
Disarming Act, the dress, and many other curiosities of the
time and place. He seemed moderate: blaming Parliament
in several points, and especially because they had framed
the Act more severely against those who wore the dress
than against those who carried weapons.

This moderation put it in my mind to question him of
the Red Fox and the Appin tenants: questions which, I
thought, would seem natural enough in the mouth of one
travelling to that country.

He said it was a bad business. 'It's wonderful,' said he,
'where the tenants find the money, for their life is mere
starvation. (Ye don't carry such a thing as snuff, do ye,
Mr Balfour? No. Well, I'm better wanting it.) But these
tenants (as I was saying) are doubtless partly driven to
it. James Stewart in Duror (that's him they call James of
the Glens) is half-brother to Ardshiel, the captain of the
clan; and he is a man much looked up to, and drives very
hard. And then there's one they call Alan Breck.'

'Ah!' cried I, 'what of him?'

'What of the wind that bloweth where it listeth?' said

Henderland. 'He's here and awa; here to-day and gone tomorrow: a fair heather-cat. He might be glowering at the two of us out of yon whin-bush, and I wouldnae wonder! Ye'll no carry such a thing as snuff, will ye?'

I told him no, and that he had asked the same thing more than once.

'It's highly possible,' said he, sighing. 'But it seems strange ye shouldnae carry it. However, as I was saying, this Alan Breck is a bold, desperate customer, and well kent to be James's right hand. His life is forfeit already; he would boggle at naething; and maybe, if a tenant-body was to hang back, he would get a dirk in his wame.'

'You make a poor story of it all, Mr Henderland,' said I. 'If it is all fear upon both sides, I care to hear no more of it.'

'Na,' said Mr Henderland, 'but there's love too, and self-denial that should put the like of you and me to shame. There's something fine about it; no perhaps Christian, but humanly fine. Even Alan Breck, by all that I hear, is a chield to be respected. There's many a lying sneck-draw sits close in kirk in our own part of the country, and stands well in the world's eye, and maybe is a far worse man, Mr Balfour, than yon misguided shedder of man's blood. Ay, ay, we might take a lesson by them—Ye'll perhaps think I've been too long in the Hielands?' he added, smiling to me.

I told him not at all; that I had seen much to admire among the Highlanders; and if he came to that, Mr Campbell himself was a Highlander.

'Ay,' said he, 'that's true. It's a fine blood.'

'And what is the King's agent about?' I asked.

'Colin Campbell?' says Henderland. 'Putting his head in a bees' byke!'

'He is to turn the tenants out by force, I hear?' said I.

'Yes,' says he, 'but the business has gone back and forth, as folk say. First, James of the Glens rode to Edinburgh and got some lawyer (a Stewart, nae doubt—they all hing together like bats in a steeple) and had the proceedings stayed. And then Colin Campbell cam' in again, and had the upper-hand before the Barons of Exchequer. And now they tell me the first of the tenants are to flit to-morrow. It's to begin at Duror under James's very windows, which doesnae seem wise by my humble way of it.'

'Do you think they'll fight?' I asked.

'Well,' says Henderland, 'they're disarmed—or supposed to be—for there's still a good deal of cold iron lying by in quiet places. And then Colin Campbell has the sogers coming. But for all that, if I was his lady wife, I wouldnae be well pleased till I got him home again. They're queer customers, the Appin Stewarts.'

I asked if they were worse than their neighbours.

'No they,' said he. 'And that's the worst part of it. For if Colin Roy can get his business done in Appin, he has it all to begin again in the next country, which they call Mamore, and which is one of the countries of the Camerons. He's King's factor upon both, and from both he has to drive out the tenants; and indeed, Mr Balfour (to be open with ye) it's my belief that if he escapes the one lot, he'll get his death by the other.'

So we continued talking and walking the great part of the day; until at last, Mr Henderland, after expressing his delight in my company, and satisfaction at meeting with a friend of Mr Campbell's ('whom,' says he, 'I will make bold to call that sweet singer of our covenanted Zion') proposed that I should make a short stage, and lie the night in his house a little beyond Kingairloch. To say truth, I was overjoyed; for I had no great desire for John of the Claymore, and since my double misadventure, first with the guide and next with the gentleman skipper, I stood in some fear of any Highland stranger. Accordingly we shook hands upon the bargain, and came in the afternoon to a small house, standing alone by the shore of the Linnhe Loch. The sun was already gone from the desert mountains of Ardgour upon the hither side, but shone on those of Appin on the farther; the loch lay as still as a lake, only the gulls were crying round the sides of it; and the whole place seemed solemn and uncouth.

We had no sooner come to the door of Mr Henderland's dwelling, than to my great surprise (for I was now used to the politeness of Highlanders) he burst rudely past me, dashed into the room, caught up a jar and a small horn spoon, and began ladling snuff into his nose in most excessive quantities. Then he had a hearty fit of sneezing, and looked round upon me with a rather silly smile.

'It's a vow I took,' says he. 'I took a vow upon me that I wouldnae carry it. Doubtless it's a great privation; but when I think upon the martyrs, not only to the Scottish Covenant but to other points of Christianity, I think shame to mind it.'

As soon as we had eaten (and porridge and whey was the best of the good man's diet) he took a grave face and said he had a duty to perform by Mr Campbell, and that was to inquire into my state of mind towards God. I was inclined to smile at him, since the business of the snuff; but he had not spoken long before he brought the tears into my eyes. There are two things that men should never weary of, goodness and humility; we get none too much of them in this rough world and among cold, proud people; but Mr Henderland had their very speech upon his tongue. And though I was a good deal puffed up with my adventures and with having come off, as the saying is, with flying colours; yet he soon had me on my knees beside a simple, poor old man, and both proud and glad to be there.

Before we went to bed he offered me sixpence to help me on my way, out of a scanty store he kept in the turf wall of his house; at which excess of goodness I knew not what to do. But at last he was so earnest with me, that I thought it the more mannerly part to let him have his way, and so left him poorer than myself.

THE NEXT DAY Mr Henderland found for me a man who had a boat of his own and was to cross the Linnhe Loch that afternoon into Appin, fishing. Him he prevailed on to take me, for he was one of his flock; and in this way I saved a long day's travel and the price of the two public ferries I must otherwise have passed.

It was near noon before we set out; a dark day, with clouds, and the sun shining upon little patches. The sea was here very deep and still, and had scarce a wave upon it; so that I must put the water to my lips before I could believe it to be truly salt. The mountains on either side were high, rough and barren, very black and gloomy in the shadow of the clouds, but all silver-laced with little watercourses where the sun shone upon them. It seemed a hard country, this of Appin, for people to care as much about as Alan did.

There was but one thing to mention. A little after we had started, the sun shone upon a little moving clump of scarlet close in along the waterside to the north. It was much of the same red as soldiers' coats; every now and then, too, there came little sparks and lightnings, as though the sun had struck upon bright steel.

I asked my boatman what it should be; and he answered he supposed it was some of the red soldiers coming from Fort William into Appin, against the poor tenantry of the country. Well, it was a sad sight to me; and whether it was because of my thoughts of Alan, or from something prophetic in my bosom, although this was but the second time I had seen King George's troops, I had no good will to them.

At last we came so near the point of land at the entering in of Loch Leven that I begged to be set on shore. My boatman (who was an honest fellow and mindful of his promise to the catechist) would fain have carried me on to Balachulish; but as this was to take me farther from my secret destination, I insisted, and was set on shore at last under the wood of Lettermore (or Lettervore, for I have heard it both ways) in Alan's country of Appin.

This was a wood of birches, growing on a steep, craggy side of a mountain that overhung the loch. It had many openings and ferny dells; and a road or bridle track ran north and south through the midst of it, by the edge of which, where was a spring, I sat down to eat some oat-bread of Mr Henderland's, and think upon my situation.

Here I was not only troubled by a cloud of stinging midges, but far more by the doubts of my mind. What I ought to do, why I was going to join myself with an outlaw and a would-be murderer like Alan, whether I should not be acting more like a man of sense to tramp back to the south country direct, by my own guidance and at my own charges, and what Mr Campbell or even Mr Henderland would think of me if they should ever learn my folly and presumption: these were the doubts that now began to come in on me stronger than ever.

As I was so sitting and thinking, a sound of men and horses came to me through the wood; and presently after, at a turning of the road, I saw four travellers come into view. The way was in this part so rough and narrow that they came single and led their horses by the reins. The first was a great, red-headed gentleman, of an imperious and flushed face, who carried his hat in his hand and fanned himself, for he was in a breathing heat. The second, by his decent black garb and white wig, I correctly took to be a lawyer. The third was a servant, and wore some part of his clothes in tartan, which showed that his master was of a Highland family, and either an outlaw or else in singular good odour with the Government, since the wearing of tartan was against the Act. If I had been better versed in these things, I would have known the tartan to be of the Argyle (or Campbell) colours. This servant had a good-sized portmanteau strapped on his horse, and a net of lemons (to brew punch with) hanging at the saddle-bow; as was often enough the custom with luxurious travellers in that part of the country.

As for the fourth, who brought up the tail, I had seen

his like before, and knew him at once to be a sheriff's officer.

I had no sooner seen these people coming than I made up my mind (for no reason that I can tell) to go through with my adventure; and when the first came alongside of me, I rose up from the bracken and asked him the way to Aucharn.

He stopped and looked at me, as I thought, a little oddly; and then, turning to the lawyer, 'Mungo,' said he, 'there's many a man would think this more of a warning than two pyats. Here am I on my road to Duror on the job ye ken; and here is a young lad starts up out of the bracken, and speers if I am on the way to Aucharn.'

'Glenure,' said the other, 'this is an ill subject for jesting.'

These two had now drawn close up and were gazing at me, while the two followers had halted about a stone-cast in the rear.

'And what seek ye in Aucharn?' said Colin Roy Campbell of Glenure; him they called the Red Fox; for he it was that I had stopped.

'The man that lives there,' said I.

'James of the Glens,' says Glenure, musingly; and then to the lawyer: 'Is he gathering his people, think ye?'

'Anyway,' says the lawyer, 'we shall do better to bide where we are, and let the soldiers rally us.'

'If you are concerned for me,' said I, 'I am neither of his people nor yours, but an honest subject of King George, owing no man and fearing no man.'

'Why, very well said,' replies the Factor. 'But if I may make so bold as ask, what does this honest man so far from his country? and why does he come seeking the brother of Ardshiel? I have power here, I must tell you. I am King's Factor upon several of these estates, and have twelve files of soldiers at my back.'

'I have heard a waif word in the country,' said I, a little nettled, 'that you were a hard man to drive.'

He still kept looking at me, as if in doubt.

'Well,' said he, at last, 'your tongue is bold; but I am no unfriend to plainness. If ye had asked me the way to the door of James Stewart on any other day but this, I would have set ye right and bidden ye God speed. But to-day—eh, Mungo?' And he turned again to look at the lawyer.

But just as he turned there came the shot of a firelock from higher up the hill; and with the very sound of it Glenure fell upon the road.

'Oh, I am dead!' he cried, several times over.

The lawyer had caught him up and held him in his arms, the servant standing over and clasping his hands. And now the wounded man looked from one to another with scared eyes, and there was a change in his voice that went to the heart.

'Take care of yourselves,' says he. 'I am dead.'

He tried to open his clothes as if to look for the wound, but his fingers slipped on the buttons. With that he gave a great sigh, his head rolled on his shoulder, and he passed away.

The lawyer said never a word, but his face was as sharp as a pen and as white as the dead man's; the servant broke out into a great noise of crying and weeping, like a child; and I, on my side, stood staring at them in a kind of horror. The sheriff's officer had run back at the first sound of the shot, to hasten the coming of the soldiers.

At last the lawyer laid down the dead man in his blood upon the road, and got to his own feet with a kind of stagger.

I believe it was his movement that brought me to my senses; for he had no sooner done so than I began to scramble up the hill, crying out, 'The murderer! the murderer!'

So little a time had elapsed, that when I got to the top of the first steepness, and could see some part of the open mountain, the murderer was still moving away at no great distance. He was a big man, in a black coat, with metal buttons, and carried a long fowling-piece.

'Here!' I cried. 'I see him!'

At that the murderer gave a little, quick look over his shoulder, and began to run. The next moment he was lost in a fringe of birches; then he came out again on the upper side, where I could see him climbing like a jackanapes, for that part was again very steep; and then he dipped behind a shoulder, and I saw him no more.

All this time I had been running on my side, and had got a good way up, when a voice cried upon me to stand.

I was at the edge of the upper wood, and so now, when

I halted and looked back, I saw all the open part of the hill below me.

The lawyer and the sheriff's officer were standing just above the road, crying and waving on me to come back; and on their left, the redcoats, musket in hand, were beginning to struggle singly out of the lower wood.

'Why should I come back?' I cried. 'Come you on!'

'Ten pounds if ye take that lad!' cried the lawyer. 'He's an accomplice. He was posted here to hold us in talk.'

At that word (which I could hear quite plainly, though it was to the soldiers and not to me that he was crying it) my heart came in my mouth with quite a new kind of terror. Indeed, it is one thing to stand the danger of your life, and quite another to run the peril of both life and character. The thing, besides, had come so suddenly, like thunder out of a clear sky, that I was all amazed and helpless.

The soldiers began to spread, some of them to run, and others to put up their pieces and cover me; and still I stood.

'Jouk in here among the trees,' said a voice, close by.

Indeed, I scarce knew what I was doing, but I obeyed; and as I did so, I heard the firelocks bang and the balls whistle in the birches.

Just inside the shelter of the trees I found Alan Breck standing, with a fishing-rod. He gave me no salutation; indeed it was no time for civilities; only 'Come!' says he, and set off running along the side of the mountain towards Balachulish; and I, like a sheep, to follow him.

Now we ran among the birches; now stooping behind low humps upon the mountain side; now crawling on all fours among the heather. The pace was deadly; my heart seemed bursting against my ribs; and I had neither time to think nor breath to speak with. Only I remember seeing with wonder, that Alan every now and then would straighten himself to his full height and look back; and every time he did so, there came a great far-away cheering and crying of the soldiers. Quarter of an hour later, Alan stopped, clapped down flat in the heather, and turned to me.

'Now,' said he, 'it's earnest. Do as I do for your life.'

And at the same speed, but now with infinitely more precaution, we traced back again across the mountain side by the same way that we had come, only perhaps higher; till at last Alan threw himself down in the upper wood of

Lettermore, where I had found him at the first, and lay, with his face in the bracken, panting like a dog.

My own sides so ached, my head so swam, my tongue so hung out of my mouth with heat and dryness, that I lay beside him like one dead.

ALAN WAS THE first to come round. He rose, went to the border of the wood, peered out a little, and then returned and sat down.

'Well,' said he, 'yon was a hot burst, David.'

I said nothing, nor so much as lifted my face. I had seen murder done, and a great, ruddy, jovial gentleman struck out of life in a moment; the pity of that sight was still sore within me, and yet that was but a part of my concern. Here was murder done upon the man Alan hated; here was Alan skulking in the trees and running from the troops; and whether his was the hand that fired or only the head that ordered, signified but little. By my way of it, my only friend in that wild country was blood-guilty in the first degree; I held him in horror; I could not look upon his face; I would have rather lain alone in the rain on my cold isle, than in that warm wood beside a murderer.

'Are ye still wearied?' he asked again.

'No,' said I, still with my face in the bracken; 'no, I am not wearied now, and I can speak. You and me must twine,' I said. 'I liked you very well, Alan; but your ways are not mine, and they're not God's; and the short and the long of it is just that we must twine.'

'I will hardly twine from ye, David, without some kind of reason for the same,' said Alan, mighty gravely. 'If ye ken anything against my reputation, it's the least thing that ye should do, for old acquaintance sake, to let me hear the name of it; and if ye have only taken a distaste to my society, it will be proper for me to judge if I'm insulted.'

'Alan,' said I, 'what is the sense of this? Ye ken very well yon Campbell-man lies in his blood upon the road.'

He was silent for a little; then says he, 'Did ever ye hear tell of the story of the Man and the Good People?'—by which he meant the fairies.

'No,' said I, 'nor do I want to hear it.'

'With your permission, Mr Balfour, I will tell it you, whatever,' says Alan. 'The man, ye should ken, was cast upon a rock in the sea, where it appears the Good People were in use to come and rest as they went through to Ireland. The name of this rock is called the Skerryvore, and it's not far from where we suffered shipwreck. Well, it seems the man cried so sore, if he could just see his little bairn before he died! that at last the king of the Good People took peety upon him, and sent one flying that brought back the bairn in a poke and laid it down beside the man where he lay sleeping. So when the man woke, there was a poke beside him and something into the inside of it that moved. Well, it seems he was one of these gentry that think aye the worst of things; and for greater security, he stuck his dirk throughout that poke before he opened it, and there was his bairn dead. I am thinking to myself, Mr Balfour, that you and the man are very much alike.'

'Do you mean you had no hand in it?' cried I, sitting up.

'I will tell you first of all, Mr Balfour of Shaws, as one friend to another,' said Alan, 'that if I were going to kill a gentleman, it would not be in my own country, to bring trouble on my clan; and I would not go wanting sword and gun, and with a long fishing-rod upon my back.'

'Well,' said I, 'that's true!'

'And now,' continued Alan, taking out his dirk and laying his hand upon it in a certain manner, 'I swear upon the Holy Iron I had neither art nor part, act nor thought in it.'

'I thank God for that!' cried I, and offered him my hand.

He did not appear to see it.

'And here is a great deal of work about a Campbell!' said he. 'They are not so scarce, that I ken!'

'At least,' said I, 'you cannot justly blame me, for you know very well what you told me in the brig. But the temptation and the act are different, I thank God again for that. We may all be tempted; but to take a life in cold blood, Alan!' And I could say no more for the moment. 'And do you know who did it?' I added. 'Do you know that man in the black coat?'

'I have nae clear mind about his coat,' said Alan, cunningly; 'but it sticks in my head that it was blue.'

'Blue or black, did ye know him?' said I.

'I couldnae just conscientiously swear to him,' says Alan. 'He gaed very close by me, to be sure, but it's a strange thing that I should just have been tying my brogues.'

'Can you swear that you don't know him, Alan?' I cried, half angered, half in a mind to laugh at his evasions.

'Not yet,' says he; 'but I've a grand memory for forgetting, David.'

'And yet there was one thing I saw clearly,' said I; 'and that was, that you exposed yourself and me to draw the soldiers.'

'It's very likely,' said Alan; 'and so would any gentleman. You and me were innocent of that transaction.'

'The better reason, since we were falsely suspected, that we should get clear,' I cried. 'The innocent should surely come before the guilty.'

'Why, David,' said he, 'the innocent have aye a chance to get assoiled in court; but for the lad that shot the bullet, I think the best place for him will be the heather. Them that havenae dipped their hands in any little difficulty, should be very mindful of the case of them that have. And that is the good Christianity. For if it was the other way round about, and the lad whom I couldnae just clearly see had been in our shoes, and we in his (as might very well have been) I think we would be a good deal obliged to him oursel's if he would draw the soldiers.'

When it came to this, I gave Alan up. But he looked so innocent all the time, and was in such clear good faith in what he said, and so ready to sacrifice himself for what he deemed his duty, that my mouth was closed. Mr Henderland's words came back to me: that we ourselves might take a lesson by these wild Highlanders. Well, here I had taken mine. Alan's morals were all tail-first; but he was ready to give his life for them, such as they were.

'Alan,' said I, 'I'll not say it's the good Christianity as I understand it, but it's good enough. And here I offer ye my hand for the second time.'

Whereupon he gave me both of his, saying surely I had cast a spell upon him, for he could forgive me anything. Then he grew very grave, and said we had not much time to throwaway, but must both flee that country: he, because he was a deserter, and the whole of Appin would now be searched like a chamber, and every one obliged to give a good account of himself; and I, because I was certainly involved in the murder.

'Oh!' says I, willing to give him a little lesson, 'I have no fear of the justice of my country.'

'As if this was your country!' said he. 'Or as if ye would be tried here, in a country of Stewarts!'

'It's all Scotland,' said I.

'Man, I whiles wonder at ye,' said Alan. 'This is a Campbell that's been killed. Well, it'll be tried in Inverara, the Campbell's head place; with fifteen Campbells in the jury-box, and the biggest Campbell of all (and that's the Duke) sitting cocking on the bench. Justice, David? The same justice, by all the world, as Glenure found a while ago at the roadside.'

This frighted me a little, I confess, and would have frighted me more if I had known how nearly exact were Alan's predictions; indeed it was but in one point that he exaggerated, there being but eleven Campbells on the jury; though as the other four were equally in the Duke's dependance, it mattered less than might appear. Still, I cried out that he was unjust to the Duke of Argyle who (for all he was a Whig), was yet a wise and honest nobleman.

'Hoot!' said Alan, 'the man's a Whig, nae doubt; but I would never deny he was a good chieftain to his clan. And what would the clan think if there was a Campbell shot and naebody hanged, and their own chief the Justice General? But I have often observed,' says Alan, 'that you Low-country bodies have no clear idea of what's right and wrong.'

At this I did at last laugh out aloud; when to my surprise, Alan joined in and laughed as merrily as myself.

'Na, na,' said he, 'we're in the Hielands, David; and when I tell ye to run, take my word and run. Nae doubt it's a hard thing to skulk and starve in the heather, but it's harder yet to lie shackled in a redcoat prison.'

I asked him whither we should flee; and as he told me 'to the Lowlands', I was a little better inclined to go with him; for indeed I was growing impatient to get back and have the upper-hand of my uncle. Besides, Alan made so sure there would be no question of justice in the matter, that I began to be afraid he might be right. Of all deaths, I would truly like least to die by the gallows; and the picture of that uncanny instrument came into my head with extraordinary clearness (as I had once seen it engraved at the top of a pedlar's ballad) and took away my appetite for courts of justice.

'I'll chance it, Alan,' said I. 'I'll go with you.'

'But mind you,' said Alan, 'it's no small thing. Ye maun lie bare and hard, and brook many an empty belly. Your bed shall be the moorcock's, and your life shall be like the hunted deer's, and ye shall sleep with your hand upon your weapons. Ay, man, ye shall taigle many a weary foot, or we get clear! I tell ye this at the start, for it's a life that I ken well. But if ye ask what other chance ye have, I answer: Nane. Either take to the heather with me, or else hang.'

'And that's a choice very easily made,' said I; and we shook hands upon it.

'And now let's take another keek at the redcoats,' says Alan, and he led me to the north-eastern fringe of the wood.

Looking out between the trees, we could see a great side of mountain, running down exceeding steep into the waters of the loch. It was a rough part, all hanging stone, and heather, and bit scrags of birchwood; and away at the far end towards Balachulish, little wee red soldiers were dipping up and down over hill and howe, and growing smaller every minute. There was no cheering now, for I think they had other uses for what breath was left them; but they still stuck to the trail, and doubtless thought that we were close in front of them.

Alan watched them, smiling to himself.

'Ay,' said he, 'they'll be gey weary before they've got to the end of that employ! And so you and me, David, can sit down and eat a bite, and breathe a bit longer, and take a dram from my bottle. Then we'll strike for Aucharn, the house of my kinsman, James of the Glens, where I must get my clothes, and my arms, and money to carry us along; and then David, we'll cry "Forth, Fortune!" and take a cast among the heather.'

So we sat again and ate and drank, in a place whence we could see the sun going down into a field of great, wild and houseless mountains, such as I was now condemned to wander in with my companion. Partly as we so sat, and partly

afterwards, on the way to Aucharn, each of us narrated his
adventures; and I shall here set down so much of Alan's
as seems either curious or needful.

It appears he ran to the bulwarks as soon as the wave
was passed; saw me, and lost me, and saw me again, as
I tumbled in the roost; and at last had one glimpse of me
clinging on the yard. It was this that put him in some hope
I would maybe get to land after all, and made him leave
those clues and messages which had brought me (for my
sins) to that unlucky country of Appin.

In the meanwhile, those still on the brig had got the skiff
launched, and one or two were on board of her already,
when there came a second wave greater than the first, and
heaved the brig out of her place, and would certainly have
sent her to the bottom, had she not struck and caught on
some projection of the reef. When she had struck first,
it had been bows-on, so that the stern had hitherto been
lowest. But now her stern was thrown in the air, and the
bows plunged under the sea; and with that, the water
began to pour into the forescuttle like the pouring of a
mill-dam.

It took the colour out of Alan's face, even to tell what
followed. For there were still two men lying impotent in
their bunks; and these, seeing the water pour in and
thinking the ship had foundered, begun to cry out aloud,
and that with such harrowing cries that all who were on
deck tumbled one after another into the skiff and fell to
their oars. They were not two hundred yards away, when
there came a third great sea; and at that the brig lifted
clean over the reef; her canvas filled for a moment, and
she seemed to sail in chase of them, but settling all the
while; and presently she drew down and down, as if a hand
was drawing her; and the sea closed over the *Covenant* of
Dysart.

Never a word they spoke as they pulled ashore, being
stunned with the horror of that screaming; but they had
scarce set foot upon the beach when Hoseason woke up, as
if out of a muse, and bade them lay hands upon Alan. They
hung back indeed, having little taste for the employment;
but Hoseason was like a fiend; crying that Alan was alone,
that he had a great sum about him, that he had been the
means of losing the brig and drowning all their comrades,

and that here was both revenge and wealth upon a single cast. It was seven against one; in that part of the shore there was no rock that Alan could set his back to; and the sailors began to spread out and come behind him.

'And then,' said Alan, 'the little man with the red head—I havenae mind of the name that he is called.'

'Riach,' said I.

'Ay,' said Alan, 'Riach! Well, it was him that took up the clubs for me, asked the men if they werenae feared of a judgment, and says he, "Dod, I'll put my back to the Hielandman's mysel'." That's none such an entirely bad little man, yon little man with the red head,' said Alan. 'He has some spunks of decency.'

'Well,' said I, 'he was kind to me in his way.'

'And so he was to Alan,' said he; 'and by my troth, I found his way a very good one! But ye see, David, the loss of the ship and the cries of these poor lads sat very ill upon the man; and I'm thinking that would be the cause of it.'

'Well, I would think so,' says I; 'for he was as keen as any of the rest at the beginning. But how did Hoseason take it?'

'It sticks in my mind that he would take it very ill,' says Alan. 'But the little man cried to me to run, and indeed I thought it was a good observe, and ran. The last that I saw they were all in a knot upon the beach, like folk that were not agreeing very well together.'

'What do you mean by that?' said I.

'Well, the fists were going,' said Alan; 'and I saw one man go down like a pair of breeks. But I thought it would be better no to wait. Ye see there's a strip of Campbells in that end of Mull, which is no good company for a gentleman like me. If it hadnae been for that I would have waited and looked for ye mysel', let alone giving a hand to the little man.' (It was droll how Alan dwelt on Mr Riach's stature, for, to say the truth, the one was not much smaller than the other.) 'So,' says he, continuing. 'I set my best foot forward, and whenever I met in with any one I cried out there was a wreck ashore. Man, they didnae stop to fash with me! Ye should have seen them linking for the beach! And when they got there they found they had had the pleasure of a run, which is aye good for a

Campbell. I'm thinking it was a judgment on the clan that the brig went down in the lump and didnae break. But it was a very unlucky thing for you, that same; for if any wreck had come ashore they would have hunted high and low, and would soon have found ye.'

NIGHT FELL AS WE were walking, and the clouds, which had broken up in the afternoon, settled in and thickened, so that it fell, for the season of the year, extremely dark. The way we went was over rough mountain sides; and though Alan pushed on with an assured manner, I could by no means see how he directed himself.

At last, about half-past ten of the clock, we came to the top of a brae, and saw lights below us. It seemed a house door stood open and let out a beam of fire and candle-light; and all round the house and steading five or six persons were moving hurriedly about, each carrying a lighted brand.

'James must have tint his wits,' said Alan. 'If this was the soldiers instead of you and me, he would be in a bonny mess. But I dare say he'll have a sentry on the road, and he would ken well enough no soldiers would find the way that we came.'

Hereupon he whistled three times, in a particular manner. It was strange to see how, at the first sound of it, all the moving torches came to a stand, as if the bearers were affrighted; and how, at the third, the bustle began again as before.

Having thus set folks' minds at rest, we came down the brae, and were met at the yard gate (for this place was like a well-doing farm) by a tall, handsome man of more than fifty, who cried out to Alan in the Gaelic.

'James Stewart,' said Alan, 'I will ask ye to speak in Scotch, for here is a young gentleman with me that has nane of the other. This is him,' he added, putting his arm through mine, 'a young gentleman of the lowlands, and a laird in his country too, but I am thinking it will be the better for his health if we give his name the go-by.'

James of the Glens turned to me for a moment, and

greeted me courteously enough; the next he had turned to Alan.

'This has been a dreadful accident,' he cried. 'It will bring trouble on the country.' And he wrung his hands.

'Hoots!' said Alan, 'ye must take the sour with the sweet, man. Colin Roy is dead, and be thankful for that!'

'Ay,' said James, 'and by my troth, I wish he was alive again! It's all very fine to blow and boast beforehand; but now it's done, Alan; and who's to bear the wyte of it? The accident fell out in Appin—mind ye that, Alan; it's Appin that must pay; and I am a man that has a family.'

While this was going on I looked about me at the servants. Some were on ladders, digging in the thatch of the house or the farm buildings, from which they brought out guns, swords, and different weapons of war; others carried them away; and by the sound of mattock blows from somewhere further down the brae, I suppose they buried them. Though they were all so busy, there prevailed no kind of order in their efforts; men struggled together for the same gun and ran into each other with their burning torches; and James was continually turning about from his talk with Alan, to cry out orders which were apparently never understood. The faces in the torchlight were like those of people overborne with hurry and panic; and though none spoke above his breath, their speech sounded both anxious and angry.

It was about this time that a lassie came out of the house carrying a pack or bundle; and it has often made me smile to think how Alan's instinct awoke at the mere sight of it.

'What's that the lassie has?' he asked.

'We're just setting the house in order, Alan,' said James, in his frightened and somewhat fawning way. 'They'll search Appin with candles, and we must have all things straight. We're digging the bit guns and swords into the moss, ye see; and these, I am thinking, will be your ain French clothes.'

'Bury my French clothes!' cried Alan. 'Troth, no!' And he laid hold upon the packet and retired into the barn to shift himself, recommending me in the meanwhile to his kinsman.

James carried me accordingly into the kitchen, and sat down with me at table, smiling and talking at first in a very hospitable manner. But presently the gloom returned upon him; he sat frowning, and biting his fingers; only remembered me from time to time; and then gave me but a word or two and a poor smile, and back into his private terrors. His wife sat by the fire and wept, with her face in her hands; his eldest son was crouched upon the floor, running over a great mass of papers and now and again setting one alight and burning it to the bitter end; all the while a servant lass with a red face was rummaging about the room, in a blind hurry of fear, and whimpering as she went; and every now and again one of the men would thrust in his face from the yard, and cry for orders.

At last James could keep his seat no longer, and begged my permission to be so unmannerly as walk about. 'I am but poor company altogether, sir,' says he, 'but I can think of nothing but this dreadful accident, and the trouble it is like to bring upon quite innocent persons.'

A little after he observed his son burning a paper, which he thought should have been kept; and at that his excitement burst out so that it was painful to witness. He struck the lad repeatedly.

'Are you gone gyte?' he cried. 'Do you wish to hang your father?' and forgetful of my presence, carried on at him a long time together in the Gaelic, the young man answering nothing; only the wife, at the name of hanging, throwing her apron over her face and sobbing out louder than before.

This was all wretched for a stranger like myself to hear and see; and I was right glad when Alan returned, looking like himself in his fine French clothes, though (to be sure) they were now grown almost too battered and withered to deserve the name of fine. I was then taken out in my turn by another of the sons, and given that change of clothing of which I had stood so long in need, and a pair of Highland brogues made of deer-leather, rather strange at first, but after a little practice very easy to the feet.

By the time I came back Alan must have told his story; for it seemed understood that I was to fly with him, and they were all busy upon our equipment. They gave us each a sword and pistols, though I professed my inability to use the former; and with these, and some ammunition, a bag of oatmeal, an iron pan, and a bottle of right French brandy, we were ready for the heather. Money, indeed, was lacking. I had about two guineas left; Alan's belt having been despatched by another hand, that trusty messenger had no more than seventeen pence to his whole fortune; and as for James, it appears he had brought himself so low with journeys to Edinburgh and legal expenses on behalf of the tenants, that he could only scrape together three-and-fivepence-halfpenny, the most of it in coppers.

'This'll no do,' said Alan.

'Ye must find a safe bit somewhere near by,' said James, 'and get word sent to me. Ye see, ye'll have to get this business prettily off, Alan. This is no time to be stayed for a guinea or two. They're sure to get wind of ye, sure to seek ye, and by my way of it, sure to lay on ye the wyte of this day's accident. If it falls on you, it falls on me that am your near kinsman and harboured ye while ye were in the country. And if it comes on me—' he paused, and bit his fingers, with a white face. 'It would be a painful thing for our friends if I was to hang,' said he.

'It would be an ill day for Appin,' says Alan.

'It's a day that sticks in my throat,' said James. 'Oh man, man, man—man Alan! you and me have spoken like two fools!' he cried, striking his hand upon the wall so that the house rang again.

'Well, and that's true, too,' said Alan; 'and my friend from the lowlands here' (nodding at me) 'gave me a good word upon that head, if I would only have listened to him.'

'But see here,' said James, returning to his former manner, 'if they lay me by the heels, Alan, it's then that you'll be needing the money. For with all that I have said and that you have said, it will look very black against the two of us; do ye mark that? Well, follow me out, and ye'll see that I'll have to get a paper out against ye mysel'; I'll have to offer a reward for ye; ay, will I! It's a sore thing to do between such near friends; but if I get the dirdum of this dreadful accident, I'll have to fend for myself, man. Do ye see that?'

He spoke with a pleading earnestness, taking Alan by the breast of the coat.

'Ay,' said Alan, 'I see that.'

'And ye'll have to be clear of the country, Alan—ay, and clear of Scotland—you and your friend from the lowlands, too. For I'll have to paper your friend from the lowlands. Ye see that, Alan—say that ye see that!'

I thought Alan flushed a bit. 'This is unco hard on me that brought him here, James,' said he, throwing his head back. 'It's like making me a traitor!'

'Now, Alan, man!' cried James. 'Look things in the face! He'll be papered anyway; Mungo Campbell'll be sure to paper him; what matters if I paper him too? And then, Alan, I am a man that has a family.' And then, after a little pause on both sides: 'And, Alan, it'll be a jury of Campbells,' said he.

'There's one thing,' said Alan, musingly, 'that naebody kens his name.'

'Nor yet they shallnae, Alan! There's my hand on that,' cried James, for all the world as if he had really known my name and was foregoing some advantage. 'But just the habit he was in, and what he looked like, and his age, and the like? I couldnae well do less.'

'I wonder at your father's son,' cried Alan, sternly. 'Would ye sell the lad with a gift? would ye change his clothes and then betray him?'

'No, no, Alan,' said James. 'No, no: the habit he took off—the habit Mungo saw him in.' But I thought he seemed crestfallen; indeed, he was clutching at every straw, and all the time, I dare say, saw the faces of his hereditary foes on the bench and in the jury-box, and the gallows in the background.

'Well, sir,' says Alan, turning to me, 'what say ye to that? Ye are here under the safeguard of my honour; and it's my part to see nothing done but what shall please you.'

'I have but one word to say,' said I; 'for to all this dispute I am a perfect stranger. But the plain common sense is to set the blame where it belongs, and that is on the man that fired the shot. Paper him, as ye call it, set the hunt on him; and let honest, innocent folk show their faces in safety.'

But at this both Alan and James cried out in horror; bidding me hold my tongue, for that was not to be thought of, and asking me 'What the Camerons would think?' (which confirmed me, it must have been a Cameron from Mamore that did the act) and if I did not see that the lad might be caught? 'Ye havenae surely thought of that?' said they, with such innocent earnestness, that my hands dropped at my side and I despaired of argument.

'Very well, then,' said I, 'paper me, if you please, paper

Alan, paper King George! We're all three innocent, and that seems to be what's wanted! But at least, sir,' said I to James, recovering from my little fit of annoyance, 'I am Alan's friend, and if I can be helpful to friends of his, I will not stumble at the risk.'

I thought it best to put a fair face on my consent, for I saw Alan troubled; and besides (thinks I to myself) as soon as my back is turned, they will paper me, as they call it, whether I consent or not. But in this I saw I was wrong; for I had no sooner said the words, than Mrs Stewart leaped out of her chair, came running over to us, and wept first upon my neck and then on Alan's, blessing God for our goodness to her family.

'As for you, Alan, it was no more than your bounden duty,' she said. 'But for this lad that has come here and seen us at our worst, and seen the good-man fleeching like a suitor, him that by rights should give his commands like any king—as for you, my lad,' she says, 'my heart is wae not to have your name, but I have your face; and as long as my heart beats under my bosom, I will keep it, and think of it, and bless it.' And with that she kissed me, and burst once more into such sobbing, that I stood abashed.

'Hoot, hoot,' said Alan, looking mighty silly. 'The day comes unco soon in this month of July; and to-morrow there'll be a fine to-do in Appin, a fine riding of dragoons, and crying of "Cruachan!" and running of redcoats; and it behoves you and me to be the sooner gone.'

Thereupon we said farewell, and set out again, bending somewhat eastward, in a fine mild dark night, and over much the same broken country as before.

SOMETIMES WE WALKED, sometimes ran; and
as it drew on to morning, walked ever the less and ran the
more. Though, upon its face, that country appeared to be
a desert, yet there were huts and houses of the people, of
which we must have passed more than twenty, hidden in
quiet places of the hills. When we came to one of these,
Alan would leave me in the way, and go himself and rap
upon the side of the house and speak a while at the window
with some sleeper awakened. This was to pass the news;
which, in that country, was so much of a duty that Alan
must pause to attend to it even while fleeing for his life;
and so well attended to by others, that in more than half of
the houses where we called they had heard already of the
murder. In the others, as well as I could make out (standing
back at a distance and hearing a strange tongue) the news
was received with more of consternation than surprise.

For all our hurry, day began to come in while we were
still far from any shelter. It found us in a prodigious valley,
strewn with rocks and where ran a foaming river. Wild
mountains stood around it; there grew there neither grass
nor trees; and I have sometimes thought since then, that it
may have been the valley called Glencoe, where the massacre
was in the time of King William. But for the details of our
itinerary, I am all to seek; our way lying now by short
cuts, now by great detours; our pace being so hurried;
our time of journeying usually by night; and the names
of such places as I asked and heard, being in the Gaelic
tongue and the more easily forgotten.

The first peep of morning, then, showed us this horrible
place, and I could see Alan knit his brow.

'This is no fit place for you and me,' he said. 'This is a
place they're bound to watch.'

And with that he ran harder than ever down to the water

side, in a part where the river was split in two among three rocks. It went through with a horrid thundering that made my belly quake; and there hung over the lynn a little mist of spray. Alan looked neither to the right nor to the left, but jumped clean upon the middle rock and fell there on his hands and knees to check himself, for that rock was small and he might have pitched over on the far side. I had scarce time to measure the distance or to understand the peril, before I had followed him, and he had caught and stopped me.

So there we stood, side by side upon a small rock slippery with spray, a far broader leap in front of us, and the river dinning upon all sides. When I saw where I was, there came on me a deadly sickness of fear, and I put my hand over my eyes. Alan took me and shook me; I saw he was speaking, but the roaring of the falls and the trouble of my mind prevented me from hearing; only I saw his face was red with anger, and that he stamped upon the rock. The same look showed me the water raging by, and the mist hanging in the air; and with that, I covered my eyes again and shuddered.

The next minute Alan had set the brandy bottle to my lips, and forced me to drink about a gill, which sent the blood into my head again. Then, putting his hands to his mouth and his mouth to my ear, he shouted 'Hang or drown!' and turning his back upon me, leaped over the farther branch of the stream, and landed safe.

I was now alone upon the rock, which gave me the more room; the brandy was singing in my ears; I had this good example fresh before me, and just wit enough to see that if I did not leap at once, I should never leap at all. I bent low on my knees and flung myself forth, with that kind of anger of despair that has sometimes stood me in stead of courage. Sure enough, it was but my hands that reached the full length; these slipped, caught again, slipped again; and I was sliddering back into the lynn, when Alan seized me, first by the hair, then by the collar, and with a great strain dragged me into safety.

Never a word he said, but set off running again for his life, and I must stagger to my feet and run after him. I had been weary before, but now I was sick and bruised, and partly drunken with the brandy; I kept stumbling as

I ran, I had a stitch that came near to overmaster me; and when at last Alan paused under a great rock that stood there among a number of others, it was none too soon for David Balfour.

A great rock, I have said; but by rights it was two rocks leaning together at the top, both some twenty feet high, and at the first sight inaccessible. Even Alan (though you may say he had as good as four hands) failed twice in an attempt to climb them; and it was only at the third trial, and then by standing on my shoulders and leaping up with such force as I thought must have broken my collar-bone, that he secured a lodgment. Once there, he let down his leathern girdle; and with the aid of that and a pair of shallow footholds in the rock, I scrambled up beside him.

Then I saw why we had come there; for the two rocks, being both somewhat hollow on the top and sloping one to the other, made a kind of dish or saucer, where as many as three or four men might have lain hidden.

All this while Alan had not said a word, and had run and climbed with such a savage, silent frenzy of hurry, that I knew he was in mortal fear of some miscarriage. Even now we were on the rock he said nothing, nor so much as relaxed the frowning look upon his face; but clapped flat down, and keeping only one eye above the edge of our place of shelter, scouted all round the compass. The dawn had come quite clear; we could see the stony sides of the valley, and its bottom, which was bestrewed with rocks, and the river, which went from one side to another, and made white falls; but nowhere the smoke of a house, nor any living creature but some eagles screaming round a cliff.

Then at last Alan smiled.

'Ay,' said he, 'now we have a chance'; and then looking at me with some amusement, 'Ye're no very gleg at the jumping,' said he.

At this I suppose I coloured with mortification, for he added at once, 'Hoots! small blame to ye! To be feared of a thing and yet to do it, is what makes the prettiest kind of a man. And then there was water there, and water's a thing that daunts even me. No, no,' said Alan, 'it's no you that's to blame, it's me.'

I asked him why.

'Why,' said he, 'I have proved myself a gomeral this

night. For first of all I take a wrong road, and that in my own country of Appin; so that the day has caught us where we should never have been; and thanks to that, we lie here in some danger and mair discomfort. And next (which is the worst of the two, for a man that has been so much among the heather as myself) I have come wanting a water-bottle, and here we lie for a long summer's day with naething but neat spirit. Ye may think that a small matter; but before it comes night, David, ye'll give me news of it.'

I was anxious to redeem my character, and offered, if he would pour out the brandy, to run down and fill the bottle at the river.

'I wouldnae waste the good spirit either,' says he. 'It's been a good friend to you this night; or in my poor opinion, ye would still be cocking on yon stone. And what's mair,' says he, 'ye may have observed (you that's a man of so much penetration) that Alan Breck Stewart was perhaps walking quicker than his ordinar'.'

'You!' I cried, 'you were running fit to burst.'

'Was I so?' said he. 'Well, then, ye may depend upon it, there was nae time to be lost. And now here is enough said; gang you to your sleep, lad, and I'll watch.'

Accordingly, I lay down to sleep; a little peaty earth had drifted in between the top of the two rocks, and some bracken grew there, to be a bed to me; the last thing I heard was still the crying of the eagles.

I dare say it would be nine in the morning when I was roughly awakened, and found Alan's hand pressed upon my mouth.

'Wheesht!' he whispered. 'Ye were snoring.'

'Well,' said I, surprised at his anxious and dark face, 'and why not?'

He peered over the edge of the rock, and signed to me to do the like.

It was now high day, cloudless, and very hot. The valley was as clear as in a picture. About half a mile up the water was a camp of redcoats; a big fire blazed in their midst, at which some were cooking; and near by, on the top of a rock about as high as ours, there stood a sentry, with the sun sparkling on his arms. All the way down along the river-side were posted other sentries; here near together, there widelier scattered; some planted like the first, on places of command, some on the ground level and marching and counter-marching, so as to meet half way. Higher up the glen, where the ground was more open, the chain of posts was continued by horse-soldiers, whom we could see in the distance riding to and fro. Lower down, the infantry continued; but as the stream was suddenly swelled by the confluence of a considerable burn, they were more widely set, and only watched the fords and stepping-stones.

I took but one look at them, and ducked again into my place. It was strange indeed to see this valley, which had lain so solitary in the hour of dawn, bristling with arms and dotted with the red coats and breeches.

'Ye see,' said Alan, 'this was what I was afraid of, Davie: that they would watch the burn-side. They began to come in about two hours ago, and, man! but ye're a grand hand at the sleeping! We're in a narrow place. If they get up the sides of the hill, they could easy spy us with a glass; but if they'll only keep in the foot of the valley, we'll do yet. The posts are thinner down the water; and, come night, we'll try our hand at getting by them.'

'And what are we to do till night?' I asked.

'Lie here,' says he, 'and birstle.'

That one good Scotch word, 'birstle', was indeed the most of the story of the day that we had now to pass. You are to remember that we lay on the bare top of a rock, like scones upon a girdle; the sun beat upon us cruelly; the rock grew so heated, a man could scarce endure the touch of it; and the little patch of earth and fern, which kept cooler, was only large enough for one at a time. We took turn about to lie on the naked rock, which was indeed like the position of that saint that was martyred on a gridiron; and it ran in my mind how strange it was, that in the same climate and at only a few days' distance, I should have suffered so cruelly, first from cold upon my island, and now from heat upon this rock.

All the while we had no water, only raw brandy for a drink, which was worse than nothing; but we kept the bottle as cool as we could, burying it in the earth, and got some relief by bathing our breasts and temples.

The soldiers kept stirring all day in the bottom of the valley, now changing guard, now in patrolling parties hunting among the rocks. These lay round in so great a number, that

to look for men among them was like looking for a needle in
a bottle of hay; and being so hopeless a task, it was gone
about with the less care. Yet we could see the soldiers pike
their bayonets among the heather, which sent a cold thrill
into my vitals; and they would sometimes hang about our
rock, so that we scarce dared to breathe.

It was in this way that I first heard the right English
speech; one fellow as he went by actually clapping his
hand upon the sunny face of the rock on which we lay,
and plucking it off again with an oath.

'I tell you it's 'ot,' says he; and I was amazed at the
clipping tones and the odd sing-song in which he spoke,
and no less at that strange trick of dropping out the letter
h. To be sure, I had heard Ransome; but he had taken his
ways from all sorts of people, and spoke so imperfectly at
the best, that I set down the most of it to childishness. My
surprise was all the greater to hear that manner of speaking in
the mouth of a grown man; and indeed I have never grown
used to it; nor yet altogether with the English grammar,
as perhaps a very critical eye might here and there spy out
even in these memories.

The tediousness and pain of these hours upon the rock
grew only the greater as the day went on; the rock getting
still the hotter and the sun fiercer. There were giddiness, and
sickness, and sharp pangs like rheumatism, to be supported.
I minded then, and have often minded since, on the lines in
our Scotch psalm:

> The moon by night thee shall not smite,
> Nor yet the sun by day

and indeed it was only by God's blessing that we were
neither of us sun-smitten.

At last, about two, it was beyond men's bearing, and there
was now temptation to resist, as well as pain to thole. For
the sun being now got a little into the west, there came a
patch of shade on the east side of our rock, which was the
side sheltered from the soldiers.

'As well one death as another,' said Alan, and slipped over
the edge and dropped on the ground on the shadowy side.

I followed him at once, and instantly fell all my length,
so weak was I and so giddy with that long exposure. Here,
then, we lay for an hour or two, aching from head to foot, as
weak as water, and lying quite naked to the eye of any soldier

who should have strolled that way. None came, however, all passing by on the other side; so that our rock continued to be our shield even in this new position.

Presently we began again to get a little strength; and as the soldiers were now lying closer along the riverside, Alan proposed that we should try a start. I was by this time afraid of but one thing in the world; and that was to be set back upon the rock; anything else was welcome to me; so we got ourselves at once in marching order, and began to slip from rock to rock one after the other, now crawling flat on our bellies in the shade, now making a run for it, heart in mouth.

The soldiers, having searched this side of the valley after a fashion, and being perhaps somewhat sleepy with the sultriness of the afternoon, had now laid by much of their vigilance, and stood dozing at their posts or only kept a look-out along the banks of the river; so that in this way, keeping down the valley and at the same time towards the mountains, we drew steadily away from their neighbourhood. But the business was the most wearing I had ever taken part in. A man had need of a hundred eyes in every part of him, to keep concealed in that uneven country and within cry of so many and scattered sentries. When we must pass an open place, quickness was not all, but a swift judgment not only of the lie of the whole country, but of the solidity of every stone on which we must set foot; for the afternoon was now fallen so breathless that the rolling of a pebble sounded abroad like a pistol shot, and would start the echo calling among the hills and cliffs.

By sundown we had made some distance, even by our slow rate of progress, though to be sure the sentry on the rock was still plainly in our view. But now we came on something that put all fears out of season; and that was a deep rushing burn, that tore down, in that part, to join the glen river. At the sight of this we cast ourselves on the ground and plunged head and shoulders in the water; and I cannot tell which was the more pleasant, the great shock as the cool stream went over us, or the greed with which we drank of it.

We lay there (for the banks hid us), drank again and again, bathed our chests, let our wrists trail in the running water till they ached with the chill; and at last, being

wonderfully renewed, we got out the meal-bag and made
drammach in the iron pan. This, though it is but cold water
mingled with oatmeal, yet makes a good enough dish for a
hungry man; and where there are no means of making fire,
or (as in our case) good reason for not making one, it is
the chief stand-by of those who have taken to the heather.

As soon as the shadow of the night had fallen, we set
forth again, at first with the same caution, but presently
with more boldness, standing our full height and stepping
out at a good pace of walking. The way was very intricate,
lying up the steep sides of mountains and along the brows
of cliffs; clouds had come in with the sunset, and the
night was dark and cool; so that I walked without much
fatigue, but in continual fear of falling and rolling down
the mountains, and with no guess at our direction.

The moon rose at last and found us still on the road; it
was in its last quarter and was long beset with clouds; but
after a while shone out, and showed me many dark heads
of mountains, and was reflected far underneath us on the
narrow arm of a sea-loch.

At this sight we both paused: I struck with wonder to
find myself so high and walking (as it seemed to me)
upon clouds: Alan to make sure of his direction.

Seemingly he was well pleased, and he must certainly
have judged us out of ear-shot of all our enemies; for
throughout the rest of our night-march he beguiled the way
with whistling of many tunes, warlike, merry, plaintive;
reel tunes that made the foot go faster; tunes of my
own south country that made me fain to be home from
my adventures; and all these, on the great, dark, desert
mountains, making company upon the way.

EARLY AS DAY comes in the beginning of July, it was
still dark when we reached our destination, a cleft in the
head of a great mountain, with a water running through
the midst, and upon the one hand a shallow cave in a rock.
Birches grew there in a thin, pretty wood, which a little
further on was changed into a wood of pines. The burn was
full of trout; the wood of cushat-doves; on the open side
of the mountain beyond, whaups would be always whistling,
and cuckoos were plentiful. From the mouth of the cleft we
looked down upon a part of Mamore, and on the sea-loch that
divides that country from Appin; and this from so great a
height, as made it my continual wonder and pleasure to sit
and behold them.

The name of the cleft was the Heugh of Corrynakiegh;
and although from its height and being so near upon the
sea, it was often beset with clouds, yet it was on the whole
a pleasant place, and the five days we lived in it went
happily.

We slept in the cave, making our bed of heather bushes
which we cut for that purpose, and covering ourselves with
Alan's great-coat. There was a low concealed place, in a
turning of the glen, where we were so bold as to make fire:
so that we could warm ourselves when the clouds set in, and
cook hot porridge, and grill the little trouts that we caught
with our hands under the stones and overhanging banks of
the burn. This was indeed our chief pleasure and business;
and not only to save our meal against worse times, but with
a rivalry that much amused us, we spent a great part of our
days at the water side, stripped to the waist and groping
about or (as they say) guddling for these fish. The largest
we got might have been a quarter of a pound; but they were
of good flesh and flavour, and when broiled upon the coals,
lacked only a little salt to be delicious.

In any by-time Alan must teach me to use my sword, for my ignorance had much distressed him; and I think besides, as I had sometimes the upper-hand of him in the fishing, he was not sorry to turn to an exercise where he had so much the upper-hand of me. He made it somewhat more of a pain than need have been, for he stormed at me all through the lessons in a very violent manner of scolding, and would push me so close that I made sure he must run me through the body. I was often tempted to turn tail, but held my ground for all that, and got some profit of my lessons; if it was but to stand on guard with an assured countenance, which is often all that is required. So, though I could never in the least please my master, I was not altogether displeased with myself.

In the meanwhile, you are not to suppose that we neglected our chief business, which was to get away.

'It will be many a long day,' Alan said to me on our first morning, 'before the redcoats think upon seeking Corrynakiegh; so now we must get word sent to James, and he must find the siller for us.'

'And how shall we send that word?' says I. 'We are here in a desert place, which yet we dare not leave; and unless ye get the fowls of the air to be your messengers, I see not what we shall be able to do.'

'Ay?' said Alan. 'Ye're a man of small contrivance, David.'

Thereupon he fell in a muse, looking in the embers of the fire; and presently, getting a piece of wood, he fashioned it in a cross, the four ends of which he blackened on the coals. Then he looked at me a little shyly.

'Could ye lend me my button?' says he. 'It seems a strange thing to ask a gift again, but I own I am laith to cut another.'

I gave him the button; whereupon he strung it on a strip of his great-coat which he had used to bind the cross; and tying in a little sprig of birch and another of fir, he looked upon his work with satisfaction.

'Now,' said he, 'there is a little clachan' (what is called a hamlet in the English) 'not very far from Corrynakiegh, and it has the name of Koalisnacoan. There, there are living many friends of mine whom I could trust with my life, and some that I am no just so sure of. Ye see, David, there will be money set upon our heads; James himsel' is to set money on them; and as for the Campbells, they would never spare siller where there was a Stewart to be hurt. If it was otherwise, I would go down to Koalisnacoan whatever, and trust my life into these people's hands as lightly as I would trust another with my glove.'

'But being so?' said I.

'Being so,' said he, 'I would as lief they didnae see me. There's bad folk everywhere, and what's far worse, weak ones. So when it comes dark again, I will steal down into that clachan, and set this that I have been making in the window of a good friend of mine, John Breck Maccoll, a bouman of Appin's.'

'With all my heart,' says I; 'and if he finds it, what is he to think?'

'Well,' says Alan, 'I wish he was a man of more penetration, for by my troth I am afraid he will make little enough of it! But this is what I have in my mind. This cross is something in the nature of the cross-tarrie, or fiery cross, which is the signal of gathering in our clans; yet he will know well enough the clan is not to rise, for there it is standing in his window, and no word with it. So he will say to himsel', *The clan is not to rise, but there is something*. Then he will see my button, and that was Duncan Stewart's. And then he will say to himsel', *The son of Duncan is in the heather, and has need of me.*'

'Well,' said I, 'it may be. But even supposing so, there is a good deal of heather between here and the Forth.'

'And that is a very true word,' says Alan. 'But then John Breck will see the sprig of birch and the sprig of pine; and he will say to himsel' (if he is a man of any penetration at all, which I misdoubt) *Alan will be lying in a wood which is both of pines and birches*. Then he will think to himsel', *That is not so very rife hereabout;* and then he will come and give us a look up in Corrynakiegh. And if he does not, David, the devil may fly away with him, for what I care; for he will no be worth the salt to his porridge.'

'Eh, man,' said I, drolling with him a little, 'you're very ingenious! But would it not be simpler for you to write him a few words in black and white?'

'And that is an excellent observe, Mr Balfour of Shaws,' says Alan, drolling with me; 'and it would certainly be much simpler for me to write to him, but it would be a sore job for John Breck to read it. He would have to go to the school for two-three years; and it's possible we might be wearied waiting on him.'

So that night Alan carried down his fiery cross and set it in the bouman's window. He was troubled when he came back; for the dogs had barked and the folk run out from their houses; and he thought he had heard a clatter of arms and seen a redcoat come to one of the doors. On all accounts, we lay the next day in the borders of the wood and kept a close look-out; so that if it was John Breck that came, we might be ready to guide him, and if it was the redcoats, we should have time to get away.

About noon a man was to be spied, straggling up the open side of the mountain in the sun, and looking round him as he came, from under his hand. No sooner had Alan seen him than he whistled; the man turned and came a little towards us: then Alan would give another 'peep!' and the man would come still nearer; and so by the sound of whistling, he was guided to the spot where we lay.

He was a ragged, wild, bearded man, about forty, grossly disfigured with the smallpox, and looked both dull and savage. Although his English was very bad and broken, yet Alan (according to his very handsome use, whenever I was by) would suffer him to speak no Gaelic. Perhaps the strange language made him appear more backward than he really was; but I thought he had little good-will to serve us, and what he had was the child of terror.

Alan would have had him carry a message to James; but the bouman would hear of no message. 'She was forget it,' he said in his screaming voice; and would either have a letter or wash his hands of us.

I thought Alan would be gravelled at that, for we lacked the means of writing in that desert. But he was a man of more resources than I knew; searched the wood until he found a quill of a cushat-dove, which he shaped into a pen; made himself a kind of ink with gunpowder from his horn and water from the running stream; and tearing a corner from his French military commission (which he carried in his pocket, like a talisman to keep him from the gallows) he sat down and wrote as follows:

Dear Kinsman,—Please send the money by the bearer to the place he kens of.

Your affectionate cousin,

A. S.

This he entrusted to the bouman, who promised to make what manner of speed he best could, and carried it off with him down the hill.

He was three full days gone, but about five in the evening of the third, we heard a whistling in the wood, which Alan answered; and presently the bouman came up the water-side, looking for us, right and left. He seemed less sulky than before, and indeed he was no doubt well pleased to have got to the end of such a dangerous commission.

He gave us the news of the country; that it was alive with redcoats; that arms were being found, and poor folk brought in trouble daily; and that James and some of his servants were already clapped in prison at Fort William, under strong suspicion of complicity. It seemed, it was noised on all sides that Alan Breck had fired the shot; and there was a bill issued for both him and me, with one hundred pounds reward.

This was all as bad as could be; and the little note the bouman had carried us from Mrs Stewart was of a miserable sadness. In it she besought Alan not to let himself be captured, assuring him, if he fell in the hands of the troops, both he and James were no better than dead men. The money she had sent was all that she could beg or borrow, and she prayed heaven we could be doing with it. Lastly, she said she enclosed us one of the bills in which we were described.

This we looked upon with great curiosity and not a little fear, partly as a man may look in a mirror, partly as he might look into the barrel of an enemy's gun to judge if it be truly aimed. Alan was advertised as 'a small, pock-marked, active man of thirty-five or thereby, dressed in a feathered hat, a French side-coat of blue with silver buttons and lace a great deal tarnished, a red waistcoat and breeches of black shag'; and I as 'a tall strong lad of about eighteen, wearing an old blue coat, very ragged, an old Highland bonnet, a long homespun waistcoat, blue breeches; his legs bare; low-country shoes, wanting the toes; speaks like a lowlander, and has no beard.'

Alan was well enough pleased to see his finery so fully

remembered and set down; only when he came to the word tarnish, he looked upon his lace like one a little mortified. As for myself, I thought I cut a miserable figure in the bill; and yet was well enough pleased too, for since I had changed these rags, the description had ceased to be a danger and become a source of safety.

'Alan,' said I, 'you should change your clothes.'

'Na, troth!' said Alan, 'I have nae others. A fine sight I would be, if I went back to France in a bonnet!'

This put a second reflection in my mind: that if I were to separate from Alan and his tell-tale clothes I should be safe against arrest, and might go openly about my business. Nor was this all; for suppose I was arrested when I was alone, there was little against me; but suppose I was taken in company with the reputed murderer, my case would begin to be grave. For generosity's sake, I dare not speak my mind upon this head; but I thought of it none the less.

I thought of it all the more, too, when the bouman brought out a green purse with four guineas in gold, and the best part of another in small change. True, it was more than I had. But then Alan, with less than five guineas, had to get as far as France; I, with my less than two, not beyond Queensferry; so that, taking things in their proportion, Alan's society was not only a peril to my life but a burden on my purse.

But there was no thought of the sort in the honest head of my companion. He believed he was serving, helping, and protecting me. And what could I do but hold my peace, and chafe, and take my chance of it?

'It's little enough,' said Alan, putting the purse in his pocket, 'but it'll do my business. And now John Breck, if ye will hand me over my button, this gentleman and me will be for taking the road.'

But the bouman, after feeling about in a hairy purse that hung in front of him in the Highland manner (though he wore otherwise the lowland habit, with sea-trousers) began to roll his eyes strangely, and at last said, 'Her nainsel will loss it,' meaning he thought he had lost it.

'What!' cried Alan, 'you will lose my button, that was my father's before me? Now, I will tell you what is in my mind, John Breck: it is in my mind this is the worst day's work that ever ye did since ye were born.'

And as Alan spoke, he set his hands on his knees and looked at the bouman with a smiling mouth, and that dancing light in his eyes that meant mischief to his enemies.

Perhaps the bouman was honest enough; perhaps he had meant to cheat and then, finding himself alone with two of us in a desert place, cast back to honesty as being safer; at least, and all at once, he seemed to find that button and handed it to Alan.

'Well, and it is a good thing for the honour of the Maccolls,' said Alan, and then to me, 'Here is my button back again, and I thank you for parting with it, which is of a piece with all your friendships to me.' Then he took the warmest parting of the bouman. 'For,' says he, 'ye have done very well by me, and set your neck at a venture, and I will always give you the name of a good man.'

Lastly, the bouman took himself off byy one way; and Alan and I (getting our chattels together) struck into another to resume our flight.

MORE THAN ELEVEN hours of incessant, hard travelling brought us early in the morning to the end of a range
of mountains. In front of us there lay a piece of low, broken,
desert land, which we must now cross. The sun was not long
up, and shone straight in our eyes; a little, thin mist went
up from the face of the moorland like a smoke; so that
(as Alan said) there might have been twenty squadron
of dragoons there and we none the wiser.

We sat down, therefore, in a howe of the hill-side till
the mist should have risen, and made ourselves a dish of
drammach, and held a council of war.

'David,' said Alan, 'this is the kittle bit. Shall we lie here
till it comes night, or shall we risk it and stave on ahead?'

'Well,' said I, 'I am tired indeed, but I could walk as far
again, if that was all.'

'Ay, but it isnae,' said Alan, 'nor yet the half. This is
how we stand: Appin's fair death to us. To the south it's
all Campbells, and no to be thought of. To the north; well,
there's no muckle to be gained by going north; neither for
you, that wants to get to Queensferry, nor yet for me, that
wants to get to France. Well then, we'll can strike east.'

'East be it!' says I, quite cheerily; but I was thinking,
in to myself: 'Oh, man, if you would only take one point
of the compass and let me take any other, it would be the
best for both of us.'

'Well, then, east, ye see, we have the muirs,' said Alan.
'Once there, David, it's mere pitch-and-toss. Out on yon
bald, naked, flat place, where can a body turn to? Let the
redcoats come over a hill, they can spy you miles away;
and the sorrow's in their horses' heels, they would soon
ride you down. It's no good place, David; and I'm free
to say, it's worse by daylight than by dark.'

'Alan,' said I, 'hear my way of it. Appin's death for us;

we have none too much money, nor yet meal; the longer they seek, the nearer they may guess where we are; it's all a risk; and I give my word to go ahead until we drop.'

Alan was delighted. 'There are whiles,' said he, 'when ye are altogether too canny and Whiggish to be company for a gentleman like me; but there come other whiles when ye show yoursel' a mettle spark; and it's then, David, that I love ye like a brother.'

The mist rose and died away, and showed us that country lying as waste as the sea; only the moorfowl and the peewees crying upon it, and far over to the east, a herd of deer, moving like dots. Much of it was red with heather; much of the rest broken up with bogs and hags and peaty pools; some had been burnt black in a heath fire; and in another place there was quite a forest of dead firs, standing like skeletons. A wearier looking desert man never saw; but at least it was clear of troops, which was our point.

We went down accordingly into the waste, and began to make our toilsome and devious travel towards the eastern verge. There were the tops of mountains all round (you are to remember) from whence we might be spied at any moment; so it behoved us to keep in the hollow parts of the moor, and when these turned aside from our direction, to move upon its naked face with infinite care. Sometimes, for half an hour together, we must crawl from one heather bush to another, as hunters do when they are hard upon the deer. It was a clear day again, with a blazing sun; the water in the brandy bottle was soon gone; and altogether, if I had guessed what it would be to crawl half the time upon my belly and to walk much of the rest stooping nearly to the knees, I should certainly have held back from such a killing enterprise.

Toiling and resting and toiling again, we wore away the morning; and about noon lay down in a thick bush of heather to sleep. Alan took the first watch; and it seemed to me I had scarce closed my eyes before I was shaken up to take the second. We had no clock to go by; and Alan stuck a sprig of heath in the ground to serve instead; so that as soon as the shadow of the bush should fall so far to the east, I might know to rouse him. But I was by this time so weary that I could have slept twelve hours at a stretch; I had the taste of sleep in my throat; my joints slept even when my mind was waking; the hot smell of the heather, and the drone of the wild bees, were like possets to me; and every now and again I would give a jump and find I had been dozing.

The last time I woke I seemed to come back from further away, and thought the sun had taken a great start in the heavens. I looked at the sprig of heath, and at that I could have cried aloud; for I saw I had betrayed my trust. My head was nearly turned with fear and shame; and at what I saw, when I looked out around me on the moor, my heart was like dying in my body. For sure enough, a body of horse-soldiers had come down during my sleep, and were drawing near to us from the south-east, spread out in the shape of a fan and riding their horses to and fro in the deep parts of the heather.

When I waked Alan, he glanced first at the soldiers, then at the mark and the position of the sun, and knitted his brows with a sudden, quick look, both ugly and anxious, which was all the reproach I had of him.

'What are we to do now?' I asked.

'We'll have to play at being hares,' said he. 'Do ye see yon mountain?' pointing to one on the north-eastern sky.

'Ay,' said I.

'Well, then,' says he, 'let us strike for that. Its name is Ben Alder; it is a wild, desert mountain full of hills and hollows, and if we can win to it before the morn, we may do yet.'

'But, Alan,' cried I, 'that will take us across the very coming of the soldiers!'

'I ken that fine,' said he; 'but if we are driven back on Appin, we are two dead men. So now, David, man, be brisk!'

With that he began to run forward on his hands and knees with an incredible quickness, as though it were his natural way of going. All the time, too, he kept winding in and out in the lower parts of the moorland where we were the best concealed. Some of these had been burned or at least scathed with fire; and there rose in our faces (which were close to the ground) a blinding, choking dust as fine as smoke. The water was long out; and this posture of running on the hands and knees brings an overmastering weakness and weariness, so that the joints ache and the wrists faint under your weight.

Now and then, indeed, where was a big bush of heather, we lay a while, and panted, and putting aside the leaves, looked back at the dragoons. They had not spied us, for they held straight on; a half-troop, I think, covering about two miles of ground, and beating it mighty thoroughly as they went. I had awakened just in time; a little later, and we must have fled in front of them, instead of escaping on one side. Even as it was, the least misfortune might betray us; and now and again, when a grouse rose out of the heather with a clap of wings, we lay as still as the dead and were afraid to breathe.

The aching and faintness of my body, the labouring of my heart, the soreness of my hands, and the smarting of my throat and eyes in the continual smoke of dust and ashes, had soon grown to be so unbearable that I would gladly have given up. Nothing but the fear of Alan lent me enough of a false kind of courage to continue. As for himself (and you are to bear in mind that he was cumbered with a great-coat) he had first turned crimson, but as time went on, the redness began to be mingled with patches of white; his breath cried and whistled as it came; and his voice, when he whispered his observations in my ear during our halts, sounded like nothing human. Yet he seemed in no way dashed in spirits, nor did he at all abate in his activity; so that I was driven to marvel at the man's endurance.

At length, in the first gloaming of the night, we heard a trumpet sound, and looking back from among the heather, saw the troop beginning to collect. A little after, they had built a fire and camped for the night, about the middle of the waste.

At this I begged and besought that we might lie down and sleep.

'There shall be no sleep the night!' said Alan. 'From now on, these weary dragoons of yours will keep the crown of the muirland, and none will get out of Appin but winged fowls. We got through in the nick of time, and shall we jeopard what we've gained? Na, na, when the day comes, it shall find you and me in a fast place on Ben Alder.'

'Alan,' I said, 'it's not the want of will: it's the strength that I want. If I could, I would; but as sure as I'm alive I cannot.'

'Very well, then,' said Alan. 'I'll carry ye.'

I looked to see if he were jesting; but no, the little man was in dead earnest; and the sight of so much resolution shamed me.

'Lead away!' said I. 'I'll follow.'

He gave me one look, as much as to say 'Well done, David!' and off he set again at his top speed.

It grew cooler and even a little darker (but not much) with the coming of the night. The sky was cloudless; it was still early in July, and pretty far north; in the darkest part of that night, you would have needed pretty good eyes to read, but for all that, I have often seen it darker in a winter midday. Heavy dew fell and drenched the moor like rain; and this refreshed me for a while. When we stopped to breathe, and I had time to see all about me, the clearness and sweetness of the night, the shapes of the hills like things asleep, and the fire dwindling away behind us, like a bright spot in the midst of the moor, anger would come upon me in a clap that I must still drag myself in agony and eat the dust like a worm.

By what I have read in books, I think few that have held a pen were ever really wearied, or they would write of it more strongly. I had no care of my life, neither past nor future, and I scarce remembered there was such a lad as David Balfour. I did not think of myself, but just of each fresh step which I was sure would be my last, with despair—and of Alan, who was the cause of it, with hatred. Alan was in the right trade as a soldier; this is the officer's part to make men continue to do things, they know not wherefore, and when, if the choice was offered, they would lie down where they were and be killed. And I dare say I would have made a good enough private; for in these last hours, it never occurred to me that I had any choice, but just to obey as long as I was able, and die obeying.

Day began to come in, after years, I thought; and by that time we were past the greatest danger, and could walk upon our feet like men, instead of crawling like brutes. But, dear heart have mercy! what a pair we must have made, going double like old grandfathers, stumbling like babes, and as white as dead folk. Never a word passed between us; each set his mouth and kept his eyes in front of him, and lifted up his foot and set it down again, like people lifting weights

at a country play; all the while, with the moorfowl crying
'peep!' in the heather, and the light coming slowly clearer
in the east.

I say Alan did as I did. Not that ever I looked at him,
for I had enough ado to keep my feet; but because it is
plain he must have been as stupid with weariness as myself,
and looked as little where we were going, or we should not
have walked into an ambush like blind men.

It fell in this way. We were going down a heathery brae,
Alan leading and I following a pace or two behind, like a
fiddler and his wife; when upon a sudden the heather gave
a rustle, three or four ragged men leaped out, and the next
moment we were lying on our backs, each with a dirk at
his throat.

I don't think I cared: the pain of this rough handling
was quite swallowed up by the pains of which I was already
full; and I was too glad to have stopped walking to mind
about a dirk. I lay looking up in the face of the man that
held me; and I mind his face was black with the sun and
his eyes very light, but I was not afraid of him. I heard Alan
and another whispering in the Gaelic; and what they said
was all one to me.

Then the dirks were put up, our weapons were taken
away, and we were set face to face, sitting in the heather.

'They are Cluny's men,' said Alan. 'We couldnae have
fallen better. We're just to bide here with these, which are
his out-sentries, till they can get word to the chief of my
arrival.'

Now Cluny Macpherson, the chief of the clan Vourich,
had been one of the leaders of the great rebellion six years
before; there was a price on his life; and I had supposed
him long ago in France, with the rest of the heads of that
desperate party. Even tired as I was, the surprise of what
I heard half wakened me.

'What?' I cried. 'Is Cluny still here?'

'Ay is he so!' said Alan. 'Still in his own country and
kept by his own clan. King George can do no more.'

I think I would have asked farther, but Alan gave me the
put-off. 'I am rather wearied,' he said, 'and I would like fine
to get a sleep.' And without more words, he rolled on his
face in a deep heather bush, and seemed to sleep at once.

There was no such thing possible for me. You have heard

grasshoppers whirring in the grass in the summer time? Well, I had no sooner closed my eyes, than my body, and above all my head, belly, and wrists, seemed to be filled with whirring grasshoppers; and I must open my eyes again at once, and tumble and toss, and sit up and lie down; and look at the sky which dazzled me, or at Cluny's wild and dirty sentries, peering out over the top of the brae and chattering to each other in the Gaelic.

That was all the rest I had, until the messenger returned; when, as it appeared that Cluny would be glad to receive us, we must get once more upon our feet and set forward. Alan was in excellent good spirits, much refreshed by his sleep, very hungry, and looking pleasantly forward to a dram and a dish of hot collops, of which, it seems, the messenger had brought him word. For my part, it made me sick to hear of eating. I had been dead-heavy before, and now I felt a kind of dreadful lightness, which would not suffer me to walk. I drifted like a gossamer; the ground seemed to me a cloud, the hills a feather-weight, the air to have a current, like a running burn, which carried me to and fro. With all that, a sort of horror of despair sat on my mind, so that I could have wept at my own helplessness.

I saw Alan knitting his brows at me, and supposed it was in anger; and that gave me a pang of light-headed fear, like what a child may have. I remember, too, that I was smiling, and could not stop smiling, hard as I tried; for I thought it was out of place at such a time. But my good companion had nothing in his mind but kindness; and the next moment, two of the gillies had me by the arms, and I began to be carried forward with great swiftness (or so it appeared to me, although I dare say it was slowly enough in truth) through a labyrinth of dreary glens and hollows and into the heart of that dismal mountain of Ben Alder.

WE CAME AT last to the foot of an exceeding steep wood, which scrambled up a craggy hillside, and was crowned by a naked precipice.

'It's here,' said one of the guides, and we struck up hill.

The trees clung upon the slope, like sailors on the shrouds a ship; and their trunks were like the rounds of a ladder, by which we mounted.

Quite at the top, and just before the rocky face of the cliff sprang above the foliage, we found that strange house which was known in the country as 'Cluny's Cage'. The trunks of several trees had been wattled across, the intervals strengthened with stakes, and the ground behind this barricade levelled up with earth to make the floor. A tree, which grew out from the hillside, was the living centre-beam of the roof. The walls were of wattle and covered with moss. The whole house had something of an egg shape; and it half hung, half stood in that steep, hillside thicket, like a wasp's nest in a green hawthorn.

Within, it was large enough to shelter five or six persons with some comfort. A projection of the cliff had been cunningly employed to be the fireplace; and the smoke rising against the face of the rock, and being not dissimilar in colour, readily escaped notice from below.

This was but one of Cluny's hiding places; he had caves, besides, and underground chambers in several parts of his country; and following the reports of his scouts, he moved from one to another as the soldiers drew near or moved away. By this manner of living, and thanks to the affection of his clan, he had not only stayed all this time in safety, while so many others had fled or been taken and slain; but stayed four or five years longer, and only went to France at last by the express command of his master. There he soon died; and it is strange to reflect that he may have regretted his Cage upon Ben Alder.

When we came to the door he was seated by his rock chimney, watching a gillie about some cookery. He was mighty plainly habited, with a knitted nightcap drawn over his ears, and smoked a foul cutty pipe. For all that he had the manners of a king, and it was quite a sight to see him rise out of his place to welcome us.

'Well, Mr Stewart, come awa' sir!' said he, 'and bring in your friend that as yet I dinna ken the name of.'

'And how is yourself, Cluny?' said Alan. 'I hope ye do brawly, sir. And I am proud to see ye, and to present to ye my friend the Laird of Shaws, Mr David Balfour.'

Alan never referred to my estate without a touch of a sneer, when we were alone; but with strangers, he rang the words out like a herald.

'Step in by, the both of ye, gentlemen,' says Cluny. 'I make ye welcome to my house, which is a queer, rude place for certain, but one where I have entertained a royal personage, Mr Stewart—ye doubtless ken the personage I have in my eye. We'll take a dram for luck, and as soon as this handless man of mine has the collops ready, we'll dine and take a hand at the cartes as gentlemen should. My life is a bit driegh,' says he, pouring out the brandy; 'I see little company, and sit and twirl my thumbs, and mind upon a great day that is gone by, and weary for another great day that we all hope will be upon the road. And so here's a toast to ye: The Restoration!'

Thereupon we all touched glasses and drank. I am sure I wished no ill to King George; and if he had been there himself in proper person, it's like he would have done as I did. No sooner had I taken out the dram than I felt hugely better, and could look on and listen, still a little mistily perhaps, but no longer with the same groundless horror and distress of mind.

It was certainly a strange place, and we had a strange host. In his long hiding, Cluny had grown to have all manner of precise habits, like those of an old maid. He had a particular place, where no one else must sit; the Cage was arranged in a particular way, which none must disturb; cookery was one of his chief fancies, and even while he was greeting us in, he kept an eye to the collops.

It appears, he sometimes visited or received visits from his wife and one or two of his nearest friends, under the cover of night; but for the more part lived quite alone, and communicated only with his sentinels and the gillies that waited on him in the Cage. The first thing in the morning, one of them, who was a barber, came and shaved him, and gave him the news of the country, of which he was immoderately greedy. There was no end to his questions; he put them as earnestly as a child; and at some of the answers, laughed out of all bounds of reason, and would break out again laughing at the mere memory, hours after the barber was gone.

To be sure, there might have been a purpose in his questions; for though he was thus sequestered, and like the other landed gentlemen of Scotland, stripped by the late Act of Parliament of legal powers, he still exercised a patriarchal justice in his clan. Disputes were brought to him in his hiding-hole to be decided; and the men of his country, who would have snapped their fingers at the Court of Session, laid aside revenge and paid down money at the bare word of this forfeited and hunted outlaw. When he was angered, which was often enough, he gave his commands and breathed threats of punishment like any king; and his gillies trembled and crouched away from him like children before a hasty father. With each of them, as he entered, he ceremoniously shook hands, both parties touching their bonnets at the same time in a military manner. Altogether, I had a fair chance to see some of the inner workings of a Highland clan; and this with a proscribed, fugitive chief; his country conquered; the troops riding upon all sides in quest of him, sometimes within a mile of where he lay; and when the least of the ragged fellows whom he rated and threatened, could have made a fortune by betraying him.

On that first day, as soon as the collops were ready, Cluny gave them with his own hand a squeeze of a lemon (for he was well supplied with luxuries) and bade us draw in to our meal.

'They,' said he, meaning the collops, 'are such as I gave His Royal Highness in this very house; bating the lemon juice, for at that time we were glad to get the meat and never fashed for kitchen. Indeed, there were mair dragoons than lemons in my country in the year forty-six.'

I do not know if the collops were truly very good, but my heart rose against the sight of them, and I could eat but little. All the while Cluny entertained us with stories of Prince Charlie's stay in the Cage, giving us the very words of the speakers, and rising from his place to show us where they stood. By these, I gathered the Prince was a gracious, spirited boy, like the son of a race of polite kings, but not so wise as Solomon. I gathered, too, that while he was in the Cage, he was often drunk; so the fault that has since, by all accounts, made such a wreck of him, had even then begun to show itself.

We were no sooner done eating than Cluny brought out an old, thumbed, greasy pack of cards, such as you may find in a mean inn; and his eyes brightened in his face as he proposed that we should fall to playing.

Now this was one of the things I had been brought up to eschew like disgrace; it being held by my father neither the part of a Christian nor yet of a gentleman, to set his own livelihood and fish for that of others, on the cast of painted pasteboard. To be sure, I might have pleaded my fatigue, which was excuse enough; but I thought it behoved that I should bear a testimony. I must have got very red in the face, but I spoke steadily, and told them I had no call to be a judge of others, but for my own part, it was a matter in which I had no clearness.

Cluny stopped mingling the cards. 'What in deil's name is this?' says he. 'What kind of Whiggish, canting talk is this, for the house of Cluny Macpherson?'

'I will put my hand in the fire for Mr Balfour,' says Alan. 'He is an honest and a mettle gentleman, and I would have ye bear in mind who says it. I bear a king's name,' says he, cocking his hat; 'and I and any that I call friend are company for the best. But the gentleman is tired, and should sleep; if he has no mind to the cartes, it will never hinder you and me. And I'm fit and willing, sir, to play ye any game that ye can name.'

'Sir,' says Cluny, 'in this poor house of mine I would have you to ken that any gentleman may follow his pleasure. If your friend would like to stand on his head, he is welcome. And if either he, or you, or any other man, is not preceesely satisfied, I will be proud to step outside with him.'

I had no will that these two friends should cut their throats for my sake.

'Sir,' said I, 'I am very wearied, as Alan says; and what's

more, as you are a man that likely has sons of your own, I may tell you it was a promise to my father.'

'Say nae mair, say nae mair,' said Cluny, and pointed me to a bed of heather in a corner of the Cage. For all that he was displeased enough, looked at me askance, and grumbled when he looked. And indeed it must be owned that both my scruples and the words in which I declared them, smacked somewhat of the Covenanter, and were little in their place among wild Highland Jacobites.

What with the brandy and the venison, a strange heaviness had come over me; and I had scarce lain down upon the bed before I fell into a kind of trance, in which I continued almost the whole time of our stay in the Cage. Sometimes I was broad awake and understood what passed; sometimes I only heard voices or men snoring, like the voice of a silly river; and the plaids upon the wall dwindled down and swelled out again, like firelight shadows on the roof. I must sometimes have spoken or cried out, for I remember I was now and then amazed at being answered; yet I was conscious of no particular nightmare, only of a general, black, abiding horror—a horror of the place I was in, and the bed I lay in, and the plaids on the wall, and the voices, and the fire, and myself.

The barber-gillie, who was a doctor too, was called in to prescribe for me; but as he spoke in the Gaelic, I understood not a word of his opinion, and was too sick even to ask for a translation. I knew well enough I was ill, and that was all I cared about.

I paid little heed while I lay in this poor pass. But Alan and Cluny were most of the time at the cards, and I am clear that Alan must have begun by winning; for I remember sitting up, and seeing them hard at it, and a great glittering pile of as much as sixty or a hundred guineas on the table. It looked strange enough, to see all this wealth in a nest upon a cliff-side, wattled about growing trees. And even then, I thought it seemed deep water for Alan to be riding, who had no better battle-horse than a green purse and a matter of five pounds.

The luck, it seems, changed on the second day. About noon I was wakened as usual for dinner, and as usual refused to eat, and was given a dram with some bitter infusion which the barber had prescribed. The sun was shining in at the open door of the Cage, and this dazzled and offended me. Cluny sat at the table, biting the pack of cards. Alan had stooped over the bed, and had his face close to my eyes; to which, troubled as they were with the fever, it seemed of the most shocking bigness.

He asked me for a loan of my money.

'What for?' said I.

'Oh, just for a loan,' said he.

'But why?' I repeated. 'I don't see.'

'Hut, David!' said Alan, 'ye wouldnae grudge me a loan?'

I would though, if I had had my senses! But all I thought of then was to get his face away, and I handed him my money.

On the morning of the third day, when we had been forty-eight hours in the Cage, I awoke with a great relief of spirits, very weak and weary indeed, but seeing things of the right size and with their honest, everyday appearance. I had a mind to eat, moreover; rose from bed of my own movement; and as soon as we had breakfasted, stepped to the entry of the Cage and sat down outside in the top of the wood. It was a grey day with a cool, mild air: and I sat in a dream all morning, only disturbed by the passing by of Cluny's scouts and servants coming with provisions and reports; for as the coast was at that time clear, you might almost say he held court openly.

When I returned, he and Alan had laid the cards aside, and were questioning a gillie; and the chief turned about and spoke to me in the Gaelic.

'I have no Gaelic, sir,' said I.

Now since the card question, everything I said or did had the power of annoying Cluny, 'Your name has more sense than yourself, then,' said he, angrily; 'for it's good Gaelic. But the point is this. My scout reports all clear in the south, and the question is have ye the strength to go?'

I saw cards on the table, but no gold; only a heap of little written papers, and these all on Cluny's side. Alan, besides, had an odd look, like a man not very well content; and I began to have a strong misgiving.

'I do not know if I am as well as I should be,' said I, looking at Alan; 'but the little money we have has a long way to carry us.'

Alan took his under-lip into his mouth, and looked upon the ground.

'David,' says he, at last, 'I've lost it; there's the naked truth.'

'My money too?' said I.

'Your money too,' says Alan, with a groan. 'Ye shouldnae have given it me. I'm daft when I get to the cartes.'

'Hoot-toot, hoot-toot,' said Cluny. 'It was all daffing; it's all nonsense. Of course, ye'll have your money back again, and the double of it, if ye'll make so free with me. It would be a singular thing for me to keep it. It's not to be supposed that I would be any hindrance to gentlemen in your situation; that would be a singular thing!' cries he, and began to pull gold out of his pocket, with a mighty red face.

Alan said nothing, only looked on the ground.

'Will you step to the door with me, sir?' said I.

Cluny said he would be very glad, and followed me readily enough, but he looked flustered and put out.

'And now, sir,' says I, 'I must first acknowledge your generosity.'

'Nonsensical nonsense!' cries Cluny. 'Where's the generosity? This is just a most unfortunate affair; but what would ye have me do—boxed up in this bee-skep of a cage of mine—but just set my friends to the cartes, when I can get them? And if they lose, of course, it's not to be supposed—' And here he came to a pause.

'Yes,' said I, 'if they lose, you give them back their money; and if they win, they carry away yours in their pouches! I have said before that I grant your generosity; but to me, sir, it's a very painful thing to be placed in this position.'

There was a little silence, in which Cluny seemed always as if he was about to speak, but said nothing. All the time he grew redder and redder in the face.

'I am a young man,' said I, 'and I ask your advice. Advise me as you would your son. My friend fairly lost this money, after having fairly gained a far greater sum of yours; can I accept it back again? would that be the right part for me to play? Whatever I do, you can see for yourself it must be hard upon a man of any pride.'

'It's rather hard on me, too, Mr Balfour,' said Cluny, 'and

ye give me very much the look of a man that has entrapped poor people to their hurt. I wouldnae have my friends come to any house of mine to accept affronts; no,' he cried, with a sudden heat of anger, 'nor yet to give them!'

'And so you see, sir,' said I, 'there is something to be said upon my side; and this gambling is a very poor employ for gentlefolks. But I am still waiting your opinion.'

I am sure if ever Cluny hated any man it was David Balfour. He looked me all over with a warlike eye, and I saw the challenge at his lips. But either my youth disarmed him, or perhaps his own sense of justice. Certainly it was a mortifying matter for all concerned, and not least for Cluny; the more credit that he took it as he did.

'Mr Balfour,' said he, 'I think you are too nice and covenanting, but for all that you have the spirit of a very pretty gentleman. Upon my honest word, ye may take this money—it's what I would tell my son—and here's my hand along with it!'

ALAN AND I were put across Loch Errocht under cloud of night, and went down its eastern shore to another hiding place near the head of Loch Rannoch, whither we were led by one of the gillies from the Cage. This fellow carried all our luggage and Alan's great-coat in the bargain, trotting along under the burthen, far less than the half of which used to weigh me to the ground, like a stout hill pony with a feather; yet he was a man that, in plain contest, I could have broken on my knee.

Doubtless it was a great relief to walk disencumbered; and perhaps without that relief, and the consequent sense of liberty and lightness, I could not have walked at all. I was but new risen from a bed of sickness; and there was nothing in the state of our affairs to hearten me for much exertion; travelling, as we did, over the most dismal deserts in Scotland, under a cloudy heaven, and with divided hearts among the travellers.

For long, we said nothing; marching alongside or one behind the other, each with a set countenance; I, angry and proud, and drawing what strength I had from these two violent and sinful feelings: Alan angry and ashamed, ashamed that he had lost my money, angry that I should take it so ill.

The thought of a separation ran always the stronger in my mind; and the more I approved of it, the more ashamed I grew of my approval. It would be a fine, handsome, generous thing, indeed, for Alan to turn round and say to me: 'Go, I am in the most danger, and my company only increases yours.' But for me to turn to the friend who certainly loved me, and say to him: 'You are in great danger, I am in but little; your friendship is a burden; go take your risks and bear your hardships alone—' no, that was impossible; and even to think of it privily to myself, made my cheeks to burn.

And yet Alan had behaved like a child and (what is worse) a treacherous child. Wheedling my money from me while I lay half-conscious, was scarce better than theft; and yet here he was trudging by my side, without a penny to his name, and by what I could see, quite blithe to sponge upon the money he had driven me to beg. True, I was ready to share it with him; but it made me rage to see him count upon my readiness.

These were the two things uppermost in my mind; and I could open my mouth upon neither without black ungenerosity. So I did the next worst, and said nothing, nor so much as looked once at my companion, save with the tail of my eye.

At last, upon the other side of Loch Errocht, going over a smooth, rushy place, where the walking was easy, he could bear it no longer, and came close to me.

'David,' says he, 'this is no way for two friends to take a small accident. I have to say that I'm sorry; and so that's said. And now if you have anything, ye'd better say it.'

'Oh,' says I, 'I have nothing.'

He seemed disconcerted; at which I was meanly pleased.

'No,' said he, with rather a trembling voice, 'but when I say I was to blame?'

'Why, of course, ye were to blame,' said I, coolly; 'and you will bear me out that I have never reproached you.'

'Never,' says he; 'but ye ken very well that ye've done worse. Are we to part? Ye said so once before. Are ye to say it again? There's hills and heather enough between here and the two seas, David; and I will own I'm no very keen to stay where I'm no wanted.'

This pierced me like a sword, and seemed to lay bare my private disloyalty.

'Alan Breck!' I cried; and then: 'Do you think I am one to turn my back on you in your chief need? You dursn't say it to my face. My whole conduct's there to give the lie to it. It's true, I fell asleep upon the muir; but that was from weariness, and you do wrong to cast it up to me.'

'Which is what I never did,' said Alan.

'But aside from that,' I continued, 'what have I done that you should even me to dogs by such a supposition? I never yet failed a friend, and it's not likely I'll begin with you.

There are things between us that I can never forget, even
if you can.'

'I will only say this to ye, David,' said Alan, very quietly,
'that I have long been owing ye my life, and now I owe ye
money. Ye should try to make that burden light for me.'

This ought to have touched me, and in a manner it did,
but the wrong manner. I felt I was behaving badly; and
was now not only angry with Alan, but angry with myself
in the bargain; and it made me the more cruel.

'You asked me to speak,' said I. 'Well, then, I will. You
own yourself that you have done me a disservice; I have
had to swallow an affront; I have never reproached you,
I never named the thing till you did. And now you blame
me,' cried I, 'because I cannae laugh and sing as if I was
glad to be affronted. The next thing will be that I'm to go
down upon my knees and thank you for it! Ye should think
more of others, Alan Breck. If ye thought more of others,
ye would perhaps speak less about yourself; and when a
friend that likes you very well, has passed over an offence
without a word, you would be blithe to let it lie, instead of
making it a stick to break his back with. By your own way
of it, it was you that was to blame; then it shouldnae be
you to seek the quarrel.'

'Aweel,' said Alan, 'say nae mair.'

And we fell back into our former silence; and came to our
journey's end, and supped, and lay down to sleep, without
another word.

The gillie put us across Loch Rannoch in the dusk of the
next day, and gave us his opinion as to our best route. This
was to get us up at once into the tops of the mountains:
to go round by a circuit, turning the heads of Glen Lyon,
Glen Lochay, and Glen Dochart, and come down upon the
lowlands by Kippen and the upper waters of the Forth.
Alan was little pleased with a route which led us through
the country of his blood-foes, the Glenorchy Campbells. He
objected that by turning to the east, we should come almost
at once among the Athole Stewarts, a race of his own name
and lineage although following a different chief, and come
besides by a far easier and swifter way to the place whither
we were bound. But the gillie, who was indeed the chief
man of Cluny's scouts, had good reasons to give him on
all hands, naming the force of troops in every district, and

alleging finally (as well as I could understand) that we should nowhere be so little troubled as in a country of the Campbells.

Alan gave way at last, but with only half a heart. 'It's one of the dowiest countries in Scotland,' said he. 'There's naething there that I ken, but heath, and crows, and Campbells. But I see that ye're a man of some penetration; and be it as ye please!'

We set forth accordingly by this itinerary; and for the best part of three nights travelled on eerie mountains and among the well-heads of wild rivers; often buried in mist, almost continually blown and rained upon, and not once cheered by any glimpse of sunshine. By day, we lay and slept in the drenching heather; by night, incessantly clambered upon breakneck hills and among rude crags. We often wandered; we were often so involved in fog, that we must lie quiet till it lightened. A fire was never to be thought of. Our only food was drammach and a portion of cold meat that we had carried from the Cage; and as for drink, Heaven knows we had no want of water.

This was a dreadful time, rendered the more dreadful by the gloom of the weather and the country. I was never warm; my teeth chattered in my head; I was troubled with a very sore throat, such as I had on the isle; I had a painful stitch in my side, which never left me; and when I slept in my wet bed, with the rain beating above and the mud oozing below me, it was to live over again in fancy the worst part of my adventures—to see the tower of Shaws lit by lightning, Ransome carried below on the men's backs, Shuan dying on the round-house floor, or Colin Campbell grasping at the bosom of his coat. From such broken slumbers, I would be aroused in the gloaming, to sit up in the same puddle where I had slept, and sup cold drammach; the rain driving sharp in my face or running down my back in icy trickles; the mist enfolding us like as in a gloomy chamber—or perhaps, if the wind blew, falling suddenly apart and showing us the gulf of some dark valley where the streams were crying aloud.

The sound of an infinite number of rivers came up from all round. In this steady rain the springs of the mountain were broken up; every glen gushed water like a cistern; every stream was in high spate, and had filled and overflowed its channel. During our night tramps, it was solemn to hear the voice of them below in the valleys, now booming like thunder, now with an angry cry. I could well understand the story of the Water Kelpie, that demon of the streams, who is fabled to keep wailing and roaring at the ford until the coming of the doomed traveller. Alan I saw believed it, or half believed it; and when the cry of the river rose more than usually sharp, I was little surprised (though, of course, I would still be shocked) to see him cross himself in the manner of the Catholics.

During all these horrid wanderings we had no familiarity, scarcely even that of speech. The truth is that I was sickening for my grave, which is my best excuse. But besides that I was of an unforgiving disposition from my birth, slow to take offence, slower to forget it, and now incensed both against my companion and myself. For the best part of two days he was unweariedly kind; silent, indeed, but always ready to help, and always hoping (as I could very well see) that my displeasure would blow by. For the same length of time I stayed in myself, nursing my anger, roughly refusing his services, and passing him over with my eyes as if he had been a bush or a stone.

The second night, or rather the peep of the third day, found us upon a very open hill, so that we could not follow our usual plan and lie down immediately to eat and sleep. Before we had reached a place of shelter, the grey had come pretty clear, for though it still rained, the clouds ran higher; and Alan, looking in my face, showed some marks of concern.

'Ye had better let me take your pack,' said he, for perhaps the ninth time since we had parted from the scout beside Loch Rannoch.

'I do very well, I thank you,' said I, as cold as ice.

Alan flushed darkly. 'I'll not offer it again,' he said. 'I'm not a patient man, David.'

'I never said you were,' said I, which was exactly the rude, silly speech of a boy of ten.

Alan made no answer at the time, but his conduct answered for him. Henceforth, it is to be thought, he quite forgave himself for the affair at Cluny's; cocked his hat again, walked jauntily, whistled airs, and looked at me upon one side with a provoking smile.

The third night we were to pass through the western end of the country of Balquidder. It came clear and cold, with a touch in the air like frost, and a northerly wind that blew the clouds away and made the stars bright. The streams were full, of course, and still made a great noise among the hills; but I observed that Alan thought no more upon the Kelpie, and was in high good spirits. As for me, the change of weather came too late; I had lain in the mire so long that (as the Bible has it) my very clothes 'abhorred me'; I was dead weary, deadly sick and full of pains and shiverings; the chill of the wind went through me, and the sound of it confused my ears. In this poor state I had to bear from my companion something in the nature of a persecution. He spoke a good deal, and never without a taunt. 'Whig' was the best name he had to give me. 'Here,' he would say, 'here's a dub for ye to jump, my Whiggie! I ken you're a fine jumper!' And so on; all the time with a gibing voice and face.

I knew it was my own doing, and no one else's; but I was too miserable to repent. I felt I could drag myself but little farther; pretty soon, I must lie down and die on these wet mountains like a sheep or a fox, and my bones must whiten there like the bones of a beast. My head was light, perhaps; but I began to love the prospect, I began to glory in the thought of such a death, alone in the desert, with the wild eagles besieging my last moments. Alan would repent then, I thought; he would remember, when I was dead, how much he owed me, and the remembrance would be torture. So I went like a sick, silly, and bad-hearted schoolboy, feeding my anger against a fellow-man, when I would have been better on my knees, crying on God for mercy. And at each of Alan's taunts, I hugged myself. 'Ah!' thinks I to myself, 'I have a better taunt in readiness; when I lie down and die, you will feel it like a buffet in your face; ah, what a revenge! ah, how you will regret your ingratitude and cruelty!'

All the while, I was growing worse and worse. Once I had fallen, my legs simply doubling under me, and this had struck Alan for the moment; but I was afoot so briskly, and set off again with such a natural manner, that he soon forgot the incident. Flushes of heat went over me, and then spasms of shuddering. The stitch in my side was hardly bearable. At last I began to feel that I could trail myself no farther: and with that, there came on me all at once the wish to have it out with Alan, let my anger blaze, and be done with my life in a more sudden manner. He had just called me 'Whig'. I stopped.

'Mr Stewart,' said I, in a voice that quivered like a fiddle-string, 'you are older than I am, and should know your manners. Do you think it either very wise or very witty to cast my politics in my teeth? I thought, where folk differed, it was the part of gentlemen to differ civilly; and if I did not, I may tell you I could find a better taunt than some of yours.'

Alan had stopped opposite to me, his hat cocked, his hands in his breeches pockets, his head a little on one side. He listened, smiling evilly, as I could see by the starlight; and when I had done he began to whistle a Jacobite air. It was the air made in mockery of General Cope's defeat at Preston Pans:

> Hey, Johnnie Cope, are ye waukin' yet?
> And are your drums a-beatin' yet?

And it came in my mind that Alan, on the day of that battle, had been engaged upon the royal side.

'Why do ye take that air, Mr Stewart?' said I. 'Is that to remind me you have been beaten on both sides?'

The air stopped on Alan's lips. 'David!' said he.

'But it's time these manners ceased,' I continued; 'and I mean you shall henceforth speak civilly of my King and my good friends the Campbells.'

'I am a Stewart—' began Alan.

'Oh!' says I, 'I ken ye bear a king's name. But you are to remember, since I have been in the Highlands, I have seen a good many of those that bear it; and the best I can say of them is this, that they would be none the worse of washing.'

'Do you know that you insult me?' said Alan, very low.

'I am sorry for that,' said I, 'for I am not done; and if you distaste the sermon, I doubt the pirliecue will please you as little. You have been chased in the field by the grown men of my party; it seems a poor kind of pleasure to outface a boy. Both the Campbells and the Whigs have beaten you; you have run before them like a hare. It behoves you to speak of them as of your betters.'

Alan stood quite still, the tails of his great-coat clapping behind him in the wind.

'This is a pity,' he said at last. 'There are things said that cannot be passed over.'

'I never asked you to,' said I. 'I am as ready as yourself.'

'Ready?' said he.

'Ready,' I repeated. 'I am no blower and boaster like some that I could name. Come on!' And drawing my sword, I fell on guard as Alan himself had taught me.

'David!' he cried. 'Are ye daft? I cannae draw upon ye, David. It's fair murder.'

'That was your look-out when you insulted me,' said I.

'It's the truth!' cried Alan, and he stood for a moment, wringing his mouth in his hand like a man in sore perplexity. 'It's the bare truth,' he said, and drew his sword. But before I could touch his blade with mine, he had thrown it from him and fallen to the ground. 'Na, na,' he kept saying, 'na, na—I cannae, I cannae.'

At this the last of my anger oozed all out of me; and I found myself only sick, and sorry, and blank, and wondering at myself. I would have given the world to take back what I had said; but a word once spoken, who can re-capture it? I minded me of all Alan's kindness and courage in the past, how he had helped and cheered and borne with me in our evil days; and then recalled my own insults, and saw that I had lost for ever that doughty friend. At the same time, the sickness that hung upon me seemed to redouble, and the pang in my side was like a sword for sharpness. I thought I must have swooned where I stood.

This it was that gave me a thought. No apology could blot out what I had said; it was needless to think of one, none could cover the offence; but where an apology was vain, a mere cry for help might bring Alan back to my side. I put my pride away from me. 'Alan!' I said; 'if you cannae help me, I must just die here.'

He started up sitting, and looked at me.

'It's true,' said I. 'I'm by with it. Oh, let me get into the bield of a house—I'll can die there easier.' I had no need to pretend; whether I chose or not, I spoke in a weeping voice that would have melted a heart of stone.

'Can ye walk?' asked Alan.

'No,' said I, 'not without help. This last hour, my legs

have been fainting under me; I've a stitch in my side like a red-hot iron; I cannae breathe right. If I die, ye'll can forgive me, Alan? In my heart, I liked ye fine—even when I was the angriest.'

'Wheesht, wheesht!' cried Alan. 'Dinnae say that! David man, ye ken—' He shut his mouth upon a sob. 'Let me get my arm about ye,' he continued; 'that's the way! Now lean upon me hard. Gude kens where there's a house! We're in Balwhidder, too; there should be no want of houses, no, nor friends' houses here. Do ye gang easier so, Davie?'

'Ay,' said I, 'I can be doing this way'; and I pressed his arm with my hand.

Again he came near sobbing. 'Davie,' said he, 'I'm no a right man at all; I have neither sense nor kindness; I couldnae remember ye were just a bairn, I couldnae see ye were dying on your feet; Davie, ye'll have to try and forgive me.'

'Oh, man, let's say no more about it!' said I. 'We're neither one of us to mend the other—that's the truth! We must just bear and forbear, man Alan! Oh, but my stitch is sore! Is there nae house?'

'I'll find a house to ye, David,' he said, stoutly. 'We'll follow down the burn, where there's bound to be houses. My poor man, will ye no be better on my back?'

'Oh, Alan,' says I, 'and me a good twelve inches taller?'

'Ye're no such a thing,' cried Alan, with a start. 'There may be a trifling matter of an inch or two; I'm no saying I'm just exactly what ye would call a tall man, whatever; and I dare say,' he added, his voice tailing off in a laughable manner, 'now when I come to think of it, I dare say ye'll be just about right. Ay, it'll be a foot, or near hand; or may be even mair!'

It was sweet and laughable to hear Alan eat his words up in the fear of some fresh quarrel. I could have laughed, had not my stitch caught me so hard; but if I had laughed, I think I must have wept too.

'Alan,' cried I, 'what makes ye so good to me? what makes ye care for such a thankless fellow?'

'Deed, and I don't know,' said Alan. 'For just precisely what I thought I liked about ye, was that ye never quarrelled;—and now I like ye better!'

AT THE DOOR of the first house we came to, Alan knocked, which was no very safe enterprise in such a part of the Highlands as the Braes of Balquidder. No great clan held rule there; it was filled and disputed by small septs, and broken remnants, and what they call 'chiefless folk', driven into the wild country about the springs of Forth and Teith by the advance of the Campbells. Here were Stewarts and Maclarens, which came to the same thing, for the Maclarens followed Alan's chief in war, and made but one clan with Appin. Here, too, were many of that old, proscribed, nameless, red-handed clan of the Macgregors. They had always been ill considered, and now worse than ever, having credit with no side or party in the whole country of Scotland. Their chief, Macgregor of Macgregor, was in exile; the more immediate leader of that part of them about Balquidder, James More, Rob Roy's eldest son, lay waiting his trial in Edinburgh Castle; they were in ill-blood with Highlander and Lowlander, with the Grahames, the Maclarens and the Stewarts; and Alan, who took up the quarrel of any friend however distant, was extremely wishful to avoid them.

Chance served us very well; for it was a household of Maclarens that we found, where Alan was not only welcome for his name's sake but known by reputation. Here then I was got to bed without delay, and a doctor fetched, who found me in a sorry plight. But whether because he was a very good doctor, or I a very young, strong man, I lay bed-ridden for no more than a week, and before a month I was able to take the road again with a good heart.

All this time Alan would not leave me; though I often pressed him, and indeed his foolhardiness in staying was a common subject of outcry with the two or three friends that were let into the secret. He hid by day in a hole of the braes under a little wood; and at night when the coast was clear, would come into the house to visit me. I need not say if I was pleased to see him; Mrs Maclaren, our hostess, thought nothing good enough for such a guest; and as Duncan Dhu (which was the name of our host) had a pair of pipes in his house and was much of a lover of music, the time of my recovery was quite a festival, and we commonly turned night into day.

The soldiers let us be; although once a party of two companies and some dragoons went by in the bottom of the valley, where I could see them through the window as I lay in bed. What was much more astonishing, no magistrate came near me, and there was no question put of whence I came or whither I was going; and in that time of excitement, I was as free of all inquiry as though I had lain in a desert. Yet my presence was known before I left to all the people in Balquidder and the adjacent parts; many coming about the house on visits and these (after the custom of the country) spreading the news among their neighbours. The bills, too, had now been printed. There was one pinned near the foot of my bed, where I could read my own not very flattering portrait and, in larger characters, the amount of the blood money that had been set upon my life. Duncan Dhu and the rest that knew that I had come there in Alan's company, could have entertained no doubt of who I was; and many others must have had their guess. For though I had changed my clothes, I could not change my age or person; and lowland boys of eighteen were not so rife in these parts of the world, and above all about that time, that they could fail to put one thing with another and connect me with the bill. So it was, at least. Other folk keep a secret among two or three near friends, and somehow it leaks out; but among these clansmen, it is told to a whole countryside, and they will keep it for a century.

There was but one thing happened worth narrating; and that is the visit I had of Robin Oig, one of the sons of the notorious Rob Roy. He was sought upon all sides on a charge of carrying a young woman from Balfron and marrying her (as was alleged) by force; yet he stepped about Balquidder like a gentleman in his own walled policy. It was he who had shot James Maclaren at the plough stilts, a quarrel never satisfied; yet he walked into the house of his blood enemies as a rider might into a public inn.

Duncan had time to pass me word of who it was; and we looked at one another in concern. You should understand, it was then close upon the time of Alan's coming; the two were little likely to agree; and yet if we sent word or sought to make a signal, it was sure to arouse suspicion in a man under so dark a cloud as the Macgregor.

He came in with a great show of civility, but like a man among inferiors; took off his bonnet to Mrs Maclaren, but clapped it on his head again to speak to Duncan; and having thus set himself (as he would have thought) in a proper light, came to my bedside and bowed.

'I am given to know, sir,' says he, 'that your name is Balfour.'

'They call me David Balfour,' said I, 'at your service.'

'I would give ye my name in return, sir,' he replied, 'but it's one somewhat blown upon of late days; and it'll perhaps suffice if I tell ye that I am own brother to James More Drummond or Macgregor, of whom ye will scarce have failed to hear.'

'No, sir,' said I, a little alarmed; 'nor yet of your father, Macgregor-Campbell.' And I sat up and bowed in bed; for I thought best to compliment him, in case he was proud of having had an outlaw to his father.

He bowed in return. 'But what I am come to say, sir,' he went on, 'is this. In the year '45, my brother raised a part of the 'Gregara', and marched six companies to strike a stroke for the good side; and the surgeon that marched with our clan and cured my brother's leg when it was broken in the brush at Preston Pans, was a gentleman of the same name precisely as yourself. He was brother to Balfour of Baith; and if you are in any reasonable degree of nearness one of that gentleman's kin, I have come to put myself and my people at your command.'

You are to remember that I knew no more of my descent than any cadger's dog; my uncle, to be sure, had prated of some of our high connections, but nothing to the present purpose; and there was nothing left me but that bitter disgrace of owning that I could not tell.

Robin told me shortly he was sorry he had put himself about, turned his back upon me without a sign of salutation, and as he went towards the door, I could hear him telling Duncan that I was 'only some kinless loon that didn't know his own father'. Angry as I was at these words and ashamed of my own ignorance, I could scarce keep from smiling that a man who was under the lash of the law (and was indeed hanged some three years later) should be so nice as to the descent of his acquaintances.

Just in the door, he met Alan coming in; and the two drew back and looked at each other like strange dogs. They were neither of them big men, but they seemed fairly to swell out with pride. Each wore a sword, and by a movement of his haunch, thrust clear the hilt of it, so that it might be the more readily grasped and the blade drawn.

'Mr Stewart, I am thinking,' says Robin.

'Troth, Mr Macgregor, it's not a name to be ashamed of,' answered Alan.

'I did not know ye were in my country, sir,' says Robin.

'It sticks in my mind that I am in the country of my friends the Maclarens,' says Alan.

'That's a kittle point,' returned the other. 'There may be two words to say to that. But I think I will have heard that you are a man of your sword?'

'Unless ye were born deaf, Mr Macgregor, ye will have heard a good deal more than that,' says Alan. 'I am not the only man that can draw steel in Appin; and when my kinsman and captain, Ardshiel, had a talk with a gentleman of your name, not so many years back, I could never hear that the Macgregor had the best of it.'

'Do ye mean my father, sir?' says Robin.

'Well, I wouldnae wonder,' said Alan. 'The gentleman I have in my mind had the ill-taste to clap Campbell to his name.'

'My father was an old man,' returned Robin. 'The match was unequal. You and me would make a better pair, sir.'

'I was thinking that,' said Alan.

I was half out of bed, and Duncan had been hanging at the elbow of these fighting cocks, ready to intervene upon the least occasion. But when that word was uttered, it was a case of now or never; and Duncan, with something of a white face to be sure, thrust himself between.

'Gentlemen,' said he, 'I will have been thinking of a very different matter, whateffer. Here are my pipes, and here are you two gentlemen who are baith acclaimed pipers. It's an auld dispute which one of ye's the best. Here will be a braw chance to settle it.'

'Why, sir,' said Alan, still addressing Robin, from whom indeed he had not so much as shifted his eyes, nor yet Robin from him, 'why, sir,' says Alan, 'I think I will have heard some sough of the sort. Have ye music, as folk say? Are ye a bit of a piper?'

'I can pipe like a Macrimmon!' cries Robin.

'And that is a very bold word,' quoth Alan.

'I have made bolder words good before now,' returned Robin, 'and that against better adversaries.'

'It is easy to try that,' says Alan.

Duncan Dhu made haste to bring out the pair of pipes that was his principal possession, and to set before his guests a mutton-ham and a bottle of that drink which they call Athole brose, and which is made of old whiskey, strained honey and sweet cream, slowly beaten together in the right order and proportion. The two enemies were still on the very breach of a quarrel; but down they sat, one upon each side of the peat fire, with a mighty show of politeness. Maclaren pressed them to taste his mutton-ham and 'the wife's brose', reminding them the wife was out of Athole and had a name far and wide for her skill in that confection. But Robin put aside these hospitalities as bad for the breath.

'I would have ye to remark, sir,' said Alan, 'that I havenae broken bread for near upon ten hours, which will be worse for the breath than any brose in Scotland.'

'I will take no advantages, Mr Stewart,' replied Robin. 'Eat and drink; I'll follow you.'

Each ate a small portion of the ham and drank a glass of the brose to Mrs Maclaren; and then after a great number of civilities, Robin took the pipes and played a little spring in a very ranting manner.

'Ay, ye can blow,' said Alan; and taking the instrument from his rival, he first played the same spring in a manner identical with Robin's; and then wandered into variations, which, as he went on, he decorated with a perfect flight of grace-notes, such as pipers love, and call the 'warblers'.

I had been pleased with Robin's playing, Alan's ravished me.

'That's no very bad, Mr Stewart,' said the rival, 'but ye show a poor device in your warblers.'

'Me!' cried Alan, the blood starting to his face. 'I give ye the lie.'

'Do ye own yourself beaten at the pipes, then,' said Robin, 'that ye seek to change them for the sword?'

'And that's very well said, Mr Macgregor,' returned Alan; 'and in the meantime' (laying a strong accent on the word) 'I take back the lie. I appeal to Duncan.'

'Indeed, ye need appeal to naebody,' said Robin. 'Ye're a far better judge than any Maclaren in Balquidder: for it's a God's truth that you're a very creditable piper for a Stewart. Hand me the pipes.'

Alan did as he asked; and Robin proceeded to imitate and correct some part of Alan's variations, which it seemed that he remembered perfectly.

'Ay, ye have music,' said Alan, gloomily.

'And now be the judge yourself, Mr Stewart,' said Robin; and taking up the variations from the beginning, he worked them throughout to so new a purpose, with such ingenuity and sentiment, and with so odd a fancy and so quick a knack in the grace-notes, that I was amazed to hear him.

As for Alan, his face grew dark and hot, and he sat and gnawed his fingers, like a man under some deep affront. 'Enough!' he cried. 'Ye can blow the pipes—make the most of that.' And he made as if to rise.

But Robin only held out his hand as if to ask for silence, and struck into the slow measure of a pibroch. It was a fine piece of music in itself, and nobly played; but it seems besides it was a piece peculiar to the Appin Stewarts and a chief favourite with Alan. The first notes were scarce out, before there came a change in his face; when the time quickened, he seemed to grow restless in his seat; and long before that piece was at an end, the last signs of his anger died from him, and he had no thought but for the music.

'Robin Oig,' he said, when it was done, 'ye are a great piper. I am not fit to blow in the same kingdom with ye. Body of me! ye have mair music in your sporran than I have in my head! And though it still sticks in my mind that I could maybe show ye another of it with the cold steel, I warn ye before hand—it'll no be fair! It would go against my heart to haggle a man that can blow the pipes as you can!'

Thereupon that quarrel was made up; all night long the brose was going and the pipes changing hands; and the day had come pretty bright, and the three men were none the better for what they had been taking, before Robin as much as thought upon the road.

It was the last I saw of him, for I was in the Low Countries at the University of Leyden, when he stood his trial, and was hanged in the Grassmarket. And I have told this at so great length, partly because it was the last incident of any note that befell me on the wrong side of the Highland Line, and partly because (as the man came to be hanged) it's in a manner history.

THE MONTH, AS I HAVE said, was not yet out, but it was already far through August, and beautiful warm weather, with every sign of an early and great harvest, when I was pronounced able for my journey. Our money was now run to so low an ebb that we must think first of all on speed; for if we came not soon to Mr Rankeillor's, or if when we came there he should fail to help me, we must surely starve. In Alan's view, besides, the hunt must have now greatly slackened; and the line of the Forth and even Stirling Bridge, which is the main pass over that river, would be watched with little interest.

'It's a chief principle in military affairs,' said he, 'to go where ye are least expected. Forth is our trouble; ye ken the saying, "Forth bridles the wild Hielandman." Well, if we seek to creep round about the head of that river and come down by Kippen or Balfron, it's just precisely there that they'll be looking to lay hands on us. But if we stave on straight to the auld Brig' of Stirling, I'll lay my sword they let us pass unchallenged.'

The first night, accordingly, we pushed to the house of a Maclaren in Strathire, a friend of Duncan's, where we slept the twenty-first of the month, and whence we set forth again about the fall of night to make another easy stage. The twenty-second we lay in a heather bush on a hillside in Uam Var, within view of a herd of deer, the happiest ten hours of sleep in a fine, breathing sunshine and on bone-dry ground, that I have ever tasted. That night we struck Allan Water, and followed it down; and coming to the edge of the hills saw the whole Carse of Stirling underfoot, as flat as a pancake, with the town and castle on a hill in the midst of it, and the moon shining on the Links of Forth.

'Now,' said Alan, 'I kenna if ye care, but ye're in your

171

own land again. We passed the Hieland Line in the first
hour; and now if we could but pass yon crooked water,
we might cast our bonnets in the air.'

In Allan Water, near by where it falls into the Forth,
we found a little sandy islet, overgrown with burdock,
butterbur and the like low plants, that would just cover
us if we lay flat. Here it was we made our camp, within
plain view of Stirling Castle, whence we could hear the
drums beat as some part of the garrison paraded. Shearers
worked all day in a field on one side of the river, and we
could hear the stones going on the hooks and the voices
and even the words of the men talking. It behoved to lie
close and keep silent. But the sand of the little isle was
sun-warm, the green plants gave us shelter for our heads,
we had food and drink in plenty; and to crown all, we
were within sight of safety.

As soon as the shearers quit their work and the dusk
began to fall, we waded ashore and struck for the Bridge
of Stirling, keeping to the fields and under the field fences.

The bridge is close under the castle hill, an old, high,
narrow bridge with pinnacles along the parapet; and you
may conceive with how much interest I looked upon it, not
only as a place famous in history, but as the very doors of
salvation to Alan and myself. The moon was not yet up
when we came there; a few lights shone along the front
of the fortress, and lower down a few lighted windows in
the town; but it was all mighty still, and there seemed to
be no guard upon the passage.

I was for pushing straight across; but Alan was more
wary.

'It looks unco' quiet,' said he; 'but for all that we'll lie
down here cannily behind a dyke, and make sure.'

So we lay for about a quarter of an hour, whiles whispering,
whiles lying still and hearing nothing earthly but the washing
of the water on the piers. At last there came by an old,
hobbling woman with a crutch stick; who first stopped a
little, close to where we lay, and bemoaned herself and the
long way she had travelled; and then set forth again up the
steep spring of the bridge. The woman was so little, and the
night still so dark, that we soon lost sight of her; only heard
the sound of her steps, and her stick, and a cough that she
had by fits, draw slowly farther away.

'She's bound to be across now,' I whispered.

'Na,' said Alan, 'her foot still sounds boss upon the bridge.'

And just then—'Who goes?' cried a voice, and we heard the butt of a musket rattle on the stones. I must suppose the sentry had been sleeping, so that had we tried, we might have passed unseen; but he was awake now, and the chance forfeited.

'This'll never do,' said Alan. 'This'll never, never do for us, David.'

And without another word, he began to crawl away through the fields; and a little after, being well out of eye-shot, got to his feet again, and struck along a road that led to the eastward. I could not conceive what he was doing; and indeed I was so sharply cut by the disappointment, that I was little likely to be pleased with anything. A moment back, and I had seen myself knocking at Mr Rankeillor's door to claim my inheritance, like a hero in a ballad; and here was I back again, a wandering, hunted blackguard, on the wrong side of Forth.

'Well?' said I.

'Well,' said Alan, 'what would ye have? They're none such fools as I took them for. We have still the Forth to pass, Davie—weary fall the rains that fed and the hillsides that guided it!'

'And why go east?' said I.

'Ou, just upon the chance!' said he. 'If we cannae pass the river, we'll have to see what we can do for the firth.'

'There are fords upon the river, and none upon the firth,' said I.

'To be sure there are fords, and a bridge forbye,' quoth Alan; 'and of what service, when they are watched?'

'Well,' said I, 'but a river can be swum.'

'By them that have the skill of it,' returned he; 'but I have yet to hear that either you or me is much of a hand at that exercise; and for my own part, I swim like a stone.'

'I'm not up to you in talking back, Alan,' I said; 'but I can see we're making bad worse. If it's hard to pass a river, it stands to reason it must be worse to pass a sea.'

'But there's such a thing as a boat,' says Alan, 'or I'm the more deceived.'

'Ay, and such a thing as money,' says I. 'But for us that

have neither one nor other, they might just as well not have been invented.'

'Ye think so?' said Alan.

'I do that,' said I.

'David,' says he, 'ye're a man of small invention and less faith. But let me set my wits upon the hone, and if I cannae beg, borrow, nor yet steal a boat, I'll make one!'

'I think I see ye!' said I. 'And what's more than all that: if ye pass a bridge, it can tell no tales; but if we pass the firth, there's the boat on the wrong side—somebody must have brought it—the countryside will all be in a bizz—'

'Man!' cried Alan, 'if I make a boat, I'll make a body to take it back again! So deave me with no more of your nonsense, but walk (for that's what you've got to do)—and let Alan think for ye.'

All night, then, we walked through the north side of the Carse under the high line of the Ochil mountains; and by Alloa and Clackmannan and Culross, all of which we avoided; and about ten in the morning, mighty hungry and tired, came to the little clachan of Limekilns. This is a place that sits near in by the waterside, and looks across the Hope to the town of the Queensferry. Smoke went up from both of these, and from other villages and farms upon all hands. The fields were being reaped; two ships lay anchored, and boats were coming and going on the Hope. It was altogether a right pleasant sight to me; and I could not take my fill of gazing at these comfortable, green, cultivated hills and the busy people both of the field and sea.

For all that, there was Mr Rankeillor's house on the south shore, where I had no doubt wealth awaited me; and here was I upon the north, clad in poor enough attire of an outlandish fashion, with three silver shillings left to me of all my fortune, a price set upon my head, and an outlawed man for my sole company.

'O, Alan!' said I, 'to think of it! Over there, there's all that heart could want waiting me; and the birds go over, and the boats go over—all that please can go, but just me only! O, man, but it's a heartbreak!'

In Limekilns we entered a small change-house, which we only knew to be a public by the wand over the door, and bought some bread and cheese from a good-looking lass that was the servant. This we carried with us in a bundle, meaning to sit and eat it in a bush of wood on the sea-shore, that we saw some third part of a mile in front. As we went, I kept looking across the water and sighing to myself; and though I took no heed of it, Alan had fallen into a muse. At last he stopped in the way.

'Did ye take heed of the lass we bought this of?' says he, tapping on the bread and cheese.

'To be sure,' said I, 'and a bonny lass she was.'

'Ye thought that?' cries he. 'Man David, that's good news.'

'In the name of all that's wonderful, why so?' says I. 'What good can that do?'

'Well,' said Alan, with one of his droll looks, 'I was rather in hopes it would maybe get us that boat.'

'If it were the other way about, it would be liker it,' said I.

'That's all that you ken, ye see,' said Alan. 'I don't want the lass to fall in love with ye, I want her to be sorry for ye, David; to which end, there is no manner of need that she should take you for a beauty. Let me see' (looking me curiously over). 'I wish ye were a wee thing paler; but apart from that ye'll do fine for my purpose—ye have a fine, hang-dog, rag-and-tatter, clappermaclaw kind of a look to ye, as if ye had stolen the coat from a potato-bogle. Come; right about, and back to the change-house for that boat of ours.'

I followed him laughing.

'David Balfour,' said he, 'Ye're a very funny gentleman by your way of it, and this is a very funny employ for ye, no doubt. For all that, if ye have any affection for my neck (to say nothing of your own) ye will perhaps be kind enough to take this matter responsibly. I am going to do a bit of play-acting, the bottom ground of which is just exactly as serious as the gallows for the pair of us. So bear it, if ye please, in mind, and conduct yourself according.'

'Well, well,' said I, 'have it as you will.'

As we got near the clachan, he made me take his arm and hang upon it like one almost helpless with weariness; and by the time he pushed open the change-house door, he seemed to be half carrying me. The maid appeared surprised (as well she might be) at our speedy return; but Alan had no words to spare for her in explanation, helped me to a chair, called for a tass of brandy with which he fed me in little sips, and then breaking up the bread and cheese helped me to eat it like a nursery-lass; the whole with that grave, concerned, affectionate countenance, that might have imposed upon a judge. It was small wonder if the maid were taken with the picture we presented, of a poor, sick, overwrought lad and his most tender comrade. She drew quite near, and stood leaning with her back on the next table.

'What's like wrong with him?' said she at last.

Alan turned upon her, to my great wonder, with a kind of fury. 'Wrong?' cries he. 'He's walked more hundreds of miles than he has hairs upon his chin, and slept oftener in wet heather than dry sheets. Wrong, quo' she! Wrong enough, I would think! Wrong, indeed!' and he kept grumbling to himself, as he fed me, like a man ill-pleased.

'He's young for the like of that,' said the maid.

'Ower young,' said Alan, with his back to her.

'He would be better riding,' says she.

'And where could I get a horse to him?' cried Alan, turning on her with the same appearance of fury. 'Would ye have me steal?'

I thought this roughness would have sent her off in dudgeon, as indeed it closed her mouth for the time. But my companion knew very well what he was doing; and for as simple as he was in some things of life, had a great fund of roguishness in such affairs as these.

'Ye neednae tell me,' she said at last—'ye're gentry.'

'Well,' said Alan, softened a little (I believe against his will) by this artless comment, 'and suppose we were? did ever you hear that gentrice put money in folk's pockets?'

She sighed at this, as if she were herself some disinherited great lady. 'No,' says she, 'that's true indeed.'

I was all this while chafing at the part I played, and sitting tongue-tied between shame and merriment; but somehow at this I could hold in no longer, and bade Alan let me be, for I was better already. My voice stuck in my throat, for I ever hated to take part in lies; but my very embarrassment helped on the plot, for the lass no doubt set down my husky voice to sickness and fatigue.

'Has he nae friends?' said she, in a tearful voice.

'That has he so!' cried Alan, 'if we could but win to

them!—friends and rich friends, beds to lie in, food to eat, doctors to see him—and here he must tramp in the dubs and sleep in the heather like a beggarman.'

'And why that?' says the lass.

'My dear,' says Alan, 'I cannae very safely say; but I'll tell ye what I'll do instead,' says he, 'I'll whistle ye a bit tune.' And with that he leaned pretty far over the table, and in a mere breath of a whistle, but with a wonderful pretty sentiment, gave her a few bars of 'Charlie is my darling'.

'Wheesht,' says she, and looked over her shoulder to the door.

'That's it,' said Alan.

'And him so young!' cries the lass.

'He's old enough to—' and Alan struck his forefinger on the back part of his neck, meaning that I was old enough to lose my head.

'It would be a black shame,' she cried, flushing high.

'It's what will be, though,' said Alan, 'unless we manage the better.'

At this the lass turned and ran out of that part of the house, leaving us alone together, Alan in high good humour at the furthering of his schemes, and I in bitter dudgeon at being called a Jacobite and treated like a child.

'Alan,' I cried, 'I can stand no more of this.'

'Ye'll have to sit it then, Davie,' said he. 'For if ye upset the pot now, ye may scrape your own life out of the fire, but Alan Breck is a dead man.'

This was so true that I could only groan; and even my groan served Alan's purpose, for it was overheard by the lass as she came flying in again with a dish of white puddings and a bottle of strong ale.

'Poor lamb!' says she, and had no sooner set the meat before us, than she touched me on the shoulder with a little friendly touch, as much as to bid me cheer up. Then she told us to fall to, and there would be no more to pay; for the inn was her own, or at least her father's, and he was gone for the day to Pittencrieff. We waited for no second bidding, for bread and cheese is but cold comfort and the puddings smelt excellently well; and while we sat and ate, she took up that same place by the next table, looking on, and thinking, and frowning to herself, and drawing the string of her apron through her hand.

'I'm thinking ye have rather a long tongue,' she said at last to Alan.

'Ay,' said Alan; 'but ye see I ken the folk I speak to.'

'I would never betray ye,' said she, 'if ye mean that.'

'No,' said he, 'ye're not that kind. But I'll tell ye what ye would do, ye would help.'

'I couldnae,' said she, shaking her head. 'Na, I couldnae.'

'No,' said he, 'but if ye could?'

She answered him nothing.

'Look here, my lass,' said Alan, 'there are boats in the kingdom of Fife for I saw two (no less) upon the beach, as I came in by your town's end. Now if we could have the use of a boat to pass under cloud of night into Lothian, and some secret, decent kind of a man to bring that boat back again and keep his counsel, there would be two souls saved—mine to all likelihood—his to a dead surety. If we lack that boat, we have but three shillings left in this wide world; and where to go, and how to do, and what other place there is for us except the chains of a gibbet—I give you my naked word, I kenna! Shall we go wanting, lassie? Are ye to lie in your warm bed and think upon us, when the wind gowls in the chimney and the rain tirls on the roof? Are ye to eat your meat by the cheeks of a red fire, and think upon this poor sick lad of mine, biting his finger ends on a blae muir for cauld and hunger? Sick or sound, he must aye be moving; with the death grapple at his throat he must aye be trailing in the rain on the lang roads; and when he gants his last on a rickle of cauld stanes, there will be nae friends near him but only me and God.'

At this appeal, I could see the lass was in great trouble of mind, being tempted to help us, and yet in some fear she might be helping malefactors; and so now I determined to step in myself and to allay her scruples with a portion of the truth.

'Did ever you hear,' said I, 'of Mr Rankeillor of the Ferry?'

'Rankeillor the writer?' said she. 'I daursay that!'

'Well,' said I, 'it's to his door that I am bound, so you may judge by that if I am an ill-doer; and I will tell you more, that though I am indeed, by a dreadful error, in some peril of my life, King George has no truer friend in all Scotland than myself.'

Her face cleared up mightily at this, although Alan's darkened.

'That's more than I would ask,' said she. 'Mr Rankeillor is a kennt man.' And she bade us finish our meat, get clear of the Clachan as soon as might be, and lie close in the bit wood on the sea beach. 'And ye can trust me,' says she, 'I'll find some means to put you over.'

At this we waited for no more, but shook hands with her upon the bargain, made short work of the puddings, and set forth again from Limekilns as far as to the wood. It was a small piece of perhaps a score of elders and hawthorns and a few young ashes, not thick enough to veil us from passers-by upon the road or beach. Here we must lie, however, making the best of the brave warm weather and the good hopes we now had of a deliverance, and planning more particularly what remained for us to do.

We had but one trouble all day: when a strolling piper came and sat in the same wood with us; a red-nosed, blear-eyed, drunken dog, with a great bottle of whiskey in his pocket, and a long story of wrongs that had been done him by all sorts of persons, from the Lord President of the Court of Session who had denied him justice, down to the Baillies of Inverkeithing who had given him more of it than he desired. It was impossible but he should conceive some suspicion of two men lying all day concealed in a thicket and having no business to allege. As long as he stayed there, he kept us in hot water with prying questions; and after he was gone, as he was a man not very likely to hold his tongue, we were in the greater impatience to be gone ourselves.

The day came to an end with the same brightness; the night fell quiet and clear; lights came out in houses and hamlets and then, one after another, began to be put out; but it was past eleven, and we were long since strangely tortured with anxieties, before we heard the grinding of oars upon the rowing pins. At that, we looked out and saw the lass herself coming rowing to us in a boat. She had trusted no one with our affairs, not even her sweetheart, if she had one; but as soon as her father was asleep, had left the house by a window, stolen a neighbour's boat, and come to our assistance single-handed.

I was abashed how to find expression for my thanks; but she was no less abashed at the thought of hearing them;

begged us to lose no time and to hold our peace, saying
(very properly) that the heart of our matter was in haste
and silence; and so, what with one thing and another, she
had set us on the Lothian shore not far from Carriden, had
shaken hands with us, and was out again at sea and rowing
for Limekilns, before there was one word said either of her
service or our gratitude.

Even after she was gone, we had nothing to say, as indeed
nothing was enough for such a kindness. Only Alan stood a
great while upon the shore shaking his head.

'It is a very fine lass,' he said at last. 'David, it is a very
fine lass.' And a matter of an hour later, as we were lying
in a den on the seashore and I had been already dozing, he
broke out again in commendations of her character. For my
part, I could say nothing, she was so simple a creature that
my heart smote me both with remorse and fear; remorse
because we had traded upon her ignorance; and fear lest
we should have anyway involved her in the dangers of our
situation.

THE NEXT DAY it was agreed that Alan should fend for himself till sunset; but as soon as it began to grow dark, he should lie in the fields by the roadside near to Newhalls, and stir for naught until he heard me whistling. At first I proposed I should give him for a signal the 'Bonnie House of Airlie', which was a favourite of mine; but he objected that as the piece was very commonly known, any ploughman might whistle it by accident; and taught me instead a little fragment of a Highland air, which has run in my head from that day to this, and will likely run in my head when I lie dying. Every time it comes to me, it takes me off to that last day of my uncertainty, with Alan sitting up in the bottom of the den, whistling and beating the measure with a finger, and the grey of the dawn coming on his face.

I was in the long street of Queensferry before the sun was up. It was a fairly built burgh, the houses of good stone, many slated; the town-hall not so fine, I thought, as that of Peebles, nor yet the street so noble; but take it altogether, it put me to shame for my foul tatters.

As the morning went on, and the fires began to be kindled, and the windows to open, and the people to appear out of the houses, my concern and despondency grew ever the blacker. I saw now that I had no grounds to stand upon; and no clear proof of my rights, nor so much as of my own identity. If it was all a bubble, I was indeed sorely cheated and left in a sore pass. Even if things were as I conceived, it would in all likelihood take time to establish my contentions; and what time had I to spare with less than three shillings in my pocket, and a condemned, hunted man upon my hands to ship out of the country? Truly, if my hope broke with me, it might come to the gallows yet for both of us. And as I continued to walk up and down, and saw people looking askance at me upon the street or out of windows, and nudging or speaking one to another with smiles, I began to take a fresh apprehension: that it might be no easy matter even to come to speech of the lawyer, far less to convince him of my story.

For the life of me I could not muster up the courage to address any of these reputable burghers; I thought shame even to speak with them in such a pickle of rags and dirt; and if I had asked for the house of such a man as Mr Rankeillor, I supposed they would have burst out laughing in my face. So I went up and down, and through the street, and down to the harbour-side, like a dog that has lost its master, with a strange gnawing in my inwards, and every now and then a movement of despair. It grew to be high day at last, perhaps nine in the forenoon; and I was worn with these wanderings, and chanced to have stopped in front of a very good house on the landward side, a house with beautiful, clear glass windows, flowering knots upon the sills, the walls new-harled, and a chase-dog sitting yawning on the step like one that was at home. Well, I was even envying this dumb brute, when the door fell open and there issued forth a shrewd, ruddy, kindly consequential man in a well-powdered wig and spectacles. I was in such a plight that no one set eyes on me once, but he looked at me again; and this gentleman, as it proved, was so much struck with my poor appearance that he came straight up to me and asked me what I did.

I told him I was come to the Queensferry on business, and taking heart of grace, asked him to direct me to the house of Mr Rankeillor.

'Why,' said he, 'that is his house that I have just come out of; and for a rather singular chance, I am that very man.'

'Then, sir,' said I, 'I have to beg the favour of an interview.'

'I do not know your name,' said he, 'nor yet your face.'

'My name is David Balfour,' said I.

'David Balfour?' he repeated, in rather a high tone, like one surprised. 'And where have you come from, Mr David Balfour?' he asked, looking me pretty drily in the face.

'I have come from a great many strange places, sir,' said I; 'but I think it would be as well to tell you where and how in a more private manner.'

He seemed to muse awhile, holding his lip in his hand, and looking now at me and now upon the causeway of the street.

'Yes,' says he, 'that will be the best, no doubt.' And he led me back with him into his house, cried out to some one whom I could not see that he would be engaged all morning, and brought me into a little dusty chamber full of books and documents. Here he sate down, and bade me be seated; though I thought he looked a little ruefully from his clean chair to my muddy rags. 'And now,' says he, 'if you have any business, pray be brief and come swiftly to the point. *Nec germino bellum Trojanum orditur ab ovo*—do you understand that?' says he, with a keen look.

'I will even do as Horace says, sir,' I answered, smiling, 'and carry you *in medias res*.' He nodded as if he was well pleased, and indeed his scrap of Latin had been set to test me. For all that, and though I was somewhat encouraged, the blood came in my face when I added: 'I have reason to believe myself some rights on the estate of Shaws.'

He got a paper book out of a drawer and set it before him open. 'Well?' said he.

But I had shot my bolt and sat speechless.

'Come, come, Mr Balfour,' said he, 'you must continue. Where were you born?'

'In Essendean, sir,' said I, 'the year 1734, the 12th of March.'

He seemed to follow this statement in his paper book; but what that meant I knew not. 'Your father and mother?' said he.

'My father was Alexander Balfour, schoolmaster of that place,' said I, 'and my mother Grace Pitarrow; I think her people were from Angus.'

'Have you any papers proving your identity?' asked Mr Rankeillor.

'No, sir,' said I, 'but they are in the hands of Mr Campbell, the minister, and could be readily produced. Mr Campbell, too, would give me his word; and for that matter, I do not think my uncle would deny me.'

'Meaning Mr Ebenezer Balfour?' says he.

'The same,' said I.

'Whom you have seen?' he asked.

'By whom I was received into his own house,' I answered.

'Did you ever meet a man of the name of Hoseason?' asked Mr Rankeillor.

'I did so, sir, for my sins,' said I; 'for it was by his means and the procurement of my uncle, that I was kidnapped within sight of this town, carried to sea, suffered shipwreck and a hundred other hardships, and stand before you to-day in this poor accoutrement.'

'You say you were shipwrecked,' said Rankeillor; 'where was that?'

'Off the south end of the Isle of Mull,' said I. 'The name of the isle on which I was cast up is the Island Earraid.'

'Ah!' says he, smiling, 'you are deeper than me in the geography. But so far, I may tell you, this agrees pretty exactly with other informations that I hold. But you say you were kidnapped; in what sense?'

'In the plain meaning of the word, sir,' said I. 'I was on my way to your house, when I was trepanned on board the brig, cruelly struck down, thrown below, and knew no more of anything till we were far at sea. I was destined for the plantations; a fate that, in God's providence, I have escaped.'

'The brig was lost on June the 27th,' says he, looking in his book, 'and we are now at August the 24th. Here is a considerable hiatus, Mr Balfour, of near upon two months. It has already caused a vast amount of trouble to your friends; and I own I shall not be very well contented until it is set right.'

'Indeed, sir,' said I, 'these months are very easily filled up; but yet before I told my story, I would be glad to know that I was talking to a friend.'

'This is to argue in a circle,' said the lawyer. 'I cannot be convinced till I have heard you. I cannot be your friend till I am properly informed. If you were more trustful, it would better befit your time of life. And you know, Mr Balfour, we have a proverb in the country that evil-doers are aye evil-dreaders.'

'You are not to forget, sir,' said I, 'that I have already suffered by my trustfulness; and was shipped off to be a slave by the very man that (if I rightly understand) is your employer.'

All this while, I had been gaining ground with Mr Rankeillor, and in proportion as I gained ground, gaining confidence. But at this sally, which I made with something of a smile myself, he fairly laughed aloud.

'No, no,' said he, 'it is not so bad as that. *Fui, non sum.* I *was* indeed your uncle's man of business; but while you (*imberbis juvenis custode remoto*) were gallivanting in the west, a good deal of water has run under the bridges; and if your ears did not sing, it was not for lack of being talked about. On the very day of your sea disaster, Mr Campbell stalked into my office, demanding you from all the winds. I had never heard of your existence; but I had known your father; and from matters in my competence (to be touched upon hereafter) I was disposed to fear the worst. Mr Ebenezer admitted having seen you; declared (what seemed improbable) that he had given you considerable sums; and that you had started for the continent of Europe, intending to fulfil your education, which was probable and praiseworthy. Interrogated how you had come to send no word to Mr Campbell, he deponed that you had expressed a great desire to break with your past life. Further interrogated where you now were, protested ignorance, but believed you were in Leyden. That is a close sum of his replies. I am not exactly sure that any one believed him,' continued Mr Rankeillor with a smile; 'and in particular he so much disrelished some expressions of mine that (in a word) he showed me to the door. We were then at a full stand; for whatever shrewd suspicions we might entertain, we had no shadow of probation. In the very article, comes Captain Hoseason with the story of your drowning; whereupon all fell through; with no consequences but concern to Mr Campbell, injury to my pocket, and another blot upon your uncle's character, which could very ill afford it. And now, Mr Balfour,' said he, 'you understand the whole process of these matters, and can judge for yourself to what extent I may be trusted.'

Indeed he was more pedantic than I can represent him, and placed more scraps of Latin in his speech; but it was all uttered with a fine geniality of eye and manner which went far to conquer my distrust. Moreover, I could see he now treated me as if I was myself beyond a doubt; so that first point of my identity seemed fully granted.

'Sir,' said I, 'if I tell you my story, I must commit a friend's life to your discretion. Pass me your word it shall be sacred; and for what touches myself, I will ask no better guarantee than just your face.'

He passed me his word very seriously. 'But,' said he, 'these are rather alarming prolocutions; and if there are in your story any little jostles to the law, I would beg you to bear in mind that I am a lawyer, and pass lightly.'

Thereupon I told him my story from the first, he listening with his spectacles thrust up and his eyes closed, so that I sometimes feared he was asleep. But no such matter! he heard every word (as I found afterward) with such quickness of hearing and precision of memory as often surprised me. Even strange, outlandish Gaelic names, heard for that time only, he remembered and would remind me of, years after. Yet when I called Alan Breck in full, we had an odd scene. The name of Alan had of course rung through Scotland, with the news of the Appin murder and the offer of the reward; and it had no sooner escaped me than the lawyer moved in his seat and opened his eyes.

'I would name no unnecessary names, Mr Balfour,' said he; 'above all of Highlanders, many of whom are obnoxious to the law.'

'Well, it might have been better not,' said I; 'but since I have let it slip, I may as well continue.'

'Not at all,' said Mr Rankeillor. 'I am somewhat dull of hearing, as you may have remarked; and I am far from sure I caught the name exactly. We will call your friend, if you please, Mr Thomson—that there may be no reflections. And in future, I would take some such way with any Highlander that you may have to mention—dead or alive.'

By this, I saw he must have heard the name all too clearly and had already guessed I might be coming to the murder. If he chose to play this part of ignorance, it was no matter of mine; so I smiled, said it was no very Highland-sounding name, and consented. Through all the rest of my story Alan was Mr Thomson; which amused me the more, as it was a piece of policy after his own heart. James Stewart, in like manner, was mentioned under the style of Mr Thomson's kinsman; Colin Campbell passed as a Mr Glen; and to Cluny, when I came to that part of my tale, I gave the name of 'Mr Jameson, a Highland chief'. It was truly the most open farce, and I wondered that the lawyer should care to keep it up; but after all it was quite in the taste of that age, when there were two parties in the state, and quiet persons, with no very high opinions of their own, sought out every cranny to avoid offence to either.

'Well, well,' said the lawyer, when I had quite done, 'this is a great epic, a great Odyssey of yours. You must tell it, sir, in a sound Latinity when your scholarship is riper; or in English if you please, though for my part I prefer the stronger tongue. You have rolled much; *quæ regio in terris*—what parish in Scotland (to make a homely translation) has not been filled with your wanderings? You have shown, besides, a singular aptitude for getting into false positions; and, yes, upon the whole, for behaving well in them. This Mr Thomson seems to me a gentleman of some choice qualities, though perhaps a trifle bloody-minded. It would please me none the worse, if (with all his merits) he were soused in the North Sea; for the man, Mr David, is a sore embarrassment. But you are doubtless quite right to adhere to him; indubitably, he adhered to you. *It comes*—we may say—he was your true companion; nor less, *paribus curis vestigia figit*, for I daresay you would both take an orra thought upon the gallows. Well, well, these days are fortunately by; and I think (speaking humanly) that you are near the end of your troubles.'

As he thus moralised on my adventures, he looked upon me with so much humour and benignity that I could scarce contain my satisfaction. I had been so long wandering with lawless people, and making my bed upon the hills and under the bare sky, that to sit once more in a clean, covered house, and to talk amicably with a gentleman in broadcloth, seemed mighty elevations. Even as I thought so, my eye fell on my unseemly tatters, and I was once more plunged in confusion. But the lawyer saw and understood me. He rose, called over the stair to lay another plate, for Mr Balfour would stay to dinner, and led me into a bedroom in the upper part of the house. Here he set before me water and soap and a comb; and laid out some clothes that belonged to his son; and here, with another apposite tag, he left me to my toilet.

I MADE WHAT change I could in my appearance; and blithe was I to look in the glass and find the beggar-man a thing of the past, and David Balfour come to life again. And yet I was ashamed of the change too, and above all, of the borrowed clothes. When I had done, Mr Rankeillor caught me on the stair, made me his compliments, and had me again into the cabinet.

'Sit ye down, Mr David,' said he, 'and now that you are looking a little more like yourself, let me see if I can find you any news. You will be wondering, no doubt, about your father and your uncle? To be sure it is a singular tale; and the explanation is one that I blush to have to offer you. For,' says he, really with embarrassment, 'the matter hinges on a love affair.'

'Truly,' said I, 'I cannot very well join that notion with my uncle.'

'But your uncle, Mr David, was not always old,' replied the lawyer, 'and what may perhaps surprise you more, not always ugly. He had a fine, gallant air; people stood in their doors to look after him, as he went by upon a mettle horse. I have seen it with these eyes, and I ingenuously confess, not altogether without envy; for I was a plain lad myself and a plain man's son; and in those days, it was a case of *Odi te, qui bellus es, Sabelle.*'

'It sounds like a dream,' said I.

'Ay, ay,' said the lawyer, 'that is how it is with youth and age. Nor was that all, but he had a spirit of his own that seemed to promise great things in the future. In 1715, what must he do but run away to join the rebels? It was your father that pursued him, found him in a ditch, and brought him back *multum gementem;* to the mirth of the whole county. However, *majora canamus*—the two lads fell in love, and that with the same lady. Mr Ebenezer, who was the admired and the beloved, and the spoiled one, made, no doubt, mighty certain of the victory; and when he found he had deceived himself, screamed like a peacock. The whole country heard of it; now he lay sick at home, with his silly family standing round the bed in tears; now he rode from public house to public house and shouted his sorrows into the lug of Tom, Dick, and Harry. Your father, Mr David, was a kind gentleman; but he was weak, dolefully weak; took all this folly with a long countenance; and one day—by your leave!—resigned the lady. She was no such fool, however; it's from her you must inherit your excellent good sense; and she refused to be bandied from one to another. Both got upon their knees to her; and the upshot of the matter for that while, was that she showed both of them the door. That was in August; dear me! the same year I came from college. The scene must have been highly farcical.'

I thought myself it was a silly business, but I could not forget my father had a hand in it. 'Surely, sir, it had some note of tragedy,' said I.

'Why, no, sir, not at all,' returned the lawyer. 'For tragedy implies some ponderable matter in dispute, some *dignus vindice nodus;* and this piece of work was all about the petulance of a young ass that had been spoiled, and wanted nothing so much as to be tied up and soundly belted. However, that was not your father's view; and the end of it was, that from concession to concession on your father's part, and from one height to another of squalling, sentimental selfishness upon your uncle's, they came at last to drive a sort of bargain, from whose ill-results you have recently been smarting. The one man took the lady, the other the estate. Now, Mr David, they talk a great deal of charity and generosity; but in this disputable state of life, I often think the happiest consequences seem to flow when a gentleman consults his lawyer and takes all the law allows him. Anyhow, this piece of Quixotry upon your father's part, as it was unjust in itself, has brought forth a monstrous family of injustices. Your father and mother lived and died poor folk; you were poorly reared; and in the meanwhile, what a time it has been for the tenants on the estate of Shaws! And I might add (if it was a matter I cared much about) what a time for Mr Ebenezer!'

'And yet that is certainly the strangest part of all,' said I, 'that a man's nature should thus change.'

'True,' said Mr Rankeillor. 'And yet I imagine it was natural enough. He could not think that he had played a handsome part. Those who knew the story gave him the cold shoulder; those who knew it not, seeing one brother disappear, and the other succeed in the estate, raised a cry of murder; so that upon all sides, he found himself evited. Money was all he got by his bargain; well, he came to think the more of money. He was selfish when he was young, he is selfish now that he is old; and the latter end of all these pretty manners and fine feelings, you have seen for yourself.'

'Well sir,' said I, 'and in all this, what is my position?'

'The estate is yours beyond a doubt,' replied the lawyer. 'It matters nothing what your father signed, you are the heir of entail. But your uncle is a man to fight the indefensible; and it would be likely your identity that he would call in question. A lawsuit is always expensive, and a family lawsuit always scandalous; besides which, if any of your doings with your friend Mr Thomson were to come out, we might find that we had burned our fingers. The kidnapping, to be sure, would be a court card upon our side, if we could only prove it. But it may be difficult to prove; and my advice (upon the whole) is to make a very easy bargain with your uncle, perhaps even leaving him at Shaws where he has taken root for a quarter of a century, and contenting yourself in the meanwhile with a fair provision.'

I told him I was very willing to be easy, and that to carry family concerns before the public was a step from which I was naturally much averse. In the meantime (thinking to myself) I began to see the outlines of that scheme on which we afterwards acted.

'The great affair,' I asked, 'is to bring home to him the kidnapping?'

'Surely,' said Mr Rankeillor, 'and if possible, out of court. For mark you here, Mr David: we could no doubt find some men of the *Covenant* who would swear to your reclusion; but once they were in the box, we could no longer check their testimony, and some word of your friend Mr Thomson must certainly crop out. Which (from what you have let fall) I cannot think to be desirable.'

'Well, sir,' said I, 'here is my way of it.' And I opened my plot to him.

'But this would seem to involve my meeting the man Thomson?' says he, when I had done.

'I think so, indeed, sir,' said I.

'Dear doctor!' cries he, rubbing his brow. 'Dear doctor! No, Mr David, I am afraid your scheme is inadmissible. I say nothing against your friend Mr Thomson; I know nothing against him; and if I did—mark this, Mr David!—it would be my duty to lay hands on him. Now I put it to you: is it wise to meet? He may have matters to his charge. He may not have told you all. His name may not be even Thomson!' cries the lawyer, twinkling; 'for some of these fellows will pick up names by the roadside as another would gather haws.'

'You must be the judge, sir,' said I.

But it was clear my plan had taken hold upon his fancy, for he kept musing to himself till we were called to dinner and the company of Mrs Rankeillor; and that lady had scarce left us again to ourselves and a bottle of wine, ere he was back harping on my proposal. When and where was I to meet my friend Mr Thomson; was I sure of Mr T.'s discretion; supposing we could catch the old fox tripping, would I consent to such and such a term of an agreement—these and the like questions he kept asking at long intervals, while he thoughtfully rolled his wine upon his tongue. When I had answered all of them, seemingly to his contentment, he fell into a still deeper muse, even the claret being now forgotten. Then he got a sheet of paper and a pencil, and set to work writing and weighing every word; and at last touched a bell and had his clerk into the chamber.

'Torrance,' said he, 'I must have this written out fair against to-night; and when it is done, you will be so kind as put on your hat and be ready to come along with this gentleman and me, for you will probably be wanted as a witness.'

'What, sir,' cried I, as soon as the clerk was gone, 'are you to venture it?'

'Why, so it would appear,' says he, filling his glass. 'But let us speak no more of business. The very sight of Torrance brings in my head a little, droll matter of some years ago,

when I had made a tryst with the poor oaf at the cross of
Edinburgh. Each had gone his proper errand; and when it
came four o'clock, Torrance had been taking a glass and did
not know his master, and I, who had forgot my spectacles,
was so blind without them, that I give you my word I did not
know my own clerk.' And thereupon he laughed heartily.

I said it was an odd chance, and smiled out of politeness;
but what held me all the afternoon in wonder, he kept
returning and dwelling on this story, and telling it again
with fresh details and laughter; so that I began at last
to be quite put of countenance and feel ashamed for my
friend's folly.

Towards the time I had appointed with Alan, we set
out from the house, Mr Rankeillor and I arm in arm, and
Torrance following behind with the deed in his pocket and
a covered basket in his hand. All through the town, the
lawyer was bowing right and left, and continually being
button-holed by gentlemen on matters of burgh or private
business; and I could see he was one greatly looked up to
in the county. At last we were clear of the houses, and began
to go along the side of the haven and towards the Hawes Inn
and the ferry pier, the scene of my misfortune. I could not
look upon the place without emotion, recalling how many
that had been there with me that day were now no more:
Ransome taken, I could hope, from the evil to come;
Shuan passed where I dared not follow him; and the poor
souls that had gone down with the brig in her last plunge.
All these, and the brig herself, I had outlived; and come
through these hardships and fearful perils without scathe.
My only thought should have been of gratitude; and yet
I could not behold the place without sorrow for others and
a chill of recollected fear.

I was so thinking when, upon a sudden, Mr Rankeillor
cried out, clapped his hand to his pockets, and began to
laugh.

'Why,' he cries, 'if this be not a farcical adventure! After
all that I said, I have forgot my glasses!'

At that, of course, I understood the purpose of his
anecdote, and knew that if he had left his spectacles at
home, it had been done on purpose, so that he might
have the benefit of Alan's help without the awkwardness
of recognising him. And indeed it was well thought upon;

for now (suppose things to go the very worst) how could Rankeillor swear to my friend's identity, or how be made to bear damaging evidence against myself? For all that, he had been a long while of finding out his want, and had spoken to and recognised a good few persons as we came through the town; and I had little doubt myself that he saw reasonably well.

As soon as we were past the Hawes (where I recognised the landlord smoking his pipe in the door, and was amazed to see him look no older) Mr Rankeillor changed the order of march, walking behind with Torrance and sending me forward in the manner of a scout. I went up the hill, whistling from time to time my Gaelic air; and at length I had the pleasure to hear it answered and to see Alan rise from behind a bush. He was somewhat dashed in spirits, having passed a long day alone skulking in the county, and made but a poor meal in an alehouse near Dundas. But at the mere sight of my clothes, he began to brighten up; and as soon as I had told him in what a forward state our matters were and the part I looked to him to play in what remained, he sprang into a new man.

'And that is a very good notion of yours,' says he; 'and I dare to say that you could lay your hands upon no better man to put it through, than Alan Breck. It is not a thing (mark ye) that anyone could do, but takes a gentleman of penetration. But it sticks in my head your lawyer-man will be somewhat wearying to see me,' says Alan.

Accordingly I cried and waved on Mr Rankeillor, who came up alone and was presented to my friend, Mr Thomson.

'Mr Thomson, I am pleased to meet you,' said he. 'But I have forgotten my glasses; and our friend, Mr David here' (clapping me on the shoulder) 'will tell you that I am little better than blind, and that you must not be surprised if I pass you by to-morrow.'

This he said, thinking that Alan would be pleased; but the Highlandman's vanity was ready to startle at a less matter than that.

'Why, sir,' says he, stiffly, 'I would say it mattered the less as we are met here for a particular end, to see justice done to Mr Balfour; and by what I can see, not very likely to have much else in common. But I accept your apology, which was a very proper one to make.'

'And that is more than I could look for, Mr Thomson,' said Rankeillor, heartily. 'And now as you and I are the chief actors in this enterprise, I think we should come into a nice agreement; to which end, I propose that you should lend me your arm, for (what with the dusk and the want of my glasses) I am not very clear as to the path; and as for you, Mr David, you will find Torrance a pleasant kind of body to speak with. Only let me remind you, it's quite needless he should hear more of your adventures or those of—ahem—Mr Thomson.'

Accordingly these two went on ahead in very close talk, and Torrance and I brought up the rear.

Night was quite come when we came in view of the house of Shaws. Ten had been gone some time; it was dark and mild, with a pleasant, rustling wind in the south-west that covered the sound of our approach; and as we drew near we saw no glimmer of light in any portion of the building. It seemed my uncle was already in bed, which was indeed the best thing for our arrangements. We made our last whispered consultations some fifty yards away; and then the lawyer and Torrance and I crept quietly up and crouched down beside the corner of the house; and as soon as we were in our places, Alan strode to the door without concealment and began to knock.

FOR SOME TIME Alan volleyed upon the door, and his knocking only roused the echoes of the house and neighbourhood. At last, however, I could hear the noise of a window gently thrust up, and knew that my uncle had come to his observatory. By what light there was, he would see Alan standing, like a dark shadow, on the steps; the three witnesses were hidden quite out of his view; so that there was nothing to alarm an honest man in his own house. For all that, he studied his visitor awhile in silence, and when he spoke his voice had a quaver of misgiving.

'What's this?' says he. 'This is nae kind of time of night for decent folk; and I hae nae trokings wi' night-hawks. What brings ye here? I have a blunderbush.'

'Is that yoursel', Mr Balfour?' returned Alan, stepping back and looking up into the darkness. 'Have a care of that blunderbuss; they're nasty things to burst.'

'What brings ye here? and whae are ye?' says my uncle, angrily.

'I have no manner of inclination to rowt out my name to the countryside,' said Alan; 'but what brings me here is another story, being more of your affairs than mine; and if ye're sure it's what ye would like, I'll set it to a tune and sing it to you.'

'And what is't?' asked my uncle.

'David,' says Alan.

'What was that?' cried my uncle, in a mighty changed voice.

'Shall I give ye the rest of the name, then?' said Alan.

There was a pause; and then, 'I'm thinking I'll better let ye in,' says my uncle, doubtfully.

'I daresay that,' said Alan; 'but the point is, Would I go? Now I will tell you what I am thinking. I am thinking that it is here upon this doorstep that we must confer upon this business; and it shall be here or nowhere at all whatever; for I would have you to understand that I am as stiffnecked as yoursel', and a gentleman of better family.'

This change of note disconcerted Ebenezer; he was a little while digesting it; and then says he, 'Weel, weel, what must be must,' and shut the window. But it took him a long time to get down stairs, and a still longer to undo the fastenings, repenting (I daresay) and taken with fresh claps of fear at every second step and every bolt and bar. At last, however, we heard the creak of the hinges, and it seems my uncle slipped gingerly out and (seeing that Alan had stepped back a pace or two) sate him down on the top doorstep with the blunderbuss ready in his hands.

'And now,' says he, 'mind I have my blunderbush, and if ye take a step nearer ye're as good as deid.'

'And a very civil speech,' says Alan, 'to be sure.'

'Na,' says my uncle, 'but this is no a very chancy kind of a proceeding, and I'm bound to be prepared. And now that we understand each other, ye'll can name your business.'

'Why,' says Alan, 'you that are a man of so much understanding, will doubtless have perceived that I am a Hieland gentleman. My name has nae business in my story; but the county of my friends is no very far from the Isle of Mull, of which ye will have heard. It seems there was a ship lost in those parts; and the next day a gentleman of my family was seeking wreck-wood for his fire along the sands, when he came upon a lad that was half drowned. Well, he brought him to; and he and some other gentlemen took and clapped him in an auld, ruined castle, where from that day to this he has been a great expense to my friends. My friends are a wee wild-like, and not so particular about the law as some that I could name; and finding that the lad owned some decent folk, and was your born nephew, Mr Balfour, they asked me to give ye a bit call and to confer upon the matter. And I may tell ye at the off-go, unless we can agree upon some terms, ye are little likely to set eyes upon him. For my friends,' added Alan, simply, 'are no very well off.'

My uncle cleared his throat. 'I'm no very caring,' says

he. 'He wasnae a good lad at the best of it, and I've nae call to interfere.'

'Ay, ay,' said Alan, 'I see what ye would be at: pretending ye don't care, to make the ransome smaller.'

'Na,' said my uncle, 'it's the mere truth. I take nae manner of interest in the lad, and I'll pay nae ransome, and ye can make a kirk and a mill of him for what I care.'

'Hoot, sir,' says Alan. 'Blood's thicker than water, in the deil's name! Ye cannae desert your brother's son for the fair shame of it; and if ye did, and it came to be kennt, ye wouldnae be very popular in your countryside, or I'm the more deceived.'

'I'm no just very popular the way it is,' returned Ebenezer; 'and I dinnae see how it would come to be kennt. No by me, onyway; nor yet by you or your friends. So that's idle talk, my buckie,' says he.

'Then it'll have to be David that tells it,' said Alan.

'How that?' says my uncle, sharply.

'Ou, just this way,' says Alan. 'My friends would doubtless keep your nephew as long as there was any likelihood of siller to be made of it, but if there was nane, I am clearly of opinion they would let him gang where he pleased, and be damned to him!'

'Ay, but I'm no very caring about that either,' said my uncle. 'I wouldnae be muckle made up with that.'

'I was thinking that,' said Alan.

'And what for why?' asked Ebenezer.

'Why, Mr Balfour,' replied Alan, 'by all that I could hear, there were two ways of it: either ye liked David and would pay to get him back; or else ye had very good reasons for not wanting him, and would pay for us to keep him. It seems it's not the first; well then, it's the second; and blythe am I to ken it, for it should be a pretty penny in my pocket and the pockets of my friends.'

'I dinnae follow ye there,' said my uncle.

'No?' said Alan. 'Well, see here: you dinnae want the lad back; well, what do ye want done with him, and how much will ye pay?'

My uncle made no answer, but shifted uneasily on his seat.

'Come, sir,' cried Alan. 'I would have ye to ken that I am a gentleman; I bear a king's name; I am nae rider to kick my shanks at your hall door. Either give me an answer in civility, and that out of hand; or by the top of Glencoe, I will ram three feet of iron through your vitals.'

'Eh, man,' cried my uncle, scrambling to his feet, 'give me a meenit! What's like wrong with ye? I'm just a plain man, and nae dancing master; and I'm trying to be as ceevil as it's morally possible. As for that wild talk, it's fair disreputable. Vitals, says you! And where would I be with my blunderbush?' he snarled.

'Powder and your auld hands are but as the snail to the swallow against the bright steel in the hands of Alan,' said the other. 'Before your jottering finger could find the trigger, the hilt would dirl on your breast bane.'

'Eh, man, whae's denying it?' said my uncle. 'Pit it as ye please, hae't your ain way; I'll do naething to cross ye. Just tell me what like ye'll be wanting, and ye'll see that we'll can agree fine.'

'Troth, sir,' said Alan, 'I ask for nothing but plain dealing. In two words: do ye want the lad killed or kept?'

'O, sirs!' cried Ebenezer. 'O, sirs, me! that's no kind of language!'

'Killed or kept?' repeated Alan.

'O keepit, keepit!' wailed my uncle. 'We'll have nae bloodshed, if you please.'

'Well,' says Alan, 'as ye please; that'll be the dearer.'

'The dearer?' cries Ebenezer. 'Would ye fyle your hands wi' crime?'

'Hoot!' said Alan, 'they're baith crime, whatever! And the killing's easier, and quicker, and surer. Keeping the lad'll be a fashious job, a fashious, kittle business.'

'I'll have him keepit, though,' returned my uncle. 'I never had naething to do with onything morally wrong; and I'm no gaun to begin to pleasure a wild Hielandman.'

'Ye're unco scrupulous,' sneered Alan.

'I'm a man o' principle,' said Ebenezer simply; 'and if I have to pay for it, I'll have to pay for it. And besides,' says he, 'ye forget the lad's my brother's son.'

'Well, well,' said Alan, 'and now about the price. It's no very easy for me to set a name upon it; I would first have to ken some small matters. I would have to ken, for instance, what ye gave Hoseason at the first off-go?'

'Hoseason?' cries my uncle, struck aback. 'What for?'

'For kidnapping David,' says Alan.

'It's a lee, it's a black lee!' cried my uncle. 'He was never kidnapped. He leed in his throat that tauld ye that. Kidnapped? He never was!'

'That's no fault of mine nor yet of yours,' said Alan; 'nor yet of Hoseason's, if he's a man that can be trusted.'

'What do ye mean?' cried Ebenezer. 'Did Hoseason tell ye?'

'Why, ye donnered auld runt, how else would I ken?' cried Alan. 'Hoseason and I are partners; we gang shares; so ye can see for yoursel', what good ye can do leeing. And I must plainly say ye drove a fool's bargain when ye let a man like the sailor-man so far forward in your private matters. But that's past praying for; and ye must lie on your bed the way ye made it. And the point in hand is just this: what did ye pay him?'

'Has he tauld ye himsel',' asked my uncle.

'That's my concern,' said Alan.

'Weel,' said my uncle, 'I dinnae care what he said, he leed, and the solemn God's truth is this, that I gave him twenty pound. But I'll be perfec'ly honest with ye: forby that, he was to have the selling of the lad in Caroliny, whilk would be as muckle mair, but no from my pocket, ye see.'

'Thank you, Mr Thomson. That will do excellently well,' said the lawyer, stepping forward; and then mighty civilly, 'Good evening, Mr Balfour,' said he.

And, 'Good evening, uncle Ebenezer,' said I.

And 'It's a braw nicht, Mr Balfour,' added Torrance.

Never a word said my uncle, neither black nor white; but just sat where he was on the top doorstep and stared upon us like a man turned to stone. Alan filched away his blunderbuss; and the lawyer, taking him by the arm, plucked him up from the doorstep, led him into the kitchen, whither we all followed, and set him down in a chair beside the hearth, where the fire was out and only a rushlight burning.

There we all looked upon him for awhile, exulting greatly in our success, but yet with a sort of pity for the man's shame.

'Come, come, Mr Ebenezer,' said the lawyer, 'you must not be down-hearted, for I promise you we shall make easy terms. In the meanwhile give us the cellar key, and Torrance shall draw us a bottle of your father's wine in honour of the event.' Then, turning to me and taking me by the hand, 'Mr David,' says he, 'I wish you all joy in your good fortune, which I believe to be deserved.' And then to Alan, with a spice of drollery, 'Mr Thomson, I pay you my compliment; it was most artfully conducted; but in one point you somewhat outran my comprehension. Do I understand your name to be James? or Charles? or is it George perhaps?'

'And why should it be any of the three, sir?' quoth Alan, drawing himself up, like one who smelt an offence.

'Only, sir, that you mentioned a king's name,' replied Rankeillor; 'and as there has never yet been a King Thomson, or his fame at least has never come my way, I judged you must refer to that you had in baptism.'

This was just the stab that Alan would feel keenest, and I am free to confess he took it very ill. Not a word would he answer, but stept off to the far end of the kitchen, and sat down and sulked; and it was not till I stepped after him, and gave him my hand, and thanked him by title as the chief spring of my success, that he began to smile a bit, and was at last prevailed upon to join our party.

By that time we had the fire lighted, and a bottle of wine uncorked; a good supper came out of the basket, to which Torrance and I and Alan set ourselves down; while the lawyer and my uncle passed into the next chamber to consult. They stayed there closeted about an hour; at the end of which period they had come to a good understanding, and my uncle and I set our hands to the agreement in a formal manner. By the terms of this, my uncle bound himself to satisfy Rankeillor as to his intromissions, and to pay me two clear thirds of the yearly income of Shaws.

So the beggar in the ballad had come home; and when I lay down that night on the kitchen chests, I was a man of means and had a name in the country. Alan and Torrance and Rankeillor slept and snored on their hard beds; but for me, who had laid out under heaven and upon dirt and stones, so many days and nights, and often with an empty belly, and in fear of death, this good change in my case unmanned me more than any of the former evil ones; and I lay till dawn, looking at the fire on the roof and planning the future.

SO FAR AS I was concerned myself, I had come to port; but I had still Alan, to whom I was so much beholden, on my hands; and I felt besides a heavy charge in the matter of the murder and James of the Glens. On both these heads I unbosomed to Rankeillor the next morning, walking to and fro about six of the clock before the house of Shaws, and with nothing in view but the fields and woods that had been my ancestors' and were now mine. Even as I spoke on these grave subjects, my eye would take a glad bit of a run over the prospect, and my heart jump with pride.

About my clear duty to my friend, the lawyer had no doubt; I must help him out of the county at whatever risk; but in the case of James, he was of a different mind.

'Mr Thomson,' says he, 'is one thing, Mr Thomson's kinsman quite another. I know little of the facts; but I gather that a great noble (whom we will call, if you like, the D. of A.) has some concern and is even supposed to feel some animosity in the matter. The D. of A. is doubtless an excellent nobleman; but, Mr David, *timeo qui nocuere deos*. If you interfere to baulk his vengeance, you should remember there is one way to shut your testimony out; and that is to put you in the dock. There, you would be in the same pickle as Mr Thomson's kinsman. You will object that you are innocent; well, but so is he. And to be tried for your life before a Highland jury, on a Highland quarrel, and with a Highland judge upon the bench, would be a brief transition to the gallows.'

Now I had made all these reasonings before and found no very good reply to them; so I put on all the simplicity I could. 'In that case, sir,' said I, 'I would just have to be hanged—would I not?'

'My dear boy,' cries he, 'go in God's name, and do what you think is right. It is a poor thought that at my time of life

I should be advising you to choose the safe and shameful; and I take it back with an apology. Go and do your duty; and be hanged, if you must, like a gentleman. There are worse things in the world than to be hanged.'

'Not many, sir,' said I, smiling.

'Why, yes, sir,' he cried, 'very many. And it would be ten times better for your uncle (to go no farther afield) if he were dangling decently upon a gibbet.'

Thereupon he turned into the house (still in a great fervour of mind, so that I saw I had pleased him heartily) and there he wrote me two letters, making his comments on them as he wrote.

'This,' says he, 'is to my bankers, the British Linen Company, placing a credit to your name. Consult Mr Thomson; he will know of ways; and you, with this credit, can supply the means. I trust you will be a good husband of your money; but in the affair of a friend like Mr Thomson, I would be even prodigal. Then, for his kinsman, there is no better way than that you should seek the Advocate, tell him your tale, and offer testimony; whether he may take it or not, is quite another matter, and will turn on the D. of A. Now that you may reach the Lord Advocate well recommended, I give you here a letter to a namesake of your own, the learned Mr Balfour of Pilrig, a man whom I esteem. It will look better that you should be presented by one of your own name; and the laird of Pilrig is much looked up to in the Faculty and stands well with Lord Advocate Grant. I would not trouble him, if I were you, with any particulars; and (do you know?) I think it would be needless to refer to Mr Thomson. Form yourself upon the laird, he is a good model; when you deal with the Advocate, be discreet; and in all these matters, may the Lord guide you, Mr David!'

Thereupon he took his farewell, and set out with Torrance for the Ferry, while Alan and I turned our faces for the city of Edinburgh. As we went by the footpath and beside the gateposts and the unfinished lodge, we kept looking back at the house of my fathers. It stood there, bare and great and smokeless, like a place not lived in; only in one of the top windows, there was the peak of a nightcap bobbing up and down and back and forward, like the head of a rabbit from a burrow. I had little welcome when I came, and less kindness while I stayed; but at least I was watched as I went away.

Alan and I went slowly forward upon our way, having little heart either to walk or speak. The same thought was uppermost in both, that we were near the time of our parting; and remembrance of all the by-gone days sate upon us sorely. We talked indeed of what should be done; and it was resolved that Alan should keep to the county, biding now here, now there, but coming once in the day to a particular place where I might be able to communicate with him, either in my own person or by messenger. In the meanwhile, I was to seek out a lawyer, who was an Appin Stewart, and a man therefore to be wholly trusted; and it should be his part to find a ship and to arrange for Alan's safe embarkation. No sooner was this business done, than the words seemed to leave us; and though I would seek to jest with Alan under the name of Mr Thomson, and he with me on my new clothes and my estate, you could feel very well that we were nearer tears than laughter.

We came the by-way over the hill of Corstorphine; and when we got near to the place called Rest-and-be-Thankful, and looked down on Corstorphine bogs and over to the city and the castle on the hill, we both stopped, for we both knew without a word said, that we had come to where our ways parted. Here he repeated to me once again what had been agreed upon between us: the address of the lawyer, the daily hour at which Alan might be found, and the signals that were to be made by any that came seeking him. Then I gave what money I had (a guinea or two of Rankeillor's) so that he should not starve in the meanwhile; and then we stood a space, and looked over at Edinburgh in silence.

'Well, good-bye,' said Alan, and held out his left hand.

'Good-bye,' said I, and gave the hand a little grasp, and went off down hill.

Neither one of us looked the other in the face, nor so long as he was in my view did I take one back glance at the friend I was leaving. But as I went on my way to the city, I felt so lost and lonesome, that I could have found it in my heart to sit down by the dyke, and cry and weep like any baby.

It was coming near noon when I passed in by the West Kirk and the Grassmarket into the streets of the capital.

The huge height of the buildings, running up to ten and fifteen storeys, the narrow arched entries that continually vomited passengers, the wares of the merchants in their windows, the hubbub and endless stir, the foul smells and the fine clothes, and a hundred other particulars too small to mention, struck me into a kind of stupor of surprise, so that I let the crowd carry me to and fro; and yet all the time what I was thinking of was Alan at Rest-and-be-Thankful; and all the time (although you would think I would not choose but be delighted with these braws and novelties) there was a cold gnawing in my inside like a remorse for something wrong.

The hand of Providence brought me in my drifting to the very doors of the British Linen Company's bank.

[Just there, with his hand upon his fortune, the present editor inclines for the time to say farewell to David. How Alan escaped, and what was done about the murder, with a variety of other delectable particulars, may be some day set forth. That is a thing, however, that hinges on the public fancy. The editor has a great kindness for both Alan and David, and would gladly spend much of his life in their society; but in this he may find himself to stand alone. In the fear of which, and lest any one should complain of scurvy usage, he hastens to protest that all went well with both, in the limited and human sense of the word 'well'; that whatever befell them, it was not dishonour, and whatever failed them, they were not found wanting to themselves.]

A sequel to 'Kidnapped'

CATRIONA

BEING MEMOIRS OF THE FURTHER ADVENTURES
OF DAVID BALFOUR AT HOME AND ABROAD.
IN WHICH ARE SET FORTH HIS MISFORTUNES
ANENT THE APPIN MURDER;
HIS TROUBLES WITH LORD ADVOCATE GRANT;
CAPTIVITY ON THE BASS ROCK;
JOURNEY INTO HOLLAND AND FRANCE;
AND SINGULAR RELATIONS WITH
JAMES MORE DRUMMOND OR MACGREGOR,
A SON OF THE NOTORIOUS ROB ROY,
AND HIS DAUGHTER CATRIONA.

WRITTEN BY HIMSELF, AND NOW SET FORTH BY
ROBERT LOUIS STEVENSON

━━

Introduced by Jenni Calder

Contents

Introduction

David Balfour was first introduced to the world in Robert Louis Stevenson's novel *Kidnapped*, published in 1886. The five years that passed before Stevenson wrote again about his hero took him a great distance from the country of his and David's origin. In 1887 he left Scotland and would never return. When he next took up the narrative of David's adventures, which he had always intended to do, he was in the South Pacific, thousands of miles away from the sights and sounds he brought to life in the pages of *Catriona*.

Both novels are dedicated to Stevenson's close friend Charles Baxter, an Edinburgh lawyer. 'You are still . . . in the venerable city which I must always think of as my home,' he wrote, referring to Edinburgh. 'And I have come so far; and the sights and thoughts of my youth pursue me.' The action of *Catriona* takes David Balfour to the Bass Rock, back to the Highlands, territory of much of *Kidnapped*, and across to the Low Countries. But the evocation of Edinburgh remains one of the novel's most distinctive features. The sense of the city seems to have haunted Stevenson's consciousness, and his memory reconstructs it with a clarity that is both visual and psychological.

David is a country boy, and does not much care for the 'old, black city', though he finds it an exciting place. But in fact his cautious and sceptical response is as illuminating as the more subjective account Stevenson gives in his *Edinburgh: Picturesque Notes*. Stevenson transports his own profound knowledge and understanding of the city one hundred years into the past, for he is describing the Edinburgh of the 1750s, in the years following the Jacobite Rising. It is a city of crude violence and mistrust and superstition, as well as sophistication, commerce and respectability. The tensions and contrasts that David encounters contribute essentially to the novel's ambience.

In *Kidnapped* Stevenson left David on the brink of a new life. In *Catriona* David enters that life, yet cannot abandon entirely his encounter with the Highlands and the influence of his exuberant Jacobite friend Alan Breck. The episode of the killing of the Red Fox, almost incidental in *Kidnapped* (though it puts the brand of outlaw on David), leaps into the foreground, and tests both the character and the morality of David. Stevenson was far too intrigued by the incident, with its moral as well as its historical dimensions, to let it go. There is a kind of inevitability in the murder's magnetic effect on David. His chance encounter with an unknown Highland girl combined with his loyalty to Alan makes it impossible for him to turn his back on the lingering aftermath of the Forty-Five.

David's meeting with Catriona captivates him at once, and is in effect the start of two stories. The one, in his anxiety for Alan and in pursuit of justice, takes him through the risks and intricacies of the law and politics. It has him criss-crossing Edinburgh and its environs, giving Stevenson the opportunity to fill in his picture of the city. It leads him to the East Lothian coast and imprisonment on the Bass Rock, followed by a hazardous escape and his desperate ride to Inveraray and trial for the murder of the Red Fox. The second makes him the protector of the destitute Catriona, follows his fortunes in Holland as student and lover, and brings him back to take up residence in his rightful home, the House of Shaws.

In some ways the two stories sit uneasily together. The first explores the essential dilemma of David Balfour, as introduced by *Kidnapped*. The Highlands hold no magic for David, no romantic or heroic appeal. He is a Whig and a Protestant, and temperamentally as well as politically out of tune with both the Jacobites and the fabric of Highland life. Yet he is loyal and conscientious, and recognizes the passion and principles of both Catriona and Alan even though he finds it difficult to respond to them in a way they understand. David's dilemma lies in the fact that he is a man of reason, and knows how to conduct himself as such. But he is also a man of feeling, and there he is vulnerable and lacking in confidence. That vulnerability saves him from being a prig, but it does not increase his self-awareness.

David's problem is brilliantly summed up by the Inveraray

episode. David, who in *Kidnapped* witnessed the Appin murder, feels impelled to bear witness to prevent a miscarriage of justice. Yet by telling the truth he will throw suspicion on Alan Breck and expose the father of the woman he loves. With sharply-focused yet delicate irony Stevenson rescues his hero from this conflict between conscience and self-interest by interposing a father-figure, the influential and shrewd Prestongrange, who persuades David that nothing he can say will influence events. David, who has shown considerable courage in getting himself to the trial, does not resist this persuasion. 'I came away, vastly pleased to have my peace made, yet a little concerned in conscience; nor could I help wondering, as I went back, whether, perhaps, I had not been a scruple too good-natured. But there was the fact, that this was a man who might have been my father, an able man, a great dignitary, and one that in the hour of my need, had reached a hand to my assistance.' Just as in *Kidnapped* David had returned with relief to the world of solid houses, authority and order, so in *Catriona* he turns away from Highland disorder and impenetrability. Prestongrange represents the world that he admires, to which he aspires. To attain this world he has to say goodbye to Highland adventures, even if he can't quite ever say goodbye to Alan Breck.

So, in a sense, the ride to Inveraray is a diversion, though it follows so readily from *Kidnapped*. The route that David takes leads him instead to a lowland adventure, in Holland, with Catriona Drummond, whom he befriends, protects and falls in love with. Stevenson clearly wanted to expand and develop the scope of David's actions, though it is an essential part of his character that he does not change significantly. He also wanted to write a love story, which he had not done before. The only female character of any substance who features in his fiction up to the writing of *Catriona* is Alison Graeme in *The Master of Ballantrae* (1889), but although she is a pivot for the rivalry of the brothers James and Henry she is subservient to it. Catriona is at the forefront of at least part of the novel that bears her name.

Stevenson was inhibited in writing about relations between men and women, for he felt that in order to do so honestly entailed exploring sexuality and sexual behaviour. In the 1880s to tackle this with any frankness was difficult: the climate of opinion was against it. In *Catriona* he solves the

problem. In a Victorian context it is a highly unconventional
tale: a young girl and a young man share a home, the situation
contained, but not defused, by innocence on the one hand
and a highly developed sense of responsibility and respectability on the other. David sets out to be 'wise for the pair of
us'. Stevenson is able to describe an awakening sexuality
without compromising either of his characters, for David is
not only too prim he is also too bashful to confess his love,
and in fact his wooing is done for him by Alan Breck.

Catriona and Alan have much in common; they share not
only a Highland background but the same pride and touchi-
ness. The Highland girl we meet first in Edinburgh, out of
her element in the city streets, has a vulnerable dignity, and
this is part of the attraction for David. But Stevenson does
not build on that. In fact, the Catriona of the latter part of the
novel is less self-possessed, less appealing—in fact, less
adult. The reason that Stevenson allowed his heroine to
become more dependent and more of a child, once transported even further from her home, is not hard to find: a more
sophisticated and mature young woman would have been
only too aware of the impropriety of sharing lodgings with a
young man. In those circumstances it would have been difficult for Stevenson to throw his two young people together
and allow them to learn about each other.

Stevenson creates an intriguing situation, but he is not able
to explore it fully, nor to draw it successfully into the main
current of the story of David Balfour. What is crucial is
that David cannot shake off his Highland adventure, that
although at the end of *Kidnapped* he cheerfully embraces
his future as a man of property with a profession, his link
with the landless and the outlawed will never be severed.
Catriona, of course, becomes part of this link. But at the end
of the novel she has been placed firmly in the context of
David's new and sober existence, and it is Alan Breck, 'a
little, lean, lively gentleman in a scratch-wig and a wraprascal', who visits late at night and has the Balfour family
'drinking the king's health *across the water*'.

Catriona, though part of the novel takes place in Holland,
is as much about Scotland as *Kidnapped*, and David Balfour
is as much about Stevenson himself as about the son of a
village schoolmaster accidentally caught up in the turbulence
of Scottish history. But if David Balfour is that part of

Stevenson which recognized that the passionate contentions of Scotland's history were barriers to progress, Alan Breck is the part that responded to every possibility of commitment and courage. Stevenson was fascinated by what he saw as the split personality at the heart of the Scottish character and the Scottish experience. In other novels and stories he described antipathy and mutual destruction. In *Kidnapped* and *Catriona* he was able, after a fashion, to reconcile opposites. Catriona herself does play a part in this reconciliation, but in the end it is the friendship and the unlikely alliance of David and Alan that dominates.

Catriona was the last complete novel of Scotland that Stevenson wrote. When he died, in 1894, he was part way through *Weir of Hermiston* and had written fragments of two other Scottish novels. *St Ives* was also left unfinished. Although he was also writing about his experiences in Samoa and the Pacific, and writing with extraordinary perception and sympathy, his thoughts and his imagination returned continually to Scotland. All his life he had struggled to confront and explain his own background and the country that had shaped him, and the need to do that did not diminish with distance. He looked at the harshest and most un-compromising features of his heritage with generosity, sensitivity, affection and irony, and all of these are present in *Catriona*.

Jenni Calder

Dedication
TO CHARLES BAXTER, WRITER TO THE SIGNET.

My dear Charles,

It is the fate of sequels to disappoint those who have waited for them; and my David, having been left to kick his heels for more than a lustre in the British Linen Company's office, must expect his late re-appearance to be greeted with hoots, if not with missiles. Yet, when I remember the days of our explorations, I am not without hope. There should be left in our native city some seed of the elect; some long-legged, hot-headed youth must repeat to-day our dreams and wanderings of so many years ago; he will relish the pleasure, which should have been ours, to follow among named streets and numbered houses the country walks of David Balfour, to identify Dean, and Silvermills, and Broughton, and Hope Park, and Pilrig, and poor old Lochend—if it still be standing and the Figgate Whins—if there be any of them left; or to push (on a long holiday) so far afield as Gillane or the Bass. So, perhaps, his eye shall be opened to behold the series of the generations, and he shall weigh with surprise his momentous and nugatory gift of life.

You are still—as when first I saw, as when I last addressed you—in the venerable city which I must always think of as my home. And I have come so far; and the sights and thoughts of my youth pursue me; and I see like a vision the youth of my father, and of his father, and the whole stream of lives flowing down there far in the north, with the sound of laughter and tears, to cast me out in the end, as by a sudden freshet, on these ultimate islands. And I admire and bow my head before the romance of destiny.

Vailima, Upolu, Samoa, 1892   R. L. S.

Summary
OF THE EARLIER ADVENTURES OF DAVID BALFOUR
AS SET FORTH IN 'KIDNAPPED'

ALEXANDER AND Ebenezer Balfour, brothers, of the house of Shaws near Cramond in the Forest of Ettrick, being in love with the same lady, and she preferring the elder brother, Alexander, it was agreed between them that Alexander should take the lady, and Ebenezer, as amends for his disappointment, the estate of Shaws. Alexander and his wife removed to Essendean, where they lived obscurely, Alexander in the character of village schoolmaster and where an only son was born to them, namely David Balfour, the hero of this history. David, brought up in ignorance of the family affairs and of his own claim on the estates, and losing both parents before he was eighteen, was left with no other fortune than a sealed letter from his father addressed to his uncle Ebenezer, which was handed him by the minister of Essendean, Mr Campbell. Proceeding to deliver it, David found his uncle living childless and a miser at Shaws; who received him ill, and after vainly endeavouring to compass his death, had him trepanned on board the brig *Covenant*, Captain Hoseason, bound to Carolina, to the end that he might be sold to labour in the plantations. But early in the voyage, the *Covenant*, running through the Minch, struck and sent to the bottom an open boat, from which there saved himself and came on board one Alan Breck Stewart, a Highland gentleman banished after the '45, and now engaged in smuggling rents from his clansmen, the Appin Stewarts, to their chief Ardshiel, living in exile in France. Hoseason and his crew, learning that Alan had gold about him, conspired to rob and murder him; but David, being made privy to the plot, put Alan on his guard and promised to stand by him.

Favoured by the shelter of the round-house, and by Alan's courage and skill of fence, the two got the better of their assailants in the attack which followed, killing or maiming more than half of them; whereby Captain Hoseason was disabled from prosecuting his voyage, and came to terms with Alan, agreeing to land him on a part of the coast whence he might best make his way to his own country of Appin. But in attempting this the *Covenant* took ground and sank off the coast of Mull. Those on board saved themselves as they best could, David separately; being first cast on the Isle of Earraid, and thence making his way across Mull. Alan had passed before by the same road, and left word that David should follow and rejoin him in his own country at the house of his kinsman, James Stewart of the Glens. On his way to keep this tryst, David found himself in Appin on the same day when the King's Factor, Colin Roy Campbell of Glenure, came with a force of red-coats to drive out the tenants from the fortified estates of Ardshiel, and was present when Glenure was slain upon the roadside by a shot out of a neighbouring wood. Suspected of complicity at the moment when he was in the act of giving chase to the unknown murderer, David betook himself to flight, and was quickly joined by Alan Breck, who, though he had not fired the shot, was lurking not far off. The two now lived the life of hunted men upon the moors, the outcry on account of the murder being very great, and its guilt being declared to rest on James Stewart of the Glens, the already outlawed Alan Breck, and a lad unknown, being no other than David Balfour; for whose apprehension blood-money was offered and the country scoured by soldiery. In the course of their wanderings, David and Alan visited James Stewart at Aucharn, were concealed in Cluny Macpherson's cage, and suffered to rest during sickness in the house of Duncan Dhu Maclaren in Balwhidder, where Alan played a match upon the pipes against Robin Oig, the son of Rob Roy. At last, after much peril and suffering, they made their way down to the Highland Line and the Forth; which, however, they dared not cross for fear of arrest until an innkeeper's daughter of Limekilns, Alison Hastie, was prevailed on to row them over to the Lothian shore under cover of night. Here Alan again went into hiding, while David made himself known to Mr Hope of Rankeillor, lawyer and lately agent to the Shaws estate; who promptly took up his cause and contrived a plan whereby, with the help of Alan, Ebenezer Balfour was compelled to recognise his nephew's title as heir to the estate, and in the meantime to make him a suitable allowance from its income.

David Balfour, having thus come to his own, proposes to go and complete his education at the University of Leyden; but must first satisfy the claims of friendship, by helping Alan out of Scotland, and of conscience, by testifying to the innocence of James Stewart of the Glens, now a prisoner awaiting his trial for the Appin murder.

Part One. The Lord Advocate

THE 25th DAY OF August, 1751, about two in the afternoon, I, David Balfour, came forth of the British Linen Company, a porter attending me with a bag of money, and some of the chief of these merchants bowing me from their doors. Two days before, and even so late as yestermorning, I was like a beggarman by the wayside, clad in rags, brought down to my last shillings, my companion a condemned traitor, a price set on my own head for a crime with the news of which the country rang. To-day I was served heir to my position in life, a landed laird, a bank porter by me carrying my gold, recommendations in my pocket, and (in the words of the saying) the ball directly at my foot.

There were two circumstances that served me as ballast to so much sail. The first was the very difficult and deadly business I had still to handle; the second, the place that I was in. The tall, black city, and the numbers and movement and noise of so many folk, made a new world for me, after the moorland braes, the sea-sands, and the still country-sides that I had frequented up to then. The throng of the citizens in particular abashed me. Rankeillor's son was short and small in the girth; his clothes scarce held on me; and it was plain I was ill qualified to strut in the front of a bank-porter. It was plain, if I did so, I should but set folk laughing, and (what was worse in my case) set them asking questions. So that I behooved to come by some clothes of my own, and in the meanwhile to walk by the porter's side, and put my hand on his arm as though we were a pair of friends.

At a merchant's in the Luckenbooths, I had myself fitted out: none too fine, for I had no idea to appear like a beggar on horseback; but comely and responsible, so that servants should respect me. Thence to an armourer's, where I got a plain sword, to suit with my degree in life. I felt safer with the

3

weapon, though (for one so ignorant of defence) it might be called an added danger. The porter, who was naturally a man of some experience, judged my accoutrement to be well chosen.

'Naething kenspeckle,' said he; 'plain, dacent claes. As for the rapier, nae doubt it sits wi' your degree; but an I had been you, I would hae waired my siller better-gates than that.' And he proposed I should buy winter-hosen from a wife in the Cowgate-back, that was a cousin of his own, and made them 'extraordinar endurable'.

But I had other matters on my hand more pressing. Here I was in this old, black city, which was for all the world like a rabbit-warren, not only by the number of its indwellers, but the complication of its passages and holes. It was indeed a place where no stranger had a chance to find a friend, let be another stranger. Suppose him even to hit on the right close, people dwelt so thronged in these tall houses, he might very well seek a day before he chanced on the right door. The ordinary course was to hire a lad they called a *caddie*, who was like a guide or pilot, led you where you had occasion, and (your errands being done) brought you again where you were lodging. But these caddies, being always employed in the same sort of services, and having it for obligation to be well informed of every house and person in the city, had grown to form a brotherhood of spies; and I knew from tales of Mr Campbell's how they communicated one with another, what a rage of curiosity they conceived as to their employer's business, and how they were like eyes and fingers to the police. It would be a piece of little wisdom, the way I was now placed, to tack such a ferret to my tails. I had three visits to make, all immediately needful: to my kinsman Mr Balfour of Pilrig, to Stewart the Writer that was Appin's agent, and to William Grant Esquire of Prestongrange, Lord Advocate of Scotland. Mr Balfour's was a non-committal visit; and besides (Pilrig being in the country) I made bold to find the way to it myself, with the help of my two legs and a Scots tongue. But the rest were in a different case. Not only was the visit to Appin's agent, in the midst of the cry about the Appin murder, dangerous in itself, but it was highly inconsistent with the other. I was like to have a bad enough time of it with my Lord Advocate Grant, the best of ways; but to go to him hot-foot from Appin's agent, was little likely to mend my own affairs, and might prove the mere ruin of friend Alan's. The whole thing, besides, gave me a look of running with the hare and hunting with the hounds that was little to my fancy. I determined, therefore, to be done at once with Mr Stewart and the whole Jacobitical side of my business, and to profit for that purpose by the guidance of the porter at my side. But it chanced I had scarce given him the address, when there came a sprinkle of rain—nothing to hurt, only for my new clothes—and we took shelter under a pend at the head of a close or alley.

Being strange to what I saw, I stepped a little farther in. The narrow paved way descended swiftly. Prodigious tall houses sprang upon each side and bulged out, one storey beyond another, as they rose. At the top only a ribbon of sky showed in. By what I could spy in the windows, and by the respectable persons that passed out and in, I saw the houses to be very well occupied; and the whole appearance of the place interested me like a tale.

I was still gazing, when there came a sudden brisk tramp of feet in time and clash of steel behind me. Turning quickly, I was aware of a party of armed soldiers, and, in their midst, a tall man in a great-coat. He walked with a stoop that was like a piece of courtesy, genteel and insinuating: he waved his hands plausibly as he went, and his face was sly and handsome. I thought his eye took me in, but could not meet it. This procession went by to a door in the close, which a serving-man in a fine livery set open; and two of the soldier-lads carried the prisoner within, the rest lingering with their firelocks by the door.

There can nothing pass in the streets of a city without some following of idle folk and children. It was so now; but the more part melted away incontinent until but three were left. One was a girl; she was dressed like a lady, and had a screen of the Drummond colours on her head; but her comrades or (I should say) followers were ragged gillies, such as I had seen the matches of by the dozen in my Highland journey. They all spoke together earnestly in Gaelic, the sound of which was pleasant in my ears for the sake of Alan; and though the rain was by again, and my porter plucked at me to be going, I even drew nearer where they were, to listen. The lady scolded sharply, the others making apologies and cringeing before her, so that I made sure she was come of a chief's house. All the while the three of them sought in their pockets, and by what I could make out, they had the matter of half a farthing among the party; which made me smile a little to see all Highland folk alike for fine obeisances and empty sporrans.

It chanced the girl turned suddenly about, so that I saw her face for the first time. There is no greater wonder than the way the face of a young woman fits in a man's mind, and stays there, and he could never tell you why; it just seems it was the thing he wanted. She had wonderful bright eyes like stars, and I daresay the eyes had a part in it; but what I remember the most clearly was the way her lips were a trifle open as she turned. And whatever was the cause, I stood there staring like a fool. On her side, as she had not known there was anyone so near, she looked at me a little longer, and perhaps with more surprise, than was entirely civil.

It went through my country head she might be wondering at my new clothes; with that, I blushed to my hair, and at the sight of my colouring it is to be supposed she drew her own conclusions, for she moved her gillies farther down the close, and they fell again to this dispute where I could hear no more of it.

I had often admired a lassie before then, if scarce so sudden and strong; and it was rather my disposition to withdraw than to come forward, for I was much in fear of mockery from the womenkind. You would have thought I had now all the more reason to pursue my common practice, since I had met this young lady in the city street, seemingly following a prisoner, and accompanied with two very ragged indecent-like Highlandmen. But there was here a different ingredient; it was plain the girl thought I had been prying in her secrets; and with my new clothes and sword, and at the top of my new fortunes, this was more than I could swallow. The beggar on horseback could not bear to be thrust down so low, or at the least of it, not by this young lady.

I followed, accordingly, and took off my new hat to her, the best that I was able.

'Madam,' said I, 'I think it only fair to myself to let you understand I have no Gaelic. It is true I was listening, for I have friends of my own across the Highland line, and the sound of that tongue comes friendly; but for your private affairs, if you had spoken Greek, I might have had more guess at them.'

She made me a little, distant curtsey. 'There is no harm done,' said she, with a pretty accent, most like the English (but more agreeable). 'A cat may look at a king.'

'I do not mean to offend,' said I. 'I have no skill of city manners; I never before this day set foot inside the doors of Edinburgh. Take me for a country lad—it's what I am; and I would rather I told you than you found it out.'

'Indeed, it will be a very unusual thing for strangers to be speaking to each other on the causeway,' she replied. 'But if you are landward bred it will be different. I am as landward as yourself; I am Highland as you see, and think myself the farther from my home.'

'It is not yet a week since I passed the line,' said I. 'Less than a week ago I was on the braes of Balwhidder.'

'Balwhither?' she cries. 'Come ye from Balwhither? The name of it makes all there is of me rejoice. You will not have been long there, and not known some of our friends or family?'

'I lived with a very honest, kind man called Duncan Dhu Maclaren,' I replied.

'Well I know Duncan, and you give him the true name!' she said; 'and if he is an honest man, his wife is honest indeed.'

'Ay,' said I, 'they are fine people, and the place is a bonny place.'

'Where in the great world is such another?' she cries; 'I am loving the smell of that place and the roots that grow there.'

I was infinitely taken with the spirit of the maid. 'I could be wishing I had brought you a spray of that heather,' says I. 'And though I did ill to speak with you at the first, now it seems we have common acquaintance, I make it my petition you will not forget me. David Balfour is the name I am known by. This is my lucky day, when I have just come into a landed estate, and am not very long out of a deadly peril. I wish you would keep my name in mind for the sake of Balwhidder,' said I, 'and I will yours for the sake of my lucky day.'

'My name is not spoken,' she replied, with a great deal of haughtiness. 'More than a hundred years it has not gone upon men's tongues, save for a blink. I am nameless like the Folk of Peace. Catriona Drummond is the one I use.'

Now indeed I knew where I was standing. In all broad Scotland there was but the one name proscribed, and that was the name of the Macgregors. Yet so far from fleeing this undesirable acquaintancy, I plunged the deeper in.

'I have been sitting with one who was in the same case with yourself,' said I, 'and I think he will be one of your friends. They called him Robin Oig.'

'Did ye so?' cries she. 'Ye met Rob?'

'I passed the night with him,' said I.

'He is a fowl of the night,' said she.

'There was a set of pipes there,' I went on, 'so you may judge if the time passed.'

'You should be no enemy, at all events,' said she. 'That was his brother there a moment since, with the red soldiers round him. It is him that I call father.'

'Is it so?' cried I. 'Are you a daughter of James More's?'

'All the daughter that he has,' says she: 'the daughter of a prisoner; that I should forget it so, even for one hour, to talk with strangers!'

Here one of the gillies addressed her in what he had of English, to know what 'she' (meaning by that himself) was to do about 'ta sneeshin'. I took some note of him for a short, bandy-legged, red-haired, big-headed man, that I was to know more of to my cost.

'There can be none the day, Neil,' she replied. 'How will you get "sneeshin", wanting siller? It will teach you another time to be more careful; and I think James More will not be very well pleased with Neil of the Tom.'

'Miss Drummond,' I said, 'I told you I was in my lucky day. Here I am, and a bank-porter at my tail. And remember I have had the hospitality of your own country of Balwhidder.'

'It was not one of my people gave it,' said she.

'Ah, well,' said I, 'but I am owing your uncle at least for some springs upon the pipes. Besides which, I have offered myself to be your friend, and you have been so forgetful that you did not refuse me in the proper time.'

'If it had been a great sum, it might have done you honour,' said she; 'but I will tell you what this is. James More lies shackled in prison; but this time past, they will be bringing him down here daily to the Advocate's. . . .'

'The Advocate's?' I cried. 'Is that . . . ?'

'It is the house of the Lord Advocate Grant of Preston-grange,' said she. 'There they bring my father one time and another, for what purpose I have no thought in my mind; but it seems there is some hope dawned for him. All this same time they will not let me be seeing him, nor yet him write; and we wait upon the King's street to catch him; and now we give him his snuff as he goes by, and now something else. And here is this son of trouble, Neil, son of Duncan, has lost my fourpenny-piece that was to buy that snuff, and James More must go wanting, and will think his daughter has forgotten him.'

I took sixpence from my pocket, gave it to Neil, and bade him go about his errand. Then to her, 'That sixpence came with me by Balwhidder,' said I.

'Ah!' she said, 'you are a friend to the Gregara!'

'I would not like to deceive you either,' said I. 'I know very little of the Gregara and less of James More and his doings, but since the while I have been standing in this close, I seem to know something of yourself; and if you will just say "a friend to Miss Catriona" I will see you are the less cheated.'

'The one cannot be without the other,' said she.

'I will even try,' said I.

'And what will you be thinking of myself?' she cried, 'to be holding my hand to the first stranger!'

'I am thinking nothing but that you are a good daughter,' said I.

'I must not be without repaying it,' she said; 'Where is it you stop?'

'To tell the truth, I am stopping nowhere yet,' said I, 'being not full three hours in the city; but if you will give me your direction, I will be so bold as come seeking my sixpence for myself.'

'Will I can trust you for that?' she asked.

'You need have little fear,' said I.

'James More could not bear it else,' said she. 'I stop beyond the village of Dean, on the north side of the water, with Mrs Drummond-Ogilvy of Allardyce, who is my near friend and will be glad to thank you.'

'You are to see me then, so soon as what I have to do permits,' said I; and the remembrance of Alan rolling in again upon my mind, I made haste to say farewell.

I could not but think, even as I did so, that we had made extraordinary free upon short acquaintance, and that a really wise young lady would have shown herself more backward. I think it was the bank-porter that put me from this ungallant train of thought.

'I thoucht ye had been a lad of some kind o' sense,' he began, shooting out his lips. 'Ye're no likely to gang far this gate. A fule and his siller's shune parted. Eh, but ye're a green callant!' he cried, 'an' a veecious, tae! Cleikin' up wi' baubee-joes!'

'If you dare to speak of the young lady. . . . ' I began.

'Leddy!' he cried. 'Haud us and safe us, whatten leddy? Ca' *thon* a leddy? The toun's fu' o' them. Leddies! Man, it's weel seen ye're no very acquant in Embro!'

A clap of anger took me.

'Here,' said I, 'lead me where I told you, and keep your foul mouth shut!'

He did not wholly obey me, for though he no more addressed me directly, he sang at me as he went in a very impudent manner of innuendo, and with an exceedingly ill voice and ear:

'As Mally Lee cam doun the street, her capuchin did flee,
She cuist a look ahint her to see her negligee.
And we're a' gaun east and wast, we're a' gaun ajee,
We're a' gaun east and wast courtin' Mally Lee.'

MR CHARLES STEWART the Writer dwelt at the top of the longest stair that ever mason set a hand to; fifteen flights of it, no less; and when I had come to his door, and a clerk had opened it, and told me his master was within, I had scarce breath enough to send my porter packing.

'Awa' east and wast wi' ye!' said I, took the money bag out of his hands, and followed the clerk in.

The outer room was an office with the clerk's chair at a table spread with law papers. In the inner chamber, which opened from it, a little brisk man sat poring on a deed, from which he scarce raised his eyes upon my entrance; indeed, he still kept his finger in the place, as though prepared to show me out and fall again to his studies. This pleased me little enough; and what pleased me less, I thought the clerk was in a good posture to overhear what should pass between us.

I asked if he was Mr Charles Stewart the Writer.

'The same,' says he; 'and if the question is equally fair, who may you be yourself?'

'You never heard tell of my name nor of me either,' said I, 'but I bring you a token from a friend that you know well. That you know well,' I repeated, lowering my voice, 'but maybe are not just so keen to hear from at this present being. And the bits of business that I have to propone to you are rather in the nature of being confidential. In short, I would like to think we were quite private.'

He rose without more words, casting down his paper like a man ill-pleased, sent forth his clerk of an errand, and shut to the house-door behind him.

'Now, sir,' said he, returning, 'speak out your mind and fear nothing; though before you begin,' he cries out, 'I tell you mine misgives me! I tell you beforehand, ye're either a Stewart or a Stewart sent ye. A good name it is, and one it would ill-become my father's son to lightly. But I begin to grue at the sound of it.'

'My name is called Balfour,' said I, 'David Balfour of Shaws. As for him that sent me, I will let his token speak.' And I showed the silver button.

'Put it in your pocket, sir!' cries he. 'Ye need name no names. The deevil's buckie, I ken the button of him! And de'il hae't! Where is he now?'

I told him I knew not where Alan was, but he had some sure place (or thought he had) about the north side, where he was to lie until a ship was found for him; and how and where he had appointed to be spoken with.

'It's been always my opinion that I would hang in a tow for this family of mine,' he cried, 'and, dod! I believe the day's come now! Get a ship for him, quot' he! And who's to pay for it? The man's daft!'

'That is my part of the affair, Mr Stewart,' said I. 'Here is a bag of good money, and if more be wanted, more is to be had where it came from.'

'I needn't ask your politics,' said he.

'Ye need not,' said I, smiling, 'for I'm as big a Whig as grows.'

'Stop a bit, stop a bit,' says Mr Stewart. 'What's all this? A Whig? Then why are you here with Alan's button? and what kind of a black-foot traffic is this that I find ye out in, Mr Whig? Here is a forfeited rebel and an accused murderer, with two hundred pounds on his life, and ye ask me to meddle in his business, and then tell me ye're a Whig: I have no mind of any such Whigs before, though I've kent plenty of them.'

'He's a forfeited rebel, the more's the pity,' said I, 'for the man's my friend. I can only wish he had been better guided. And an accused murderer, that he is too, for his misfortune; but wrongfully accused.'

'I hear you say so,' said Stewart.

'More than you are to hear me say so, before long,' said I. 'Alan Breck is innocent, and so is James.'

'Oh!' says he, 'the two cases hang together. If Alan is out, James can never be in.'

Hereupon I told him briefly of my acquaintance with Alan, of the accident that brought me present at the Appin murder, and the various passages of our escape among the heather, and my recovery of my estate. 'So, sir, you have now the whole train of these events,' I went on, 'and can see for yourself how I come to be so much mingled up with the affairs of your family and friends, which (for all of our sakes) I wish had been plainer and less bloody. You can see for yourself, too, that I have certain pieces of business depending, which were scarcely fit to lay before a lawyer chosen at random. No more remains, but to ask if you will undertake my service?'

'I have no great mind to it; but coming as you do with Alan's button, the choice is scarcely left me,' said he. 'What are your instructions?' he added, and took up his pen.

'The first point is to smuggle Alan forth of this country,' said I, 'but I need not be repeating that.'

'I am little likely to forget it,' said Stewart.

'The next thing is the bit money I am owing to Cluny,' I went on. 'It would be ill for me to find a conveyance, but that should be no stick to you. It was two pounds five shillings and three-halfpence farthing sterling.'

He noted it.

'Then,' said I, 'there's a Mr Henderland, a licensed preacher and missionary in Ardgour, that I would like well to get some snuff into the hands of; and as I daresay you keep touch with your friends in Appin (so near by), it's a job you could doubtless overtake with the other.'

'How much snuff are we to say?' he asked.

'I was thinking of two pounds,' said I.

'Two,' said he.

'Then there's the lass Alison Hastie, in Limekilns,' said I. 'Her that helped Alan and me across the Forth. I was thinking if I could get her a good Sunday gown, such as she could wear with decency in her degree, it would be an ease to my conscience; for the mere truth is, we owe her our two lives.'

'I am glad to see you are thrifty, Mr Balfour,' says he, making his notes.

'I would think shame to be otherwise the first day of my

fortune,' said I. 'And now, if you will compute the outlay and your own proper charges, I would be glad to know if I could get some spending-money back. It's not that I grudge the whole of it to get Alan safe; it's not that I lack more; but having drawn so much the one day, I think it would have a very ill appearance if I was back again seeking, the next. Only be sure you have enough,' I added, 'for I am very undesirous to meet with you again.'

'Well, and I'm pleased to see you're cautious too,' said the Writer. 'But I think ye take a risk to lay so considerable a sum at my discretion.'

He said this with a plain sneer.

'I'll have to run the hazard,' I replied. 'O, and there's another service I would ask, and that's to direct me to a lodging, for I have no roof to my head. But it must be a lodging I may seem to have hit upon by accident, for it would never do if the Lord Advocate were to get any jealousy of our acquaintance.'

'Ye may set your weary spirit at rest,' said he. 'I will never name your name, sir; and it's my belief the Advocate is still so much to be sympathised with that he doesnae ken of your existence.'

I saw I had got to the wrong side of the man.

'There's a braw day coming for him, then,' said I, 'for he'll have to learn of it on the deaf side of his head no later than tomorrow, when I call on him.'

'When ye *call* on him!' repeated Mr Stewart. 'Am I daft, or are you? What takes ye near the Advocate?'

'O, just to give myself up,' said I.

'Mr Balfour,' he cried, 'are ye making a mock of me?'

'No, sir,' said I, 'though I think you have allowed yourself some such freedom with myself. But I give you to understand once and for all that I am in no jesting spirit.'

'Nor yet me,' says Stewart. 'And I give you to understand (if that's to be the word) that I like the looks of your behaviour less and less. You come here to me with all sorts of propositions, which will put me in a train of very doubtful acts and bring me among very undesirable persons this many a day to come. And then you tell me you're going straight out of my office to make your peace with the Advocate! Alan's button here or Alan's button there, the four quarters of Alan wouldnae bribe me further in.'

'I would take it with a little more temper,' said I, 'and perhaps we can avoid what you object to. I can see no way for it but to give myself up, but perhaps you can see another; and if you could, I could never deny but what I would be rather relieved. For I think my traffic with his lordship is little likely to agree with my health. There's just the one thing clear, that I have to give my evidence; for I hope it'll save Alan's character (what's left of it), and James's neck, which is the more immediate.'

He was silent for a breathing-space, and then, 'My man,' said he, 'you'll never be allowed to give such evidence.'

'We'll have to see about that,' said I; 'I'm stiff-necked when I like.'

'Ye muckle ass!' cried Stewart, 'it's James they want; James has got to hang—Alan too, if they could catch him—but James whatever! Go near the Advocate with any such business, and you'll see! he'll find a way to muzzle ye.'

'I think better of the Advocate than that,' said I.

'The Advocate be damned!' cries he. 'It's the Campbells, man! You'll have the whole clanjamfry of them on your back; and so will the Advocate too, poor body! It's extraordinar ye cannot see where ye stand! If there's no fair way to stop your gab, there's a foul one gaping. They can put ye in the dock, do ye no see that?' he cried, and stabbed me with one finger in the leg.

'Ay,' said I, 'I was told that same no further back than this morning by another lawyer.'

'And who was he?' asked Stewart. 'He spoke sense at least.'

I told I must be excused from naming him, for he was a decent stout old Whig, and had little mind to be mixed up in such affairs.

'I think all the world seems to be mixed up in it!' cries Stewart. 'But what said you?'

I told him what had passed between Rankeillor and myself before the house of Shaws.

'Well, and so ye will hang!' said he.' Ye'll hang beside James Stewart. There's your fortune told.'

'I hope better of it yet than that,' said I; 'but I could never deny there was a risk.'

'Risk!' says he, and then sat silent again. 'I ought to thank you for your staunchness to my friends, to whom you show a very good spirit,' he says, 'if you have the strength to stand by it. But I warn you that you're wading deep. I wouldn't put myself in your place (me that's a Stewart born!) for all the Stewarts that ever there were since Noah. Risk? ay, I take over-many: but to be tried in court before a Campbell jury and a Campbell judge, and that in a Campbell country and upon a Campbell quarrel—think what you like of me, Balfour, it's beyond me.'

'It's a different way of thinking, I suppose,' said I; 'I was brought up to this one by my father before me.'

'Glory to his bones! he has left a decent son to his name,' says he. 'Yet I would not have you judge me over-sorely. My case is dooms hard. See, sir, ye tell me ye're a Whig: I wonder what I am. No Whig to be sure; I couldnae be just that. But—laigh in your ear, man—I'm maybe no very keen on the other side.'

'Is that a fact?' cried I. 'It's what I would think of a man of your intelligence.'

'Hut! none of your whillywhas!' cries he. 'There's intelligence upon both sides. But for my private part I have no particular desire to harm King George; and as for King James, God bless him! he does very well for me across the water. I'm a lawyer, ye see: fond of my books and my bottle, a good plea, a well-drawn deed, a crack in the Parliament House with other lawyer bodies, and perhaps a turn at the golf on a Saturday at e'en. Where do ye come in with your Hieland plaids and claymores?'

'Well,' said I, 'it's a fact ye have little of the wild Highlandman.'

'Little?' quoth he. 'Nothing, man! And yet I'm Hieland born, and when the clan pipes, who but me has to dance? The clan and the name, that goes by all. It's just what you said yourself; my father learned it to me, and a bonny trade I have of it. Treason and traitors, and the smuggling of them out and in; and the French recruiting, weary fall it! and the smuggling through of the recruits; and their pleas—a sorrow of their pleas! Here have I been moving one for young Ardshiel, my cousin; claimed the estate under the marriage contract—a forfeited estate! I told them it was nonsense: muckle they cared! And there was I cocking behind a yadvocate that liked the business as little as myself, for it was fair ruin to the pair of us—a black mark, *disaffected*, branded on our hurdies like folk's names upon their kye! And what can I do? I'm a Stewart, ye see, and must fend for my clan and family. Then no later by than yesterday there was one of our Stewart lads carried to the Castle. What for? I ken fine: Act of 1736: recruiting for King Lewie. And you'll see, he'll whistle me in to be his lawyer, and there'll be another black mark on my chara'ter! I tell you fair: if I but kent the heid of a Hebrew word from the hurdies of it, be dammed but I would fling the whole thing up and turn minister!'

'It's rather a hard position,' said I.

'Dooms hard!' cries he. 'And that's what makes me think so much of ye—you that's no Stewart—to stick your head so deep in Stewart business. And for what, I do not know: unless it was the sense of duty.'

'I hope it will be that,' said I.

'Well,' says he, 'it's a grand quality. But here is my clerk back; and, by your leave, we'll pick a bit of dinner, all the three of us. When that's done, I'll give you the direction of a very decent man, that'll be very fain to have you for a lodger. And I'll fill your pockets to ye, forbye, out of your ain bag. For this business'll not be near as dear as ye suppose—not even the ship part of it.'

I made him a sign that his clerk was within hearing.

'Hoot, ye neednae mind for Robbie,' cries he. 'A Stewart, too, puir deevil! and has smuggled out more French recruits and trafficking Papists than what he has hairs upon his face. Why it's Robin that manages that branch of my affairs. Who will we have now, Rob, for across the water?'

'There'll be Andie Scougal, in the *Thristle*,' replied Rob. 'I saw Hoseason the other day, but it seems he's wanting the ship. Then there'll be Tam Stobo; but I'm none so sure of Tam. I've seen him colloguing with some gey queer acquaintances; and if was anybody important, I would give Tam the go-by.'

'The head's worth two hundred pounds, Robin,' said Stewart.

'Gosh, that'll no be Alan Breck?' cried the clerk.

'Just Alan,' said his master.

'Weary winds! that's sayrious,' cried Robin. 'I'll try Andie, then; Andie'll be the best.'

'It seems it's quite a big business,' I observed.

'Mr Balfour, there's no end to it,' said Stewart.

'There was a name your clerk mentioned,' I went on: 'Hoseason. That must be my man, I think: Hoseason, of the brig *Covenant*. Would you set your trust on him?'

'He didnae behave very well to you and Alan,' said Mr Stewart; 'but my mind of the man in general is rather otherwise. If he had taken Alan on board his ship on an agreement, it's my notion he would have proved a just dealer. How say ye, Rob?'

'No more honest skipper in the trade than Eli,' said the clerk. 'I would lippen to Eli's word—ay, if it was the Chevalier, or Appin himsel',' he added.

'And it was him that brought the doctor, wasnae't?' asked the master.

'He was the very man,' said the clerk.

'And I think he took the doctor back?' says Stewart.

'Ay, with his sporran full!' cried Robin. 'And Eli kent of that!'*

'Well it seems it's hard to ken folk rightly,' said I.

'That was just what I forgot when ye came in, Mr Balfour!' says the Writer.

* This must have reference to Dr Cameron on his first visit D.B.

THE NEXT MORNING, I was no sooner awake in my new lodging than I was up and into my new clothes; and no sooner the breakfast swallowed, than I was forth on my adventures. Alan, I could hope, was fended for; James was like to be a more difficult affair, and I could not but think that enterprise might cost me dear, even as everybody said to whom I had opened my opinion. It seemed I was come to the top of the mountain only to cast myself down; that I had clambered up, through so many and hard trials, to be rich, to be recognised, to wear city clothes and a sword to my side, all to commit mere suicide at the last end of it, and the worst kind of suicide besides, which is to get hanged at the King's charges.

What was I doing it for? I asked, as I went down the High Street and out north by Leith Wynd. First I said it was to save James Stewart; and no doubt the memory of his distress, and his wife's cries, and a word or so I had let drop on that occasion worked upon me strongly. At the same time I reflected that it was (or ought to be) the most indifferent matter to my father's son, whether James died in his bed or from a scaffold. He was Alan's cousin, to be sure; but so far as regarded Alan, the best thing would be to lie low, and let the King, and his Grace of Argyll, and the corbie crows, pick the bones of his kinsman their own way. Nor could I forget that, while we were all in the pot together, James had shown no such particular anxiety whether for Alan or me.

Next it came upon me I was acting for the sake of justice: and I thought that a fine word, and reasoned it out that (since we dwelt in polities, at some discomfort to each one of us) the main thing of all must still be justice, and the death of any innocent man a wound upon the whole community. Next, again, it was the Accuser of the Brethren that gave me a turn of his argument; bade me think shame for pretending myself concerned in these high matters, and told me I was but a prating vain child, who had spoken big words to Rankeillor and to Stewart, and held myself bound upon my vanity to make good that boastfulness. Nay, and he hit me with the other end of the stick; for he accused me of a kind of artful cowardice, going about at the expense of a little risk to purchase greater safety. No doubt, until I had declared and cleared myself, I might any day encounter Mungo Campbell or the sheriff's officer, and be recognised, and dragged into the Appin murder by the heels; and, no doubt, in case I could manage my declaration with success, I should breathe more free for ever after. But when I looked this argument full in the face I could see nothing to be ashamed of. As for the rest, 'Here are the two roads,' I thought, 'and both go to the same place. It's unjust that James should hang if I can save him; and it would be ridiculous in me to have talked so much and then do nothing. It's lucky for James of the Glens that I have boasted beforehand; and none so unlucky for myself, because now I'm committed to do right. I have the name of a gentleman and the means of one; it would be a poor discovery that I was wanting in the essence.' And then I thought this was a Pagan spirit, and said a prayer in to myself, asking for what courage I might lack, and that I might go straight to my duty like a soldier to battle, and come off again scatheless as so many do.

This train of reasoning brought me to a more resolved complexion; though it was far from closing up my sense of the dangers that surrounded me, nor of how very apt I was (if I went on) to stumble on the ladder of the gallows. It was a plain, fair morning, but the wind in the east. The little chill of it sang in my blood, and gave me a feeling of the autumn, and the dead leaves, and dead folks' bodies in their graves. It seemed the devil was in it, if I was to die in that tide of my fortunes and for other folks' affairs. On the top of the Calton Hill, though it was not the customary time of year for that diversion, some children were crying and running with their kites. These toys appeared very plain against the sky; I remarked a great one soar on the wind to a high altitude and then plump among the whins; and I thought to myself at sight of it, 'There goes Davie.'

My way lay over Mouter's Hill, and through an end of a clachan on the braeside among fields. There was a whirr of looms in it went from house to house; bees hummed in the gardens; the neighbours that I saw at the doorsteps talked in a strange tongue; and I found out later that this was Picardy, a village where the French weavers wrought for the Linen Company. Here I got a fresh direction for Pilrig, my destination; and a little beyond, on the wayside, came by a gibbet and two men hanged in chains. They were dipped in tar, as the manner is; the wind span them, the chains clattered, and the birds hung about the uncanny jumping-jacks and cried. The sight coming on me suddenly, like an illustration of my fears, I could scarce be done with examining it and drinking in discomfort. And as I thus turned and turned about the gibbet, what should I strike on, but a weird old wife, that sat behind a leg of it, and nodded, and talked aloud to herself with becks and courtesies.

'Who are these two, mother?' I asked, and pointed to the corpses.

'A blessing on your precious face!' she cried. 'Twa joes o' mine: just twa o' my old joes, my hinny dear.'

'What did they suffer for?' I asked.

'Ou, just for the guid cause,' said she. 'Aften I spaed to them the way that it would end. Twa shillin' Scots: no pickle mair; and there are twa bonny callants hingin' for 't! They took it frae a wean belanged to Brouchton.'

'Ay!' said I to myself, and not to the daft limmer, 'and did they come to such a figure for so poor a business? This is to lose all indeed.'

'Gie's your loof, hinny,' says she, 'and let me spae your weird to ye.'

'No, mother,' said I, 'I see far enough the way I am. It's an unco thing to see too far in front.'

'I read it in your bree,' she said. 'There's a bonnie lassie that has bricht een, and there's a wee man in a braw coat, and a big man in a pouthered wig, and there's the shadow of the wuddy, joe, that lies braid across your path.

Gie's your loof, hinny, and let Auld Merren spae it to ye bonny.'

The two chance shots that seemed to point at Alan and the daughter of James More, struck me hard; and I fled from the eldritch creature, casting her a baubee, which she continued to sit and play with under the moving shadows of the hanged.

My way down the causeway of Leith Walk would have been more pleasant to me but for this encounter. The old rampart ran among fields, the like of them I had never seen for artfulness of agriculture; I was pleased, besides, to be so far in the still countryside; but the shackles of the gibbet clattered in my head; and the mops and mows of the old witch, and the thought of the dead men, hag-rode my spirits. To hang on a gallows, that seemed a hard case; and whether a man came to hang there for two shillings Scots, or (as Mr Stewart had it) from the sense of duty, once he was tarred and shackled and hung up, the difference seemed small. There might David Balfour hang, and other lads pass on their errands and think light of him; and old daft limmers sit at a leg-foot and spae their fortunes; and the clean genty maids go by, and look to the other side, and hold a nose. I saw them plain, and they had grey eyes, and their screens upon their heads were of the Drummond colours.

I was thus in the poorest of spirits, though still pretty resolved, when I came in view of Pilrig, a pleasant gabled house set by the walkside among some brave young woods. The laird's horse was standing saddled at the door as I came up, but himself was in the study, where he received me in the midst of learned works and musical instruments, for he was not only a deep philosopher but much of a musician. He greeted me at first pretty well, and when he had read Rankeillor's letter, placed himself obligingly at my disposal.

'And what is it, cousin David?' says he—'since it appears that we are cousins—what is this that I can do for you? A word to Prestongrange? Doubtless that is easily given. But what should be the word?'

'Mr Balfour,' said I, 'if I were to tell you my whole story the way it fell out, it's my opinion (and it was Rankeillor's before me) that you would be very little made up with it.'

'I am sorry to hear this of you, kinsman,' says he.

'I must not take that at your hands, Mr Balfour,' said I; 'I have nothing to my charge to make me sorry, or you for me, but just the common infirmities of mankind. "The guilt of Adam's first sin, the want of original righteousness, and the corruption of my whole nature," so much I must answer for, and I hope I have been taught where to look for help,' I said; for I judged from the look of the man he would think the better of me if I knew my questions. 'But in the way of worldly honour I have no great stumble to reproach myself with; and my difficulties have befallen me very much against my will and (by all that I can see) without my fault. My trouble is to have become dipped in a political complication, which it is judged you would be blythe to avoid a knowledge of.'

'Why, very well, Mr David,' he replied, 'I am pleased to see you are all that Rankeillor represented. And for what you say of political complications, you do me no more than justice. It is my study to be beyond suspicion, and indeed outside the field of it. The question is,' says he, 'how, if I am to know nothing of the matter, I can very well assist you?'

'Why, sir,' said I, 'I propose you should write to his lordship, that I am a young man of reasonable good family and of good means: both of which I believe to be the case.'

'I have Rankeillor's word for it,' said Mr Balfour, 'and I count that a warrandice against all deadly.'

'To which you might add (if you will take my word for so much) that I am a good churchman, loyal to King George, and so brought up,' I went on.

'None of which will do you any harm,' said Mr Balfour.

'Then you might go on to say that I sought his lordship on a matter of great moment, connected with His Majesty's service and the administration of justice,' I suggested.

'As I am not to hear the matter,' says the laird, 'I will not take upon myself to qualify its weight. "Great moment" therefore falls, and "moment" along with it. For the rest I might express myself much as you propose.'

'And then, sir,' said I, and rubbed my neck a little with my thumb, 'then I would be very desirous if you could slip in a word that might perhaps tell for my protection.'

'Protection?' says he, 'for your protection? Here is a phrase that somewhat dampens me. If the matter be so dangerous, I own I would be a little loath to move in it blindfold.'

'I believe I could indicate in two words where the thing sticks,' said I.

'Perhaps that would be the best,' said he.

'Well, it's the Appin murder,' said I.

He held up both the hands. 'Sirs! sirs!' cried he.

I thought by the expression of his face and voice that I had lost my helper.

'Let me explain . . .' I began.

'I thank you kindly, I will hear no more of it,' says he. 'I decline *in toto* to hear more of it. For your name's sake and Rankeillor's, and perhaps a little for your own, I will do what I can to help you; but I will hear no more upon the facts. And it is my first clear duty to warn you. These are deep waters, Mr David, and you are a young man. Be cautious and think twice.'

'It is to be supposed I will have thought oftener than that, Mr Balfour,' said I, 'and I will direct your attention again to Rankeillor's letter, where (I hope and believe) he has registered his approval of that which I design.'

'Well, well,' said he; and then again, 'Well, well! I will do what I can for you.' Therewith he took a pen and paper, sat awhile in thought, and began to write with much consideration. 'I understand that Rankeillor approves of what you have in mind?' he asked presently.

'After some discussion, sir, he bade me to go forward in God's name,' said I.

'That is the name to go in,' said Mr Balfour, and resumed his writing. Presently, he signed, re-read what he had written, and addressed me again. 'Now here, Mr David,' said he, 'is a letter of introduction, which I will seal without closing, and give into your hands open, as the form requires. But since I am acting in the dark, I will just read it to you, so that you may see if it will secure your end:

Pilrig, *August 26th*,1751

My Lord,—This is to bring to your notice my namesake and cousin, David Balfour Esquire of Shaws, a young gentleman of unblemished descent and good estate. He has enjoyed besides the more valuable advantages of a godly training, and his political principles are all that your lordship can desire. I am not in Mr Balfour's confidence, but I understand him to have a matter to declare, touching His Majesty's service and the administration of justice: purposes for which your Lordship's zeal is known. I should add that the young gentleman's intention is known to and approved by some of his friends, who will watch with hopeful anxiety the event of his success or failure.

'Whereupon,' continued Mr Balfour, 'I have subscribed myself with the usual compliments. You observe I have said "some of your friends"; I hope you can justify my plural?'

'Perfectly, sir; my purpose is known and approved by more than one,' said I. 'And your letter, which I take a pleasure to thank you for, is all I could have hoped.'

'It was all I could squeeze out,' said he; 'and from what I know of the matter you design to meddle in, I can only pray God that it may prove sufficient.'

4. LORD ADVOCATE PRESTONGRANGE

MY KINSMAN KEPT me to a meal, 'for the honour of the roof', he said; and I believe I made the better speed on my return. I had no thought but to be done with the next stage, and have myself fully committed; to a person circumstanced as I was, the appearance of closing a door on hesitation and temptation was itself extremely tempting; and I was the more disappointed, when I came to Prestongrange's house, to be informed he was abroad. I believe it was true at the moment, and for some hours after; and then I have no doubt the Advocate came home again, and enjoyed himself in a neighbouring chamber among friends, while perhaps the very fact of my arrival was forgotten. I would have gone away a dozen times, only for this strong drawing to have done with my declaration out of hand and be able to lay me down to sleep with a free conscience. At first I read, for the little cabinet where I was left contained a variety of books. But I fear I read with little profit; and the weather falling cloudy, the dusk coming up earlier than usual, and my cabinet being lighted with but a loophole of a window, I was at last obliged to desist from this diversion (such as it was), and pass the rest of my time of waiting in a very burthensome vacuity. The sound of people talking in a near chamber, the pleasant note of a harpsichord, and once the voice of a lady singing, bore me a kind of company.

I do not know the hour, but the darkness was long come, when the door of the cabinet opened, and I was aware, by the light behind him, of a tall figure of a man upon the threshold. I rose at once.

'Is anybody there?' he asked. 'Who is that?'

'I am bearer of a letter from the laird of Pilrig to the Lord Advocate,' said I.

'Have you been here long?' he asked.

'I would not like to hazard an estimate of how many hours,' said I.

'It is the first I hear of it,' he replied, with a chuckle. 'The lads must have forgotten you. But you are in the bit at last, for I am Prestongrange.'

So saying, he passed before me into the next room, whither (upon his sign) I followed him, and where he lit a candle and took his place before a business-table. It was a long room, of a good proportion, wholly lined with books. That small spark of light in a corner struck out the man's handsome person and strong face. He was flushed, his eye watered and sparkled, and before he sat down I observed him to sway back and forth. No doubt he had been supping liberally; but his mind and tongue were under full control.

'Well, sir, sit ye down,' said he, 'and let us see Pilrig's letter.'

He glanced it through in the beginning carelessly, looking up and bowing when he came to my name; but at the last words I thought I observed his attention to redouble, and I made sure he read them twice. All this while you are to suppose my heart was beating, for I had now crossed my Rubicon and was come fairly on the field of battle.

'I am pleased to make your acquaintance, Mr Balfour,' he said, when he had done. 'Let me offer you a glass of claret.'

'Under your favour, my lord, I think it would scarce be fair on me,' said I. 'I have come here, as the letter will have mentioned, on a business of some gravity to myself; and as I am little used with wine, I might be the sooner affected.'

'You shall be the judge,' said he. 'But if you will permit, I believe I will even have the bottle in myself.'

He touched a bell, and a footman came, as at a signal, bringing wine and glasses.

'You are sure you will not join me?' asked the Advocate. 'Well, here is to our better acquaintance! In what way can I serve you?'

'I should perhaps begin by telling you, my lord, that I am here at your own pressing invitation,' said I.

'You have the advantage of me somewhere,' said he, 'for I profess I think I never heard of you before this evening.'

'Right, my lord, the name is indeed new to you,' said I.

'And yet you have been for some time extremely wishful to make my acquaintance, and have declared the same in public.'

'I wish you would afford me a clue,' says he. 'I am no Daniel.'

'It will perhaps serve for such,' said I, 'that if I was in a jesting humour—which is far from the case—I believe I might lay a claim on your lordship for two hundred pounds.'

'In what sense?' he inquired.

'In the sense of rewards offered for my person,' said I.

He thrust away his glass once and for all, and sat straight up in the chair where he had been previously lolling. 'What am I to understand?' said he.

'*A tall strong lad of about eighteen*,' I quoted, '*speaks like a Lowlander, and has no beard.*'

'I recognise those words,' said he, 'which, if you have come here with any ill-judged intention of amusing yourself, are like to prove extremely prejudicial to your safety.'

'My purpose in this,' I replied, 'is just entirely as serious as life and death, and you have understood me perfectly. I am the boy who was speaking with Glenure when he was shot.'

'I can only suppose (seeing you here) that you claim to be innocent,' said he.

'The inference is clear,' I said. 'I am a very loyal subject to King George, but if I had anything to reproach myself with, I would have had more discretion than to walk into your den.'

'I am glad of that,' said he. 'This horrid crime, Mr Balfour, is of a dye which cannot permit any clemency. Blood has been barbarously shed. It has been shed in direct opposition to his Majesty and our whole frame of laws, by those who are their known and public oppugnants. I take a very high sense of this. I will not deny that I consider the crime as directly personal to his Majesty.'

'And unfortunately, my lord,' I added, a little drily, 'directly personal to another great personage who may be nameless.'

'If you mean anything by those words, I must tell you I consider them unfit for a good subject; and were they spoke publicly I should make it my business to take note

of them,' said he. 'You do not appear to me to recognise
the gravity of your situation, or you would be more careful
not to pejorate the same by words which glance upon the
purity of justice. Justice, in this country, and in my poor
hands, is no respecter of persons.'

'You give me too great a share in my own speech, my
lord,' said I. 'I did but repeat the common talk of the
country, which I have heard everywhere, and from men
of all opinions as I came along.'

'When you are come to more discretion you will understand such talk is not to be listened to, how much less
repeated,' says the Advocate. 'But I acquit you of an ill
intention. That nobleman, whom we all honour, and who has
indeed been wounded in a near place by the late barbarity,
sits too high to be reached by these aspersions. The Duke of
Argyle—you see that I deal plainly with you—takes it
to heart as I do, and as we are both bound to do by our judicial
functions and the service of his Majesty; and I could wish
that all hands, in this ill age, were equally clean of family rancour. But from the accident that this is a Campbell who has
fallen martyr to his duty—as who else but the Campbells
have ever put themselves foremost on that path?—I may
say it, who am no Campbell—and that the chief of that
great house happens (for all our advantages) to be the
present head of the College of Justice, small minds and
disaffected tongues are set agog in every changehouse in
the country; and I find a young gentleman like Mr Balfour
so ill-advised as to make himself their echo.' So much he
spoke with a very oratorical delivery, as if in court, and
then declined again upon the manner of a gentleman. 'All
this apart,' said he. 'It now remains that I should learn what
I am to do with you.'

'I had thought it was rather I that should learn the same
from your lordship,' said I.

'Ay, true,' says the Advocate. 'But, you see, you come
to me well recommended. There is a good honest Whig
name to this letter,' says he, picking it up a moment from
the table. 'And—extra-judicially, Mr Balfour—there
is always the possibility of some arrangement. I tell you,
and I tell you beforehand that you may be the more upon

your guard, your fate lies with me singly. In such a matter (be it said with reverence) I am more powerful than the king's Majesty; and should you please me—and of course satisfy my conscience—in what remains to be held of our interview, I tell you it may remain between ourselves.'

'Meaning how?' I asked.

'Why, I mean it thus, Mr Balfour,' said he, 'that if you give satisfaction, no soul need know so much as that you visited my house; and you may observe that I do not even call my clerk.'

I saw what way he was driving. 'I suppose it is needless anyone should be informed upon my visit,' said I, 'though the precise nature of my gains by that I cannot see. I am not at all ashamed of coming here.'

'And have no cause to be,' says he, encouragingly. 'Nor yet (if you are careful) to fear the consequences.'

'My lord,' said I, 'speaking under your correction I am not very easy to be frightened.'

'And I am sure I do not seek to frighten you,' says he. 'But to the interrogation; and let me warn you to volunteer nothing beyond the questions I shall ask you. It may consist very immediately with your safety. I have a great discretion, it is true, but there are bounds to it.'

'I shall try to follow your lordship's advice,' said I.

He spread a sheet of paper on the table and wrote a heading. 'It appears you were present, by the way, in the wood of Lettermore at the moment of the fatal shot,' he began. 'Was this by accident?'

'By accident,' said I.

'How came you in speech with Colin Campbell?' he asked.

'I was inquiring my way of him to Aucharn,' I replied.

I observed he did not write this answer down.

'H'm, true,' said he, 'I had forgotten that. And do you know, Mr Balfour, I would dwell, if I were you, as little as might be on your relations with these Stewarts? It might be found to complicate our business. I am not yet inclined to regard these matters as essential.'

'I had thought, my lord, that all points of fact were equally material in such a case,' said I.

'You forget we are now trying these Stewarts,' he replied, with great significance. 'If we should ever come to be trying you, it will be very different; and I shall press these very questions that I am now willing to glide upon. But to resume: I have it here in Mr Mungo Campbell's precognition that you ran immediately up the brae. How came that?'

'Not immediately, my lord, and the cause was my seeing of the murderer.'

'You saw him, then?'

'As plain as I see your lordship, though not so near hand.'

'You know him?'

'I should know him again.'

'In your pursuit you were not so fortunate, then, as to overtake him?'

'I was not.'

'Was he alone?'

'He was alone.'

'There was no one else in that neighbourhood?'

'Alan Breck Stewart was not far off, in a piece of a wood.'

The Advocate laid his pen down. 'I think we are playing at cross purposes,' said he, 'which you will find to prove a very ill amusement for yourself.'

'I content myself with following your lordship's advice, and answering what I am asked,' said I.

'Be so wise as to bethink yourself in time,' said he, 'I use you with the most anxious tenderness, which you scarce seem to appreciate, and which (unless you be more careful) may prove to be in vain.'

'I do appreciate your tenderness, but conceive it to be mistaken,' I replied, with something of a falter, for I saw we were come to grips at last. 'I am here to lay before you certain information, by which I shall convince you Alan had no hand whatever in the killing of Glenure.'

The Advocate appeared for a moment at a stick, sitting with pursed lips, and blinking his eyes upon me like an angry cat. 'Mr Balfour,' he said at last, 'I tell you pointedly you go an ill way for your own interests.'

'My lord,' I said, 'I am as free of the charge of considering my own interests in this matter as your lordship. As God judges me, I have but the one design, and that is to see

justice executed and the innocent go clear. If in pursuit of
that I come to fall under your lordship's displeasure, I must
bear it as I may.'

At this he rose from his chair, lit a second candle, and
for a while gazed upon me steadily. I was surprised to see
a great change of gravity fallen upon his face, and I could
have almost thought he was a little pale.

'You are either very simple, or extremely the reverse, and
I see that I must deal with you more confidentially,' says he.
'This is a political case—ah, yes, Mr Balfour! whether
we like it or no, the case is political—and I tremble when
I think what issues may depend from it. To a political case, I
need scarce tell a young man of your education, we approach
with very different thoughts from one which is criminal only.
Salus populi suprema lex is a maxim susceptible of great abuse,
but it has that force which we find elsewhere only in the laws
of nature: I mean it has the force of necessity. I will open
this out to you, if you will allow me, at more length. You
would have me believe—'

'Under your pardon, my lord, I would have you to believe
nothing but that which I can prove,' said I.

'Tut! tut! young gentleman,' says he, 'be not so prag-
matical, and suffer a man who might be your father (if it
was nothing more) to employ his own imperfect language,
and express his own poor thoughts, even when they have the
misfortune not to coincide with Mr Balfour's. You would
have me to believe Breck innocent. I would think this of
little account, the more so as we cannot catch our man.
But the matter of Breck's innocence shoots beyond itself.
Once admitted, it would destroy the whole presumptions
of our case against another and a very different criminal; a
man grown old in treason, already twice in arms against his
king and already twice forgiven; a fomenter of discontent,
and (whoever may have fired the shot) the unmistakable
original of the deed in question. I need not tell you that I
mean James Stewart.'

'And I can just say plainly that the innocence of Alan and
of James is what I am here to declare in private to your
lordship, and what I am prepared to establish at the trial
by my testimony,' said I.

'To which I can only answer by an equal plainness, Mr Balfour,' said he, 'that (in that case) your testimony will not be called by me, and I desire you to withhold it altogether.'

'You are at the head of Justice in this country,' I cried, 'and you propose to me a crime!'

'I am a man nursing with both hands the interests of this country,' he replied, 'and I press on you a political necessity. Patriotism is not always moral in the formal sense. You might be glad of it I think: it is your own protection; the facts are heavy against you; and if I am still trying to except you from a very dangerous place, it is in part of course because I am not insensible to your honesty in coming here; in part because of Pilrig's letter; but in part, and in chief part, because I regard in this matter my political duty first and my judicial duty only second. For the same reason—I repeat it to you in the same frank words—I do not want your testimony.'

'I desire not to be thought to make a repartee, when I express only the plain sense of our position,' said I. 'But if your lordship has no need of my testimony, I believe the other side would be extremely blythe to get it.'

Prestongrange arose and began to pace to and fro in the room. 'You are not so young,' he said, 'but what you must remember very clearly the year '45 and the shock that went about the country. I read in Pilrig's letter that you are sound in Kirk and State. Who saved them in that fatal year? I do not refer to His Royal Highness and his ramrods, which were extremely useful in their day; but the country had been saved and the field won before ever Cumberland came upon Drummossie. Who saved it? I repeat; who saved the Protestant religion and the whole frame of our civil institutions? The late Lord President Culloden, for one; he played a man's part, and small thanks he got for it—even as I, whom you see before you, straining every nerve in the same service, look for no reward beyond the conscience of my duties done. After the President, who else? You know the answer as well as I do; 'tis partly a scandal, and you glanced at it yourself, and I reproved you for it, when you first came in. It was the Duke and the great clan of Campbell. Now here is a Campbell foully murdered, and that in the King's service. The Duke and I are Highlanders. But we are Highlanders civilised, and it is not so with the great mass of our clans and families. They have still savage virtues and defects. They are still barbarians, like these Stewarts; only the Campbells were barbarians on the right side, and the Stewarts were barbarians on the wrong. Now be you the judge. The Campbells expect vengeance. If they do not get it—if this man James escape—there will be trouble with the Campbells. That means disturbance in the Highlands, which are uneasy and very far from being disarmed: the disarming is a farce. . . .'

'I can bear you out in that,' said I.

'Disturbance in the Highlands makes the hour of our old watchful enemy,' pursued his lordship, holding out a finger as he paced; 'and I give you my word we may have a '45 again with the Campbells on the other side. To protect the life of this man Stewart—which is forfeit already on half-a-dozen different counts if not on this—do you propose to plunge your country in war, to jeopardise the faith of your fathers, and to expose the lives and fortunes of how many thousand innocent persons? . . . These are considerations that weigh with me, and that I hope will weigh no less with yourself, Mr Balfour, as a lover of your country, good government, and religious truth.'

'You deal with me very frankly, and I thank you for it,' said I. 'I will try on my side to be no less honest. I believe your policy to be sound. I believe these deep duties may lie upon your lordship; I believe you may have laid them on your conscience when you took the oaths of the high office which you hold. But for me, who am just a plain man—or scarce a man yet—the plain duties must suffice. I can think but of two things, of a poor soul in the immediate and unjust danger of a shameful death, and of the cries and tears of his wife that still tingle in my head. I cannot see beyond, my lord. It's the way that I am made. If the country has to fall, it has to fall. And I pray God, if this be wilful blindness, that He may enlighten me before too late.'

He had heard me motionless, and stood so a while longer.

'This is an unexpected obstacle,' says he, aloud, but to himself.

'And how is your lordship to dispose of me?' I asked.

'If I wished,' said he, 'you know that you might sleep in gaol?'

'My lord,' said I, 'I have slept in worse places.'

'Well; my boy,' said he, 'there is one thing appears very plainly from our interview, that I may rely on your pledged word. Give me your honour that you will be wholly secret, not only on what has passed to-night, but in the matter of the Appin case, and I let you go free.'

'I will give it till to-morrow or any other near day that you may please to set,' said I. 'I would not be thought too wily; but if I gave the promise without qualification your lordship would have attained his end.'

'I had no thought to entrap you,' said he.

'I am sure of that,' said I.

'Let me see,' he continued. 'To-morrow is the Sabbath. Come to me on Monday by eight in the morning, and give me your promise until then.'

'Freely given, my lord,' said I. 'And with regard to what has fallen from yourself, I will give it for as long as it shall please God to spare your days.'

'You will observe,' he said next, 'that I have made no employment of menaces.'

'It was like your lordship's nobility,' said I. 'Yet I am not altogether so dull but what I can perceive the nature of those you have not uttered.'

'Well,' said he, 'good-night to you. May you sleep well, for I think it is more than I am like to do.'

With that he sighed, took up a candle, and gave me his conveyance as far as the street door.

THE NEXT DAY, Sabbath, August 27th, I had the occasion I had long looked forward to, to hear some of the famous Edinburgh preachers, all well known to me already by the report of Mr Campbell. Alas! and I might just as well have been at Essendean, and sitting under Mr Campbell's worthy self! the turmoil of my thoughts, which dwelt continually on the interview with Prestongrange, inhibiting me from all attention. I was indeed much less impressed by the reasoning of the divines than by the spectacle of the thronged congregation in the churches, like what I imagined of a theatre or (in my then disposition) of an assize of trial; above all at the West Kirk, with its three tiers of galleries, where I went in the vain hope that I might see Miss Drummond.

On the Monday I betook me for the first time to a barber's, and was very well pleased with the result. Thence to the Advocate's, where the red coats of the soldiers showed again about his door, making a bright place in the close. I looked about for the young lady and her gillies: there was never a sign of them. But I was no sooner shown into the cabinet or antechamber where I had spent so wearyful a time upon the Saturday, than I was aware of the tall figure of James More in a corner. He seemed a prey to a painful uneasiness, reaching forth his feet and hands, and his eyes speeding here and there without rest about the walls of the small chamber, which recalled to me with a sense of pity the man's wretched situation. I suppose it was partly this, and partly my strong continuing interest in his daughter, that moved me to accost him.

'Give you a good-morning, sir,' said I.

'And a good-morning to you, sir,' said he.

'You bide tryst with Prestongrange?' I asked.

'I do, sir, and I pray your business with that gentleman be more agreeable than mine,' was his reply.

'I hope at least that yours will be brief, for I suppose you pass before me,' said I.

'All pass before me,' he said, with a shrug and a gesture upward of the open hands. 'It was not always so, sir, but times change. It was not so when the sword was in the scale, young gentleman, and the virtues of the soldier might sustain themselves.'

There came a kind of Highland snuffle out of the man that raised my dander strangely.

'Well, Mr Macgregor,' said I, 'I understand the main thing for a soldier is to be silent, and the first of his virtues never to complain.'

'You have my name, I perceive'—he bowed to me with his arms crossed—'though it's one I must not use myself. Well, there is a publicity—I have shown my face and told my name too often in the beards of my enemies. I must not wonder if both should be known to many that I know not.'

'That you know not in the least, sir,' said I, 'nor yet anybody else; but the name I am called, if you care to hear it, is Balfour.'

'It is a good name,' he replied, civilly; 'there are many decent folk that use it. And now that I call to mind, there was a young gentleman, your namesake, that marched surgeon in the year '45 with my battalion.'

'I believe that would be a brother to Balfour of Baith,' said I, for I was ready for the surgeon now.

'The same, sir,' said James More. 'And since I have been fellow-soldier with your kinsman, you must suffer me to grasp your hand.'

He shook hands with me long and tenderly, beaming on me the while as though he had found a brother.

'Ah!' says he, 'these are changed days since your cousin and I heard the balls whistle in our lugs.'

'I think he was a very far-away cousin,' said I, drily, 'and I ought to tell you that I never clapped eyes upon the man.'

'Well, well,' said he, 'it makes no change. And you—I do not think you were out yourself, sir—I have no clear mind of your face, which is one not probable to be forgotten.'

'In the year you refer to, Mr Macgregor, I was getting skelped in the parish school,' said I.

'So young!' cries he. 'Ah, then, you will never be able to think what this meeting is to me. In the hour of my adversity, and here in the house of my enemy, to meet in with the blood of an old brother-in-arms—it heartens me, Mr Balfour, like the skirling of the Highland pipes! Sir, this is a sad look-back that many of us have to make: some with falling tears. I have lived in my own country like a king; my sword, my mountains, and the faith of my friends and kinsmen sufficed for me. Now I lie in a stinking dungeon; and do you know, Mr Balfour,' he went on, taking my arm and beginning to lead me about, 'do you know, sir, that I lack mere necessaries? The malice of my foes has quite sequestered my resources. I lie, as you know, sir, on a trumped-up charge, of which I am as innocent as yourself. They dare not bring me to my trial, and in the meanwhile I am held naked in my prison. I could have wished it was your cousin I had met, or his brother Baith himself. Either would, I know, have been rejoiced to help me; while a comparative stranger like yourself—'

I would be ashamed to set down all he poured out to me in this beggarly vein, or the very short and grudging answers that I made to him. There were times when I was tempted to stop his mouth with some small change; but whether it was from shame or pride—whether it was for my own sake or Catriona's—whether it was because I thought him no fit father for his daughter, or because I resented that grossness of immediate falsity that clung about the man himself—the thing was clean beyond me. And I was still being wheedled and preached to, and still being marched to and fro, three steps and a turn, in that small chamber, and had already, by some very short replies, highly incensed, although not finally discouraged, my beggar, when Prestongrange appeared in the doorway and bade me eagerly into his big chamber.

'I have a moment's engagement,' said he; 'and that you may not sit empty-handed I am going to present you to my three braw daughters, of whom perhaps you may have heard, for I think they are more famous than papa. This way.'

He led me into another long room above, where a dry old lady sat at a frame of embroidery, and the three handsomest young women (I suppose) in Scotland stood together by a window.

'This is my new friend, Mr Balfour,' said he, presenting me by the arm. 'David, here is my sister, Miss Grant, who is so good as keep my house for me, and will be very pleased if she can help you. And here,' says he, turning to the three younger ladies, 'here are my *three braw dauchters*. A fair question to ye, Mr Davie: which of the three is the best favoured? And I wager he will never have the impudence to propound honest Alan Ramsay's answer!'

Hereupon all three, and the old Miss Grant as well, cried out against this sally, which (as I was acquainted with the verses he referred to) brought shame into my own cheek. It seemed to me a citation unpardonable in a father, and I was amazed that these ladies could laugh even while they reproved, or made believe to.

Under cover of this mirth, Prestongrange got forth of the chamber, and I was left, like a fish upon dry land, in that very unsuitable society. I could never deny, in looking back upon what followed, that I was eminently stockish; and I must say the ladies were well drilled to have so long a patience with me. The aunt indeed sat close at her embroidery, only looking now and again and smiling; but the misses, and especially the eldest, who was besides the most handsome, paid me a score of attentions which I was very ill able to repay. It was all in vain to tell myself I was a young fellow of some worth as well as a good estate, and had no call to feel abashed before these lasses, the eldest not so much older than myself, and no one of them by any probability half as learned. Reasoning would not change the fact; and there were times when the colour came into my face to think I was shaved that day for the first time.

The talk going, with all their endeavours, very heavily, the eldest took pity on my awkwardness, sat down to her instrument, of which she was a passed mistress, and entertained me for a while with playing and singing, both in the Scots and in the Italian manners; this put me more at my ease, and being reminded of Alan's air that he had taught me in the hole near Carriden, I made so bold as to whistle a bar or two, and ask if she knew that.

She shook her head. 'I never heard a note of it,' said she. 'Whistle it all through. And now once again,' she added, after I had done so.

Then she picked it out upon the keyboard, and (to my surprise) instantly enriched the same with well-sounding chords, and sang, as she played, with a very droll expression and broad accent:

> Haenae I got just the lilt of it?
> Isnae this the tune that ye whustled?

'You see,' she says, 'I can do the poetry too, only it won't rhyme. And then again:

> I am Miss Grant, sib to the Advocate:
> You, I believe, are Dauvit Balfour.

I told her how much astonished I was by her genius.

'And what do you call the name of it?' she asked.

'I do not know the real name,' said I. 'I just call it *Alan's air*.'

She looked at me directly in the face. 'I shall call it *David's air*,' said she; 'though if it's the least like what your namesake of Israel played to Saul I would never wonder that the king got little good by it, for it's but melancholy music. Your other name I do not like; so if you was ever wishing to hear your tune again you are to ask for it by mine.'

This was said with a significance that gave my heart a jog. 'Why that, Miss Grant?' I asked.

'Why,' says she, 'if ever you should come to get hanged, I will set your last dying speech and confession to that tune and sing it.'

This put it beyond a doubt that she was partly informed of my story and peril. How, or just how much, it was more difficult to guess. It was plain she knew there was something of danger in the name of Alan, and thus warned me to leave it out of reference; and plain she knew that I stood under some criminal suspicion. I judged besides that the harshness of her last speech (which besides she had followed up immediately with a very noisy piece of music) was to put an end to the present conversation. I stood beside her, affecting to listen and admire, but truly whirled away by my own thoughts. I have always found this young lady to be a lover of the mysterious; and certainly this first interview made a mystery that was beyond my plummet. One thing I learned long after, the hours of the Sunday had been well employed, the bank porter had been found and examined, my visit to Charles Stewart was discovered, and the deduction made that I was pretty deep with James and Alan, and most likely in a continued correspondence with the last. Hence this broad hint that was given me across the harpsichord.

In the midst of the piece of music, one of the younger misses, who was at a window over the close, cried on her sisters to come quick, for there was 'Grey eyes again'. The whole family trooped there at once, and crowded one another for a look. The window whither they ran was in an odd corner of that room, gave above the entrance door, and flanked up the close.

'Come, Mr Balfour,' they cried, 'come and see. She is the most beautiful creature! She hangs round the close-head these last days, always with some wretched-like gillies, and yet seems quite a lady.'

I had no need to look; neither did I look twice, or long. I was afraid she might have seen me there, looking down upon her from that chamber of music, and she without, and her father in the same house, perhaps begging for his life with tears, and myself come but newly from rejecting his petitions. But even that glance set me in a better conceit of myself, and much less awe of the young ladies. They were beautiful, that was beyond question, but Catriona was beautiful too, and had a kind of brightness in her like a coal of fire. As much as the others cast me down, she lifted me up. I remembered I had talked easily with her. If I could make no hand of it with these fine maids, it was perhaps something their own fault. My embarrassment began to be a little mingled and lightened with a sense of fun; and when the aunt smiled at me from her embroidery, and the three daughters unbent to me like a baby, all with 'papa's orders' written on their faces, there were times when I could have found it in my heart to smile myself.

Presently papa returned, the same kind, happy-like, pleasant-spoken man.

'Now, girls,' said he, 'I must take Mr Balfour away again; but I hope you have been able to persuade him to return where I shall be always gratified to find him.'

So they each made me a little farthing compliment, and I was led away.

If this visit to the family had been meant to soften my resistance, it was the worst of failures. I was no such ass but what I understood how poor a figure I had made, and that the girls would be yawning their jaws off as soon as my stiff back was turned. I felt I had shown how little I had in me of what was soft and graceful; and I longed for a chance to prove that I had something of the other stuff, the stern and dangerous.

Well, I was to be served to my desire, for the scene to which he was conducting me was of a different character.

THERE WAS A man waiting us in Prestongrange's study, whom I distasted at the first look, as we distaste a ferret or an earwig. He was bitter ugly, but seemed very much of a gentleman; had still manners, but capable of sudden leaps and violences; and a small voice, which could ring out shrill and dangerous when he so desired.

The Advocate presented us in a familiar, friendly way.

'Here, Fraser,' said he, 'here is Mr Balfour whom we talked about. Mr David, this is Mr Simon Fraser, whom we used to call by another title, but that is an old song. Mr Fraser has an errand to you.'

With that he stepped aside to his book-shelves, and made believe to consult a quarto volume in the far end.

I was thus left (in a sense) alone with perhaps the last person in the world I had expected. There was no doubt upon the terms of introduction; this could be no other than the forfeited Master of Lovat and chief of the great clan Fraser. I knew he had led his men in the Rebellion; I knew his father's head—my old lord's, that grey fox of the mountains—to have fallen on the block for that offence, the lands of the family to have been seized, and their nobility attainted. I could not conceive what he should be doing in Grant's house; I could not conceive that he had been called to the bar, had eaten all his principles, and was now currying favour with the Government even to the extent of acting Advocate-Depute in the Appin murder.

'Well, Mr Balfour,' said he, 'what is all this I hear of ye?'

'It would not become me to prejudge,' said I, 'but if the Advocate was your authority he is fully possessed of my opinions.'

'I may tell you I am engaged in the Appin case,' he went on; 'I am to appear under Prestongrange; and from my study of the precognitions I can assure you your opinions are erroneous. The guilt of Breck is manifest; and your testimony, in which you admit you saw him on the hill at the very moment, will certify his hanging.'

'It will be rather ill to hang him till you catch him,' I observed. 'And for other matters I very willingly leave you to your own impressions.'

'The Duke has been informed,' he went on. 'I have just come from his Grace, and he expressed himself before me with an honest freedom like the great nobleman he is. He spoke of you by name, Mr Balfour, and declared his gratitude beforehand in case you would be led by those who understand your own interests and those of the country so much better than yourself. Gratitude is no empty expression in that mouth: *experto crede*. I daresay you know something of my name and clan, and the damnable example and lamented end of my late father, to say nothing of my own errata. Well, I have made my peace with that good Duke; he has intervened for me with our friend Prestongrange; and here I am with my foot in the stirrup again and some of the responsibility shared into my hand of prosecuting King George's enemies and avenging the late daring and barefaced insult to his Majesty.'

'Doubtless a proud position for your father's son,' says I.

He wagged his bald eyebrows at me. 'You are pleased to make experiments in the ironical, I think,' said he. 'But I am here upon duty, I am here to discharge my errand in good faith, it is in vain you think to divert me. And let me tell you, for a young fellow of spirit and ambition like yourself, a good shove in the beginning will do more than ten years' drudgery. The shove is now at your command; choose what you will to be advanced in, the Duke will watch upon you with the affectionate disposition of a father.'

'I am thinking that I lack the docility of the son,' says I.

'And do you really suppose, sir, that the whole policy of this country is to be suffered to trip up and tumble down for an ill-mannered colt of a boy?' he cried. 'This has been made a test case, all who would prosper in the future must put a shoulder to the wheel. Look at me! Do you suppose it is for my pleasure that I put myself in the highly invidious position of prosecuting a man that I have drawn the sword alongside of? The choice is not left me.'

'But I think, sir, that you forfeited your choice when you mixed in with that unnatural rebellion,' I remarked. 'My case is happily otherwise; I am a true man, and can look either the Duke or King George in the face without concern.'

'Is it so the wind sits?' says he. 'I protest you are fallen in the worst sort of error. Prestongrange has been hitherto so civil (he tells me) as not to combat your allegations; but you must not think they are not looked upon with strong suspicion. You say you are innocent. My dear sir, the facts declare you guilty.'

'I was waiting for you there,' said I.

'The evidence of Mungo Campbell; your flight after the completion of the murder; your long course of secrecy—my good young man!' said Mr Simon, 'here is enough evidence to hang a bullock, let be a David Balfour! I shall be upon that trial; my voice shall be raised; I shall then speak much otherwise from what I do to-day, and far less to your gratification, little as you like it now! Ah, you look white!' cries he. 'I have found the key of your impudent heart. You look pale, your eyes waver, Mr David! You see the grave and the gallows nearer by than you had fancied.'

'I own to a natural weakness,' said I. 'I think no shame for that. Shame . . .' I was going on.

'Shame waits for you on the gibbet,' he broke in.

'Where I shall but be even'd with my lord your father,' said I.

'Aha, but not so!' he cried, 'and you do not yet see to the bottom of this business. My father suffered in a great cause, and for dealing in the affairs of kings. You are to hang for a dirty murder about boddle-pieces. Your personal part in it, the treacherous one of holding the poor wretch in talk, your accomplices a pack of ragged Highland gillies. And it can be shown, my great Mr Balfour—it can be shown, and it *will* be shown, trust *me* that has a finger in the pie—it can be shown, and shall be shown, that you were paid to do it. I think I can see the looks go round the court when I adduce my evidence, and it shall appear that you, a young man of education, let yourself be corrupted to this shocking act for a suit of cast clothes, a bottle of Highland spirits, and three-and-fivepence-halfpenny in copper money.'

There was a touch of the truth in these words that knocked me like a blow: clothes, a bottle of *usquebaugh*, and three-and-fivepence-halfpenny in change made up, indeed, the most of what Alan and I had carried from Aucharn; and I saw that some of James's people had been blabbing in their dungeons.

'You see I know more than you fancied,' he resumed in triumph. 'And as for giving it this turn, great Mr David, you must not suppose the Government of Great Britain and Ireland will ever be stuck for want of evidence. We have men here in prison who will swear out their lives as we direct them; as I direct, if you prefer the phrase. So now you are to guess your part of glory if you choose to die. On the one hand, life, wine, women, and a duke to be your hand-gun: on the other, a rope to your craig, and a gibbet to clatter your bones on, and the lousiest, lowest story to hand down to your namesakes in the future that was ever told about a hired assassin. And see here!' he cried, with a formidable shrill voice, 'see this paper that I pull out of my pocket. Look at the name there: it is the name of the great David, I believe, the ink scarce dry yet. Can you guess its nature? It is the warrant for your arrest, which I have but to touch this bell beside me to have executed on the spot. Once in the Tolbooth upon this paper, may God help you, for the die is cast!'

I must never deny that I was greatly horrified by so much baseness, and much unmanned by the immediacy and ugliness of my danger. Mr Simon had already gloried in the changes of my hue; I make no doubt I was now no ruddier than my shirt; my speech besides trembled.

'There is a gentleman in this room,' cried I. 'I appeal to him. I put my life and credit in his hands.'

Prestongrange shut his book with a snap. 'I told you so, Simon,' said he; 'you have played your hand for all it was worth, and you have lost. Mr David,' he went on, 'I wish you to believe it was by no choice of mine you were subjected to this proof. I wish you could understand how glad I am you should come forth from it with so much credit. You may not quite see how, but it is a little of a service to myself. For had our friend here been more successful than I was last night, it might have appeared that he was a better judge of men than I; it might have appeared we were altogether in the wrong situations, Mr Simon and myself. And I know our friend Simon to be ambitious,' says he, striking lightly on Fraser's shoulder. 'As for this stage play, it is over; my sentiments are very much engaged in your behalf; and whatever issue we can find to this unfortunate affair, I shall make it my business to see it is adopted with tenderness to you.'

These were very good words, and I could see besides that there was little love, and perhaps a spice of genuine ill-will, between those two who were opposed to me. For all that, it was unmistakable this interview had been designed, perhaps rehearsed, with the consent of both; it was plain my adversaries were in earnest to try me by all methods; and now (persuasion, flattery, and menaces, having been tried in vain) I could not but wonder what would be their next expedient. My eyes besides were still troubled, and my knees loose under me, with the distress of the late ordeal; and I could do no more than stammer the same form of words: 'I put my life and credit in your hands.'

'Well, well,' says he, 'we must try to save them. And in the meanwhile let us return to gentler methods. You must not bear any grudge upon my friend, Mr Simon, who did but speak by his brief. And even if you did conceive some malice against myself, who stood by and seemed rather to hold a candle, I must not let that extend to innocent members of my family. These are greatly engaged to see more of you, and I cannot consent to have my young womenfolk disappointed. Tomorrow they will be going to Hope Park, where I think it very proper you should make your bow. Call for me first, when I may possibly have something for your private hearing; then you shall be turned abroad again under the conduct of my misses; and until that time repeat to me your promise of secrecy.'

I had done better to have instantly refused, but in truth I

was beside the power of reasoning; did as I was bid; took my leave I know not how; and when I was forth again in the close, and the door had shut behind me, was glad to lean on a house wall and wipe my face. That horrid apparition (as I may call it) of Mr Simon rang in my memory, as a sudden noise rings after it is over in the ear. Tales of the man's father, of his falseness, of his manifold perpetual treacheries, rose before me from all that I had heard and read, and joined on with what I had just experienced of himself. Each time it occurred to me, the ingenious foulness of that calumny he had proposed to nail upon my character startled me afresh. The case of the man upon the gibbet by Leith Walk appeared scarce distinguishable from that I was now to consider as my own. To rob a child of so little more than nothing was certainly a paltry enterprise for two grown men; but my own tale, as it was to be represented in a court by Simon Fraser, appeared a fair second in every possible point of view of sordidness and cowardice.

The voices of two of Prestongrange's liveried men upon his doorstep recalled me to myself.

'Ha'e,' said the one, 'this billet as fast as ye can link to the captain.'

'Is that for the cateran back again?' asked the other.

'It would seem sae,' returned the first. 'Him and Simon are seeking him.'

'I think Prestongrange is gane gyte,' says the second. 'He'll have James More in bed with him next.'

'Weel, it's neither your affair nor mine's,' says the first.

And they parted, the one upon his errand, and the other back into the house.

This looked as ill as possible. I was scarce gone and they were sending already for James More, to whom I thought Mr Simon must have pointed when he spoke of men in prison and ready to redeem their lives by all extremities. My scalp curdled among my hair, and the next moment the blood leaped in me to remember Catriona. Poor lass! her father stood to be hanged for pretty indefensible misconduct. What was yet more unpalatable, it now seemed he was prepared to save his four quarters by the worst of shame and the most foul of cowardly murders—murder by the false oath; and to complete our misfortunes, it seemed myself was picked out to be the victim.

I began to walk swiftly and at random, conscious only of a desire for movement, air, and the open country.

I CAME FORTH, I vow I know not how, on the *Lang Dykes*. This is a rural road which runs on the north side over against the city. Thence I could see the whole black length of it tail down, from where the castle stands upon its crags above the loch in a long line of spires and gable ends, and smoking chimneys, and at the sight my heart swelled in my bosom. My youth, as I have told, was already inured to dangers; but such danger as I had seen the face of but that morning, in the midst of what they call the safety of a town, shook me beyond experience. Peril of slavery, peril of shipwreck, peril of sword and shot, I had stood all of these without discredit; but the peril there was in the sharp voice and the fat face of Simon, properly Lord Lovat, daunted me wholly.

I sat by the lake side in a place where the rushes went down into the water, and there steeped my wrists and laved my temples. If I could have done so with any remains of self-esteem I would now have fled from my foolhardy enterprise. But (call it courage or cowardice, and I believe it was both the one and the other) I decided I was ventured out beyond the possibility of a retreat. I had out-faced these men, I would continue to out-face them; come what might, I would stand by the word spoken.

The sense of my own constancy somewhat uplifted my spirits, but not much. At the best of it there was an icy place about my heart, and life seemed a black business to be at all engaged in. For two souls in particular my pity flowed. The one was myself, to be so friendless and lost among dangers. The other was the girl, the daughter of James More. I had seen but little of her; yet my view was taken and my judgment made. I thought her a lass of a clean honour, like a man's; I thought her one to die of a disgrace; and now I believed her father to be at that moment bargaining his vile life for mine. It made a bond in my thoughts betwixt the girl and me. I had seen her before only as a wayside appearance, though one that pleased me strangely; I saw her now in a sudden nearness of relation, as the daughter of my blood foe, and I might say, my murderer. I reflected it was hard I should be so plagued and persecuted all my days for other folks' affairs, and have no manner of pleasure myself. I got meals and a bed to sleep in when my concerns would suffer it; beyond that my wealth was of no help to me. If I was to hang, my days were like to be short; if I was not to hang but to escape out of this trouble, they might yet seem long to me ere I was done with them. Of a sudden her face appeared in my memory, the way I had first seen it, with the parted lips; at that, weakness came in my bosom and strength into my legs; and I set resolutely forward on the way to Dean. If I was to hang to-morrow, and it was sure enough I might very likely sleep that night in a dungeon, I determined I should hear and speak once more with Catriona.

The exercise of walking and the thought of my destination braced me yet more, so that I began to pluck up a kind of spirit. In the village of Dean, where it sits in the bottom of a glen beside the river, I inquired my way of a miller's man, who sent me up the hill upon the farther side by a plain path, and so to a decent-like small house in a garden of lawns and apple-trees. My heart beat high as I stepped inside the garden hedge, but it fell low indeed when I came face to face with a grim and fierce old lady, walking there in a white mutch with a man's hat strapped upon the top of it.

'What do ye come seeking here?' she asked.

I told her I was after Miss Drummond.

'And what may be your business with Miss Drummond?' says she.

I told her I had met her on Saturday last, had been so fortunate as to render her a trifling service, and was come now on the young lady's invitation.

'O, so you're Saxpence!' she cried, with a very sneering manner. 'A braw gift, a bonny gentleman. And hae ye ony ither name and designation, or were ye bapteesed Saxpence?' she asked.

I told my name.

'Preserve me!' she cried. 'Has Ebenezer gotten a son?'

'No, ma'am,' said I. 'I am a son of Alexander's. It's I that am the Laird of Shaws.'

'Ye'll find your work cut out for ye to establish that,' quoth she.

'I perceive you know my uncle,' said I; 'and I daresay you may be the better pleased to hear that business is arranged.'

'And what brings ye here after Miss Drummond?' she pursued.

'I'm come after my saxpence, mem,' said I. 'It's to be thought, being my uncle's nephew, I would be found a careful lad.'

'So ye have a spark of sleeness in ye?' observed the old lady, with some approval. 'I thought ye had just been a cuif—you and your saxpence, and your *lucky day* and your *sake of Balwhidder*'—from which I was gratified to learn that Catriona had not forgotten some of our talk. 'But all this is by the purpose,' she resumed. 'Am I to understand that ye come here keeping company?'

'This is surely rather an early question,' said I. 'The maid is young, so am I, worse fortune. I have but seen her the once. I'll not deny,' I added, making up my mind to try her with some frankness, 'I'll not deny but she has run in my head a good deal since I met in with her. That is one thing; but it would be quite another, and I think I would look very like a fool, to commit myself.'

'You can speak out of your mouth, I see,' said the old lady. 'Praise God, and so can I! I was fool enough to take charge of this rogue's daughter: a fine charge I have gotten; but it's mine, and I'll carry it the way I want to. Do ye mean to tell me, Mr Balfour of Shaws, that you would marry James More's daughter, and him hanged? Well, then, where there's no possible marriage there shall be no manner of carryings on, and take that for said. Lasses are bruckle things,' she added, with a nod; 'and though ye would never think it by my wrunkled chafts, I was a lassie mysel', and a bonny one.'

'Lady Allardyce,' said I, 'for that I suppose to be your name, you seem to do the two sides of the talking, which is a very poor manner to come to an agreement. You give me rather a home thrust when you ask if I would marry, at the gallows' foot, a young lady whom I have seen but the once. I have told you already I would never be so untenty as to commit myself. And yet I'll go some way with you. If I continue to like the lass as well as I have reason to expect, it will be something more than her father, or the gallows either, that keeps the two of us apart. As for my family, I found it by the wayside like a lost bawbee! I owe less than nothing to my uncle; and if ever I marry, it will be to please one person: that's myself.'

'I have heard this kind of talk before ye were born,' said Mrs Ogilvy, 'which is perhaps the reason that I think of it so little. There's much to be considered. This James More is a kinsman of mine, to my shame be it spoken. But the better the family, the mair men hanged or heided, that's always been poor Scotland's story. And if it was just the hanging! For my part, I think I would be best pleased with James upon the gallows, which would be at least an end to him. Catrine's a good lass enough, and a good-hearted, and lets herself be deaved all day with a runt of an auld wife like me. But, ye see, there's the weak bit. She's daft about that long, false, fleeching beggar of a father of hers, and red-mad about the Gregara, and proscribed names, and King James, and a wheen blethers. And you might think ye could guide her, ye would find yourself sore mista'en. Ye say ye've seen her but the once. . . .'

'Spoke with her but the once, I should have said,' I interrupted. 'I saw her again this morning from a window at Prestongrange's.'

This I daresay I put in because it sounded well; but I was properly paid for my ostentation on the return.

'What's this of it?' cries the old lady, with a sudden pucker of her face. 'I think it was at the Advocate's door-cheek that ye met her first.'

I told her that was so.

'H'm,' she said; and then suddenly, upon rather a scolding tone, 'I have your bare word for it,' she cries, 'as to who and what you are. By your way of it, you're Balfour of the Shaws; but for what I ken you may be Balfour of the Deevil's oxter. It's possible ye may come here for what ye say, and it's equally possible ye may come here for deil care what! I'm good enough Whig to sit quiet, and to have keepit all my men-folk's heads upon their shoulders. But I'm not just a good enough Whig to be made a fool of neither. And I tell you fairly, there's too much Advocate's door and Advocate's window here for a man that comes taigling after a Macgregor's daughter. Ye can tell that to the Advocate that sent ye, with my fond love. And I kiss my loof to ye, Mr Balfour,' says she, suiting the action to the word; 'and a braw journey to ye back to where ye cam frae.'

'If you think me a spy,' I broke out, and speech stuck in my throat. I stood and looked murder at the old lady for a space, then bowed and turned away.

'Here! Hoots! The callant's in a creel!' she cried. 'Think ye a spy? what else would I think ye—me that kens naething by ye? But I see that I was wrong; and as I cannot fight, I'll have to apologise. A bonny figure I would be with a broadsword. Ay! ay!' she went on, 'you're none such a bad lad in your way; I think ye'll have some redeeming vices. But, O! Davit Balfour, ye're damned countryfeed. Ye'll have to win over that, lad; ye'll have to soople your back-bone, and think a wee pickle less of your dainty self; and ye'll have to try to find out that women-folk are nae grenadiers. But that can never be. To your last day you'll ken no more of women-folk than what I do of sow-gelding.'

I had never been used with such expressions from a lady's tongue, the only two ladies I had known, Mrs Campbell and my mother, being most devout and most particular women; and I suppose my amazement must have been depicted in my countenance, for Mrs Ogilvy burst forth suddenly in a fit of laughter.

'Keep me!' she cried, struggling with her mirth, 'you have the finest timber face—and you to marry the daughter of a Hieland cateran! Davie, my dear, I think we'll have to make a match of it—if it was just to see the weans. And now,' she went on, 'there's no manner of service in your daidling here, for the young woman is from home, and it's my fear that the old woman is no suitable companion for your father's son. Forbye that I have nobody but myself to look after my reputation, and have been long enough alone with a sedooctive youth. And come back another day for your saxpence!' she cried after me as I left.

My skirmish with this disconcerting lady gave my thoughts a boldness they had otherwise wanted. For two days the image of Catriona had mixed in all my meditations; she made their background, so that I scarce enjoyed my own company without a glint of her in a corner of my mind. But now she came immediately near; I seemed to touch her, whom I had never touched but the once; I let myself flow out to her in a happy weakness, and looking all about, and before and behind, saw the world like an undesirable desert, where men go as soldiers on a march, following their duty with what constancy they have, and Catriona alone there to offer me some pleasure of my days. I wondered at myself that I could dwell on such considerations in that time of my peril and disgrace; and when I remembered my youth I was ashamed. I had my studies to complete; I had to be called into some useful business; I had yet to take my part of service in a place where all must serve; I had yet to learn, and know, and prove myself a man; and I had so much sense as blush that I should be already tempted with these further-on and holier delights and duties. My education spoke home to me sharply; I was never brought up on sugar biscuits but on the hard food of the truth. I knew that he was quite unfit to be a husband who was not prepared to be a father also; and for a boy like me to play the father was a mere derision.

When I was in the midst of these thoughts and about half-way back to town I saw a figure coming to meet me, and the trouble of my heart was heightened. It seemed I had everything in the world to say to her, but nothing to say first; and remembering how tongue-tied I had been that morning at the Advocate's I made sure that I would find myself struck dumb. But when she came up my fears fled away; not even the consciousness of what I had been privately thinking disconcerted me the least; and I found I could talk with her as easily and rationally as I might with Alan.

'O!' she cried, 'you have been seeking your sixpence: did you get it?'

I told her no; but now I had met with her my walk was not in vain. 'Though I have seen you to-day already,' said I, and told her where and when.

'I did not see you,' she said. 'My eyes are big, but there are better than mine at seeing far. Only I heard singing in the house.'

'That was Miss Grant,' said I, 'the eldest and the bonniest.'

'They say they are all beautiful,' said she.

'They think the same of you, Miss Drummond,' I replied, 'and were all crowding to the window to observe you.'

'It is a pity about my being so blind,' said she, 'or I might have seen them too. And you were in the house? You must have been having the fine time with the fine music and the pretty ladies.'

'There is just where you are wrong,' said I; 'for I was as uncouth as a sea-fish upon the brae of a mountain. The truth is that I am better fitted to go about with rudas men than pretty ladies.'

'Well, I would think so too, at all events!' said she, at which we both of us laughed.

'It is a strange thing, now,' said I. 'I am not the least afraid with you, yet I could have run from the Miss Grants. And I was afraid of your cousin too.'

'O, I think any man will be afraid of her,' she cried. 'My father is afraid of her himself.'

The name of her father brought me to a stop. I looked at her as she walked by my side; I recalled the man, and the little I knew and the much I guessed of him; and comparing the one with the other, felt like a traitor to be silent.

'Speaking of which,' said I, 'I met your father no later than this morning.'

'Did you?' she cried, with a voice of joy that seemed to mock at me. 'You saw James More? You will have spoken with him, then?'

'I did even that,' said I.

Then I think things went the worst way for me that was humanly possible. She gave me a look of mere gratitude. 'Ah, thank you for that!' says she.

'You thank me for very little,' said I, and then stopped. But it seemed when I was holding back so much, something at least had to come out. 'I spoke rather ill to him,' said I; 'I did not like him very much; I spoke him rather ill, and he was angry.'

'I think you had little to do then, and less to tell it to his daughter!' she cried out. 'But those that do not love and cherish him I will not know.'

'I will take the freedom of a word yet,' said I, beginning to tremble. 'Perhaps neither your father nor I are in the best of good spirits at Prestongrange's. I daresay we both have anxious business there, for it's a dangerous house. I was sorry for him too, and spoke to him the first, if I could but have spoken the wiser. And for one thing, in my opinion, you will soon find that his affairs are mending.'

'It will not be through your friendship, I am thinking,' said she; 'and he is much made up to you for your sorrow.'

'Miss Drummond,' cried I, 'I am alone in this world. . . .'

'And I am not wondering at that,' said she.

'O, let me speak!' said I. 'I will speak but the once, and then leave you, if you will, for ever. I came this day in the hopes of a kind word that I am sore in want of. I know that what I said must hurt you, and I knew it then. It would have been easy to have spoken smooth, easy to lie to you; can you not think how I was tempted to the same? Cannot you see the truth of my heart shine out?'

'I think here is a great deal of work, Mr Balfour,' said she. 'I think we will have met but the once, and will can part like gentle folk.'

'O, let me have one to believe in me!' I pleaded, 'I cannae bear it else. The whole world is clanned against me. How am I to go through with my dreadful fate? If there's to be none to believe in me I cannot do it. The man must just die, for I cannot do it.'

She had still looked straight in front of her, head in air; but at my words or the tone of my voice she came to a stop. 'What is this you say?' she asked. 'What are you talking of?'

'It is my testimony which may save an innocent life,' said I, 'and they will not suffer me to bear it. What would you do yourself? You know what this is, whose father lies in danger. Would you desert the poor soul? They have tried all ways with me. They have sought to bribe me; they offered me hills and valleys. And to-day that sleuth-hound told me how I stood, and to what a length he would go to butcher and disgrace me. I am to be brought in a party to the murder; I am to have held Glenure in talk for money and old clothes; I am to be killed and shamed. If this is the way I am to fall, and me scarce a man—if this is the story to be told of me in all Scotland—if you are to believe it too, and my name is to be nothing but a by-word—Catriona, how can I go through with it? The thing's not possible; it's more than a man has in his heart.'

I poured my words out in a whirl, one upon the other; and when I stopped I found her gazing on me with a startled face.

'Glenure! It is the Appin murder,' she said softly, but with a very deep surprise.

I had turned back to bear her company, and we were now come near the head of the brae above Dean village. At this word I stepped in front of her like one suddenly distracted.

'For God's sake!' I cried, 'for God's sake, what is this that I have done?' and carried my fists to my temples. 'What made me do it? Sure, I am bewitched to say these things!'

'In the name of heaven, what ails you now?' she cried.

'I gave my honour,' I groaned, 'I gave my honour and now I have broke it. O, Catriona!'

'I am asking you what it is,' she said; 'was it these things you should not have spoken? And do you think *I* have no honour, then? or that I am one that would betray a friend? I hold up my right hand to you and swear.'

'O, I knew you would be true!' said I. 'It's me—it's here. I that stood but this morning and out-faced them, that risked rather to die disgraced upon the gallows than do wrong—and a few hours after I throw my honour away by the roadside in common talk! "There is one thing clear upon our interview," says he, "that I can rely

on your pledged word." Where is my word now? Who
could believe me now? *You* could not believe me. I am
clean fallen down; I had best die!' All this I said with a
weeping voice, but I had no tears in my body.

'My heart is sore for you,' said she, 'but be sure you are
too nice. I would not believe you, do you say? I would trust
you with anything. And these men? I would not be thinking
of them! Men who go about to entrap and to destroy you!
Fy! this is no time to crouch. Look up! Do you not think
I will be admiring you like a great hero of the good—and
you a boy not much older than myself? And because you
said a word too much in a friend's ear, that would die ere she
betrayed you—to make such a matter! It is one thing that
we must both forget.'

'Catriona,' said I, looking at her, hang-dog, 'is this true
of it? Would ye trust me yet?'

'Will you not believe the tears upon my face?' she cried.
'It is the world I am thinking of you, Mr David Balfour. Let
them hang you; I will never forget, I will grow old and still
remember you. I think it is great to die so; I will envy you
that gallows.'

'And maybe all this while I am but a child frighted with
bogles,' said I. 'Maybe they but make a mock of me.'

'It is what I must know,' she said. 'I must hear the
whole. The harm is done at all events, and I must hear
the whole.'

I had sat down on the wayside, where she took a place
beside me, and I told her all that matter much as I have
written it, my thoughts about her father's dealing being
alone omitted.

'Well,' she said, when I had finished, 'you are a hero,
surely, and I never would have thought that same! And
I think you are in peril, too. O, Simon Fraser! to think
upon that man! For his life and the dirty money, to be
dealing in such traffic!' And just then she called out aloud
with a queer word that was common with her, and belongs, I
believe, to her own language. 'My torture!' says she, 'look
at the sun!'

Indeed, it was already dipping towards the mountains.

She bid me come again soon, gave me her hand, and left

me in a turmoil of glad spirits. I delayed to go home to my
lodging, for I had a terror of immediate arrest; but got some
supper at a change house, and the better part of that night
walked by myself in the barley-fields, and had such a sense
of Catriona's presence that I seemed to bear her in my arms.

THE NEXT DAY, August 29th, I kept my appointment at the Advocate's in a coat that I had made to my own measure, and was but newly ready.

'Aha,' says Prestongrange, 'you are very fine to-day; my misses are to have a fine cavalier. Come, I take that kind of you. I take that kind of you, Mr David. O, we shall do very well yet, and I believe your troubles are nearly at an end.'

'You have news for me?' cried I.

'Beyond anticipation,' he replied. 'Your testimony is after all to be received; and you may go, if you will, in my company to the trial, which is to be held at Inverary, Thursday, 21st *proximo*.'

I was too much amazed to find words.

'In the meanwhile,' he continued, 'though I will not ask you to renew your pledge, I must caution you strictly to be reticent. To-morrow your precognition must be taken; and outside of that, do you know, I think least said will be soonest mended.'

'I shall try to go discreetly,' said I. 'I believe it is yourself that I must thank for this crowning mercy, and I do thank you gratefully. After yesterday, my lord, this is like the doors of Heaven. I cannot find it in my heart to get the thing believed.'

'Ah, but you must try and manage, you must try and manage to believe it,' says he, soothing-like, 'and I am very glad to hear your acknowledgment of obligation, for I think you may be able to repay me very shortly'—he coughed—'or even now. The matter is much changed. Your testimony, which I shall not trouble you for to-day, will doubtless alter the complexion of the case for all concerned, and this makes it less delicate for me to enter with you on a side issue.'

'My Lord,' I interrupted, 'excuse me for interrupting you, but how has this been brought about? The obstacles you told me of on Saturday appeared even to me to be quite insurmountable; how has it been contrived?'

'My dear Mr David,' said he, 'it would never do for me to divulge (even to you, as you say) the councils of the Government; and you must content yourself, if you please, with the gross fact.'

He smiled upon me like a father as he spoke, playing the while with a new pen; methought it was impossible there could be any shadow of deception in the man: yet when he drew to him a sheet of paper, dipped his pen among the ink, and began again to address me, I was somehow not so certain, and fell instinctively into an attitude of guard.

'There is a point I wish to touch upon,' he began. 'I purposely left it before upon one side, which need be now no longer necessary. This is not, of course, a part of your examination, which is to follow by another hand; this is a private interest of my own. You say you encountered Alan Breck upon the hill?'

'I did, my lord,' said I.

'This was immediately after the murder?'

'It was.'

'Did you speak to him?'

'I did.'

'You had known him before, I think?' says my lord, carelessly.

'I cannot guess your reason for so thinking, my lord,' I replied, 'but such is the fact.'

'And when did you part with him again?' said he.

'I reserve my answer,' said I. 'The question will be put to me at the assize.'

'Mr Balfour,' said he, 'will you not understand that all this is without prejudice to yourself? I have promised you life and honour; and, believe me, I can keep my word. You are therefore clear of all anxiety. Alan, it appears, you suppose you can protect; and you talk to me of your gratitude, which I think (if you push me) is not ill-deserved. There are a great many different considerations all pointing the same way; and I will never be persuaded that you could not help us (if you chose) to put salt on Alan's tail.'

'My lord,' said I, 'I give you my word I do not so much as guess where Alan is.'

He paused a breath. 'Nor how he might be found?' he asked.

I sat before him like a log of wood.

'And so much for your gratitude, Mr David!' he observed. Again there was a piece of silence. 'Well,' said he, rising, 'I am not fortunate, and we are a couple at cross purposes. Let us speak of it no more; you will receive notice when, where, and by whom, we are to take your precognition. And in the meantime, my misses must be waiting you. They will never forgive me if I detain their cavalier.'

Into the hands of these Graces I was accordingly offered up, and found them dressed beyond what I had thought possible, and looking fair as a posy.

As we went forth from the doors a small circumstance occurred which came afterwards to look extremely big. I heard a whistle sound loud and brief like a signal, and looking all about, spied for one moment the red head of Neil of the Tom, the son of Duncan. The next moment he was gone again, nor could I see so much as the skirt-tail of Catriona, upon whom I naturally supposed him to be then attending.

My three keepers led me out by Bristo and the Bruntsfield Links; whence a path carried us to Hope Park, a beautiful pleasance, laid with gravel-walks, furnished with seats and summer-sheds, and warded by a keeper. The way there was a little longsome; the two younger misses affected an air of genteel weariness that damped me cruelly, the eldest considered me with something that at times appeared like mirth; and though I thought I did myself more justice than the day before, it was not without some effort. Upon our reaching the park I was launched on a bevy of eight or ten young gentlemen (some of them cockaded officers, the rest chiefly advocates) who crowded to attend upon these beauties; and though I was presented to all of them in very good words, it seemed I was by all immediately forgotten. Young folk in a company are like to savage animals: they fall upon or scorn a stranger without civility, or I may say, humanity; and I am sure, if I had been among baboons, they would have shown me quite as much of both. Some of the advocates set up to be wits, and some of the soldiers to be rattles; and I could not tell which of these extremes annoyed me most. All had a manner of handling their swords and coat-skirts, for the which (in mere black envy) I could have kicked them from that park. I daresay, upon their side, they grudged me extremely the fine company in which I had arrived; and altogether I had soon fallen behind, and stepped stiffly in the rear of all that merriment with my own thoughts.

From these I was recalled by one of the officers, Lieutenant Hector Duncansby, a gawky, leering Highland boy, asking if my name was not 'Palfour'.

I told him it was, not very kindly, for his manner was scant civil.

'Ha, Palfour,' says he, and then, repeating it, 'Palfour, Palfour!'

'I am afraid you do not like my name, sir,' says I, annoyed with myself to be annoyed with such a rustical fellow.

'No,' says he, 'but I wass thinking.'

'I would not advise you to make a practice of that, sir,' says I. 'I feel sure you would not find it to agree with you.'

'Tit you effer hear where Alan Grigor fand the tangs?' said he.

I asked him what he could possibly mean, and he answered, with a heckling laugh, that he thought I must have found the poker in the same place and swallowed it.

There could be no mistake about this, and my cheek burned.

'Before I went about to put affronts on gentlemen,' said I, 'I think I would learn the English language first.'

He took me by the sleeve with a nod and a wink, and led me quietly outside Hope Park. But no sooner were we beyond the view of the promenaders, than the fashion of his countenance changed. 'You tam lowland scoon'rel!' cries he, and hit me a buffet on the jaw with his closed fist.

I paid him as good or better on the return; whereupon he stepped a little back and took off his hat to me decorously.

'Enough plows I think,' says he. 'I will be the offended shentleman, for who effer heard of such suffeeciency as tell a shentlemans that is the king's officer he cannae speak Cot's English? We have swords at our hurdies, and here is the King's Park at hand. Will ye walk first, or let me show ye the way?'

I returned his bow, told him to go first, and followed him. As he went I heard him grumble to himself about *Cot's English* and the *King's coat*, so that I might have supposed him to be seriously offended. But his manner at the beginning of our interview was there to belie him. It was manifest he had come prepared to fasten a quarrel on me, right or wrong; manifest that I was taken in a fresh contrivance of my enemies; and to me (conscious as I was of my deficiencies) manifest enough that I should be the one to fall in our encounter.

As we came into that rough rocky desert of the King's Park I was tempted half-a-dozen times to take to my heels and run for it, so loath was I to show my ignorance in fencing, and so much averse to die or even to be wounded. But I considered if their malice went as far as this, it would likely stick at nothing; and that to fall by the sword, however ungracefully, was still an improvement on the gallows. I considered besides that by the unguarded pertness of my words and the quickness of my blow I had put myself quite out of court; and that even if I ran, my adversary would probably pursue and catch me, which would add disgrace to my misfortune. So that, taking all in all, I continued marching behind him, much as a man follows the hangman, and certainly with no more hope.

We went about the end of the long craigs, and came into the Hunter's Bog. Here, on a piece of fair turf, my adversary drew. There was nobody there to see us but some birds; and no resource for me but to follow his example, and stand on guard with the best face I could display. It seems it was not good enough for Mr Duncansby, who spied some flaw in my manœuvres, paused, looked upon me sharply, and came off and on, and menaced me with his blade in the air. As I had seen no such proceedings from Alan, and was besides a good deal affected with the proximity of death, I grew quite bewildered, stood helpless, and could have longed to run away.

'Fat deil ails her?' cries the lieutenant.

And suddenly engaging, he twitched the sword out of my grasp and sent it flying far among the rushes.

Twice was this manœuvre repeated; and the third time when I brought back my humiliated weapon, I found he had returned his own to the scabbard, and stood awaiting me with a face of some anger, and his hands clasped under his skirt.

'Pe tamned if I touch you!' he cried, and asked me bitterly what right I had to stand up before 'shentlemans' when I did not know the back of a sword from the front of it.

I answered that was the fault of my upbringing; and would he do me the justice to say I had given him all the satisfaction it was unfortunately in my power to offer, and had stood up like a man?

'And that is the truth,' said he. 'I am fery prave myself, and pold as a lions. But to stand up there—and you ken naething of fence!—the way that you did, I declare it was peyond me. And I am sorry for the plow; though I declare I pelief your own was the elder brother, and my heid still sings with it. And I declare if I had kent what way it wass, I would not put a hand to such a piece of pusiness.'

'That is handsomely said,' I replied, 'and I am sure you will not stand up a second time to be the actor for my private enemies.'

'Indeed, no, Palfour,' said he; 'and I think I was used extremely suffeeciently myself to be set up to fecht with an auld wife, or all the same as a bairn whateffer! And I will tell the Master so, and fecht him, by Cot, himself!'

'And if you knew the nature of Mr Simon's quarrel with me,' said I, 'you would be yet the more affronted to be mingled up with such affairs.'

He swore he could well believe it; that all the Lovats were made of the same meal and the devil was the miller that ground that; then suddenly shaking me by the hand, he vowed I was a pretty enough fellow after all, that it was a thousand pities I had been neglected, and that if he could find the time, he would give an eye himself to have me educated.

'You can do me a better service than even what you propose,' said I; and when he had asked its nature—'Come with me to the house of one of my enemies, and testify how I have carried myself this day,' I told him. 'That will be the true service. For though he has sent me a gallant adversary for the first, the thought in Mr Simon's mind is merely murder. There will be a second and then a third; and by what you have seen of my cleverness with the cold steel, you can judge for yourself what is like to be the upshot.'

'And I would not like it myself, if I was no more of a man than what you wass!' he cried. 'But I will do you right, Palfour. Lead on!'

If I had walked slowly on the way into that accursed park my heels were light enough on the way out. They kept time to a very good old air, that is as ancient as the Bible, and the words of it are: *Surely the bitterness of death is passed.* I mind that I was extremely thirsty, and had a drink at Saint Margaret's well on the road down, and the sweetness of that water passed belief. We went through the sanctuary, up the Canongate, in by the Netherbow, and straight to Prestongrange's door, talking as we came and arranging the details of our affair. The footman owned his master was at home, but declared him engaged with other gentlemen on very private business, and his door forbidden.

'My business is but for three minutes, and it cannot wait,' said I. 'You may say it is by no means private, and I shall be even glad to have some witnesses.'

As the man departed unwillingly enough upon this errand, we made so bold as to follow him to the antechamber, whence I could hear for a while the murmuring of several voices in the room within. The truth is, they were three at the one table—Prestongrange, Simon Fraser, and Mr Erskine, Sheriff of Perth; and as they were met in consultation on the very business of the Appin murder, they were a little disturbed at my appearance, but decided to receive me.

'Well, well, Mr Balfour, and what brings you here again? and who is this you bring with you?' says Prestongrange.

As for Fraser, he looked before him on the table.

'He is here to bear a little testimony in my favour, my

lord, which I think it very needful you should hear,' said
I, and turned to Duncansby.

'I have only to say this,' said the lieutenant, 'that I stood
up this day with Palfour in the Hunter's Pog, which I am
now fery sorry for, and he behaved himself as pretty as a
shentlemans could ask it. And I have creat respects for
Palfour,' he added.

'I thank you for your honest expressions,' said I.

Whereupon Duncansby made his bow to the company,
and left the chamber, as we had agreed upon before.

'What have I to do with this?' says Prestongrange.

'I will tell your lordship in two words,' said I. 'I have
brought this gentleman, a King's officer, to do me so much
justice. Now I think my character is covered, and until a
certain date, which your lordship can very well supply, it
will be quite in vain to despatch against me any more officers.
I will not consent to fight my way through the garrison of the
castle.'

The veins swelled on Prestongrange's brow, and he
regarded me with fury.

'I think the devil uncoupled this dog of a lad between
my legs!' he cried; and then, turning fiercely on his
neighbour, 'This is some of your work, Simon,' he said.
'I spy your hand in the business, and, let me tell you,
I resent it. It is disloyal, when we are agreed upon one
expedient, to follow another in the dark. You are disloyal
to me. What! you let me send this lad to the place with
my very daughters! And because I let drop a word to you
. . . Fy, sir, keep your dishonours to yourself!'

Simon was deadly pale. 'I will be a kick-ball between you
and the Duke no longer,' he exclaimed. 'Either come to
an agreement, or come to a differ, and have it out among
yourselves. But I will no longer fetch and carry, and get
your contrary instructions, and be blamed by both. For if
I were to tell you what I think of all your Hanover business
it would make your head sing.'

But Sheriff Erskine had preserved his temper, and now
intervened smoothly. 'And in the meantime,' says he, 'I
think we should tell Mr Balfour that his character for valour
is quite established. He may sleep in peace. Until the date

he was so good as to refer to it shall be put to the proof no more.'

His coolness brought the others to their prudence; and they made haste, with a somewhat distracted civility, to pack me from the house.

9. THE HEATHER ON FIRE

WHEN I LEFT Prestongrange that afternoon I was for the first time angry. The Advocate had made a mock of me. He had pretended my testimony was to be received and myself respected; and in that very hour, not only was Simon practising against my life by the hands of the Highland soldier, but (as appeared from his own language) Prestongrange himself had some design in operation. I counted my enemies: Prestongrange with all the King's authority behind him; and the Duke with the power of the West Highlands; and the Lovat interest by their side to help them with so great a force in the north, and the whole clan of old Jacobite spies and traffickers. And when I remembered James More, and the red head of Neil the son of Duncan, I thought there was perhaps a fourth in the confederacy, and what remained of Rob Roy's old desperate sept of caterans would be banded against me with the others. One thing was requisite—some strong friend or wise adviser. The country must be full of such, both able and eager to support me, or Lovat and the Duke and Prestongrange had not been nosing for expedients; and it made me rage to think that I might brush against my champions in the street and be no wiser.

And just then (like an answer) a gentleman brushed against me going by, gave me a meaning look, and turned into a close. I knew him with the tail of my eye—it was Stewart the Writer; and, blessing my good fortune, turned in to follow him. As soon as I had entered the close I saw him standing in the mouth of a stair, where he made me a signal and immediately vanished. Seven storeys up, there he was again in a house door, the which he locked behind us after we had entered. The house was quite dismantled, with not a stick of furniture; indeed, it was one of which Stewart had the letting in his hands.

'We'll have to sit upon the floor,' said he; 'but we're safe here for the time being, and I've been wearying to see ye, Mr Balfour.'

'How's it with Alan?' I asked.

'Brawly,' said he. 'Andie picks him up at Gillane sands tomorrow, Wednesday. He was keen to say good-bye to ye, but the way that things were going, I was feared the pair of ye was maybe best apart. And that brings me to the essential: how does your business speed?'

'Why,' said I, 'I was told only this morning that my testimony was accepted, and I was to travel to Inverary with the Advocate, no less.'

'Hout awa!' cried Stewart. 'I'll never believe that.'

'I have maybe a suspicion of my own,' says I, 'but I would like fine to hear your reasons.'

'Well, I tell ye fairly, I'm horn-mad,' cries Stewart. 'If my one hand could pull their Government down I would pluck it like a rotten apple. I'm doer for Appin and for James of the Glens; and, of course, it's my duty to defend my kinsman for his life. Hear how it goes with me, and I'll leave the judgment of it to yourself. The first thing they have to do is to get rid of Alan. They cannae bring in James as art and part until they've brought in Alan first as principal; that's sound law: they could never put the cart before the horse.'

'And how are they to bring in Alan till they can catch him?' says I.

'Ah, but there is a way to evite that arrestment,' said he. 'Sound law, too. It would be a bonny thing if, by the escape of one ill-doer another was to go scatheless, and the remeid is to summon the principal and put him to outlawry for the non-compearance. Now there's four places where a person can be summoned: at his dwelling-house; at a place where he has resided forty days; at the head burgh of the shire where he ordinarily resorts; or lastly (if there be ground to think him forth of Scotland) *at the cross of Edinburgh, and the pier and shore of Leith, for sixty days*. The purpose of which last provision is evident upon its face: being that outgoing ships may have time to carry news of the transaction, and the summonsing be something other than a form. Now take the case of Alan. He had no dwelling-house that ever I could hear of; I would be obliged if anyone would show me where he has lived forty days together since the '45; there is no shire where he resorts whether ordinarily or extraordinarily; if he has a domicile at all, which I misdoubt, it must be with his regiment in France; and if he is not yet forth of Scotland (as we happen to know and they happen to guess) it must be evident to the most dull it's what he's aiming for. Where, then, and what way should he be summoned? I ask it at yourself, a layman.'

'You have given the very words,' said I. 'Here at the cross, and at the pier and shore of Leith, for sixty days.'

'Ye're a sounder Scots lawyer than Prestongrange, then!' cries the Writer. 'He has had Alan summoned once; that was on the twenty-fifth, the day that we first met. Once, and done with it. And where? Where, but at the cross of Inverary, the head burgh of the Campbells? A word in your ear, Mr Balfour—they're not seeking Alan.'

'What do you mean?' I cried. 'Not seeking him?'

'By the best that I can make of it,' said he. 'Not wanting to find him, in my poor thought. They think perhaps he might set up a fair defence, upon the back of which James, the man they're really after, might climb out. This is not a case, ye see, it's a conspiracy.'

'Yet I can tell you Prestongrange asked after Alan keenly,' said I; 'though, when I come to think of it, he was something of the easiest put by.'

'See that!' says he. 'But there! I may be right or wrong, that's guesswork at the best, and let me get to my facts again. It comes to my ears that James and the witnesses—the witnesses, Mr Balfour!—lay in close dungeons, and shackled forbye, in the military prison at Fort William; none allowed in to them, nor they to write. The witnesses, Mr Balfour; heard ye ever the match of that? I assure ye, no old, crooked Stewart of the gang ever out-faced the law more impudently. It's clean in the two eyes of the Act of Parliament of 1700, anent wrongous imprisonment. No sooner did I get the news than I petitioned the Lord Justice Clerk. I have his word to-day. There's law for ye! here's justice!'

He put a paper in my hand, that same mealy-mouthed,

false-faced paper that was printed since in the pamphlet 'by a bystander', for behoof (as the title says) of James's 'poor widow and five children'.

'See,' said Stewart, 'he couldn't dare to refuse me access to my client, so he *recommends the commanding officer to let me in*. Recommends!—the Lord Justice Clerk of Scotland recommends. Is not the purpose of such language plain? They hope the officer may be so dull, or so very much the reverse, as to refuse the recommendation. I would have to make the journey back again betwixt here and Fort William. Then would follow a fresh delay till I got fresh authority, and they had disavowed the officer—military man, notoriously ignorant of the law, and that—I ken the cant of it. Then the journey a third time; and there we should be on the immediate heels of the trial before I had received my first instruction. Am I not right to call this a conspiracy?'

'It will bear that colour,' said I.

'And I'll go on to prove it you outright,' said he. 'They have the right to hold James in prison, yet they cannot deny me to visit him. They have no right to hold the witnesses; but am I to get a sight of them, that should be as free as the Lord Justice Clerk himself? See—read: *For the rest, refuses to give any orders to keepers of prisons who are not accused as having done anything contrary to the duties of their office.* Anything contrary! Sirs! And the Act of seventeen hunner? Mr Balfour, this makes my heart to burst; the heather is on fire inside my wame.'

'And the plain English of that phrase,' said I, 'is that the witnesses are still to lie in prison and you are not to see them?'

'And I am not to see them until Inverary, when the court is set!' cries he, 'and then to hear Prestongrange upon *the anxious responsibilities of his office and the great facilities afforded the defence!* But I'll begowk them there, Mr David. I have a plan to waylay the witnesses upon the road, and see if I cannae get a little harle of justice out of the *military man notoriously ignorant of the law* that shall command the party.'

It was actually so—it was actually on the wayside near Tynedrum, and by the connivance of a soldier officer, that Mr Stewart first saw the witnesses upon the case.

'There is nothing that would surprise me in this business,'
I remarked.

'I'll surprise you ere I'm done!' cries he. 'Do ye see
this?'—producing a print still wet from the press. 'This
is the libel: see, there's Prestongrange's name to the list of
witnesses, and I find no word of any Balfour. But here is not
the question. Who do ye think paid for the printing of this
paper?'

'I suppose it would likely be King George,' said I.

'But it happens it was me!' he cried. 'Not but it was
printed by and for themselves, for the Grants and the
Erskines, and yon thief of the black midnight, Simon
Fraser. But could *I* win to get a copy? No! I was to
go blindfold to my defence; I was to hear the charges for
the first time in court alongst the jury.'

'Is not this against the law?' I asked.

'I cannot say so much,' he replied. 'It was a favour so natural and so constantly rendered (till this nonesuch business)
that the law has never looked to it. And now admire the hand
of Providence! A stranger is in Fleming's printing house,
spies a proof on the floor, picks it up, and carries it to me.
Of all things, it was just this libel. Whereupon I had it set
again—printed at the expense of the defence: *sumptibus
moesti rei*; heard ever man the like of it?—and here it is
for anybody, the muckle secret out—all may see it now.
But how do you think I would enjoy this, that has the life
of my kinsman on my conscience?'

'Troth, I think you would enjoy it ill,' said I.

'And now you see how it is,' he concluded, 'and why when
you tell me your evidence is to be let in, I laugh aloud in
your face.'

It was now my turn. I laid before him in brief Mr Simon's
threats and offers, and the whole incident of the bravo, with
the subsequent scene at Prestongrange's. Of my first talk,
according to promise, I said nothing, nor indeed was it
necessary. All the time I was talking Stewart nodded his
head like a mechanical figure; and no sooner had my voice
ceased, than he opened his mouth and gave me his opinion
in two words, dwelling strong on both of them.

'Disappear yourself,' said he.

'I do not take you,' said I.

'Then I'll carry you there,' said he. 'By my view of it you're to disappear whatever. O, that's outside debate. The Advocate, who is not without some spunks of a remainder decency, has wrung your life-safe out of Simon and the Duke. He has refused to put you on your trial, and refused to have you killed; and there is the clue to their ill words together, for Simon and the Duke can keep faith with neither friend nor enemy. Ye're not to be tried then, and ye're not to be murdered; but I'm in bitter error if ye're not to be kidnapped and carried away like the Lady Grange. Bet me what ye please—there was their *expedient*!'

'You make me think,' said I, and told him of the whistle and the red-headed retainer, Neil.

'Wherever James More is there's one big rogue, never be deceived on that,' said he. 'His father was none so ill a man, though a kenning on the wrong side of the law, and no friend to my family, that I should waste my breath to be defending him! But as for James he's a brock and a blagyard. I like the appearing of, this red-headed Neil as little as yourself. It looks uncanny: fiegh! it smells bad. It was old Lovat that managed the Lady Grange affair; if young Lovat is to handle yours, it'll be all in the family. What's James More in prison for? The same offence: abduction. His men have had practice in the business. He'll be to lend them to be Simon's instruments; and the next thing we'll be hearing, James will have made his peace, or else he'll have escaped; and you'll be in Benbecula or Applecross.'

'Ye make a strong case,' I admitted.

'And what I want,' he resumed, 'is that you should disappear yourself ere they can get their hands upon ye. Lie quiet until just before the trial, and spring upon them at the last of it when they'll be looking for you least. This is always supposing, Mr Balfour, that your evidence is worth so very great a measure of both risk and fash.'

'I will tell you one thing,' said I. 'I saw the murderer and it was not Alan.'

'Then, by God, my cousin's saved!' cried Stewart. 'You have his life upon your tongue; and there's neither time, risk, nor money to be spared to bring you to the trial.' He emptied his pockets on the floor. 'Here is all that I have by me,' he went on. 'Take it, ye'll want it ere ye're through. Go straight down this close, there's a way out by there to the Lang Dykes, and by my will of it! see no more of Edinburgh till the clash is over.'

'Where am I to go, then?' I inquired.

'And I wish that I could tell ye!' says he, 'but all the places that I could send ye to, would be just the places they would seek. No, ye must fend for yourself, and God be your guiding! Five days before the trial, September the sixteen, get word to me at the *King's Arms* in Stirling; and if ye've managed for yourself as long as that, I'll see that ye reach Inverary.'

'One thing more,' said I. 'Can I no see Alan?'

He seemed boggled. 'Hech, I would rather you wouldnae,' said he. 'But I can never deny that Alan is extremely keen of it, and is to lie this night by Silvermills on purpose. If you're sure that you're not followed, Mr Balfour—but make sure of that— lie in a good place and watch your road for a clear hour before ye risk it. It would be a dreadful business if both you and him was to miscarry!'

10. THE RED-HEADED MAN

IT WAS ABOUT half-past three when I came forth on the Lang Dykes. Dean was where I wanted to go. Since Catriona dwelled there, and her kinsfolk the Glengyle Macgregors appeared almost certainly to be employed against me, it was just one of the few places I should have kept away from; and being a very young man, and beginning to be very much in love, I turned my face in that direction without pause. As a salve to my conscience and common sense, however, I took a measure of precaution. Coming over the crown of a bit of a rise in the road, I clapped down suddenly among the barley and lay waiting. After a while, a man went by that looked to be a Highlandman, but I had never seen him till that hour. Presently after came Neil of the red head. The next to go past was a miller's cart, and after that nothing but manifest country people. Here was enough to have turned the most foolhardy from his purpose, but my inclination ran too strong the other way. I argued it out that if Neil was on that road, it was the right road to find him in, leading direct to his chief's daughter; as for the other Highlandman, if I was to be startled off by every Highlandman I saw, I would scarce reach anywhere. And having quite satisfied myself with this disingenuous debate, I made the better speed of it, and came a little after four to Mrs Drummond-Ogilvy's.

Both ladies were within the house; and upon my perceiving them together by the open door, I plucked off my hat and said, 'Here was a lad come seeking saxpence,' which I thought might please the dowager.

Catriona ran out to greet me heartily, and, to my surprise, the old lady seemed scarce less forward than herself. I learned long afterwards that she had despatched a horseman by daylight to Rankeillor at the Queensferry, whom she knew to be

77

the doer for Shaws, and had then in her pocket a letter from
that good friend of mine, presenting, in the most favourable
view, my character and prospects. But had I read it I could
scarce have seen more clear in her designs. Maybe I was
countryfeed; at least, I was not so much so as she thought;
and it was plain enough, even to my homespun wits, that she
was bent to hammer up a match between her cousin and a
beardless boy that was something of a laird in Lothian.

'Saxpence had better take his broth with us, Catrine,' says
she. 'Run and tell the lasses.'

And for the little while we were alone was at a good deal
of pains to flatter me; always cleverly, always with the
appearance of a banter, still calling me Saxpence, but with
such a turn that should rather uplift me in my own opinion.
When Catriona returned, the design became if possible more
obvious; and she showed off the girl's advantages like a
horse-couper with a horse. My face flamed that she should
think me so obtuse. Now I would fancy the girl was being
innocently made a show of, and then I could have beaten the
old carline wife with a cudgel; and now, that perhaps these
two had set their heads together to entrap me, and at that I
sat and gloomed betwixt them like the very image of ill-will.
At last the match-maker had a better device, which was to
leave the pair of us alone. When my suspicions are anyway
roused it is sometimes a little the wrong side of easy to allay
them. But though I knew what breed she was of, and that
was a breed of thieves, I could never look in Catriona's face
and disbelieve her.

'I must not ask?' says she, eagerly, the same moment we
were left alone.

'Ah, but to-day I can talk with a free conscience,' I replied.
'I am lightened of my pledge, and indeed (after what has
come and gone since morning) I would not have renewed
it were it asked.'

'Tell me,' she said. 'My cousin will not be so long.'

So I told her the tale of the lieutenant from the first step
to the last of it, making it as mirthful as I could, and, indeed,
there was matter of mirth in that absurdity.

'And I think you will be as little fitted for the rudas men
as for the pretty ladies, after all!' says she, when I had

done. 'But what was your father that he could not learn you to draw the sword? It is most ungentle; I have not heard the match of that in anyone.'

'It is most misconvenient at least,' said I; 'and I think my father (honest man!) must have been wool-gathering to learn me Latin in the place of it. But you see I do the best I can, and just stand up like Lot's wife and let them hammer at me.'

'Do you know what makes me smile?' said she. 'Well, it is this. I am made this way, that I should have been a man child. In my own thoughts it is so I am always; and I go on telling myself about this thing that is to befall and that. Then it comes to the place of the fighting, and it comes over me that I am only a girl at all events, and cannot hold a sword or give one good blow; and then I have to twist my story round about, so that the fighting is to stop, and yet me have the best of it, just like you and the lieutenant; and I am the boy that makes the fine speeches all through, like Mr David Balfour.'

'You are a bloodthirsty maid,' said I.

'Well, I know it is good to sew and spin, and to make samplers,' she said, 'but if you were to do nothing else in the great world, I think you will say yourself it is a driech business; and it is not that I want to kill, I think. Did ever you kill anyone?'

'That I have, as it chances. Two, no less, and me still a lad that should be at the college,' said I. 'But yet, in the look-back, I take no shame for it.'

'But how did you feel, then—after it?' she asked.

''Deed, I sat down and grat like a bairn,' said I.

'I know that, too,' she cried. 'I feel where these tears should come from. And at any rate, I would not wish to kill, only to be Catherine Douglas that put her arm through the staples of the bolt, where it was broken. That is my chief hero. Would you not love to die so—for your king?' she asked.

'Troth,' said I, 'my affection for my king, God bless the puggy face of him, is under more control; and I thought I saw death so near to me this day already, that I am rather taken up with the notion of living.'

'Right,' she said, 'the right mind of a man! Only you must learn arms; I would not like to have a friend that cannot strike. But it will not have been with the sword that you killed these two?'

'Indeed, no,' said I, 'but with a pair of pistols. And a fortunate thing it was the men were so near-hand to me, for I am about as clever with the pistols as I am with the sword.'

So then she drew from me the story of our battle in the brig, which I had omitted in my first account of my affairs.

'Yes,' said she, 'you are brave. And your friend, I admire and love him.'

'Well, and I think any one would!' said I. 'He has his faults like other folk; but he is brave and staunch and kind, God bless him! That will be a strange day when I forget Alan.' And the thought of him, and that it was within my choice to speak with him that night, had almost overcome me.

'And where will my head be gone that I have not told my news!' she cried, and spoke of a letter from her father, bearing that she might visit him to-morrow in the castle whither he was now transferred, and that his affairs were mending. 'You do not like to hear it,' said she. 'Will you judge my father and not know him?'

'I am a thousand miles from judging,' I replied. 'And I give you my word I do rejoice to know your heart is lightened. If my face fell at all, as I suppose it must, you will allow this is rather an ill day for compositions, and the people in power extremely ill persons to be compounding with. I have Simon Fraser extremely heavy on my stomach still.'

'Ah!' she cried, 'you will not be evening these two; and you should bear in mind that Prestongrange and James More, my father, are of the one blood.'

'I never heard tell of that,' said I.

'It is rather singular how little you are acquainted with,' said she. 'One part may call themselves Grant, and one Macgregor, but they are still of the same clan. They are all the sons of Alpin, from whom, I think, our country has its name.'

'What country is that?' I asked.

'My country and yours,' said she.

'This is my day for discoveries, I think,' said I, 'for I always thought the name of it was Scotland.'

'Scotland is the name of what you call Ireland,' she replied. 'But the old ancient true name of this place that we have our foot-soles on, and that our bones are made of, will be Alban. It was Alban they called it when our forefathers will be fighting for it against Rome and Alexander; and it is called so still in your own tongue that you forget.'

'Troth,' said I, 'and that I never learned!' For I lacked heart to take her up about the Macedonian.

'But your fathers and mothers talked it, one generation with another,' said she. 'And it was sung about the cradles before you or me were ever dreamed of; and your name remembers it still. Ah, if you could talk that language you would find me another girl. The heart speaks in that tongue.'

I had a meal with the two ladies, all very good, served in fine old plate, and the wine excellent, for it seems that Mrs Ogilvy was rich. Our talk, too, was pleasant enough; but as soon as I saw the sun decline sharply and the shadows to run out long, I rose to take my leave. For my mind was now made up to say farewell to Alan; and it was needful I should see the trysting wood, and reconnoitre it, by daylight. Catriona came with me as far as to the garden gate.

'It is long till I see you now?' she asked.

'It is beyond my judging,' I replied. 'It will be long, it may be never.'

'It may be so,' said she. 'And you are sorry?'

I bowed my head, looking upon her.

'So am I, at all events,' said she. 'I have seen you but a small time, but I put you very high. You are true, you are brave; in time I think you will be more of a man yet. I will be proud to hear of that. If you should speed worse, if it will come to fall as we are afraid—O well! think you have the one friend. Long after you are dead and me an old wife, I will be telling the bairns about David Balfour, and my tears running. I will be telling how we parted, and what I said to you, and did to you. *God go with you and guide you, prays your little friend*: so I said—I will be telling them—and here is what I did.'

She took up my hand and kissed it. This so surprised my
spirits that I cried out like one hurt. The colour came strong
in her face, and she looked at me and nodded.

'O yes, Mr David,' said she, 'that is what I think of you.
The heart goes with the lips.'

I could read in her face high spirit, and a chivalry like a
brave child's; not anything besides. She kissed my hand, as
she had kissed Prince Charlie's, with a higher passion than
the common kind of clay has any sense of. Nothing before
had taught me how deep I was her lover, nor how far I had
yet to climb to make her think of me in such a character.
Yet I could tell myself I had advanced some way, and that
her heart had beat and her blood flowed at thoughts of me.

After that honour she had done me I could offer no more
trivial civility. It was even hard for me to speak; a certain
lifting in her voice had knocked directly at the door of my
own tears.

'I praise God for your kindness, dear,' said I. 'Farewell,
my little friend!' giving her that name which she had given
to herself; with which I bowed and left her.

My way was down the glen of the Leith River, towards
Stockbridge and Silvermills. A path led in the foot of it,
the water bickered and sang in the midst; the sunbeams
overhead struck out of the west among long shadows and
(as the valley turned) made like a new scene and a new
world of it at every corner. With Catriona behind and Alan
before me, I was like one lifted up. The place besides, and
the hour, and the talking of the water, infinitely pleased me;
and I lingered in my steps and looked before and behind me
as I went. This was the cause, under Providence, that I spied
a little in my rear a red head among some bushes.

Anger sprang in my heart, and I turned straight about
and walked at a stiff pace to where I came from. The path
lay close by the bushes where I had remarked the head. The
cover came to the wayside, and as I passed I was all strung
up to meet and to resist an onfall. No such thing befell, I
went by unmeddled with; and at that fear increased upon
me. It was still day indeed, but the place exceeding solitary.
If my haunters had let slip that fair occasion I could but judge
they aimed at something more than David Balfour. The lives

of Alan and James weighed upon my spirit with the weight of two grown bullocks.

Catriona was yet in the garden walking by herself.

'Catriona,' said I, 'you see me back again.'

'With a changed face,' said she.

'I carry two men's lives besides my own,' said I. 'It would be a sin and a shame not to walk carefully. I was doubtful whether I did right to come here. I would like it ill, if it was by that means we were brought to harm.'

'I could tell you one that would be liking it less, and will like little enough to hear you talking at this very same time,' she cried. 'What have I done, at all events?'

'O, you! you are not alone,' I replied. 'But since I went off I have been dogged again, and I can give you the name of him that follows me. It is Neil, son of Duncan, your man or your father's.'

'To be sure you are mistaken there,' she said, with a white face. 'Neil is in Edinburgh on errands from my father.'

'It is what I fear,' said I, 'the last of it. But for his being in Edinburgh I think I can show you another of that. For sure you have some signal, a signal of need, such as would bring him to your help, if he was anywhere within the reach of ears and legs?'

'Why, how will you know that?' says she.

'By means of a magical talisman God gave to me when I was born, and the name they call it by is Common-sense,' said I. 'Oblige me so far as make your signal, and I will show you the red head of Neil.'

No doubt but I spoke bitter and sharp. My heart was bitter. I blamed myself and the girl and hated both of us: her for the vile crew that she was come of, myself for my wanton folly to have stuck my head in such a byke of wasps.

Catriona set her fingers to her lips and whistled once, with an exceeding clear, strong, mounting note, as full as a ploughman's. A while we stood silent; and I was about to ask her to repeat the same, when I heard the sound of some one bursting through the bushes below on the braeside. I pointed in that direction with a smile, and presently Neil leaped into the garden. His eyes burned, and he had a black knife (as they call it on the Highland side) naked in his hand; but, seeing me beside his mistress, stood like a man struck.

'He has come to your call,' said I; 'judge how near he was to Edinburgh, or what was the nature of your father's errands. Ask himself. If I am to lose my life, or the lives of those that hang by me, through the means of your clan, let me go where I have to go with my eyes open.'

She addressed him tremulously in the Gaelic. Remembering Alan's anxious civility in that particular, I could have laughed out loud for bitterness; here, sure, in the midst of these suspicions, was the hour she should have stuck by English.

Twice or thrice they spoke together, and I could make out that Neil (for all his obsequiousness) was an angry man.

Then she turned to me. 'He swears it is not,' she said.

'Catriona,' said I, 'do you believe the man yourself?'

She made a gesture like wringing the hands.

'How will I can know?' she cried.

'But I must find some means to know,' said I. 'I cannot continue to go dovering round in the black night with two men's lives at my girdle! Catriona, try to put yourself in my place, as I vow to God I try hard to put myself in yours. This is no kind of talk that should ever have fallen between me and you; no kind of talk; my heart is sick with it. See, keep him here till two of the morning, and I care not. Try him with that.'

They spoke together once more in the Gaelic.

'He says he has James More my father's errand,' said she. She was whiter than ever, and her voice faltered as she said it.

'It is pretty plain now,' said I, 'and may God forgive the wicked!'

She said never anything to that, but continued gazing at me with the same white face.

'This is a fine business,' said I again. 'Am I to fall, then, and those two along with me?'

'O, what am I to do?' she cried. 'Could I go against my father's orders, and him in prison, in the danger of his life?'

'But perhaps we go too fast,' said I. 'This may be a lie too. He may have no right orders; all may be contrived by Simon, and your father knowing nothing.'

She burst out weeping between the pair of us; and my heart smote me hard, for I thought this girl was in a dreadful situation.

'Here,' said I, 'keep him but the one hour; and I'll chance it, and say God bless you.'

She put out her hand to me. 'I will be needing one good word,' she sobbed.

'The full hour, then?' said I, keeping her hand in mine. 'Three lives of it, my lass!'

'The full hour!' she said, and cried aloud on her Redeemer to forgive her.

I thought it no fit place for me, and fled.

I LOST NO time, but down through the valley and by
Stockbrig and Silvermills as hard as I could stave. It was
Alan's tryst to lie every night between twelve and two 'in
a bit scrog of wood by east of Silvermills and by south the
south mill-lade'. This I found easy enough, where it grew on
a steep brae, with the mill-lade flowing swift and deep along
the foot of it; and here I began to walk slower and to reflect
more reasonably on my employment. I saw I had made but a
fool's bargain with Catriona. It was not to be supposed that
Neil was sent alone upon his errand, but perhaps he was
the only man belonging to James More; in which case, I
should have done all I could to hang Catriona's father, and
nothing the least material to help myself. To tell the truth,
I fancied neither one of these ideas. Suppose, by holding
back Neil, the girl should have helped to hang her father,
I thought she would never forgive herself this side of time.
And suppose there were others pursuing me that moment,
what kind of a gift was I come bringing to Alan? and how
would I like that?

I was up with the west end of that wood when these two
considerations struck me like a cudgel. My feet stopped of
themselves and my heart along with them. 'What wild game
is this that I have been playing?' thought I; and turned
instantly upon my heels to go elsewhere.

This brought my face to Silvermills; the path came
past the village with a crook, but all plainly visible; and,
Highland or Lowland, there was nobody stirring. Here was
my advantage, here was just such a conjuncture as Stewart
had counselled me to profit by, and I ran by the side of the
mill-lade, fetched about beyond the east corner of the wood,
threaded through the midst of it, and returned to the west
selvage, whence I could again command the path, and yet be

myself unseen. Again it was all empty, and my heart began to rise.

For more than an hour I sat close in the border of the trees, and no hare or eagle could have kept a more particular watch. When that hour began the sun was already set, but the sky still all golden and the daylight clear; before the hour was done it had fallen to be half mirk, the images and distances of things were mingled, and observation began to be difficult. All that time not a foot of man had come east from Silvermills, and the few that had gone west were honest countryfolk and their wives upon the road to bed. If I were tracked by the most cunning spies in Europe, I judged it was beyond the course of nature they could have any jealousy of where I was; and going a little further home into the wood I lay down to wait for Alan.

The strain of my attention had been great, for I had watched not the path only, but every bush and field within my vision. That was now at an end. The moon, which was in her first quarter, glinted a little in the wood; all round there was a stillness of the country; and as I lay there on my back, the next three or four hours, I had a fine occasion to review my conduct.

Two things became plain to me first: that I had had no right to go that day to Dean, and (having gone there) had now no right to be lying where I was. This (where Alan was to come) was just the one wood in all broad Scotland that was, by every proper feeling, closed against me; I admitted that, and yet stayed on, wondering at myself. I thought of the measure with which I had meted to Catriona that same night; how I had prated of the two lives I carried, and had thus forced her to enjeopardy her father's; and how I was here exposing them again, it seemed in wantonness. A good conscience is eight parts of courage. No sooner had I lost conceit of my behaviour, than I seemed to stand disarmed amidst a throng of terrors. Of a sudden I sat up. How if I went now to Prestongrange, caught him (as I still easily might) before he slept, and made a full submission? Who could blame me? Not Stewart the Writer; I had but to say that I was followed, despaired of getting clear, and so gave in. Not Catriona: here, too, I had my answer ready; that I could not bear she should expose her father. So, in a moment, I could lay all these troubles by, which were after all and truly none of mine; swim clear of the Appin murder; get forth out of hand-stroke of all the Stewarts and Campbells, all the Whigs and Tories, in the land; and live thenceforth to my own mind, and be able to enjoy and to improve my fortunes, and devote some hours of my youth to courting Catriona, which would be surely a more suitable occupation than to hide and run and be followed like a hunted thief, and begin over again the dreadful miseries of my escape with Alan.

At first I thought no shame of this capitulation; I was only amazed I had not thought upon the thing and done it earlier; and began to inquire into the causes of the change. These I traced to my lowness of spirits, that back to my late recklessness, and that again to the common, old, public, disconsidered sin of self-indulgence. Instantly the text came in my head, *How can Satan cast out Satan?* What? (I thought) I had, by self-indulgence, and the following of pleasant paths, and the lure of a young maid, cast myself wholly out of conceit with my own character, and jeopardised the lives of James and Alan? And I was to seek the way out by the same road as I had entered in? No; the hurt that had been caused by self-indulgence must be cured by self-denial; the flesh I had pampered must be crucified. I looked about me for that course which I least liked to follow: this was to leave the wood without waiting to see Alan, and go forth again alone, in the dark and in the midst of my perplexed and dangerous fortunes.

I have been the more careful to narrate this passage of my reflections, because I think it is of some utility, and may serve as an example to young men. But there is reason (they say) in planting kale, and even in ethic and religion, room for common sense. It was already close on Alan's hour, and the moon was down. If I left (as I could not very decently whistle to my spies to follow me) they might miss me in the dark and tack themselves to Alan by mistake. If I stayed, I could at the least of it set my friend upon his guard which might prove his mere salvation. I had adventured other peoples' safety in a course of self-indulgence; to have endangered them again, and now on a mere design

of penance, would have been scarce rational. Accordingly,
I had scarce risen from my place ere I sat down again, but
already in a different frame of spirits, and equally marvelling
at my past weakness and rejoicing in my present composure.

Presently after came a crackling in the thicket. Putting my
mouth near down to the ground, I whistled a note or two of
Alan's air; an answer came, in the like guarded tone, and
soon we had knocked together in the dark.

'Is this you at last, Davie?' he whispered.

'Just myself,' said I.

'God, man, but I've been wearying to see ye!' says he.
'I've had the longest kind of a time. A' day, I've had my
dwelling into the inside of a stack of hay, where I couldnae
see the nebs of my ten fingers; and then two hours of it
waiting here for you, and you never coming! Dŏd, and
ye're none too soon the way it is, with me to sail the morn!
The morn? what am I saying?—the day, I mean.'

'Ay, Alan, man, the day, sure enough,' said I. 'It's past
twelve now, surely, and ye sail the day. This'll be a long
road you have before you.'

'We'll have a long crack of it first,' said he.

'Well, indeed, and I have a good deal it will be telling you
to hear,' said I.

And I told him what behooved, making rather a jumble
of it, but clear enough when done. He heard me out with
very few questions, laughing here and there like a man
delighted: and the sound of his laughing (above all there,
in the dark, where neither one of us could see the other)
was extraordinary friendly to my heart.'

'Ay, Davie, ye're a queer character,' says he, when I had
done: 'a queer bitch after a', and I have no mind of meeting
with the like of ye. As for your story, Prestongrange is a
Whig like yoursel', so I'll say the less of him; and, dod!
I believe he was the best friend ye had, if ye could only trust
him. But Simon Fraser and James More are my ain kind of
cattle, and I'll give them the name that they deserve. The
muckle black deil was father to the Frasers, a'body kens
that; and as for the Gregara, I never could abye the reek
of them since I could stotter on two feet. I bloodied the nose
of one, I mind, when I was still so wambly on my legs that

I cowped upon the top of him. A proud man was my father that day, God rest him! and I think he had the cause. I'll never can deny but what Robin was something of a piper,' he added; 'but as for James More, the deil guide him for me!'

'One thing we have to consider,' said I. 'Was Charles Stewart right or wrong? Is it only me they're after, or the pair of us?'

'And what's your ain opinion, you that's a man of so much experience?' said he.

'It passes me,' said I.

'And me too,' says Alan. 'Do ye think this lass would keep her word to ye?' he asked.

'I do that,' said I.

'Well, there's nae telling,' said he. 'And anyway, that's over and done: he'll be joined to the rest of them lang syne.'

'How many would ye think there would be of them?' I asked.

'That depends,' said Alan. 'If it was only you, they would likely send two-three lively, brisk young birkies, and if they thought that I was to appear in the employ, I daresay ten or twelve,' said he.

It was no use, I gave a little crack of laughter.

'And I think your own two eyes will have seen me drive that number, or the double of it, nearer hand!' cries he.

'It matters the less,' said I, 'because I am well rid of them for this time.'

'Nae doubt that's your opinion,' said he; 'but I wouldnae be the least surprised if they were hunkering this wood. Ye see, David man, they'll be Hieland folk. There'll be some Frasers, I'm thinking, and some of the Gregara; and I would never deny but what the both of them, and the Gregara in especial, were clever experienced persons. A man kens little till he's driven a spreagh of neat cattle (say) ten miles through a throng lowland country and the black soldiers maybe at his tail. It's there that I learned a great part of my penetration. And ye need nae tell me: it's better than war; which is the next best, however, though generally rather a bauchle of a business. Now the Gregara have had grand practice.'

'No doubt that's a branch of education that was left out with me,' said I.

'And I can see the marks of it upon ye constantly,' said Alan. 'But that's the strange thing about you folk of the college learning: ye're ignorant, and ye cannae see 't. Wae's me for my Greek and Hebrew; but, man, I ken that I dinnae ken them—there's the differ of it. Now, here's you. Ye lie on your wame a bittie in the bield of this wood, and ye tell me that ye've cuist off these Frasers and Macgregors. Why! *Because I couldnae see them*, says you. Ye blockhead, that's their livelihood.'

'Take the worst of it,' said I, 'and what are we to do?'

'I am thinking of that same,' said he. 'We might twine. It wouldnae be greatly to my taste; and forbye that, I see reasons against it. First, it's now unco dark, and it's just humanly possible we might give them the clean slip. If we keep together, we make but the ae line of it; if we gang separate, we make twae of them: the more likelihood to stave in upon some of these gentry of yours. And then, second, if they keep the track of us, it may come to a fecht for it yet, Davie; and then, I'll confess I would be blythe to have you at my oxter, and I think you would be none the worse of having me at yours. So, by my way of it, we should creep out of this wood no further gone than just the inside of next minute, and hold away east for Gillane, where I'm to find my ship. It'll be like old days while it lasts, Davie; and (come the time) we'll have to think what you should be doing. I'm wae to leave ye here, wanting me.'

'Have with ye, then!' says I. 'Do ye gang back where you were stopping.'

'Deil a fear!' said Alan. 'They were good folks to me, but I think they would be a good deal disappointed if they saw my bonny face again. For (the way times go) I amnae just what ye could call a Walcome Guest. Which makes me the keener for your company, Mr David Balfour of the Shaws, and set ye up! For, leave aside twa cracks here in the wood with Charlie Stewart, I have scarce said black or white since the day we parted at Corstorphine.'

With which he rose from his place, and we began to move quietly eastward through the wood.

IT WAS LIKELY between one and two; the moon (as
I have said) was down; a strongish wind, carrying a heavy
wrack of cloud, had set in suddenly from the west; and we
began our movement in as black a night as ever a fugitive
or a murderer wanted. The whiteness of the path guided
us into the sleeping town of Broughton, thence through
Picardy, and beside my old acquaintance the gibbet of the
two thieves. A little beyond we made a useful beacon, which
was a light in an upper window of Lochend. Steering by this,
but a good deal at random, and with some trampling of the
harvest, and stumbling and falling down upon the bauks,
we made our way across country, and won forth at last upon
the linky, boggy muirland that they call the Figgate Whins.
Here, under a bush of whin, we lay down the remainder of
that night and slumbered.

The day called us about five. A beautiful morning it was,
the high westerly wind still blowing strong, but the clouds
all blown away to Europe. Alan was already sitting up and
smiling to himself. It was my first sight of my friend since
we were parted, and I looked upon him with enjoyment. He
had still the same big great-coat on his back; but (what was
new) he had now a pair of knitted boot-hose drawn above
the knee. Doubtless these were intended for disguise; but as
the day promised to be warm, he made a most unseasonable
figure.

'Well, Davie,' said he, 'is this no a bonny morning? Here
is a day that looks the way that a day ought to. This is a great
change of it from the belly of my haystack; and while you
were there sottering and sleeping I have done a thing that
maybe I do over seldom.'

'And what was that?' said I.

'O, just said my prayers,' said he.

'And where are my gentry, as ye call them?' I asked.

'Gude kens,' says he; 'and the short and the long of it is that we must take our chance of them. Up with your foot-soles, Davie! Forth, Fortune, once again of it! And a bonny walk we are like to have.'

So we went east by the beach of the sea, towards where the salt-pans were smoking in by the Esk mouth. No doubt there was a by-ordinary bonny blink of morning sun on Arthur's Seat and the green Pentlands; and the pleasantness of the day appeared to set Alan among nettles.

'I feel like a gomeral,' says he, 'to be leaving Scotland on a day like this. It sticks in my head; I would maybe like it better to stay here and hing.'

'Ay, but ye wouldnae, Alan,' said I.

'No but what France is a good place too,' he explained; 'but it's some way no the same. It's brawer, I believe, but it's no Scotland. I like it fine when I'm there, man; yet I kind of weary for Scots divots and the Scots peat-reek.'

'If that's all you have to complain of, Alan, it's no such great affair,' said I.

'And it sets me ill to be complaining, whatever,' said he, 'and me but new out of yon deil's haystack.'

'And so you were unco' weary of your haystack?' I asked.

'Weary's nae word for it,' said he. 'I'm not just precisely a man that's easily cast down; but I do better with caller air and the lift above my head. I'm like the auld Black Douglas (wasnae't?) that likit better to hear the lav-erock sing than the mouse cheep. And yon place, ye see, Davie—whilk was a very suitable place to hide in, as I'm free to own—was pit mirk from dawn to gloaming. There were days (or nights, for how would I tell one from other?) that seemed to me as long as a long winter.'

'How did you know the hour to bide your tryst?' I asked.

'The goodman brought me my meat and a drop brandy, and a candle-dowp to eat it by, about eleeven,' said he. 'So, when I had swallowed a bit, it would be time to be getting to the wood. There I lay and wearied for ye sore, Davie,' says he, laying his hand on my shoulder, 'and guessed when the two hours would be about by—unless Charlie Stewart would come and tell me on his watch—and then back to

the dooms haystack. Na, it was a driech employ, and praise
the Lord that I have warstled through with it!'

'What did you do with yourself?' I asked.

'Faith,' said he, 'the best I could! Whiles I played at
the knucklebones. I'm an extraordinar good hand at the
knuckle-bones, but it's a poor piece of business playing with
naebody to admire ye. And whiles I would make songs.'

'What were they about?' says I.

'O, about the deer and the heather,' says he, 'and about
the ancient old chiefs that are all by with it long syne, and
just about what songs are about in general. And then whiles
I would make believe I had a set of pipes and I was playing.
I played some grand springs, and I thought I played them
awful bonny; I vow whiles that I could hear the squeal of
them! But the great affair is that it's done with.'

With that he carried me again to my adventures, which
he heard all over again with more particularity, and extraordinary approval, swearing at intervals that I was 'a queer
character of a callant'.

'So ye were frich'ened of Sim Fraser?' he asked once.

'In troth was I!' cried I.

'So would I have been, Davie,' said he. 'And that is indeed
a dreidful man. But it is only proper to give the deil his due;
and I can tell you he is a most respectable person on the field
of war.'

'Is he so brave?' I asked.

'Brave!' said he. 'He is as brave as my steel sword.'

The story of my duel set him beside himself.

'To think of that!' he cried. 'I showed ye the trick
in Corrynakiegh too. And three times—three times disarmed! It's a disgrace upon my character that learned ye!
Here, stand up, out with your airn; ye shall walk no step
beyond this place upon the road till ye can do yoursel' and
me mair credit.'

'Alan,' said I, 'this is midsummer madness. Here is no
time for fencing lessons.'

'I cannae well say no to that,' he admitted. 'But three
times, man! And you standing there like a straw bogle
and rinning to fetch your ain sword like a doggie with
a pocket-napkin! David, this man Duncansby must be

something altogether by-ordinar! He maun be extraordinar skilly. If I had the time, I would gang straight back and try a turn at him mysel'. The man must be a provost.'

'You silly fellow,' said I, 'you forget it was just me.'

'Na,' said he, 'but three times!'

'When ye ken yourself that I am fair incompetent,' I cried.

'Well, I never heard tell the equal of it,' said he.

'I promise you the one thing, Alan,' said I. 'The next time that we forgather, I'll be better learned. You shall not continue to bear the disgrace of a friend that cannot strike.'

'Ay, the next time!' says he. 'And when will that be, I would like to ken?'

'Well, Alan, I have had some thoughts of that, too,' said I; 'and my plan is this. It's my opinion to be called an advocate.'

'That's but a weary trade, Davie,' says Alan, 'and rather a blagyard one forbye. Ye would be better in a king's coat than that.'

'And no doubt that would be the way to have us meet,' cried I. 'But as you'll be in King Lewie's coat, and I'll be in King Geordie's, we'll have a dainty meeting of it.'

'There's some sense in that,' he admitted.

'An advocate, then, it'll have to be,' I continued, 'and I think it a more suitable trade for a gentleman that was *three times* disarmed. But the beauty of the thing is this: that one of the best colleges for that kind of learning—and the one where my kinsman, Pilrig, made his studies—is the college of Leyden in Holland. Now, what say you, Alan? Could not a cadet of *Royal Ecossais* get a furlough, slip over the marches, and call in upon a Leyden student!'

'Well, and I would think he could!' cried he. 'Ye see, I stand well in with my colonel, Count Drummond-Melfort; and, what's mair to the purpose, I have a cousin of mine lieutenant-colonel in a regiment of the Scots-Dutch. Naething could be mair proper than what I would get a leave to see Lieutenant-Colonel Stewart of Halkett's. And Lord Melfort, who is a very scienteefic kind of a man, and writes books like Cæsar, would be doubtless very pleased to have the advantage of my observes.'

'Is Lord Melfort an author, then?' I asked, for much as

Alan thought of soldiers, I thought more of the gentry that write books.

'The very same, Davie,' said he. 'One would think a colonel would have something better to attend to. But what can I say that make songs?'

'Well, then,' said I, 'it only remains you should give me an address to write you at in France; and as soon as I am got to Leyden I will send you mine.'

'The best will be to write me in the care of my chieftain,' said he, 'Charles Stewart, of Ardsheil, Esquire, at the town of Melons, in the Isle of France. It might take long, or it might take short, but it would aye get to my hands at the last of it.'

We had a haddock to our breakfast in Musselburgh, where it amused me vastly to hear Alan. His great-coat and boot-hose were extremely remarkable this warm morning, and perhaps some hint of an explanation had been wise; but Alan went into that matter like a business, or I should rather say, like a diversion. He engaged the goodwife of the house with some compliments upon the rizzoring of our haddocks; and the whole of the rest of our stay held her in talk about a cold he had taken on his stomach, gravely relating all manner of symptoms and sufferings, and hearing with a vast show of interest all the old wives' remedies she could supply him with in return.

We left Musselburgh before the first ninepenny coach was due from Edinburgh, for (as Alan said) that was a rencounter we might very well avoid. The wind, although still high, was very mild, the sun shone strong, and Alan began to suffer in proportion. From Prestonpans he had me aside to the field of Gladsmuir, where he exerted himself a great deal more than needful to describe the stages of the battle. Thence, at his old round pace, we travelled to Cockenzie. Though they were building herring-busses there at Mrs Cadell's, it seemed a desert-like, back-going town, about half full of ruined houses; but the ale-house was clean, and Alan, who was now in a glowing heat, must indulge himself with a bottle of ale, and carry on to the new luckie with the old story of the cold upon his stomach, only now the symptoms were all different.

I sat listening; and it came in my mind that I had scarce ever heard him address three serious words to any woman, but he was always drolling and fleering and making a private mock of them, and yet brought to that business a remarkable degree of energy and interest. Something to this effect I remarked to him, when the good-wife (as chanced) was called away.

'What do ye want?' says he. 'A man should aye put his best foot forrit with the womenkind; he should aye give them a bit of a story to divert them, the poor lambs! It's what ye should learn to attend to, David; ye should get the principles, it's like a trade. Now, if this had been a young lassie, or onyways bonnie, she would never have heard tell of my stomach, Davie. But aince they're too old to be seeking joes, they a' set up to be apotecaries. Why? What do I ken? They'll be just the way God made them, I suppose. But I think a man would be a gomeral that didnae give his attention to the same.'

And here, the luckie coming back, he turned from me as if with impatience to renew their former conversation. The lady had branched some while before from Alan's stomach to the case of a goodbrother of her own in Aberlady, whose last sickness and demise she was describing at extraordinary length. Sometimes it was merely dull, sometimes both dull and awful, for she talked with unction. The upshot was that I fell in a deep muse, looking forth of the window on the road, and scarce marking what I saw. Presently had any been looking they might have seen me to start.

'We pit a fomentation to his feet,' the goodwife was saying, 'and a het stane to his wame, and we gied him hyssop and water of pennyroyal, and fine, clean balsam of sulphur for the hoast. . . .'

'Sir,' says I, cutting very quietly in, 'there's a friend of mine gone by the house.'

'Is that e'en sae?' replies Alan, as though it were a thing of small account. And then, 'Ye were saying, mem?' says he; and the wearyful wife went on.

Presently, however, he paid her with a half-crown piece, and she must go forth after the change.

'Was it him with the red head?' asked Alan.

'Ye have it,' said I.

'What did I tell you in the wood?' he cried. 'And yet it's strange he should be here too! Was he his lane?'

'His lee-lane for what I could see,' said I.

'Did he gang by?' he asked.

'Straight by,' said I, 'and looked neither to the right nor left.'

'And that's queerer yet,' said Alan. 'It sticks in my mind, Davie, that we should be stirring. But where to?—deil hae't! This is like old days fairly,' cries he.

'There is one big differ, though,' said I, 'that now we have money in our pockets.'

'And another big differ, Mr Balfour,' says he, 'that now we have dogs at our tail. They're on the scent; they're in full cry, David. It's a bad business and be damned to it.' And he sat thinking hard with a look of his that I knew well.

'I'm saying, Luckie,' says he, when the goodwife returned, 'have ye a back road out of this change house?'

She told him there was and where it led to.

'Then, sir,' says he to me, 'I think that will be the shortest road for us. And here's good-bye to ye, my braw woman; and I'll no forget thon of the cinnamon water.'

We went out by way of the woman's kale yard, and up a lane among fields. Alan looked sharply to all sides, and seeing we were in a little hollow place of the country, out of view of men, sat down.

'Now for a council of war, Davie,' said he. 'But first of all, a bit lesson to ye. Suppose that I had been like you, what would yon old wife have minded of the pair of us? Just that we had gone out by the back gate. And what does she mind now? A fine, canty, friendly, cracky man, that suffered with the stomach, poor body! and was real ta'en up about the goodbrother. O man, David, try and learn to have some kind of intelligence!'

'I'll try, Alan,' said I.

'And now for him of the red head,' says he; 'was he gaun fast or slow?'

'Betwixt and between,' said I.

'No kind of a hurry about the man?' he asked.

'Never a sign of it,' said I.

'Nhm!' said Alan, 'it looks queer. We saw nothing of them this morning on the Whins; he's passed us by, he doesnae seem to be looking, and yet here he is on our road! Dod, Davie, I begin to take a notion. I think it's no you they're seeking, I think it's me; and I think they ken fine where they're gaun.'

'They ken?' I asked.

'I think Andie Scougal's sold me—him or his mate wha kent some part of the affair—or else Chairlie's clerk callant, which would be a pity too,' says Alan; 'and if you askit me for just my inward private conviction, I think there'll be heads cracked on Gillane sands.'

'Alan,' I cried, 'if you're at all right there'll be folk there and to spare. It'll be small service to crack heads.'

'It would aye be a satisfaction though,' says Alan. 'But bide a bit, bide a bit; I'm thinking—and thanks to this bonny westland wind, I believe I've still a chance of it. It's this way, Davie. I'm no trysted with this man Scougal till the gloaming comes. *But*, says he, *if I can get a bit of a wind out of the west I'll be there long or that*, he says, *and lie-to for ye behind the Isle of Fidra*. Now if your gentry kens the place, they ken the time forbye. Do ye see me coming, Davie? Thanks to Johnnie Cope and other red-coat gomerals, I should ken this country like the back of my hand; and if ye're ready for another bit run with Alan Breck, we'll can cast back inshore, and come down to the seaside again by Dirleton. If the ship's there, we'll try and get on board of her. If she's no there, I'll just have to get back to my weary hay-stack. But either way of it, I think we will leave your gentry whistling on their thumbs.'

'I believe there's some chance in it,' said I. 'Have on with ye Alan!'

I DID NOT profit by Alan's pilotage as he had done by his marchings under General Cope; for I can scarce tell what way we went. It is my excuse that we travelled exceeding fast. Some part we ran, some trotted, and the rest walked at a vengeance of a pace. Twice, while we were at top speed, we ran against country-folk; but though we plumped into the first from round a corner, Alan was as ready as a loaded musket.

'Hae ye seen my horse?' he gasped.

'Na, man, I haenae seen nae horse the day,' replied the countryman.

And Alan spared the time to explain to him that we were travelling 'ride and tie'; that our charger had escaped, and it was feared he had gone home to Linton. Not only that, but he expended some breath (of which he had not very much left) to curse his own misfortune and my stupidity which was said to be its cause.

'Them that cannae tell the truth,' he observed to myself as we went on again, 'should be aye mindful to leave an honest, handy lee behind them. If folk dinnae ken what ye're doing, Davie, they're terrible taken up with it; but if they think they ken, they care nae mair for it than what I do for pease porridge.'

As we had first made inland, so our road came in the end to lie very near due north; the old Kirk of Aberlady for a landmark on the left; on the right, the top of the Berwick Law; and it was thus we struck the shore again, not far from Dirleton. From North Berwick west to Gillane Ness there runs a string of four small islets, Craiglieth, the Lamb, Fidra, and Eyebrough, notable by their diversity of size and shape. Fidra is the most particular, being a strange grey islet of two humps, made the more conspicuous by a piece of ruin; and I mind that (as we drew closer to it) by some door or window of these ruins the sea peeped through like a man's eye. Under the lee of Fidra there is a good anchorage in westerly winds, and there, from a far way off, we could see the *Thistle* riding.

The shore in face of these islets is altogether waste. Here is no dwelling of man, and scarce any passage, or at most of vagabond children running at their play. Gillane is a small place on the far side of the Ness, the folk of Dirleton go to their business in the inland fields, and those of North Berwick straight to the sea-fishing from their haven; so that few parts of the coast are lonelier. But I mind, as we crawled upon our bellies into that multiplicity of heights and hollows, keeping a bright eye upon all sides, and our hearts hammering at our ribs, there was such a shining of the sun and the sea, such a stir of the wind in the bent grass, and such a bustle of down-popping rabbits and up-flying gulls, that the desert seemed to me like a place alive. No doubt it was in all ways well chosen for a secret embarcation, if the secret had been kept; and even now that it was out, and the place watched, we were able to creep unperceived to the front of the sandhills, where they look down immediately on the beach and sea.

But here Alan came to a full stop.

'Davie,' said he, 'this is a kittle passage! As long as we lie here we're safe; but I'm nane sae muckle nearer to my ship or the coast of France. And as soon as we stand up and signal the brig, it's another matter. For where will your gentry be, think ye?'

'Maybe they're no come yet,' said I. 'And even if they are, there's one clear matter in our favour. They'll be all arranged to take us, that's true. But they'll have arranged for our coming from the west and here we are upon their east.'[1]

'Ay,' says Alan, 'I wish we were in some force, and this was a battle, we would have bonnily out-manœuvred them! But it isnae, Davit; and the way it is, is a wee thing less inspiring to Alan Breck. I swither, Davie.'

---

[1] The first edition reads '. . . from the east and here we are upon their west' which is evidently a mistake—*Editor's Note*.

'Time flies, Alan,' said I.

'I ken that,' said Alan. 'I ken naething else, as the French folk say. But this is a dreidful case of heids or tails. O! if I could but ken where your gentry were!'

'Alan,' said I, 'this is no like you. It's got to be now or never.'

'This is no me, quo' he,'

sang Alan, with a queer face betwixt shame and drollery,

Neither you nor me, quo' he, neither you nor me,
Wow, na, Johnnie man! neither you nor me.

And then of a sudden he stood straight up where he was, and with a handkerchief flying in his right hand, marched down upon the beach. I stood up myself, but lingered behind him, scanning the sand hills to the east. His appearance was at first unremarked: Scougal not expecting him so early, and *my gentry* watching on the other side. Then they awoke on board the *Thistle*, and it seemed they had all in readiness, for there was scarce a second's bustle on the deck before we saw a skiff put round her stern and begin to pull lively for the coast. Almost at the same moment of time, and perhaps half a mile away towards Gillane Ness, the figure of a man appeared for a blink upon a sandhill, waving with his arms; and though he was gone again in the same flash, the gulls in that part continued a little longer to fly wild.

Alan had not seen this, looking straight to seaward at the ship and skiff.

'It maun be as it will!' said he, when I had told him. 'Weel may yon boatie row, or my craig'll have to thole a raxing.'

That part of the beach was long and flat, and excellent walking when the tide was down; a little cressy burn flowed over it in one place to the sea; and the sandhills ran along the head of it like the rampart of a town. No eye of ours could spy what was passing behind there in the bents, no hurry of ours could mend the speed of the boat's coming: time stood still with us through that uncanny period of waiting.

'There is one thing I would like to ken,' says Alan. 'I would like fine to ken these gentry's orders. We're worth four hunner pound the pair of us: how if they took the guns to us, Davie? They would get a bonny shot from the top of that lang sandy bauk.'

'Morally impossible,' said I. 'The point is that they can have no guns. This thing has been gone about too secret; pistols they may have, but never guns.'

'I believe ye'll be in the right,' says Alan. 'For all which I am wearying a good deal for yon boat.'

And he snapped his fingers and whistled to it like a dog.

It was now perhaps a third of the way in, and we ourselves already hard on the margin of the sea, so that the soft sand rose over my shoes. There was no more to do whatever but to wait, to look as much as we were able at the creeping nearer of the boat, and as little as we could manage at the long impenetrable front of the sandhills, over which the gulls twinkled and behind which our enemies were doubtless marshalling.

'This is a fine, bright, caller place to get shot in,' says Alan, suddenly; 'and, man, I wish that I had your courage!'

'Alan!' I cried, 'what kind of talk is this of it? You're just made of courage; it's the character of the man, as I could prove myself if there was nobody else.'

'And you would be the more mistaken,' said he. 'What makes the differ with me is just my great penetration and knowledge of affairs. But for auld, cauld, dour, deidly courage, I am not fit to hold a candle to yourself. Look at us two here upon the sands. Here am I, fair hotching to be off; here's you (for all that I ken) in two minds of it whether you'll no stop. Do you think that I could do that, or would? No me! Firstly, because I havenae got the courage and wouldnae daur; and secondly, because I am a man of so much penetration and would see ye damned first.'

'It's there ye're coming, is it?' I cried. 'Ah, man Alan, you can wile your old wives, but you never can wile me.'

Remembrance of my temptation in the wood made me strong as iron.

'I have a tryst to keep,' I continued. 'I am trysted with your cousin Charlie; I have passed my word.'

'Braw trysts that you'll can keep,' said Alan. 'Ye'll just mistryst aince and for a' with the gentry in the bents. And what for?' he went on with an extreme threatening gravity.

'Just tell me that, my mannie! Are ye to be speerited away like Lady Grange? Are they to drive a dirk in your inside and bury ye in the bents? Or is it to be the other way, and are they to bring ye in with James? Are they folk to be trustit? Would ye stick your head in the mouth of Sim Fraser and the ither Whigs?' he added with extraordinary bitterness.

'Alan,' cried I, 'they're all rogues and liars, and I'm with ye there. The more reason there should be one decent man in such a land of thieves! My word is passed, and I'll stick to it. I said long syne to your kinswoman that I would stumble at no risk. Do ye mind of that?—the night Red Colin fell, it was. No more I will, then. Here I stop. Prestongrange promised me my life; if he's to be mansworn, here I'll have to die.'

'Aweel, aweel,' said Alan.

All this time we had seen or heard no more of our pursuers. In truth we had caught them unawares; their whole party (as I was to learn afterwards) had not yet reached the scene; what there was of them was spread among the bents towards Gillane. It was quite an affair to call them in and bring them over, and the boat was making speed. They were besides but cowardly fellows: a mere leash of Highland cattle-thieves, of several clans, no gentleman there to be the captain: and the more they looked at Alan and me upon the beach, the less (I must suppose) they liked the looks of us.

Whoever had betrayed Alan it was not the captain: he was in the skiff himself, steering and stirring up his oarsmen, like a man with his heart in his employ. Already he was near in, and the boat scouring—already Alan's face had flamed crimson with the excitement of his deliverance, when our friends in the bents, either in despair to see their prey escape them or with some hope of scaring Andie, raised suddenly a shrill cry of several voices.

This sound, arising from what appeared to be a quite deserted coast, was really very daunting, and the men in the boat held water instantly.

'What's this of it?' sings out the captain; for he was come within an easy hail.

'Freens o' mine,' says Alan, and began immediately to wade forth in the shallow water towards the boat. 'Davie,' he said, pausing, 'Davie, are ye no coming? I am swier to leave ye.'

'Not a hair of me,' said I.

He stood part of a second where he was to his knees in the salt water, hesitating.

'He that will to Cupar, maun to Cupar,' said he, and swashing in deeper than his waist, was hauled into the skiff, which was immediately directed for the ship.

I stood where he had left me, with my hands behind my back; Alan sat with his head turned watching me; and the boat drew smoothly away. Of a sudden I came the nearest hand to shedding tears, and seemed to myself the most deserted, solitary lad in Scotland. With that I turned my back upon the sea and faced the sandhills. There was no sight or sound of man; the sun shone on the wet sand and the dry, the wind blew in the bents, the gulls made a dreary piping. As I passed higher up the beach, the sand-lice were hopping nimbly about the stranded tangles. The devil any other sight or sound in that unchancy place. And yet I knew there were folk there, observing me, upon some secret purpose. They were no soldiers, or they would have fallen on and taken us ere now; doubtless they were some common rogues hired for my undoing, perhaps to kidnap, perhaps to murder me outright. From the position of those engaged, the first was the more likely; from what I knew of their character and ardency in this business, I thought the second very possible; and the blood ran cold about my heart.

I had a mad idea to loosen my sword in the scabbard; for though I was very unfit to stand up like a gentleman blade to blade, I thought I could do some scathe in a random combat. But I perceived in time the folly of resistance. This was no doubt the joint 'expedient' on which Prestongrange and Fraser were agreed. The first, I was very sure, had done something to secure my life; the second was pretty likely to have slipped in some contrary hints into the ears of Neil and his companions; and if I were to show bare steel I might play straight into the hands of my worst enemy and seal my own doom.

These thoughts brought me to the head of the beach. I cast a look behind, the boat was nearing the brig, and Alan flew his handkerchief for a farewell, which I replied to with the waving of my hand. But Alan himself was shrunk to a small thing in my view, alongside of this pass that lay in front of me. I set my hat hard on my head, clenched my teeth, and went right before me up the face of the sand-wreath. It made a hard climb, being steep, and the sand like water underfoot. But I caught hold at last by the long bent-grass on the brae-top, and pulled myself to a good footing. The same moment men stirred and stood up here and there, six or seven of them, ragged-like knaves, each with a dagger in his hand. The fair truth is, I shut my eyes and prayed. When I opened them again, the rogues were crept the least thing nearer without speech or hurry. Every eye was upon mine, which struck me with a strange sensation of their brightness, and of the fear with which they continued to approach me. I held out my hands empty: whereupon one asked, with a strong Highland brogue, if I surrendered.

'Under protest,' said I, 'if ye ken what that means, which I misdoubt.'

At that word, they came all in upon me like a flight of birds upon a carrion, seized me, took my sword, and all the money from my pockets, bound me hand and foot with some strong line, and cast me on a tussock of bent. There they sat about their captive in a part of a circle and gazed upon him silently like something dangerous, perhaps a lion or a tiger on the spring. Presently this attention was relaxed. They drew nearer together, fell to speech in the Gaelic, and very cynically divided my property before my eyes. It was my diversion in this time that I could watch from my place the progress of my friend's escape. I saw the boat come to the brig and be hoisted in, the sails fill, and the ship pass out seaward behind the isles and by North Berwick.

In the course of two hours or so, more and more ragged Highlandmen kept collecting, Neil among the first, until the party must have numbered near a score. With each new arrival there was a fresh bout of talk, that sounded like complaints and explanations; but I observed one thing, none of those that came late had any share in the division of my spoils. The last discussion was very violent and eager, so that once I thought they would have quarrelled; on the heels of which their company parted, the bulk of them returning westward in a troop, and only three, Neil and two others, remaining sentries on the prisoner.

'I could name one who would be very ill pleased with your day's work, Neil Duncanson,' said I, when the rest had moved away.

He assured me in answer I should be tenderly used, for he knew he was 'acquent wi' the leddy'.

This was all our talk, nor did any other son of man appear upon that portion of the coast until the sun had gone down among the Highland mountains, and the gloaming was beginning to grow dark. At which hour I was aware of a long, lean, bony-like Lothian man of a very swarthy countenance, that came towards us among the bents on a farm horse.

'Lads,' cried he, 'hae ye a paper like this?' and held up one in his hand. Neil produced a second, which the new-comer studied through a pair of horn spectacles, and saying all was right and we were the folk he was seeking, immediately dismounted. I was then set in his place, my feet tied under the horse's belly, and we set forth under the guidance of the Lowlander. His path must have been very well chosen, for we met but one pair—a pair of lovers—the whole way, and these, perhaps taking us to be free-traders, fled on our approach. We were at one time close at the foot of Berwick Law on the south side; at another, as we passed over some open hills, I spied the lights of a clachan and the old tower of a church among some trees not far off, but too far to cry for help, if I had dreamed of it. At last we came again within sound of the sea. There was moonlight, though not much; and by this I could see the three huge towers and broken battlements of Tantallon, that old chief place of the Red Douglases. The horse was picketed in the bottom of the ditch to graze, and I was led within, and forth into the court, and thence into a tumble-down stone hall. Here my conductors built a brisk fire in the midst of the pavement, for there was a chill in the night. My hands were loosed, I was set by the wall in the inner end, and (the Lowlander having produced provisions) I was given oatmeal bread and a pitcher of French brandy. This done, I was left once more alone with my three Highlandmen. They sat close by the fire drinking and talking; the wind blew in by the breaches, cast about the smoke and flames, and sang in the tops of the towers; I could hear the sea under the cliffs, and my mind being reassured as to my life, and my body and spirits wearied with the day's employment, I turned upon one side and slumbered.

I had no means of guessing at what hour I was wakened, only the moon was down and the fire low. My feet were now loosed, and I was carried through the ruins and down the cliff-side by a precipitous path to where I found a fisher's boat in a haven of the rocks. This I was had on board of, and we began to put forth from the shore in a fine starlight.

I HAD NO thought where they were taking me; only looked here and there for the appearance of a ship; and there ran the while in my head a word of Ransome's—the *twenty-pounders*. If I were to be exposed a second time to that same former danger of the plantations, I judged it must turn ill with me; there was no second Alan, and no second shipwreck and spare yard to be expected now; and I saw myself hoe tobacco under the whip's lash. The thought chilled me; the air was sharp upon the water, the stretchers of the boat drenched with a cold dew; and I shivered in my place beside the steersman. This was the dark man whom I have called hitherto the Lowlander; his name was Dale, ordinarily called Black Andie. Feeling the thrill of my shiver, he very kindly handed me a rough jacket full of fish-scales, with which I was glad to cover myself.

'I thank you for this kindness,' said I, 'and will make so free as to repay it with a warning. You take a high responsibility in this affair. You are not like these ignorant, barbarous Highlanders, but know what the law is and the risks of those that break it.'

'I am no just exactly what ye would ca' an extremist for the law,' says he, 'at the best of times; but in this business I act with a good warranty.'

'What are you going to do with me?' I asked.

'Nae harm,' said he, 'nae harm ava'. Ye'll hae strong freens, I'm thinking. Ye'll be richt eneuch yet.'

There began to fall a greyness on the face of the sea; little dabs of pink and red, like coals of slow fire, came in the east; and at the same time the geese awakened, and began crying about the top of the Bass. It is just the one crag of rock, as everybody knows, but great enough to carve a city from. The sea was extremely little, but there went a hollow plowter round the base of it. With the growing of the dawn I could see it clearer and clearer; the straight crags painted with sea-birds' droppings like a morning frost, the sloping top of it green with grass, the clan of white geese that cried about the sides, and the black, broken buildings of the prison sitting close on the sea's edge.

At the sight the truth came in upon me in a clap.

'It's there you're taking me!' I cried.

'Just to the Bass, mannie,' said he: 'Whaur the auld sants were afore ye, and I misdoubt if ye have come so fairly by your preeson.'

'But none dwells there now,' I cried; 'the place is long a ruin.'

'It'll be the mair pleisand a change for the solan geese, then,' quoth Andie dryly.

The day coming slowly brighter I observed on the bilge, among the big stones with which fisherfolk ballast their boats, several kegs and baskets, and a provision of fuel. All these were discharged upon the crag. Andie, myself, and my three Highlanders (I call them mine, although it was the other way about), landed along with them. The sun was not yet up when the boat moved away again, the noise of the oars on the tholepins echoing from the cliffs, and left us in our singular reclusion.

Andie Dale was the Prefect (as I would jocularly call him) of the Bass, being at once the shepherd and the gamekeeper of that small and rich estate. He had to mind the dozen or so of sheep that fed and fattened on the grass of the sloping part of it, like beasts grazing the roof of a cathedral. He had charge besides of the solan geese that roosted in the crags; and from these an extraordinary income is derived. The young are dainty eating, as much as two shillings a-piece being a common price, and paid willingly by epicures; even the grown birds are valuable for their oil and feathers; and a part of the minister's stipend of North Berwick is paid to this day in solan geese, which makes it (in some folks' eyes) a parish to be coveted. To perform these several businesses, as well as to protect the geese from poachers, Andie had frequent occasion to sleep and pass days together on the crag; and we found the man at home there like a farmer in his steading. Bidding us all shoulder some of the packages, a matter in which I made haste to bear a hand, he led us in by a locked gate, which was the only admission to the island, and through the ruins of the fortress, to the governor's house. There we saw, by the ashes in the chimney and a standing bed-place in one corner, that he made his usual occupation.

This bed he now offered me to use, saying he supposed I would set up to be gentry.

'My gentrice has nothing to do with where I lie,' said I. 'I bless God I have lain hard ere now, and can do the same again with thankfulness. While I am here, Mr Andie, if that be your name, I will do my part and take my place beside the rest of you; and I ask you on the other hand to spare me your mockery, which I own I like ill.'

He grumbled a little at this speech, but seemed upon reflection to approve it. Indeed, he was a long-headed, sensible man, and a good Whig and Presbyterian; read daily in a pocket Bible, and was both able and eager to converse seriously on religion, leaning more than a little towards the Cameronian extremes. His morals were of a more doubtful colour. I found he was deep in the free trade, and used the ruins of Tantallon for a magazine of smuggled merchandise. As for a gauger, I do not believe he valued the life of one at half-a-farthing. But that part of the coast of Lothian is to this day as wild a place, and the commons there as rough a crew, as any in Scotland.

One incident of my imprisonment is made memorable by a consequence it had long after. There was a warship at this time stationed in the Firth, the *Seahorse*, Captain Palliser. It chanced she was cruising in the month of September, plying between Fife and Lothian, and sounding for sunk dangers. Early one fine morning she was seen about two miles to east of us, where she lowered a boat, and seemed to examine the Wildfire Rocks and Satan's Bush, famous dangers of that coast. And presently after having got her boat again, she came before the wind and was headed directly for the Bass. This was very troublesome to Andie and the Highlanders; the whole business of my sequestration was designed for privacy, and here, with a navy captain perhaps blundering ashore, it looked to become public enough, if it were nothing worse. I was in a minority of one, I am no Alan to fall upon so many, and I was far from sure that a warship was the least likely to improve my condition. All which considered, I gave Andie my parole of good behaviour and obedience, and was had briskly to the summit of the rock, where we all lay down, at the cliff's edge, in different places of observation and concealment. The *Seahorse* came straight on till I thought she would have struck, and we (looking giddily down) could see the ship's company at their quarters and hear the leadsman singing at the lead. Then she suddenly wore and let fly a volley of I know not how many great guns. The rock was shaken with the thunder of the sound, the smoke flowed over our heads, and the geese rose in number beyond computation or belief. To hear their screaming and to see the twinkling of their wings, made a most inimitable curiosity; and I suppose it was after this somewhat childish pleasure that Captain Palliser had come so near the Bass. He was to pay dear for it in time. During his approach I had the opportunity to make a remark upon the rigging of that ship by which I ever after knew it miles away; and this was a means (under Providence) of my averting from a friend a great calamity, and inflicting on Captain Palliser himself a sensible disappointment.

All the time of my stay on the rock we lived well. We had small ale and brandy, and oatmeal of which we made our porridge night and morning. At times a boat came from the Castleton and brought us a quarter of mutton, for the sheep upon the rock we must not touch, these being specially fed to market. The geese were unfortunately out of season, and we let them be. We fished ourselves, and yet more often made the geese to fish for us: observing one when he had made a capture and scaring him from his prey ere he had swallowed it.

The strange nature of this place, and the curiosities with which it abounded, held me busy and amused. Escape being impossible, I was allowed my entire liberty, and continually explored the surface of the isle wherever it might support the foot of man. The old garden of the prison was still to be observed, with flowers and pot-herbs running wild, and some ripe cherries on a bush. A little lower stood a chapel or a hermit's cell; who built or dwelt in it, none may know, and the thought of its age made a ground of many meditations. The prison too, where I now bivouacked with Highland cattle-thieves, was a place full of history, both human and divine. I thought it strange so many saints and martyrs should have gone by there so recently, and left not so much as a leaf out of their Bibles, or a name carved upon the wall, while the rough soldier lads that mounted guard upon the battlements had filled the neighbourhood with their mementoes—broken tobacco-pipes for the most part, and that in a surprising plenty, but also metal buttons from their coats. There were times when I thought I could have heard the pious sound of psalms out of the martyrs' dungeons, and seen the soldiers tramp the ramparts with their glinting pipes, and the dawn rising behind them out of the North Sea.

No doubt it was a good deal Andie and his tales that put these fancies in my head. He was extraordinary well acquainted with the story of the rock in all particulars, down to the names of private soldiers, his father having served there in that same capacity. He was gifted besides with a natural genius for narration, so that the people seemed to speak and the things to be done before your face. This gift of his and my assiduity to listen brought us the more close together. I could not honestly deny but what I liked him; I soon saw that he liked me; and indeed, from the first I had set myself out to capture his good will. An odd circumstance (to be told presently) effected this beyond my expectation; but even in early days we made a friendly pair to be a prisoner and his gaoler.

I should trifle with my conscience if I pretended my stay upon the Bass was wholly disagreeable. It seemed to me a safe place, as though I was escaped there out of my troubles. No harm was to be offered me; a material impossibility, rock and the deep sea, prevented me from fresh attempts; I felt I had my life safe and my honour safe, and there were times when I allowed myself to gloat on them like stolen waters. At other times my thoughts were very different. I recalled how strong I had expressed myself both to Rankeillor and to Stewart; I reflected that my captivity upon the Bass, in view of a great part of the coasts of Fife and Lothian, was a thing I should be thought more likely to have invented than endured; and in the eyes of these two gentlemen, at least, I must pass for a boaster and a coward. Now I would take this lightly enough; tell myself that so long as I stood well with Catriona Drummond, the opinion of the rest of man was but moonshine and spilled water; and thence pass off into those meditations of a lover which are so delightful to himself and must always appear so surprisingly idle to a reader. But anon the fear would take me otherwise; I would be shaken with a perfect panic of self-esteem, and these supposed hard judgments appear an injustice impossible to be supported. With that another train of thought would be presented, and I had scarce begun to be concerned about men's judgments of myself, than I was haunted with the remembrance of James Stewart in his dungeon and the lamentations of his wife. Then, indeed, passion began to work in me; I could not forgive myself to sit there idle; it seemed (if I were a man at all) that I could fly or swim out of my place of safety; and it was in such humours and to amuse my self-reproaches that I would set the more particularly to win the good side of Andie Dale.

At last, when we two were alone on the summit of the rock on a bright morning, I put in some hint about a bribe. He looked at me, cast back his head, and laughed out loud.

'Ay, you're funny, Mr Dale,' said I, 'but perhaps if you'll glance an eye upon that paper you may change your note.'

The stupid Highlanders had taken from me at the time of my seizure nothing but hard money, and the paper I now showed Andie was an acknowledgment from the British Linen Company for a considerable sum.

He read it. 'Troth, and ye're nane sae ill aff,' said he.

'I thought that would maybe vary your opinions,' said I.

'Hout!' said he. 'It shows me ye can bribe; but I'm no to be bribit.'

'We'll see about that yet a while,' says I. 'And first, I'll show you that I know what I am talking. You have orders to detain me here till after Thursday, 21st September.'

'Ye're no a'thegether wrong either,' says Andie. 'I'm to let ye gang, bar orders contrair, on Saturday, the 23rd.'

I could not but feel there was something extremely insidious in this arrangement. That I was to reappear precisely
in time to be too late would cast the more discredit on my
tale, if I were minded to tell one; and this screwed me to
fighting point.

'Now then, Andie, you that kens the world, listen to me,
and think while ye listen,' said I. 'I know there are great folks
in the business, and I make no doubt you have their names
to go upon. I have seen some of them myself since this affair
began, and said my say into their faces too. But what kind of
a crime would this be that I had committed? or what kind of
a process is this that I am fallen under? To be apprehended
by some ragged John-Hielandmen on August 30th, carried
to a rickle of old stones that is now neither fort nor gaol
(whatever it once was) but just the gamekeeper's lodge
of the Bass Rock, and set free again, September 23rd, as
secretly as I was first arrested—does that sound like law
to you? or does it sound like justice? or does it not sound
honestly like a piece of some low dirty intrigue, of which the
very folk that meddle with it are ashamed?'

'I canna gainsay ye, Shaws. It looks unco underhand,'
says Andie. 'And werenae the folk guid sound Whigs and
true-blue Presbyterians I would hae seen them ayont Jordan
and Jeroozlem or I would have set hand to it.'

'The Master of Lovat'll be a braw Whig,' says I, 'and a
grand Presbyterian.'

'I ken naething by him,' said he. 'I hae nae trokings wi'
Lovats.'

'No, it'll be Prestongrange that you'll be dealing with,'
said I.

'Ah, but I'll no tell ye that,' said Andie.

'Little need when I ken,' was my retort.

'There's just the ae thing ye can be fairly sure of, Shaws,'
says Andie. 'And that is that (try as ye please) I'm no
dealing wi' yoursel'; nor yet I amnae goin' to,' he added.

'Well, Andie, I see I'll have to be speak out plain with
you,' I replied. And I told him so much as I thought needful
of the facts.

He heard me out with serious interest, and when I had
done, seemed to consider a little with himself.

'Shaws,' said he at last, 'I'll deal with the naked hand. It's a queer tale, and no very creditable, the way you tell it; and I'm far frae minting that is other than the way that ye believe it. As for yoursel', ye seem to me rather a dacent-like young man. But me, that's aulder and mair judeecious, see perhaps a wee bit further forrit in the job than what ye can dae. And here is the maitter clear and plain to ye. There'll be nae skaith to yoursel' if I keep ye here; far frae that, I think ye'll be a hantle better by it. There'll be nae skaith to the kintry—just ae mair Hielantman hangit—Gude kens, a guid riddance! On the ither hand, it would be considerable skaith to me if I would let you free. Sae, speakin as a guid Whig, an honest freen' to you, and an anxious freen' to my ainsel', the plain fact is that I think ye'll just have to bide here wi' Andie an' the solans.'

'Andie,' said I, laying my hand upon his knee, 'this Hielantman's innocent.'

'Ay, it's a peety about that,' said he. 'But ye see, in this warld, the way God made it, we cannae just get a'thing that we want.'

I HAVE YET said little of the Highlanders. They were all three of the followers of James More, which bound the accusation very tight about their master's neck. All understood a word or two of English; but Neil was the only one who judged he had enough of it for general converse, in which (when once he got embarked) his company was often tempted to the contrary opinion. They were tractable, simple creatures; showed much more courtesy than might have been expected from their raggedness and their uncouth appearance, and fell spontaneously to be like three servants for Andie and myself.

Dwelling in that isolated place, in the old falling ruins of a prison, and among endless strange sounds of the sea and the sea-birds, I thought I perceived in them early the effects of superstitious fear. When there was nothing doing they would either lie and sleep, for which their appetite appeared insatiable, or Neil would entertain the others with stories which seemed always of a terrifying strain. If neither of these delights were within reach—if perhaps two were sleeping and the third could find no means to follow their example—I would see him sit and listen and look about him in a progression of uneasiness, starting, his face blenching, his hands clutched, a man strung like a bow. The nature of these fears I had never an occasion to find out, but the sight of them was catching, and the nature of the place that we were in favourable to alarms. I can find no word for it in the English, but Andie had an expression for it in the Scots from which he never varied.

'Ay,' he would say, '*it's an unco place, the Bass.*'

It is so I always think of it. It was an unco place by night, unco by day; and these were unco sounds, of the calling of the solans, and the plash of the sea and the rock

echoes, that hung continually in our ears. It was chiefly so
in moderate weather. When the waves were anyway great
they roared about the rock like thunder and the drums of
armies, dreadful but merry to hear; and it was in the calm
days that a man could daunt himself with listening—not
a Highlandman only, as I several times experimented on
myself, so many still, hollow noises haunted and reverber-
ated in the porches of the rock.

This brings me to a story I heard, and a scene I took part
in, which quite changed our terms of living, and had a great
effect on my departure. It chanced one night I fell in a muse
beside the fire and (that little air of Alan's coming back to
my memory) began to whistle. A hand was laid upon my
arm, and the voice of Neil bade me to stop, for it was not
'canny musics'.

'Not canny?' I asked. 'How can that be?'

'Na,' said he; 'it will be made by a bogle and her wanting
ta heid upon his body.'*

'Well,' said I, 'there can be no bogles here, Neil; for
it's not likely they would fash themselves to frighten solan
geese.'

'Ay?' says Andie, 'is that what ye think of it? But I'll
can tell ye there's been waur nor bogles here.'

'What's waur than bogles, Andie?' said I.

'Warlocks,' said he. 'Or a warlock at the least of it. And
that's a queer tale, too,' he added. 'And if ye would like,
I'll tell it ye.'

To be sure we were all of the one mind, and even the
Highlander that had the least English of the three set himself
to listen with all his might.

THE TALE OF TOD LAPRAIK

My faither, Tam Dale, peace to his banes, was a wild,
sploring lad in his young days, wi' little wisdom and less

---

* A learned folklorist of my acquaintance hereby identifies Alan's
air. It has been printed (it seems) in Campbell's *Tales of the West
Highlands*, vol. 11, p.91. Upon examination it would really seem
as if Miss Grant's unrhymed doggrel (see chapter 5) would fit
with a little humouring to the notes in question.

grace. He was fond of a lass and fond of a glass, and fond of a ran-dan; but I could never hear tell that he was muckle use for honest employment. Frae ae thing to anither, he listed at last for a sodger and was in the garrison of this fort, which was the first way that ony of the Dales cam to set foot upon the Bass. Sorrow upon that service! The governor brewed his ain ale; it seems it was the warst conceivable. The rock was proveesioned frae the shore with vivers, the thing was ill-guided, and there were whiles when they but to fish and shoot solans for their diet. To crown a', thir was the Days of the Persecution. The perishin' cauld chalmers were all occupeed wi' sants and martyrs, the saut of the yearth, of which it wasnae worthy. And though Tam Dale carried a firelock there, a single sodger, and liked a lass and a glass, as I was sayin', the mind of the man was mair just than set with his position. He had glints of the glory of the kirk; there were whiles when his dander rase to see the Lord's sants misguided, and shame covered him that he should be haulding a can'le (or carrying a firelock) in so black a business. There were nights of it when he was here on sentry, the place a' wheesht, the frosts o' winter maybe riving in the wa's, and he would hear ane o' the prisoners strike up a psalm, and the rest join in, and the blessed sounds rising from the different chalmers—or dungeons, I would raither say—so that this auld craig in the sea was like a pairt of Heev'n. Black shame was on his saul; his sins hove up before him muckle as the Bass, and above a', that chief sin, that he should have a hand in hagging and hashing at Christ's Kirk. But the truth is that he resisted the spirit. Day cam, there were the rousing compainions, and his guid resolves depairtit.

In thir days, dwalled upon the Bass a man of God, Peden the Prophet was his name. Ye'll have heard tell of Prophet Peden. There was never the wale of him sinsyne, and it's a question wi' mony if there ever was his like afore. He was wild's a peat-hag, fearsome to look at, fearsome to hear, his face like the day of judgment. The voice of him was like a solan's and dinnle'd in folks' lugs, and the words of him like coals of fire.

Now there was a lass on the rock, and I think she had

little to do, for it was nae place far dacent weemen; but it seems she was bonny, and her and Tam Dale were very well agreed. It befell that Peden was in the gairden his lane at the praying when Tam and the lass cam by; and what should the lassie do but mock with laughter at the sant's devotions? He rose and lookit at the twa o' them, and Tam's knees knoitered thegether at the look of him. But whan he spak, it was mair in sorrow than in anger. 'Poor thing, poor thing!' says he, and it was the lass he lookit at, 'I hear you skirl and laugh,' he says, 'but the Lord has a deid shot prepared for you, and at that surprising judgment ye shall skirl but the ae time!' Shortly thereafter she was daundering on the craigs wi' twa-three sodgers, and it was a blawy day. There cam a gowst of wind, claught her by the coats, and awa' wi' her bag and baggage. And it was remarked by the sodgers that she gied but the ae skirl.

Nae doubt this judgment had some weicht upon Tam Dale; but it passed again and him none the better. Ae day he was flyting wi' anither sodger-lad. 'Deil hae me!' quo' Tam, for he was a profane swearer. And there was Peden glowering at him, gash an' waefu'; Peden wi' his lang chafts an' luntin' een, the maud happed about his kist, and the hand of him held out wi' the black nails upon the finger-nebs—for he had nae care of the body. 'Fy, fy, poor man!' cries he, 'the poor fool man! *Deil hae me*, quo' he; an' I see the deil at his oxter.' The conviction of guilt and grace cam in on Tam like the deep sea; he flang doun the pike that was in his hands—'I will nae mair lift arms against the cause o' Christ!' says he, and was as gude's word. There was a sair fyke in the beginning, but the governor, seeing him resolved, gied him his dischairge, and he went and dwallt and married in North Berwick, and had aye a gude name with honest folk frae that day on.

It was in the year seeventeen hunner and sax that the Bass cam in the hands o' the Da'rymples, and there was twa men soucht the chairge of it. Baith were weel qualified, for they had baith been sodgers in the garrison, and kent the gate to handle solans, and the seasons and values of them. Forbye that they were baith—or they baith seemed—earnest professors and men of comely conversation. The first of them was just Tam Dale, my faither. The second was ane Lapraik, whom the folk ca'd Tod Lapraik maistly, but whether for his name or his nature I could never hear tell. Weel, Tam gaed to see Lapraik upon this business, and took me, that was a toddlin' laddie, by the hand. Tod had his dwallin' in the lang loan benorth the kirkyaird. It's a dark uncanny loan, forbye that the kirk has aye had an ill name since the days o' James the Saxt and the deevil's cantrips played therein when the Queen was on the seas; and as for Tod's house, it was in the mirkest end, and was little liked by some that kenned the best. The door was on the sneck that day, and me and my faither gaed straucht in. Tod was a wabster to his trade; his loom stood in the but. There he sat, a muckle fat, white hash of a man like creish, wi' a kind of a holy smile that gart me scunner. The hand of him aye cawed the shuttle, but his een was steeked. We cried to him by his name, we skirled in the deid lug of him, we shook him by the shou'ther. Nae mainner o' service! There he sat on his dowp, an' cawed the shuttle and smiled like creish.

'God be guid to us,' says Tam Dale, 'this is no canny!'

He had jimp said the word, when Tod Lapraik cam to himsel'.

'Is this you, Tam?' says he. 'Haith, man! I'm blythe to see ye. I whiles fa' into a bit dwam like this,' he says; 'it's frae the stamach.'

Weel, they began to crack about the Bass and which of them twa was to get the warding o't, and by little and little cam to very ill words, and twined in anger. I mind weel, that as my faither and me gaed hame again, he cam ower and ower the same expression, how little he likit Tod Lapraik and his dwams.

'Dwam!' says he. 'I think folk hae brunt far dwams like yon.'

Aweel, my faither got the Bass and Tod had to go wantin'. It was remembered sinsyne what way he had ta'en the thing. 'Tam,' says he, 'ye hae gotten the better o' me aince mair, and I hope,' says he, 'ye'll find at least a' that ye expeckit at the Bass.' Which have since been thought remarkable expressions. At last the time came for Tam Dale to take young solans. This was a business he was weel used wi', he had been a craigsman frae a laddie, and trustit nane but himsel'. So there was he hingin' by a line an' speldering on the craig face, whaur it's hieest and steighest. Fower tenty lads were on the tap, hauldin' the line and mindin' for his signals. But whaur Tam hung there was naething but the craig, and the sea belaw, and the solans skirling and flying. It was a braw spring morn, and Tam whustled as he claught in the young geese. Mony's the time I heard him tell of this experience, and aye the swat ran upon the man.

It chanced, ye see, that Tam keeked up, and he was awaur of a muckle solan, and the solan pyking at the line. He thocht this by-ordinar and outside the creature's habits. He minded that ropes was unco saft things, and the solan's neb and the Bass Rock unco hard, and that twa hunner feet were raither mair than he would care to fa'.

'Shoo!' says Tam. 'Awa', bird! Shoo, awa' wi' ye!' says he.

The solan keekit doun into Tam's face, and there was something unco in the creature's ee. Just the ae keek it gied, and back to the rope. But now it wroucht and warstl't like a thing dementit. There never was the solan made that wroucht as that solan wroucht; and it seemed to understand its employ brawly, birzing the saft rope between the neb of it and a crunkled jag o' stane.

There gaed a cauld stend o' fear into Tam's heart. 'This thing is nae bird,' thinks he. His een turnt backward in his heid and the day gaed black about him. 'If I get a dwam here,' he thocht, 'it's by wi' Tam Dale.' And he signalled for the lads to pu' him up.

And it seemed the solan understood about signals. For nae sooner was the signal made than he let be the rope, spried his wings, squawked out loud, took a turn flying, and dashed straucht at Tam Dale's een. Tam had a knife, he gart the cauld steel glitter. And it seemed the solan understood about knives, for nae suner did the steel glint in the sun than he gied the ae squawk, but laigher, like a body disappointit, and flegged aff about the roundness of the craig, and Tam saw him nae mair. And as sune as that thing was gane, Tam's heid drapt upon his shouther, and they pu'd him up like a deid corp, dadding on the craig.

A dram of brandy (which he went never without) broucht him to his mind, or what was left of it. Up he sat.

'Rin, Geordie, rin to the boat, mak' sure of the boat, man—rin!' he cries, 'or yon solan'll have it awa',' says he.

The fower lads stared at ither, an' tried to whillywha him to be quiet. But naething would satisfy Tam Dale, till ane o' them had startit on aheid to stand sentry on the boat. The ithers askit if he was for down again.

'Na,' says he, 'and niether you nor me,' says he, 'and as sune as I can win to stand on my twa feet we'll be aff frae this craig o' Sawtan.'

Sure eneuch, nae time was lost, and that was ower muckle; for before they won to North Berwick Tam was in a crying fever. He lay a' the simmer; and wha was sae kind as come speiring for him, but Tod Lapraik! Folk thocht afterwards that ilka time Tod cam near the house the fever had worsened. I kenna for that; but what I ken the best, that was the end of it.

It was about this time o' the year; my grandfaither was out at the white fishing; and like a bairn, I but to gang wi' him. We had a grand take, I mind, and the way that the fish lay broucht us near in by the Bass, whaur we forgaithered wi' anither boat that belanged to a man Sandie Fletcher in Castleton. He's no lang deid neither, or ye could speir at himsel'. Weel, Sandie hailed.

'What's yon on the Bass?' says he.

'On the Bass?' says grandfaither.

'Ay,' says Sandie, 'on the green side o't.'

'Whatten kind of a thing?' says grandfaither. 'There cannae be naething on the Bass but just the sheep.'

'It looks unco like a body,' quo' Sandie, who was nearer in.

'A body!' says we, and we nane of us likit that. For there was nae boat that could have broucht a man, and the key o' the prison yett hung ower my faither's heid at hame in the press bed.

We keepit the twa boats closs for company, and crap in nearer hand. Grandfaither had a gless, for he had been a sailor, and the captain of a smack, and had lost her on the sands of Tay. And when we took the gless to it, sure eneuch

there was a man. He was in a crunkle o' green brae, a wee
below the chaipel, a' by his lee lane, and lowped and flang
and danced like a daft quean at a waddin'.

'It's Tod,' says grandfaither, and passed the gless to
Sandie.

'Ay, it's him,' says Sandie.

'Or ane in the likeness o' him,' says grandfaither.

'Sma' is the differ,' quo' Sandie. 'De'il or warlock, I'll try
the gun at him,' quo' he, and broucht up a fowling-piece
that he aye carried, for Sandie was a notable famous shot
in all that country.

'Haud your hand, Sandie,' says grandfaither; 'we maun
see clearer first,' says he, 'or this may be a dear day's wark
to the baith of us.'

'Hout!' says Sandie, 'this is the Lord's judgments surely,
and be damned to it!' says he.

'Maybe ay, and maybe no,' says my grandfaither, worthy
man! 'But have you a mind of the Procurator Fiscal, that
I think ye'll have forgaithered wi' before,' says he.

This was ower true, and Sandie was a wee thing set ajee.
'Aweel, Edie,' says he, 'and what would be your way of it?'

'Ou, just this,' says grandfaither. 'Let me that has the
fastest boat gang back to North Berwick, and let you bide
here and keep an eye on Thon. If I cannae find Lapraik,
I'll join ye and the twa of us'll have a crack wi' him. But if
Lapraik's at hame, I'll rin up the flag at the harbour, and
ye can try Thon Thing wi' the gun.'

Aweel, so it was agreed between them twa. I was just a
bairn, an' clum in Sandie's boat, whaur I thoucht I would
see the best of the employ. My grandsire gied Sandie a siller
tester to pit in his gun wi' the leid draps, bein' mair deidly
again bogles. And then the ae boat set aff for North Berwick,
an' the tither lay whaur it was and watched the wanchancy
thing on the brae-side.

A' the time we lay there it lowped and flang and capered
and span like a teetotum, and whiles we could hear it skelloch
as it span. I hae seen lassies, the daft queans, that would lowp
and dance a winter's nicht, and still be lowping and dancing
when the winter's day cam in. But there would be folk there
to hauld them company, and the lads to egg them on; and

this thing was its lee-lane. And there would be a fiddler diddling his elbock in the chimney-side; and this thing had nae music but the skirling of the solans. And the lassies were bits o' young things wi' the reid life dinnling and stending in their members; and this was a muckle, fat, crieshy man, and him fa'n in the vale o' years. Say what ye like, I maun say what I believe. It was joy was in the creature's heart; the joy o' hell, I daursay: joy whatever. Mony a time I have askit mysel', why witches and warlocks should sell their sauls (whilk are their maist dear possessions) and be auld, duddy, wrunkl't wives or auld, feckless, doddered men; and then I mind upon Tod Lapraik dancing a' they hours by his lane in the black glory of his heart. Nae doubt they burn for it in muckle hell, but they have a grand time here of it, whatever!—and the Lord forgie us!

Weel, at the hinder end, we saw the wee flag yirk up to the mast-heid upon the harbour rocks. That was a' Sandie waited for. He up wi' the gun, took a deleeberate aim, an' pu'd the trigger. There cam' a bang and then ae waefu' skirl frae the Bass. And there were we rubbin' our een and lookin' at ither like daft folk. For wi' the bang and the skirl the thing had clean disappeared. The sun glintit, the wund blew, and there was the bare yaird whaur the Wonder had been lowping and flinging but ae second syne.

The hale way hame I roared and grat wi' the terror of that dispensation. The grawn folk were nane sae muckle better; there was little said in Sandie's boat but just the name of God; and when we won in by the pier, the harbour rocks were fair black wi' the folk waitin' us. It seems they had fund Lapraik in ane of his dwams, cawing the shuttle and smiling. Ae lad they sent to hoist the flag, and the rest abode there in the wabster's house. You may be sure they liked it little; but it was a means of grace to severals that stood there praying in to themsel's (for nane cared to pray out loud) and looking on thon awesome thing as it cawed the shuttle. Syne, upon a suddenty, and wi' the ae dreidfu' skelloch, Tod sprang up frae his hinderlands and fell forrit on the wab, a bluidy corp.

When the corp was examined the leid draps hadnae played buff upon the warlock's body; sorrow a leid drap was to be fund; but there was grandfaither's siller tester in the puddock's heart of him.

Andie had scarce done when there befell a mighty silly affair that had its consequence. Neil, as I have said, was himself a great narrator. I have heard since that he knew all the stories in the Highlands; and thought much of himself, and was thought much of by others, on the strength of it. Now Andie's tale reminded him of one he had already heard.

'She would ken that story afore,' he said. 'She was the story of Uistean More M'Gillie Phadrig and the Gavar Vore.'

'It is no sic a thing,' cried Andie. 'It is the story of my faither (now wi' God) and Tod Lapraik. And the same in your beard,' says he; 'and keep the tongue of ye inside your Hielant chafts!'

In dealing with Highlanders it will be found, and has been shown in history, how well it goes with Lowland gentlefolk; but the thing appears scarce feasible for Lowland commons. I had already remarked that Andie was continually on the point of quarrelling with our three Macgregors, and now, sure enough, it was to come.

'Thir will be no words to use to shentlemans,' says Neil.

'Shentlemans!' cries Andie. 'Shentlemans, ye hielant stot! If God would give ye the grace to see yoursel' the way that ithers see ye, ye would throw your denner up.'

There came some kind of a Gaelic oath from Neil, and the black knife was in his hand that moment.

There was no time to think; and I caught the Highlander by the leg, and had him down, and his armed hand pinned out, before I knew what I was doing. His comrades sprang to rescue him, Andie and I were without weapons, the Gregara three to two. It seemed we were beyond salvation, when Neil screamed in his own tongue, ordering the others back, and made his submission to myself in a manner the most abject, even giving me up his knife which (upon a repetition of his promises) I returned to him on the morrow.

Two things I saw plain: the first, that I must not build too high on Andie, who had shrunk against the wall and stood there, as pale as death, till the affair was over; the second, the strength of my own position with the High-landers, who must have received extraordinary charges to be tender of my safety. But if I thought Andie came not very well out in courage, I had no fault to find with him upon the account of gratitude. It was not so much that he troubled me with thanks, as that his whole mind and manner appeared changed; and as he preserved ever after a great timidity of our companions, he and I were yet more constantly together.

ON THE SEVENTEENTH, the day I was trysted with the Writer, I had much rebellion against fate. The thought of him waiting in the *King's Arms*, and of what he would think, and what he would say when next we met, tormented and oppressed me. The truth was unbelievable, so much I had to grant, and it seemed cruel hard I should be posted as a liar and a coward, and have never consciously omitted what it was possible that I should do. I repeated this form of words with a kind of bitter relish, and re-examined in that light the steps of my behaviour. It seemed I had behaved to James Stewart as a brother might; all the past was a picture that I could be proud of, and there was only the present to consider. I could not swim the sea, nor yet fly in the air, but there was always Andie. I had done him a service, he liked me; I had a lever there to work on; if it were just for decency, I must try once more with Andie.

It was late afternoon; there was no sound in all the Bass but the lap and bubble of a very quiet sea; and my four companions were all crept apart, the three Macgregors higher on the rock, and Andie with his Bible to a sunny place among the ruins; there I found him in deep sleep, and, as soon as he was awake, appealed to him with some fervour of manner and a good show of argument.

'If I thoucht it was to do guid to ye, Shaws!' said he, staring at me over his spectacles.

'It's to save another,' said I, 'and to redeem my word. What would be more good than that? Do ye no mind the scripture, Andie? And you with the Book upon your lap! *What shall it profit a man if he gain the whole world?*'

'Ay,' said he, 'that's grand for you. But where do I come in? I have my word to redeem the same's yoursel'. And what are ye asking me to do, but just to sell it ye for siller?'

'Andie! have I named the name of siller?' cried I.

'Ou, the name's naething,' said he; 'the thing is there, whatever. It just comes to this; if I am to service ye the way that you propose, I'll lose my lifelihood. Then it's clear ye'll have to make it up to me, and a pickle mair, for your ain credit like. And what's that but just a bribe? And if even I was certain of the bribe! But by a' that I can learn, it's far frae that; and if *you* were to hang, where would *I* be? Na: the thing's no possible. And just awa' wi' ye like a bonny lad! and let Andie read his chapter.'

I remember I was at bottom a good deal gratified with this result; and the next humour I fell into was one (I had near said) of gratitude to Prestongrange, who had saved me, in this violent, illegal manner, out of the midst of my dangers, temptations, and perplexities. But this was both too flimsy and too cowardly to last me long, and the remembrance of James began to succeed to the possession of my spirits. The 21st, the day set for the trial, I passed in such misery of mind as I can scarce recall to have endured, save perhaps upon Isle Earraid only. Much of the time I lay on a brae-side betwixt sleep and waking, my body motionless, my mind full of violent thoughts. Sometimes I slept indeed; but the court-house of Inverary and the prisoner glancing on all sides to find his missing witness, followed me in slumber; and I would wake again with a start to darkness of spirit and distress of body. I thought Andie seemed to observe me, but I paid him little heed. Verily, my bread was bitter to me, and my days a burthen.

Early the next morning (Friday, 22nd) a boat came with provisions, and Andie placed a packet in my hand. The cover was without address but sealed with a Government seal. It enclosed two notes. 'Mr Balfour can now see for himself it is too late to meddle. His conduct will be observed and his discretion rewarded.' So ran the first, which seemed to be laboriously writ with the left hand. There was certainly nothing in these expressions to compromise the writer, even if that person could be found; the seal, which formidably served instead of signature, was affixed to a separate sheet on which there was no scratch of writing; and I had to confess that (so far) my adversaries knew what they were doing, and to digest as well as I was able the threat that peeped under the promise.

But the second enclosure was by far the more surprising. It was in a lady's hand of writ. '*Maister Dauvit Balfour is informed a friend was speiring for him, and her eyes were of the grey,*' it ran—and seemed so extraordinary a piece to come to my hands at such a moment and under cover of a Government seal, that I stood stupid. Catriona's grey eyes shone in my remembrance. I thought with a bound of pleasure, she must be the friend. But who should the writer be, to have her billet thus enclosed with Prestongrange's? And of all wonders, why was it thought needful to give me this pleasing but most inconsequential intelligence upon the Bass? For the writer, I could hit upon none possible except Miss Grant. Her family, I remembered, had remarked on Catriona's eyes and even named her for their colour; and she herself had been much in the habit to address me with a broad pronunciation, by way of a sniff, I supposed, at my rusticity. No doubt, besides, but she lived in the same house as this letter came from. So there remained but one step to be accounted for; and that was how Prestongrange should have permitted her at all in an affair so secret, or let her daft-like billet go in the same cover with his own. But even here I had a glimmering. For, first of all, there was something rather alarming about the young lady, and papa might be more under her domination than I knew. And second, there was the man's continual policy to be remembered, how his conduct had been continually mingled with caresses, and he had scarce ever, in the midst of so much contention, laid aside a mask of friendship. He must conceive that my imprisonment had incensed me. Perhaps this little jesting, friendly message was intended to disarm my rancour?

I will be honest—and I think it did. I felt a sudden warmth towards that beautiful Miss Grant, that she should stoop to so much interest in my affairs. The summoning up of Catriona moved me of itself to milder and more cowardly counsels. If the Advocate knew of her and of our acquaintance—if I should please him by some of that 'discretion' at which his letter pointed—to what might not this lead? *In vain is the net spread in the sight of any fowl*, the scripture says. Well, fowls must be wiser than folk! For I thought I perceived the policy, and yet fell in with it.

I was in this frame, my heart beating, the grey eyes plain before me like two stars, when Andie broke in upon my musing.

'I see ye hae gotten guid news,' said he.

I found him looking curiously in my face; with that there came before me like a vision of James Stewart and the court of Inverary; and my mind turned at once like a door upon its hinges. Trials, I reflected, sometimes draw out longer than is looked for. Even if I came to Inverary just too late, something might yet be attempted in the interests of James—and in those of my own character, the best would be accomplished. In a moment, it seemed without thought, I had a plan devised.

'Andie,' said I, 'is it still to be to-morrow?'

He told me nothing was changed.

'Was anything said about the hour?' I asked.

He told me it was to be two o'clock afternoon.

'And about the place?' I pursued.

'Whatten place?' says Andie.

'The place I'm to be landed at,' said I.

He owned there was nothing as to that.

'Very well, then,' I said, 'this shall be mine to arrange. The wind is in the east, my road lies westward; keep your boat, I hire it; let us work up the Forth all day; and land me at two o'clock to-morrow at the westmost we'll can have reached.'

'Ye daft callant!' he cried, 'ye would try for Inverary after a'!'

'Just that, Andie,' says I.

'Weel, ye're ill to beat!' says he. 'And I was kind o' sorry for ye a' day yesterday,' he added. 'Ye see, I was never entirely sure till then, which way of it ye really wantit.'

Here was a spur to a lame horse!

'A word in your ear, Andie,' said I. 'This plan of mine has another advantage yet. We can leave these Hielandmen behind us on the rock, and one of your boats from the Castleton can bring them off to-morrow. Yon Neil has a

queer eye when he regards you; maybe, if I was once out
of the gate there might be knives again; these red-shanks
are unco grudgeful. And if there should come to be any
question, here is your excuse. Our lives were in danger by
these savages; being answerable for my safety, you chose
the part to bring me from their neighbourhood and detain
me the rest of the time on board your boat: and do you
know, Andie?' says I, with a smile, 'I think it was very
wisely chosen.'

'The truth is I have nae goo for Neil,' says Andie, 'nor
he for me, I'm thinking; and I would like ill to come to
my hands wi' the man. Tam Anster will make a better hand
of it with the cattle onyway.' (For this man, Anster, came
from Fife, where the Gaelic is still spoken.) 'Ay, ay!' says
Andie, 'Tam'll can deal with them the best. And troth!
the mair I think of it, the less I see what way we would
be required. The place—ay, feggs! they had forgot the
place. Eh, Shaws, ye're a lang-heided chield when ye like!
Forbye that I'm awing ye my life,' he added, with more
solemnity, and offered me his hand upon the bargain.

Whereupon, with scarce more words, we stepped suddenly on board the boat, cast off, and set the lug. The
Gregara were then busy upon breakfast, for the cookery
was their usual part; but, one of them stepping to the
battlements, our flight was observed before we were twenty
fathoms from the rock; and the three of them ran about
the ruins and the landing-shelf, for all the world like ants
about a broken nest, hailing and crying on us to return. We
were still in both the lee and the shadow of the rock, which
last lay broad upon the waters, but presently came forth in
almost the same moment into the wind and sunshine; the
sail filled, the boat heeled to the gunwale, and we swept
immediately beyond sound of the men's voices. To what
terrors they endured upon the rock, where they were now
deserted without the countenance of any civilised person or
so much as the protection of a Bible, no limit can be set;
nor had they any brandy left to be their consolation, for
even in the haste and secrecy of our departure Andie had
managed to remove it.

It was our first care to set Anster ashore in a cove by the

Glenteithy Rocks, so that the deliverance of our maroons might be duly seen to the next day. Thence we kept away up Firth. The breeze, which was then so spirited, swiftly declined, but never wholly failed us. All day we kept moving, though often not much more; and it was after dark ere we were up with the Queensferry. To keep the letter of Andie's engagement (or what was left of it) I must remain on board, but I thought no harm to communicate with the shore in writing. On Prestongrange's cover, where the Government seal must have a good deal surprised my correspondent, I writ, by the boat's lantern, a few necessary words and Andie carried them to Rankeillor. In about an hour he came aboard again, with a purse of money and the assurance that a good horse should be standing saddled for me by two to-morrow at Clackmannan Pool. This done, and the boat riding by her stone anchor, we lay down to sleep under the sail.

We were in the Pool the next day long ere two; and there was nothing left for me but sit and wait. I felt little alacrity upon my errand. I would have been glad of any passable excuse to lay it down; but none being to be found, my uneasiness was no less great than if I had been running to some desired pleasure. By shortly after one the horse was at the waterside, and I could see a man walking it to and fro till I should land, which vastly swelled my impatience. Andie ran the moment of my liberation very fine, showing himself a man of his bare word, but scarce serving his employers with a heaped measure; and by about fifty seconds after two I was in the saddle and on the full stretch for Stirling. In a little more than an hour I had passed that town, and was already mounting Alan Water side, when the weather broke in a small tempest. The rain blinded me, the wind had nearly beat me from the saddle, and the first darkness of the night surprised me in a wilderness still some way east of Balwhidder, not very sure of my direction and mounted on a horse that began already to be weary.

In the press of my hurry, and to be spared the delay and annoyance of a guide, I had followed (so far as it was possible for any horseman) the line of my journey with Alan. This I did with open eyes, foreseeing a great risk in it, which the tempest had now brought to a reality. The last that I knew of where I was, I think it must have been about Uam Var; the hour perhaps six at night. I must still think it great good fortune that I got about eleven to my destination, the house of Duncan Dhu. Where I had wandered in the interval perhaps the horse could tell. I know we were twice down, and once over the saddle and for a moment carried away in a roaring burn. Steed and rider were bemired up to the eyes.

From Duncan I had news of the trial. It was followed in all these Highland regions with religious interest; news of it spread from Inverary as swift as men could travel; and I was rejoiced to learn that, up to a late hour that Saturday, it was not yet concluded; and all men began to suppose it must spread over to the Monday. Under the spur of this intelligence I would not sit to eat; but, Duncan having agreed to be my guide, took the road again on foot, with the piece in my hand and munching as I went. Duncan brought with him a flask of usquebaugh and a hand-lantern; which last enlightened us just so long as we could find houses where to rekindle it, for the thing leaked outrageously and blew out with every gust. The more part of the night we walked blindfold among sheets of rain, and day found us aimless on the mountains. Hard by we struck a hut on a burn-side, where we got a bite and a direction; and, a little before the end of the sermon, came to the kirk doors of Inverary.

The rain had somewhat washed the upper parts of me, but I was still bogged as high as to the knees; I streamed water; I was so weary I could hardly limp, and my face was like a ghost's. I stood certainly more in need of a change of raiment and a bed to lie on, than of all the benefits in Christianity. For all which (being persuaded the chief point for me was to make myself immediately public) I set the door open, entered that church with the dirty Duncan at my tails, and finding a vacant place hard by, sat down.

'Thirteenthly, my brethren, and in parenthesis, the law itself must be regarded as a means of grace,' the minister was saying, in the voice of one delighting to pursue an argument.

The sermon was in English on account of the assize. The judges were present with their armed attendants, the halberts glittered in a corner by the door, and the seats were thronged beyond custom with the array of lawyers. The text was in Romans 5th and 13th—the minister a skilled hand; and the whole of that able churchful—from Argyle, and my Lords Elchies and Kilkerran, down to the halbertmen that came in their attendance—was sunk with gathered brows in a profound critical attention. The minister himself and a sprinkling of those about the door observed our entrance at the moment and immediately forgot the same; the rest either did not hear or would not heed; and I sat there amongst my friends and enemies unremarked.

The first that I singled out was Prestongrange. He sat well forward, like an eager horseman in the saddle, his lips moving with relish, his eyes glued on the minister: the doctrine was clearly to his mind. Charles Stewart, on the other hand, was half asleep, and looked harassed and pale. As for Simon Fraser, he appeared like a blot, and almost a scandal, in the midst of that attentive congregation, digging his hands in his pockets, shifting his legs, clearing his throat, rolling up his bald eyebrows and shooting out his eyes to right and left, now with a yawn, now with a secret smile. At times too, he would take the Bible in front of him, run it through, seem to read a bit, run it through again, and stop and yawn prodigiously: the whole as if for exercise.

In the course of this restlessness his eye alighted on myself. He sat a second stupefied, then tore a half leaf out of the Bible, scrawled upon it with a pencil, and passed it with a whispered word to his next neighbour. The note came to Prestongrange, who gave me but the one look; thence it voyaged to the hands of Mr Erskine; thence again to Argyle, where he sat between the other two lords of session, and his Grace turned and fixed me with an arrogant eye. The last of those interested to observe my presence was Charlie Stewart, and he too began to pencil and hand about despatches, none of which I was able to trace to their destination in the crowd.

But the passage of these notes had aroused notice; all who were in the secret (or supposed themselves to be so) were whispering information—the rest questions; and the minister himself seemed quite discountenanced by the flutter in the church and sudden stir and whispering. His voice changed, he plainly faltered, nor did he again recover the easy conviction and full tones of his delivery. It would be a puzzle to him till his dying day, why a sermon that had gone with triumph through four parts, should thus miscarry in the fifth.

As for me, I continued to sit there, very wet and weary, and a good deal anxious as to what should happen next, but greatly exulting in my success.

THE LAST WORD of the blessing was scarce out of the minister's mouth before Stewart had me by the arm. We were the first to be forth of the church, and he made such extraordinary expedition that we were safe within the four walls of a house before the street had begun to be thronged with the home-going congregation.

'Am I yet in time?' I asked.

'Ay and no,' said he. 'The case is over; the jury is enclosed, and will be so kind as let us ken their view of it to-morrow in the morning, the same as I could have told it my own self three days ago before the play began. The thing has been public from the start. The panel kent it. *Ye may do what ye will for me*, whispers he two days ago. *I ken my fate by what the Duke of Argyle has just said to Mr Macintosh.* O, it's been a scandal!

The great Argyle he gaed before,
He gart the cannons and guns to roar,

and the very macer cried "Cruachan!" But now that I have got you again I'll never despair. The oak shall go over the myrtle yet; we'll ding the Campbells yet in their own town. Praise God that I should see the day!'

He was leaping with excitement, emptied out his mails upon the floor that I might have a change of clothes, and incommoded me with his assistance as I changed. What remained to be done, or how I was to do it, was what he never told me nor, I believe, so much as thought of. 'We'll ding the Campbells yet!' that was still his overcome. And it was forced home upon my mind how this, that had the externals of a sober process of law, was in its essence a clan battle between savage clans. I thought my friend the Writer none of the least savage. Who, that had only seen him at a counsel's back before the Lord Ordinary or following a golf

137

ball and laying down his clubs on Bruntsfield links, could
have recognised for the same person this voluble and violent
clansman?

James Stewart's counsel were four in number—Sheriffs
Brown of Colstoun and Miller, Mr Robert Macintosh and Mr
Stewart younger of Stewart Hall. These were covenanted to
dine with the Writer after sermon, and I was very obligingly
included of the party. No sooner the cloth lifted, and the
first bowl very artfully compounded by Sheriff Miller, than
we fell to the subject in hand. I made a short narration
of my seizure and captivity, and was then examined and
re-examined upon the circumstances of the murder. It will
be remembered this was the first time I had had my say
out, or the matter at all handled, among lawyers; and the
consequence was very dispiriting to the others and (I must
own) disappointing to myself.

'To sum up,' said Colstoun, 'you prove that Alan was
on the spot; you have heard him proffer menaces against
Glenure; and though you assure us he was not the man who
fired, you leave a strong impression that he was in league with
him, and consenting, perhaps immediately assisting, in the
act. You show him besides, at the risk of his own liberty,
actively furthering the criminal's escape. And the rest of
your testimony (so far as the least material) depends on
the bare word of Alan or of James, the two accused. In short,
you do not at all break, but only lengthen by one personage,
the chain that binds our client to the murderer; and I need
scarcely say that the introduction of a third accomplice rather
aggravates that appearance of a conspiracy which has been
our stumbling block from the beginning.'

'I am of the same opinion,' said Sheriff Miller. 'I think we
may all be very much obliged to Prestongrange for taking a
most uncomfortable witness out of our way. And chiefly, I
think, Mr Balfour himself might be obliged. For you talk
of a third accomplice, but Mr Balfour (in my view) has
very much the appearance of a fourth.'

'Allow me, sirs!' interposed Stewart the Writer. 'There is
another view. Here we have a witness—never fash whether
material or not—a witness in this cause, kidnapped by that
old, lawless, bandit crew of the Glengyle Macgregors, and

sequestered for near upon a month in a bourock of old cold
ruins on the Bass. Move that and see what dirt you fling on
the proceedings! Sirs, this is a tale to make the world ring
with! It would be strange, with such a grip as this, if we
couldnae squeeze out a pardon for my client.'

'And suppose we took up Mr Balfour's cause to-morrow?'
said Stewart Hall. 'I am much deceived or we should find so
many impediments thrown in our path, as that James should
have been hanged before we had found a court to hear us.
This is a great scandal, but I suppose we have none of
us forgot a greater still, I mean the matter of the Lady
Grange. The woman was still in durance; my friend Mr
Hope of Rankeillor did what was humanly possible; and
how did he speed? He never got a warrant! Well, it'll
be the same now; the same weapons will be used. This
is a scene, gentlemen, of clan animosity. The hatred of the
name which I have the honour to bear, rages in high quarters.
There is nothing here to be viewed but naked Campbell spite
and scurvy Campbell intrigue.'

You may be sure this was to touch a welcome topic, and I
sat for some time in the midst of my learned counsel, almost
deaved with their talk but extremely little the wiser for its
purport. The Writer was led into some hot expressions;
Colstoun must take him up and set him right; the rest
joined in on different sides, but all pretty noisy; the Duke of
Argyle was beaten like a blanket; King George came in for
a few digs in the by-going and a great deal of rather elaborate
defence: and there was only one person that seemed to be
forgotten, and that was James of the Glens.

Through all this Mr Miller sat quiet. He was a slip of
an oldish gentleman, ruddy and twinkling; he spoke in
a smooth rich voice, with an infinite effect of pawkiness,
dealing out each word the way an actor does, to give the
most expression possible; and even now, when he was
silent, and sat there with his wig laid aside, his glass in
both hands, his mouth funnily pursed, and his chin out,
he seemed the mere picture of a merry slyness. It was plain
he had a word to say, and waited for the fit occasion.

It came presently. Colstoun had wound up one of his
speeches with some expression of their duty to their

client. His brother sheriff was pleased, I suppose, with the transition. He took the table in his confidence with a gesture and a look.

'That suggests to me a consideration which seems overlooked,' said he. 'The interest of our client goes certainly before all, but the world does not come to an end with James Stewart.' Whereat he cocked his eye. 'I might condescend, *exempli gratia*, upon a Mr George Brown, a Mr Thomas Miller, and a Mr David Balfour. Mr David Balfour has a very good ground of complaint, and I think, gentlemen—if his story was properly redd out—I think there would be a number of wigs on the green.'

The whole table turned to him with a common movement.

'Properly handled and carefully redd out, his is a story that could scarcely fail to have some consequence,' he continued. 'The whole administration of justice, from its highest officer downward, would be totally discredited; and it looks to me as if they would need to be replaced.' He seemed to shine with cunning as he said it. 'And I need not point out to ye that this of Mr Balfour's would be a remarkable bonny cause to appear in,' he added.

Well, there they all were started on another hare; Mr Balfour's cause, and what kind of speeches could be there delivered, and what officials could be thus turned out, and who would succeed to their positions. I shall give but the two specimens. It was proposed to approach Simon Fraser, whose testimony, if it could be obtained, would prove certainly fatal to Argyle and Prestongrange. Miller highly approved of the attempt. 'We have here before us a dreeping roast,' said he, 'here is cut-and-come-again for all.' And methought all licked their lips. The other was already near the end. Stewart the Writer was out of the body with delight, smelling vengeance on his chief enemy, the Duke.

'Gentlemen,' cried he, charging his glass, 'here is to Sheriff Miller. His legal abilities are known to all. His culinary, this bowl in front of us is here to speak for. But when it comes to the poleetical!'—cries he, and drains the glass.

'Ay, but it will hardly prove politics in your meaning, my friend,' said the gratified Miller. 'A revolution, if you like, and I think I can promise you that historical writers shall date from Mr Balfour's cause. But properly guided, Mr Stewart, tenderly guided, it shall prove a peaceful revolution.'

'And if the damned Campbells get their ears rubbed, what care I?' cries Stewart, smiting down his fist.

It will be thought I was not very well pleased with all this, though I could scarce forbear smiling at a kind of innocency in these old intriguers. But it was not my view to have undergone so many sorrows for the advancement of Sheriff Miller or to make a revolution in the Parliament House: and I interposed accordingly with as much simplicity of manner as I could assume.

'I have to thank you, gentlemen, for your advice,' said I. 'And now I would like, by your leave, to set you two or three questions. There is one thing that has fallen rather on one side, for instance: Will this cause do any good to our friend James of the Glens?'

They seemed all a hair set back, and gave various answers, but concurring practically in one point, that James had now no hope but in the King's mercy.

'To proceed, then,' said I, 'will it do any good to Scotland? We have a saying that it is an ill bird that fouls his own nest. I remember hearing we had a riot in Edinburgh when I was an infant child, which gave occasion to the late Queen to call this country barbarous; and I always understood that we had rather lost than gained by that. Then came the year 'Forty-five, which made Scotland to be talked of everywhere; but I never heard it said we had any way gained by the 'Forty-five. And now we come to this cause of Mr Balfour's, as you call it. Sheriff Miller tells us historical writers are to date from it, and I would not wonder. It is only my fear they would date from it as a period of calamity and public reproach.'

The nimble-witted Miller had already smelt where I was travelling to, and made haste to get on the same road. 'Forcibly put, Mr Balfour,' says he. 'A weighty observe, sir.'

'We have next to ask ourselves if it will be good for King George,' I pursued. 'Sheriff Miller appears pretty easy upon this; but I doubt you will scarce be able to pull down the house from under him, without his Majesty coming by a knock or two, one of which might easily prove fatal.'

I gave them a chance to answer, but none volunteered.

'Of those for whom the case was to be profitable,' I went on, 'Sheriff Miller gave us the names of several, among the which he was good enough to mention mine. I hope he will pardon me if I think otherwise. I believe I hung not the least back in this affair while there was life to be saved; but I own I thought myself extremely hazarded, and I own I think it would be a pity for a young man, with some idea of coming to the bar, to ingrain upon himself the character of a turbulent, factious fellow before he was yet twenty. As for James, it seems—at this date of the proceedings, with the sentence as good as pronounced—he has no hope but in the King's mercy. May not his Majesty, then, be more pointedly addressed, the characters of these high officers sheltered from the public, and myself kept out of a position which I think spells ruin for me?'

They all sat and gazed into their glasses and I could see they found my attitude on the affair unpalatable. But Miller was ready at all events.

'If I may be allowed to put our young friend's notion in more formal shape,' says he, 'I understand him to propose that we should embody the fact of his sequestration, and perhaps some heads of the testimony he was prepared to offer, in a memorial to the Crown. This plan has elements of success. It is as likely as any other (and perhaps likelier) to help our client. Perhaps his Majesty would have the goodness to feel a certain gratitude to all concerned in such a memorial, which might be construed into an expression of a very delicate loyalty; and I think, in the drafting of the same, this view might be brought forward.'

They all nodded to each other, not without sighs, for the former alternative was doubtless more after their inclination.

'Paper then, Mr Stewart, if you please,' pursued Miller; 'and I think it might very fittingly be signed by the five of us here present, as procurators for the "condemned man".'

'It can do none of us any harm at least,' says Colstoun, heaving another sigh, for he had seen himself Lord Advocate the last ten minutes.

Thereupon they set themselves, not very enthusiastically, to draft the memorial—a process in the course of which they soon caught fire; and I had no more ado but to sit looking on and answer an occasional question. The paper was very well expressed; beginning with a recitation of the facts about myself, the reward offered for my apprehension, my surrender, the pressure brought to bear upon me; my sequestration; and my arrival at Inverary in time to be too late; going on to explain the reasons of loyalty and public interest for which it was agreed to waive any right of action; and winding up with a forcible appeal to the King's mercy on behalf of James.

Methought I was a good deal sacrificed, and rather represented in the light of a firebrand of a fellow whom my cloud of lawyers had restrained with difficulty from extremes. But I let it pass, and made but the one suggestion, that I should be described as ready to deliver my own evidence and adduce that of others before any commission of inquiry—and the one demand, that I should be immediately furnished with a copy.

Colstoun hummed and hawed. 'This is a very confidential document,' said he.

'And my position towards Prestongrange is highly peculiar,' I replied. 'No question but I must have touched his heart at our first interview, so that he has since stood my friend consistently. But for him, gentlemen, I must now be lying dead or awaiting my sentence alongside poor James. For which reason I choose to communicate to him the fact of this memorial as soon as it is copied. You are to consider also that this step will make for my protection. I have enemies here accustomed to drive hard; his Grace is in his own country, Lovat by his side; and if there should hang any ambiguity over our proceedings I think I might very well awake in gaol.'

Not finding any very ready answer to these considerations, my company of advisers were at the last persuaded to consent, and made only this condition that I was to lay the paper before Prestongrange with the express compliments of all concerned.

The Advocate was at the castle dining with his Grace. By

the hand of one of Colstoun's servants I sent him a billet asking for an interview, and received a summons to meet him at once in a private house of the town. Here I found him alone in a chamber; from his face there was nothing to be gleaned; yet I was not so unobservant but what I spied some halberts in the hall, and not so stupid but what I could gather he was prepared to arrest me there and then, should it appear advisable.

'So, Mr David, this is you?' said he.

'Where I fear I am not overly welcome, my lord,' said I. 'And I would like before I go further to express my sense of your lordship's continued good offices, even should they now cease.'

'I have heard of your gratitude before,' he replied drily, 'and I think this can scarce be the matter you called me from my wine to listen to. I would remember also, if I were you, that you still stand on a very boggy foundation.'

'Not now, my lord, I think,' said I; 'and if your lordship will but glance an eye along this, you will perhaps think as I do.'

He read it sedulously through, frowning heavily; then turned back to one part and another which he seemed to weigh and compare the effect of. His face a little lightened.

'This is not so bad but what it might be worse,' said he; 'though I am still likely to pay dear for my acquaintance with Mr David Balfour.'

'Rather for your indulgence to that unlucky young man, my lord,' said I.

He still skimmed the paper, and all the while his spirits seemed to mend.

'And to whom am I indebted for this?' he asked presently. 'Other counsels must have been discussed, I think. Who was it proposed this private method? Was it Miller?'

'My lord, it was myself,' said I. 'These gentlemen have shown me no such consideration, as that I should deny myself any credit I can fairly claim, or spare them any responsibility they should properly bear. And the mere truth is, that they were all in favour of a process which should have remarkable consequences in the Parliament House, and prove for them (in one of their own expressions) a dripping roast. Before I intervened, I think they were on the point of sharing out the different law appointments. Our friend Mr Simon was to be taken in upon some composition.'

Prestongrange smiled. 'These are our friends!' said he. 'And what were your reasons for dissenting, Mr David?'

I told them without concealment, expressing, however, with more force and volume those which regarded Prestongrange himself.

'You do me no more than justice,' said he. 'I have fought as hard in your interest as you have fought against mine. And how came you here to-day?' he asked. 'As the case drew out, I began to grow uneasy that I had clipped the period so fine, and I was even expecting you to-morrow. But to-day—I never dreamed of it.'

I was not, of course, going to betray Andie.

'I suspect there is some very weary cattle by the road,' said I.

'If I had known you were such a mosstrooper you should have tasted longer of the Bass,' says he.

'Speaking of which, my lord, I return your letter.' And I gave him the enclosure in the counterfeit hand.

'There was the cover also with the seal,' said he.

'I have it not,' said I. 'It bore nought but the address, and could not compromise a cat. The second enclosure I have, and with your permission, I desire to keep it.'

I thought he winced a little, but he said nothing to the point. 'To-morrow,' he resumed, 'our business here is to be finished, and I proceed by Glasgow. I would be very glad to have you of my party, Mr David.'

'My lord . . .' I began.

'I do not deny it will be of service to me,' he interrupted. 'I desire even that, when we shall come to Edinburgh you should alight at my house. You have very warm friends in the Miss Grants, who will be overjoyed to have you to themselves. If you think I have been of use to you, you can thus easily repay me, and so far from losing, may reap some advantage by the way. It is not every strange young man who is presented in society by the King's Advocate.'

Often enough already (in our brief relations) this gentleman had caused my head to spin; no doubt but what for a moment he did so again now. Here was the old fiction still maintained of my particular favour with his daughters, one of whom had been so good as laugh at me, while the other two had scarce deigned to remark the fact of my existence. And now I was to ride with my lord to Glasgow; I was to dwell with him in Edinburgh; I was to be brought into society under his protection! That he should have so much good-nature as to forgive me was surprising enough; that he could wish to take me up and serve me seemed impossible; and I began to seek for some ulterior meaning. One was plain. If I became his guest, repentance was excluded; I could never think better of my present design and bring any action. And besides, would not my presence in his house draw out the whole pungency of the memorial? For that complaint could not be very seriously regarded, if the person chiefly injured was the guest of the official most incriminated. As I thought upon this, I could not quite refrain from smiling.

'This is in the nature of a countercheck to the memorial?' said I.

'You are cunning, Mr David,' said he, 'and you do not wholly guess wrong; the fact will be of use to me in my defence. Perhaps, however, you underrate my friendly sentiments, which are perfectly genuine. I have a respect for you, Mr David, mingled with awe,' says he, smiling.

'I am more than willing, I am earnestly desirous to meet your wishes,' said I. 'It is my design to be called to the bar, where your lordship's countenance would be invaluable; and I am besides sincerely grateful to yourself and family for different marks of interest and of indulgence. The difficulty is here. There is one point in which we pull two ways. You are trying to hang James Stewart, I am trying to save him. In so far as my riding with you would better your lordship's defence, I am at your lordship's orders; but in so far as it would help to hang James Stewart, you see me at a stick.'

I thought he swore to himself. 'You should certainly be called; the bar is the true scene for your talents,' says he, bitterly, and then fell a while silent. 'I will tell you,' he presently resumed, 'there is no question of James Stewart, for or against. James is a dead man; his life is given and taken—bought (if you like it better) and sold; no memorial can help—no defalcation of a faithful Mr David hurt him. Blow high, blow low, there will be no pardon for James Stewart: and take that for said! The question is now of myself: am I to stand or fall? and I do not deny to you that I am in some danger. But will Mr David Balfour consider why? It is not because I have pushed the case unduly against James; for that, I am sure of condonation. And it is not because I have sequestered Mr David on a rock, though it will pass under that colour; but because I did not take the ready and plain path, to which I was pressed repeatedly, and send Mr David to his grave or to the gallows. Hence the scandal—hence this damned memorial,' striking the paper on his leg. 'My tenderness for you has brought me in this difficulty. I wish to know if your tenderness to your own conscience is too great to let you help me out of it?'

No doubt but there was much of the truth in what he said; if James was past helping, whom was it more natural that I should turn to help than just the man before me, who had helped myself so often, and was even now setting me a pattern of patience? I was besides not only weary, but beginning to be ashamed of my perpetual attitude of suspicion and refusal.

'If you will name the time and place, I will be punctually ready to attend your lordship,' said I.

He shook hands with me. 'And I think my misses have some news for you,' says he, dismissing me.

I came away, vastly pleased to have my peace made, yet a little concerned in conscience; nor could I help wondering, as I went back, whether, perhaps, I had not been a scruple too good-natured. But there was the fact, that this was a man that might have been my father, an able man, a great dignitary, and one that, in the hour of my need, had reached a hand to my assistance. I was in the better humour to enjoy the remainder of that evening, which I passed with the advocates, in excellent company no doubt, but perhaps with rather more than a sufficiency of punch: for though I went early to bed I have no clear mind of how I got there.

ON THE MORROW, from the justices' private room, where none could see me, I heard the verdict given in and judgment rendered upon James. The Duke's words I am quite sure I have correctly; and since that famous passage has been made a subject of dispute, I may as well commemorate my version. Having referred to the year '45, the chief of the Campbells, sitting as Justice-General upon the bench, thus addressed the unfortunate Stewart before him: 'If you had been successful in that rebellion, you might have been giving the law where you have now received the judgment of it; we, who are this day your judges, might have been tried before one of your mock courts of judicature; and then you might have been satiated with the blood of any name or clan to which you had an aversion.'

'This is to let the cat out of the bag, indeed,' thought I. And that was the general impression. It was extraordinary how the young advocate lads took hold and made a mock of this speech, and how scarce a meal passed but what some one would get in the words: 'And then you might have been satiated'. Many songs were made in that time for the hour's diversion, and are near all forgot. I remember one began:

> What do ye want the bluid of, bluid of?
> Is it a name, or is it a clan,
> Or is it an aefauld Hielandman,
> That ye want the bluid of, bluid of?

Another went to my old favourite air, *The House of Airlie*, and began thus:

> It fell on a day when Argyle was on the bench,
> That they served him a Stewart for his denner.

And one of the verses ran:

> Then up and spak the Duke, and flyted on his cook,
> I regaird it as a sensible aspersion,

That I would sup ava', an' satiate my maw,
With the bluid of ony clan of my aversion.

James was as fairly murdered as though the Duke had got a fowling-piece and stalked him. So much of course I knew: but others knew not so much, and were more affected by the items of scandal that came to light in the progress of the cause. One of the chief was certainly this sally of the justice's. It was run hard by another of a juryman, who had struck into the midst of Colstoun's speech for the defence with a 'Pray, sir, cut it short, we are quite weary,' which seemed the very excess of impudence and simplicity. But some of my new lawyer friends were still more staggered with an innovation that had disgraced and even vitiated the proceedings. One witness was never called. His name, indeed, was printed, where it may still be seen on the fourth page of the list: 'James Drummond, *alias* Macgregor, *alias* James More, late tenant in Inveronachile'; and his precognition had been taken, as the manner is, in writing. He had remembered or invented (God help him) matter which was lead in James Stewart's shoes, and I saw was like to prove wings to his own. This testimony it was highly desirable to bring to the notice of the jury, without exposing the man himself to the perils of cross-examination; and the way it was brought about was a matter of surprise to all. For the paper was handed round (like a curiosity) in court; passed through the jury-box, where it did its work; and disappeared again (as though by accident) before it reached the counsel for the prisoner. This was counted a most insidious device; and that the name of James More should be mingled up with it filled me with shame for Catriona and concern for myself.

The following day, Prestongrange and I, with a considerable company, set out for Glasgow, where (to my impatience) we continued to linger some time in a mixture of pleasure and affairs. I lodged with my lord, with whom I was encouraged to familiarity; had my place at entertainments; was presented to the chief guests; and altogether made more of than I thought accorded either with my parts or station; so that, on strangers being present, I would often blush for Prestongrange. It must be owned the view I had taken of the world in these last months was fit to cast a gloom upon my character. I had met many men, some of them leaders in Israel whether by their birth or talents; and who among them all had shown clean hands? As for the Browns and Millers, I had seen their self-seeking, I could never again respect them. Prestongrange was the best yet; he had saved me, had spared me rather, when others had it in their minds to murder me outright; but the blood of James lay at his door; and I thought his present dissimulation with myself a thing below pardon. That he should affect to find pleasure in my discourse almost surprised me out of my patience. I would sit and watch him with a kind of a slow fire of anger in my bowels, 'Ah, friend, friend,' I would think to myself, 'if you were but through with this affair of the memorial, would you not kick me in the streets?' Here I did him, as events have proved, the most grave injustice; and I think he was at once far more sincere, and a far more artful performer than I supposed.

But I had some warrant for my incredulity in the behaviour of that court of young advocates that hung about him in the hope of patronage. The sudden favour of a lad not previously heard of troubled them at first out of measure; but two days were not gone by before I found myself surrounded with flattery and attention. I was the same young man, and neither better nor bonnier, that they had rejected a month before; and now there was no civility too fine for me! The same, do I say? It was not so; and the by-name by which I went behind my back confirmed it. Seeing me so firm with the Advocate, and persuaded that I was to fly high and far, they had taken a word from the golfing green, and called me *the Tee'd Ball*. I was told I was now 'one of themselves'; I was to taste of their soft lining, who had already made my own experience of the roughness of the outer husk; and one, to whom I had been presented in Hope Park, was so assured as even to remind me of that meeting. I told him I had not the pleasure of remembering it.

'Why,' says he, 'it was Miss Grant herself presented me! My name is so-and-so.'

'It may very well be, sir,' said I; 'but I have kept no mind of it.'

At which he desisted; and in the midst of the disgust that commonly overflowed my spirits I had a glisk of pleasure.

But I have not patience to dwell upon that time at length. When I was in company with these young politics I was borne down with shame for myself and my own plain ways, and scorn for them and their duplicity. Of the two evils, I thought Prestongrange to be the least; and while I was always as stiff as buckram to the young bloods, I made rather a dissimulation of my hard feelings towards the Advocate, and was (in old Mr Campbell's word) 'soople to the laird'. Himself commented on the difference, and bid me be more of my age, and make friends with my young comrades.

I told him I was slow of making friends.

'I will take the word back,' said he. 'But there is such a thing as *Fair gude e'en and fair gude day*, Mr David. These are the same young men with whom you are to pass your days and get through life: your backwardness has a look of arrogance; and unless you can assume a little more lightness of manner, I fear you will meet difficulties in the path.'

'It will be an ill job to make a silk purse of a sow's ear,' said I.

On the morning of October 1st I was awakened by the clattering in of an express; and getting to my window almost before he had dismounted, I saw the messenger had ridden hard. Somewhile after I was called to Prestongrange, where he was sitting in his bedgown and nightcap, with his letters round him.

'Mr David,' said he, 'I have a piece of news for you. It concerns some friends of yours, of whom I sometimes think you are a little ashamed, for you have never referred to their existence.'

I suppose I blushed.

'I see you understand, since you make the answering signal,' said he. 'And I must compliment you on your excellent taste in beauty. But do you know, Mr David, this seems to me a very enterprising lass? She crops up from every side. The Government of Scotland appears unable to proceed for Mistress Katrine Drummond, which was somewhat the case (no great while back) with a certain Mr David Balfour. Should not these make a good match?

Her first intromission in politics—but I must not tell you that story, the authorities have decided you are to hear it otherwise and from a livelier narrator. This new example is more serious, however; and I am afraid I must alarm you with the intelligence that she is now in prison.'

I cried out.

'Yes,' said he, 'the little lady is in prison. But I would not have you to despair. Unless you (with your friends and memorials) shall procure my downfall, she is to suffer nothing.'

'But what has she done? What is her offence?' I cried.

'It might be almost construed a high treason,' he returned, 'for she has broke the King's Castle of Edinburgh.'

'The lady is much my friend,' I said. 'I know you would not mock me if the thing were serious.'

'And yet it is serious in a sense,' said he; 'for this rogue of a Katrine—or Cateran, as we may call her—has set adrift again upon the world that very doubtful character, her papa.'

Here was one of my previsions justified: James More was once again at liberty. He had lent his men to keep me a prisoner; he had volunteered his testimony in the Appin case, and the same (no matter by what subterfuge) had been employed to influence the jury. Now came his reward, and he was free. It might please the authorities to give to it the colour of an escape; but I knew better—I knew it must be the fulfilment of a bargain. The same course of thought relieved me of the least alarm for Catriona. She might be thought to have broke prison for her father; she might have believed so herself. But the chief hand in the whole business was that of Prestongrange; and I was sure, so far from letting her come to punishment, he would not suffer her to be even tried. Whereupon thus came out of me the not very politic ejaculation:

'Ah! I was expecting that!'

'You have at times a great deal of discretion too!' says Prestongrange.

'And what is my lord pleased to mean by that?' I asked.

'I was just marvelling,' he replied, 'that being so clever as to draw these inferences, you should not be clever enough to keep them to yourself. But I think you would like to hear the details of the affair. I have received two versions: and the least official is the more full and far the more entertaining, being from the lively pen of my eldest daughter. "Here is all the town bizzing with a fine piece of work," she writes, "and what would make the thing more noted (if it were only known) the malefactor is a *protégée* of his lordship my papa. I am sure your heart is too much in your duty (if it were nothing else) to have forgotten Grey Eyes. What does she do, but get a broad hat with the flaps open, a long hairy-like man's great-coat, and a big gravatt; kilt her coats up to *Gude kens whaur*, clap two pair of boot-hose upon her legs, take a pair of *clouted brogues* in her hand, and off to the Castle! Here she gives herself out to be a soutar in the employ of James More, and gets admitted to his cell, the lieutenant (who seems to have been full of pleasantry) making sport among his soldiers of the soutar's great-coat. Presently they hear disputation and the sound of blows inside. Out flies the cobbler, his coat flying, the flaps of his hat beat about his face, and the lieutenant and his soldiers mock at him as he runs off. They laughed not so hearty the next time they had occasion to visit the cell, and found nobody but a tall, pretty, grey-eyed lass in the female habit! As for the cobbler, he was 'over the hills ayont Dumblane', and it's thought that poor Scotland will have to console herself without him. I drank Catriona's health this night in public. Indeed, the whole town admires her; and I think the beaux would wear bits of her garters in their button-holes if they could only get them. I would have gone to visit her in prison too, only I remembered in time I was papa's daughter; so I wrote her a billet instead, which I entrusted to the faithful Doig, and I hope you will admit I can be political when I please. The same faithful gomeral is to despatch this letter by the express along with those of the wiseacres, so that you may hear Tom Fool in company with Solomon. Talking of *gomerals*, do tell *Dauvit Balfour*. I would I could see the face of him at the thought of a long-legged lass in such a predicament! to say nothing of the levities of your affectionate daughter, and his respectful friend." So my rascal signs herself!' continued Prestongrange. 'And you see, Mr David, it is quite true what I tell you, that my daughters regard you with the most affectionate playfulness.'

'The gomeral is much obliged,' said I.

'And was not this prettily done?' he went on. 'Is not this Highland maid a piece of a heroine?'

'I was always sure she had a great heart,' said I. 'And I wager she guessed nothing. . . . But I beg your pardon, this is to tread upon forbidden subjects.'

'I will go bail she did not,' he returned, quite openly. 'I will go bail she thought she was flying straight into King George's face.'

Remembrance of Catriona, and the thought of her lying in captivity, moved me strangely. I could see that even Prestongrange admired, and could not withhold his lips from smiling when he considered her behaviour. As for Miss Grant, for all her ill habit of mockery, her admiration shone out plain. A kind of a heat came on me.

'I am not your lordship's daughter . . .' I began.

'That I know of!' he put in smiling.

'I speak like a fool,' said I; 'or rather I began wrong. It would doubtless be unwise in Mistress Grant to go to her in prison; but for me, I think I would look like a half-hearted friend if I did not fly there instantly.'

'So-ho, Mr David,' says he; 'I thought that you and I were in a bargain?'

'My lord,' I said, 'when I made that bargain I was a good deal affected by your goodness, but I'll never can deny that I was moved besides by my own interest. There was self-seeking in my heart, and I think shame of it now. It may be for your lordship's safety to say this fashious Davie Balfour is your friend and housemate. Say it then; I'll never contradict you. But as for your patronage, I give it all back. I ask but the one thing—let me go, and give me a pass to see her in her prison.'

He looked at me with a hard eye. 'You put the cart before the horse, I think,' says he. 'That which I had given was a portion of my liking, which your thankless nature does not seem to have remarked. But for my patronage, it is not given, nor (to be exact) is it yet offered.' He paused a bit. 'And I warn you, you do not know yourself,' he added. 'Youth is a hasty season; you will think better of all this before a year.'

'Well, and I would like to be that kind of youth!' I cried. 'I have seen too much of the other party in these young advocates that fawn upon your lordship and are even at the pains to fawn on me. And I have seen it in the old ones also. They are all for by-ends, the whole clan of them! It's this that makes me seem to misdoubt your lordship's liking. Why would I think that you would like me? But ye told me yourself ye had an interest!'

I stopped at this, confounded that I had run so far; he was observing me with an unfathomable face.

'My lord, I ask your pardon,' I resumed. 'I have nothing in my chafts but a rough country tongue. I think it would be only decent-like if I would go to see my friend in her captivity; but I'm owing you my life—I'll never forget that; and if it's for your lordship's good, here I'll stay. That's barely gratitude.'

'This might have been reached in fewer words,' says Prestongrange grimly. 'It is easy, and it is at times gracious, to say a plain Scots "ay".'

'Ah, but, my lord, I think ye take me not yet entirely!' cried I. 'For *your* sake, for my life-safe, and the kindness that ye say ye bear to me—for these, I'll consent; but not for any good that might be coming to myself. If I stand aside when this young maid is in her trial, it's a thing I will be noways advantaged by; I will lose by it, I will never gain. I would rather make a shipwreck wholly than to build on that foundation.'

He was a minute serious, then smiled. 'You mind me of the man with the long nose,' said he; 'was you to look at the moon by a telescope, you would see David Balfour there! But you shall have your way of it, I will ask at you one service, and then set you free. My clerks are overdriven; be so good as copy me these few pages,' says he, visibly swithering among some huge rolls of manuscripts, 'and when that is done, I shall bid you God speed! I would never charge myself with Mr David's conscience; and if you could cast some part of it (as you went by) in a moss hag, you would find yourself to ride much easier without it.'

'Perhaps not just entirely in the same direction though, my lord!' says I.

'And you shall have the last word, too!' cries he gaily.

Indeed he had some cause for gaiety, having now found the means to gain his purpose. To lessen the weight of the memorial, or to have a readier answer at his hand, he desired I should appear publicly in the character of his intimate. But if I were to appear with the same publicity as a visitor to Catriona in her prison the world would scarce stint to draw conclusions, and the true nature of James More's escape must become evident to all. This was the little problem I had set him of a sudden, and to which he had so briskly found an answer. I was to be tethered in Glasgow by that job of copying, which in mere outward decency I could not well refuse; and during these hours of my employment Catriona was privately got rid of. I think shame to write of this man that loaded me with so many goodnesses. He was kind to me as any father, yet I ever thought him as false as a cracked bell.

THE COPYING WAS a weary business, the more so as I perceived very early there was no sort of urgency in the matters treated, and began very early to consider my employment a pretext. I had no sooner finished, than I got to horse, used what remained of daylight to the best purpose, and being at last fairly benighted, slept in a house by Almond-Water side. I was in the saddle again before the day, and the Edinburgh booths were just opening when I clattered in by the West Bow and drew up a smoking horse at my lord Advocate's door. I had a written word for Doig, my lord's private hand that was thought to be in all his secrets—a worthy, little plain man, all fat and snuff and self-sufficiency. Him I found already at his desk and already bedabbled with maccabaw, in the same ante-room where I rencountered with James More. He read the note scrupulously through like a chapter in his Bible.

'H'm,' says he; 'ye come a wee thing ahint-hand, Mr Balfour. The bird's flaen—we hae letten her out.'

'Miss Drummond is set free?' I cried.

'Achy!' said he. 'What would we keep her for, ye ken? To hae made a steer about the bairn would hae pleased naebody.'

'And where'll she be now?' says I.

'Gude kens!' says Doig, with a shrug.

'She'll have gone home to Lady Allardyce, I'm thinking,' said I.

'That'll be it,' said he.

'Then I'll gang there straight,' says I.

'But ye'll be for a bite or ye go?' said he.

'Neither bite nor sup,' said I. 'I had a good waucht of milk in by Ratho.'

'Aweel, aweel,' says Doig. 'But ye'll can leave your horse

here and your bags, for it seems we're to have your up-put.'

'Na, na,' said I. 'Tamson's mear would never be the thing for me this day of all days.'

Doig speaking somewhat broad, I had been led by imitation into an accent much more countrified than I was usually careful to affect—a good deal broader indeed than I have written it down; and I was the more ashamed when another voice joined in behind me with a scrap of a ballad.

> Gae saddle me the bonny black,
> Gae saddle sune and mak' him ready,
> Far I will down the Gatehope-slack,
> And a' to see my bonny leddy.

The young lady, when I turned to her, stood in a morning gown, and her hands muffled in the same, as if to hold me at a distance. Yet I could not but think there was kindness in the eye with which she saw me.

'My best respects to you, Mistress Grant,' said I, bowing.

'The like to yourself, Mr David,' she replied, with a deep courtesy. 'And I beg to remind you of an old musty saw, that meat and mass never hindered man. The mass I cannot afford you, for we are all good Protestants. But the meat I press on your attention. And I would not wonder but I could find something for your private ear that would be worth the stopping for.'

'Mistress Grant,' said I, 'I believe I am already your debtor for some merry words—and I think they were kind too—on a piece of unsigned paper.'

'Unsigned paper?' says she, and made a droll face, which was likewise wondrous beautiful, as of one trying to remember.

'Or else I am the more deceived,' I went on. 'But to be sure, we shall have the time to speak of these, since your father is so good as to make me for a while your inmate; and the *gomeral* begs you at this time only for the favour of his liberty.'

'You give yourself hard names,' said she.

'Mr Doig and I would be blythe to take harder at your clever pen,' says I.

'Once more I have to admire the discretion of all menfolk,' she replied. 'But if you will not eat, off with you at once; you will be back the sooner, for you go on a fool's errand. Off with you, Mr David,' she continued, opening the door.

> He has lowpen on his bonny grey,
> He rade the richt gate and the ready;
> I trow he would neither stint nor stay,
> Far he was seeking his bonny leddy.

I did not wait to be twice bidden, and did justice to Miss Grant's citation on the way to Dean.

Old Lady Allardyce walked there alone in the garden, in her hat and mutch, and having a silver-mounted staff of some black wood to lean upon. As I alighted from my horse, and drew near to her with *congees*, I could see the blood come in her face, and her head fling into the air like what I had conceived of empresses.

'What brings you to my poor door?' she cried, speaking high through her nose. 'I cannot bar it. The males of my house are dead and buried; I have neither son nor husband to stand in the gate for me; any beggar can pluck me by the baird—and a baird there is, and that's the worst of it yet!' she added, partly to herself.

I was extremely put out at this reception, and the last remark, which seemed like a daft wife's, left me near hand speechless.

'I see I have fallen under your displeasure, ma'am,' said I. 'Yet I will still be so bold as ask after Mistress Drummond.'

She considered me with a burning eye, her lips pressed close together into twenty creases, her hand shaking on her staff. 'This cows all!' she cried. 'Ye come to me to speir for her? Would God I knew!'

'She is not here?' I cried.

She threw up her chin and made a step and a cry at me, so that I fell back incontinent.

'Out upon your leeing throat!' she cried. 'What! ye come and speir at me! She's in jyle, whaur ye took her to—that's all there is to it. And of a' the beings ever I beheld in breeks, to think it should be you! Ye timmer scoun'rel, if I had a male left my name I would have your jaicket dustit till ye raired.'

I thought it not good to delay longer in that place, because

I remarked her passion to be rising. As I turned to the horse-post she even followed me; and I make no shame to confess that I rode away with the one stirrup on and scrambling for the other.

As I knew no other quarter where I could push my inquiries, there was nothing left me but to return to the Advocate's. I was well received by the four ladies, who were now in company together, and must give the news of Prestongrange and what word went in the west country, at the most inordinate length and with great weariness to myself; while all the time that young lady, with whom I so much desired to be alone again, observed me quizzically and seemed to find pleasure in the sight of my impatience. At last, after I had endured a meal with them, and was come very near the point of appealing for an interview before her mother, she went and stood by the music-case, and picking out a tune, sang to it on a high key—'He that will not when he may, When he will he shall have nay.' But this was the end of her rigours, and presently, after making some excuse of which I have no mind, she carried me away in private to her father's library. I should not fail to say that she was dressed to the nines, and appeared extraordinary handsome.

'Now, Mr David, sit ye down here and let us have a two-handed crack,' said she. 'For I have much to tell you, and it appears besides that I have been grossly unjust to your good taste.'

'In what manner, Mistress Grant?' I asked. 'I trust I have never seemed to fail in due respect.'

'I will be your surety, Mr David,' said she. 'Your respect, whether to yourself or your poor neighbours, has been always and most fortunately beyond imitation. But that is by the question. You got a note from me?' she asked.

'I was so bold as to suppose so upon inference,' said I, 'and it was kindly thought upon.'

'It must have prodigiously surprised you,' said she. 'But let us begin with the beginning. You have not perhaps forgot a day when you were so kind as to escort three very tedious misses to Hope Park? I have the less cause to forget it myself, because you was so particular obliging as to introduce me to some of the principles of the Latin grammar, a thing which wrote itself profoundly on my gratitude.'

'I fear I was sadly pedantical,' said I, overcome with confusion at the memory. 'You are only to consider I am quite unused with the society of ladies.'

'I will say the less about the grammar then,' she replied. 'But how came you to desert your charge? "He has thrown her out, overboard his ain, dear Annie!"' she hummed; 'and his ain dear Annie and her two sisters had to taigle home by theirselves like a string of green geese! It seems you returned to my papa's, where you showed yourself excessively martial, and then on to realms unknown, with an eye (it appears) to the Bass Rock; solan geese being perhaps more to your mind than bonny lasses.'

Through all this raillery there was something indulgent in the lady's eye which made me suppose there might be better coming.

'You take a pleasure to torment me,' said I, 'and I make a very feckless plaything; but let me ask you to be more merciful. At this time there is but the one thing that I care to hear of, and that will be news of Catriona.'

'Do you call her by that name to her face, Mr Balfour?' she asked.

'In troth, and I am not very sure,' I stammered.

'I would not do so in any case to strangers,' said Miss Grant. 'And why are you so much immersed in the affairs of this young lady?'

'I heard she was in prison,' said I.

'Well, and now you hear that she is out of it,' she replied, 'and what more would you have? She has no need of any further champion.'

'I may have the greater need of her, ma'am,' said I.

'Come, this is better!' says Miss Grant. 'But look me fairly in the face; am I not bonnier than she?'

'I would be the last to be denying it,' said I. 'There is not your marrow in all Scotland.'

'Well, here you have the pick of the two at your hand, and must needs speak of the other,' said she. 'This is never the way to please the ladies, Mr Balfour.'

'But, mistress,' said I, 'there are surely other things besides mere beauty.'

'By which I am to understand that I am no better than I should be, perhaps?' she asked.

'By which you will please understand that I am like the cock in the midden in the fable book,' said I. 'I see the braw jewel—and I like fine to see it too—but I have more need of the pickle corn.'

'Bravissimo!' she cried. 'There is a word well said at last, and I will reward you for it with my story. That same night of your desertion I came late from a friend's house—where I was excessively admired, whatever you may think of it—and what should I hear but that a lass in a tartan screen desired to speak with me? She had been there an hour or better, said the servant-lass, and she grat in to herself as she sat waiting. I went to her direct; she rose as I came in, and I knew her at a look. "*Grey Eyes!*" says I to myself, but was more wise than to let on. *You will be Miss Grant at last!* she says, rising and looking at me hard and pitiful. *Ay, it was true he said, you are bonny at all events.—The way God made me, my dear*, I said, *but I would be gey and obliged if ye could tell me what brought you here at such a time of the night.—Lady*, she said, *we are kinsfolk, we are both come of the blood of the sons of Alpin.—My dear*, I replied, *I think no more of Alpin or his sons than what I do of a kalestock. You have a better argument in these tears upon your bonny face.* And at that I was so weak-minded as to kiss her, which is what you would like to do dearly, and I wager will never find the courage of. I say it was weak-minded of me, for I knew no more of her than the outside; but it was the wisest stroke I could have hit upon. She is a very staunch, brave nature, but I think she has been little used with tenderness; and at that caress (though to say the truth, it was but lightly given) her heart went out to me. I will never betray the secrets of my sex, Mr Davie; I will never tell you the way she turned me round her thumb, because it is the same she will use to twist yourself. Ay, it is a fine lass! She is as clean as hill well water.'

'She is e'en't!' I cried.

'Well, then, she told me her concerns,' pursued Miss Grant, 'and in what a swither she was in about her papa, and what a taking about yourself, with very little cause, and in what a perplexity she had found herself after you was gone away. *And then I minded at long last*, says she, *that we were kinswomen, and that Mr David should have given you the name of the bonniest of the bonny, and I was thinking to myself "If she is so bonny she will be good at all events"; and I took up my foot soles out of that.* That was when I forgave yourself, Mr Davie. When you was in my society, you seemed upon hot iron: by all marks, if ever I saw a young man that wanted to be gone, it was yourself, and I and my two sisters were the ladies you were so desirous to be gone from; and now it appeared you had given me some notice in the bygoing, and was so kind as to comment on my attractions! From that hour you may date our friendship, and I began to think with tenderness upon the Latin grammar.'

'You will have many hours to rally me in,' said I; 'and I think besides you do yourself injustice. I think it was Catriona turned your heart in my direction. She is too simple to perceive as you do the stiffness of her friend.'

'I would not like to wager upon that, Mr David,' said she. 'The lasses have clear eyes. But at least she is your friend entirely, as I was to see. I carried her in to his lordship my papa; and his Advocacy, being in a favourable stage of claret, was so good as to receive the pair of us. *Here is Grey Eyes that you have been deaved with these days past*, said I, *she is come to prove that we spoke true, and I lay the prettiest lass in the three Lothians at your feet*—making a papistical reservation of myself. She suited her action to my words: down she went upon her knees to him—I would not like to swear but he saw two of her, which doubtless made her appeal the more irresistible, for you are all a pack of Mahomedans—told him what had passed that night, and how she had withheld her father's man from following of you, and what a case she was in about her father, and what a flutter for yourself; and begged with weeping for the lives of both of you (neither of which was in the slightest danger), till I vow I was proud of my sex because it was done so pretty, and ashamed for it because of the smallness of the occasion. She had not gone far, I assure you, before the Advocate was wholly sober, to see his inmost politics ravelled out by a young lass and discovered to the most unruly of his daughters. But we took him in hand, the pair of us, and brought that matter straight. Properly managed—and that means managed by me—there is no one to compare with my papa.'

'He has been a good man to me,' said I.

'Well, he was a good man to Katrine, and I was there to see to it,' said she.

'And she pled for me!' say I.

'She did that, and very movingly,' said Miss Grant. 'I would not like to tell you what she said—I find you vain enough already.'

'God reward her for it!' cried I.

'With Mr David Balfour, I suppose?' says she.

'You do me too much injustice at the last!' I cried. 'I would tremble to think of her in such hard hands. Do you think I would presume, because she begged my life? She would do that for a new whelped puppy! I have had more than that to set me up, if you but ken'd. She kissed that hand of mine. Ay, but she did. And why? because she thought I was playing a brave part and might be going to my death. It was not for my sake—but I need not be telling that to you, that cannot look at me without laughter. It was for the love of what she thought was bravery. I believe there is none but me and poor Prince Charlie had that honour done them. Was this not to make a god of me? and do you not think my heart would quake when I remember it?'

'I do laugh at you a good deal, and a good deal more than is quite civil,' said she; 'but I will tell you one thing: if you speak to her like that, you have some glimmerings of a chance.'

'Me?' I cried, 'I would never dare. I can speak to you, Miss Grant, because it's a matter of indifference what ye think of me. But her? no fear!' said I.

'I think you have the largest feet in all broad Scotland,' says she.

'Troth, they are no very small,' said I, looking down.

'Ah, poor Catriona!' cries Miss Grant.

And I could but stare upon her; for though I now see very well what she was driving at (and perhaps some justification for the same), I was never swift at the uptake in such flimsy talk.

'Ah well, Mr David,' she said, 'it goes sore against my conscience, but I see I shall have to be your speaking board. She shall know you came to her straight upon the news of her imprisonment; she shall know you would not pause to eat; and of our conversation she shall hear just so much as I think convenient for a maid of her age and inexperience. Believe me, you will be in that way much better served than you could serve yourself, for I will keep the big feet out of the platter.'

'You know where she is, then?' I exclaimed.

'That I do, Mr David, and will never tell,' said she.

'Why that?' I asked.

'Well,' she said, 'I am a good friend, as you will soon discover; and the chief of those that I am friend to is my papa. I assure you, you will never heat nor melt me out of that, so you may spare me your sheep's eyes; and adieu to your David-Balfourship for the now.'

'But there is yet one thing more,' I cried. 'There is one thing that must be stopped, being mere ruin to herself, and to me too.'

'Well,' she said, 'be brief; I have spent half the day on you already.'

'My Lady Allardyce believes,' I began—'she suppos-es—she thinks that I abducted her.'

The colour came into Miss Grant's face, so that at first I was quite abashed to find her ear so delicate, till I bethought me she was struggling rather with mirth, a notion in which I was altogether confirmed by the shaking of her voice as she replied—

'I will take up the defence of your reputation,' said she. 'You may leave it in my hands.'

And with that she withdrew out of the library.

FOR ABOUT EXACTLY two months I remained a guest in Prestongrange's family, where I bettered my acquaintance with the bench, the bar, and the flower of Edinburgh company. You are not to suppose my education was neglected; on the contrary, I was kept extremely busy. I studied the French, so as to be more prepared to go to Leyden; I set myself to the fencing, and wrought hard, sometimes three hours in the day, with notable advancement; at the suggestion of my cousin, Pilrig, who was an apt musician, I was put to a singing class; and by the orders of my Miss Grant, to one for the dancing, at which I must say I proved far from ornamental. However, all were good enough to say it gave me an address a little more genteel; and there is no question but I learned to manage my coat-skirts and sword with more dexterity, and to stand in a room as though the same belonged to me. My clothes themselves were all earnestly re-ordered; and the most trifling circumstance, such as where I should tie my hair, or the colour of my ribbon, debated among the three misses like a thing of weight. One way with another, no doubt I was a good deal improved to look at, and acquired a bit of a modish air that would have surprised the good folks at Essendean.

The two younger misses were very willing to discuss a point of my habiliment, because that was in the line of their chief thoughts. I cannot say that they appeared any other way conscious of my presence; and though always more than civil, with a kind of heartless cordiality, could not hide how much I wearied them. As for the aunt, she was a wonderful still woman; and I think she gave me much the same attention as she gave the rest of the family, which was little enough. The eldest daughter and the Advocate himself

166

were thus my principal friends, and our familiarity was much increased by a pleasure that we took in common. Before the court met we spent a day or two at the house of Grange, living very nobly with an open table, and here it was that we three began to ride out together in the fields, a practice afterwards maintained in Edinburgh, so far as the Advocate's continual affairs permitted. When we were put in a good frame by the briskness of the exercise, the difficulties of the way, or the accidents of bad weather, my shyness wore entirely off; we forgot that we were strangers, and speech not being required, it flowed the more naturally on. Then it was that they had my story from me, bit by bit, from the time that I left Essendean, with my voyage and battle in the *Covenant*, wanderings in the heather, etc.; and from the interest they found in my adventures sprung the circumstance of a jaunt we made a little later on, on a day when the courts were not sitting, and of which I will tell a trifle more at length.

We took horse early, and passed first by the house of Shaws, where it stood smokeless in a great field of white frost, for it was yet early in the day. Here Prestongrange alighted down, gave me his horse, and proceeded alone to visit my uncle. My heart, I remember, swelled up bitter within me at the sight of that bare house and the thought of the old miser sitting chittering within in the cold kitchen.

'There is my home,' said I; 'and my family.'

'Poor David Balfour!' said Miss Grant.

What passed during the visit I have never heard; but it would doubtless not be very agreeable to Ebenezer, for when the Advocate came forth again his face was dark.

'I think you will soon be the laird indeed, Mr Davie,' says he, turning half about with the one foot in the stirrup.

'I will never pretend sorrow,' said I; and, to say the truth, during his absence Miss Grant and I had been embellishing the place in fancy with plantations, parterres, and a terrace—much as I have since carried out in fact.

Thence we pushed to the Queensferry, where Rankeillor gave us a good welcome, being indeed out of the body to receive so great a visitor. Here the Advocate was so unaffectedly good as to go quite fully over my affairs, sitting perhaps two hours with the Writer in his study, and expressing (I was told) a great esteem for myself and concern for my fortunes. To while this time, Miss Grant and I and young Rankeillor took boat and passed the Hope to Limekilns. Rankeillor made himself very ridiculous (and, I thought, offensive) with his admiration for the young lady, and to my wonder (only it is so common a weakness of her sex) she seemed, if anything, to be a little gratified. One use it had: for when we were come to the other side, she laid her commands on him to mind the boat, while she and I passed a little further to the alehouse. This was her own thought, for she had been taken with my account of Alison Hastie, and desired to see the lass herself. We found her once more alone—indeed, I believe her father wrought all day in the fields—and she curtsied dutifully to the gentry-folk and the beautiful young lady in the riding coat.

'Is this all the welcome I am to get?' said I, holding out my hand. 'And have you no more memory of old friends?'

'Keep me! wha's this of it?' she cried, and then, 'God's truth, it's the tautit laddie!'

'The very same,' says I.

'Mony's the time I've thocht upon you and your freen, and blythe am I to see in your braws,' she cried. 'Though I kent ye were come to your ain folk by the grand present that ye sent me and that I thank ye for with a' my heart.'

'There,' said Miss Grant to me, 'run out by with ye, like a good bairn. I didnae come here to stand and haud a candle; it's her and me that are to crack.'

I suppose she stayed ten minutes in the house, but when she came forth I observed two things—that her eyes were reddened, and a silver brooch was gone out of her bosom. This very much affected me.

'I never saw you so well adorned,' said I.

'O Davie man, dinna be a pompous gowk!' said she, and was more than usually sharp to me the remainder of the day.

About candlelight we came home from this excursion.

For a good while I heard nothing further of Catriona— my Miss Grant remaining quite impenetrable, and stopping my mouth with pleasantries. At last, one day that she returned from walking and found me alone in the parlour over my French, I thought there was something unusual in her looks; the colour heightened, the eyes sparkling high, and a bit of a smile continually bitten in as she regarded me. She seemed indeed like the very spirit of mischief, and, walking briskly in the room, had soon involved me in a kind of quarrel over nothing and (at the least) with nothing intended on my side. I was like Christian in the slough—the more I tried to clamber out upon the side, the deeper I became involved; until at last I heard her declare, with a great deal of passion, that she would take that answer at the hands of none, and I must down upon my knees for pardon.

The causelessness of all this fuff stirred my own bile. 'I have said nothing you can properly object to,' said I, 'and as for my knees, that is an attitude I keep for God.'

'And as a goddess I am to be served!' she cried, shaking her brown locks at me and with a bright colour. 'Every man that comes within waft of my petticoats shall use me so!'

'I will go so far as ask your pardon for the fashion's sake, although I vow I know not why,' I replied. 'But for these play-acting postures, you can go to others.'

'O Davie!' she said. 'Not if I was to beg you?'

I bethought me I was fighting with a woman, which is the same as to say a child, and that upon a point entirely formal.

'I think it a bairnly thing,' I said, 'not worthy in you to ask, or me to render. Yet I will not refuse you, neither,' said I; 'and the stain, if there be any, rests with yourself.' And at that I kneeled fairly down.

'There!' she cried. 'There is the proper station, there is where I have been manœuvring to bring you.' And then, suddenly, 'Kep,' said she, flung me a folded billet, and ran from the apartment laughing.

The billet had neither place nor date. 'Dear Mr David,' it began, 'I get your news continually by my cousin, Miss Grant, and it is a pleisand hearing. I am very well, in a good place, among good folk, but necessitated to be quite private, though I am hoping that at long last we may meet again. All your friendships have been told me by my loving cousin, who loves us both. She bids me to send you this writing, and oversees the same. I will be asking you to do all her commands, and rest your affectionate friend,

Catriona Macgregor-Drummond. P.S.—Will you not see my cousin, Allardyce?'

I think it not the least brave of my campaigns (as the soldiers say) that I should have done as I was here bidden and gone forthright to the house by Dean. But the old lady was now entirely changed and supple as a glove. By what means Miss Grant had brought this round I could never guess; I am sure, at least, she dared not to appear openly in the affair, for her papa was compromised in it pretty deep. It was he, indeed, who had persuaded Catriona to leave, or rather, not to return, to her cousin's, placing her instead with a family of Gregorys—decent people, quite at the Advocate's disposition, and in whom she might have the more confidence because they were of her own clan and family. These kept her private till all was ripe, heated and helped her to attempt her father's rescue, and after she was discharged from prison received her again into the same secrecy. Thus Prestongrange obtained and used his instrument; nor did there leak out the smallest word of his acquaintance with the daughter of James More. There was some whispering, of course, upon the escape of that discredited person; but the Government replied by a show of rigour, one of the cell porters was flogged, the lieutenant of the guard (my poor friend, Duncansby) was broken of his rank, and as for Catriona, all men were well enough pleased that her fault should be passed by in silence.

I could never induce Miss Grant to carry back an answer. 'No,' she would say, when I persisted, 'I am going to keep the big feet out of the platter.' This was the more hard to bear, as I was aware she saw my little friend many times in the week, and carried her my news whenever (as she said) I 'had behaved myself'. At last she treated me to what she called an indulgence, and I thought rather more of a banter. She was certainly a strong, almost a violent, friend to all she liked, chief among whom was a certain frail old gentlewoman, very blind and very witty, who dwelt in the top of a tall land on a strait close, with a nest of linnets in a cage, and thronged all day with visitors. Miss Grant was very fond to carry me there and put me to entertain her friend with the narrative of my misfortunes; and Miss

Tibbie Ramsay (that was her name) was particular kind, and told me a great deal that was worth knowledge of old folks and past affairs in Scotland. I should say that from her chamber window, and not three feet away, such is the straitness of that close, it was possible to look into a barred loophole lighting the stairway of the opposite house.

Here, upon some pretext, Miss Grant left me one day alone with Miss Ramsay. I mind I thought that lady inattentive and like one preoccupied. I was besides very uncomfortable, for the window, contrary to custom, was left open and the day was cold. All at once the voice of Miss Grant sounded in my ears as from a distance.

'Here, Shaws!' she cried, 'keek out of the window and see what I have broughten you.'

I think it was the prettiest sight that ever I beheld. The well of the close was all in clear shadow where a man could see distinctly, the walls very black and dingy; and there from the barred loophole I saw two faces smiling across at me—Miss Grant's and Catriona's.

'There!' says Miss Grant, 'I wanted her to see you in your braws like the lass of Limekilns. I wanted her to see what I could make of you, when I buckled to the job in earnest!'

It came in my mind she had been more than common particular that day upon my dress: and I think that some of the same care had been bestowed upon Catriona. For so merry and sensible a lady, Miss Grant was certainly wonderful taken up with duds.

'Catriona!' was all I could get out.

As for her, she said nothing in the world, but only waved her hand and smiled to me, and was suddenly carried away again from before the loop-hole.

That vision was no sooner lost than I ran to the house door, where I found I was locked in; thence back to Miss Ramsay, crying for the key, but might as well have cried upon the castle rock. She had passed her word, she said, and I must be a good lad. It was impossible to burst the door, even if it had been mannerly; it was impossible I should leap from the window, being seven storeys above ground. All I could do was to crane over the close and

watch for their reappearance from the stair. It was little to
see, being no more than the tops of their two heads each on
a ridiculous bobbin of skirts, like to a pair of pincushions.
Nor did Catriona so much as look up for a farewell; being
prevented (as I heard afterwards) by Miss Grant, who told
her folk were never seen to less advantage than from above
downward.

On the way home, as soon as I was set free, I upbraided
Miss Grant with her cruelty.

'I am sorry you was disappointed,' says she demurely.
'For my part I was very pleased. You looked better than I
dreaded; you looked—if it will not make you vain—a
mighty pretty young man when you appeared in the window.
You are to remember that she could not see your feet,' says
she, with the manner of one reassuring me.

'O!' cried I, 'leave my feet be—they are no bigger
than my neighbour's.'

'They are even smaller than some,' said she, 'but I speak
in parables like a Hebrew prophet.'

'I marvel little they were sometimes stoned!' says I. 'But,
you miserable girl, how could you do it? Why should you
care to tantalise me with a moment?'

'Love is like folk,' says she; 'it needs some kind of vivers.'

'O, Barbara, let me see her properly!' I pleaded. '*You*
can—you see her when you please; let me have half an
hour.'

'Who is it that is managing this love affair? You? Or
me?' she asked, and as I continued to press her with
my instances, fell back upon a deadly expedient: that of
imitating the tones of my voice when I called on Catriona
by name; with which, indeed, she held me in subjection
for some days to follow.

There was never the least word heard of the memorial, or
none by me. Prestongrange and his grace the Lord President
may have heard of it (for what I know) on the deafest sides
of their heads; they kept it to themselves, at least—the
public was none the wiser; and in course of time, on
November 8th, and in the midst of a prodigious storm of
wind and rain, poor James of the Glens was duly hanged at
Lettermore by Ballachulish.

So there was the final upshot of my politics! Innocent men have perished before James, and are like to keep on perishing (in spite of all our wisdom) till the end of time. And till the end of time young folk (who are not yet used with the duplicity of life and men) will struggle as I did, and make heroical resolves, and take long risks; and the course of events will push them upon the one side and go on like a marching army. James was hanged; and here was I dwelling in the house of Prestongrange, and grateful to him for his fatherly attention. He was hanged; and behold! when I met Mr Simon in the causeway, I was fain to pull off my beaver to him like a good little boy before his dominie. He had been hanged by fraud and violence, and the world wagged along, and there was not a pennyweight of difference; and the villains of that horrid plot were decent, kind, respectable fathers of families, who went to kirk and took the sacrament!

But I had had my view of that detestable business they call politics—I had seen it from behind, when it is all bones and blackness; and I was cured for life of any temptations to take part in it again. A plain, quiet, private path was that which I was ambitious to walk in, when I might keep my head out of the way of dangers and my conscience out of the road of temptation. For, upon a retrospect, it appeared I had not done so grandly, after all; but with the greatest possible amount of big speech and preparation, had accomplished nothing.

The 25th of the same month a ship was advertised to sail from Leith; and I was suddenly recommended to make up my mails for Leyden. To Prestongrange I could, of course, say nothing; for I had already been a long while sorning on his house and table. But with his daughter I was more open, bewailing my fate that I should be sent out of the country, and assuring her, unless she should bring me to farewell with Catriona, I would refuse at the last hour.

'Have I not given you my advice?' she asked.

'I know you have,' said I, 'and I know how much I am beholden to you already, and that I am bidden to obey your orders. But you must confess you are something too merry a lass at times to lippen to entirely.'

'I will tell you, then,' said she. 'Be you on board by nine o'clock forenoon; the ship does not sail before one; keep your boat alongside; and if you are not pleased with my farewells when I shall send them, you can come ashore again and seek Katrine for yourself.'

Since I could make no more of her, I was fain to be content with this.

The day came round at last when she and I were to separate. We had been extremely intimate and familiar; I was much in her debt; and what way we were to part was a thing that put me from my sleep, like the vails I was to give to the domestic servants. I knew she considered me too backward, and rather desired to rise in her opinion on that head. Besides which, after so much affection shown and (I believe) felt upon both sides, it would have looked cold-like to be anyways stiff. Accordingly, I got my courage up and my words ready, and the last chance we were like to be alone, asked pretty boldly to be allowed to salute her in farewell.

'You forget yourself strangely, Mr Balfour,' said she. 'I cannot call to mind that I have given you any right to presume on our acquaintancy.'

I stood before her like a stopped clock, and knew not what to think, far less to say, when of a sudden she cast her arms about my neck and kissed me with the best will in the world.

'You inimitable bairn!' she cried. 'Did you think that I would let us part like strangers? Because I can never keep my gravity at you five minutes on end, you must not dream I do not love you very well: I am all love and laughter, every time I cast an eye on you! And now I will give you an advice to conclude your education, which you will have need of before it's very long. Never *ask* women-folk. They're bound to answer "No"; God never made the lass that could resist the temptation. It's supposed by divines to be the curse of Eve: because she did not say it when the devil offered her the apple, her daughters can say nothing else.'

'Since I am so soon to lose my bonny professor,' I began.

'This is gallant, indeed,' says she curtseying.

'—I would put the one question,' I went on: 'May I ask a lass to marry me?'

'You think you could not marry her without?' she asked. 'Or else get her to offer?'

'You see you cannot be serious,' said I.

'I shall be very serious in one thing, David,' said she: 'I shall always be your friend.'

As I got to my house the next morning, the four ladies were all at that same window whence we had once looked down on Catriona, and all cried farewell and waved their pocket napkins as I rode away. One out of the four I knew was truly sorry; and at the thought of that, and how I had come to the door three months ago for the first time, sorrow and gratitude made a confusion in my mind.

Part Two. Father and Daughter

THE SHIP LAY at a single anchor, well outside the pier of Leith, so that all we passengers must come to it by the means of skiffs. This was very little troublesome, for the reason that the day was a flat calm, very frosty and cloudy, and with a low shifting fog upon the water. The body of the vessel was thus quite hid as I drew near, but the tall spars of her stood high and bright in a sunshine like the flickering of a fire. She proved to be a very roomy, commodious merchant, but somewhat blunt in the bows, and loaden extraordinary deep with salt, salted salmon, and fine white linen stockings for the Dutch. Upon my coming on board, the captain welcomed me—one Sang (out of Lesmahago, I believe), a very hearty, friendly tarpaulin of a man, but at the moment in rather of a bustle. There had no other of the passengers yet appeared, so that I was left to walk about upon the deck, viewing the prospect and wondering a good deal what these farewells should be which I was promised.

All Edinburgh and the Pentland Hills glinted above me in a kind of smuisty brightness, now and again overcome with blots of cloud; of Leith there was no more than the tops of chimneys visible, and on the face of the water, where the haar lay, nothing at all. Out of this I was presently aware of a sound of oars pulling, and a little after (as if out of the smoke of a fire) a boat issued. There sat a grave man in the stern sheets, well muffled from the cold, and by his side a tall, pretty, tender figure of a maid that brought my heart to a stand. I had scarce the time to catch my breath in, and be ready to meet her, as she stepped upon the deck, smiling, and making my best bow, which was now vastly finer than some months before, when first I made it to her ladyship. No doubt we were both a good deal changed: she seemed to have shot up taller, like a young, comely tree. She had now a kind of pretty backwardness that became her well, as of one that regarded herself more highly and was fairly woman; and for another thing, the hand of the same magician had been at work upon the pair of us, and Miss Grant had made us both *braw*, if she could make but the one *bonny*.

The same cry, in words not very different, came from both of us, that the other was come in compliment to say farewell, and then we perceived in a flash we were to ship together.

'O, why will not Baby have been telling me!' she cried; and then remembered a letter she had been given, on the condition of not opening it till she was well on board. Within was an enclosure for myself, and ran thus:

> Dear Davie,—What do you think of my farewell? and what do you say to your fellow-passenger? Did you kiss, or did you ask? I was about to have signed here, but that would leave the purport of my question doubtful; and in my own case *I ken the answer*. So fill up here with good advice. Do not be too blate, and for God's sake do not try to be too forward; nothing sets you worse. I am
>
> > Your affectionate friend and governess,
> >
> > > Barbara Grant

I wrote a word of answer and compliment on a leaf out of my pocketbook, put it in with another scratch from Catriona, sealed the whole with my new signet of the Balfour arms, and despatched it by the hand of Prestongrange's servant that still waited in my boat.

Then we had time to look upon each other more at leisure, which we had not done for a piece of a minute before (upon a common impulse) we shook hands again.

'Catriona!' said I. It seemed that was the first and last word of my eloquence.

'You will be glad to see me again?' says she.

'And I think that is an idle word,' said I. 'We are too deep friends to make speech upon such trifles.'

'Is she not the girl of all the world?' she cried again. 'I was never knowing such a girl, so honest and so beautiful.'

'And yet she cared no more for Alpin than what she did for a kale-stock,' said I.

'Ah, she will say so indeed!' cries Catriona. 'Yet it was for the name and the gentle kind blood that she took me up and was so good to me.'

'Well, I will tell you why it was,' said I. 'There are all sorts of people's faces in this world. There is Barbara's face, that everyone must look at and admire, and think her a fine, brave, merry girl. And then there is your face, which is quite different—I never knew how different till to-day. You cannot see yourself, and that is why you do not understand; but it was for the love of your face that she took you up and was so good to you. And everybody in the world would do the same.'

'Everybody?' says she.

'Every living soul!' said I.

'Ah, then, that will be why the soldiers at the castle took me up!' she cried.

'Barbara has been teaching you to catch me,' said I.

'She will have taught me more than that at all events. She will have taught me a great deal about Mr David—all the ill of him, and a little that was not so ill either, now and then,' she said, smiling. 'She will have told me all there was of Mr David, only just that he would sail upon this very same ship. And why it is you go?'

I told her.

'Ah, well,' said she, 'we will be some days in company and then (I suppose) good-bye for altogether! I go to meet my father at a place of the name of Helvoetsluys, and from there to France, to be exiles by the side of our chieftain.'

I could say no more than just 'O!' the name of James More always drying up my very voice.

She was quick to perceive it, and to guess some portion of my thought.

'There is one thing I must be saying first of all, Mr David,' said she. 'I think two of my kinsfolk have not behaved to you altogether very well. And the one of them two is James More, my father, and the other is the Laird of Prestongrange. Prestongrange will have spoken by himself, or his daughter in the place of him. But for James More, my father, I have this much to say: he lay shackled in a prison; he is a plain honest soldier and a plain Highland gentleman; what they would be after he would never be guessing; but if he had understood it was to be some prejudice to a young gentleman like yourself, he would have died first. And for the sake of all your friendships, I will be asking you to pardon my father and family for that same mistake.'

'Catriona,' said I, 'what that mistake was I do not care to know. I know but the one thing—that you went to Prestongrange and begged my life upon your knees. O, I ken well it was for your father that you went, but when you were there you pleaded for me also. It is a thing I cannot speak of. There are two things I cannot think of in to myself: and the one is your good words when you called yourself my little friend, and the other that you pleaded for my life. Let us never speak more, we two, of pardon or offence.'

We stood after that silent, Catriona looking on the deck and I on her; and before there was more speech, a little wind having sprung up in the nor'-west, they began to shake out the sails and heave in upon the anchor.

There were six passengers besides our two selves, which made of it a full cabin. Three were solid merchants out of Leith, Kirkcaldy, and Dundee, all engaged in the same adventure into High Germany. One was a Hollander returning; the rest worthy merchants' wives, to the charge of one of whom Catriona was recommended. Mrs Gebbie (for that was her name) was by great good fortune heavily incommoded by the sea, and lay day and night on the broad of her back. We were besides the only creatures at all young on board the *Rose*, except a white-faced boy that did my old duty to attend upon the table; and it came about that Catriona and I were left almost entirely to ourselves. We had the next seats together at the table, where I waited on her with extraordinary pleasure. On deck, I made her a soft place with my cloak; and the weather being singularly fine for that season, with bright frosty days and nights, a steady, gentle wind, and scarce a sheet started all the way through the North Sea, we sat there (only now and again walking to and fro for warmth) from the first blink of the sun till eight or nine at night under the clear stars. The merchants or Captain Sang would sometimes glance and smile upon us, or pass a merry word or two and give us the go-by again; but the most part of the time they were deep in herring and chintzes and linen, or in computations of the slowness of the passage, and left us to our own concerns, which were very little important to any but ourselves.

At the first, we had a great deal to say, and thought ourselves pretty witty; and I was at a little pains to be the *beau*, and she (I believe) to play the young lady of experience. But soon we grew plainer with each other. I laid aside my high, clipped English (what little there was of it) and forgot to make my Edinburgh bows and scrapes; she, upon her side, fell into a sort of kind familiarity; and we dwelt together like those of the same household, only (upon my side) with a more deep emotion. About the same time, the bottom seemed to fall out of our conversation, and neither one of us the less pleased. Whiles she would tell me old wives' tales, of which she had a wonderful variety, many of them from my friend red-headed Neil. She told them very pretty, and they were pretty enough childish tales; but the pleasure to myself was in the sound of her voice, and the thought that she was telling and I listening. Whiles, again, we would sit entirely silent, not communicating even with a look, and tasting pleasure enough in the sweetness of that neighbourhood. I speak here only for myself. Of what was in the maid's mind, I am not very sure that ever I asked myself; and what was in my own, I was afraid to consider. I need make no secret of it now, either to myself or to the reader: I was fallen totally in love. She came between me and the sun. She had grown suddenly taller, as I say, but with a wholesome growth; she seemed all health, and lightness, and brave spirits; and I thought she walked like a young deer, and stood like a birch upon the mountains. It was enough for me to sit near by her on the deck; and I declare I scarce spent two thoughts upon the future, and was so well content with what I then enjoyed that I was never at the pains to imagine any further step; unless perhaps that I would be sometimes tempted to take her hand in mine and hold it there. But I was too like a miser of what joys I had, and would venture nothing on a hazard.

What we spoke was usually of ourselves or of each other, so that if anyone had been at so much pains as overhear us, he must have supposed us the most egotistical persons in the world. It befell one day when we were at this practice, that we came on a discourse of friends and friendship, and I think now that we were sailing near the wind. We said what a fine thing friendship was, and how little we had guessed of it, and how it made life a new thing, and a thousand covered things of the same kind that will have been said, since the foundation of the world, by young folk in the same predicament. Then we remarked upon the strangeness of that circumstance, that friends came together in the beginning as if they were there for the first time, and yet each had been alive a good while, losing time with other people.

'It is not much that I have done,' said she, 'and I could be telling you the five-fifths of it in two-three words. It is only a girl I am, and what can befall a girl, at all events? But I went with the clan in the year '45. The men marched with swords and firelocks, and some of them in brigades in the same set of tartan; they were not backward at the marching, I can tell you. And there were gentlemen from the Low Country, with their tenants mounted and trumpets to sound, and there was a grand skirling of war-pipes. I rode on a little Highland horse on the right hand of my father, James More, and of Glengyle himself. And here is one fine thing that I remember, that Glengyle kissed me in the face, because (says he) "my kinswoman, you are the only lady of the clan that has come out", and me a little maid of maybe twelve years old! I saw Prince Charlie too, and the blue eyes of him; he was pretty indeed! I had his hand to kiss in the front of the army. O, well, these were the good days, but it is all like a dream that I have seen and then awakened. It went what way you very well know; and these were the worst days of all, when the red-coat soldiers were out, and my father and my uncles lay in the hill, and I was to be carrying them their meat in the middle night, or at the short side of day when the cocks crow. Yes, I have walked in the night, many's the time, and my heart great in me for terror of the darkness. It is a strange thing I will never have been meddled with a bogle; but they say a maid goes safe. Next there was my uncle's marriage, and that was a dreadful affair beyond all. Jean Kay was that woman's name; and she had me in the room with her that night at Inversnaid, the night we took her from her friends in the old, ancient manner. She would and she wouldn't; she was for marrying Rob the one minute, and the next she would be for none of him. I will never have seen such a feckless creature of a woman; surely all there was of her would tell her ay or no. Well, she was a widow, and I can never be thinking a widow a good woman.'

'Catriona!' says I, 'how do you make out that?'

'I do not know,' said she; 'I am only telling you the seeming in my heart. And then to marry a new man! Fy! But that was her; and she was married again upon my Uncle Robin, and went with him awhile to kirk and market; and then wearied, or else her friends got claught of her and talked her round, or maybe she turned ashamed; at the least of it, she ran away, and went back to her own folk, and said we had held her in the lake, and I will never tell you all what. I have never thought much of any females since that day. And so in the end my father, James More, came to be cast in prison, and you know the rest of it as well as me.'

'And through all you had no friends?' said I.

'No,' said she; 'I have been pretty chief with two-three lasses on the braes, but not to call it friends.'

'Well, mine is a plain tale,' said I. 'I never had a friend to my name till I met in with you.'

'And that brave Mr Stewart?' she asked.

'O, yes, I was forgetting him,' I said. 'But he is a man, and that is very different.'

'I would think so,' said she. 'O, yes, it is quite different.'

'And then there was one other,' said I. 'I once thought I had a friend, but it proved a disappointment.'

She asked me who she was?

'It was a he, then,' said I. 'We were the two best lads at my father's school, and we thought we loved each other dearly. Well, the time came when he went to Glasgow to a merchant's house, that was his second cousin once removed; and wrote me two-three times by the carrier;

and then he found new friends, and I might write till I was tired, he took no notice. Eh, Catriona, it took me a long while to forgive the world. There is not anything more bitter than to lose a fancied friend.'

Then she began to question me close upon his looks and character, for we were each a great deal concerned in all that touched the other; till at last, in a very evil hour, I minded of his letters and went and fetched the bundle from the cabin.

'Here are his letters,' said I, 'and all the letters that ever I got. That will be the last I'll can tell of myself; you know the lave as well as I do.'

'Will you let me read them, then?' says she.

I told her, *if she would be at the pains*; and she bade me go away and she would read them from the one end to the other. Now, in this bundle that I gave her, there were packed together not only all the letters of my false friend, but one or two of Mr Campbell's when he was in town at the Assembly, and to make a complete roll of all that ever was written to me, Catriona's little word, and the two I had received from Miss Grant, one when I was on the Bass and one on board that ship. But of these last I had no particular mind at the moment.

I was in that state of subjection to the thought of my friend that it mattered not what I did, nor scarce whether I was in her presence or out of it; I had caught her like some kind of a noble fever that lived continually in my bosom, by night and by day, and whether I was waking or asleep. So it befell that after I was come into the fore-part of the ship where the broad bows splashed into the billows, I was in no such hurry to return as you might fancy; rather prolonged my absence like a variety in pleasure. I do not think I am by nature much of an Epicurean; and there had come till then so small a share of pleasure in my way that I might be excused perhaps to dwell on it unduly.

When I returned to her again, I had a faint, painful impression as of a buckle slipped, so coldly she returned the packet.

'You have read them?' said I; and I thought my voice sounded not wholly natural, for I was turning in my mind for what could ail her.

'Did you mean me to read all?' she asked.

I told her 'Yes,' with a drooping voice.

'The last of them as well?' said she.

I knew where we were now; yet I would not lie to her either. 'I gave them all without afterthought,' I said, 'as I supposed that you would read them. I see no harm in any.'

'I will be differently made,' said she. 'I thank God I am differently made. It was not a fit letter to be shown me. It was not fit to be written.'

'I think you are speaking of your own friend, Barbara Grant?' said I.

'There will not be anything as bitter as to lose a fancied friend,' said she, quoting my own expression.

'I think it is sometimes the friendship that was fancied!' I cried. 'What kind of justice do you call this, to blame me for some words that a tomfool of a madcap lass has written down upon a piece of paper? You know yourself with what respect I have behaved—and would do always.'

'Yet you would show me that same letter!' says she. 'I want no such friends. I can be doing very well, Mr Balfour, without her—or you.'

'This is your fine gratitude!' says I.

'I am very much obliged to you,' said she. 'I will be asking you to take away your—letters.' She seemed to choke upon the word, so that it sounded like an oath.

'You shall never ask twice,' said I; picked up that bundle, walked a little way forward and cast them as far as possible into the sea. For a very little more I could have cast myself after them.

The rest of the day I walked up and down raging. There were few names so ill but what I gave her them in my own mind before the sun went down. All that I had ever heard of Highland pride seemed quite out-done; that a girl (scarce grown) should resent so trifling an allusion, and that from her next friend, that she had near wearied me with praising of! I had bitter, sharp, hard thoughts of her, like an angry boy's. If I had kissed her indeed (I thought), perhaps she would have taken it pretty well; and only because it had been written down, and with a spice of jocularity, up she must fuff in this ridiculous passion. It seemed to me there was a want of penetration in the female sex, to make angels weep over the case of the poor men.

We were side by side again at supper, and what a change was there! She was like curdled milk to me; her face was like a wooden doll's; I could have indifferently smitten her or grovelled at her feet, but she gave me not the least occasion to do either. No sooner the meal done than she betook herself to attend on Mrs Gebbie, which I think she had a little neglected heretofore. But she was to make up for lost time, and in what remained of the passage was extraordinary assiduous with the old lady, and on deck began to make a great deal more than I thought wise of Captain Sang. Not but what the captain seemed a worthy, fatherly man; but I hated to behold her in the least familiarity with anyone except myself.

Altogether, she was so quick to avoid me, and so constant to keep herself surrounded with others, that I must watch a long while before I could find my opportunity; and after it was found, I made not much of it, as you are now to hear.

'I have no guess how I have offended,' said I; 'it should scarce be beyond pardon, then. O, try if you can pardon me.'

'I have no pardon to give,' said she; and the words seemed to come out of her throat like marbles. 'I will be very much obliged for all your friendships.' And she made me an eighth part of a curtsey.

But I had schooled myself beforehand to say more, and I was going to say it too.

'There is one thing,' said I. 'If I have shocked your particularity by the showing of that letter, it cannot touch Miss Grant. She wrote not to you, but to a poor, common, ordinary lad, who might have had more sense than show it. If you are to blame me—'

'I will advise you to say no more about that girl, at all events!' said Catriona. 'It is her I will never look the road of, not if she lay dying.' She turned away from me, and suddenly back. 'Will you swear you will have no more to deal with her?' she cried.

'Indeed, and I will never be so unjust then,' said I; 'nor yet so ungrateful.'

And now it was I that turned away.

THE WEATHER IN the end considerably worsened; the wind sang in the shrouds, the sea swelled higher, and the ship began to labour and cry out among the billows. The song of the leadsman in the chains was now scarce ceasing, for we thrid all the way among shoals. About nine in the morning, in a burst of wintry sun between two squalls of hail, I had my first look of Holland—a line of windmills birling in the breeze. It was besides my first knowledge of these daft-like contrivances, which gave me a near sense of foreign travel and a new world and life. We came to an anchor about half-past eleven, outside the harbour of Helvoetsluys, in a place where the sea sometimes broke and the ship pitched outrageously. You may be sure we were all on deck save Mrs Gebbie, some of us in cloaks, others mantled in the ship's tarpaulins, all clinging on by ropes, and jesting the most like old sailor-folk that we could imitate.

Presently a boat, that was backed like a partan-crab, came gingerly alongside, and the skipper of it hailed our master in the Dutch. Thence Captain Sang turned, very troubled-like, to Catriona; and the rest of us crowding about, the nature of the difficulty was made plain to all. The *Rose* was bound to the port of Rotterdam, whither the other passengers were in a great impatience to arrive, in view of a conveyance due to leave that very evening in the direction of the Upper Germany. This, with the present half-gale of wind, the captain (if no time were lost) declared himself still capable to save. Now James More had trysted in Helvoet with his daughter, and the captain had engaged to call before the port and place her (according to the custom) in a shore boat. There was the boat, to be sure, and here was Catriona ready: but both our master and the patroon of the boat scrupled at the risk, and the first was in no humour to delay.

'Your father,' said he, 'would be gey an little pleased if we was to break a leg to ye, Miss Drummond; let-a-be drowning of you. Take my way of it,' says he, 'and come on-by with the rest of us here to Rotterdam. Ye can get a passage down the Maes in a sailing scoot as far as to the Brill, and thence on again, by a place in a rattel-waggon, back to Helvoet.'

But Catriona would hear of no change. She looked white-like as she beheld the bursting of the sprays, the green seas that sometimes poured upon the forecastle, and the perpetual bounding and swooping of the boat among the billows; but she stood firmly by her father's orders. 'My father, James More, will have arranged it so,' was her first word and her last. I thought it very idle and indeed wanton in the girl to be so literal and stand opposite to so much kind advice; but the fact is she had a very good reason, if she would have told us. Sailing scoots and rattel-waggons are excellent things; only the use of them must first be paid for, and all she was possessed of in the world was just two shillings and a penny halfpenny sterling. So it fell out that captain and passengers, not knowing of her destitution—and she being too proud to tell them—spoke in vain.

'But you ken nae French and nae Dutch neither,' said one.

'It is very true,' says she, 'but since the year '46 there are so many of the honest Scots abroad that I will be doing very well, I thank you.'

There was a pretty country simplicity in this that made some laugh, others looked the more sorry, and Mr Gebbie fall outright in a passion. I believe he knew it was his duty (his wife having accepted charge of the girl) to have gone ashore with her and seen her safe: nothing would have induced him to have done so, since it must have involved the loss of his conveyance; and I think he made it up to his conscience by the loudness of his voice. At least he broke out upon Captain Sang, raging and saying the thing was a disgrace; that it was mere death to try to leave the ship, and at any event we could not cast down an innocent maid in a boatful of nasty Holland fishers, and leave her to her fate. I was thinking something of the same; took the mate upon one side, arranged with him to send on my chests by track-scoot to an address I had in Leyden, and stood up and signalled to the fishers.

'I will go ashore with the young lady, Captain Sang,' said I. 'It is all one what way I go to Leyden'; and leaped at the same time into the boat, which I managed not so elegantly but what I fell with two of the fishers in the bilge.

From the boat the business appeared yet more precarious than from the ship, she stood so high over us, swung down so swift, and menaced us so perpetually with her plunging and passaging upon the anchor cable. I began to think I had made a fool's bargain, that it was merely impossible Catriona should be got on board to me, and that I stood to be set ashore at Helvoet all by myself and with no hope of any reward but the pleasure of embracing James More, if I should want to. But this was to reckon without the lass's courage. She had seen me leap with very little appearance (however much reality) of hesitation; to be sure, she was not to be beat by her discarded friend. Up she stood on the bulwarks and held by a stay, the wind blowing in her petticoats, which made the enterprise more dangerous, and gave us rather more of a view of her stockings than would be thought genteel in cities. There was no minute lost, and scarce time given for any to interfere if they had wished the same. I stood up on the other side and spread my arms; the ship swung down on us, the patroon humoured his boat nearer in than was perhaps wholly safe, and Catriona leaped into the air. I was so happy as to catch her, and the fishers readily supporting us, escaped a fall. She held to me a moment very tight, breathing quick and deep; thence (she still clinging to me with both hands) we were passed aft to our places by the steersman; and Captain Sang and all the crew and passengers cheering and crying farewell, the boat was put about for shore.

As soon as Catriona came a little to herself she unhanded me suddenly but said no word. No more did I; and indeed the whistling of the wind and the breaching of the sprays made it no time for speech; and our crew not only toiled excessively but made extremely little way, so that the *Rose* had got her anchor and was off again before we had approached the harbour mouth.

We were no sooner in smooth water than the patroon,

according to their beastly Hollands custom, stopped his boat and required of us our fares. Two guilders was the man's demand—between three and four shillings English money—for each passenger. But at this Catriona began to cry out with a vast deal of agitation. She had asked of Captain Sang, she said, and the fare was but an English shilling. 'Do you think I will have come on board and not ask first?' cries she. The patroon scolded back upon her in a lingo where the oaths were English and the rest right Hollands; till at last (seeing her near tears) I privately slipped in the rogue's hand six shillings, whereupon he was obliging enough to receive from her the other shilling without more complaint. No doubt I was a good deal nettled and ashamed. I like to see folk thrifty, but not with so much passion; and I daresay it would be rather coldly that I asked her, as the boat moved on again for shore, where it was that she was trysted with her father.

'He is to be inquired of at the house of one Sprott, an honest Scotch merchant,' says she; and then with the same breath, 'I am wishing to thank you very much—you are a brave friend to me.'

'It will be time enough when I get you to your father,' said I, little thinking that I spoke so true. 'I can tell him a fine tale of a loyal daughter.'

'O, I do not think I will be a loyal girl, at all events,' she cried, with a great deal of painfulness in the expression. 'I do not think my heart is true.'

'Yet there are very few that would have made that leap, and all to obey a father's orders,' I observed.

'I cannot have you to be thinking of me so,' she cried again. 'When you had done that same, how would I stop behind? And at all events that was not all the reasons.' Whereupon, with a burning face, she told me the plain truth upon her poverty.

'Good guide us!' cried I, 'what kind of daft-like proceeding is this, to let yourself be launched on the continent of Europe with an empty purse—I count it hardly decent—scant decent!' I cried.

'You forget James More, my father, is a poor gentleman,' said she. 'He is a hunted exile.'

'But I think not all your friends are hunted exiles,' I exclaimed. 'And was this fair to them that care for you? Was it fair to me? was it fair to Miss Grant that counselled you to go, and would be driven fair horn-mad if she could hear of it? Was it even fair to these Gregory folk that you were living with, and used you lovingly? It's a blessing you have fallen in my hands! Suppose your father hindered by an accident, what would become of you here, and you your lee-lone in a strange place? The thought of the thing frightens me,' I said.

'I will have lied to all of them,' she replied. 'I will have told them all that I had plenty. I told *her* too. I could not be lowering James More to them.'

I found out later on that she must have lowered him in the very dust, for the lie was originally the father's, not the daughter's, and she thus obliged to persevere in it for the man's reputation. But at the time I was ignorant of this, and the mere thought of her destitution and the perils in which she must have fallen, had ruffled me almost beyond reason.

'Well, well, well,' said I, 'you will have to learn more sense.'

I left her mails for the moment in an inn upon the shore, where I got a direction for Sprott's house in my new French, and we walked there—it was some little way—beholding the place with wonder as we went. Indeed, there was much for Scots folk to admire: canals and trees being intermingled with the houses; the houses, each within itself, of a brave red brick, the colour of a rose, with steps and benches of blue marble at the cheek of every door, and the whole town so clean you might have dined upon the causeway. Sprott was within, upon his ledgers, in a low parlour, very neat and clean, and set out with china and pictures and a globe of the earth in a brass frame. He was a big-chafted, ruddy, lusty man, with a crooked hard look to him; and he made us not that much civility as offer us a seat.

'Is James More Macgregor now in Helvoet, sir?' says I.

'I ken nobody by such a name,' says he, impatient-like.

'Since you are so particular,' says I, 'I will amend my

question, and ask you where we are to find in Helvoet one James Drummond, *alias* Macgregor, *alias* James More, late tenant in Inveronachile?'

'Sir,' says he, 'he may be in Hell for what I ken, and for my part I wish he was.'

'The young lady is that gentleman's daughter, sir,' said I, 'before whom, I think you will agree with me, it is not very becoming to discuss his character.'

'I have nothing to make either with him, or her, or you!' cries he in his gross voice.

'Under your favour, Mr Sprott,' said I, 'this young lady is come from Scotland seeking him, and by whatever mistake, was given the name of your house for a direction. An error it seems to have been, but I think this places both you and me—who am but her fellow-traveller by accident—under a strong obligation to help our countrywoman.'

'Will you ding me daft?' he cries. 'I tell ye I ken naething and care less either for him or his breed. I tell ye the man owes me money.'

'That may very well be, sir,' said I, who was now rather more angry than himself. 'At least, I owe you nothing; the young lady is under my protection; and I am neither at all used with these manners, nor in the least content with them.'

As I said this, and without particularly thinking what I did, I drew a step or two nearer to his table; thus striking, by mere good fortune, on the only argument that could at all affect the man. The blood left his lusty countenance.

'For the Lord's sake dinna be hasty, sir!' he cried. 'I am truly wishfu' no to be offensive. But ye ken, sir, I'm like a wheen guid-natured, honest, canty auld fallows—my bark is waur nor my bite. To hear me, ye micht whiles fancy I was a wee thing dour; but na, na! it's a kind auld fallow at heart, Sandie Sprott! And ye could never imagine the fyke and fash this man has been to me.'

'Very good, sir,' said I. 'Then I will make that much freedom with your kindness as trouble you for your last news of Mr Drummond.'

'You're welcome, sir!' said he. 'As for the young leddy (my respec's to her!), he'll just have clean forgotten her. I ken the man, ye see; I have lost siller by him ere now. He thinks of naebody but just himsel': clan, king, or dauchter, if he can get his wameful, he would give them a' the go-by! ay, or his correspondent either. For there is a sense in whilk I may be nearly almost said to be his correspondent. The fact is, we are employed thegether in a business affair, and I think it's like to turn out a dear affair for Sandie Sprott. The man's as guid's my pairtner, and I give ye my mere word I ken naething by where he is. He micht be coming here to Helvoet; he micht come here the morn, he michtnae come for a twalmonth; I would wonder at naething—or just at the ae thing, and that's if he was to pay me my siller. Ye see what way I stand with it; and it's clear I'm no very likely to meddle up with the young leddy, as ye ca' her. She cannae stop here, that's ae thing certain sure. Dod, sir, I'm a lone man! If I was to tak her in, it's highly possible the hellicat would try and gar me marry her when he turned up.'

'Enough of this talk,' said I. 'I will take the young lady among better friends. Give me pen, ink, and paper, and I will leave here for James More the address of my correspondent in Leyden. He can inquire from me where he is to seek his daughter.'

This word I wrote and sealed; which while I was doing, Sprott of his own motion made a welcome offer, to charge himself with Miss Drummond's mails, and even send a porter for them to the inn. I advanced him to that effect a dollar or two to be a cover, and he gave me an acknowledgment in writing of the sum.

Whereupon (I giving my arm to Catriona) we left the house of this unpalatable rascal. She had said no word throughout, leaving me to judge and speak in her place; I, upon my side, had been careful not to embarrass her by a glance; and even now, although my heart still glowed inside of me with shame and anger, I made it my affair to seem quite easy.

'Now,' said I, 'let us get back to yon same inn where they can speak the French, have a piece of dinner, and inquire for conveyances to Rotterdam. I will never be easy till I have you safe again in the hands of Mrs Gebbie.'

'I suppose it will have to be,' said Catriona, 'though whoever will be pleased, I do not think it will be her.

And I will remind you this once again that I have but one shilling, and three baubees.'

'And just this once again,' said I, 'I will remind you it was a blessing that I came alongst with you.'

'What else would I be thinking all this time?' says she, and I thought weighed a little on my arm. 'It is you that are the good friend to me.'

THE RATTEL-WAGON, which is a kind of a long wagon set with benches, carried us in four hours of travel to the great city of Rotterdam. It was long past dark by then, but the streets pretty brightly lighted and thronged with wild-like, outlandish characters—bearded Hebrews, black men, and the hordes of courtesans, most indecently adorned with finery and stopping seamen by their very sleeves; the clash of talk about us made our heads to whirl; and what was the most unexpected of all, we appeared to be no more struck with all these foreigners than they with us. I made the best face I could, for the lass's sake and my own credit; but the truth is I felt like a lost sheep, and my heart beat in my bosom with anxiety. Once or twice I inquired after the harbour or the berth of the ship *Rose*; but either fell on some who spoke only Hollands, or my own French failed me. Trying a street at a venture, I came upon a lane of lighted houses, the doors and windows thronged with wauf-like painted women; these jostled and mocked upon us as we passed, and I was thankful we had nothing of their language. A little after we issued forth upon an open place along the harbour.

'We shall be doing now,' cries I, as soon as I spied masts. 'Let us walk here by the harbour. We are sure to meet some that has the English, and at the best of it we may light upon that very ship.'

We did the next best, as happened; for, about nine of the evening, whom should we walk into the arms of but Captain Sang? He told us they had made their run in the most incredible brief time, the wind holding strong till they reached port; by which means his passengers were all gone already on their further travels. It was impossible to chase after the Gebbies into the High Germany, and we had no other acquaintance to fall back upon but Captain Sang himself. It was the more gratifying to find the man friendly and wishful to assist. He made it a small affair to find some good plain family of merchants, where Catriona might harbour till the *Rose* was loaden; declared he would then blithely carry her back to Leith for nothing and see her safe in the hands of Mr Gregory; and in the meanwhile carried us to a late ordinary for the meal we stood in need of. He seemed extremely friendly, as I say, but what surprised me a good deal, rather boisterous in the bargain; and the cause of this was soon to appear. For at the ordinary, calling for Rhenish wine and drinking of it deep, he soon became unutterably tipsy. In this case, as too common with all men, but especially with those of his rough trade, what little sense or manners he possessed deserted him; and he behaved himself so scandalous to the young lady, jesting most ill-favouredly at the figure she had made on the ship's rail, that I had no resource but carry her suddenly away.

She came out of that ordinary clinging to me close. 'Take me away, David,' she said. '*You* keep me. I am not afraid with you.'

'And have no cause, my little friend!' cried I, and could have found it in my heart to weep.

'Where will you be taking me?' she said again. 'Don't leave me at all events—never leave me.'

'Where am I taking you indeed?' says I stopping, for I had been staving on ahead in mere blindness. 'I must stop and think. But I'll not leave you, Catriona; the Lord do so to me, and more also, if I should fail or fash you.'

She crept closer in to me by way of a reply.

'Here,' I said, 'is the stillest place that we have hit on yet in this busy byke of a city. Let us sit down here under yon tree and consider of our course.'

That tree (which I am little like to forget) stood hard by the harbour side. It was a black night, but lights were in the houses, and nearer hand in the quiet ships; there was a shining of the city on the one hand, and a buzz hung over it of many thousands walking and talking; on the other, it was dark and the water bubbled on the sides. I spread my cloak upon a builder's stone, and made her sit there; she would have kept her hold upon me, for she still shook with the late affronts; but I wanted to think clear, disengaged myself, and paced to and fro before her, in the manner of what we call a smuggler's walk, belabouring my brains for any remedy. By the course of these scattering thoughts I was brought suddenly face to face with a remembrance that, in the heat and haste of our departure, I had left Captain Sang to pay the ordinary. At this I began to laugh out loud, for I thought the man well served; and at the same time, by an instinctive movement, carried my hand to the pocket where my money was. I suppose it was in the lane where the women jostled us; but there is only the one thing certain, that my purse was gone.

'You will have thought of something good,' said she, observing me to pause.

At the pinch we were in, my mind became suddenly clear as a perspective glass, and I saw there was no choice of methods. I had not one doit of coin, but in my pocket-book I had still my letter on the Leyden merchant; and there was now but the one way to get to Leyden, and that was to walk on our two feet.

'Catriona,' said I, 'I know you're brave and I believe you're strong—do you think you could walk thirty miles on a plain road?' We found it, I believe, scarce the two-thirds of that, but such was my notion of the distance.

'David,' she said, 'if you will just keep near, I will go anywhere and do anything. The courage of my heart, it is all broken. Do not be leaving me in this horrible country by myself, and I will do all else.'

'Can you start now and march all night?' said I.

'I will do all that you can ask of me,' she said, 'and never ask you why. I have been a bad ungrateful girl to you; and do what you please with me now! And I think Miss Barbara Grant is the best lady in the world,' she added, 'and I do not see what she would deny you for at all events.'

This was Greek and Hebrew to me; but I had other matters to consider, and the first of these was to get clear of that city on the Leyden road. It proved a cruel problem; and it may have been one or two at night ere we had solved it. Once beyond the houses, there was neither moon nor stars to guide us; only the whiteness of the way in the midst and a blackness of an alley on both hands. The walking was besides made most extraordinary difficult by a plain black frost that fell suddenly in the small hours and turned that highway into one long slide.

'Well, Catriona,' said I, 'here we are like the king's sons and the old wives' daughters in your daft-like Highland tales. Soon we'll be going over the "*seven Bens, the seven glens, and the seven mountain moors*".' Which was a common byword or overcome in those tales of hers that had stuck in my memory.

'Ah,' says she, 'but here are no glens or mountains! Though I will never be denying but what the trees and some of the plain places hereabouts are very pretty. But our country is the best yet.'

'I wish we could say as much for our own folk,' says I, recalling Sprott and Sang, and perhaps James More himself.

'I will never complain of the country of my friend,' said she, and spoke it out with an accent so particular that I seemed to see the look upon her face.

I caught in my breath sharp and came near falling (for my pains) on the black ice.

'I do not know what *you* think, Catriona,' said I, when I was a little recovered, 'but this has been the best day yet! I think shame to say it, when you have met in with such misfortunes and disfavours; but for me, it has been the best day yet.'

'It was a good day when you showed me so much love,' said she.

'And yet I think shame to be happy too,' I went on, 'and you here on the road in the black night.'

'Where in the great world would I be else?' she cried. 'I am thinking I am safest where I am with you.'

'I am quite forgiven, then?' I asked.

'Will you not forgive me that time so much as not to take it in your mouth again?' she cried. 'There is nothing in this heart to you but thanks. But I will be honest too,' she added, with a kind of suddenness, 'and I'll never can forgive that girl.'

'Is this Miss Grant again?' said I. 'You said yourself she was the best lady in the world.'

'So she will be, indeed!' says Catriona. 'But I will never forgive her for all that. I will never, never forgive her, and let me hear tell of her no more.'

'Well,' said I, 'this beats all that ever came to my knowledge; and I wonder that you can indulge yourself in such bairnly whims. Here is a young lady that was the best friend in the world to the both of us, that learned us how to dress ourselves, and in a great manner how to behave, as anyone can see that knew us both before and after.'

But Catriona stopped square in the midst of the highway.

'It is this way of it,' said she. 'Either you will go on to speak of her, and I will go back to yon town, and let come of it what God pleases! Or else you will do me that politeness to talk of other things.'

I was the most nonplussed person in this world; but I bethought me that she depended altogether on my help, that she was of the frail sex and not so much beyond a child, and it was for me to be wise for the pair of us.

'My dear girl,' said I, 'I can make neither head nor tails of this; but God forbid that I should do anything to set you on the jee. As for talking of Miss Grant, I have no such a mind to it, and I believe it was yourself began it. My only design (if I took you up at all) was for your own improvement, for I hate the very look of injustice. Not that I do not wish you to have a good pride and a nice female delicacy; they become you well; but here you show them to excess.'

'Well, then, have you done?' said she.

'I have done,' said I.

'A very good thing,' said she, and we went on again, but now in silence.

It was an eerie employment to walk in the gross night, beholding only shadows and hearing nought but our own steps. At first, I believe our hearts burned against each other with a deal of enmity; but the darkness and the cold, and the silence, which only the cocks sometimes interrupted, or sometimes the farmyard dogs, had pretty soon brought down our pride to the dust; and for my own particular, I would have jumped at any decent opening for speech.

Before the day peeped, came on a warmish rain, and the frost was all wiped away from among our feet. I took my cloak to her and sought to hap her in the same; she bade me, rather impatiently, to keep it.

'Indeed and I will do no such thing,' said I. 'Here am I, a great, ugly lad that has seen all kinds of weather, and here are you a tender, pretty maid! My dear, you would not put me to a shame?'

Without more words she let me cover her; which as I was doing in the darkness, I let my hand rest a moment on her shoulder, almost like an embrace.

'You must try to be more patient of your friend,' said I.

I thought she seemed to lean the least thing in the world against my bosom, or perhaps it was but fancy.

'There will be no end to your goodness,' said she.

And we went on again in silence; but now all was changed; and the happiness that was in my heart was like a fire in a great chimney.

The rain passed ere day; it was but a sloppy morning as we came into the town of Delft. The red gabled houses made a handsome show on either hand of a canal; the servant lassies were out slestering and scrubbing at the very stones upon the public highway; smoke rose from a hundred kitchens; and it came in upon me strongly it was time to break our fasts.

'Catriona,' said I, 'I believe you have yet a shilling and three baubees?'

'Are you wanting it?' said she, and passed me her purse. 'I am wishing it was five pounds! What will you want it for?'

'And what have we been walking for all night, like a pair of waif Egyptians?' says I. 'Just because I was robbed of my purse and all I possessed in that unchancy town of Rotterdam. I will tell you of it now, because I think the worst is over, but we have still a good tramp before us till we get to where any money is, and if you would not buy me a piece of bread, I were like to go fasting.'

She looked at me with open eyes. By the light of the new day she was all black and pale for weariness, so that my heart smote me for her. But as for her, she broke out laughing.

'My torture! are we beggars then?' she cried. 'You too? O, I could have wished for this same thing! And

I am glad to buy your breakfast to you. But it would be pleisand if I would have had to dance to get a meal to you! For I believe they are not very well acquainted with our manner of dancing over here, and might be paying for the curiosity of that sight.'

I could have kissed her for that word, not with a lover's mind, but in a heat of admiration. For it always warms a man to see a woman brave.

We got a drink of milk from a country wife but new come to the town, and in a baker's, a piece of excellent, hot, sweet-smelling bread, which we ate upon the road as we went on. That road from Delft to the Hague is just five miles of a fine avenue shaded with trees, a canal on the one hand, on the other excellent pastures of cattle. It was pleasant here indeed.

'And now, Davie,' said she, 'what will you do with me at all events?'

'It is what we have to speak of,' said I, 'and the sooner yet the better. I can come by money in Leyden; that will be all well. But the trouble is how to dispose of you until your father come. I thought last night you seemed a little sweir to part from me?'

'It will be more than seeming then,' said she.

'You are a very young maid,' said I, 'and I am but a very young callant. This is a great piece of difficulty. What way are we to manage? Unless indeed, you could pass to be my sister?'

'And what for no?' said she, 'if you would let me!'

'I wish you were so, indeed!' I cried. 'I would be a fine man if I had such a sister. But the rub is that you are Catriona Drummond.'

'And now I will be Catrine Balfour,' she said. 'And who is to ken? They are all strange folk here.'

'If you think that it would do,' says I. 'I own it troubles me. I would like it very ill, if I advised you at all wrong.'

'David, I have no friend here but you,' she said.

'The mere truth is, I am too young to be your friend,' said I. 'I am too young to advise you, or you to be advised. I see not what else we are to do, and yet I ought to warn you.'

'I will have no choice left,' said she. 'My father James More has not used me very well, and it is not the first time. I am cast upon your hands like a sack of barley meal, and have nothing else to think of but your pleasure. If you will have me, good and well. If you will not'—she turned and touched her hand upon my arm—'David, I am afraid,' said she.

'No, but I ought to warn you,' I began; and then bethought me that I was the bearer of the purse, and it would never do to seem too churlish. 'Catriona,' said I, 'don't misunderstand me: I am just trying to do my duty by you, girl! Here am I going alone to this strange city, to be a solitary student there; and here is this chance arisen that you might dwell with me a bit, and be like my sister; you can surely understand this much, my dear, that I would just love to have you?'

'Well, and here I am,' said she. 'So that's soon settled.'

I know I was in duty bounden to have spoke more plain. I know this was a great blot on my character, for which I was lucky that I did not pay more dear. But I minded how easy her delicacy had been startled with a word of kissing her in Barbara's letter; now that she depended on me, how was I to be more bold? Besides, the truth is, I could see no other feasible method to dispose of her. And I daresay inclination pulled me very strong.

A little beyond the Hague she fell very lame and made the rest of the distance heavily enough. Twice she must rest by the wayside, which she did with pretty apologies, calling herself a shame to the Highlands and the race she came of, and nothing but a hindrance to myself. It was her excuse, she said, that she was not much used with walking shod. I would have had her strip off her shoes and stockings and go barefoot. But she pointed out to me that the women of that country, even in the landward roads, appeared to be all shod.

'I must not be disgracing my brother,' said she, and was very merry with it all, although her face told tales of her.

There is a garden in that city we were bound to, sanded below with clean sand, the trees meeting overhead, some of them trimmed, some pleached, and the whole place beautified with alleys and arbours. Here I left Catriona, and went forward by myself to find my correspondent. There

I drew on my credit, and asked to be recommended to some decent, retired lodging. My baggage not being yet arrived, I told him I supposed I should require his caution with the people of the house; and explained that, my sister being come for a while to keep house with me, I should be wanting two chambers. This was all very well; but the trouble was that Mr Balfour in his letter of recommendation had condescended on a great deal of particulars, and never a word of any sister in the case. I could see my Dutchman was extremely suspicious; and viewing me over the rims of a great pair of spectacles—he was a poor, frail body, and reminded me of an infirm rabbit—he began to question me close.

Here I fell in a panic. Suppose he accept my tale (thinks I), suppose he invite my sister to his house, and that I bring her. I shall have a fine ravelled pirn to unwind, and may end by disgracing both the lassie and myself. Thereupon I began hastily to expound to him my sister's character. She was of a bashful disposition, it appeared, and so extremely fearful of meeting strangers that I had left her at that moment sitting in a public place alone. And then, being launched upon the stream of falsehood, I must do like all the rest of the world in the same circumstance, and plunge in deeper than was any service; adding some altogether needless particulars of Miss Balfour's ill-health and retirement during childhood. In the midst of which I awoke to a sense of my behaviour, and was turned to one blush.

The old gentleman was not so much deceived but what he discovered a willingness to be quit of me. But he was first of all a man of business; and knowing that my money was good enough, however it might be with my conduct, he was so far obliging as to send his son to be my guide and caution in the matter of a lodging. This implied my presenting of the young man to Catriona. The poor, pretty child was much recovered with resting, looked and behaved to perfection, and took my arm and gave me the name of brother more easily than I could answer her. But there was one misfortune: thinking to help, she was rather towardly than otherwise to my Dutchman. And I could not but reflect that Miss Balfour had rather suddenly outgrown her bashfulness. And there was another thing, the difference of our speech. I had the Low Country tongue and dwelled upon my words; she had a hill voice, spoke with something of an English accent, only far more delightful, and was scarce quite fit to be called a deacon in the craft of talking English grammar; so that, for a brother and sister, we made a most uneven pair. But the young Hollander was a heavy dog, without so much spirit in his belly as to remark her prettiness, for which I scorned him. And as soon as he had found a cover to our heads, he left us alone, which was the greater service of the two.

THE PLACE FOUND was in the upper part of a house backed on a canal. We had two rooms, the second entering from the first; each had a chimney built out into the floor in the Dutch manner; and being alongside, each had the same prospect from the window of the top of a tree below us in a little court, of a piece of the canal, and of houses in the Hollands architecture and a church spire upon the further side. A full set of bells hung in that spire and made delightful music; and when there was any sun at all, it shone direct in our two chambers. From a tavern hard by we had good meals sent in.

The first night we were both pretty weary, and she extremely so. There was little talk between us, and I packed her off to her bed as soon as she had eaten. The first thing in the morning I wrote word to Sprott to have her mails sent on, together with a line to Alan at his chief's; and had the same despatched, and her breakfast ready, ere I waked her. I was a little abashed when she came forth in her one habit, and the mud of the way upon her stockings. By what inquiries I had made, it seemed a good few days must pass before her mails could come to hand in Leyden, and it was plainly needful she must have a shift of things. She was unwilling at first that I should go to that expense; but I reminded her she was now a rich man's sister and must appear suitably in the part, and we had not got to the second merchant's before she was entirely charmed into the spirit of the thing, and her eyes shining. It pleased me to see her so innocent and thorough in this pleasure. What was more extraordinary was the passion into which I fell on it myself; being never satisfied that I had bought her enough or fine enough, and never weary of beholding her in different attires. Indeed, I began to understand some little of Miss Grant's immersion in that interest of clothes; for the truth is, when you have the ground of a beautiful person to adorn, the whole business becomes beautiful. The Dutch chintzes I should say were extraordinary cheap and fine; but I would be ashamed to set down what I paid for stockings to her. Altogether I spent so great a sum upon this pleasuring (as I may call it) that I was ashamed for a great while to spend more; and by way of a set-off, I left our chambers pretty bare. If we had beds, if Catriona was a little braw, and I had light to see her by, we were richly enough lodged for me.

By the end of this merchandising I was glad to leave her at the door with all our purchases, and go for a long walk alone in which to read myself a lecture. Here had I taken under my roof, and as good as to my bosom, a young lass extremely beautiful, and whose innocence was her peril. My talk with the old Dutchman, and the lies to which I was constrained, had already given me a sense of how my conduct must appear to others; and now, after the strong admiration I had just experienced and the immoderacy with which I had continued my vain purchases, I began to think of it myself as very hazarded. I bethought me, if I had a sister indeed, whether I would so expose her; then, judging the case too problematical, I varied my question into this, whether I would so trust Catriona in the hands of any other Christian being: the answer to which made my face to burn. The more cause, since I had been entrapped and had entrapped the girl into an undue situation, that I should behave in it with scrupulous nicety. She depended on me wholly for her bread and shelter; in case I should alarm her delicacy, she had no retreat. Besides, I was her host and her protector; and the more irregularly I had fallen in these positions, the less excuse for me if I should profit by the same to forward even the most honest suit; for with the opportunities that I enjoyed, and which no wise parent would have suffered for a moment, even the most honest suit would be unfair. I saw I must be extremely hold-off in my relations; and yet not too much so neither; for if I had no right to appear at all in the character of a suitor, I must yet appear continually, and if possible agreeably, in that of host. It was plain I should require a great deal of tact and conduct, perhaps more than my years afforded. But I had rushed in where angels might have feared to tread, and there was no way out of that position save by behaving right while I was in it. I made a set of rules for my guidance; prayed for strength to be enabled to observe them, and as a more human aid to the same end purchased a study-book in law. This being all that I could think of, I relaxed from these grave considerations; whereupon my mind bubbled at once into an effervescency of pleasing spirits, and it was like one treading on air that I turned homeward. As I thought that name of home, and recalled the image of that figure awaiting me between four walls, my heart beat upon my bosom.

My troubles began with my return. She ran to greet me with an obvious and affecting pleasure. She was clad, besides, entirely in the new clothes that I had bought for her; looked in them beyond expression well; and must walk about and drop me curtseys to display them and to be admired. I am sure I did it with an ill grace, for I thought to have choked upon the words.

'Well,' she said, 'if you will not be caring for my pretty clothes, see what I have done with our two chambers.' And she showed me the place all very finely swept and the fires glowing in the two chimneys.

I was glad of a chance to seem a little more severe than I quite felt. 'Catriona,' said I, 'I am very much displeased with you, and you must never again lay a hand upon my room. One of us two must have the rule while we are here together; it is most fit it should be I who am both the man and the elder; and I give you that for my command.'

She dropped me one of her curtseys, which were extraordinary taking. 'If you will be cross,' said she, 'I must be making pretty manners at you, Davie. I will be very obedient, as I should be when every stitch upon all there is of me belongs to you. But you will not be very cross either, because now I have not anyone else.'

This struck me hard, and I made haste, in a kind of penitence, to blot out all the good effect of my last speech. In this direction progress was more easy, being down hill; she led me forward, smiling; at the sight of her, in the brightness of the fire and with her pretty becks and looks, my heart was altogether melted. We made our meal with infinite mirth and tenderness; and the two seemed to be commingled into one, so that our very laughter sounded like a kindness.

In the midst of which I awoke to better recollections, made a lame word of excuse, and set myself boorishly to my studies. It was a substantial, instructive book that I had bought, by the late Dr Heineccius, in which I was to do a great deal of reading these next days, and often very glad that I had no one to question me of what I read. Methought she bit her lip at me a little, and that cut me. Indeed it left her wholly solitary, the more as she was very little of a reader, and had never a book. But what was I to do?

So the rest of the evening flowed by almost without speech.

I could have beat myself. I could not lie in my bed that night for rage and repentance, but walked to and fro on my bare feet till I was nearly perished, for the chimney was gone out and the frost keen. The thought of her in the next room, the thought that she might even hear me as I walked, the remembrance of my churlishness and that I must continue to practise the same ungrateful course or be dishonoured, put me beside my reason. I stood like a man between Scylla and Charybdis: *What must she think of me?* was my one thought that softened me continually into weakness. *What is to become of us?* the other which steeled me again to resolution. This was my first night of wakefulness and divided counsels, of which I was now to pass many, pacing like a madman, sometimes weeping like a childish boy, sometimes praying (I would fain hope) like a Christian.

But prayer is not very difficult, and the hitch comes in practice. In her presence, and above all if I allowed any beginning of familiarity, I found I had very little command of what should follow. But to sit all day in the same room with her, and feign to be engaged upon Heineccius, surpassed my strength. So that I fell instead upon the expedient of absenting myself so much as I was able; taking out classes and sitting there regularly, often with small attention, the test of which I found the other day in a note-book of that period, where I had left off to follow an edifying lecture and actually scribbled in my book some very ill verses, though the Latinity is rather better than I thought I could ever have compassed. The evil of this course was unhappily near as great as its advantage. I had the less time of trial, but I believe, while that time lasted, I was tried the more extremely. For she being so much left to solitude, she came to greet my return with an increasing fervour that came nigh to overmaster me. These friendly offers I must barbarously cast back; and my rejection sometimes wounded her so cruelly that I must unbend and seek to make it up to her in kindness. So that our time passed in ups and downs, tiffs and disappointments, upon the which I could almost say (if it may be said with reverence) that I was crucified.

The base of my trouble was Catriona's extraordinary innocence, at which I was not so much surprised as filled with pity and admiration. She seemed to have no thought of our position, no sense of my struggles; welcomed any mark of my weakness with responsive joy; and when I was drove again to my retrenchments, did not always dissemble her chagrin. There were times when I have thought to myself, 'If she were over head in love, and set her cap to catch me, she would scarce behave much otherwise'; and then I would fall again into wonder at the simplicity of woman, from whom I felt (in these moments) that I was not worthy to be descended.

There was one point in particular on which our warfare turned, and of all things, this was the question of her clothes. My baggage had soon followed me from Rotterdam, and hers from Helvoet. She had now, as it were, two wardrobes; and it grew to be understood between us (I could never tell how) that when she was friendly she would wear my clothes, and when otherwise her own. It was meant for a buffet, and (as it were) the renunciation of her gratitude; and I felt it so in my bosom, but was generally more wise than to appear to have observed the circumstance.

Once, indeed, I was betrayed into a childishness greater than her own; it fell in this way. On my return from classes, thinking upon her devoutly with a great deal of love and a good deal of annoyance in the bargain, the annoyance began to fade away out of my mind; and spying in a window one of those forced flowers, of which the Hollanders are so skilled in the artifice, I gave way to an impulse and bought it for Catriona. I do not know the name of that flower, but it was of the pink colour, and I thought she would admire the same, and carried it home to her with a wonderful soft heart. I had left her in my clothes, and when I returned to find her all changed and a face to match, I cast but the one look at her from head to foot, ground my teeth together, flung the window open, and my flower into the court, and then (between rage and prudence) myself out of that room again, of which I slammed the door as I went out.

On the steep stair I came near falling, and this brought me to myself, so that I began at once to see the folly of my conduct. I went, not into the street as I had purposed, but to the house court, which was always a solitary place, and where I saw my flower (that had cost me vastly more than it was worth) hanging in the leafless tree. I stood by the side of the canal, and looked upon the ice. Country people went by on their skates, and I envied them. I could see no way out of the pickle I was in: no way so much as to return to the room I had just left. No doubt was in my mind but I had now betrayed the secret of my feelings; and to make things worse, I had shown at the same time (and that with wretched boyishness) incivility to my helpless guest.

I suppose she must have seen me from the open window. It did not seem to me that I had stood there very long before I heard the crunching of footsteps on the frozen snow, and turning somewhat angrily (for I was in no spirit to be interrupted) saw Catriona drawing near. She was all changed again, to the clocked stockings.

'Are we not to have our walk to-day?' said she.

I was looking at her in a maze. 'Where is your brooch?' says I.

She carried her hand to her bosom and coloured high. 'I will have forgotten it,' said she. 'I will run upstairs for it quick, and then surely we'll can have our walk?'

There was a note of pleading in that last that staggered me; I had neither words nor voice to utter them; I could do no more than nod by way of answer; and the moment she had left me, climbed into the tree and recovered my flower, which on her return I offered her.

'I bought it for you, Catriona,' said I.

She fixed it in the midst of her bosom with the brooch, I could have thought tenderly.

'It is none the better of my handling,' said I again, and blushed.

'I will be liking it none the worse, you may be sure of that,' said she.

We did not speak so much that day; she seemed a thought on the reserve, though not unkindly. As for me, all the time of our walking, and after we came home, and I had seen her put my flower into a pot of water, I was thinking to myself what puzzles women were. I was thinking, the one moment, it was the most stupid thing on earth she should not have perceived my love; and the next, that she had certainly perceived it long ago, and (being a wise girl with the fine female instinct of propriety) concealed her knowledge.

We had our walk daily. Out in the streets I felt more safe; I relaxed a little in my guardedness; and for one thing, there was no Heineccius. This made these periods not only a relief to myself, but a particular pleasure to my poor child. When I came back about the hour appointed, I would generally find her ready dressed and glowing with anticipation. She would prolong their duration to the extreme, seeming to dread (as I did myself) the hour of the return; and there is scarce a field or waterside near Leyden, scarce a street or lane there, where we have not lingered. Outside of these, I bade her confine herself entirely to our lodgings; this in the fear of her encountering any acquaintance, which would have rendered our position very difficult. From the same apprehension I would never suffer her to attend church, nor even go myself; but made some kind of shift to hold worship privately in our own chamber—I hope with an honest, but I am quite sure with a very much divided mind. Indeed, there was scarce anything that more affected me, than thus to kneel down alone with her before God like man and wife.

One day it was snowing downright hard. I had thought it not possible that we should venture forth, and was surprised to find her waiting for me ready dressed.

'I will not be doing without my walk,' she cried. 'You are never a good boy, Davie, in the house; I will never be caring for you only in the open air. I think we two will better turn Egyptian and dwell by the roadside.'

That was the best walk yet of all of them; she clung near to me in the falling snow; it beat about and melted on us, and the drops stood upon her bright cheeks like tears and ran into her smiling mouth. Strength seemed to come upon me with the sight like a giant's; I thought I could have caught her up and run with her into the uttermost places in the earth; and we spoke together all that time beyond belief for freedom and sweetness.

It was the dark night when we came to the house door. She pressed my arm upon her bosom. 'Thank you kindly for these same good hours,' said she, on a deep note of her voice.

The concern in which I fell instantly on this address, put me with the same swiftness on my guard; and we were no sooner in the chamber, and the light made, than she beheld the old, dour, stubborn countenance of the student of Heineccius. Doubtless she was more than usually hurt; and I know for myself, I found it more than usually difficult to maintain my strangeness. Even at the meal, I durst scarce unbuckle and scarce lift my eyes to her; and it was no sooner over than I fell again to my civilian, with more seeming abstraction and less understanding than before. Methought, as I read, I could hear my heart strike like an eight-day clock. Hard as I feigned to study, there was still some of my eyesight that spilled beyond the book upon Catriona. She sat on the floor by the side of my great mail, and the chimney lighted her up, and shone and blinked upon her, and made her glow and darken through a wonder of fine hues. Now she would be gazing in the fire, and then again at me; and at that I would be plunged in a terror of myself, and turn the pages of Heineccius like a man looking for the text in church.

Suddenly she called out aloud. 'O, why does not my father come?' she cried, and fell at once into a storm of tears.

I leaped up, flung Heineccius fairly in the fire, ran to her side, and cast an arm around her sobbing body.

She put me from her sharply. 'You do not love your friend,' says she. 'I could be so happy too, if you would let me!' And then, 'O, what will I have done that you should hate me so?'

'Hate you!' cries I, and held her firm. 'You blind lass, can you not see a little in my wretched heart? Do you think when I sit there, reading in that fool-book that I have just burned and be damned to it, I take ever the least thought of any stricken thing but just yourself? Night after night I could have grat to see you sitting there your lone. And what was I to do? You are here under my honour; would you punish me for that? Is it for that that you would spurn a loving servant?'

At the word, with a small, sudden motion, she clung near to me. I raised her face to mine, I kissed it, and she bowed her brow upon my bosom, clasping me tight. I sat in a mere whirl like a man drunken. Then I heard her voice sound very small and muffled in my clothes.

'Did you kiss her truly?' she asked.

There went through me so great a heave of surprise that I was all shook with it.

'Miss Grant!' I cried, all in a disorder. 'Yes, I asked her to kiss me good-bye, the which she did.'

'Ah, well!' said she, 'you have kissed me too, at all events.'

At the strangeness and sweetness of that word, I saw where we had fallen; rose, and set her on her feet.

'This will never do,' said I. 'This will never, never do. O Catrine, Catrine!' Then there came a pause in which I was debarred from any speaking. And then, 'Go away to your bed,' said I. 'Go away to your bed and leave me.'

She turned to obey me like a little child, and the next I knew of it, had stopped in the very doorway.

'Good night, Davie!' said she.

'And O, good night, my love!' I cried, with a great outbreak of my soul, and caught her to me again, so that it seemed I must have broken her. The next moment I had thrust her from the room, shut to the door even with violence, and stood alone.

The milk was spilt now, the word was out and the truth

told. I had crept like an untrusty man into the poor maid's
affections; she was in my hand like any frail, innocent thing
to make or mar; and what weapon of defence was left me?
It seemed like a symbol that Heineccius, my old protection,
was now burned. I repented, yet could not find it in my
heart to blame myself for that great failure. It seemed not
possible to have resisted the boldness of her innocence or
that last temptation of her weeping. And all that I had to
excuse me did but make my sin appear the greater—it
was upon a nature so defenceless, and with such advantages
of the position, that I seemed to have practised.

What was to become of us now? It seemed we could no
longer dwell in the one place. But where was I to go? or
where she? Without either choice or fault of ours, life had
conspired to wall us together in that narrow place. I had a
wild thought of marrying out of hand; and the next moment
put it from me with revolt. She was a child, she could not tell
her own heart; I had surprised her weakness, I must never
go on to build on that surprisal; I must keep her not only
clear of reproach, but free as she had come to me.

Down I sat before the fire, and reflected, and repented,
and beat my brains in vain for any means of escape. About
two of the morning, there were three red embers left and
the house and all the city was asleep, when I was aware of a
small sound of weeping in the next room. She thought that
I slept, the poor soul; she regretted her weakness—and
what perhaps (God help her!) she called her forward-
ness—and in the dead of the night solaced herself with
tears. Tender and bitter feelings, love and penitence and
pity, struggled in my soul; it seemed I was under bond
to heal that weeping.

'O, try to forgive me!' I cried out, 'try, try to forgive
me. Let us forget it all, let us try if we'll no can forget it!'

There came no answer, but the sobbing ceased. I stood
a long while with my hands still clasped as I had spoken;
then the cold of the night laid hold upon me with a shudder,
and I think my reason reawakened.

'You can make no hand of this, Davie,' thinks I. 'To bed
with you like a wise lad, and try if you can sleep. To-morrow
you may see your way.'

I WAS CALLED on the morrow out of a late and troubled slumber by a knocking on my door, ran to open it, and had almost swooned with the contrariety of my feelings, mostly painful; for on the threshold, in a rough wraprascal and an extraordinary big laced hat, there stood James More.

I ought to have been glad perhaps without admixture, for there was a sense in which the man came like an answer to prayer. I had been saying till my head was weary that Catriona and I must separate, and looking till my head ached for any possible means of separation. Here were the means come to me upon two legs, and joy was the hindmost of my thoughts. It is to be considered, however, that even if the weight of the future were lifted off me by the man's arrival, the present heaved up the more black and menacing; so that, as I first stood before him in my shirt and breeches, I believe I took a leaping step backward like a person shot.

'Ah,' said he, 'I have found you, Mr Balfour.' And offered me his large, fine hand, the which (recovering at the same time my post in the doorway, as if with some thought of resistance) I took him by doubtfully. 'It is a remarkable circumstance how our affairs appear to intermingle,' he continued. 'I am owing you an apology for an unfortunate intrusion upon yours, which I suffered myself to be entrapped into by my confidence in that false-face, Prestongrange; I think shame to own to you that I was ever trusting to a lawyer.' He shrugged his shoulders with a very French air. 'But indeed the man is very plausible,' says he. 'And now it seems that you have busied yourself handsomely in the matter of my daughter, for whose direction I was remitted to yourself.'

'I think, sir,' said I, with a very painful air, 'that it will be necessary we two should have an explanation.'

'There is nothing amiss?' he asked. 'My agent, Mr Sprott—'

'For God's sake moderate your voice!' I cried. 'She must not hear till we have had an explanation.'

'She is in this place?' cries he.

'That is her chamber door,' said I.

'You are here with her alone?' he asked.

'And who else would I have got to stay with us?' cries I.

I will do him the justice to admit that he turned pale.

'This is very unusual,' said he. 'This is a very unusual circumstance. You are right, we must hold an explanation.'

So saying, he passed me by, and I must own the tall old rogue appeared at that moment extraordinary dignified. He had now, for the first time, the view of my chamber, which I scanned (I may say) with his eyes. A bit of morning sun glinted in by the window pane, and showed it off; my bed, my mails, and washing dish, with some disorder of my clothes, and the unlighted chimney, made the only plenishing; no mistake but it looked bare and cold, and the most unsuitable, beggarly place conceivable to harbour a young lady. At the same time came in on my mind the recollection of the clothes that I had bought for her; and I thought this contrast of poverty and prodigality bore an ill appearance.

He looked all about the chamber for a seat, and finding nothing else to his purpose except my bed, took a place upon the side of it; where, after I had closed the door, I could not very well avoid joining him. For however this extraordinary interview might end, it must pass if possible without waking Catriona; and the one thing needful was that we should sit close and talk low. But I can scarce picture what a pair we made; he in his great-coat which the coldness of my chamber made extremely suitable; I shivering in my shirt and breeks; he with very much the air of a judge; and I (whatever I looked) with very much the feelings of a man who has heard the last trumpet.

'Well?' says he.

And 'Well,' I began, but found myself unable to go further.

'You tell me she is here?' said he again, but now with a spice of impatience that seemed to brace me up.

'She is in this house,' said I, 'and I knew the circumstance would be called unusual. But you are to consider how very unusual the whole business was from the beginning. Here is a young lady landed on the coast of Europe with two shillings and a penny halfpenny. She is directed to yon man Sprott in Helvoet. I hear you call him your agent. All I can say is he could do nothing but damn and swear at the mere mention of your name, and I must fee him out of my own pocket even to receive the custody of her effects. You speak of unusual circumstances, Mr Drummond, if that be the name you prefer. Here was a circumstance, if you like, to which it was barbarity to have exposed her.'

'But this is what I cannot understand the least,' said James. 'My daughter was placed into the charge of some responsible persons, whose names I have forgot.'

'Gebbie was the name,' said I; 'and there is no doubt that Mr Gebbie should have gone ashore with her at Helvoet. But he did not, Mr Drummond; and I think you might praise God that I was there to offer in his place.'

'I shall have a word to say to Mr Gebbie before long,' said he. 'As for yourself, I think it might have occurred that you were somewhat young for such a post.'

'But the choice was not between me and somebody else, it was between me and nobody,' I cried. 'Nobody offered in my place, and I must say I think you show a very small degree of gratitude to me that did.'

'I shall wait until I understand my obligation a little more in the particular,' says he.

'Indeed, and I think it stares you in the face, then,' said I. 'Your child was deserted, she was clean flung away in the midst of Europe, with scarce two shillings, and not two words of any language spoken there: I must say, a bonny business! I brought her to this place. I gave her the name and the tenderness due to a sister. All this has not gone without expense, but that I scarce need to hint at. They were services due to the young lady's character which I respect; and I think it would be a bonny business too, if I was to be singing her praises to her father.'

'You are a young man,' he began.

'So I hear you tell me,' said I, with a good deal of heat.

'You are a very young man,' he repeated, 'or you would have understood the significancy of the step.'

'I think you speak very much at your ease,' cried I. 'What else was I to do? It is a fact I might have hired some decent, poor woman to be a third to us, and I declare I never thought of it until this moment! But where was I to find her, that am a foreigner myself? And let me point out to your observation, Mr Drummond, that it would have cost me money out of my pocket. For here is just what it comes to, that I had to pay through the nose for your neglect; and there is only the one story to it, just that you were so unloving and so careless as to have lost your daughter.'

'He that lives in a glass house should not be casting stones,' says he; 'and we will finish inquiring into the behaviour of Miss Drummond before we go on to sit in judgment on her father.'

'But I will be entrapped into no such attitude,' said I. 'The character of Miss Drummond is far above inquiry, as her father ought to know. So is mine, and I am telling you that. There are but the two ways of it open. The one is to express your thanks to me as one gentleman to another, and to say no more. The other (if you are so difficult as to be still dissatisfied) is to pay me that which I have expended and be done.'

He seemed to soothe me with a hand in the air. 'There, there,' said he. 'You go too fast, you go too fast, Mr Balfour. It is a good thing that I have learned to be more patient. And I believe you forget that I have yet to see my daughter.'

I began to be a little relieved upon this speech and a change in the man's manner that I spied in him as soon as the name of money fell between us.

'I was thinking it would be more fit—if you will excuse the plainness of my dressing in your presence—that I should go forth and leave you to encounter her alone?' said I.

'What I would have looked for at your hands!' says he; and there was no mistake but what he said it civilly.

I thought this better and better still, and as I began to

pull on my hose, recalling the man's impudent mendicancy at Prestongrange's, I determined to pursue what seemed to be my victory.

'If you have any mind to stay some while in Leyden,' said I, 'this room is very much at your disposal, and I can easy find another for myself: in which way we shall have the least amount of flitting possible, there being only one to change.'

'Why, sir,' said he, making his bosom big, 'I think no shame of a poverty I have come by in the service of my king; I make no secret that my affairs are quite involved; and for the moment, it would be even impossible for me to undertake a journey.'

'Until you have occasion to communicate with your friends,' said I, 'perhaps it might be convenient for you (as of course it would be honourable to myself) if you were to regard yourself in the light of my guest?'

'Sir,' said he, 'when an offer is frankly made, I think I honour myself most to imitate that frankness. Your hand, Mr David; you have the character that I respect the most; you are one of those from whom a gentleman can take a favour and no more words about it. I am an old soldier,' he went on, looking rather disgusted-like around my chamber, 'and you need not fear I shall prove burthensome. I have ate too often at a dyke-side, drank of the ditch, and had no roof but the rain.'

'I should be telling you,' said I, 'that our breakfasts are sent customarily in about this time of morning. I propose I should go now to the tavern, and bid them add a cover for yourself and delay the meal the matter of an hour, which will give you an interval to meet your daughter in.'

Methought his nostrils wagged at this. 'O, an hour?' says he. 'That is perhaps superfluous. Half an hour, Mr David, or say twenty minutes; I shall do very well in that. And by the way,' he adds, detaining me by the coat, 'what is it you drink in the morning, whether ale or wine?'

'To be frank with you, sir,' says I, 'I drink nothing else but spare, cold water.'

'Tut-tut,' says he, 'that is fair destruction to the stomach, take an old campaigner's word for it. Our country spirit at home is perhaps the most entirely wholesome; but as that is not come-at-able, Rhenish or a white wine of Burgundy will be next best.'

'I shall make it my business to see you are supplied,' said I.

'Why, very good,' said he, 'and we shall make a man of you yet, Mr David.'

By this time, I can hardly say that I was minding him at all, beyond an odd thought of the kind of father-in-law that he was like to prove; and all my cares centred about the lass his daughter, to whom I determined to convey some warning of her visitor. I stepped to the door accordingly, and cried through the panels, knocking thereon at the same time: 'Miss Drummond, here is your father come at last.'

With that I went forth upon my errand, having (by two words) extraordinarily damaged my affairs.

WHETHER OR NOT I was to be so much blamed, or rather perhaps pitied, I must leave others to judge. My shrewdness (of which I have a good deal, too) seems not so great with the ladies. No doubt, at the moment when I awaked her, I was thinking a good deal of the effect upon James More; and similarly when I returned and we were all sat down to breakfast, I continued to behave to the young lady with deference and distance; as I still think to have been most wise. Her father had cast doubts upon the innocence of my friendship; and these, it was my first business to allay. But there is a kind of an excuse for Catriona also. We had shared in a scene of some tenderness and passion, and given and received caresses; I had thrust her from me with violence; I had called aloud upon her in the night from the one room to the other; she had passed hours of wakefulness and weeping; and it is not to be supposed I had been absent from her pillow thoughts. Upon the back of this, to be awaked, with unaccustomed formality, under the name of Miss Drummond, and to be thenceforth used with a great deal of distance and respect, led her entirely in error on my private sentiments; and she was indeed so incredibly abused as to imagine me repentant and trying to draw off!

The trouble betwixt us seems to have been this: that whereas I (since I had first set eyes on his great hat) thought singly of James More, his return and suspicions, she made so little of these that I may say she scarce remarked them, and all her troubles and doings regarded what had passed between us in the night before. This is partly to be explained by the innocence and boldness of her character; and partly because James More, having sped so ill in his interview with me, or had his mouth closed by my invitation, said no word to her upon the subject. At the breakfast, accordingly, it soon appeared we were at cross purposes. I had looked to find her in clothes of her own: I found her (as if her father were forgotten) wearing some of the best that I had bought for her and which she knew (or thought) that I admired her in. I had looked to find her imitate my affectation of distance, and be most precise and formal; instead I found her flushed and wild-like, with eyes extraordinary bright, and a painful and varying expression, calling me by name with a sort of appeal of tenderness, and referring and deferring to my thoughts and wishes like an anxious or a suspected wife.

But this was not for long. As I beheld her so regardless of her own interests, which I had jeopardised and was now endeavouring to recover, I redoubled my own coldness in the manner of a lesson to the girl. The more she came forward, the further I drew back; the more she betrayed the closeness of our intimacy, the more pointedly civil I became, until even her father (if he had not been so engrossed with eating) might have observed the opposition. In the midst of which, of a sudden, she became wholly changed, and I told myself, with a good deal of relief, that she had took the hint at last.

All day I was at my classes or in quest of my new lodging; and though the hour of our customary walk hung miserably on my hands, I cannot say but I was happy on the whole to find my way cleared, the girl again in proper keeping, the father satisfied or at least acquiescent, and myself free to prosecute my love with honour. At supper, as at all our meals, it was James More that did the talking. No doubt but he talked well, if anyone could have believed him. But I will speak of him presently more at large. The meal at an end, he rose, got his great-coat, and looking (as I thought) at me, observed he had affairs abroad. I took this for a hint that I was to be going also, and got up; whereupon the girl, who had scarce given me greeting at my entrance, turned her eyes on me wide open, with a look that bade me stay. I stood between them like a fish out of water, turning from one to the other; neither seemed to observe me, she gazing on the floor, he buttoning his coat: which vastly swelled my embarrassment. This appearance of indifference argued, upon her side, a good deal of anger very near to burst out. Upon his, I thought it horribly alarming; I made sure there was a tempest brewing there; and considering that to be the chief peril, turned towards him and put myself (so to speak) in the man's hands.

'Can I do anything for *you*, Mr Drummond?' says I.

He stifled a yawn, which again I thought to be duplicity. 'Why, Mr David,' said he, 'since you are so obliging as to propose it, you might show me the way to a certain tavern' (of which he gave the name) 'where I hope to fall in with some old companions in arms.'

There was no more to say, and I got my hat and cloak to bear him company.

'And as for you,' says he to his daughter, 'you had best go to your bed. I shall be late home, and *Early to bed and early to rise, gars bonny lasses have bright eyes.*'

Whereupon he kissed her with a good deal of tenderness, and ushered me before him from the door. This was so done (I thought on purpose) that it was scarce possible there should be any parting salutation; but I observed she did not look at me, and set it down to terror of James More.

It was some distance to that tavern. He talked all the way of matters which did not interest me the smallest, and at the door dismissed me with empty manners. Thence I walked to my new lodging, where I had not so much as a chimney to hold me warm, and no society but my own thoughts. These were still bright enough; I did not so much as dream that Catriona was turned against me; I thought we were like folk pledged; I thought we had been too near and spoke too warmly to be severed, least of all by what were only steps in a most needful policy. And the chief of my concern was only the kind of father-in-law that I was getting, which was not at all the kind I would have chosen: and the matter of how soon I ought to speak to him, which was a delicate point on several sides. In the first place, when I thought how young I was, I blushed all over, and could almost have found it in my heart to have desisted; only that if once I let them go from Leyden without explanation, I might lose her altogether. And in the second place, there was our very irregular situation to be kept in view, and the rather scant measure of satisfaction I had given James More that morning. I concluded, on the whole, that delay would not hurt anything, yet I would not delay too long neither; and got to my cold bed with a full heart.

The next day, as James More seemed a little on the complaining hand in the matter of my chamber, I offered to have in more furniture; and coming in the afternoon, with porters bringing chairs and tables, found the girl once more left to herself. She greeted me on my admission civilly, but withdrew at once to her own room, of which she shut the door. I made my disposition, and paid and dismissed the men so that she might hear them go, when I supposed she would at once come forth again to speak to me. I waited yet awhile, then knocked upon her door.

'Catriona!' said I.

The door was opened so quickly, even before I had the word out, that I thought she must have stood behind it listening. She remained there in the interval quite still; but she had a look that I cannot put a name on, as of one in a bitter trouble.

'Are we not to have our walk to-day either?' so I faltered.

'I am thanking you,' said she. 'I will not be caring much to walk, now that my father is come home.'

'But I think he has gone out himself and left you here alone,' said I.

'And do you think that was very kindly said?' she asked.

'It was not unkindly meant,' I replied. 'What ails you, Catriona? What have I done to you that you should turn from me like this?'

'I do not turn from you at all,' she said, speaking very carefully. 'I will ever be grateful to my friend that was good to me; I will ever be his friend in all that I am able. But now that my father James More is come again, there is a difference to be made, and I think there are some things said and done that would be better to be forgotten. But I will ever be your friend in all that I am able, and if that is not all that . . . if it is not so much . . . Not that you will be caring! But I would not have you think of me too hard. It was true what you said to me, that I was too young to be advised, and I am hoping you will remember I was just a child. I would not like to lose your friendship, at all events.'

She began this very pale; but before she was done, the blood was in her face like scarlet, so that not her words only, but her face and the trembling of her very hands, besought me to be gentle. I saw, for the first time, how very wrong I had done to place the child in that position, where she had been entrapped into a moment's weakness, and now stood before me like a person shamed.

'Miss Drummond,' I said, and stuck, and made the same beginning once again, 'I wish you could see into my heart,' I cried. 'You would read there that my respect is undiminished. If that were possible, I should say it was increased. This is but the result of the mistake we made; and had to come; and the less said of it now the better. Of all of our life here, I promise you it shall never pass my lips; I would like to promise you too that I would never think of it, but it's a memory that will be always dear to me. And as for a friend, you have one here that would die for you.'

'I am thanking you,' said she.

We stood awhile silent, and my sorrow for myself began to get the upper hand; for here were all my dreams come to a sad tumble, and my love lost, and myself alone again in the world as at the beginning.

'Well,' said I, 'we shall be friends always, that's a certain thing. But this is a kind of a farewell too: it's a kind of a farewell after all; I shall always ken Miss Drummond, but this is a farewell to my Catriona.'

I looked at her; I could hardly say I saw her, but she seemed to grow great and brighten in my eyes; and with that I suppose I must have lost my head, for I called out her name again and made a step at her with my hands reached forth.

She shrank back like a person struck, her face flamed; but the blood sprang no faster up into her cheeks, than what it flowed back upon my own heart, at sight of it, with penitence and concern. I found no words to excuse myself, but bowed before her very deep, and went my ways out of the house with death in my bosom.

I think it was about five days that followed without any

change. I saw her scarce ever but at meals, and then of course in the company of James More. If we were alone even for a moment, I made it my devoir to behave the more distantly and to multiply respectful attentions, having always in my mind's eye that picture of the girl shrinking and flaming in a blush, and in my heart more pity for her than I could depict in words. I was sorry enough for myself, I need not dwell on that, having fallen all my length and more than all my height in a few seconds; but, indeed, I was near as sorry for the girl, and sorry enough to be scarce angry with her save by fits and starts. Her plea was good: she was but a child; she had been placed in an unfair position; if she had deceived herself and me, it was no more than was to have been looked for.

And for another thing she was now very much alone. Her father, when he was by, was rather a caressing parent; but he was very easy led away by his affairs and pleasures, neglected her without compunction or remark, spent his nights in taverns when he had the money, which was more often than I could at all account for; and even in the course of these few days, failed once to come to a meal, which Catriona and I were at last compelled to partake of without him. It was the evening meal, and I left immediately that I had eaten, observing I supposed she would prefer to be alone; to which she agreed and (strange as it may seem) I quite believed her. Indeed, I thought myself but an eyesore to the girl, and a reminder of a moment's weakness that she now abhorred to think of. So she must sit alone in that room where she and I had been so merry, and in the blink of that chimney whose light had shone upon our many difficult and tender moments. There she must sit alone, and think of herself as of a maid who had most unmaidenly proffered her affections and had the same rejected. And in the meanwhile I would be alone some other place, and reading myself (whenever I was tempted to be angry) lessons upon human frailty and female delicacy. And altogether I suppose there were never two poor fools made themselves more unhappy in a greater misconception.

As for James, he paid not so much heed to us, or to anything in nature but his pocket, and his belly, and his own prating talk. Before twelve hours were gone he had raised a small loan of me; before thirty, he had asked for a second and been refused. Money and refusal he took with the same kind of high good-nature. Indeed, he had an outside air of magnanimity that was very well fitted to impose upon a daughter; and the light in which he was constantly presented in his talk, and the man's fine presence and great ways went together pretty harmoniously. So that a man that had no business with him, and either very little penetration or a furious deal of prejudice, might almost have been taken in. To me, after my first two interviews, he was as plain as print; I saw him to be perfectly selfish, with a perfect innocency in the same; and I would harken to his swaggering talk (of arms, and 'an old soldier', and 'a poor Highland gentleman', and 'the strength of my country and my friends') as I might to the babbling of a parrot.

The odd thing was that I fancy he believed some part of it himself, or did at times; I think he was so false all through that he scarce knew when he was lying; and for one thing, his moments of dejection must have been wholly genuine. There were times when he would be the most silent, affectionate, clinging creature possible, holding Catriona's hand like a big baby, and begging of me not to leave if I had any love to him; of which, indeed, I had none, but all the more to his daughter. He would press and indeed beseech us to entertain him with our talk, a thing very difficult in the state of our relations; and again break forth in pitiable regrets for his own land and friends, or into Gaelic singing.

'This is one of the melancholy airs of my native land,' he would say. 'You may think it strange to see a soldier weep, and indeed it is to make a near friend of you,' says he. 'But the notes of this singing are in my blood, and the words come out of my heart. And when I mind upon my red mountains and the wild birds calling there, and the brave streams of water running down, I would scarce think shame to weep before my enemies.' Then he would sing again, and translate to me pieces of the song, with a great deal of boggling and much expressed contempt against the English language. 'It says here,' he would say, 'that the sun is gone down, and the battle is at an end, and the brave chiefs are defeated. And it tells here how the stars see them fleeing into strange countries or lying dead on the red mountain; and they will never more shout the call of battle or wash their feet in the streams of the valley. But if you had only some of this language, you would weep also because the words of it are beyond all expression, and it is mere mockery to tell you it in English.'

Well, I thought there was a good deal of mockery in the business, one way and another; and yet, there was some feeling too, for which I hated him, I think, the worst of all. And it used to cut me to the quick to see Catriona so much concerned for the old rogue, and weeping herself to see him weep, when I was sure one half of his distress flowed from his last night's drinking in some tavern. There were times when I was tempted to lend him a round sum, and see the last of him for good; but this would have been to see the last of Catriona as well, for which I was scarcely so prepared; and besides, it went against my conscience to squander my good money on one who was so little of a husband.

I BELIEVE IT was about the fifth day, and I know at least that James was in one of his fits of gloom, when I received three letters. The first was from Alan, offering to visit me in Leyden; the other two were out of Scotland and prompted by the same affair, which was the death of my uncle and my own complete accession to my rights. Rankeillor's was, of course, wholly in the business view; Miss Grant's was like herself, a little more witty than wise, full of blame to me for not having written (though how was I to write with such intelligence?) and of rallying talk about Catriona, which it cut me to the quick to read in her very presence.

For it was of course in my own rooms that I found them, when I came to dinner, so that I was surprised out of my news in the very first moment of reading it. This made a welcome diversion for all three of us, nor could any have foreseen the ill consequences that ensued. It was accident that brought the three letters the same day, and that gave them into my hand in the same room with James More; and of all the events that flowed from that accident, and which I might have prevented if I had held my tongue, the truth is that they were pre-ordained before Agricola came into Scotland or Abraham set out upon his travels.

The first that I opened was naturally Alan's; and what more natural than that I should comment on his design to visit me? but I observed James to sit up with an air of immediate attention.

'Is that not Alan Breck that was suspected of the Appin accident?' he inquired.

I told him, 'Ay,' it was the same; and he withheld me some time from my other letters, asking of our acquaintance, of Alan's manner of life in France, of which I knew very little, and further of his visit as now proposed.

'All we forfeited folk hang a little together,' he explained, 'and besides I know the gentleman: and though his descent is not the thing, and indeed he has no true right to use the name of Stewart, he was very much admired in the day of Drummossie. He did there like a soldier; if some that need not be named had done as well, the upshot need not have been so melancholy to remember. There were two that did their best that day, and it makes a bond between the pair of us,' says he.

I could scarce refrain from shooting out my tongue at him, and could almost have wished that Alan had been there to have inquired a little further into that mention of his birth. Though, they tell me, the same was indeed not wholly regular.

Meanwhile, I had opened Miss Grant's, and could not withhold an exclamation.

'Catriona,' I cried, forgetting, the first time since her father was arrived, to address her by a handle, 'I am come into my kingdom fairly, I am the laird of Shaws indeed—my uncle is dead at last.'

She clapped her hands together leaping from her seat. The next moment it must have come over both of us at once what little cause of joy was left to either, and we stood opposite, staring on each other sadly.

But James showed himself a ready hypocrite. 'My daughter,' says he, 'is this how my cousin learned you to behave? Mr David has lost a near friend, and we should first condole with him on his bereavement.'

'Troth, sir,' said I, turning to him in a kind of anger, 'I can make no such faces. His death is as blithe news as ever I got.'

'It's a good soldier's philosophy,' says James. ''Tis the way of flesh, we must all go, all go. And if the gentleman was so far from your favour, why, very well! But we may at least congratulate you on your accession to your estates.'

'Nor can I say that either,' I replied, with the same heat. 'It is a good estate; what matters that to a lone man that has enough already? I had a good revenue before in my frugality; and but for the man's death—which gratifies me, shame to me that must confess it!—I see not how anyone is to be bettered by this change.'

'Come, come,' said he, 'you are more affected than you let on, or you would never make yourself out so lonely. Here are three letters; that means three that wish you well; and I could name two more, here in this very chamber. I have known you not so very long, but Catriona, when we are alone, is never done with the singing of your praises.'

She looked up at him, a little wild at that; and he slid off at once into another matter, the extent of my estate, which (during the most of the dinner time) he continued to dwell upon with interest. But it was to no purpose he dissembled; he had touched the matter with too gross a hand: and I knew what to expect. Dinner was scarce ate when he plainly discovered his designs. He reminded Catriona of an errand, and bid her attend to it. 'I do not see you should be gone beyond the hour,' he added, 'and friend David will be good enough to bear me company till you return.' She made haste to obey him without words. I do not know if she understood, I believe not; but I was completely satisfied, and sat strengthening my mind for what should follow.

The door had scarce closed behind her departure, when the man leaned back in his chair and addressed me with a good affectation of easiness. Only the one thing betrayed him, and that was his face; which suddenly shone all over with fine points of sweat.

'I am rather glad to have a word alone with you,' says he, 'because in our first interview there were some expressions you misapprehended and I have long meant to set you right upon. My daughter stands beyond doubt. So do you, and I would make that good with my sword against all gainsayers. But, my dear David, this world is a censorious place—as who should know it better than myself, who have lived ever since the days of my late departed father, God sain him! in a perfect spate of calumnies? We have to face to that; you and me have to consider of that; we have to consider of that.' And he wagged his head like a minister in a pulpit.

'To what effect, Mr Drummond?' said I. 'I would be obliged to you if you would approach your point.'

'Ay, ay,' says he, laughing, 'like your character indeed! and what I most admire in it. But the point, my worthy fellow, is sometimes in a kittle bit.' He filled a glass of wine. 'Though between you and me, that are such fast friends, it need not bother us long. The point, I need scarcely tell you, is my daughter. And the first thing is that I have no thought in my mind of blaming you. In the unfortunate circumstances, what could you do else? 'Deed, and I cannot tell.'

'I thank you for that,' said I, pretty close upon my guard.

'I have besides studied your character,' he went on; 'your talents are fair; you seem to have a moderate competence, which does no harm; and one thing with another, I am very happy to have to announce to you that I have decided on the latter of the two ways open.'

'I am afraid I am dull,' said I. 'What ways are these?'

He bent his brows upon me formidably and uncrossed his legs. 'Why, sir,' says he, 'I think I need scarce describe them to a gentleman of your condition: either that I should cut your throat or that you should marry my daughter.'

'You are pleased to be quite plain at last,' said I.

'And I believe I have been plain from the beginning!' cries he robustiously. 'I am a careful parent, Mr Balfour; but I thank God, a patient and deleeberate man. There is many a father, sir, that would have hirsled you at once either to the altar or the field. My esteem for your character—'

'Mr Drummond,' I interrupted, 'if you have any esteem for me at all, I will beg of you to moderate your voice. It is quite needless to rowt at a gentleman in the same chamber with yourself and lending you his best attention.'

'Why, very true,' says he, with an immediate change. 'And you must excuse the agitations of a parent.'

'I understand you then,' I continued—'for I will take no note of your other alternative, which perhaps it was a pity you let fall—I understand you rather to offer me encouragement in case I should desire to apply for your daughter's hand?'

'It is not possible to express my meaning better,' said he, 'and I see we shall do well together.'

'That remains to be yet seen,' said I. 'But so much I need make no secret of, that I bear the lady you refer to the most tender affection, and I could not fancy, even in a dream, a better fortune than to get her.'

'I was sure of it, I felt certain of you, David,' he cried, and reached out his hand to me.

I put it by. 'You go too fast, Mr Drummond,' said I. 'There are conditions to be made; and there is a difficulty in the path, which I see not entirely how we shall come over. I have told you that, upon my side, there is no objection to the marriage, but I have good reason to believe there will be much on the young lady's.'

'This is all beside the mark,' says he. 'I will engage for her acceptance.'

'I think you forget, Mr Drummond,' said I, 'that, even in dealing with myself you have been betrayed into two-three unpalatable expressions. I will have none such employed to the young lady. I am here to speak and think for the two of us; and I give you to understand that I would no more let a wife be forced upon myself, than what I would let a husband be forced on the young lady.'

He sat and glowered at me like one in doubt and a good deal of temper.

'So that this is to be the way of it,' I concluded. 'I will marry Miss Drummond, and that blithely, if she is entirely willing. But if there be the least unwillingness, as I have reason to fear—marry her will I never.'

'Well, well,' said he, 'this is a small affair. As soon as she returns I will sound her a bit, and hope to reassure you—'

But I cut in again. 'Not a finger of you, Mr Drummond, or I cry off, and you can seek a husband to your daughter somewhere else,' said I. 'It is I that am to be the only dealer and the only judge. I shall satisfy myself exactly; and none else shall anyways meddle—you the least of all.'

'Upon my word, sir!' he exclaimed, 'and who are you to be the judge?'

'The bridegroom, I believe,' said I.

'This is to quibble,' he cried. 'You turn your back upon the facts. The girl, my daughter, has no choice left to exercise. Her character is gone.'

'And I ask your pardon,' said I, 'but while this matter lies between her and you and me, that is not so.'

'What security have I!' he cried. 'Am I to let my daughter's reputation depend upon a chance?'

'You should have thought of all this long ago,' said I, 'before you were so misguided as to lose her; and not afterwards, when it is quite too late. I refuse to regard myself as any way accountable for your neglect, and I will be browbeat by no man living. My mind is quite made up, and come what may, I will not depart from it a hair's breadth. You and me are to sit here in company till her return; upon which, without either word or look from you, she and I are to go forth again to hold our talk. If she can satisfy me that she is willing to this step, I will then make it; and if she cannot, I will not.'

He leaped out of his seat like a man stung. 'I can spy your manœuvre,' he cried; 'you would work upon her to refuse!'

'Maybe ay, and maybe no,' said I. 'That is the way it is to be, whatever.'

'And if I refuse?' cries he.

'Then, Mr Drummond, it will have to come to the throat-cutting,' said I.

What with the size of the man, his great length of arm in which he came near rivalling his father, and his reputed skill at weapons, I did not use this word without some trepidation, to say nothing at all of the circumstance that he was Catriona's father. But I might have spared myself alarms. From the poorness of my lodging—he does not seem to have remarked his daughter's dresses, which were indeed all equally new to him—and from the fact that I had shown myself averse to lend, he had embraced a strong idea of my poverty. The sudden news of my estate convinced him of his error, and he had made but the one bound of it on this fresh venture, to which he was now so wedded, that I believe he would have suffered anything rather than fall to the alternative of fighting.

A little while longer he continued to dispute with me, until I hit upon a word that silenced him.

'If I find you so averse to let me see the lady by herself,' said I, 'I must suppose you have very good grounds to think me in the right about her unwillingness.'

He gabbled some kind of an excuse.

'But all this is very exhausting to both of our tempers,' I added, 'and I think we would do better to preserve a judicious silence.'

The which we did until the girl returned, and I must suppose would have cut a very ridiculous figure, had there been any there to view us.

I OPENED THE door to Catriona and stopped her on the threshold.

'Your father wishes us to take our walk,' said I.

She looked to James More, who nodded, and at that, like a trained soldier, she turned to go with me.

We took one of our old ways, where we had gone often together, and been more happy than I can tell of in the past. I came a half a step behind, so that I could watch her unobserved. The knocking of her little shoes upon the way sounded extraordinary pretty and sad; and I thought it a strange moment that I should be so near both ends of it at once, and walk in the midst between two destinies, and could not tell whether I was nearing these steps for the last time, or whether the sound of them was to go in and out with me till death should part us.

She avoided even to look at me, only walked before her, like one who had a guess of what was coming. I saw I must speak soon before my courage was run out, but where to begin I knew not. In this painful situation, when the girl was as good as forced into my arms and had already besought my forbearance, any excess of pressure must have seemed indecent; yet to avoid it wholly would have a very cold-like appearance. Between these extremes I stood helpless, and could have bit my fingers; so that, when at last I managed to speak at all, it may be said I spoke at random.

'Catriona,' said I, 'I am in a very painful situation; or rather, so we are both; and I would be a good deal obliged to you if you would promise to let me speak through first of all, and not to interrupt till I have done.'

She promised me that simply.

'Well,' said I, 'this that I have got to say is very difficult, and I know very well I have no right to be saying it. After what passed between the two of us last Friday, I have no manner of right. We have got so ravelled up (and all by my fault) that I know very well the least I could do is just to hold my tongue, which was what I intended fully, and there was nothing further from my thoughts than to have troubled you again. But, my dear, it has become merely necessary, and no way by it. You see, this estate of mine has fallen in, which makes of me rather a better match; and the—the business would not have quite the same ridiculous-like appearance that it would before. Besides which, it's supposed that our affairs have got so much ravelled up (as I was saying) that it would be better to let them be the way they are. In my view, this part of the thing is vastly exaggerate, and if I were you I would not wear two thoughts on it. Only it's right I should mention the same, because there's no doubt it has some influence on James More. Then I think we were none so unhappy when we dwelt together in this town before. I think we did pretty well together. If you would look back, my dear—'

'I will look neither back nor forward,' she interrupted. 'Tell me the one thing: this is my father's doing?'

'He approves of it,' said I. 'He approved that I should ask your hand in marriage,' and was going on again with somewhat more of an appeal upon her feelings; but she marked me not, and struck into the midst.

'He told you to!' she cried. 'It is no sense denying it, you said yourself that there was nothing farther from your thoughts. He told you to.'

'He spoke of it the first, if that is what you mean,' I began.

She was walking ever the faster, and looking fair in front of her; but at this she made a little noise in her head, and I thought she would have run.

'Without which,' I went on, 'after what you said last Friday, I would never have been so troublesome as make the offer. But when he as good as asked me, what was I to do?'

She stopped and turned round upon me.

'Well, it is refused at all events,' she cried, 'and there will be an end of that.'

And she began again to walk forward.

'I suppose I could expect no better,' said I, 'but I think you might try to be a little kind to me for the last end of it. I see not why you should be harsh. I have loved you very well, Catriona—no harm that I should call you so for the last time. I have done the best that I could manage, I am trying the same still, and only vexed that I can do no better. It is a strange thing to me that you can take any pleasure to be hard to me.'

'I am not thinking of you,' she said, 'I am thinking of that man, my father.'

'Well, and that way, too!' said I. 'I can be of use to you that way, too; I will have to be. It is very needful, my dear, that we should consult about your father; for the way this talk has gone, an angry man will be James More.'

She stopped again. 'It is because I am disgraced?' she asked.

'That is what he is thinking,' I replied, 'but I have told you already to make nought of it.'

'It will be all one to me,' she cried. 'I prefer to be disgraced!'

I did not know very well what to answer, and stood silent.

There seemed to be something working in her bosom after that last cry; presently she broke out, 'And what is the meaning of all this? Why is all this shame loundered on my head? How could you dare it, David Balfour?'

'My dear,' said I, 'what else was I to do?'

'I am not your dear,' she said, 'and I defy you to be calling me these words.'

'I am not thinking of my words,' said I. 'My heart bleeds for you, Miss Drummond. Whatever I may say, be sure you have my pity in your difficult position. But there is just the one thing that I wish you would bear in view, if it was only long enough to discuss it quietly; for there is going to be a collieshangie when we two get home. Take my word for it, it will need the two of us to make this matter end in peace.'

'Ay,' said she. There sprang a patch of red in either of her cheeks. 'Was he for fighting you?' said she.

'Well, he was that,' said I.

She gave a dreadful kind of laugh. 'At all events, it is complete!' she cried. And then turning on me: 'My father and I are a fine pair,' said she, 'but I am thanking the good God there will be somebody worse than what we are. I am thanking the good God that he has let me see you so. There will never be the girl made that would not scorn you.'

I had borne a good deal pretty patiently, but this was over the mark.

'You have no right to speak to me like that,' said I. 'What have I done but to be good to you, or try to be? And here is my repayment! O, it is too much.'

She kept looking at me with a hateful smile. 'Coward!' said she.

'The word in your throat and in your father's!' I cried. 'I have dared him this day already in your interest. I will dare him again, the nasty pole-cat; little I care which of us should fall! Come,' said I, 'back to the house with us; let us be done with it, let me be done with the whole Hieland crew of you! You will see what you think when I am dead.'

She shook her head at me with that same smile I could have struck her for.

'O, smile away!' I cried. 'I have seen your bonny father smile on the wrong side this day. Not that I mean he was afraid, of course,' I added hastily, 'but he preferred the other way of it.'

'What is this?' she asked.

'When I offered to draw with him,' said I.

'You offered to draw upon James More?' she cried.

'And I did so,' said I, 'and found him backward enough, or how would we be here?'

'There is a meaning upon this,' said she. 'What is it you are meaning?'

'He was to make you take me,' I replied, 'and I would not have it. I said you should be free, and I must speak with you alone; little I supposed it would be such a speaking! *And what if I refuse?* says he.—*Then it must come to the throat-cutting,* says I, *for I will no more have a husband forced on that young lady, than what I would have a wife forced upon myself.* These were my words, they were a friend's words; bonnily have I been paid for them! Now you have refused me of your own clear free will, and there lives no father in the Highlands, or out of them, that can force on this marriage. I

will see that your wishes are respected; I will make the same
my business, as I have all through. But I think you might
have that decency as to affect some gratitude. 'Deed, and I
thought you knew me better! I have not behaved quite well
to you, but that was weakness. And to think me a coward,
and such a coward as that—O, my lass, there was a stab
for the last of it!'

'Davie, how would I guess?' she cried. 'O, this is a
dreadful business! Me and mine,'—she gave a kind of
wretched cry at the word—'me and mine are not fit to
speak to you. O, I could be kneeling down to you in the
street, I could be kissing your hands for your forgiveness!'

'I will keep the kisses I have got from you already,' cried
I. 'I will keep the ones I wanted and that were something
worth; I will not be kissed in penitence.'

'What can you be thinking of this miserable girl?' says
she.

'What I am trying to tell you all this while!' said I, 'that
you had best leave me alone, whom you can make no more
unhappy if you tried, and turn your attention to James More,
your father, with whom you are like to have a queer pirn to
wind.'

'O, that I must be going out into the world alone with such
a man!' she cried, and seemed to catch herself in with a great
effort. 'But trouble yourself no more for that,' said she. 'He
does not know what kind of nature is in my heart. He will
pay me dear for this day of it; dear, dear, will he pay.'

She turned, and began to go home and I to accompany
her. At which she stopped.

'I will be going alone,' she said. 'It is alone I must be
seeing him.'

Some little while I raged about the streets, and told myself
I was the worst used lad in Christendom. Anger choked me;
it was all very well for me to breathe deep; it seemed there
was not air enough about Leyden to supply me, and I thought
I would have burst like a man at the bottom of the sea. I
stopped and laughed at myself at a street corner a minute
together, laughing out loud, so that a passenger looked at
me, which brought me to myself.

'Well,' I thought, 'I have been a gull and a ninny and

a soft Tommy long enough. Time it was done. Here is a good lesson to have nothing to do with that accursed sex, that was the ruin of the man in the beginning and will be so to the end. God knows I was happy enough before ever I saw her; God knows I can be happy enough again when I have seen the last of her.'

That seemed to me the chief affair: to see them go. I dwelled upon the idea fiercely; and presently slipped on, in a kind of malevolence, to consider how very poorly they were like to fare when Davie Balfour was no longer by to be their milk-cow; at which, to my own very great surprise, the disposition of my mind turned bottom up. I was still angry; I still hated her; and yet I thought I owed it to myself that she should suffer nothing.

This carried me home again at once, where I found the mails drawn out and ready fastened by the door, and the father and daughter with every mark upon them of a recent disagreement. Catriona was like a wooden doll; James More breathed hard, his face was dotted with white spots, and his nose upon one side. As soon as I came in, the girl looked at him with a steady, clear, dark look that might very well have been followed by a blow. It was a hint that was more contemptuous than a command, and I was surprised to see James More accept it. It was plain he had had a master talking-to; and I could see there must be more of the devil in the girl than I had guessed, and more good-humour about the man than I had given him the credit of.

He began, at least, calling me Mr Balfour, and plainly speaking from a lesson; but he got not very far, for at the first pompous swell of his voice, Catriona cut in.

'I will tell you what James More is meaning,' said she. 'He means we have come to you, beggar-folk, and have not behaved to you very well, and we are ashamed of our ingratitude and ill-behaviour. Now we are wanting to go away and be forgotten; and my father will have guided his gear so ill, that we cannot even do that unless you will give us some more alms. For that is what we are, at all events, beggar-folk and sorners.'

'By your leave, Miss Drummond,' said I, 'I must speak to your father by myself.'

She went into her own room and shut the door, without a word or a look.

'You must excuse her, Mr Balfour,' says James More. 'She has no delicacy.'

'I am not here to discuss that with you,' said I, 'but to be quit of you. And to that end I must talk of your position. Now, Mr Drummond, I have kept the run of your affairs more closely than you bargained for. I know you had money of your own when you were borrowing mine. I know you have had more since you were here in Leyden, though you concealed it even from your daughter.'

'I bid you beware. I will stand no more baiting,' he broke out. 'I am sick of her and you. What kind of a damned trade is this to be a parent! I have had expressions used to me—' There he broke off. 'Sir, this is the heart of a soldier and a parent,' he went on again, laying his hand on his bosom, 'outraged in both characters—and I bid you beware.'

'If you would have let me finish,' says I, 'you would have found I spoke for your advantage.'

'My dear friend,' he cried, 'I know I might have relied upon the generosity of your character.'

'Man! will you let me speak?' said I. 'The fact is that I cannot win to find out if you are rich or poor. But it is my idea that your means, as they are mysterious in their source, so they are something insufficient in amount; and I do not choose your daughter to be lacking. If I durst speak to herself, you may be certain I would never dream of trusting it to you; because I know you like the back of my hand, and all your blustering talk is that much wind to me. However, I believe in your way you do still care something for your daughter after all; and I must just be doing with that ground of confidence, such as it is.'

Whereupon, I arranged with him that he was to communicate with me, as to his whereabouts and Catriona's welfare, in consideration of which I was to serve him a small stipend.

He heard the business out with a great deal of eagerness; and when it was done, 'My dear fellow, my dear son,' he cried out, 'this is more like yourself than any of it yet! I will serve you with a soldier's faithfulness—'

'Let me hear no more of it!' says I. 'You have got me to

that pitch that the bare name of soldier rises on my stomach.
Our traffic is settled; I am now going forth and will return
in one half-hour, when I expect to find my chambers purged
of you.'

I gave them good measure of time; it was my one fear
that I might see Catriona again, because tears and weakness
were ready in my heart, and I cherished my anger like a piece
of dignity. Perhaps an hour went by; the sun had gone
down, a little wisp of a new moon was following it across
a scarlet sunset; already there were stars in the east, and
in my chambers, when at last I entered them, the night lay
blue. I lit a taper and reviewed the rooms; in the first there
remained nothing so much as to awake a memory of those
who were gone; but in the second, in a corner of the floor,
I spied a little heap that brought my heart into my mouth.
She had left behind at her departure all that ever she had of
me. It was the blow that I felt sorest, perhaps because it was
the last; and I fell upon that pile of clothing and behaved
myself more foolish than I care to tell of.

Late in the night, in a strict frost, and my teeth chattering,
I came again by some portion of my manhood and considered
with myself. The sight of these poor frocks and ribbons,
and her shifts, and the clocked stockings, was not to be
endured; and if I were to recover any constancy of mind,
I saw I must be rid of them ere the morning. It was my
first thought to have made a fire and burned them; but
my disposition has always been opposed to wastery, for one
thing; and for another, to have burned these things that
she had worn so close upon her body seemed in the nature
of a cruelty. There was a corner cupboard in that chamber;
there I determined to bestow them. The which I did and
made it a long business, folding them with very little skill
indeed but the more care; and sometimes dropping them
with my tears. All the heart was gone out of me, I was weary
as though I had run miles, and sore like one beaten; when,
as I was folding a kerchief that she wore often at her neck,
I observed there was a corner neatly cut from it. It was a
kerchief of a very pretty hue, on which I had frequently
remarked; and once that she had it on, I remembered
telling her (by way of a banter) that she wore my colours.

There came a glow of hope and like a tide of sweetness in my bosom; and the next moment I was plunged back in a fresh despair. For there was the corner crumpled in a knot and cast down by itself in another part of the floor.

But when I argued with myself, I grew more hopeful. She had cut that corner off in some childish freak that was manifestly tender; that she had cast it away again was little to be wondered at; and I was inclined to dwell more upon the first than upon the second, and to be more pleased that she had ever conceived the idea of that keepsake, than concerned because she had flung it from her in an hour of natural resentment.

ALTOGETHER, THEN, I was scarce so miserable the next days but what I had many hopeful and happy snatches; threw myself with a good deal of constancy upon my studies; and made out to endure the time till Alan should arrive, or I might hear word of Catriona by the means of James More. I had altogether three letters in the time of our separation. One was to announce their arrival in the town of Dunkirk in France, from which place James shortly after started alone upon a private mission. This was to England and to see Lord Holderness; and it has always been a bitter thought that my good money helped to pay the charges of the same. But he has need of a long spoon who sups with the deil, or James More either. During this absence, the time was to fall due for another letter; and as the letter was the condition of his stipend, he had been so careful as to prepare it beforehand and leave it with Catriona to be despatched. The fact of our correspondence aroused her suspicions, and he was no sooner gone than she had burst the seal. What I received began accordingly in the writing of James More:

> My dear Sir,—Your esteemed favour came to hand duly, and I have to acknowledge the inclosure according to agreement. It shall be all faithfully expended on my daughter, who is well, and desires to be remembered to her dear friend. I find her in rather a melancholy disposition, but trust in the mercy of God to see her re-established. Our manner of life is very much alone, but we solace ourselves with the melancholy tunes of our native mountains, and by walking upon the margin of the sea that lies next to Scotland. It was better days with me when I lay with five wounds upon my body on the field of Gladsmuir. I have found employment

here in the *haras* of a French nobleman, where my experience is valued. But, my dear Sir, the wages are so exceedingly unsuitable that I would be ashamed to mention them, which makes your remittances the more necessary to my daughter's comfort, though I daresay the sight of old friends would be still better.

My dear Sir,

Your affectionate, obedient servant,

James Macgregor Drummond

Below it began again in the hand of Catriona:

Do not be believing him, it is all lies together.

C. M. D.

Not only did she add this postscript, but I think she must have come near suppressing the letter; for it came long after date, and was closely followed by the third. In the time betwixt them, Alan had arrived, and made another life to me with his merry conversation; I had been presented to his cousin of the Scots-Dutch, a man that drank more than I could have thought possible and was not otherwise of interest; I had been entertained to many jovial dinners and given some myself, all with no great change upon my sorrow; and we two (by which I mean Alan and myself, and not at all the cousin) had discussed a good deal the nature of my relations with James More and his daughter. I was naturally diffident to give particulars; and this disposition was not anyway lessened by the nature of Alan's commentary upon those I gave.

'I cannae make head nor tail of it,' he would say, 'but it sticks in my mind ye've made a gowk of yourself. There's few people that has had more experience than Alan Breck; and I can never call to mind to have heard tell of a lassie like this one of yours. The way that you tell it, the thing's fair impossible. Ye must have made a terrible hash of the business, David.'

'There are whiles that I am of the same mind,' said I.

'The strange thing is that ye seem to have a kind of a fancy for her too!' said Alan.

'The biggest kind, Alan,' said I, 'and I think I'll take it to my grave with me.'

'Well, ye beat me, whatever!' he would conclude.

I showed him the letter with Catriona's postscript. 'And here again!' he cried. 'Impossible to deny a kind of decency to this Catriona, and sense forbye! As for James More, the man's as boss as a drum; he's just a wame and a wheen words; though I'll can never deny that he fought reasonably well at Gladsmuir, and it's true what he says here about the five wounds. But the loss of him is that the man's boss.'

'Ye see, Alan,' said I, 'it goes against the grain with me to leave the maid in such poor hands.'

'Ye couldnae weel find poorer,' he admitted. 'But what are ye to do with it? It's this way about a man and a woman, ye see, Davie: The weemenfolk have got no kind of reason to them. Either they like the man, and then a' goes fine; or else they just detest him, and ye may spare your breath—ye can do naething. There's just the two sets of them—them that would sell their coats for ye, and them that never look the road ye're on. That's a' that there is to women; and you seem to be such a gomeral that ye cannae tell the tane frae the tither.'

'Well, and I'm afraid that's true for me,' said I.

'And yet there's naething easier!' cried Alan. 'I could easy learn ye the science of the thing; but ye seem to me to be born blind, and there's where the deefficulty comes in!'

'And can *you* no help me?' I asked, 'you that's so clever at the trade?'

'Ye see, David, I wasnae here,' said he. 'I'm like a field officer that has naebody but blind men for scouts and *éclaireurs*; and what would he ken? But it sticks in my mind that ye'll have made some kind of bauchle; and if I was you, I would have a try at her again.'

'Would ye so, man Alan?' said I.

'I would e'en't,' says he.

The third letter came to my hand while we were deep in some such talk; and it will be seen how pat it fell to the occasion. James professed to be in some concern upon his daughter's health, which I believe was never better; abounded in kind expressions to myself; and finally proposed that I should visit them at Dunkirk.

'You will now be enjoying the society of my old comrade, Mr Stewart,' he wrote. 'Why not accompany him so far in

his return to France? I have something very particular for
Mr Stewart's ear; and, at any rate, I would be pleased
to meet in with an old fellow-soldier and one so mettle as
himself. As for you, my dear sir, my daughter and I would
be proud to receive our benefactor, whom we regard as a
brother and a son. The French nobleman has proved a
person of the most filthy avarice of character, and I have
been necessitate to leave the *haras*. You will find us, in
consequence, a little poorly lodged in the *auberge* of a man
Bazin on the dunes; but the situation is caller, and I
make no doubt but we might spend some very pleasant
days, when Mr Stewart and I could recall our services,
and you and my daughter divert yourselves in a manner
more befitting your age. I beg at least that Mr Stewart
would come here; my business with him opens a very
wide door.'

'What does the man want with me?' cried Alan, when he
had read. 'What he wants with you is clear enough—it's
siller. But what can he want with Alan Breck?'

'O, it'll be just an excuse,' said I. 'He is still after this
marriage, which I wish from my heart that we could bring
about. And he asks you because he thinks I would be less
likely to come wanting you.'

'Well, I wish that I kent,' says Alan. 'Him and me were
never onyways pack; we used to girn at ither like a pair of
pipers. "Something for my ear," quo' he! I'll maybe have
something for his hinder end, before we're through with it.
Dod, I'm thinking it would be a kind of a divertisement to
gang and see what he'll be after! Forbye that I could see
your lassie then. What say ye, Davie? Will ye ride with
Alan?'

You may be sure I was not backward, and Alan's furlough
running towards an end, we set forth presently upon this
joint adventure.

It was near dark of a January day when we rode at last
into the town of Dunkirk. We left our horses at the post,
and found a guide to Bazin's Inn, which lay beyond the
walls. Night was quite fallen, so that we were the last to
leave that fortress, and heard the doors of it close behind
us as we passed the bridge. On the other side there lay a

lighted suburb, which we thridded for a while, then turned into a dark lane, and presently found ourselves wading in the night among deep sand where we could hear a bullering of the sea. We travelled in this fashion for some while, following our conductor mostly by the sound of his voice; and I had begun to think he was perhaps misleading us, when we came to the top of a small brae, and there appeared out of the darkness a dim light in a window.

'*Voilà l'auberge à Bazin*,' says the guide.

Alan smacked his lips. 'An unco lonely bit,' said he, and I thought by his tone he was not wholly pleased.

A little after, and we stood in the lower storey of that house, which was all the one apartment, with a stair leading to the chambers at the side, benches and tables by the wall, the cooking fire at the one end of it, and shelves of bottles and the cellar-trap at the other. Here Bazin, who was an ill-looking, big man, told us the Scottish gentleman was gone abroad he knew not where, but the young lady was above, and he would call her down to us.

I took from my breast that kerchief wanting the corner, and knotted it about my throat. I could hear my heart go; and Alan patting me on the shoulder with some of his laughable expressions, I could scarce refrain from a sharp word. But the time was not long to wait. I heard her step pass overhead, and saw her on the stair. This she descended very quietly, and greeted me with a pale face and a certain seeming of earnestness, or uneasiness, in her manner that extremely dashed me.

'My father, James More, will be here soon. He will be very pleased to see you,' she said. And then of a sudden her face flamed, her eyes lightened, the speech stopped upon her lips; and I made sure she had observed the kerchief. It was only for a breath that she was discomposed; but methought it was with a new animation that she turned to welcome Alan. 'And you will be his friend, Alan Breck?' she cried. 'Many is the dozen times I will have heard him tell of you; and I love you already for all your bravery and goodness.'

'Well, well,' says Alan, holding her hand in his and viewing her, 'and so this is the young lady at the last of it! David, ye're an awful poor hand of a description.'

I do not know that ever I heard him speak so straight to people's hearts; the sound of his voice was like song.

'What? will he have been describing me?' she cried.

'Little else of it since I ever came out of France!' says he, 'forbye a bit of a speciment one night in Scotland in a shaw of wood by Silvermills. But cheer up, my dear! ye're bonnier than what he said. And now there's one thing sure: you and me are to be a pair of friends. I'm a kind of a henchman to Davie here; I'm like a tyke at his heels: and whatever he cares for, I've got to care for too—and by the holy airn! they've got to care for me! So now you can see what way you stand with Alan Breck, and ye'll find ye'll hardly lose on the transaction. He's no very bonnie, my dear, but he's leal to them he loves.'

'I thank you with my heart for your good words,' said she. 'I have that honour for a brave, honest man that I cannot find any to be answering with.'

Using travellers' freedom, we spared to wait for James More, and sat down to meat, we threesome. Alan had Catriona sit by him and wait upon his wants: he made her drink first out of his glass, he surrounded her with continual kind gallantries, and yet never gave me the most small occasion to be jealous; and he kept the talk so much in his own hand, and that in so merry a note, that neither she nor I remembered to be embarrassed. If any had seen us there, it must have been supposed that Alan was the old friend and I the stranger. Indeed, I had often cause to love and to admire the man, but I never loved or admired him better than that night; and I could not help remarking to myself (what I was sometimes rather in danger of forgetting) that he had not only much experience of life, but in his own way a great deal of natural ability besides. As for Catriona she seemed quite carried away; her laugh was like a peal of bells, her face gay as a May morning; and I own, although I was very well pleased, yet I was a little sad also, and thought myself a dull, stockish character in comparison of my friend, and very unfit to come into a young maid's life, and perhaps ding down her gaiety.

But if that was like to be my part, I found at least that I was not alone in it; for, James More returning suddenly, the girl was changed into a piece of stone. Through the rest of that evening, until she made an excuse and slipped to bed, I kept an eye upon her without cease: and I can bear testimony that she never smiled, scarce spoke, and looked mostly on the board in front of her. So that I really marvelled to see so much devotion (as it used to be) changed into the very sickness of hate.

Of James More it is unnecessary to say much; you know the man already, what there was to know of him; and I am weary of writing out his lies. Enough that he drank a great deal, and told us very little that was to any possible purpose. As for the business with Alan, that was to be reserved for the morrow and his private hearing.

It was the more easy to be put off, because Alan and I were pretty weary with our day's ride, and sat not very late after Catriona.

We were soon alone in a chamber where we were to make shift with a single bed. Alan looked on me with a queer smile.

'Ye muckle ass!' said he.

'What do ye mean by that?' I cried.

'Mean? What do I mean? It's extraordinar, David man,' says he, 'that you should be so mortal stupit.'

Again I begged him to speak out.

'Well, it's this of it,' said he. 'I told ye there were the two kinds of women—them that would sell their shifts for ye, and the others. Just you try for yoursel', my bonny man! But what's that neepkin at your craig?'

I told him.

'I thocht it was something thereabout,' said he.

Nor would he say another word though I besieged him long with importunities.

DAYLIGHT SHOWED US how solitary the inn stood.
It was plainly hard upon the sea, yet out of all view of it, and
beset on every side with scabbit hills of sand. There was,
indeed, only one thing in the nature of a prospect, where
there stood out over a brae the two sails of a windmill, like
an ass's ears, but with the ass quite hidden. It was strange
(after the wind rose, for at first it was dead calm) to
see the turning and following of each other of these great
sails behind the hillock. Scarce any road came by there;
but a number of footways travelled among the bents in all
directions up to Mr Bazin's door. The truth is, he was a
man of many trades, not any one of them honest, and the
position of his inn was the best of his livelihood. Smugglers
frequented it; political agents and forfeited persons bound
across the water came there to await their passages; and I
daresay there was worse behind, for a whole family might
have been butchered in that house and nobody the wiser.

I slept little and ill. Long ere it was day, I had slipped
from beside my bedfellow, and was warming myself at the
fire or walking to and fro before the door. Dawn broke
mighty sullen; but a little after, sprang up a wind out of
the west, which burst the clouds, let through the sun, and set
the mill to the turning. There was something of spring in the
sunshine, or else it was in my heart; and the appearing of the
great sails one after another from behind the hill, diverted me
extremely. At times I could hear a creak of the machinery;
and by half-past eight of the day, Catriona began to sing in
the house. At this I would have cast my hat in the air; and
I thought this dreary, desert place was like a paradise.

For all which, as the day drew on and nobody came near,
I began to be aware of an uneasiness that I could scarce
explain. It seemed there was trouble afoot; the sails of the

windmill, as they came up and went down over the hill, were like persons spying; and outside of all fancy, it was surely a strange neighbourhood and house for a young lady to be brought to dwell in.

At breakfast, which we took late, it was manifest that James More was in some danger or perplexity; manifest that Alan was alive to the same, and watched him close; and this appearance of duplicity upon the one side, and vigilance upon the other, held me on live coals. The meal was no sooner over than James seemed to come to a resolve, and began to make apologies. He had an appointment of a private nature in the town (it was with the French nobleman, he told me), and we would please excuse him till about noon. Meanwhile, he carried his daughter aside to the far end of the room, where he seemed to speak rather earnestly and she to listen without much inclination.

'I am caring less and less about this man James,' said Alan. 'There's something no right with the man James, and I wouldnae wonder but what Alan Breck would give an eye to him this day. I would like fine to see yon French nobleman, Davie; and I daresay you could find an employ to yoursel, and that would be to speir at the lassie for some news of your affair. Just tell it to her plainly—tell her ye're a muckle ass at the off-set; and then, if I were you, and ye could do it naitural, I would just mint to her I was in some kind of a danger; a' weemenfolk likes that.'

'I cannae lee, Alan, I cannae do it naitural,' says I, mocking him.

'The more fool you!' says he. 'Then ye'll can tell her that I recommended it; that'll set her to the laughing; and I wouldnae wonder but what that was the next best. But see to the pair of them! If I didnae feel just sure of the lassie, and that she was awful pleased and chief with Alan, I would think there was some kind of hocus-pocus about yon.'

'And is she so pleased with ye, then, Alan?' I asked.

'She thinks a heap of me,' says he. 'And I'm no like you: I'm one that can tell. That she does—she thinks a heap of Alan. And troth! I'm thinking a good deal of him mysel'; and with your permission, Shaws, I'll be getting a wee yont among the bents, so that I can see what way James goes.'

One after another went, till I was left alone beside the
breakfast table; James to Dunkirk, Alan dogging him,
Catriona up the stairs to her own chamber. I could very
well understand how she should avoid to be alone with me;
yet was none the better pleased with it for that, and bent my
mind to entrap her to an interview before the men returned.
Upon the whole, the best appeared to me to do like Alan.
If I was out of view among the sand-hills, the fine morning
would decoy her forth; and once I had her in the open, I
could please myself.

No sooner said than done; nor was I long under the
bield of a hillock before she appeared at the inn door,
looked here and there, and (seeing nobody) set out by
a path that led directly seaward, and by which I followed
her. I was in no haste to make my presence known; the
further she went I made sure of the longer hearing to my
suit; and the ground being all sandy it was easy to follow
her unheard. The path rose and came at last to the head of
a knowe. Thence I had a picture for the first time of what a
desolate wilderness that inn stood hidden in; where was no
man to be seen, nor any house of man, except just Bazin's
and the windmill. Only a little further on, the sea appeared
and two or three ships upon it, pretty as a drawing. One of
these was extremely close in to be so great a vessel; and I
was aware of a shock of new suspicion, when I recognised
the trim of the *Seahorse*. What should an English ship be
doing so near in to France? Why was Alan brought into
her neighbourhood, and that in a place so far from any
hope of rescue? and was it by accident, or by design,
that the daughter of James More should walk that day to
the seaside?

Presently I came forth behind her in the front of the sand-
hills and above the beach. It was here long and solitary;
with a man-o'-war's boat drawn up about the middle of the
prospect, and an officer in charge and pacing the sands like
one who waited. I sat immediately down where the rough
grass a good deal covered me, and looked for what should
follow. Catriona went straight to the boat; the officer met
her with civilities; they had ten words together; I saw a
letter changing hands; and there was Catriona returning.

At the same time, as if this were all her business on the Continent, the boat shoved off and was headed for the *Seahorse*. But I observed the officer to remain behind and disappear among the bents.

I liked the business little; and the more I considered of it, liked it less. Was it Alan the officer was seeking? or Catriona? She drew near with her head down, looking constantly on the sand, and made so tender a picture that I could not bear to doubt her innocence. The next, she raised her face and recognised me; seemed to hesitate, and then came on again, but more slowly, and I thought with a changed colour. And at that thought, all else that was upon my bosom—fears, suspicions, the care of my friend's life—was clean swallowed up; and I rose to my feet and stood waiting her in a drunkenness of hope.

I gave her 'good-morning' as she came up, which she returned with a good deal of composure.

'Will you forgive my having followed you?' said I.

'I know you are always meaning kindly,' she replied; and then, with a little outburst, 'but why will you be sending money to that man? It must not be.'

'I never sent it for him,' said I, 'but for you, as you know well.'

'And you have no right to be sending it to either one of us,' said she. 'David, it is not right.'

'It is not, it is all wrong,' said I; 'and I pray God he will help this dull fellow (if it be at all possible) to make it better. Catriona, this is no kind of life for you to lead; and I ask your pardon for the word, but yon man is no fit father to take care of you.'

'Do not be speaking of him, even!' was her cry.

'And I need speak of him no more; it is not of him that I am thinking, O, be sure of that!' says I. 'I think of the one thing. I have been alone now this long time in Leyden; and when I was by way of at my studies, still I was thinking of that. Next Alan came, and I went among soldier-men to their big dinners; and still I had the same thought. And it was the same before, when I had her there beside me. Catriona, do you see this napkin at my

throat? You cut a corner from it once and then cast it from
you. They're *your* colours now; I wear them in my heart.
My dear, I cannot be wanting you. O, try to put up with
me!'

I stepped before her so as to intercept her walking on.

'Try to put up with me,' I was saying, 'try and bear with
me a little.'

Still she had never the word, and a fear began to rise in
me like a fear of death.

'Catriona,' I cried, gazing on her hard, 'is it a mistake
again? Am I quite lost?'

She raised her face to me, breathless.

'Do you want me, Davie, truly?' said she, and I scarce
could hear her say it.

'I do that,' said I. 'O, sure you know it—I do that.'

'I have nothing left to give or to keep back,' said she. 'I
was all yours from the first day, if you would have had a
gift of me!' she said.

This was on the summit of a brae; the place was windy
and conspicuous, we were to be seen there even from the
English ship; but I kneeled down before her in the sand,
and embraced her knees, and burst into that storm of weeping that I thought it must have broken me. All thought
was wholly beaten from my mind by the vehemency of my
discomposure. I knew not where I was, I had forgot why I
was happy; only I knew she stooped, and I felt her cherish
me to her face and bosom, and heard her words out of a whirl.

'Davie,' she was saying, 'O, Davie, is this what you think
of me? Is it so that you were caring for poor me? O, Davie,
Davie!'

With that she wept also, and our tears were commingled
in a perfect gladness.

It might have been ten in the day before I came to a clear
sense of what a mercy had befallen me; and sitting over
against her, with her hands in mine, gazed in her face,
and laughed out loud for pleasure like a child, and called
her foolish and kind names. I have never seen the place
that looked so pretty as these bents by Dunkirk; and the
windmill sails, as they bobbed over the knowe, were like a
tune of music.

I know not how much longer we might have continued to forget all else besides ourselves, had I not chanced upon a reference to her father, which brought us to reality.

'My little friend,' I was calling her again and again, rejoicing to summon up the past by the sound of it, and to gaze across on her, and to be a little distant—'My little friend, now you are mine altogether; mine for good, my little friend; and that man's no longer at all.'

There came a sudden whiteness in her face, she plucked her hands from mine.

'Davie, take me away from him!' she cried. 'There's something wrong; he's not true. There will be something wrong; I have a dreadful terror here at my heart. What will he be wanting at all events with that King's ship? What will this word be saying?' And she held the letter forth. 'My mind misgives me, it will be some ill to Alan. Open it, Davie—open it and see.'

I took it, and looked at it, and shook my head.

'No,' said I, 'it goes against me, I cannot open a man's letter.'

'Not to save your friend?' she cried.

'I cannae tell,' said I. 'I think not. If I was only sure!'

'And you have but to break the seal!' said she.

'I know it,' said I, 'but the thing goes against me.'

'Give it here,' said she, 'and I will open it myself.'

'Nor you neither,' said I. 'You least of all. It concerns your father, and his honour, dear, which we are both misdoubting. No question but the place is dangerous-like, and the English ship being here, and your father having word from it, and yon officer that stayed ashore! He would not be alone either; there must be more along with him; I daresay we are spied upon this minute. Ay, no doubt, the letter should be opened; but somehow, not by you nor me.'

I was about thus far with it, and my spirit very much overcome with a sense of danger and hidden enemies, when I spied Alan, come back again from following James and walking by himself among the sand-hills. He was in his soldier's coat, of course, and mighty fine; but I could not avoid to shudder when I thought how little that jacket would avail him, if he were once caught and flung in a skiff, and carried on board of the *Seahorse*, a deserter, a rebel, and now a condemned murderer.

'There,' said I, 'there is the man that has the best right to open it: or not, as he thinks fit.'

With which I called upon his name, and we both stood up to be a mark for him.

'If it is so—if it be more disgrace—will you can bear it?' she asked, looking upon me with a burning eye.

'I was asked something of the same question when I had seen you but the once,' said I. 'What do you think I answered? That if I liked you as I thought I did—and O, but I like you better!—I would marry you at his gallows' foot.'

The blood rose in her face; she came close up and pressed upon me, holding my hand: and it was so that we awaited Alan.

He came with one of his queer smiles. 'What was I telling ye, David?' says he.

'There is a time for all things, Alan,' said I, 'and this time is serious. How have you sped? You can speak out plain before this friend of ours.'

'I have been upon a fool's errand,' said he.

'I doubt we have done better than you, then,' said I; 'and, at least, here is a great deal of matter that you must judge of. Do you see that?' I went on, pointing to the ship. 'That is the *Seahorse*, Captain Palliser.'

'I should ken her, too,' says Alan. 'I had fyke enough with her when she was stationed in the Forth. But what ails the man to come so close?'

'I will tell you why he came there first,' said I. 'It was to bring this letter to James More. Why he stops here now that it's delivered, what it's likely to be about, why there's an officer hiding in the bents, and whether or not it's probable that he's alone—I would rather you considered for yourself.'

'A letter to James More?' said he.

'The same,' said I.

'Well, and I can tell ye more than that,' said Alan. 'For last night, when you were fast asleep, I heard the man colloguing with some one in the French, and then the door of that inn to be opened and shut.'

'Alan!' cried I, 'you slept all night, and I am here to prove it.'

'Ay, but I would never trust Alan whether he was asleep or waking!' says he. 'But the business looks bad. Let's see the letter.'

I gave it him.

'Catriona,' said he, 'ye'll have to excuse me, my dear; but there's nothing less than my fine bones upon the cast of it, and I'll have to break this seal.'

'It is my wish,' said Catriona.

He opened it, glanced it through, and flung his hand in the air.

'The stinking brock!' says he, and crammed the paper in his pocket. 'Here, let's get our things thegether. This place is fair death to me.' And he began to walk towards the inn.

It was Catriona that spoke the first. 'He has sold you?' she asked.

'Sold me, my dear,' said Alan. 'But thanks to you and Davie, I'll can jink him yet. Just let me win upon my horse!' he added.

'Catriona must come with us,' said I. 'She can have no more traffic with that man. She and I are to be married.' At which she pressed my hand to her side.

'Are ye there with it?' says Alan, looking back. 'The best day's work that ever either of ye did yet! And I'm bound to say, my dawtie, ye make a real, bonny couple.'

The way that he was following brought us close in by the windmill, where I was aware of a man in seaman's trousers, who seemed to be spying from behind it. Only, of course, we took him in the rear.

'See, Alan!' said I.

'Wheesht!' said he, 'this is my affairs.'

The man was, no doubt, a little deafened by the clattering of the mill, and we got up close before he noticed. Then he turned, and we saw he was a big fellow with a mahogany face.

'I think, sir,' says Alan, 'that you speak the English?'

'*Non, monsieur*,' says he, with an incredible bad accent.

'*Non, monsieur*,' cries Alan, mocking him. 'Is that how

they learn you French on the *Seahorse*? Ye muckle, gutsey
hash, here's a Scots boot to your English hurdies!'

And bounding on him before he could escape, he dealt
the man a kick that laid him on his nose. Then he stood,
with a savage smile, and watched him scramble to his feet
and scamper off into the sand-hills.

'But it's high time I was clear of these empty bents!'
said Alan; and continued his way at top speed and we still
following, to the back door of Bazin's inn.

It chanced that as we entered by the one door we came
face to face with James More entering by the other.

'Here!' said I to Catriona, 'quick! upstairs with you
and make your packets; this is no fit scene for you.'

In the meanwhile James and Alan had met in the midst
of the long room. She passed them close by to reach the
stairs; and after she was some way up I saw her turn and
glance at them again, though without pausing. Indeed, they
were worth looking at. Alan wore as they met one of his best
appearances of courtesy and friendliness, yet with something
eminently warlike, so that James smelled danger off the man,
as folk smell fire in a house, and stood prepared for accidents.

Time pressed. Alan's situation in that solitary place, and
his enemies about him, might have daunted Cæsar. It made
no change in him; and it was in his old spirit of mockery
and daffing that he began the interview.

'A braw good day to ye again, Mr Drummond,' said he.
'What'll yon business of yours be just about?'

'Why, the thing being private, and rather of a long story,'
says James, 'I think it will keep very well till we have eaten.'

'I'm none so sure of that,' said Alan. 'It sticks in my mind
it's either now or never; for the fact is me and Mr Balfour
here have gotten a line, and we're thinking of the road.'

I saw a little surprise in James's eye; but he held himself
stoutly.

'I have but the one word to say to cure you of that,' said
he, 'and that is the name of my business.'

'Say it then,' says Alan. 'Hout! wha minds for Davie?'

'It is a matter that would make us both rich men,' said
James.

'Do ye tell me that?' cries Alan.

'I do sir,' said James. 'The plain fact is that it is Cluny's Treasure.'

'No!' cried Alan. 'Have ye got word of it?'

'I ken the place, Mr Stewart, and can take you there,' said James.

'This crowns all!' says Alan. 'Well, and I'm glad I came to Dunkirk. And so this was your business, was it? Halvers, I'm thinking?'

'That is the business, sir,' says James.

'Well, well,' says Alan; and then in the same tone of childlike interest, 'it has naething to do with the *Seahorse* then?' he asked.

'With what?' says James.

'Or the lad that I have just kicked the bottom of behind yon windmill?' pursued Alan. 'Hut, man! have done with your lees! I have Palliser's letter here in my pouch. You're by with it, James More. You can never show your face again with dacent folk.'

James was taken all aback with it. He stood a second, motionless and white, then swelled with the living anger.

'Do you talk to me, you bastard?' he roared out.

'Ye glee'd swine!' cried Alan, and hit him a sounding buffet on the mouth, and the next wink of time their blades clashed together.

At the first sound of the bare steel I instinctively leaped back from the collision. The next I saw, James parried a thrust so nearly that I thought him killed; and it lowed up in my mind that this was the girl's father, and in a manner almost my own, and I drew and ran in to sever them.

'Keep back, Davie! Are ye daft? Damn ye, keep back!' roared Alan. 'Your blood be on your ain heid then!'

I beat their blades down twice. I was knocked reeling against the wall; I was back again betwixt them. They took no heed of me, thrusting at each other like two furies. I can never think how I avoided being stabbed myself or stabbing one of these two Rodomonts, and the whole business turned about me like a piece of a dream; in the midst of which I heard a great cry from the stair, and Catriona sprang before her father. In the same moment the point of my sword encountered something yielding. It came back to me reddened. I saw the blood flow on the girl's kerchief, and stood sick.

'Will you be killing him before my eyes, and me his daughter after all?' she cried.

'My dear, I have done with him,' said Alan, and went and sat on a table, with his arms crossed and the sword naked in his hand.

Awhile she stood before the man, panting, with big eyes, then swung suddenly about and faced him.

'Begone!' was her word, 'take your shame out of my sight; leave me with clean folk. I am a daughter of Alpin! Shame of the sons of Alpin, begone!'

It was said with so much passion as awoke me from the horror of my own bloodied sword. The two stood facing, she with the red stain on her kerchief, he white as a rag. I knew him well enough—I knew it must have pierced him in the quick place of his soul; but he betook himself to a bravado air.

'Why,' says he, sheathing his sword, though still with a bright eye on Alan, 'if this brawl is over I will but get my portmanteau—'

'There goes no pockmantie out of this place except with me,' says Alan.

'Sir!' cries James.

'James More,' says Alan, 'this lady daughter of yours is to marry my friend Davie, upon the which account I let you pack with a hale carcase. But take you my advice of it and get that carcase out of harm's way or ower late. Little as you suppose it, there are leemits to my temper.'

'Be damned, sir, but my money's there!' said James.

'I'm vexed about that, too,' says Alan, with his funny face, 'but now, ye see, it's mines.' And then with more gravity, 'Be you advised, James More, you leave this house.'

James seemed to cast about for a moment in his mind; but it's to be thought he had enough of Alan's swordsmanship, for he suddenly put off his hat to us and (with a face like one of the damned) bade us farewell in a series. With which he was gone.

At the same time a spell was lifted from me.

'Catriona,' I cried, 'it was me—it was my sword. O, are ye much hurt?'

'I know it, Davie, I am loving you for the pain of it; it was done defending that bad man, my father. See!' she said, and showed me a bleeding scratch, 'see, you have made a man of me now. I will carry a wound like an old soldier.'

Joy that she should be so little hurt, and the love of her brave nature, transported me. I embraced her, I kissed the wound.

'And am I to be out of the kissing, me that never lost a chance?' says Alan; and putting me aside and taking Catriona by either shoulder, 'My dear,' he said, 'you're a true daughter of Alpin. By all accounts, he was a very fine man, and he may weel be proud of you. If ever I was to get married, it's the marrow of you I would be seeking for a mother to my sons. And I bear a king's name and speak the truth.'

He said it with a serious heat of admiration that was honey to the girl, and through her, to me. It seemed to wipe us clean of all James More's disgraces. And the next moment he was just himself again.

'And now by your leave, my dawties,' said he, 'this is a' very bonny; but Alan Breck'll be a wee thing nearer to the gallows than he's caring for; and Dod! I think this is a grand place to be leaving.'

The word recalled us to some wisdom. Alan ran upstairs and returned with our saddle-bags and James More's portmanteau; I picked up Catriona's bundle where she had dropped it on the stair; and we were setting forth out of that dangerous house, when Bazin stopped the way with cries and gesticulations. He had whipped under a table when the swords were drawn, but now he was as bold as a lion. There was his bill to be settled, there was a chair broken, Alan had sat among his dinner things, James More had fled.

'Here,' I cried, 'pay yourself,' and flung him down some Lewie d'ors; for I thought it was no time to be accounting.

He sprang upon that money, and we passed him by, and ran forth into the open. Upon three sides of the house were seamen hasting and closing in; a little nearer to us James

More waved his hat as if to hurry them; and right behind him, like some foolish person holding up its hands, were the sails of the windmill turning.

Alan gave but the one glance, and laid himself down to run. He carried a great weight in James More's portmanteau; but I think he would as soon have lost his life as cast away that booty which was his revenge; and he ran so that I was distressed to follow him, and marvelled and exulted to see the girl bounding at my side.

As soon as we appeared, they cast off all disguise upon the other side; and the seamen pursued us with shouts and view-hullohs. We had a start of some two hundred yards, and they were but bandy-legged tarpaulins after all, that could not hope to better us at such an exercise. I suppose they were armed, but did not care to use their pistols on French ground. And as soon as I perceived that we not only held our advantage but drew a little away, I began to feel quite easy of the issue. For all which, it was a hot, brisk bit of work, so long as it lasted; Dunkirk was still far off; and when we popped over a knowe, and found a company of the garrison marching on the other side on some manœuvre, I could very well understand the word that Alan had.

He stopped running at once; and mopping at his brow,

'They're a real bonny folk, the French nation,' says he.

NO SOONER WERE we safe within the walls of Dunkirk
than we held a very necessary council-of-war on our position.
We had taken a daughter from her father at the sword's
point; any judge would give her back to him at once, and
by all likelihood clap me and Alan into jail; and though
we had an argument upon our side in Captain Palliser's
letter, neither Catriona nor I were very keen to be using
it in public. Upon all accounts it seemed the most prudent
to carry the girl to Paris to the hands of her own chieftain,
Macgregor of Bohaldie, who would be very willing to help
his kinswoman, on the one hand, and not at all anxious to
dishonour James upon the other.

We made but a slow journey of it up, for Catriona was
not so good at the riding as the running, and had scarce
sat in a saddle since the 'Forty-five. But we made it out at
last, reached Paris early of a Sabbath morning, and made
all speed, under Alan's guidance, to find Bohaldie. He was
finely lodged, and lived in a good style, having a pension on
the Scots Fund, as well as private means; greeted Catriona
like one of his own house, and seemed altogether very civil
and discreet, but not particularly open. We asked of the
news of James More. 'Poor James!' said he, and shook his
head and smiled, so that I thought he knew further than he
meant to tell. Then we showed him Palliser's letter, and he
drew a long face at that.

'Poor James!' said he again. 'Well, there are worse folk
than James More, too. But this is dreadful bad. Tut, tut, he
must have forgot himself entirely! This is a most undesirable letter. But, for all that, gentlemen, I cannot see what we
would want to make it public for. It's an ill bird that fouls
his own nest, and we are all Scots folk and all Hieland.'

Upon this we were all agreed, save perhaps Alan; and

still more upon the question of our marriage, which Bohaldie took in his own hands, as though there had been no such person as James More, and gave Catriona away with very pretty manners and agreeable compliments in French. It was not till all was over, and our healths drunk, that he told us James was in that city, whither he had preceded us some days, and where he now lay sick, and like to die. I thought I saw by my wife's face what way her inclination pointed.

'And let us go see him, then,' said I.

'If it is your pleasure,' said Catriona. These were early days.

He was lodged in the same quarter of the city with his chief, in a great house upon a corner; and we were guided up to the garret where he lay by the sound of Highland piping. It seemed he had just borrowed a set of them from Bohaldie to amuse his sickness; though he was no such hand as was his brother Rob, he made good music of the kind; and it was strange to observe the French folk crowding on the stairs, and some of them laughing. He lay propped in a pallet. The first look of him I saw he was upon his last business; and, doubtless, this was a strange place for him to die in. But even now I find I can scarce dwell upon his end with patience. Doubtless, Bohaldie had prepared him; he seemed to know we were married, complimented us on the event, and gave us a benediction like a patriarch.

'I have been never understood,' said he. 'I forgive you both without an afterthought'; after which he spoke for all the world in his old manner, was so obliging as to play us a tune or two upon his pipes, and borrowed a small sum before I left. I could not trace even a hint of shame in any part of his behaviour; but he was great upon forgiveness; it seemed always fresh to him. I think he forgave me every time we met; and when after some four days he passed away in a kind of odour of affectionate sanctity, I could have torn my hair out for exasperation. I had him buried; but what to put upon his tomb was quite beyond me, till at last I considered the date would look best alone.

I thought it wiser to resign all thoughts of Leyden, where we had appeared once as brother and sister, and it would certainly look strange to return in a new character. Scotland would be doing for us; and thither, after I had recovered that which I had left behind, we sailed in a Low Country ship.

And now, Miss Barbara Balfour (to set the ladies first), and Mr Alan Balfour, younger of Shaws, here is the story brought fairly to an end. A great many of the folk that took a part in it, you will find (if you think well) that you have seen and spoken with. Alison Hastie in Limekilns was the lass that rocked your cradle when you were too small to know of it, and walked abroad with you in the policy when you were bigger. That very fine great lady that is Miss Barbara's name-mamma is no other than the same Miss Grant that made so much a fool of David Balfour in the house of the Lord Advocate. And I wonder whether you remember a little, lean, lively gentleman in a scratch-wig and a wraprascal, that came to Shaws very late of a dark night, and whom you were awakened out of your beds and brought down to the dining-hall to be presented to, by the name of Mr Jamieson? Or has Alan forgotten what he did at Mr Jamieson's request—a most disloyal act—for which, by the letter of the law, he might be hanged—no less than drinking the king's health *across the water*? These were strange doings in a good Whig house! But Mr Jamieson is a man privileged, and might set fire to my corn-barn; and the name they know him by now in France is the Chevalier Stewart.

As for Davie and Catriona, I shall watch you pretty close in the next days, and see if you are so bold as to be laughing at papa and mamma. It is true we were not so wise as we might have been, and made a great deal of sorrow out of nothing; but you will find as you grow up that even the artful Miss Barbara, and even the valiant Mr Alan, will be not so very much wiser than their parents. For the life of man upon this world of ours is a funny business. They talk of the angels weeping; but I think they must more often be holding their sides, as they look on; and there was one thing I determined to do when I began this long story, and that was to tell out everything as it befell.

THE MASTER
OF BALLANTRAE

A Winter's Tale

———

Introduced by Roderick Watson

Contents

Introduction

The Master of Ballantrae is a challenging book, and numerous
readers have puzzled over its dynamics. On the surface the
novel looks like an adventure epic—a marriage of *Kidnapped,
Treasure Island* and Fenimore Cooper's leatherstocking tales,
with something of the later Kipling, perhaps, in the mysterious
Secundra Dass. And yet early readers were puzzled by the
book's final effect, which did not seem to fit the adventure
conventions at all.

Andrew Lang described its spirit as 'elaborate, melancholy and almost hopeless', finding 'a very modern
gloom' within its pages. Stevenson's close friend W.E.
Henley (the model for some of Long John Silver's better
attributes) recognised the author's skill, but reckoned that
the book left 'an impression of unreality . . . as if you had
been awakened from a sinister dream'. '*The Master*', he
concluded, 'is a romance which differs from the romances
of Sir Walter [Scott] as a black marble vault differs from a
radiant palace.'

Henley thought he was criticising the text but I think he
got it exactly right with his remark, for I believe that *The
Master of Ballantrae* is in fact a subversion of romance, a dark
revision of Scott, and a left-handed reappraisal of both the
territory and the imaginative resources which had been so
successfully deployed in *Treasure Island* and *Kidnapped*. Let
us start with the novel as a subversion of *Treasure Island*.

The pirate sub-plot in *The Master of Ballantrae* may seem
like only another adventuresome twist to the tale, but in fact
it was the starting point of Stevenson's original inspiration
and it clearly demonstrates the darker side of his intention,
and why he subtitled his book 'a winter's tale'. *Treasure*

Island had its own terrors, but its characters—good or bad—were worthy of them, and the moral force of the tale survived at the end. But life under Teach's command (he is not even the 'real' Teach we are told), is a series of bungled and fruitless pursuits, with episodes of cowardly and brutal cruelty to those who are too slow or too frightened to escape from a vessel which is itself 'too foul to overhaul a bottle'.

According to Chevalier Burke the most dangerous thing about being a pirate was having to serve under their own 'lunatic' captain; or perhaps they might slip and fall when clambering aboard a surrendered vessel, despite the helpful lines cast down by 'the poor souls on board . . . so eager were they to volunteer instead of walking the plank.' There may not be much romance in this vision of feeble merchants actively helping drunken and incompetent pirates to board their vessel, but there is even less comedy, for the terrified captives were invariably put to death all the same. And all for what? 'We found many ships and took many' reflects Burke, 'yet few of them contained much money . . . what did we want with a cargo of ploughs . . . ?'

Faced with Teach's capacity for random and pointless violence the bold Chevalier quickly becomes 'crowding Pat' in order to ingratiate himself with the pirates. This vulgar parody of his own Irishness is all the more appropriate in the face of Teach's own infantile parody of 'wickedness' as he appears in a cloud of sulphur with his face blackened and his whiskers curled, chewing glass and shouting '"Hell, hell!"' Yet, monstrous as he is, Teach, too, is a feeble thing who is easily outfaced by the Master when he stamps his foot at him and commands '"Go down!"' W.E. Henley complained that the pirates in *Treasure Island* '. . . are sober, cleanly, almost respectable mariners, compared to the raving, loathsome miscreants who formed the crew of the *Sarah*', but once again this is exactly the point, for Stevenson wanted to retell his pirate tale in a darker key.

I think that Stevenson's final understanding of where such 'romance' leads us can be found in the physical descriptions of where the Master ends up. The steaming swamps and the shapeless estuaries of the Bermudas, and latterly the frozen wilderness and the night-time terrors of North America—these are the true moral landscape of the Master, an adventurer who can be all things to all men, who decides his course of action, at least three times in the book, by the toss of a coin:

> Some parts of the forest were perfectly dense down to the ground, so that we must cut our way like mites in a cheese. In some the bottom was full of deep swamp, and the whole wood entirely rotten. I have leapt on a great fallen log and sunk to the knees in touchwood. I have sought to stay myself, in falling, against what looked to be a solid trunk, and the whole thing has whiffed away at my touch like a sheet of paper.

It is Mackellar, unimaginative as he is, who senses something of this same hollowness in James Durie himself:

> . . . sometimes I would draw away as though from something partly spectral. I had moments when I thought of him as a man of pasteboard—as though, if one should strike smartly through the buckram of his countenance, there would be found a mere vacuity within.

Such essential emptiness is the very signature of Teach, the pirates, the swamps and the wilderness, and it lies at the heart of the Master too, despite the undoubted force of his will and the power of his charm. The same emptiness can be found at the heart of the Jacobite romance with which the tale begins, for *The Master of Ballantrae* undermines the world of *Kidnapped* just as effectively as it reappraises *Treasure Island*.

Ever since Walter Scott, the conflicting claims of romance and responsibility have been a thematic landmark in the field of Scottish fiction. 'Highland' versus 'Lowland'; 'past' versus 'present'; 'romance' versus 'realism' are the familiar poles of this debate, all coming down in the end to a struggle between 'disorder' and 'order'. In *Kidnapped*, Stevenson offered his own version of the theme through the characters of Alan Breck Stewart and David Balfour. It is tempting to

see the Byronic James Durie and his duller younger brother
Henry in the same roles, but this is not quite right, for
when we look more closely we see that there is little
honour on either side, nor is there any mutual learning
or rapprochement as the story progresses. On the contrary,
it ends with increasing hatred, mad obsession and a double
death in the wilderness.

In fact the House of Durrisdeer was bereft of honour
from the start, for there was no question of 'coming out'
for Charlie, but rather a kind of double insurance policy in
joining both sides of what was shaping up as civil war. It is
Henry, 'not yet very able, but an honest, solid sort of lad'
who sees how shameful this really is. James cries out in fine
style that:

> 'It is the direct heir of Durrisdeer that should ride by
> his King's bridle . . .'
> 'If we were playing a manly part', says Mr. Henry,
> 'there might be sense in such talk. But what are we
> doing? Cheating at cards!'

And who is the head of this family? He is a man grown
prematurely senile, who sits by the fire reading his books
all day; a man blind to the failings of his elder son and
careless of the virtues of the younger. He has plans to
boost his 'deeply mortgaged' estate by marrying his heir
to a wealthy orphan girl, Alison Graeme, who has been
entrusted to his care. And when James is presumed dead
at Culloden, the old lord sets out to persuade her, by what
Mackellar calls 'quiet persecution', to marry Henry, even
though she loved James.

> Day in, day out, he would work upon her, sitting by his
> chimney-side with his finger in his Latin book, and his
> eyes set upon her face with a kind of pleasant intentness
> that became the old gentleman very well. If she wept,
> he would condole with her like an ancient man that has
> seen worse times and begins to think lightly even of
> sorrow; if she raged, he would fall to his reading again
> in his Latin book but always with some civil excuse; if
> she offered, as she often did, to let them have her money

in a gift, he would show her how little it consisted with his honour . . .

The Durrisdeers had a family crest on their stained-glass window, until it was smashed by the coin that sent James to the wars. The old lord and Alison, now married to Henry, refuse to let him mend the missing window pane. Desiring neither the old identity renewed, nor a new identity defined, the pair prefer the mutual seclusion of the chimney-side where they chatter and weep together, jealous of their private heartache, watched over by a blank space. The old heraldic values have been smashed by a golden guinea and the symbolism of this could not be more pointed.

The 'old cause', too, is soon revealed as a matter for the kind of lachrimose sentimentality which is both self-serving and self-deceiving, as Tam Macmorland spreads his wild tales of betrayal, and even Jessie Broun (seduced and left pregnant by the Master) joins the drunken chorus weeping for her 'bonny laddie'. Nor is it long before the 'laddie' himself is shown in the same unflattering light, and even the Chevalier Burke's admiring narrative cannot hide the fact that his hero managed to escape after Culloden at the expense of many friends left behind. Three years after writing *Kidnapped*, Stevenson has redrawn the fierce pride and the loyalty of Alan Breck into a picture of something positively morbid.

Nothing is as it might seem in this tale, not least because it comes to us by way of three separate narrators, none of whom are wholly reliable or unbiased. But the final symbol of the Master's nature, and of how radically Stevenson has sought to subvert the conventions of his earlier fiction, can be found, once again, in the coin which set the whole affair in motion. As a symbol of gold, it smashed the blazon of the Durrisdeers; and as a symbol of blind, causeless chance, it stands for the ruling principle of James Durie's life.

The Master tosses a coin to see who will go to war, and he does it again with Burke to see whether they will be friends or foes. Even when starving in the wilderness, surrounded by possible enemies, he trusts to chance and the turn of a coin to choose his next step. On first acquaintance Burke admired the gesture as something worthy of 'the old tales of Homer and the poets'; but once again Stevenson uses James's physical position to symbolise the true status of such an act:

> . . . he suddenly plucked out his coin, shook it in his closed hands, looked at it, and then lay down with his face in the dust.

Ephraim Mackellar, sober-sided Calvinist and supporter of Mr Henry that he is, suspects the Master of Satanic powers. At least there would be *some* sort of order to the tale if James can be seen as a follower of evil, dedicated to overthrow the good and the true. But the randomness of the coin is the true symbol of James's condition. As a marker of the ultimate indifference of the universe the spinning coin stands at the heart of this tale of causeless fraternal enmity, and in the last analysis it subverts all romance, even the undeniable glamour of James himself. 'I have always done exactly as I felt inclined', the Master admits, and again: 'I go my own way with inevitable motion.' It is not just his family crest which has a blank space at the core of its being:

> 'Life is a singular thing', said he, 'and mankind a very singular people. You suppose yourself to love my brother. I assure you it is merely custom. . . . Had you instead fallen in with me, you would today be as strong upon my side.'

So it is that James and Henry uncover a loveless world, and Stevenson, the undoubted master of the dynamics of romance and dualism in his earlier books, has subverted them in *The Master of Ballantrae*. With all the apparently familiar adventure trappings of *Treasure Island*, *Kidnapped*, and even of *Jekyll and Hyde*, he has produced a memorable 'winter's tale' instead: a tale which ends in mere blankness, just as the brothers end, in a wilderness of cold and night.

Roderick Watson

Dedication

TO SIR PERCY FLORENCE AND LADY SHELLEY

Here is a tale which extends over many years and travels into many countries. By a peculiar fitness of circumstance the writer began, continued it, and concluded it among distant and diverse scenes. Above all, he was much upon the sea. The character and fortune of the fraternal enemies, the hall and shrubbery of Durrisdeer, the problem of Mackellar's homespun and how to shape it for superior flights; these were his company on deck in many star-reflecting harbours, ran often in his mind at sea to the tune of slatting canvas, and were dismissed (something of the suddenest) on the approach of squalls. It is my hope that these surroundings of its manufacture may to some degree find favour for my story with seafarers and sealovers like yourselves.

And at least here is a dedication from a great way off: written by the loud shores of a subtropical island near upon ten thousand miles from Boscombe Chine and Manor: scenes which rise before me as I write, along with the faces and voices of my friends.

Well, I am for the sea once more; no doubt Sir Percy also. Let us make the signal B.R.D.!

R.L.S.
Waikiki, May 17*th*, 1889

Preface

ALTHOUGH an old, consistent exile, the editor of the following pages revisits now and again the city of which he exults to be a native; and there are few things more strange, more painful, or more salutary, than such revisitations. Outside, in foreign spots, he comes by surprise and awakens more attention than he had expected; in his own city, the relation is reversed, and he stands amazed to be so little recollected. Elsewhere he is refreshed to see attractive faces, to remark possible friends; there he scouts the long streets, with a pang at heart, for the faces and friends that are no more. Elsewhere he is delighted with the presence of what is new, there tormented by the absence of what is old. Elsewhere he is content to be his present self; there he is smitten with an equal regret for what he once was and for what he once hoped to be.

He was feeling all this dimly, as he drove from the station, on his last visit; he was feeling it still as he alighted at the door of his friend Mr Johnstone Thomson, W.S., with whom he was to stay. A hearty welcome, a face not altogether changed, a few words that sounded of old days, a laugh provoked and shared, a glimpse in passing of the snowy cloth and bright decanters and the Piranesis on the dining-room wall, brought him to his bedroom with a somewhat lightened cheer, and when he and Mr Thomson sat down a few minutes later, cheek by jowl, and pledged the past in a preliminary bumper, he was already almost consoled, he had already almost forgiven himself his two unpardonable errors, that he should ever have left his native city or ever returned to it.

'I have something quite in your way,' said Mr Thomson. 'I

wished to do honour to your arrival; because, my dear fellow, it is my own youth that comes back along with you; in a very tattered and withered state, to be sure, but—well!—all that's left of it.'

'A great deal better than nothing,' said the editor. 'But what is this which is quite in my way?'

'I was coming to that,' said Mr Thomson: 'Fate has put it in my power to honour your arrival with something really original by way of dessert. A mystery.'

'A mystery?' I repeated.

'Yes,' said his friend, 'a mystery. It may prove to be nothing, and it may prove to be a great deal. But in the meanwhile it is truly mysterious, no eye having looked on it for near a hundred years; it is highly genteel, for it treats of a titled family; and it ought to be melodramatic, for (according to the superscription) it is concerned with death.'

'I think I rarely heard a more obscure or a more promising annunciation,' the other remarked. 'But what is It?'

'You remember my predecessor's, old Peter M'Brair's business?'

'I remember him acutely; he could not look at me without a pang of reprobation, and he could not feel the pang without betraying it. He was to me a man of a great historical interest, but the interest was not returned.'

'Ah well, we go beyond him,' said Mr Thomson. 'I daresay old Peter knew as little about this as I do. You see, I succeeded to a prodigious accumulation of old lawpapers and old tin boxes, some of them of Peter's hoarding, some of his father's, John, first of the dynasty, a great man in his day. Among other collections, were all the papers of the Durrisdeers.'

'The Durrisdeers!' cried I. 'My dear fellow, these may be of the greatest interest. One of them was out in the 'Forty-five; one had some strange passages with the devil—you will find a note of it in Law's "Memorials," I think; and there was an unexplained tragedy, I know not what, much later, about a hundred years ago——'

'More than a hundred years ago,' said Mr Thomson. 'In 1783.'

'How do you know that? I mean some death.'

'Yes, the lamentable deaths of my Lord Durrisdeer and his brother, the Master of Ballantrae (attainted in the troubles),' said Mr Thomson with something the tone of a man quoting. 'Is that it?'

'To say truth,' said I, 'I have only seen some dim reference to the things in memoirs; and heard some traditions dimmer still, through my uncle (whom I think you knew). My uncle lived when he was a boy in the neighbourhood of St Bride's; he has often told me of the avenue closed up and grown over with grass, the great gates never opened, the last lord and his old maid sister who lived in the back parts of the house, a quiet, plain, poor, humdrum couple it would seem—but pathetic too, as the last of that stirring and brave house—and, to the country folk, faintly terrible from some deformed traditions.'

'Yes,' said Mr Thomson. 'Henry Graeme Durie, the last lord, died in 1820; his sister, the Honourable Miss Katharine Durie, in 'Twenty-seven; so much I know; and by what I have been going over the last few days, they were what you say, decent, quiet people, and not rich. To say truth, it was a letter of my lord's that put me on the search for the packet we are going to open this evening. Some papers could not be found; and he wrote to Jack M'Brair suggesting they might be among those sealed up by a Mr Mackellar. M'Brair answered, that the papers in question were all in Mackellar's own hand, all (as the writer understood) of a purely narrative character; and besides, said he, "I am not bound to open them before the year 1889." You may fancy if these words struck me: I instituted a hunt through all the M'Brair repositories; and at last hit upon that packet which (if you have had enough wine) I propose to show you at once.'

In the smoking-room, to which my host now led me, was a packet, fastened with many seals and enclosed in a single sheet of strong paper thus endorsed:

Papers relating to the lives and lamentable death of the late Lord Durisdeer, and his elder brother James, commonly called Master of Ballantrae, attainted in the troubles: entrusted into the hands of John M'Brair in the Lawnmarket of Edinburgh, W.S.; this 20th day of September Anno Domini 1789; by him to be kept secret until the revolution of one hundred years complete, or until the 20th day of September 1889: the same compiled and written by me,

EPHRAIM MACKELLAR,
For near forty years Land Steward on the estates of his Lordship.

As Mr Thomson is a married man, I will not say what hour had struck when we laid down the last of the following pages; but I will give a few words of what ensued.

'Here,' said Mr Thomson, 'is a novel ready to your hand: all you have to do is to work up the scenery, develop the characters, and improve the style.'

'My dear fellow,' said I, 'they are just the three things that I would rather die than set my hand to. It shall be published as it stands.'

'But it's so bald,' objected Mr Thomson.

'I believe there is nothing so noble as baldness,' replied I, 'and I am sure there is nothing so interesting. I would have all literature bald, and all authors (if you like) but one.'

'Well, well,' said Mr Thomson, 'we shall see.'

CHAPTER ONE

Summary of Events during the Master's Wanderings

THE FULL TRUTH of this odd matter is what the world has long been looking for, and public curiosity is sure to welcome. It so befell that I was intimately mingled with the last years and history of the house; and there does not live one man so able as myself to make these matters plain, or so desirous to narrate them faithfully. I knew the Master; on many secret steps of his career I have an authentic memoir in my hand; I sailed with him on his last voyage almost alone; I made one upon that winter's journey of which so many tales have gone abroad; and I was there at the man's death. As for my late Lord Durrisdeer, I served him and loved him near twenty years; and thought more of him the more I knew of him. Altogether, I think it not fit that so much evidence should perish; the truth is a debt I owe my lord's memory; and I think my old years will flow more smoothly, and my white hair lie quieter on the pillow, when the debt is paid.

The Duries of Durrisdeer and Ballantrae were a strong family in the south-west from the days of David First. A rhyme still current in the countryside—

> Kittle folk are the Durrisdeers,
> They ride wi' ower mony spears—

bears the mark of its antiquity; and the name appears in another, which common report attributes to Thomas of Ercildoune himself—I cannot say how truly, and which some have applied—I dare not say with how much justice—to the events of this narration:

> Twa Duries in Durrisdeer,
>   Ane to tie and ane to ride.
> An ill day for the groom
>   And a waur day for the bride.

Authentic history besides is filled with their exploits, which
(to our modern eyes) seem not very commendable: and the
family suffered its full share of those ups and downs to
which the great houses of Scotland have been ever liable.
But all these I pass over, to come to that memorable year
1745, when the foundations of this tragedy were laid.

At that time there dwelt a family of four persons in the
house of Durrisdeer, near St Bride's, on the Solway shore;
a chief hold of their race since the Reformation. My old lord,
eighth of the name, was not old in years, but he suffered
prematurely from the disabilities of age; his place was at
the chimney-side; there he sat reading, in a lined gown,
with few words for any man, and wry words for none: the
model of an old retired housekeeper; and yet his mind very
well nourished with study, and reputed in the country to be
more cunning than he seemed. The Master of Ballantrae,
James in baptism, took from his father the love of serious
reading; some of his tact, perhaps, as well; but that which
was only policy in the father became black dissimulation in
the son. The face of his behaviour was merely popular and
wild: he sat late at wine, later at the cards; had the name in
the country of 'an unco man for the lasses'; and was ever
in the front of broils. But for all he was the first to go in,
yet it was observed he was invariably the best to come off;
and his partners in mischief were usually alone to pay the
piper. This luck or dexterity got him several ill-wishers,
but with the rest of the country enhanced his reputation;
so that great things were looked for in his future, when
he should have gained more gravity. One very black mark
he had to his name; but the matter was hushed up at the
time, and so defaced by legends before I came into these
parts that I scruple to set it down. If it was true, it was
a horrid fact in one so young; and if false, it was a horrid
calumny. I think it notable that he had always vaunted
himself quite implacable, and was taken at his word; so
that he had the addition among his neighbours of 'an ill
man to cross.' Here was altogether a young nobleman (not
yet twenty-four in the year 'Forty-five) who had made a
figure in the country beyond his time of life. The less marvel
if there were little heard of the second son, Mr Henry (my

late Lord Durrisdeer), who was neither very bad nor yet very able, but an honest, solid sort of lad, like many of his neighbours. Little heard, I say; but indeed it was a case of little spoken. He was known among the salmon fishers in the firth, for that was a sport that he assiduously followed; he was an excellent good horse-doctor besides; and took a chief hand, almost from a boy, in the management of the estates. How hard a part that was, in the situation of that family, none knows better than myself; nor yet with how little colour of justice a man may there acquire the reputation of a tyrant and a miser. The fourth person in the house was Miss Alison Graeme, a near kinswoman, an orphan, and the heir to a considerable fortune which her father had acquired in trade. This money was loudly called for by my lord's necessities; indeed, the land was deeply mortgaged; and Miss Alison was designed accordingly to be the Master's wife, gladly enough on her side; with how much goodwill on his is another matter. She was a comely girl, and in those days very spirited and self-willed; for the old lord having no daughter of his own, and my lady being long dead, she had grown up as best she might.

To these four came the news of Prince Charlie's landing, and set them presently by the ears. My lord, like the chimney-keeper that he was, was all for temporising. Miss Alison held the other side, because it appeared romantical; and the Master (though I have heard they did not agree often) was for this once of her opinion. The adventure tempted him, as I conceive; he was tempted by the opportunity to raise the fortunes of the house, and not less by the hope of paying off his private liabilities, which were heavy beyond all opinion. As for Mr Henry, it appears he said little enough at first; his part came later on. It took the three a whole day's disputation before they agreed to steer a middle course, one son going forth to strike a blow for King James, my lord and the other staying at home to keep in favour with King George. Doubtless this was my lord's decision; and, as is well known, it was the part played by many considerable families. But the one dispute settled, another opened. For my lord, Miss Alison, and Mr Henry all held the one view: that it was the cadet's part to go out;

and the Master, what with restlessness and vanity, would at no rate consent to stay at home. My lord pleaded, Miss Alison wept, Mr Henry was very plain spoken: all was of no avail.

'It is the direct heir of Durrisdeer that should ride by his King's bridle,' says the Master.

'If we were playing a manly part,' says Mr Henry, 'there might be sense in such talk. But what are we doing? Cheating at cards!'

'We are saving the house of Durrisdeer, Henry,' his father said.

'And see, James,' said Mr Henry, 'if I go, and the Prince has the upper hand, it will be easy to make your peace with King James. But if you go, and the expedition fails, we divide the right and the title. And what shall I be then?'

'You will be Lord Durrisdeer,' said the Master. 'I put all I have upon the table.'

'I play at no such game,' cries Mr Henry. 'I shall be left in such a situation as no man of sense and honour could endure. I shall be neither fish nor flesh!' he cried. And a little after he had another expression, plainer perhaps than he intended. 'It is your duty to be here with my father,' said he. 'You know well enough you are the favourite.'

'Ay?' said the Master. 'And there spoke Envy! Would you trip up my heels—Jacob?' said he, and dwelled upon the name maliciously.

Mr Henry went and walked at the low end of the hall without reply; for he had an excellent gift of silence. Presently he came back.

'I am the cadet, and I *should* go,' said he. 'And my lord here is the master, and he says I *shall* go. What say ye to that, my brother?'

'I say this, Harry,' returned the Master, 'that when very obstinate folk are met, there are only two ways out: Blows—and I think none of us could care to go so far; or the arbitrament of chance—and here is a guinea piece. Will you stand by the toss of the coin?'

'I will stand and fall by it,' said Mr Henry. 'Heads, I go; shield, I stay.'

The coin was spun, and it fell shield. 'So there is a lesson for Jacob,' says the Master.

'We shall live to repent of this,' says Mr Henry, and flung out of the hall.

As for Miss Alison, she caught up that piece of gold which had just sent her lover to the wars, and flung it clean through the family shield in the great painted window.

'If you loved me as well as I love you, you would have stayed,' cried she.

'"I could not love you, dear, so well, loved I not honour more,"' sang the Master.

'O!' she cried, 'you have no heart—I hope you may be killed!' and she ran from the room, and in tears, to her own chamber.

It seems the Master turned to my lord with his most comical manner, and says he, 'This looks like a devil of a wife.'

'I think you are a devil of a son to me,' cried his father, 'you that have always been the favourite, to my shame be it spoken. Never a good hour have I gotten of you since you were born; no, never one good hour,' and repeated it again the third time. Whether it was the Master's levity, or his insubordination, or Mr Henry's word about the favourite son, that had so much disturbed my lord, I do not know: but I incline to think it was the last, for I have it by all accounts that Mr Henry was more made up to from that hour.

Altogether it was in pretty ill blood with his family that the Master rode to the North; which was the more sorrowful for others to remember when it seemed too late. By fear and favour he had scraped together near upon a dozen men, principally tenants' sons; they were all pretty full when they set forth, and rode up the hill by the old abbey, roaring and singing, the white cockade in every hat. It was a desperate venture for so small a company to cross the most of Scotland unsupported; and (what made folk think so the more) even as that poor dozen was clattering up the hill, a great ship of the King's navy, that could have brought them under with a single boat, lay with her broad ensign streaming in the bay. The next afternoon, having given the Master a fair start, it was Mr Henry's turn; and he rode off, all by himself, to offer his sword and carry letters from his father to King George's Government. Miss Alison was shut in her room, and did little but weep, till both were gone; only she stitched the cockade upon the Master's hat, and (as John Paul told me) it was wetted with tears when he carried it down to him.

In all that followed, Mr Henry and my old lord were true to their bargain. That ever they accomplished anything is more than I could learn; and that they were anyway strong on the King's side, more than I believe. But they kept the letter of loyalty, corresponded with my Lord President, sat still at home, and had little or no commerce with the Master while that business lasted. Nor was he, on his side, more communicative. Miss Alison, indeed, was always sending him expresses, but I do not know if she had many answers. Macconochie rode for her once, and found the Highlanders before Carlisle, and the Master riding by the Prince's side in high favour; he took the letter (so Macconochie tells), opened it, glanced it through with a mouth like a man whistling, and stuck it in his belt, whence, on his horse passageing, it fell unregarded to the ground. It was Macconochie who picked it up; and he still kept it, and indeed I have seen it in his hands. News came to Durrisdeer of course, by the common report, as it goes travelling through a country, a thing always wonderful to me. By that means the family learned more of the Master's favour with the Prince, and the ground it was said to stand on: for by a strange condescension in a man so proud—only that he was a man still more ambitious—he was said to have crept into notability by truckling to the Irish. Sir Thomas Sullivan, Colonel Burke, and the rest, were his daily comrades, by which course he withdrew himself from his own country-folk. All the small intrigues he had a hand in fomenting; thwarted my Lord George upon a thousand points; was always for the advice that seemed palatable to the Prince, no matter if it was good or bad; and seems upon the whole (like the gambler he was all through life) to have had less regard to the chances of the campaign than to the greatness of favour he might aspire to, if, by any luck, it should succeed. For the rest, he did very well in the field; no one questioned that: for he was no coward.

The next was the news of Culloden, which was brought to Durrisdeer by one of the tenants' sons—the only survivor, he declared, of all those that had gone singing up the hill. By an unfortunate chance John Paul and Macconochie had that very morning found the guinea piece—which was the root of all the evil—sticking in a holly bush; they had been 'up the gait,' as the servants say at Durrisdeer, to the change-house; and if they had little left of the guinea, they had less of their wits. What must John Paul do but burst into the hall where the family sat at dinner, and cry the news to them that 'Tam Macmorland was but new lichtit at the door, and—wirra, wirra—there were nane to come behind him'?

They took the word in silence like folk condemned; only Mr Henry carrying his palm to his face, and Miss Alison laying her head outright upon her hands. As for my lord, he was like ashes.

'I have still one son,' says he. 'And, Henry, I will do you this justice—it is the kinder that is left.'

It was a strange thing to say in such a moment; but my lord had never forgotten Mr Henry's speech, and he had years of injustice on his conscience. Still it was a strange thing, and more than Miss Alison could let pass. She broke out and blamed my lord for his unnatural words, and Mr Henry because he was sitting there in safety when his brother lay dead, and herself because she had given her sweetheart ill words at his departure, calling him the flower of the flock, wringing her hands, protesting her love, and crying on him by his name—so that the servants stood astonished.

Mr Henry got to his feet, and stood holding his chair. It was he that was like ashes now.

'O!' he burst out suddenly, 'I know you loved him.'

'The world knows that, glory be to God!' cries she; and then to Mr Henry: 'There is none but me to know one thing—that you were a traitor to him in your heart.'

'God knows,' groans he, 'it was lost love on both sides.'

Time went by in the house after that without much change; only they were now three instead of four, which was a perpetual reminder of their loss. Miss Alison's money, you are to bear in mind, was highly needful for the estates; and the one brother being dead, my old lord soon set his heart upon her marrying the other. Day in, day out, he would work upon her, sitting by the chimney-side with his finger in his Latin book, and his eyes set upon her face with a kind of pleasant intentness that became the old gentleman very well. If she wept, he would condole with her like an ancient man that has seen worse times and begins to think lightly even of sorrow; if she raged, he would fall to reading again in his Latin book, but always with some civil excuse; if she offered, as she often did, to let them have her money in a gift, he would show her how little it consisted with his honour, and remind her, even if he should consent, that Mr Henry would certainly refuse. *Non vi sed sæpe cadendo* was a favourite word of his; and no doubt this quiet persecution wore away much of her resolve; no doubt, besides, he had a great influence on the girl, having stood in the place of both her parents; and, for that matter, she was herself filled with the spirit of the Duries, and would have gone a great way for the glory of Durrisdeer; but not so far, I think, as to marry my poor patron, had it not been—strangely enough—for the circumstance of his extreme unpopularity.

This was the work of Tam Macmorland. There was not much harm in Tam; but he had that grievous weakness, a long tongue; and as the only man in that country who had been out—or, rather, who had come in again—he was sure of listeners. Those that have the underhand in any fighting, I have observed, are ever anxious to persuade themselves they were betrayed. By Tam's account of it, the rebels had been betrayed at every turn and by every officer they had; they had been betrayed at Derby, and betrayed at Falkirk; the night march was a step of treachery of my Lord George's; and Culloden was lost by the treachery of the Macdonalds. This habit of imputing treason grew upon the fool, till at last he must have in Mr Henry also. Mr Henry (by his account) had betrayed the lads of Durrisdeer; he had promised to follow with more men, and instead of that he had ridden to King George. 'Ay, and the next day!' Tam would cry. 'The puir bonny Master, and the puir kind lads that rade wi' him, were hardly ower the scaur or he was aff—the Judis! Ay, weel—he has his way o't: he's to be my lord, nae less, and there's mony a cold corp amang the Hieland heather!' And at this, if Tam had been drinking, he would begin to weep.

Let any one speak long enough, he will get believers. This view of Mr Henry's behaviour crept about the country by little and little; it was talked upon by folk that knew the contrary, but were short of topics; and it was heard and believed and given out for gospel by the ignorant and the ill-willing. Mr Henry began to be shunned; yet a while, and the commons began to murmur as he went by, and the women (who are always the most bold because they are the most safe) to cry out their reproaches to his face. The Master was cried up for a saint. It was remembered how he had never any hand in pressing the tenants; as, indeed, no more he had, except to spend the money. He was a little wild perhaps, the folk said; but how much better was a natural, wild lad that would soon have settled down, than a skinflint and a sneckdraw, sitting with his nose in an account book to persecute poor tenants! One trollop, who had had a child to the Master, and by all accounts been very badly used, yet made herself a kind of champion of his memory. She flung a stone one day at Mr Henry.

'Whaur's the bonny lad that trustit ye?' she cried.

Mr Henry reined in his horse and looked upon her, the blood flowing from his lip. 'Ay, Jess,' says he. 'You too? And yet ye should ken me better.' For it was he who had helped her with money.

The woman had another stone ready, which she made as if she would cast; and he, to ward himself, threw up the hand that held his riding rod.

'What, would ye beat a lassie, ye ugly—?' cries she, and ran away screaming as though he had struck her.

Next day word went about the country like wildfire that Mr Henry had beaten Jessie Broun within an inch of her life. I give it as one instance of how this snowball grew, and one calumny brought another; until my poor patron was so perished in reputation that he began to keep the house like my lord. All this while, you may be very sure, he uttered no complaints at home; the very ground of the scandal was too sore a matter to be handled; and Mr Henry was very proud, and strangely obstinate in silence. My old lord must have heard of it, by John Paul, if by no one else; and he must at least have remarked the altered habits of his son. Yet even he, it is probable, knew not how high the feeling ran; and as for Miss Alison, she was ever the last person to hear news, and the least interested when she heard them.

In the height of the ill-feeling (for it died away as it came, no man could say why) there was an election forward in the town of St Bride's, which is the next to Durrisdeer, standing on the Water of Swift; some grievance was fermenting, I forget what, if ever I heard: and it was currently said there would be broken heads ere night, and that the sheriff had sent as far as Dumfries for soldiers. My lord moved that Mr Henry should be present, assuring him it was necessary to appear, for the credit of the house. 'It will soon be reported,' said he, 'that we do not take the lead in our own country.'

'It is a strange lead that I can take,' said Mr Henry; and when they had pushed him further, 'I tell you the plain truth,' he said: 'I dare not show my face.'

'You are the first of the house that ever said so,' cries Miss Alison.

'We will go all three,' said my lord; and sure enough he got into his boots (the first time in four years—a sore business John Paul had to get them on), and Miss Alison into her riding coat, and all three rode together to St Bride's.

The streets were full of the riff-raff of all the countryside, who had no sooner clapped eyes on Mr Henry than the hissing began, and the hooting, and the cries of 'Judas!' and 'Where was the Master?' and 'Where were the poor lads that rode with him?' Even a stone was cast; but the more part cried shame at that, for my old lord's sake, and Miss Alison's. It took not ten minutes to persuade my lord that Mr Henry had been right. He said never a word, but turned his horse about, and home again, with his chin upon his bosom. Never a word said Miss Alison; no doubt she thought the more; no doubt her pride was stung, for she was a bone-bred Durie; and no doubt her heart was touched to see her cousin so unjustly used. That night she was never in bed; I have often blamed my lady—when I call to mind that night I readily forgive her all; and the first thing in the morning she came to the old lord in his usual seat.

'If Henry still wants me,' said she, 'he can have me now.' To himself she had a different speech: 'I bring you no love, Henry; but God knows, all the pity in the world.'

June the 1st, 1748, was the day of their marriage. It was December of the same year that first saw me alighting at the doors of the great house; and from there I take up the history of events as they befell under my own observation, like a witness in a court.

CHAPTER TWO

Summary of Events (continued)

I MADE THE last of my journey in the cold end of December, in a mighty dry day of frost, and who should be my guide but Patey Macmorland, brother of Tam! For a tow-headed, bare-legged brat of ten, he had more ill tales upon his tongue than ever I heard the match of; having drunken betimes in his brother's cup. I was still not so old myself; pride had not yet the upper hand of curiosity; and indeed it would have taken any man, that cold morning, to hear all the old clashes of the country, and be shown all the places by the way where strange things had fallen out. I had tales of Claverhouse as we came through the bogs, and tales of the devil as we came over the top of the scaur. As we came in by the abbey I heard somewhat of the old monks, and more of the freetraders, who use its ruins for a magazine, landing for that cause within a cannon-shot of Durrisdeer; and along all the road the Duries and poor Mr Henry were in the first rank of slander. My mind was thus highly prejudiced against the family I was about to serve, so that I was half surprised when I beheld Durrisdeer itself, lying in a pretty, sheltered bay, under the Abbey Hill; the house most commodiously built in the French fashion, or perhaps Italianate, for I have no skill in these arts; and the place the most beautified with gardens, lawns, shrubberies, and trees I had ever seen. The money sunk here unproductively would have quite restored the family; but as it was, it cost a revenue to keep it up.

Mr Henry came himself to the door to welcome me: a tall dark young gentleman (the Duries are all black men) of a plain and not cheerful face, very strong in body, but not so strong in health; taking me by the hand without any pride, and putting me at home with plain kind speeches. He led me into the hall, booted as I was, to present me to my lord. It was still daylight; and the first thing I observed was a lozenge of clear glass in the midst of the shield in the painted window, which I remember thinking a blemish on a room otherwise so handsome, with its family portraits, and the pargeted ceiling with pendants, and the carved chimney, in one corner of which my old lord sat reading in his Livy. He was like Mr Henry, with much the same plain countenance, only more subtle and pleasant, and his talk a thousand times more entertaining. He had many questions to ask me, I remember, of Edinburgh College, where I had just received my mastership of arts, and of the various professors, with whom and their proficiency he seemed well acquainted; and thus, talking of things that I knew, I soon got liberty of speech in my new home.

In the midst of this came Mrs Henry into the room; she was very far gone, Miss Katharine being due in about six weeks, which made me think less of her beauty at the first sight; and she used me with more of condescension than the rest; so that, upon all accounts, I kept her in the third place of my esteem.

It did not take long before all Patey Macmorland's tales were blotted out of my belief, and I was become, what I have ever since remained, a loving servant of the house of Durrisdeer. Mr Henry had the chief part of my affection. It was with him I worked; and I found him an exacting master, keeping all his kindness for those hours in which we were unemployed, and in the steward's office not only loading me with work, but viewing me with a shrewd supervision. At length one day he looked up from his paper with a kind of timidness, and says he, 'Mr Mackellar, I think I ought to tell you that you do very well.' That was my first word of commendation; and from that day his jealousy of my performance was relaxed; soon it was 'Mr Mackellar' here, and 'Mr Mackellar' there, with the whole family; and for much of my service at Durrisdeer I have transacted everything at my own time, and to my own fancy, and never a farthing challenged. Even while he was driving me, I had begun to find my heart go out to Mr Henry; no doubt, partly in pity, he was a man so palpably unhappy. He would fall into a deep muse over our accounts, staring at the page or out of the window; and at those times the look of his face, and the sigh that would break from him, awoke in me strong feelings of curiosity and commiseration. One day, I remember, we were late upon some business in the steward's room. This room is in the top of the house, and has a view upon the bay, and over a little wooded cape, on the long sands; and there, right over against the sun, which was then dipping, we saw the free-traders, with a great force of men and horses, scouring on the beach. Mr Henry had been staring straight west, so that I marvelled he was not blinded by the sun; suddenly he frowns, rubs his hand upon his brow, and turns to me with a smile.

'You would not guess what I was thinking,' says he. 'I was thinking I would be a happier man if I could ride and run the danger of my life with these lawless companions.'

I told him I had observed he did not enjoy good spirits; and that it was a common fancy to envy others and think we should be the better of some change; quoting Horace to the point, like a young man fresh from college.

'Why, just so,' said he. 'And with that we may get back to our accounts.'

It was not long before I began to get wind of the causes that so much depressed him. Indeed, a blind man must have soon discovered there was a shadow on that house, the shadow of the Master of Ballantrae. Dead or alive (and he was then supposed to be dead) that man was his brother's rival: his rival abroad, where there was never a good word for Mr Henry, and nothing but regret and praise for the Master; and his rival at home, not only with his father and his wife, but with the very servants.

They were two old serving men that were the leaders. John Paul, a little, bald, solemn, stomachy man, a great professor of piety and (take him for all in all) a pretty faithful servant, was the chief of the Master's faction. None durst go so far as John. He took a pleasure in disregarding Mr Henry publicly, often with a slighting comparison. My lord and Mrs Henry took him up, to be sure, but never so resolutely as they should; and he had only to pull his weeping face and begin his lamentations for the Master—'his laddie,' as he called him—to have the whole condoned. As for Henry, he let these things pass in silence, sometimes with a sad

and sometimes with a black look. There was no rivalling
the dead, he knew that; and how to censure an old serving
man for a fault of loyalty was more than he could see. His
was not the tongue to do it.

Macconochie was chief upon the other side; an old,
ill-spoken, swearing, ranting, drunken dog; and I have often
thought it an odd circumstance in human nature that these
two serving-men should each have been the champion of his
contrary, and blackened their own faults, and made light
of their own virtues, when they beheld them in a master.
Macconochie had soon smelled out my secret inclination,
took me much into his confidence, and would rant against
the Master by the hour, so that even my work suffered.
'They're a' daft here,' he would cry, 'and be damned to
them! The Master—the deil's in their thrapples that should
call him sae! It's Mr Henry should be master now! They
were nane sae fond o' the Master when they had him, I'll
can tell ye that. Sorrow on his name! Never a guid word
did I hear on his lips, nor naebody else, but just fleering
and flyting and profane cursing—deil hae him! There's
nane kent his wickedness: him a gentleman! Did ever ye
hear tell, Mr Mackellar, o' Wully White the wabster? No?
Aweel, Wully was an unco praying kind o' man; a dreigh
body, nane o' my kind, I never could abide the sight o'
him; onyway he was a great hand by his way of it, and he
up and rebukit the Master for some of his ongoings. It was
a grand thing for the Master o' Ball'ntrae to tak' up a feud
wi' a wabster, wasnae't?' Macconochie would sneer; indeed,
he never took the full name upon his lips but with a sort of a
whine of hatred. 'But he did! A fine employ it was: chapping
at the man's door, and crying "boo" in his lum, and puttin'
poother in his fire, and pee-oys in his window; till the man
thocht it was Auld Hornie was come seekin' him. Weel, to
mak a lang story short, Wully gaed gyte. At the hinder end
they couldnae get him frae his knees, but he just roared
and prayed and grat straucht on, till he got his release. It
was fair murder, a'body said that. Ask John Paul—he was
brawly ashamed o' that game, him that's sic a Christian
man! Grand doin's for the Master o' Ball'ntrae! 'I asked
him what the Master had thought of it himself. 'How would

I ken?' says he; 'He never said naething.' And on again in
his usual manner of banning and swearing, with every now
and again a 'Master of Ballantrae' sneered through his nose.
It was in one of these confidences that he showed me the
Carlisle letter, the print of the horseshoe still stamped in
the paper. Indeed, that was our last confidence; for he then
expressed himself so ill-naturedly of Mrs Henry that I had
to reprimand him sharply, and must thenceforth hold him
at a distance.

My old lord was uniformly kind to Mr Henry; he had
even pretty ways of gratitude, and would sometimes clap
him on the shoulder and say, as if to the world at large:
'This is a very good son to me.' And grateful he was, no
doubt, being a man of sense and justice. But I think that
was all, and I am sure Mr Henry thought so. The love
was all for the dead son. Not that this was often given
breath to; indeed, with me but once. My lord had asked
me one day how I got on with Mr Henry, and I had told
him the truth.

'Ay,' said he, looking sideways on the burning fire, 'Henry
is a good lad, a very good lad,' said he. 'You have heard,
Mr Mackellar, that I had another son? I am afraid he was
not so virtuous a lad as Mr Henry; but dear me, he's dead,
Mr Mackellar! and while he lived we were all very proud of
him, all very proud. If he was not all he should have been
in some ways, well, perhaps we loved him better!' This last
he said looking musingly in the fire; and then to me, with
a great deal of briskness, 'But I am rejoiced you do so well
with Mr Henry. You will find him a good master.' And with
that he opened his book, which was the customary signal of
dismission. But it would be little that he read, and less that
he understood; Culloden field and the Master, these would
be the burthen of his thought; and the burthen of mine was
an unnatural jealousy of the dead man for Mr Henry's sake,
that had even then begun to grow on me.

I am keeping Mrs Henry for the last, so that this expression of my sentiment may seem unwarrantably strong: the
reader shall judge for himself when I have done. But I
must first tell of another matter, which was the means of
bringing me more intimate. I had not yet been six months

at Durrisdeer when it chanced that John Paul fell sick and must keep his bed; drink was the root of his malady, in my poor thought; but he was tended, and indeed carried himself, like an afflicted saint; and the very minister, who came to visit him, professed himself edified when he went away. The third morning of his sickness Mr Henry comes to me with something of a hang-dog look.

'Mackellar,' says he, 'I wish I could trouble you upon a little service. There is a pension we pay; it is John's part to carry it, and now that he is sick I know not to whom I should look, unless it was yourself. The matter is very delicate; I could not carry it with my own hand for a sufficient reason; I dare not send Macconochie, who is a talker, and I am—I have—I am desirous this should not come to Mrs Henry's ears,' says he, and flushed to his neck as he said it.

To say truth, when I found I was to carry money to one Jessie Broun, who was no better than she should be, I supposed it was some trip of his own that Mr Henry was dissembling. I was the more impressed when the truth came out.

It was up a wynd off a side street in St Bride's that Jessie had her lodging. The place was very ill inhabited, mostly by the free-trading sort. There was a man with a broken head at the entry; half-way up, in a tavern, fellows were roaring and singing, though it was not yet nine in the day. Altogether, I had never seen a worse neighbourhood, even in the great city of Edinburgh, and I was in two minds to go back. Jessie's room was of a piece with her surroundings, and herself no better. She would not give me the receipt (which Mr Henry had told me to demand, for he was very methodical) until she had sent out for spirits, and I had pledged her in a glass; and all the time she carried on in a light-headed, reckless way—now aping the manners of a lady, now breaking into unseemly mirth, now making coquettish advances that oppressed me to the ground. Of the money she spoke more tragically.

'It's blood-money!' said she; 'I take it for that: blood-money for the betrayed! See what I'm brought down to! Ah, if the bonny lad were back again, it would be changed days.

But he's deid—he's lyin' deid amang the Hieland hills—the bonny lad, the bonny lad!'

She had a rapt manner of crying on the bonny lad, clasping her hands and casting up her eyes, that I think she must have learned of strolling players; and I thought her sorrow very much of an affectation, and that she dwelled upon the business because her shame was now all she had to be proud of. I will not say I did not pity her, but it was a loathing pity at the best; and her last change of manner wiped it out. This was when she had had enough of me for an audience, and had set her name at last to the receipt. 'There!' says she, and, taking the most unwomanly oaths upon her tongue, bade me begone and carry it to the Judas who had sent me. It was the first time I had heard the name applied to Mr Henry; I was staggered besides at her sudden vehemence of word and manner, and got forth from the room, under this shower of curses, like a beaten dog. But even then I was not quit, for the vixen threw up her window, and, leaning forth, continued to revile me as I went up the wynd; the free-traders, coming to the tavern door, joined in the mockery, and one had even the inhumanity to set upon me a very savage small dog, which bit me in the ankle. This was a strong lesson, had I required one, to avoid ill company; and I rode home in much pain from the bite, and considerable indignation of mind.

Mr Henry was in the steward's room, affecting employment, but I could see he was only impatient to hear of my errand.

'Well?' says he, as soon as I came in; and when I had told him something of what passed, and that Jessie seemed an undeserving woman, and far from grateful: 'She is no friend to me,' said he; 'but indeed, Mackellar, I have few friends to boast of, and Jessie has some cause to be unjust. I need not dissemble what all the country knows: she was not very well used by one of our family.' This was the first time I had heard him refer to the Master, even distantly; and I think he found his tongue rebellious even for that much, but presently he resumed—'This is why I would have nothing said. It would give pain to Mrs Henry . . . and to my father,' he added, with another flush.

'Mr Henry,' said I, 'if you will take a freedom at my hands, I would tell you to let that woman be. What service is your money to the like of her? She has no sobriety and no economy—as for gratitude, you will as soon get milk from a whinstone; and if you will pretermit your bounty, it will make no change at all but just to save the ankles of your messengers.'

Mr Henry smiled. 'But I am grieved about your ankle,' said he the next moment, with a proper gravity.

'And observe,' I continued, 'I give you this advice upon consideration; and yet my heart was touched for the woman in the beginning.'

'Why, there it is, you see!' said Mr Henry. 'And you are to remember that I knew her once a very decent lass. Besides which, although I speak little of my family, I think much of its repute.'

And with that he broke up the talk, which was the first we had together in such confidence. But the same afternoon I had the proof that his father was perfectly acquainted with the business, and that it was only from his wife that Mr Henry kept it secret.

'I fear you had a painful errand today,' says my lord to me, 'for which, as it enters in no way among your duties, I wish to thank you, and to remind you at the same time (in case Mr Henry should have neglected) how very desirable it is that no word of it should reach my daughter. Reflections on the dead, Mr Mackellar, are doubly painful.'

Anger glowed in my heart; and I could have told my lord to his face how little he had to do, bolstering up the image of the dead in Mrs Henry's heart, and how much better he were employed to shatter that false idol; for by this time I saw very well how the land lay between my patron and his wife.

My pen is clear enough to tell a plain tale; but to render the effect of an infinity of small things, not one great enough in itself to be narrated; and to translate the story of looks, and the message of voices when they are saying no great matter; and to put in half a page the essence of near eighteen months—this is what I despair to accomplish. The fault, to be very blunt, lay all in Mrs Henry. She felt it a merit to have consented to the marriage, and she took it like a martyrdom; in which my old lord, whether he knew it or not, fomented her. She made a merit, besides, of her constancy to the dead, though its name, to a nicer conscience, should have seemed rather disloyalty to the living; and here also my lord gave her his countenance. I suppose he was glad to talk of his loss, and ashamed to dwell on it with Mr Henry. Certainly, at least, he made a little coterie apart in that family of three, and it was the husband who was shut out. It seems it was an old custom when the family were alone in Durrisdeer, that my lord should take his wine to the chimney-side, and Miss Alison, instead of withdrawing, should bring a stool to his knee, and chatter to him privately; and after she had become my patron's wife the same manner of doing was continued. It should have been pleasant to behold this ancient gentleman so loving with his daughter, but I was too much a partisan of Mr Henry's to be anything but wroth at his exclusion. Many's the time I have seen him make an obvious resolve, quit the table, and go and join himself to his wife and my Lord Durrisdeer; and on their part, they were never backward to make him welcome, turned to him smilingly as to an intruding child, and took him into their talk with an effort so ill-concealed that he was soon back again beside me at the table, whence (so great is the hall of Durrisdeer) we could but hear the murmur of voices at the chimney. There he would sit and watch, and I along with him; and sometimes by my lord's head sorrowfully shaken, or his hand laid on Mrs Henry's head, or hers upon his knee as if in consolation, or sometimes by an exchange of tearful looks, we would draw our conclusion that the talk had gone to the old subject and the shadow of the dead was in the hall.

I have hours when I blame Mr Henry for taking all too patiently; yet we are to remember he was married in pity, and accepted his wife upon that term. And, indeed, he had small encouragement to make a stand. Once, I remember, he announced he had found a man to replace the pane of the stained window, which, as it was he that managed all the business, was a thing clearly within his attributions. But to the Master's fanciers that pane was like a relic;

and on the first word of any change the blood flew to Mrs Henry's face.

'I wonder at you!' she cried.

'I wonder at myself,' says Mr Henry, with more of bitterness than I had ever heard him to express.

Thereupon my old lord stepped in with his smooth talk, so that before the meal was at an end all seemed forgotten; only that, after dinner, when the pair had withdrawn as usual to the chimney-side, we could see her weeping with her head upon his knee. Mr Henry kept up the talk with me upon some topic of the estates—he could speak of little else but business, and was never the best of company; but he kept it up that day with more continuity, his eye straying ever and again to the chimney, and his voice changing to another key, but without check of delivery. The pane, however, was not replaced; and I believe he counted it a great defeat.

Whether he was stout enough or no, God knows he was kind enough. Mrs Henry had a manner of condescension with him, such as (in a wife) would have pricked my vanity into an ulcer; he took it like a favour. She held him at the staff's end; forgot and then remembered and unbent to him, as we do to children; burthened him with cold kindness; reproved him with a change of colour and a bitten lip, like one shamed by his disgrace: ordered him with a look of the eye, when she was off her guard; when she was on the watch, pleaded with him for the most natural attentions, as though they were unheard-of favours. And to all this he replied with the most unwearied service; loving, as folk say, the very ground she trod on, and carrying that love in his eyes as bright as a lamp. When Miss Katharine was to be born, nothing would serve but he must stay in the room behind the head of the bed. There he sat, as white (they tell me) as a sheet, and the sweat dropping from his brow; and the handkerchief he had in his hand was crushed into a little ball no bigger than a musket bullet. Nor could he bear the sight of Miss Katharine for many a day; indeed, I doubt if he was ever what he should have been to my young lady; for the which want of natural feeling he was loudly blamed.

Such was the state of this family down to the 7th April 1749, when there befell the first of that series of events which were to break so many hearts and lose so many lives.

On that day I was sitting in my room a little before supper, when John Paul burst open the door with no civility of knocking, and told me there was one below that wished to speak with the steward; sneering at the name of my office.

I asked what manner of man, and what his name was; and this disclosed the cause of John's ill-humour; for it appeared the visitor refused to name himself except to me, a sore affront to the major-domo's consequence.

'Well,' said I, smiling a little, 'I will see what he wants.'

I found in the entrance-hall a big man, very plainly habited, and wrapped in a sea-cloak, like one new landed, as indeed he was. Not far off Macconochie was standing, with his tongue out of his mouth and his hand upon his chin, like a dull fellow thinking hard; and the stranger, who had brought his cloak about his face, appeared uneasy. He had no sooner seen me coming than he went to meet me with an effusive manner.

'My dear man,' said he, 'a thousand apologies for disturbing you, but I'm in the most awkward position. And there's a son of a ramrod there that I should know the looks of, and more, betoken, I believe that he knows mine. Being in this family, sir, and in a place of some responsibility (which was the cause I took the liberty to send for you), you are doubtless of the honest party?'

'You may be sure at least,' says I, 'that all of that party are quite safe in Durrisdeer.'

'My dear man, it is my very thought,' says he. 'You see, I have just been set on shore here by a very honest man, whose name I cannot remember, and who is to stand off and on for me till morning, at some danger to himself; and, to be clear with you, I am a little concerned lest it should be at some to me. I have saved my life so often, Mr——, I forget your name, which is a very good one—that, faith, I would be very loth to lose it after all.

And the son of a ramrod, whom I believe I saw before Carlisle . . .'

'O, sir,' said I, 'you can trust Macconochie until to-morrow.'

'Well, and it's a delight to hear you say so,' says the stranger. 'The truth is, that my name is not a very suitable one in this country of Scotland. With a gentleman like you, my dear man, I would have no concealments of course; and by your leave I'll just breathe it in your ear. They call me Francis Burke—Colonel Francis Burke; and I am here, at a most damnable risk to myself, to see your masters—if you'll excuse me, my good man, for giving them the name, for I'm sure it's a circumstance I would never have guessed from your appearance. And if you would just be so very obliging as to take my name to them, you might say that I come bearing letters which I am sure they will be very rejoiced to have the reading of.'

Colonel Francis Burke was one of the Prince's Irishmen, that did his cause such an infinity of hurt, and were so much distasted of the Scots at the time of the rebellion; and it came at once into my mind how the Master of Ballantrae had astonished all men by going with that party. In the same moment a strong foreboding of the truth possessed my soul.

'If you will step in here,' said I, opening a chamber door, 'I will let my lord know.'

'And I am sure it's very good of you, Mr What's-your-name,' says the Colonel.

Up to the hall I went, slow-footed. There they were, all three—my old lord in his place, Mrs Henry at work by the window, Mr Henry (as was much his custom) pacing the low end. In the midst was the table laid for supper. I told them briefly what I had to say. My old lord lay back in his seat. Mrs Henry sprang up standing with a mechanical motion, and she and her husband stared at each other's eyes across the room; it was the strangest, challenging look these two exchanged, and as they looked, the colour faded in their faces. Then Mr Henry turned to me; not to speak, only to sign with his finger; but that was enough, and I went down again for the Colonel.

When we returned, these three were in much the same position I had left them in; I believe no word had passed.

'My Lord Durrisdeer, no doubt?' says the Colonel, bowing, and my lord bowed in answer. 'And this,' continues the Colonel, 'should be the Master of Ballantrae?'

'I have never taken that name,' said Mr Henry; 'but I am Henry Durie, at your service.'

Then the Colonel turns to Mrs Henry, bowing with his hat upon his heart and the most killing airs of gallantry. 'There can be no mistake about so fine a figure of a lady,' says he. 'I address the seductive Miss Alison, of whom I have so often heard?'

Once more husband and wife exchanged a look.

'I am Mrs Henry Durie,' said she; 'but before my marriage my name was Alison Graeme.'

Then my lord spoke up. 'I am an old man, Colonel Burke,' said he, 'and a frail one. It will be mercy on your part to be expeditious. Do you bring me news of—' he hesitated, and then the words broke from him with a singular change of voice—'my son?'

'My dear lord, I will be round with you like a soldier,' said the Colonel. 'I do.'

My lord held out a wavering hand; he seemed to wave a signal, but whether it was to give him time or to speak on, was more than we could guess. At length he got out the one word, 'Good?'

'Why, the very best in the creation!' cries the Colonel. 'For my good friend and admired comrade is at this hour in the fine city of Paris, and as like as not, if I know anything of his habits, he will be drawing in his chair to a piece of dinner.—Bedad, I believe the lady's fainting.'

Mrs Henry was indeed the colour of death, and drooped against the window frame. But when Mr Henry made a movement as if to run to her, she straightened with a sort of shiver. 'I am well,' she said, with her white lips.

Mr Henry stopped, and his face had a strong twitch of anger. The next moment he had turned to the Colonel. 'You must not blame yourself,' says he, 'for this effect on Mrs Durie. It is only natural; we were all brought up like brother and sister.'

Mrs Henry looked at her husband with something like relief, or even gratitude. In my way of thinking, that speech was the first step he made in her good graces.

'You must try to forgive me, Mrs Durie, for indeed and I am just an Irish savage,' said the Colonel; 'and I deserve to be shot for not breaking the matter more artistically to a lady.—But here are the Master's own letters; one for each of the three of you; and to be sure (if I know anything of my friend's genius) he will tell his own story with a better grace.'

He brought the three letters forth as he spoke, arranged them by their superscriptions, presented the first to my lord, who took it greedily, and advanced towards Mrs Henry holding out the second.

But the lady waved it back. 'To my husband,' says she, with a choked voice.

The Colonel was a quick man, but at this he was somewhat nonplussed. 'To be sure!' says he; 'how very dull of me! To be sure!' But he still held the letter.

At last Mr Henry reached forth his hand, and there was nothing to be done but give it up. Mr Henry took the letters (both hers and his own), and looked upon their outside, with his brows knit hard, as if he were thinking. He had surprised me all through by his excellent behaviour; but he was to excel himself now.

'Let me give you a hand to your room,' said he to his wife. 'This has come something of the suddenest; and, at any rate, you will wish to read your letter by yourself.'

Again she looked upon him with the same thought of wonder; but he gave her no time, coming straight to where she stood. 'It will be better so, believe me,' said he; 'and Colonel Burke is too considerate not to excuse you.' And with that he took her hand by the fingers, and led her from the hall.

Mrs Henry returned no more that night; and when Mr Henry went to visit her next morning, as I heard long afterwards, she gave him the letter again, still unopened.

'O, read it and be done!' he had cried.

'Spare me that,' said she.

And by these two speeches, to my way of thinking, each

undid a great part of what they had previously done well. But the letter, sure enough, came into my hands, and by me was burned, unopened.

To be very exact as to the adventures of the Master after Culloden, I wrote not long ago to Colonel Burke, now a Chevalier of the Order of St Louis, begging him for some notes in writing, since I could scarce depend upon my memory at so great an interval. To confess the truth, I have been somewhat embarrassed by his response; for he sent me the complete memoirs of his life, touching only in places on the Master; running to a much greater length than my whole story, and not everywhere (as it seems to me) designed for edification. He begged in his letter, dated from Ettenheim, that I would find a publisher for the whole, after I had made what use of it I required; and I think I shall best answer my own purpose and fulfil his wishes by giving certain parts of it in full. In this way my readers will have a detailed and, I believe, a very genuine account of some essential matters; and if any publisher should take a fancy to the Chevalier's manner of narration, he knows where to apply for the rest, of which there is plenty at his service. I put in my first extract here, so that it may stand in the place of what the Chevalier told us over our wine in the hall of Durrisdeer; but you are to suppose it was not the brutal fact, but a very varnished version that he offered to my lord.

CHAPTER THREE

The Master's Wanderings

FROM THE MEMOIRS OF THE CHEVALIER DE BURKE

. . . I LEFT RUTHVEN (it's hardly necessary to remark) with much greater satisfaction than I had come to it; but whether I missed my way in the deserts, or whether my companions failed me, I soon found myself alone. This was a predicament very disagreeable; for I never understood this horrid country or savage people, and the last stroke of the Prince's withdrawal had made us of the Irish more unpopular than ever. I was reflecting on my poor chances, when I saw another horseman on the hill, whom I supposed at first to have been a phantom, the news of his death in the very front at Culloden being current in the army generally. This was the Master of Ballantrae, my Lord Durrisdeer's son, a young nobleman of the rarest gallantry and parts, and equally designed by nature to adorn a Court and to reap laurels in the field. Our meeting was the more welcome to both, as he was one of the few Scots who had used the Irish with consideration, and as he might now be of very high utility in aiding my escape. Yet what founded our particular friendship was a circumstance, by itself as romantic as any fable of King Arthur.

This was on the second day of our flight, after we had slept one night in the rain upon the inclination of a mountain. There was an Appin man, Alan Black Stewart (or some such name,[1] but I have seen him since in France) who chanced to be passing the same way, and had a jealousy of my companion. Very uncivil expressions were exchanged; and Stewart calls upon the Master to alight and have it out.

1. *Note by Mr Mackellar.*—Should not this be Alan *Breck* Stewart, afterwards notorious as the Appin murderer? The Chevalier is sometimes very weak on names.

'Why, Mr Stewart,' says the Master, 'I think at the present time I would prefer to run a race with you.' And with the word claps spurs to his horse.

Stewart ran after us, a childish thing to do, for more than a mile; and I could not help laughing, as I looked back at last and saw him on a hill, holding his hand to his side, and nearly burst with running.

'But, all the same,' I could not help saying to my companion, 'I would let no man run after me for any such proper purpose, and not give him his desire. It was a good jest, but it smells a trifle cowardly.'

He bent his brows at me. 'I do pretty well,' says he, 'when I saddle myself with the most unpopular man in Scotland, and let that suffice for courage.'

'O, bedad,' says I, 'I could show you a more unpopular with the naked eye. And if you like not my company, you can "saddle" yourself on some one else.'

'Colonel Burke,' says he, 'do not let us quarrel; and, to that effect, let me assure you I am the least patient man in the world.'

'I am as little patient as yourself,' said I. 'I care not who knows that.'

'At this rate,' says he, reining in, 'we shall not go very far. And I propose we do one of two things upon the instant: either quarrel and be done; or make a sure bargain to bear everything at each other's hands.'

'Like a pair of brothers?' said I.

'I said no such foolishness,' he replied. 'I have a brother of my own, and I think no more of him than of a coleworth. But if we are to have our noses rubbed together in this course of flight, let us each dare to be ourselves like savages, and each swear that he will neither resent nor deprecate the other. I am a pretty bad fellow at bottom, and I find the pretence of virtues very irksome.'

'O, I am as bad as yourself,' said I. 'There is no skim milk in Francis Burke. But which is it to be? Fight or make friends?'

'Why,' says he, 'I think it will be the best manner to spin a coin for it.'

This proposition was too highly chivalrous not to take

my fancy; and, strange as it may seem of two well-born gentlemen of today, we span a half-crown (like a pair of ancient paladins) whether we were to cut each other's throats or be sworn friends. A more romantic circumstance can rarely have occurred; and it is one of those points in my memoirs, by which we may see the old tales of Homer and the poets are equally true today—at least, of the noble and genteel. The coin fell for peace, and we shook hands upon our bargain. And then it was that my companion explained to me his thought in running away from Mr Stewart, which was certainly worthy of his political intellect. The report of his death, he said, was a great guard to him; Mr Stewart having recognised him, had become a danger; and he had taken the briefest road to that gentleman's silence. 'For,' says he, 'Alan Black is too vain a man to narrate any such story of himself.'

Towards afternoon we came down to the shores of that loch for which we were heading; and there was the ship, but newly come to anchor. She was the *Sainte-Marie-des-Anges*, out of the port of Havre-de-Grace. The Master, after we had signalled for a boat, asked me if I knew the captain. I told him he was a countryman of mine, of the most unblemished integrity, but, I was afraid, a rather timorous man.

'No matter,' says he. 'For all that, he should certainly hear the truth.'

I asked him if he meant about the battle; for if the captain once knew the standard was down, he would certainly put to sea again at once.

'And even then!' said he; 'the arms are now of no sort of utility.'

'My dear man,' said I, 'who thinks of the arms? But, to be sure, we must remember our friends. They will be close upon our heels, perhaps the Prince himself, and if the ship be gone, a great number of valuable lives may be imperilled.'

'The captain and the crew have lives also, if you come to that,' says Ballantrae.

This I declared was but a quibble, and that I would not hear of the captain being told; and then it was that Ballantrae made me a witty answer, for the sake of which (and also because I have been blamed myself in this business of the *Sainte-Marie-des-Anges*) I have related the whole conversation as it passed.

'Frank,' says he, 'remember our bargain. I must not object to your holding your tongue, which I hereby even encourage you to do; but, by the same terms, you are not to resent my telling.'

I could not help laughing at this; though I still forewarned him what would come of it.

'The devil may come of it for what I care,' says the reckless fellow. 'I have always done exactly as I felt inclined.'

As is well known, my prediction came true. The captain had no sooner heard the news than he cut his cable and to sea again; and before morning broke we were in the Great Minch.

The ship was very old; and the skipper, although the most honest of men (and Irish too), was one of the least capable. The wind blew very boisterous, and the sea raged extremely. All that day we had little heart whether to eat or drink; went early to rest in some concern of mind; and (as if to give us a lesson) in the night the wind chopped suddenly into the north-east, and blew a hurricane. We were awaked by the dreadful thunder of the tempest and the stamping of the mariners on deck; so that I supposed our last hour was certainly come; and the terror of my mind was increased out of all measure by Ballantrae, who mocked at my devotions. It is in hours like these that a man of any piety appears in his true light, and we find (what we are taught as babes) the small trust that can be set in worldly friends: I would be unworthy of my religion if I let this pass without particular remark. For three days we lay in the dark in the cabin, and had but a biscuit to nibble. On the fourth the wind fell, leaving the ship dismasted and heaving on vast billows. The captain had not a guess of whither we were blown; he was stark ignorant of his trade, and could do naught but bless the Holy Virgin; a very good thing too, but scarce the whole of seamanship. It seemed, our one hope was to be picked up by another vessel; and if that should prove to be an English ship, it might be no great blessing to the Master and myself.

The fifth and sixth days we tossed there helpless. The seventh some sail was got on her, but she was an unwieldy vessel at the best, and we made little but leeway. All the time, indeed, we had been drifting to the south and west, and during the tempest must have driven in that direction with unheard-of violence. The ninth dawn was cold and black, with a great sea running, and every mark of foul weather. In this situation we were overjoyed to sight a small ship on the horizon, and to perceive her go about and head for the *Sainte-Marie*. But our gratification did not very long endure; for when she had laid-to and lowered a boat, it was immediately filled with disorderly fellows, who sang and shouted as they pulled across to us, and swarmed in on our deck with bare cutlasses, cursing loudly. Their leader was a horrible villain, with his face blacked and his whiskers curled in ringlets; Teach his name; a most notorious pirate. He stamped about the deck, raving and crying out that his name was Satan, and his ship was called Hell. There was something about him like a wicked child or a half-witted person, that daunted me beyond expression. I whispered in the ear of Ballantrae that I would not be the last to volunteer, and only prayed God they might be short of hands; he approved my purpose with a nod.

'Bedad,' said I to Master Teach, 'if you are Satan, here is a devil for ye.'

The word pleased him; and (not to dwell upon these shocking incidents) Ballantrae and I and two others were taken for recruits, while the skipper and all the rest were cast into the sea by the method of walking the plank. It was the first time I had seen this done; my heart died within me at the spectacle; and Master Teach or one of his acolytes (for my head was too much lost to be precise) remarked upon my pale face in a very alarming manner. I had the strength to cut a step or two of a jig, and cry out some ribaldry, which saved me for that time; but my legs were like water when I must get down into the skiff among these miscreants; and what with my horror of my company and fear of the monstrous billows, it was all I could do to keep an Irish tongue and break a jest or two as we were pulled aboard. By the blessing of God there was a fiddle in the pirate ship, which I had no sooner seen than I fell upon; and in my quality of crowder I had the heavenly good luck to get favour in their eyes. 'Crowding Pat' was the name they dubbed me with: and it was little I cared for a name so long as my skin was whole.

What kind of a pandemonium that vessel was I cannot describe, but she was commanded by a lunatic, and might be called a floating Bedlam. Drinking, roaring, singing, quarrelling, dancing, they were never all sober at one time; and there were days together when, if a squall had supervened, it must have sent us to the bottom; or if a King's ship had come along, it would have found us quite helpless for defence. Once or twice we sighted a sail, and, if we were sober enough, overhauled it, God forgive us! and if we were all too drunk, she got away, and I would bless the saints under my breath. Teach ruled, if you can call that rule which brought no order, by the terror he created; and I observed the man was very vain of his position. I have known marshals of France—ay, and even Highland chieftains—that were less openly puffed up; which throws a singular light on the pursuit of honour and glory. Indeed, the longer we live the more we perceive the sagacity of Aristotle and the other old philosophers; and though I have all my life been eager for legitimate distinctions, I can lay my hand upon my heart, at the end of my career, and declare there is not one—no, nor yet life itself—which is worth acquiring or preserving at the slightest cost of dignity.

It was long before I got private speech of Ballantrae; but at length one night we crept out upon the boltsprit, when the rest were better employed, and commiserated our position.

'None can deliver us but the saints,' said I.

'My mind is very different,' said Ballantrae; 'for I am going to deliver myself. This Teach is the poorest creature possible; we make no profit of him, and lie continually open to capture; and,' says he, 'I am not going to be a tarry pirate for nothing, nor yet to hang in chains if I can help it.' And he told me what was in his mind to better the state of the ship in the way of discipline, which would give us safety for the present, and a sooner hope of deliverance when they should have gained enough and should break up their company.

I confessed to him ingenuously that my nerve was quite

shook amid these horrible surroundings, and I durst scarce tell him to count upon me.

'I am not very easy frightened,' said he, 'nor very easy beat.'

A few days after there befell an accident which had nearly hanged us all; and offers the most extraordinary picture of the folly that ruled in our concerns. We were all pretty drunk: and some bedlamite spying a sail, Teach put the ship about in chase without a glance, and we began to bustle up the arms and boast of the horrors that should follow. I observed Ballantrae stood quiet in the bows, looking under the shade of his hand; but for my part, true to my policy among these savages, I was at work with the busiest, and passing Irish jests for their diversion.

'Run up the colours!' cries Teach. 'Show the——s the Jolly Roger!'

It was the merest drunken braggadocio at such a stage, and might have lost us a valuable prize; but I thought it no part of mine to reason, and I ran up the black flag with my own hand.

Ballantrae steps presently aft with a smile upon his face.

'You may perhaps like to know, you drunken dog,' says he, 'that you are chasing a King's ship.'

Teach roared him the lie; but he ran at the same time to the bulwarks, and so did they all. I have never seen so many drunken men struck suddenly sober. The cruiser had gone about, upon our impudent display of colours; she was just then filling on the new tack; her ensign blew out quite plain to see; and even as we stared, there came a puff of smoke, and then a report, and a shot plunged in the waves a good way short of us. Some ran to the ropes, and got the *Sarah* round with an incredible swiftness. One fellow fell on the rum barrel, which stood broached upon the deck, and rolled it promptly overboard. On my part, I made for the Jolly Roger, struck it, tossed it in the sea; and could have flung myself after, so vexed was I with our mismanagement. As for Teach, he grew as pale as death, and incontinently went down to his cabin. Only twice he came on deck that afternoon; went to the taffrail; took a long look at the King's ship, which was still on the horizon heading after us; and then, without speech, back to his cabin. You may say he deserted us; and if it had not been for one very capable sailor we had on board, and for the lightness of the airs that blew all day, we must certainly have gone to the yard arm.

It is to be supposed Teach was humiliated, and perhaps alarmed for his position with the crew; and the way in which he set about regaining what he had lost was highly characteristic of the man. Early next day we smelled him burning sulphur in his cabin and crying out of 'Hell, hell!' which was well understood among the crew, and filled their minds with apprehension. Presently he comes on deck, a perfect figure of fun, his face blacked, his hair and whiskers curled, his belt stuck full of pistols; chewing bits of glass so that the blood ran down his chin, and brandishing a dirk. I do not know if he had taken these manners from the Indians of America, where he was a native; but such was his way, and he would always thus announce that he was wound up to horrid deeds. The first that came near him was the fellow who had sent the rum overboard the day before; him he stabbed to the heart, damning him for a mutineer; and then capered about the body, raving and swearing and daring us to come on. It was the silliest exhibition; and yet dangerous too, for the cowardly fellow was plainly working himself up to another murder.

All of a sudden Ballantrae stepped forth. 'Have done with this play-acting,' says he. 'Do you think to frighten us with making faces? We saw nothing of you yesterday, when you were wanted; and we did well without you, let me tell you that.'

There was a murmur and a movement in the crew, of pleasure and alarm, I thought, in nearly equal parts. As for Teach, he gave a barbarous howl, and swung his dirk to fling it, an art in which (like many seamen) he was very expert.

'Knock that out of his hand!' says Ballantrae, so sudden and sharp that my arm obeyed him before my mind had understood.

Teach stood like one stupid, never thinking on his pistols.

'Go down to your cabin,' cries Ballantrae, 'and come on

deck again when you are sober. Do you think we are going to hang for you, you black-faced, half-witted, drunken brute and butcher? Go down!' And he stamped his foot at him with such a sudden smartness that Teach fairly ran for it to the companion.

'And now, mates,' says Ballantrae, 'a word with you. I don't know if you are gentlemen of fortune for the fun of the thing, but I am not. I want to make money, and get ashore again, and spend it like a man. And on one thing my mind is made up: I will not hang if I can help it. Come, give me a hint; I'm only a beginner! Is there no way to get a little discipline and common sense about this business?'

One of the men spoke up: he said by rights they should have a quartermaster; and no sooner was the word out of his mouth than they were all of that opinion. The thing went by acclamation; Ballantrae was made quartermaster, the rum was put in his charge, laws were passed in imitation of those of a pirate by the name of Roberts, and the last proposal was to make an end of Teach. But Ballantrae was afraid of a more efficient captain, who might be a counterweight to himself, and he opposed this stoutly. Teach, he said, was good enough to board ships and frighten fools with his blacked face and swearing; we could scarce get a better man than Teach for that; and besides, as the man was now disconsidered, and as good as deposed, we might reduce his proportion of the plunder. This carried it; Teach's share was cut down to a mere derision, being actually less than mine; and there remained only two points: whether he would consent, and who was to announce to him this resolution.

'Do not let that stick you,' says Ballantrae; 'I will do that.'

And he stepped to the companion and down alone into the cabin to face that drunken savage.

'This is the man for us,' cried one of the hands. 'Three cheers for the quartermaster!' which were given with a will, my own voice among the loudest, and I daresay these plaudits had their effect on Master Teach in the cabin, as we have seen of late days how shouting in the streets may trouble even the minds of legislators.

What passed precisely was never known, though some of

the heads of it came to the surface later on; and we were all amazed, as well as gratified, when Ballantrae came on deck with Teach upon his arm, and announced that all had been consented.

I pass swiftly over those twelve or fifteen months in which we continued to keep the sea in the North Atlantic, getting our food and water from the ships we overhauled, and doing on the whole a pretty fortunate business. Sure, no one could wish to read anything so ungenteel as the memoirs of a pirate, even an unwilling one like me! Things went extremely better with our designs, and Ballantrae kept his lead, to my admiration, from that day forth. I would be tempted to suppose that a gentleman must everywhere be first, even aboard a rover; but my birth is every whit as good as any Scottish lord's, and I am not ashamed to confess that I stayed Crowding Pat until the end, and was not much better than the crew's buffoon. Indeed, it was no scene to bring out my merits. My health suffered from a variety of reasons; I was more at home to the last on a horse's back than a ship's deck; and, to be ingenuous, the fear of the sea was constantly in my mind, battling with the fear of my companions. I need not cry myself up for courage; I have done well on many fields under the eyes of famous generals, and earned my late advancement by an act of the most distinguished valour before many witnesses. But when we must proceed on one of our abordages, the heart of Francis Burke was in his boots; the little eggshell skiff in which we must set forth, the horrible heaving of the vast billows, the height of the ship that we must scale, the thought of how many might be there in garrison upon their legitimate defence, the scowling heavens which (in that climate) so often looked darkly down upon our exploits, and the mere crying of the wind in my ears, were all considerations most unpalatable to my valour. Besides which, as I was always a creature of the nicest sensibility, the scenes that must follow on our success tempted me as little as the chances of defeat. Twice we found women on board; and though I have seen towns sacked, and of late days in France some very horrid public tumults, there was something in the smallness of the numbers engaged, and the bleak dangerous sea surroundings, that made these acts of piracy far the most revolting. I confess ingenuously I could never proceed unless I was three parts drunk; it was the same even with the crew; Teach himself was fit for no enterprise till he was full of rum; and it was one of the most difficult parts of Ballantrae's performance to serve us with liquor in the proper quantities. Even this he did to admiration; being upon the whole the most capable man I ever met with, and the one of the most natural genius. He did not even scrape favour with the crew, as I did, by continual buffoonery made upon a very anxious heart; but preserved on most occasions a great deal of gravity and distance; so that he was like a parent among a family of young children, or a schoolmaster with his boys. What made his part the harder to perform, the men were most inveterate grumblers; Ballantrae's discipline, little as it was, was yet irksome to their love of licence; and, what was worse, being kept sober they had time to think. Some of them accordingly would fall to repenting their abominable crimes; one in particular, who was a good Catholic, and with whom I would sometimes steal apart for prayer; above all in bad weather, fogs, lashing rain, and the like, when we would be the less observed; and I am sure no two criminals in the cart have ever performed their devotions with more anxious sincerity. But the rest, having no such grounds of hope, fell to another pastime, that of computation. All day long they would be telling up their shares or glooming over the result. I have said we were pretty fortunate. But an observation falls to be made: that in this world, in no business that I have tried, do the profits rise to a man's expectations. We found many ships, and took many; yet few of them contained much money, their goods were usually nothing to our purpose—what did we want with a cargo of ploughs, or even of tobacco?—and it is quite a painful reflection how many whole crews we have made to walk the plank for no more than a stock of biscuit or an anker or two of spirits.

In the meanwhile our ship was growing very foul, and it was high time we should make for our *port de carénage*, which was in the estuary of a river among swamps. It was openly understood that we should then break up and go

and squander our proportions of the spoil; and this made
every man greedy of a little more, so that our decision was
delayed from day to day. What finally decided matters was
a trifling accident, such as an ignorant person might suppose
incidental to our way of life. But here I must explain: on
only one of all the ships we boarded, the first on which we
found women, did we meet with any genuine resistance. On
that occasion we had two men killed and several injured,
and if it had not been for the gallantry of Ballantrae we
had surely been beat back at last. Everywhere else the
defence (where there was any at all) was what the worst
troops in Europe would have laughed at; so that the most
dangerous part of our employment was to clamber up the
side of the ship: and I have even known the poor souls on
board to cast us a line, so eager were they to volunteer
instead of walking the plank. This constant immunity had
made our fellows very soft, so that I understood how Teach
had made so deep a mark upon their minds; for indeed the
company of that lunatic was the chief danger in our way of
life. The accident to which I have referred was this:—We
had sighted a little full-rigged ship very close under our
board in a haze; she sailed near as well as we did—I should
be nearer truth if I said, near as ill; and we cleared the
bow-chaser to see if we could bring a spar or two about
their ears. The swell was exceedingly great; the motion
of the ship beyond description; it was little wonder if our
gunners should fire thrice and be still quite broad of what
they aimed at. But in the meanwhile the chase had cleared
a stern gun, the thickness of the air concealing them; and
being better marksmen, their first shot struck us in the
bows, knocked our two gunners into mincemeat, so that
we were all sprinkled with the blood, and plunged through
the deck into the forecastle where we slept. Ballantrae would
have held on; indeed, there was nothing in this *contretemps* to
affect the mind of any soldier; but he had a quick perception
of the men's wishes, and it was plain this lucky shot had
given them a sickener of their trade. In a moment they were
all of one mind: the chase was drawing away from us, it was
needless to hold on, the *Sarah* was too foul to overhaul a
bottle, it was mere foolery to keep the sea with her; and

on these pretended grounds her head was incontinently put about and the course laid for the river. It was strange to see what merriment fell on that ship's company, and how they stamped about the deck jesting, and each computing what increase had come to his share by the death of the two gunners.

We were nine days making our port, so light were the airs we had to sail on, so foul the ship's bottom; but early on the tenth, before dawn, and in a light lifting haze, we passed the head. A little after, the haze lifted, and fell again, showing us a cruiser very close. This was a sore blow, happening so near our refuge. There was a great debate of whether she had seen us, and if so whether it was likely they had recognised the *Sarah*. We were very careful, by destroying every member of those crews we overhauled, to leave no evidence as to our own persons; but the appearance of the *Sarah* herself we could not keep so private; and above all of late, since she had been foul, and we had pursued many ships without success, it was plain that her description had been often published. I supposed this alert would have made us separate upon the instant. But here again that original genius of Ballantrae's had a surprise in store for me. He and Teach (and it was the most remarkable step of his success) had gone hand in hand since the first day of his appointment. I often questioned him upon the fact, and never got an answer but once, when he told me he and Teach had an understanding 'which would very much surprise the crew if they should hear of it, and would surprise himself a good deal if it was carried out.' Well, here again he and Teach were of a mind; and by their joint procurement the anchor was no sooner down than the whole crew went off upon a scene of drunkenness indescribable. By afternoon we were a mere shipful of lunatical persons, throwing of things overboard, howling of different songs at the same time, quarrelling and falling together, and then forgetting our quarrels to embrace. Ballantrae had bidden me drink nothing, and feign drunkenness, as I valued my life; and I have never passed a day so wearisomely, lying the best part of the time upon the forecastle and watching the swamps and thickets by which our little basin was entirely surrounded for the eye. A little after dusk Ballantrae stumbled up to my side, feigned to fall, with a drunken laugh, and before he got to his feet again, whispered me to 'reel down into the cabin and seem to fall asleep upon a locker, for there would be need of me soon.' I did as I was told, and coming into the cabin, where it was quite dark, let myself fall on the first locker. There was a man there already: by the way he stirred and threw me off, I could not think he was much in liquor; and yet when I had found another place, he seemed to continue to sleep on. My heart now beat very hard, for I saw some desperate matter was in act. Presently down came Ballantrae, lit the lamp, looked about the cabin, nodded as if pleased, and on deck again without a word. I peered out from between my fingers, and saw there were three of us slumbering, or feigning to slumber, on the lockers: myself, one Dutton, and one Grady, both resolute men. On deck the rest were got to a pitch of revelry quite beyond the bounds of what is human; so that no reasonable name can describe the sounds they were now making. I have heard many a drunken bout in my time, many on board that very *Sarah*, but never anything the least like this, which made me early suppose the liquor had been tampered with. It was a long while before these yells and howls died out into a sort of miserable moaning, and then to silence; and it seemed a long while after that before Ballantrae came down again, this time with Teach upon his heels. The latter cursed at the sight of us three upon the lockers.

'Tut,' says Ballantrae, 'you might fire a pistol at their ears. You know what stuff they have been swallowing.'

There was a hatch in the cabin floor, and under that the richest part of the booty was stored against the day of division. It fastened with a ring and three padlocks, the keys (for greater security) being divided; one to Teach, one to Ballantrae, and one to the mate, a man called Hammond. Yet I was amazed to see they were now all in the one hand; and yet more amazed (still looking through my fingers) to observe Ballantrae and Teach bring up several packets, four of them in all, very carefully made up, and with a loop for carriage.

'And now,' says Teach, 'let us be going.'

'One word,' says Ballantrae. 'I have discovered there is another man besides yourself who knows a private path across the swamp; and it seems it is shorter than yours.'

Teach cried out, in that case, they were undone.

'I do not know for that,' says Ballantrae. 'For there are several other circumstances with which I must acquaint you. First of all, there is no bullet in your pistols, which (if you remember) I was kind enough to load for both of us this morning. Secondly, as there is some one else who knows a passage, you must think it highly improbable I should saddle myself with a lunatic like you. Thirdly, these gentlemen (who need no longer pretend to be asleep) are those of my party, and will now proceed to gag and bind you to the mast; and when your men awaken (if they ever do awake after the drugs we have mingled in their liquor), I am sure they will be so obliging as to deliver you, and you will have no difficulty, I daresay, to explain the business of the keys.'

Not a word said Teach, but looked at us like a frightened baby as we gagged and bound him.

'Now you see, you moon-calf,' says Ballantrae, why we made four packets. Heretofore you have been called Captain Teach, but I think you are now rather Captain Learn.'

That was our last word on board the *Sarah*. We four, with our four packets, lowered ourselves softly into a skiff, and left that ship behind us as silent as the grave, only for the moaning of some of the drunkards. There was a fog about breast-high on the waters; so that Dutton, who knew the passage, must stand on his feet to direct our rowing; and this, as it forced us to row gently, was the means of our deliverance. We were yet but a little way from the ship, when it began to come grey, and the birds to fly abroad upon the water. All of a sudden Dutton clapped down upon his hams, and whispered us to be silent for our lives, and hearken. Sure enough, we heard a little faint creak of oars upon one hand, and then again, and farther off, a creak of oars upon the other. It was clear we had been sighted yesterday in the morning; here were the cruiser's boats to cut us out; here were we defenceless in their very midst. Sure, never were poor souls more perilously placed; and as we lay there on our oars, praying God the mist might hold, the sweat poured from my brow. Presently we heard one of the boats where we might have thrown a biscuit in her. 'Softly, men,' we heard an officer whisper; and I marvelled they could not hear the drumming of my heart.

'Never mind the path,' says Ballantrae; 'we must get shelter anyhow; let us pull straight ahead for the sides of the basin.'

This we did with the most anxious precaution, rowing, as best we could, upon our hands, and steering at a venture in the fog, which was (for all that) our only safety. But Heaven guided us; we touched ground at a thicket; scrambled ashore with our treasure; and having no other way of concealment, and the mist beginning already to lighten, hove down the skiff and let her sink. We were still but new under cover when the sun rose; and at the same time, from the midst of the basin, a great shouting of seamen sprang up, and we knew the *Sarah* was being boarded. I heard afterwards the officer that took her got great honour; and it's true the approach was creditably managed, but I think he had an easy capture when he came to board.[1]

I was still blessing the saints for my escape, when I became aware we were in trouble of another kind. We were here landed at random in a vast and dangerous swamp; and how to come at the path was a concern of doubt, fatigue, and peril. Dutton, indeed, was of opinion we should wait until the ship was gone, and fish up the skiff; for any delay would be more wise than to go blindly ahead in that morass. One went back accordingly to the basin-side and (peering through the thicket) saw the fog already quite drunk up, and English colours flying on the *Sarah*, but no movement made to get her under way. Our situation was now very doubtful. The swamp was an unhealthful place to linger in; we had

1. *Note by Mr Mackellar.*—This Teach of the *Sarah* must not be confused with the celebrated *Blackbeard*. The dates and facts by no means tally. It is possible the second Teach may have at once borrowed the name and imitated the more excessive part of his manners from the first. Even the Master of Ballantrae could make admirers.

been so greedy to bring treasures that we had brought but little food; it was highly desirable, besides, that we should get clear of the neighbourhood and into the settlements before the news of the capture went abroad; and against all these considerations there was only the peril of the passage on the other side. I think it not wonderful we decided on the active part.

It was already blistering hot when we set forth to pass the marsh, or rather to strike the path, by compass. Dutton took the compass, and one or other of us three carried his proportion of the treasure. I promise you he kept a sharp eye to his rear, for it was like the man's soul that he must trust us with. The thicket was as close as a bush; the ground very treacherous, so that we often sank in the most terrifying manner, and must go round about; the heat, besides, was stifling, the air singularly heavy, and the stinging insects abounded in such myriads that each of us walked under his own cloud. It has often been commented on, how much better gentlemen of birth endure fatigue than persons of the rabble; so that walking officers, who must tramp in the dirt beside their men, shame them by their constancy. This was well to be observed in the present instance; for here were Ballantrae and I, two gentlemen of the highest breeding, on the one hand; and on the other, Grady, a common mariner, and a man nearly a giant in physical strength. The case of Dutton is not in point, for I confess he did as well as any of us.[1] But as for Grady, he began early to lament his case, tailed in the rear, refused to carry Dutton's packet when it came his turn, clamoured continually for rum (of which we had too little), and at last even threatened us from behind with a cocked pistol, unless we should allow him rest. Ballantrae would have fought it out, I believe; but I prevailed with him the other way; and we made a stop and ate a meal. It seemed to benefit Grady little; he was in the rear again at once, growling and bemoaning his lot; and at last, by some carelessness, not having followed

1. *Note by Mr Mackellar.*—And is not this the whole explanation? since this Dutton, exactly like the officers, enjoyed the stimulus of some responsibility.

properly in our tracks, stumbled into a deep part of the
slough where it was mostly water, gave some very dreadful
screams, and before we could come to his aid had sunk
along with his booty. His fate, and above all these screams
of his, appalled us to the soul; yet it was on the whole a
fortunate circumstance, and the means of our deliverance,
for it moved Dutton to mount into a tree, whence he was
able to perceive and to show me, who had climbed after him,
a high piece of the wood, which was a landmark for the path.
He went forward the more carelessly, I must suppose; for
presently we saw him sink a little down, draw up his feet
and sink again, and so twice. Then he turned his face to us,
pretty white.

'Lend a hand,' said he, 'I am in a bad place.'

'I don't know about that,' says Ballantrae, standing still.

Dutton broke out into the most violent oaths, sinking a
little lower as he did, so that the mud was nearly to his
waist, and plucking a pistol from his belt, 'Help me,' he
cries, 'or die and be damned to you!'

'Nay,' says Ballantrae, 'I did but jest. I am coming.' And
he set down his own packet and Dutton's, which he was then
carrying. 'Do not venture near till we see if you are needed,'
said he to me, and went forward alone to where the man was
bogged. He was quiet now, though he still held the pistol;
and the marks of terror in his countenance were very moving
to behold.

'For the Lord's sake,' says he, 'look sharp.'

Ballantrae was now got close up. 'Keep still,' says he,
and seemed to consider; and then, 'Reach out both your
hands!'

Dutton laid down his pistol, and so watery was the top
surface that it went clear out of sight; with an oath he
stooped to snatch it; and as he did so, Ballantrae leaned
forth and stabbed him between the shoulders. Up went his
hands over his head—I know not whether with the pain or
to ward himself; and the next moment he doubled forward
in the mud.

Ballantrae was already over the ankles; but he plucked
himself out, and came back to me, where I stood with my
knees smiting one another. 'The devil take you, Francis!'

says he. 'I believe you are a half-hearted fellow, after all. I have only done justice on a pirate. And here we are quite clear of the *Sarah*! Who shall now say that we have dipped our hands in any irregularities?'

I assured him he did me injustice; but my sense of humanity was so much affected by the horridness of the fact that I could scarce find breath to answer with.

'Come,' said he, 'you must be more resolved. The need for this fellow ceased when he had shown you where the path ran; and you cannot deny I would have been daft to let slip so fair an opportunity.'

I could not deny but he was right in principle; nor yet could I refrain from shedding tears, of which I think no man of valour need have been ashamed; and it was not until I had a share of the rum that I was able to proceed. I repeat, I am far from ashamed of my generous emotion; mercy is honourable in the warrior; and yet I cannot altogether censure Ballantrae, whose step was really fortunate, as we struck the path without further misadventure, and the same night, about sundown, came to the edge of the morass.

We were too weary to seek far; on some dry sands, still warm with the day's sun, and close under a wood of pines, we lay down and were instantly plunged in sleep.

We awaked the next morning very early, and began with a sullen spirit a conversation that came near to end in blows. We were now cast on shore in the southern provinces, thousands of miles from any French settlement; a dreadful journey and a thousand perils lay in front of us; and sure, if there was ever need for amity, it was in such an hour. I must suppose that Ballantrae had suffered in his sense of what is truly polite; indeed, and there is nothing strange in the idea, after the sea wolves we had consorted with so long; and as for myself, he fubbed me off unhandsomely, and any gentleman would have resented his behaviour.

I told him in what light I saw his conduct; he walked a little off, I following to upbraid him; and at last he stopped me with his hand.

'Frank,' says he, 'you know what we swore; and yet there is no oath invented would induce me to swallow such expressions, if I did not regard you with sincere affection.

It is impossible you should doubt me there: I have given proofs. Dutton I had to take, because he knew the pass, and Grady because Dutton would not move without him; but what call was there to carry you along? You are a perpetual danger to me with your cursed Irish tongue. By rights you should now be in irons in the cruiser. And you quarrel with me like a baby for some trinkets!'

I considered this one of the most unhandsome speeches ever made; and indeed to this day I can scarce reconcile it to my notion of a gentleman that was my friend. I retorted upon him with his Scots accent, of which he had not so much as some, but enough to be very barbarous and disgusting, as I told him plainly; and the affair would have gone to a great length, but for an alarming intervention.

We had got some way off upon the sand. The place where we had slept, with the packets lying undone and the money scattered openly, was now between us and the pines; and it was out of these the stranger must have come. There he was at least, a great hulking fellow of the country, with a broad axe on his shoulder, looking open-mouthed, now at the treasure, which was just at his feet, and now at our disputation, in which we had gone far enough to have weapons in our hands. We had no sooner observed him than he found his legs and made off again among the pines.

This was no scene to put our minds at rest: a couple of armed men in sea clothes found quarrelling over a treasure, not many miles from where a pirate had been captured—here was enough to bring the whole country about our ears. The quarrel was not even made up; it was blotted from our minds; and we got our packets together in the twinkling of an eye, and made off, running with the best will in the world. But the trouble was, we did not know in what direction, and must continually return upon our steps. Ballantrae had indeed collected what he could from Dutton; but it's hard to travel upon hearsay; and the estuary, which spreads into a vast irregular harbour, turned us off upon every side with a new stretch of water.

We were near beside ourselves, and already quite spent with running, when, coming to the top of a dune, we saw we were again cut off by another ramification of the bay. This was a creek, however, very different from those that had arrested us before; being set in rocks, and so precipitously deep that a small vessel was able to lie alongside, made fast with a hawser; and her crew had laid a plank to the shore. Here they had lighted a fire, and were sitting at their meal. As for the vessel herself, she was one of those they build in the Bermudas.

The love of gold and the great hatred that everybody has to pirates were motives of the most influential, and would certainly raise the country in our pursuit. Besides, it was now plain we were on some sort of straggling peninsula, like the fingers of a hand; and the wrist, or passage to the mainland, which we should have taken at the first, was by this time not improbably secured. These considerations put us on a bolder counsel. For as long as we dared, looking every moment to hear sounds of the chase, we lay among some bushes on the top of the dune; and having by this means secured a little breath and recomposed our appearance, we strolled down at last, with a great affectation of carelessness, to the party by the fire.

It was a trader and his negroes, belonging to Albany, in the province of New York, and now on the way home from the Indies with a cargo; his name I cannot recall. We were amazed to learn he had put in here from terror of the *Sarah*; for we had no thought our exploits had been so notorious. As soon as the Albanian heard she had been taken the day before, he jumped to his feet, gave us a cup of spirits for our good news, and sent his negroes to get sail on the Bermudan. On our side, we profited by the dram to become more confidential, and at last offered ourselves as passengers. He looked askance at our tarry clothes and pistols, and replied civilly enough that he had scarce accommodation for himself; nor could either our prayers or our offers of money, in which we advanced pretty far, avail to shake him.

'I see, you think ill of us,' says Ballantrae, 'but I will show you how well we think of you by telling you the truth. We are Jacobite fugitives, and there is a price upon our heads.'

At this the Albanian was plainly moved a little. He asked us many questions as to the Scots war, which Ballantrae very patiently answered. And then, with a wink, in a vulgar manner, 'I guess you and your Prince Charlie got more than you cared about,' said he.

'Bedad, and that we did,' said I. 'And, my dear man, I wish you would set a new example, and give us just that much.'

This I said in the Irish way, about which there is allowed to be something very engaging. It's a remarkable thing, and a testimony to the love with which our nation is regarded, that this address scarce ever fails in a handsome fellow. I cannot tell how often I have seen a private soldier escape the horse, or a beggar wheedle out a good alms, by a touch of the brogue. And, indeed, as soon as the Albanian had laughed at me I was pretty much at rest. Even then, however, he made many conditions, and—for one thing—took away our arms, before he suffered us aboard; which was the signal to cast off; so that in a moment after we were gliding down the bay with a good breeze, and blessing the name of God for our deliverance. Almost in the mouth of the estuary, we passed the cruiser, and a little after the poor *Sarah* with her prize crew; and these were both sights to make us tremble. The Bermudan seemed a very safe place to be in, and our bold stroke to have been fortunately played, when we were thus reminded of the case of our companions. For all that, we had only exchanged traps, jumped out of the frying pan into the fire, run from the yard arm to the block, and escaped the open hostility of the man-of-war to lie at the mercy of the doubtful faith of our Albanian merchant.

From many circumstances, it chanced we were safer than we could have dared to hope. The town of Albany was at that time much concerned in contraband trade across the desert with the Indians and the French. This, as it was highly illegal, relaxed their loyalty, and as it brought them in relation with the politest people on the earth, divided even their sympathies. In short, they were like all the smugglers in the world, spies and agents ready-made for either party. Our Albanian, besides, was a very honest man indeed, and very greedy; and, to crown our luck, he conceived a great delight in our society. Before we had reached the town of New York we had come to a full agreement, that he should carry us as far as Albany upon his ship, and thence put us on a way to pass the boundaries and join the French. For all this we were to pay at a high rate; but beggars cannot be choosers, nor outlaws bargainers.

We sailed, then, up the Hudson River, which, I protest, is a very fine stream, and put up at the 'King's Arms' in Albany. The town was full of the militia of the province, breathing slaughter against the French. Governor Clinton was there himself, a very busy man, and, by what I could learn, very near distracted by the factiousness of his Assembly. The Indians on both sides were on the warpath; we saw parties of them bringing in prisoners and (what was much worse) scalps, both male and female, for which they were paid at a fixed rate; and I assure you the sight was not encouraging. Altogether, we could scarce have come at a period more unsuitable for our designs; our position in the chief inn was dreadfully conspicuous; our Albanian fubbed us off with a thousand delays, and seemed upon the point of a retreat from his engagements; nothing but peril appeared to environ the poor fugitives, and for some time we drowned our concern in a very irregular course of living.

This, too, proved to be fortunate; and it's one of the remarks that fall to be made upon our escape, how providentially our steps were conducted to the very end. What a humiliation to the dignity of man! My philosophy, the extraordinary genius of Ballantrae, our valour, in which I grant that we were equal—all these might have proved insufficient without the Divine blessing on our efforts. And how true it is, as the Church tells us, that the Truths of Religion are, after all, quite applicable even to daily affairs! At least, it was in the course of our revelry that we made the acquaintance of a spirited youth by the name of Chew. He was one of the most daring of the Indian traders, very well acquainted with the secret paths of the wilderness, needy, dissolute, and, by a last good fortune, in some disgrace with his family. Him we persuaded to come to our relief; he privately provided what was needful for our flight, and one day we slipped out of Albany, without a word to our former friend, and embarked, a little above, in a canoe.

To the toils and perils of this journey it would require a

pen more elegant than mine to do full justice. The reader must conceive for himself the dreadful wilderness which we had now to thread; its thickets, swamps, precipitous rocks, impetuous rivers, and amazing waterfalls. Among these barbarous scenes we must toil all day, now paddling, now carrying our canoe upon our shoulders; and at night we slept about a fire, surrounded by the howling of wolves and other savage animals. It was our design to mount the headwaters of the Hudson, to the neighbourhood of Crown Point, where the French had a strong place in the woods, upon Lake Champlain. But to have done this directly were too perilous; and it was accordingly gone upon by such a labyrinth of rivers, lakes, and portages as makes my head giddy to remember. These paths were in ordinary times entirely desert; but the country was now up, the tribes on the warpath, the woods full of Indian scouts. Again and again we came upon these parties when we least expected them; and one day, in particular, I shall never forget how, as dawn was coming in, we were suddenly surrounded by five or six of these painted devils, uttering a very dreary sort of cry, and brandishing their hatchets. It passed off harmlessly, indeed, as did the rest of our encounters; for Chew was well known and highly valued among the different tribes. Indeed, he was a very gallant, respectable young man; but even with the advantage of his companionship, you must not think these meetings were without sensible peril. To prove friendship on our part, it was needful to draw upon our stock of rum—indeed, under whatever disguise, that is the true business of the Indian trader, to keep a travelling public house in the forest; and when once the braves had got their bottle of *scaura* (as they call this beastly liquor), it behoved us to set forth and paddle for our scalps. Once they were a little drunk, goodbye to any sense or decency; they had but the one thought, to get more *scaura*. They might easily take it in their heads to give us chase, and had we been overtaken, I had never written these memoirs.

We were come to the most critical portion of our course, where we might equally expect to fall into the hands of French or English, when a terrible calamity befell us. Chew was taken suddenly sick with symptoms like those

of poison, and in the course of a few hours expired in the
bottom of the canoe. We thus lost at once our guide, our
interpreter, our boatman, and our passport, for he was all
these in one; and found ourselves reduced, at a blow, to the
most desperate and irremediable distress. Chew, who took a
great pride in his knowledge, had indeed often lectured us
on the geography; and Ballantrae, I believe, would listen.
But for my part I have always found such information
highly tedious; and beyond the fact that we were now in
the country of the Adirondack Indians, and not so distant
from our destination, could we but have found the way, I
was entirely ignorant. The wisdom of my course was soon
the more apparent; for, with all his pains, Ballantrae was no
further advanced than myself. He knew we must continue
to go up one stream; then, by way of a portage, down
another; and then up a third. But you are to consider,
in a mountain country, how many streams come rolling in
from every hand. And how is a gentleman, who is a perfect
stranger in that part of the world, to tell any one of them
from any other? Nor was this our only trouble. We were
great novices, besides, in handling a canoe; the portages
were almost beyond our strength, so that I have seen us
sit down in despair for half an hour at a time without one
word; and the appearance of a single Indian, since we had
now no means of speaking to them, would have been in all
probability the means of our destruction. There is altogether
some excuse if Ballantrae showed something of a glooming
disposition; his habit of imputing blame to others, quite as
capable as himself, was less tolerable, and his language it
was not always easy to accept. Indeed, he had contracted
on board the pirate ship a manner of address which was
in a high degree unusual between gentlemen; and now,
when you might say he was in a fever, it increased upon
him hugely.

The third day of these wanderings, as we were carrying
the canoe upon a rocky portage, she fell, and was entirely
bilged. The portage was between two lakes, both pretty
extensive; the track, such as it was, opened at both ends
upon the water, and on both hands was enclosed by the
unbroken woods; and the sides of the lakes were quite

impassable with bog: so that we beheld ourselves not only condemned to go without our boat and the greater part of our provisions, but to plunge at once into impenetrable thickets and to desert what little guidance we still had—the course of the river. Each stuck his pistols in his belt, shouldered an axe, made a pack of his treasure and as much food as he could stagger under; and deserting the rest of our possessions, even to our swords, which would have much embarrassed us among the woods, we set forth on this deplorable adventure. The labours of Hercules, so finely described by Homer, were a trifle to what we now underwent. Some parts of the forest were perfectly dense down to the ground, so that we must cut our way like mites in a cheese. In some the bottom was full of deep swamp, and the whole wood entirely rotten. I have leaped on a great fallen log and sunk to the knees in touchwood; I have sought to stay myself, in falling, against what looked to be a solid trunk, and the whole thing has whiffed at my touch like a sheet of paper. Stumbling, falling, bogging to the knees, hewing our way, our eyes almost put out with twigs and branches, our clothes plucked from our bodies, we laboured all day, and it is doubtful if we made two miles. What was worse, as we could rarely get a view of the country, and were perpetually justled from our path by obstacles, it was impossible even to have a guess in what direction we were moving.

A little before sundown, in an open place with a stream, and set about with barbarous mountains, Ballantrae threw down his pack. 'I will go no further,' said he, and bade me light the fire, damning my blood in terms not proper for a chairman.

I told him to try to forget he had ever been a pirate, and to remember he had been a gentleman.

'Are you mad?' he cried. 'Don't cross me here!'

And then, shaking his fist at the hills, 'To think,' cries he, 'that I must leave my bones in this miserable wilderness! Would God I had died upon the scaffold like a gentleman!' This he said ranting like an actor; and then sat biting his fingers and staring on the ground, a most unchristian object.

I took a certain horror of the man, for I thought a soldier and a gentleman should confront his end with more philosophy. I made him no reply, therefore, in words; and presently the evening fell so chill that I was glad, for my own sake, to kindle a fire. And yet God knows, in such an open spot, and the country alive with savages, the act was little short of lunacy. Ballantrae seemed never to observe me; but at last, as I was about parching a little corn, he looked up.

'Have you ever a brother?' said he.

'By the blessing of Heaven,' said I, 'not less than five.'

'I have the one,' said he, with a strange voice; and then presently, 'He shall pay me for all this,' he added. And when I asked him what was his brother's part in our distress, 'What!' he cried, 'he sits in my place, he bears my name, he courts my wife; and I am here alone with a damned Irishman in this tooth-chattering desert! O, I have been a common gull!' he cried.

The explosion was in all ways so foreign to my friend's nature that I was daunted out of all my just susceptibility. Sure, an offensive expression, however vivacious, appears a wonderfully small affair in circumstances so extreme! But here there is a strange thing to be noted. He had only once before referred to the lady with whom he was contracted. That was when we came in view of the town of New York, when he had told me, if all had their rights, he was now in sight of his own property, for Miss Graeme enjoyed a large estate in the province. And this was certainly a natural occasion; but now here she was named a second time; and what is surely fit to be observed, in this very month, which was November, 'Forty-seven, and *I believe upon that very day as we sat among these barbarous mountains*, his brother and Miss Graeme were married. I am the least superstitious of men; but the hand of Providence is here displayed too openly not to be remarked.[1]

The next day, and the next, were passed in similar

1. *Note by Mr Mackellar.*—A complete blunder: there was at this date no word of the marriage: see above in my own narration.

labours; Ballantrae often deciding on our course by the spinning of a coin; and once, when I expostulated on this childishness, he had an odd remark that I never have forgotten. 'I know no better way,' said he, 'to express my scorn of human reason.' I think it was the third day that we found the body of a Christian, scalped and most abominably mangled, and lying in a pudder of his blood; the birds of the desert screaming over him, as thick as flies. I cannot describe how dreadfully this sight affected us; but it robbed me of all strength and all hope for this world. The same day, and only a little after, we were scrambling over a part of the forest that had been burned, when Ballantrae, who was a little ahead, ducked suddenly behind a fallen trunk. I joined him in this shelter, whence we could look abroad without being seen ourselves; and in the bottom of the next vale beheld a large war party of the savages going by across our line. There might be the value of a weak battalion present; all naked to the waist, blacked with grease and soot, and painted with white lead and vermilion, according to their beastly habits. They went one behind another like a string of geese, and at a quickish trot; so that they took but a little while to rattle by, and disappear again among the woods. Yet I suppose we endured a greater agony of hesitation and suspense in these few minutes than goes usually to a man's whole life. Whether they were French or English Indians, whether they desired scalps or prisoners, whether we should declare ourselves upon the chance, or lie quiet and continue the heart-breaking business of our journey: sure, I think these were questions to have puzzled the brains of Aristotle himself. Ballantrae turned to me with a face all wrinkled up, and his teeth showing in his mouth, like what I have read of people starving; he said no word, but his whole appearance was a kind of dreadful question.

'They may be of the English side,' I whispered; 'and think! the best we could then hope is to begin this over again.'

'I know—I know,' he said. 'Yet it must come to a plunge at last.' And he suddenly plucked out his coin, shook it in his closed hands, looked at it, and then lay down with his face in the dust.

Addition by Mr Mackellar.—I drop the Chevalier's narration at this point because the couple quarrelled and separated the same day; and the Chevalier's account of the quarrel seems to me (I must confess) quite incompatible with the nature of either of the men. Henceforth they wandered alone, undergoing extraordinary sufferings; until first one and then the other was picked up by a party from Fort St Frederick. Only two things are to be noted. And first (as most important for my purpose) that the Master, in the course of his miseries, buried his treasure, at a point never since discovered, but of which he took a drawing in his own blood on the lining of his hat. And second, that on his coming thus penniless to the Fort, he was welcomed like a brother by the Chevalier, who thence paid his way to France. The simplicity of Mr Burke's character leads him at this point to praise the Master exceedingly; to an eye more worldly wise, it would seem it was the Chevalier alone that was to be commended. I have the more pleasure in pointing to this really very noble trait of my esteemed correspondent, as I fear I may have wounded him immediately before. I have refrained from comments on any of his extraordinary and (in my eyes) immoral opinions, for I know him to be jealous of respect. But his version of the quarrel is really more than I can reproduce; for I knew the Master myself, and a man more insusceptible of fear is not conceivable. I regret this oversight of the Chevalier's, and all the more because the tenor of his narrative (set aside a few flourishes) strikes me as highly ingenuous.

CHAPTER FOUR

Persecutions Endured by
Mr Henry

YOU CAN GUESS on what part of his adventures the Colonel
principally dwelled. Indeed, if we had heard it all, it is to be
thought the current of this business had been wholly altered;
but the pirate ship was very gently touched upon. Nor did
I hear the Colonel to an end even of that which he was
willing to disclose; for Mr Henry, having for some while
been plunged in a brown study, rose at last from his seat
and (reminding the Colonel there were matters that he must
attend to) bade me follow him immediately to the office.

Once there, he sought no longer to dissemble his concern,
walking to and fro in the room with a contorted face, and
passing his hand repeatedly upon his brow.

'We have some business,' he began at last; and there broke
off, declared we must have wine, and sent for a magnum
of the best. This was extremely foreign to his habitudes;
and, what was still more so, when the wine had come, he
gulped down one glass upon another like a man careless of
appearances. But the drink steadied him.

'You will scarce be surprised, Mackellar,' says he, 'when
I tell you that my brother—whose safety we are all rejoiced
to learn—stands in some need of money.'

I told him I had misdoubted as much; but the time was
not very fortunate, as the stock was low.

'Not mine,' said he. 'There is the money for the mortgage.'

I reminded him it was Mrs Henry's.

'I will be answerable to my wife,' he cried violently.

'And then,' said I, 'there is the mortgage.'

'I know,' said he; 'it is on that I would consult you.'

I showed him how unfortunate a time it was to divert this
money from its destination; and how, by so doing, we must
lose the profit of our past economies, and plunge back the

estate into the mire. I even took the liberty to plead with
him; and when he still opposed me with a shake of the head
and a bitter dogged smile, my zeal quite carried me beyond
my place. 'This is midsummer madness,' cried I; 'and I for
one will be no party to it.'

'You speak as though I did it for my pleasure,' says he.
'But I have a child now; and, besides, I love order; and to
say the honest truth, Mackellar, I had begun to take a pride
in the estates.' He gloomed for a moment. 'But what would
you have?' he went on. 'Nothing is mine, nothing. This
day's news has knocked the bottom out of my life. I have
only the name and the shadow of things—only the shadow;
there is no substance in my rights.'

'They will prove substantial enough before a court,' said I.

He looked at me with a burning eye, and seemed to
repress the word upon his lips; and I repented what I
had said, for I saw that while he spoke of the estate he
had still a side-thought to his marriage. And then, of a
sudden, he twitched the letter from his pocket, where it
lay all crumpled, smoothed it violently on the table, and
read these words to me with a trembling tongue:—'"My
dear Jacob"—This is how he begins!' cries he—'"My dear
Jacob, I once called you so, you may remember; and you
have now done the business, and flung my heels as high as
Criffel." What do you think of that, Mackellar,' says he,
'from an only brother? I declare to God I liked him very
well; I was always staunch to him; and this is how he writes!
But I will not sit down under the imputation'—walking to
and fro—'I am as good as he; I am a better man than he, I
call on God to prove it! I cannot give him all the monstrous
sum he asks; he knows the estate to be incompetent; but I
will give him what I have, and it is more than he expects. I
have borne all this too long. See what he writes further on;
read it for yourself: "I know you are a niggardly dog." A
niggardly dog! I niggardly? Is that true, Mackellar? You
think it is?' I really thought he would have struck me at
that. 'O, you all think so! Well, you shall see, and he shall
see, and God shall see. If I ruin the estate and go barefoot,
I shall stuff this bloodsucker. Let him ask all—all, and he
shall have it! It is all his by rights. Ah!' he cried, 'and I

foresaw all this, and worse, when he would not let me go.'
He poured out another glass of wine, and was about to carry
it to his lips, when I made so bold as to lay a finger on his
arm. He stopped a moment. 'You are right,' said he, and
flung glass and all in the fireplace. 'Come, let us count
the money.'

I durst no longer oppose him; indeed, I was very much
affected by the sight of so much disorder in a man usually
so controlled; and we sat down together, counted the money,
and made it up in packets for the greater ease of Colonel
Burke, who was to be the bearer. This done, Mr Henry
returned to the hall, where he and my old lord sat all night
through with their guest.

A little before dawn I was called and set out with the
Colonel. He would scarce have liked a less responsible
convoy, for he was a man who valued himself; nor could
we afford him one more dignified, for Mr Henry must not
appear with the free-traders. It was a very bitter morning
of wind, and as we went down through the long shrubbery
the Colonel held himself muffled in his cloak.

'Sir,' said I, 'this is a great sum of money that your friend
requires. I must suppose his necessities to be very great.'

'We must suppose so,' says he, I thought drily, but
perhaps it was the cloak about his mouth.

'I am only a servant of the family,' said I. 'You may deal
openly with me. I think we are likely to get little good
by him?'

'My dear man,' said the Colonel, 'Ballantrae is a gentleman of the most eminent natural abilities, and a man that
I admire, and that I revere, to the very ground he treads
on.' And then he seemed to me to pause like one in a
difficulty.

'But for all that,' said I, 'we are likely to get little good
by him?'

'Sure, and you can have it your own way, my dear man,'
says the Colonel.

By this time we had come to the side of the creek, where
the boat awaited him. 'Well,' said he, 'I am sure I am very
much your debtor for all your civility, Mr Whatever-your-
name-is; and just as a last word, and since you show so much

intelligent interest, I will mention a small circumstance that
may be of use to the family. For I believe my friend omitted
to mention that he has the largest pension on the Scots
Fund of any refugee in Paris; and it's the more disgraceful,
sir,' cries the Colonel, warming, 'because there's not one
dirty penny for myself.'

He cocked his hat at me, as if I had been to blame for
this partiality; then changed again into his usual swaggering
civility, shook me by the hand, and set off down to the boat,
with the money under his arms, and whistling as he went
the pathetic air of 'Shule Aroon.' It was the first time I had
heard that tune; I was to hear it again, words and all, as you
shall learn, but I remember how that little stave of it ran in
my head after the free-traders had bade him 'Wheesht, in
the deil's name,' and the grating of the oars had taken its
place, and I stood and watched the dawn creeping on the
sea, and the boat drawing away, and the lugger lying with
her foresail backed awaiting it.

The gap made in our money was a sore embarrassment, and,
among other consequences, it had this: that I must ride to
Edinburgh, and there raise a new loan on very questionable
terms to keep the old afloat; and was thus, for close upon
three weeks, absent from the house of Durrisdeer.

What passed in the interval I had none to tell me, but
I found Mrs Henry, upon my return, much changed in
her demeanour. The old talks with my lord for the most
part pretermitted; a certain deprecation visible towards her
husband, to whom I thought she addressed herself more
often; and, for one thing, she was now greatly wrapped
up in Miss Katharine. You would think the change was
agreeable to Mr Henry; no such matter! To the contrary,
every circumstance of alteration was a stab to him; he read
in each the avowal of her truant fancies. That constancy to
the Master of which she was proud while she supposed him
dead, she had to blush for now she knew he was alive, and
these blushes were the hated spring of her new conduct.
I am to conceal no truth; and I will here say plainly, I
think this was the period in which Mr Henry showed the
worst. He contained himself, indeed, in public; but there

was a deep-seated irritation visible underneath. With me, from whom he had less concealment, he was often grossly unjust, and even for his wife he would sometimes have a sharp retort: perhaps when she had ruffled him with some unwonted kindness; perhaps upon no tangible occasion, the mere habitual tenor of the man's annoyance bursting spontaneously forth. When he would thus forget himself (a thing so strangely out of keeping with the terms of their relation), there went a shock through the whole company, and the pair would look upon each other in a kind of pained amazement.

All the time, too, while he was injuring himself by this defect of temper, he was hurting his position by a silence, of which I scarce know whether to say it was the child of generosity or pride. The free-traders came again and again, bringing messengers from the Master, and none departed empty-handed. I never durst reason with Mr Henry; he gave what was asked of him in a kind of noble rage. Perhaps because he knew he was by nature inclining to the parsimonious, he took a backforemost pleasure in the recklessness with which he supplied his brother's exigence. Perhaps the falsity of the position would have spurred a humbler man into the same excess. But the estate (if I may say so) groaned under it; our daily expenses were shorn lower and lower; the stables were emptied, all but four roadsters; servants were discharged, which raised a dreadful murmuring in the country, and heated up the old disfavour upon Mr Henry; and at last the yearly visit to Edinburgh must be discontinued.

This was in 1756. You are to suppose that for seven years this bloodsucker had been drawing the life's blood from Durrisdeer, and that all this time my patron had held his peace. It was an effect of devilish malice in the Master that he addressed Mr Henry alone upon the matter of his demands, and there was never a word to my lord. The family had looked on, wondering at our economies. They had lamented, I have no doubt, that my patron had become so great a miser—a fault always despicable, but in the young abhorrent, and Mr Henry was not yet thirty years of age. Still, he had managed the business of Durrisdeer almost from a boy; and they bore with these changes in a silence as proud and bitter as his own, until the coping-stone of the Edinburgh visit.

At this time I believe my patron and his wife were rarely together, save at meals. Immediately on the back of Colonel Burke's announcement Mrs Henry made palpable advances; you might say she had laid a sort of timid court to her husband, different, indeed, from her former manner of unconcern and distance. I never had the heart to blame Mr Henry because he recoiled from these advances; nor yet to censure the wife, when she was cut to the quick by their rejection. But the result was an entire estrangement, so that (as I say) they rarely spoke, except at meals. Even the matter of the Edinburgh visit was first broached at table, and it chanced that Mrs Henry was that day ailing and querulous. She had no sooner understood her husband's meaning than the red flew in her face.

'At last,' she cried; 'this is too much! Heaven knows what pleasure I have in my life, that I should be denied my only consolation. These shameful proclivities must be trod down; we are already a mark and an eyesore in the neighbourhood. I will not endure this fresh insanity.'

'I cannot afford it,' says Mr Henry.

'Afford?' she cried. 'For shame! But I have money of my own.'

'That is all mine, madam, by marriage,' he snarled, and instantly left the room.

My old lord threw up his hands to Heaven, and he and his daughter, withdrawing to the chimney, gave me a broad hint to be gone. I found Mr Henry in his usual retreat, the steward's room, perched on the end of the table, and plunging his penknife in it with a very ugly countenance.

'Mr Henry,' said I, 'you do yourself too much injustice, and it is time this should cease.'

'O!' cries he, 'nobody minds here. They think it only natural. I have shameful proclivities. I am a niggardly dog,' and he drove his knife up to the hilt.

'But I will show that fellow,' he cried with an oath, 'I will show him which is the more generous.'

'This is no generosity,' said I; 'this is only pride.'

'Do you think I want morality?' he asked.

I thought he wanted help, and I should give it him, willy-nilly; and no sooner was Mrs Henry gone to her room than I presented myself at her door and sought admittance.

She openly showed her wonder. 'What do you want with me, Mr Mackellar?' said she.

'The Lord knows, madam,' says I, 'I have never troubled you before with any freedoms; but this thing lies too hard upon my conscience, and it will out. Is it possible that two people can be so blind as you and my lord? and have lived all these years with a noble gentleman like Mr Henry, and understand so little of his nature?'

'What does this mean?' she cried.

'Do you not know where his money goes to? his—and yours—and the money for the very wine he does not drink at table?' I went on. 'To Paris—to that man! Eight thousand pounds has he had of us in seven years, and my patron fool enough to keep it secret!'

'Eight thousand pounds!' she repeated. 'It is impossible; the estate is not sufficient.'

'God knows how we have sweated farthings to produce it,' said I. 'But eight thousand and sixty is the sum, beside odd shillings. And if you can think my patron miserly after that, this shall be my last interference.'

'You need say no more, Mr Mackellar,' said she. 'You have done most properly in what you too modestly call your interference. I am much to blame; you must think me indeed a very unobservant wife' (looking upon me with a strange smile), 'but I shall put this right at once. The Master was always of a very thoughtless nature; but his heart is excellent; he is the soul of generosity. I shall write to him myself. You cannot think how you have pained me by this communication.'

'Indeed, madam, I had hoped to have pleased you,' said I, for I raged to see her still thinking of the Master.

'And pleased,' said she, 'and pleased me of course.'

That same day (I will not say but what I watched) I had the satisfaction to see Mr Henry come from his wife's room in a state most unlike himself; for his face was all bloated with weeping, and yet he seemed to me to walk upon the air. By this, I was sure his wife had made him full amends for once. 'Ah,' thought I to myself, 'I have done a brave stroke this day.'

On the morrow, as I was seated at my books, Mr Henry came in softly behind me, took me by the shoulders and shook me in a manner of playfulness. 'I find you are a faithless fellow after all,' says he, which was his only reference to my part; but the tone he spoke in was more to me than any eloquence of protestation. Nor was this all I had effected; for when the next messenger came (as he did, not long afterwards) from the Master, he got nothing away with him but a letter. For some while back it had been I myself who had conducted these affairs; Mr Henry not setting pen to paper, and I only in the driest and most formal terms. But this letter I did not even see; it would scarce be pleasant reading, for Mr Henry felt he had his wife behind him for once, and I observed, on the day it was despatched, he had a very gratified expression.

Things went better now in the family, though it could scarce be pretended they went well. There was now at least no misconception; there was kindness upon all sides; and I believe my patron and his wife might again have drawn together if he could but have pocketed his pride, and she forgot (what was the ground of all) her brooding on another man. It is wonderful how a private thought leaks out; it is wonderful to me now how we should all have followed the current of her sentiments; and though she bore herself quietly, and had a very even disposition, yet we should have known whenever her fancy ran to Paris. And would not any one have thought that my disclosure must have rooted up that idol? I think there is the devil in women: all these years passed, never a sight of the man, little enough kindness to remember (by all accounts) even while she had him, the notion of his death intervening, his heartless rapacity laid bare to her; that all should not do, and she must still keep the best place in her heart for this accursed fellow, is a thing to make a plain man rage. I had never much natural sympathy for the passion of love; but this unreason in my patron's wife disgusted me outright with the whole matter.

I remember checking a maid because she sang some bairnly kickshaw while my mind was thus engaged; and my asperity brought about my ears the enmity of all the petticoats about the house; of which I recked very little, but it amused Mr Henry, who rallied me much upon our joint unpopularity. It is strange enough (for my own mother was certainly one of the salt of the earth, and my Aunt Dickson, who paid my fees at the University, a very notable woman), but I have never had much toleration for the female sex, possibly not much understanding; and being far from a bold man, I have ever shunned their company. Not only do I see no cause to regret this diffidence in myself, but have invariably remarked the most unhappy consequences follow those who were less wise. So much I thought proper to set down, lest I show myself unjust to Mrs Henry. And, besides, the remark arose naturally, on a re-perusal of the letter which was the next step in these affairs, and reached me, to my sincere astonishment, by a private hand, some week or so after the departure of the last messenger.

Letter from Colonel BURKE (*afterwards Chevalier*) *to* MR MACKELLAR.

TROYES IN CHAMPAGNE, *July* 12, 1756.
My Dear Sir,—You will doubtless be surprised to receive a communication from one so little known to you; but on the occasion I had the good fortune to encounter you at Durrisdeer, I remarked you for a young man of a solid gravity of character: a qualification which I profess I admire and revere next to natural genius or the bold chivalrous spirit of the soldier. I was, besides, interested in the noble family which you have the honour to serve, or (to speak more by the book) to be the humble and respected friend of; and a conversation I had the pleasure to have with you very early in the morning has remained much upon my mind.

Being the other day in Paris, on a visit from this famous city, where I am in garrison, I took occasion to inquire your name (which I profess I had forgot) at my friend, the Master of B.; and, a fair opportunity occurring, I write to inform you of what's new.

The Master of B. (when we had last some talk of him together) was in receipt, as I think I then told you, of a highly advantageous pension on the Scots Fund. He next received a company, and was soon after advanced to a regiment of his own. My dear sir, I do not offer to explain this circumstance; any more than why I myself, who have rid at the right hand of Princes, should be fubbed off with a pair of colours and sent to rot in a hole at the bottom of the province. Accustomed as I am to Courts, I cannot but feel it is no atmosphere for a plain soldier; and I could never hope to advance by similar means, even could I stoop to the endeavour. But our friend has a particular aptitude to succeed by the means of ladies; and if all be true that I have heard, he enjoyed a remarkable protection. It is like this turned against him; for when I had the honour to shake him by the hand, he was but newly released from the Bastille, where he had been cast on a sealed letter; and, though now released, has both lost his regiment and his pension. My dear sir, the loyalty of a plain Irishman will ultimately succeed in the place of craft; as I am sure a gentleman of your probity will agree.

Now, sir, the Master is a man whose genius I admire beyond expression, and, besides, he is my friend; but I thought a little word of this revolution in his fortunes would not come amiss, for, in my opinion, the man's desperate. He spoke, when I saw him, of an adventure upon India (whither I am myself in some hope of accompanying my illustrious countryman, Mr Lally); but for this he would require (as I understood) more money than was readily at his command. You may have heard a military proverb: that it is a good thing to make a bridge of gold to a flying enemy? I trust you will take my meaning, and I subscribe myself, with proper respects to my Lord Durrisdeer, to his son, and to the beauteous Mrs Durie,

My dear Sir,

Your obedient humble Servant,

FRANCIS BURKE.

This missive I carried at once to Mr Henry; and I think there was but the one thought between the two of us: that it had come a week too late. I made haste to send an answer to Colonel Burke, in which I begged him, if he should see the Master, to assure him his next messenger would be attended to. But with all my haste I was not in time to avert what was impending: the arrow had been drawn, it must now fly. I could almost doubt the power of Providence (and certainly His will) to stay the issue of events; and it is a strange thought, how many of us had been storing up the elements of this catastrophe, for how long a time, and with how blind an ignorance of what we did.

From the coming of the Colonel's letter, I had a spyglass in my room, began to drop questions to the tenant folk, and as there was no great secrecy observed, and the free trade (in our part) went by force as much as stealth, I had soon got together a knowledge of the signals in use, and knew pretty well to an hour when any messenger might be expected. I say, I questioned the tenants; for with the traders themselves, desperate blades that went habitually armed, I could never bring myself to meddle willingly. Indeed, by what proved in the sequel an unhappy chance, I was an object of scorn to some of these braggadocios; who had not only gratified me with a nickname, but catching me one night upon a by-path, and being all (as they would have said) somewhat merry, had caused me to dance for their diversion. The method employed was that of cruelly chipping at my toes with naked cutlasses, shouting at the same time 'Square-toes'; and though they did me no bodily mischief, I was none the less deplorably affected, and was indeed for several days confined to my bed: a scandal on the state of Scotland on which no comment is required.

It happened on the afternoon of November 7th, in this same unfortunate year, that I espied, during my walk, the smoke of a beacon fire upon the Muckleross. It was drawing near time for my return; but the uneasiness upon my spirits was that day so great that I must burst through the thickets

to the edge of what they call the Craig Head. The sun was
already down, but there was still a broad light in the west,
which showed me some of the smugglers treading out their
signal fire upon the Ross, and in the bay the lugger lying
with her sails brailed up. She was plainly but new come to
anchor, and yet the skiff was already lowered and pulling
for the landing place at the end of the long shrubbery. And
this I knew could signify but one thing,—the coming of a
messenger for Durrisdeer.

I laid aside the remainder of my terrors, clambered
down the brae—a place I had never ventured through
before—and was hid among the shoreside thickets in time
to see the boat touch. Captain Crail himself was steering,
a thing not usual; by his side there sat a passenger; and
the men gave way with difficulty, being hampered with
near upon half a dozen portmanteaus, great and small.
But the business of landing was briskly carried through;
and presently the baggage was all tumbled on shore, the
boat on its return voyage to the lugger, and the passenger
standing alone upon the point of rock, a tall slender figure of
a gentleman, habited in black, with a sword by his side and
a walking cane upon his wrist. As he so stood, he waved the
cane to Captain Crail by way of salutation, with something
both of grace and mockery that wrote the gesture deeply on
my mind.

No sooner was the boat away with my sworn enemies
than I took a sort of half courage, came forth to the
margin of the thicket, and there halted again, my mind
being greatly pulled about between natural diffidence and
a dark foreboding of the truth. Indeed, I might have stood
there swithering all night, had not the stranger turned,
spied me through the mists, which were beginning to fall,
and waved and cried on me to draw near. I did so with a
heart like lead.

'Here, my good man,' said he, in the English accent, 'here
are some things for Durrisdeer.'

I was now near enough to see him, a very handsome
figure and countenance, swarthy, lean, long, with a quick,
alert, black look, as of one who was a fighter, and accustomed to command; upon one cheek he had a mole, not

unbecoming; a large diamond sparkled on his hand; his clothes, although of the one hue, were of a French and foppish design; his ruffles, which he wore longer than common, of exquisite lace; and I wondered the more to see him in such a guise when he was but newly landed from a dirty smuggling lugger. At the same time he had a better look at me, toised me a second time sharply, and then smiled.

'I wager, my friend,' says he, 'that I know both your name and your nickname. I divined these very clothes upon your hand of writing, Mr Mackellar.'

At these words I fell to shaking.

'O,' says he, 'you need not be afraid of me. I bear no malice for your tedious letters; and it is my purpose to employ you a good deal. You may call me Mr Bally: it is the name I have assumed; or rather (since I am addressing so great a precisian) it is so I have curtailed my own. Come now, pick up that, and that'—indicating two of the portmanteaus. 'That will be as much as you are fit to bear, and the rest can very well wait. Come, lose no more time, if you please.'

His tone was so cutting that I managed to do as he bid by a sort of instinct, my mind being all the time quite lost. No sooner had I picked up the portmanteaus than he turned his back and marched off through the long shrubbery, where it began already to be dusk, for the wood is thick and evergreen. I followed behind, loaded almost to the dust, though I profess I was not conscious of the burthen; being swallowed up in the monstrosity of this return, and my mind flying like a weaver's shuttle.

On a sudden I set the portmanteaus to the ground and halted. He turned and looked back at me.

'Well?' said he.

'You are the Master of Ballantrae?'

'You will do me the justice to observe,' says he, 'that I have made no secret with the astute Mackellar.'

'And in the name of God,' cries I, 'what brings you here? Go back, while it is yet time.'

'I thank you,' said he. 'Your master has chosen this way, and not I; but since he has made the choice, he (and you also) must abide by the result.—And now pick up these things of mine, which you have set down in a very boggy place, and attend to that which I have made your business.'

But I had no thought now of obedience; I came straight up to him. 'If nothing will move you to go back,' said I; 'though, sure, under all the circumstances, any Christian, or even any gentleman, would scruple to go forward . . .'

'These are gratifying expressions,' he threw in.

'If nothing will move you to go back,' I continued, 'there are still some decencies to be observed. Wait here with your baggage, and I will go forward and prepare your family. Your father is an old man; and . . .' I stumbled . . . 'there are decencies to be observed.'

'Truly,' said he, 'this Mackellar improves upon acquaintance. But look you here, my man, and understand it once for all—you waste your breath upon me, and I go my own way with inevitable motion.'

'Ah!' says I. 'Is that so? We shall see then!'

And I turned and took to my heels for Durrisdeer. He clutched at me, and cried out angrily, and then I believe I heard him laugh, and then I am certain he pursued me for a step or two, and (I suppose) desisted. One thing at least is sure, that I came but a few minutes later to the door of the great house, nearly strangled for the lack of breath, but quite alone. Straight up the stair I ran, and burst into the hall, and stopped before the family without the power of speech; but I must have carried my story in my looks, for they rose out of their places and stared on me like changelings.

'He has come,' I panted out at last.

'He?' said Mr Henry.

'Himself,' said I.

'My son?' cried my lord. 'Imprudent, imprudent boy! O, could he not stay where he was safe!'

Never a word says Mrs Henry; nor did I look at her, I scarce knew why.

'Well,' said Mr Henry, with a very deep breath, 'and where is he?'

'I left him in the long shrubbery,' said I.

'Take me to him,' said he.

So we went out together, he and I, without another word from any one; and in the midst of the gravelled plot encountered the Master strolling up, whistling as he came, and beating the air with his cane. There was still light enough overhead to recognise, though not to read, a countenance.

'Ah! Jacob,' says the Master. 'So here is Esau back.'

'James,' says Mr Henry, 'for God's sake, call me by my name. I will not pretend that I am glad to see you; but I would fain make you as welcome as I can in the house of our fathers.'

'Or in *my* house? or *yours*?' says the Master. 'Which were you about to say? But this is an old sore, and we need not rub it. If you would not share with me in Paris, I hope you will yet scarce deny your elder brother a corner of the fire at Durrisdeer?'

'That is very idle speech,' replied Mr Henry. 'And you understand the power of your position excellently well.'

'Why, I believe I do,' said the other, with a little laugh. And this, though they had never touched hands, was (as we may say) the end of the brothers' meeting; for at this the Master turned to me and bade me fetch his baggage.

I, on my side, turned to Mr Henry for a confirmation; perhaps with some defiance.

'As long as the Master is here, Mr Mackellar, you will very much oblige me by regarding his wishes as you would my own,' says Mr Henry. 'We are constantly troubling you: will you be so good as send one of the servants?'—with an accent on the word.

If this speech were anything at all, it was surely a well-deserved reproof upon the stranger; and yet, so devilish was his impudence, he twisted it the other way.

'And shall we be common enough to say, "Sneck up"?' inquires he softly, looking upon me sideways.

Had a kingdom depended on the act, I could not have trusted myself in words; even to call a servant was beyond me; I had rather serve the man myself than speak; and I turned away in silence and went into the long shrubbery, with a heart full of anger and despair. It was dark under the trees, and I walked before me and forgot what business I was come upon, till I nearly broke my shin on the portmanteaus. Then it was that I remarked a strange particular; for whereas I had before carried both and scarce observed it, it was now as much as I could do to manage one. And this, as it forced me to make two journeys, kept me the longer from the hall.

When I got there, the business of welcome was over long ago; the company was already at supper; and, by an oversight that cut me to the quick, my place had been forgotten. I had seen one side of the Master's return; now I was to see the other. It was he who first remarked my coming in and standing back (as I did) in some annoyance. He jumped from his seat.

'And if I have not got the good Mackellar's place!' cries he. 'John, lay another for Mr Bally; I protest he will disturb no one, and your table is big enough for all.'

I could scarce credit my ears, nor yet my senses, when he took me by the shoulders and thrust me, laughing, into my own place—such an affectionate playfulness was in his voice. And while John laid the fresh place for him (a thing on which he still insisted), he went and leaned on his father's chair and looked down upon him, and the old man turned about and looked upwards on his son, with such a pleasant mutual tenderness that I could have carried my hand to my head in mere amazement.

Yet all was of a piece. Never a harsh word fell from him, never a sneer showed upon his lip. He had laid aside even his cutting English accent, and spoke with the kindly Scots tongue, that set a value on affectionate words; and though his manners had a graceful elegance mighty foreign to our ways in Durrisdeer, it was still a homely courtliness, that did not shame but flattered us. All that he did throughout the meal, indeed, drinking wine with me with a notable respect, turning about for a pleasant word with John, fondling his father's hand, breaking into little merry tales of his adventures, calling up the past with happy reference—all he did was so becoming, and himself so handsome, that I could scarce wonder if my lord and Mrs Henry sat about the board with radiant faces, or if John waited behind with dropping tears.

As soon as supper was over, Mrs Henry rose to with-draw.

'This was never your way, Alison,' said he.

'It is my way now,' she replied: which was notoriously false, 'and I will give you a goodnight, James, and a welcome—from the dead,' said she, and her voice dropped and trembled.

Poor Mr Henry, who had made rather a heavy figure through the meal, was more concerned than ever; pleased to see his wife withdraw, and yet half displeased, as he thought upon the cause of it; and the next moment altogether dashed by the fervour of her speech.

On my part, I thought I was now one too many; and was stealing after Mrs Henry, when the Master saw me.

'Now, Mr Mackellar,' says he, 'I take this near on an unfriendliness. I cannot have you go: this is to make a stranger of the prodigal son; and let me remind you where—in his own father's house! Come, sit ye down, and drink another glass with Mr Bally.'

'Ay, ay, Mr Mackellar,' says my lord, 'we must not make a stranger either of him or you. I have been telling my son,' he added, his voice brightening as usual on the word, 'how much we valued all your friendly service.'

So I sat there, silent, till my usual hour; and might have been almost deceived in the man's nature but for one passage, in which his perfidy appeared too plain. Here was the passage; of which, after what he knows of the brothers' meeting, the reader shall consider for himself. Mr Henry sitting somewhat dully, in spite of his best endeavours to carry things before my lord, up jumps the Master, passes about the board, and claps his brother on the shoulder.

'Come, come, *Hairry lad*,' says he, with a broad accent, such as they must have used together when they were boys, 'you must not be downcast because your brother has come home. All's yours, that's sure enough, and little I grudge it you. Neither must you grudge me my place beside my father's fire.'

'And that is too true, Henry,' says my old lord, with a

little frown, a thing rare with him. 'You have been the elder brother of the parable in the good sense; you must be careful of the other.'

'I am easily put in the wrong,' said Mr Henry.

'Who puts you in the wrong?' cried my lord, I thought very tartly for so mild a man. 'You have earned my gratitude and your brother's many thousand times: you may count on its endurance; and let that suffice.'

'Ay, Harry, that you may,' said the Master; and I thought Mr Henry looked at him with a kind of wildness in his eye.

On all the miserable business that now followed, I have four questions that I asked myself often at the time, and ask myself still:—Was the man moved by a particular sentiment against Mr Henry? or by what he thought to be his interest? or by a mere delight in cruelty such as cats display and theologians tell us of the devil? or by what he would have called love? My common opinion halts among the three first; but perhaps there lay at the spring of his behaviour an element of all. As thus:—Animosity to Mr Henry would explain his hateful usage of him when they were alone; the interests he came to serve would explain his very different attitude before my lord; that and some spice of a design of gallantry, his care to stand well with Mrs Henry; and the pleasure of malice for itself, the pains he was continually at to mingle and oppose these lines of conduct.

Partly because I was a very open friend to my patron, partly because in my letters to Paris I had often given myself some freedom of remonstrance, I was included in his diabolical amusement. When I was alone with him, he pursued me with sneers; before the family he used me with the extreme of friendly condescension. This was not only painful in itself; not only did it put me continually in the wrong; but there was in it an element of insult indescribable. That he should thus leave me out in his dissimulation, as though even my testimony were too despicable to be considered, galled me to the blood. But what it was to me is not worth notice. I make but memorandum of it here; and chiefly for this reason, that it had one good result, and gave me the quicker sense of Mr Henry's martyrdom.

It was on him the burthen fell. How was he to respond to the public advances of one who never lost a chance of gibing him in private? How was he to smile back on the deceiver and the insulter? He was condemned to seem ungracious. He was condemned to silence. Had he been less proud, had he spoken, who would have credited the truth? The acted calumny had done its work; my lord and Mrs Henry were the daily witnesses of what went on; they could have sworn in court that the Master was a model of long-suffering good nature, and Mr Henry a pattern of jealousy and thanklessness. And ugly enough as these must have appeared in any one, they seemed tenfold uglier in Mr Henry; for who could forget that the Master lay in peril of his life, and that he had already lost his mistress, his title, and his fortune?

'Henry, will you ride with me?' asks the Master one day.

And Mr Henry, who had been goaded by the man all morning, raps out: 'I will not.'

'I sometimes wish you would be kinder, Henry,' says the other wistfully.

I give this for a specimen; but such scenes befell continually. Small wonder if Mr Henry was blamed; small wonder if I fretted myself into something near upon a bilious fever; nay, and at the mere recollection feel a bitterness in my blood.

Sure, never in this world was a more diabolical contrivance: so perfidious, so simple, so impossible to combat. And yet I think again, and I think always, Mrs Henry might have read between the lines; she might have had more knowledge of her husband's nature; after all these years of marriage she might have commanded or captured his confidence. And my old lord, too—that very watchful gentleman—where was all his observation? But, for one thing, the deceit was practised by a master hand, and might have gulled an angel. For another (in the case of Mrs Henry), I have observed there are no persons so far away as those who are both married and estranged, so that they seem out of earshot, or to have no common tongue. For a third (in the case of both of these spectators) they were blinded by old ingrained predilection. And for a fourth, the risk the Master was supposed to stand in (supposed, I say—you will soon hear why) made it seem the more ungenerous to criticise; and, keeping them in a perpetual tender solicitude about his life, blinded them the more effectually to his faults.

It was during this time that I perceived most clearly the effect of manner, and was led to lament most deeply the plainness of my own. Mr Henry had the essence of a gentleman; when he was moved, when there was any call of circumstance, he could play his part with dignity and spirit; but in the day's commerce (it is idle to deny it) he fell short of the ornamental. The Master (on the other hand) had never a movement but it commended him. So it befell that when the one appeared gracious and the other ungracious, every trick of their bodies seemed to call out confirmation. Not that alone: but the more deeply Mr Henry floundered in his brother's toils, the more clownish he grew; and the more the Master enjoyed his spiteful entertainment, the more engagingly, the more smilingly, he went! So that the plot, by its own scope and progress, furthered and confirmed itself.

It was one of the man's arts to use the peril in which (as I say) he was supposed to stand. He spoke of it to those who loved him with a gentle pleasantry, which made it the more touching. To Mr Henry he used it as a cruel weapon of offence. I remember his laying his finger on the clean lozenge of the painted window one day when we three were alone together in the hall. 'Here went your lucky guinea, Jacob,' said he. And when Mr Henry only looked upon him darkly, 'O!' he added, 'you need not look such impotent malice, my good fly. You can be rid of your spider when you please. How long, O Lord? When are you to be wrought to the point of a denunciation, scrupulous brother? It is one of my interests in this dreary hole. I ever loved experiment.' Still Mr Henry only stared upon him with a glooming brow, and a changed colour; and at last the Master broke out in a laugh and clapped him on the shoulder, calling him a sulky dog. At this my patron leaped back with a gesture I thought very dangerous; and I must suppose the Master thought so too, for he looked the least in the world discountenanced, and I do not remember him again to have laid hands on Mr Henry.

But though he had his peril always on his lips in the one way or the other, I thought his conduct strangely incautious, and began to fancy the Government—who had set a price upon his head—was gone sound asleep. I will not deny I was tempted with the wish to denounce him; but two thoughts withheld me: one, that if he were thus to end his life upon an honourable scaffold, the man would be canonised for good in the minds of his father and my patron's wife; the other, that if I was anyway mingled in the matter, Mr Henry himself would scarce escape some glancings of suspicion. And in the meanwhile our enemy went in and out more than I could have thought possible, the fact that he was home again was buzzed about all the countryside, and yet he was never stirred. Of all those so many and so different persons who were acquainted with his presence, none had the least greed—as I used to say in my annoyance—or the least loyalty; and the man rode here and there—fully more welcome, considering the lees of old unpopularity, than Mr Henry—and, considering the free-traders, far safer than myself.

Not but what he had a trouble of his own; and this, as it brought about the gravest consequences, I must now relate. The reader will scarce have forgotten Jessie Broun; her way of life was much among the smuggling party; Captain Crail himself was of her intimates; and she had early word of Mr Bally's presence at the house. In my opinion, she had long ceased to care two straws for the Master's person; but it was become her habit to connect herself continually with the Master's name; that was the ground of all her play-acting; and so now, when he was back, she thought she owed it to herself to grow a haunter of the neighbourhood of Durrisdeer. The Master could scarce go abroad but she was there in wait for him; a scandalous figure of a woman, not often sober; hailing him wildly as 'her bonny laddie,' quoting pedlar's poetry, and, as I receive the story, even seeking to weep upon his neck. I own I rubbed my hands over this persecution; but the Master, who laid so much upon others, was himself the least patient of men. There were strange scenes enacted in the policies. Some say he took his cane to her, and Jessie fell back upon her former weapons—stones. It is certain at least that he made a motion to Captain Crail to have the woman trepanned, and that the Captain refused the proposition with uncommon vehemence. And the end of the matter was victory for Jessie. Money was got together; an interview took place, in which my proud gentleman must consent to be kissed and wept upon; and the woman was set up in a public of her own, somewhere on Solway side (but I forget where), and, by the only news I ever had of it, extremely ill-frequented.

This is to look forward. After Jessie had been but a little while upon his heels, the Master comes to me one day in the steward's office, and with more civility than usual, 'Mackellar,' says he, 'there is a damned crazy wench comes about here. I cannot well move in the matter myself, which brings me to you. Be so good as to see to it: the men must have a strict injunction to drive the wench away.'

'Sir,' said I, trembling a little, 'you can do your own dirty errands for yourself.'

He said not a word to that, and left the room.

Presently came Mr Henry. 'Here is news!' cried he. 'It seems all is not enough, and you must add to my wretchedness. It seems you have insulted Mr Bally.'

'Under your kind favour, Mr Henry,' said I, 'it was he that insulted me, and, as I think, grossly. But I may have been careless of your position when I spoke; and if you think so when you know all, my dear patron, you have but to say the word. For you I would obey in any point whatever, even to sin, God pardon me!' And thereupon I told him what had passed.

Mr Henry smiled to himself; a grimmer smile I never witnessed. 'You did exactly well,' said he. 'He shall drink his Jessie Broun to the dregs.' And then, spying the Master outside, he opened the window, and, crying to him by the name of Mr Bally, asked him to step up and have a word.

'James,' said he, when our persecutor had come in and closed the door behind him, looking at me with a smile, as if he thought I was to be humbled, 'you brought me a complaint against Mr Mackellar, into which I have inquired. I need not tell you I would always take his word against yours; for we are alone, and I am going to use something of your own freedom. Mr Mackellar is a gentleman I value; and you must contrive, so long as you are under this roof, to bring yourself into no more collisions with one whom I will support at any possible cost to me or mine. As for the errand upon which you came to him, you must deliver yourself from the consequences of your own cruelty, and none of my servants shall be at all employed in such a case.'

'My father's servants, I believe,' said the Master.

'Go to him with this tale,' said Mr Henry.

The Master grew very white. He pointed at me with his finger. 'I want that man discharged,' he said.

'He shall not be,' said Mr Henry.

'You shall pay pretty dear for this,' says the Master.

'I have paid so dear already for a wicked brother,' said Mr Henry, 'that I am bankrupt even of fears. You have no place left where you can strike me.'

'I will show you about that,' says the Master, and went softly away.

'What will he do next, Mackellar?' cries Mr Henry.

'Let me go away,' said I. 'My dear patron, let me go away; I am but the beginning of fresh sorrows.'

'Would you leave me quite alone?' said he.

We were not long in suspense as to the nature of the new assault. Up to that hour the Master had played a very close game with Mrs Henry; avoiding pointedly to be alone with her, which I took at the time for an effect of decency, but now think to have been a most insidious art; meeting her, you may say, at mealtime only; and behaving, when he did so, like an affectionate brother. Up to that hour, you may say he had scarce directly interfered between Mr Henry and his wife; except in so far as he had manoeuvred the one quite forth from the good graces of the other. Now all that was to be changed; but whether really in revenge, or because he was wearying of

Durrisdeer, and looked about for some diversion, who but the devil shall decide?

From that hour, at least, began the siege of Mrs Henry; a thing so deftly carried on that I scarce know if she was aware of it herself, and that her husband must look on in silence. The first parallel was opened (as was made to appear) by accident. The talk fell, as it did often, on the exiles in France; so it glided to the matter of their songs.

'There is one,' says the Master, 'if you are curious in these matters, that has always seemed to me very moving. The poetry is harsh; and yet, perhaps because of my situation, it has always found the way to my heart. It is supposed to be sung, I should tell you, by an exile's sweetheart; and represents perhaps not so much the truth of what she is thinking, as the truth of what he hopes of her, poor soul! in these far lands.' And here the Master sighed. 'I protest it is a pathetic sight when a score of rough Irish, all common sentinels, get to this song; and you may see, by their falling tears, how it strikes home to them. It goes thus, father,' says he, very adroitly taking my lord for his listener, 'and if I cannot get to the end of it, you must think it is a common case with us exiles.' And thereupon he struck up the same air as I had heard the Colonel whistle; but now to words, rustic indeed, yet most pathetically setting forth a poor girl's aspirations for an exiled lover; of which one verse indeed (or something like it) still sticks by me:—

> O, I will dye my petticoat red,
> With my dear boy I'll beg my bread,
> Though all my friends should wish me dead,
> For Willie among the rushes, O!

He sang it well, even as a song; but he did better yet as a performer. I have heard famous actors, when there was not a dry eye in the Edinburgh theatre; a great wonder to behold; but no more wonderful than how the Master played upon that little ballad, and on those who heard him, like an instrument, and seemed now upon the point of failing, and now to conquer his distress, so that words and music seemed to pour out of his own heart and his own past, and to be aimed directly at Mrs Henry. And his art went further yet; for all was so delicately touched, it seemed impossible to suspect him of the least design; and so far from making a parade of emotion, you would have sworn he was striving to be calm. When it came to an end, we all sat silent for a time; he had chosen the dusk of the afternoon, so that none could see his neighbour's face; but it seemed as if we held our breathing; only my old lord cleared his throat. The first to move was the singer, who got to his feet suddenly and softly, and went and walked softly to and fro in the low end of the hall, Mr Henry's customary place. We were to suppose that he there struggled down the last of his emotion; for he presently returned and launched into a disquisition on the nature of the Irish (always so much miscalled, and whom he defended) in his natural voice; so that, before the lights were brought, we were in the usual course of talk. But even then, methought Mrs Henry's face was a shade pale; and for another thing, she withdrew almost at once.

The next sign was a friendship this insidious devil struck up with innocent Miss Katharine; so that they were always together, hand in hand, or she climbing on his knee, like a pair of children. Like all his diabolical acts, this cut in several ways. It was the last stroke to Mr Henry, to see his own babe debauched against him; it made him harsh with the poor innocent, which brought him still a peg lower in his wife's esteem; and (to conclude) it was a bond of union between the lady and the Master. Under this influence, their old reserve melted by daily stages. Presently there came walks in the long shrubbery, talks in the Belvedere, and I know not what tender familiarity. I am sure Mrs Henry was like many a good woman; she had a whole conscience, but perhaps by the means of a little winking. For even to so dull an observer as myself, it was plain her kindness was of a more moving nature than the sisterly. The tones of her voice appeared more numerous; she had a light and softness in her eye; she was more gentle with all of us, even with Mr Henry, even with myself; methought she breathed of some quiet melancholy happiness.

To look on at this, what a torment it was for Mr Henry! And yet it brought our ultimate deliverance, as I am soon to tell.

The purport of the Master's stay was no more noble (gild it as they might) than to wring money out. He had some design of a fortune in the French Indies, as the Chevalier wrote me; and it was the sum required for this that he came seeking. For the rest of the family it spelled ruin; but my lord, in his incredible partiality, pushed ever for the granting. The family was now so narrowed down (indeed, there were no more of them than just the father and the two sons) that it was possible to break the entail and alienate a piece of land. And to this, at first by hints, and then by open pressure, Mr Henry was brought to consent. He never would have done so, I am very well assured, but for the weight of the distress under which he laboured. But for his passionate eagerness to see his brother gone, he would not thus have broken with his own sentiment and the traditions of his house. And even so, he sold them his consent at a dear rate, speaking for once openly, and holding the business up in its own shameful colours.

'You will observe,' he said, 'this is an injustice to my son, if ever I have one.'

'But that you are not likely to have,' said my lord.

'God knows!' says Mr Henry. 'And considering the cruel falseness of the position in which I stand to my brother, and that you, my lord, are my father, and have the right to command me, I set my hand to this paper. But one thing I will say first: I have been ungenerously pushed, and when next, my lord, you are tempted to compare your sons, I call on you to remember what I have done and what he has done. Acts are the fair test.'

My lord was the most uneasy man I ever saw; even in his old face the blood came up. 'I think this is not a very wisely chosen moment, Henry, for complaints,' said he. 'This takes away from the merit of your generosity.'

'Do not deceive yourself, my lord,' said Mr Henry. 'This injustice is not done from generosity to him, but in obedience to yourself.'

'Before strangers . . .' begins my lord, still more unhappily affected.

'There is no one but Mackellar here,' said Mr Henry; 'he

is my friend. And, my lord, as you make him no stranger to your frequent blame, it were hard if I must keep him one to a thing so rare as my defence.'

Almost I believe my lord would have rescinded his decision; but the Master was on the watch.

'Ah! Henry, Henry,' says he, 'you are the best of us still. Rugged and true! Ah! man, I wish I was as good.'

And at that instance of his favourite's generosity my lord desisted from his hesitation, and the deed was signed.

As soon as it could be brought about, the land of Ochterhall was sold for much below its value, and the money paid over to our leech and sent by some private carriage into France. And now here was all the man's business brought to a successful head, and his pockets once more bulging with our gold; and yet the point for which we had consented to this sacrifice was still denied us, and the visitor still lingered on at Durrisdeer. Whether in malice, or because the time was not yet come for his adventure to the Indies, or because he had hopes of his design on Mrs Henry, or from the orders of the Government, who shall say? but linger he did, and that for weeks.

You will observe I say: 'from the orders of the Government'; for about this time the man's disreputable secret trickled out.

The first hint I had was from a tenant, who commented on the Master's stay, and yet more on his security; for this tenant was a Jacobitish sympathiser, and had lost a son at Culloden, which gave him the more critical eye. 'There is one thing,' said he, 'that I cannot but think strange; and that is how he got to Cockermouth.'

'To Cockermouth?' said I, with a sudden memory of my first wonder on beholding the man disembark so *point-device* after so long a voyage.

'Why, yes,' says the tenant, 'it was there he was picked up by Captain Crail. You thought he had come from France by sea? And so we all did.'

I turned this news a little in my head, and then carried it to Mr Henry. 'Here is an odd circumstance,' said I, and told him.

'What matters how he came, Mackellar, so long as he is here?' groans Mr Henry.

'No, sir,' said I, 'but think again! Does not this smack a little of some Government connivance? You know how much we have wondered already at the man's security.'

'Stop,' said Mr Henry. 'Let me think of this.' And as he thought, there came that grim smile upon his face that was a little like the Master's. 'Give me paper,' said he. And he sat without another word and wrote to a gentleman of his acquaintance—I will name no unnecessary names, but he was one in a high place. This letter I despatched by the only hand I could depend upon in such a case—Macconochie's; and the old man rode hard, for he was back with the reply before even my eagerness had ventured to expect him. Again, as he read it, Mr Henry had the same grim smile.

'This is the best you have done for me yet, Mackellar,' says he. 'With this in my hand I will give him a shog. Watch for us at dinner.'

At dinner accordingly Mr Henry proposed some very public appearance for the Master; and my lord, as he had hoped, objected to the danger of the course.

'O!' says Mr Henry, very easily, 'you need no longer keep this up with me. I am as much in the secret as yourself.'

'In the secret?' says my lord. 'What do you mean, Henry? I give you my word, I am in no secret from which you are excluded.'

The Master had changed countenance, and I saw he was struck in a joint of his harness.

'How?' says Mr Henry, turning to him with a huge appearance of surprise. 'I see you serve your masters very faithfully; but I had thought you would have been humane enough to set your father's mind at rest.'

'What are you talking of? I refuse to have my business publicly discussed. I order this to cease,' cries the Master very foolishly and passionately, and indeed more like a child than a man.

'So much discretion was not looked for at your hands, I can assure you,' continued Mr Henry. 'For see what my correspondent writes'—unfolding the paper—'"It is, of course, in the interests both of the Government and the gentleman whom we may perhaps best continue to call Mr Bally, to keep this understanding secret; but it was never meant his own family should continue to endure the suspense you paint so feelingly; and I am pleased mine should be the hand to set these fears at rest. Mr Bally is as safe in Great Britain as yourself.'"

'Is this possible?' cries my lord, looking at his son, with a great deal of wonder, and still more of suspicion in his face.

'My dear father,' says the Master, already much recovered. 'I am overjoyed that this may be disclosed. My own instructions, direct from London, bore a very contrary sense, and I was charged to keep the indulgence secret from every one, yourself not excepted, and indeed yourself expressly named—as I can show in black and white, unless I have destroyed the letter. They must have changed their mind very swiftly, for the whole matter is still quite fresh; or rather, Henry's correspondent must have misconceived that part, as he seems to have misconceived the rest. To tell you the truth, sir,' he continued, getting visibly more easy, 'I had supposed this unexplained favour to a rebel was the effect to some application from yourself; and the injunction to secrecy among my family the result of a desire on your part to conceal your kindness. Hence I was the more careful to obey orders. It remains now to guess by what other channel indulgence can have flowed on so notorious an offender as myself; for I do not think your son need defend himself from what seems hinted at in Henry's letter. I have never yet heard of a Durrisdeer who was a turncoat or a spy,' says he proudly.

And so it seemed he had swum out of this danger unharmed; but this was to reckon without a blunder he had made, and without the pertinacity of Mr Henry, who was now to show he had something of his brother's spirit.

'You say the matter is still fresh?' says Mr Henry.

'It is recent,' says the Master, with a fair show of stoutness, and yet not without a quaver.

'Is it so recent as that?' asks Mr Henry, like a man a little puzzled, and spreading his letter forth again.

In all the letter there was no word as to the date; but how was the Master to know that?

'It seemed to come late enough for me,' says he, with a laugh. And at the sound of that laugh, which rang false, like a cracked bell, my lord looked at him again across the table, and I saw his old lips draw together close.

'No,' said Mr Henry, still glancing on his letter, 'but I remember your expression. You said it was very fresh.'

And here we had a proof of our victory, and the strongest instance yet of my lord's incredible indulgence; for what must he do but interfere to save his favourite from exposure!

'I think, Henry,' says he, with a kind of pitiful eagerness, 'I think we need dispute no more. We are all rejoiced at last to find your brother safe; we are all at one on that; and, as grateful subjects, we can do no less than drink to the King's health and bounty.'

Thus was the Master extricated; but at least he had been put to his defence, he had come lamely out, and the attraction of his personal danger was now publicly plucked away from him. My lord, in his heart of hearts, now knew his favourite to be a Government spy; and Mrs Henry (however she explained the tale) was notably cold in her behaviour to the discredited hero of romance. Thus in the best fabric of duplicity there is some weak point, if you can strike it, which will loosen all; and if, by this fortunate stroke, we had not shaken the idol, who can say how it might have gone with us at the catastrophe?

And yet at the time we seemed to have accomplished nothing. Before a day or two he had wiped off the ill results of his discomfiture, and, to all appearance, stood as high as ever. As for my Lord Durrisdeer, he was sunk in parental partiality; it was not so much love, which should be an active quality, as an apathy and torpor of his other powers; and forgiveness (so to misapply a noble word) flowed from him in sheer weakness, like the tears of senility. Mrs Henry's was a different case; and Heaven alone knows what he found to say to her, or how he persuaded her from her contempt. It is one of the worst things of sentiment, that the voice grows to be more important than the words, and the speaker than that which is spoken. But some excuse the Master must have found, or perhaps he had even struck upon some art to wrest this exposure to his own advantage; for after a time of coldness, it seemed as if things went worse than ever between him and Mrs Henry. They were then constantly together. I would not be thought to cast one shadow of blame, beyond what is due to a half-wilful blindness, on that unfortunate lady; but I do think, in these last days, she was playing very near the fire; and whether I be wrong or not in that, one thing is sure and quite sufficient: Mr Henry thought so. The poor gentleman sat for days in my room, so great a picture of distress that I could never venture to address him; yet it is to be thought he found some comfort even in my presence and the knowledge of my sympathy. There were times, too, when we talked, and a strange manner of talk it was; there was never a person named, nor an individual circumstance referred to; yet we had the same matter in our minds, and we were each aware of it. It is a strange art that can thus be practised; to talk for hours of a thing, and never name nor yet so much as hint at it. And I remember I wondered if it was by some such natural skill that the Master made love to Mrs Henry all day long (as he manifestly did), yet never startled her into reserve.

To show how far affairs had gone with Mr Henry, I will give some words of his, uttered (as I have cause not to forget) upon the 26th of February 1757. It was unseasonable weather, a cast back into winter: windless, bitter cold, the world all white with rime, the sky low and grey: the sea black and silent like a quarry hole. Mr Henry sat close by the fire, and debated (as was now common with him) whether 'a man' should 'do things,' whether 'interference was wise,' and the like general propositions, which each of us particularly applied. I was by the window, looking out, when there passed below me the Master, Mrs Henry, and Miss Katharine, that now constant trio. The child was running to and fro, delighted with the frost; the Master spoke close in the lady's ear with what seemed (even from so far) a devilish grace of insinuation; and she on her part looked on the ground like a person lost in listening. I broke out of my reserve.

'If I were you, Mr Henry,' said I, 'I would deal openly with my lord.'

'Mackellar, Mackellar,' says he, 'you do not see the weakness of my ground. I can carry no such base thoughts to any one—to my father least of all; that would be to fall into the bottom of his scorn. The weakness of my ground,' he continued, 'lies in myself, that I am not one who engages love. I have their gratitude, they all tell me that; I have a rich estate of it! But I am not present in their minds; they are moved neither to think with me nor to think for me. There is my loss!' He got to his feet, and trod down the fire. 'But some method must be found, Mackellar,' said he, looking at me suddenly over his shoulder; 'some way must be found. I am a man of a great deal of patience—far too much—far too much. I begin to despise myself. And yet, sure, never was a man involved in such a toil!' He fell back to his brooding.

'Cheer up,' said I. 'It will burst of itself.'

'I am far past anger now,' says he, which had so little coherency with my own observation that I let both fall.

CHAPTER FIVE

Account of All that Passed on the Night of February 27th, 1757

ON THE EVENING of the interview referred to, the Master went abroad; he was abroad a great deal of the next day also, that fatal 27th; but where he went, or what he did, we never concerned ourselves to ask until next day. If we had done so, and by any chance found out, it might have changed all. But as all we did was done in ignorance, and should be so judged, I shall so narrate these passages as they appeared to us in the moment of their birth, and reserve all that I since discovered for the time of its discovery. For I have now come to one of the dark parts of my narrative, and must engage the reader's indulgence for my patron.

All the 27th that rigorous weather endured: a stifling cold; the folk passing about like smoking chimneys; the wide hearth in the hall piled high with fuel; some of the spring birds that had already blundered north into our neighbourhood besieging the windows of the house or trotting on the frozen turf like things distracted. About noon there came a blink of sunshine; showing a very pretty, wintry, frosty landscape of white hills and woods, with Crail's lugger waiting for a wind under the Craig Head, and the smoke mounting straight into the air from every farm and cottage. With the coming of night, the haze closed in overhead; it fell dark and still and starless, and exceeding cold: a night the most unseasonable, fit for strange events.

Mrs Henry withdrew, as was now her custom, very early. We had set ourselves of late to pass the evening with a game of cards; another mark that our visitor was wearying mightily of the life at Durrisdeer; and we had not been long at this when my old lord slipped from his place beside the fire, and was off without a word to seek the warmth of bed. The three thus left together had neither love nor courtesy to share; not one of us would have sat up one instant to oblige another; yet from the influence of custom, and as the cards had just been dealt, we continued the form of playing out the round. I should say we were late sitters; and though my lord had departed earlier than was his custom, twelve was already gone some time upon the clock, and the servants long ago in bed. Another thing I should say, that although I never saw the Master anyway affected with liquor, he had been drinking freely, and was perhaps (although he showed it not) a trifle heated.

Anyway, he now practised one of his transitions; and so soon as the door closed behind my lord, and without the smallest change of voice, shifted from ordinary civil talk into a stream of insult.

'My dear Henry, it is yours to play,' he had been saying, and now continued: 'It is a very strange thing how, even in so small a matter as a game of cards, you display your rusticity. You play, Jacob, like a bonnet-laird, or a sailor in a tavern. The same dullness, the same petty greed, *cette lenteur d'hébété qui me fait rager;* it is strange I should have such a brother. Even Square-toes has a certain vivacity when his stake is imperilled; but the dreariness of a game with you I positively lack language to depict.'

Mr Henry continued to look at his cards, as though very maturely considering some play; but his mind was elsewhere.

'Dear God, will this never be done?' cries the Master. '*Quel lourdaud!* But why do I trouble you with French expressions, which are lost on such an ignoramus? A *lourdaud*, my dear brother, is as we might say a bumpkin, a clown, a clodpole: a fellow without grace, lightness, quickness; any gift of pleasing, any natural brilliancy: such a one as you shall see, when you desire, by looking in the mirror. I tell you these things for your good, I assure you; and besides, Square-toes' (looking at me and stifling a yawn), 'It is one of my diversions in this very dreary spot to toast you and your master at the fire like chestnuts. I have great pleasure in your case, for I observe the nickname (rustic as it is) has always the power to make you writhe. But sometimes I have more trouble with this dear fellow here, who seems to have gone to sleep upon his cards.—Do you not see the applicability of the epithet I have just explained, dear Henry? Let me show you. For instance, with all those solid qualities which I delight to recognise in you, I never knew a woman who did not prefer me—nor, I think,' he continued, with the most silken deliberation, 'I think—who did not continue to prefer me.'

Mr Henry laid down his cards. He rose to his feet very softly, and seemed all the while like a person in deep thought. 'You coward!' he said gently, as if to himself. And then, with neither hurry nor any particular violence, he struck the Master in the mouth.

The Master sprang to his feet like one transfigured; I had never seen the man so beautiful. 'A blow!' he cried. 'I would not take a blow from God Almighty!'

'Lower your voice,' said Mr Henry. 'Do you wish my father to interfere for you again?'

'Gentlemen, gentlemen,' I cried, and sought to come between them.

The Master caught me by the shoulder, held me at arm's length, and still addressing his brother: 'Do you know what this means?' said he.

'It was the most deliberate act of my life,' says Mr Henry.

'I must have blood, I must have blood for this,' says the Master.

'Please God it shall be yours,' said Mr Henry; and he went to the wall and took down a pair of swords that hung there with others, naked. These he presented to the Master by the points. 'Mackellar shall see us play fair,' said Mr Henry. 'I think it very needful.'

'You need insult me no more,' said the Master, taking one of the swords at random. 'I have hated you all my life.'

'My father is but newly gone to bed,' said Mr Henry. 'We must go somewhere forth of the house.'

'There is an excellent place in the long shrubbery,' said the Master.

'Gentlemen,' said I, 'shame upon you both! Sons of the same mother, would you turn against the life she gave you?'

'Even so, Mackellar,' said Mr Henry, with the same perfect quietude of manner he had shown throughout.

'It is what I will prevent,' said I.

And now here is a blot upon my life. At these words of mine the Master turned his blade against my bosom; I saw the light run along the steel; and I threw up my arms and fell to my knees before him on the floor. 'No, no,' I cried, like a baby.

'We shall have no more trouble with him,' said the Master. 'It is a good thing to have a coward in the house.'

'We must have light,' said Mr Henry, as though there had been no interruption.

'This trembler can bring a pair of candles,' said the Master.

To my shame be it said, I was still so blinded with the flashing of that bare sword that I volunteered to bring a lantern.

'We do not need a l-l-lantern,' says the Master, mocking me. 'There is no breath of air. Come, get to your feet, take a pair of lights, and go before. I am close behind with this'—making the blade glitter as he spoke.

I took up the candlesticks and went before them, steps that I would give my hands to recall; but a coward is a slave at the best; and even as I went, my teeth smote each other in my mouth. It was as he had said: there was no breath stirring; a windless stricture of frost had bound the air; and as we went forth in the shine of the candles, the blackness was like a roof over our heads. Never a word was said; there was never a sound but the creaking of our steps along the frozen path. The cold of the night fell about me like a bucket of water; I shook as I went with more than terror; but my companions, bare-headed like myself, and fresh from the warm hall, appeared not even conscious of the change.

'Here is the place,' said the Master. 'Set down the candles.'

I did as he bid me, and presently the flames went up, as steady as in a chamber, in the midst of the frosted trees, and I beheld these two brothers take their places.

'The light is something in my eyes,' said the Master.

'I will give you every advantage,' replied Mr Henry, shifting his ground, 'for I think you are about to die.' He spoke rather sadly than otherwise, yet there was a ring in his voice.

'Henry Durie,' said the Master, 'two words before I begin. You are a fencer, you can hold a foil; you little know what a change it makes to hold a sword! And by that I know you are to fall. But see how strong is my situation! If you fall, I shift out of this country to where my money is before me. If I fall, where are you? My father, your wife—who is in love with me, as you very well know—your child even, who prefers me to yourself:—how will these avenge me! Had you thought of that, dear Henry?' He looked at his brother with a smile; then made a fencing room salute.

Never a word said Mr Henry, but saluted too, and the swords rang together.

I am no judge of the play; my head, besides, was gone with cold and fear and horror; but it seems that Mr Henry took and kept the upper hand from the engagement, crowding in upon his foe with a contained and glowing fury. Nearer and nearer he crept upon the man, till of a sudden the Master leaped back with a little sobbing oath; and I believe the movement brought the light once more against his eyes. To it they went again, on the fresh ground; but now methought closer, Mr Henry pressing more outrageously, the Master beyond doubt with shaken confidence. For it is beyond doubt he now recognised himself for lost, and had some taste of the cold agony of fear; or he had never attempted the foul stroke. I cannot say I followed it, my untrained eye was never quick enough to seize details, but it appears he caught his brother's blade with his left hand, a practice not permitted. Certainly Mr Henry only saved himself by leaping on one side; as certainly the Master, lungeing in the air, stumbled on his knee, and before he could move, the sword was through his body.

I cried out with a stifled scream, and ran in; but the body was already fallen to the ground, where it writhed a moment like a trodden worm, and then lay motionless.

'Look at his left hand,' said Mr Henry.

'It is all bloody,' said I.

'On the inside?' said he.

'It is cut on the inside,' said I.

'I thought so,' said he, and turned his back.

I opened the man's clothes; the heart was quite still, it gave not a flutter.

'God forgive us, Mr Henry!' said I. 'He is dead.'

'Dead?' he repeated, a little stupidly; and then, with a rising tone, 'Dead? dead?' says he, and suddenly cast his bloody sword upon the ground.

'What must we do?' said I. 'Be yourself, sir. It is too late now: you must be yourself.'

He turned and stared at me. 'O, Mackellar!' says he, and put his face in his hands.

I plucked him by the coat. 'For God's sake, for all our sakes, be more courageous!' said I. 'What must we do?'

He showed me his face with the same stupid stare. 'Do?' says he. And with that his eye fell on the body, and 'O!' he cries out, with his hand to his brow, as if he had never remembered; and, turning from me, made off towards the house of Durrisdeer at a strange stumbling run.

I stood a moment mused; then it seemed to me my duty lay most plain on the side of the living; and I ran after him, leaving the candles on the frosty ground and the body lying in their light under the trees. But run as I pleased, he had the start of me, and was got into the house, and up to the hall, where I found him standing before the fire with his face once more in his hands, and as he so stood he visibly shuddered.

'Mr Henry, Mr Henry,' I said, 'this will be the ruin of us all.'

'What is this that I have done?' cries he, and then looking upon me with a countenance that I shall never forget, 'Who is to tell the old man?' he said.

The word knocked at my heart; but it was no time for weakness. I went and poured him out a glass of brandy. 'Drink that,' said I, 'drink it down.' I forced him to swallow it like a child; and, being still perished with the cold of the night, I followed his example.

'It has to be told, Mackellar,' said he. 'It must be told.' And he fell suddenly in a seat—my old lord's seat by the chimney-side—and was shaken with dry sobs.

Dismay came upon my soul; it was plain there was no help

in Mr Henry. 'Well,' said I, 'sit there, and leave all to me.'
And taking a candle in my hand, I set forth out of the room
in the dark house. There was no movement; I must suppose
that all had gone unobserved; and I was now to consider how
to smuggle through the rest with the like secrecy. It was no
hour for scruples; and I opened my lady's door without so
much as a knock, and passed boldly in.

'There is some calamity happened,' she cried, sitting
up in bed.

'Madam,' said I, 'I will go forth again into the passage;
and do you get as quickly as you can into your clothes. There
is much to be done.'

She troubled me with no questions, nor did she keep me
waiting. Ere I had time to prepare a word of that which
I must say to her, she was on the threshold signing me
to enter.

'Madam,' said I, 'if you cannot be very brave, I must go
elsewhere; for if no one helps me tonight, there is an end
of the house of Durrisdeer.'

'I am very courageous,' said she; and she looked at
me with a sort of smile, very painful to see, but very
brave too.

'It has come to a duel,' said I.

'A duel?' she repeated. 'A duel! Henry and——'

'And the Master,' said I. 'Things have been borne so long,
things of which you know nothing, which you would not
believe if I should tell. But tonight it went too far, and
when he insulted you—'

'Stop,' said she. 'He? Who?'

'O! madam,' cried I, my bitterness breaking forth, 'do you
ask me such a question? Indeed, then, I may go elsewhere
for help; there is none here!'

'I do not know in what I have offended you,' said she.
'Forgive me; put me out of this suspense.'

But I dared not tell her yet; I felt not sure of her; and
at the doubt, and under the sense of impotence it brought
with it, I turned on the poor woman with something near
to anger.

'Madam,' said I, 'we are speaking of two men: one of
them insulted you, and you ask me which. I will help you

to the answer. With one of these men you have spent all your hours: has the other reproached you? To one you have been always kind; to the other, as God sees me and judges between us two, I think not always: has his love ever failed you? Tonight one of these two men told the other, in my hearing—the hearing of a hired stranger,—that you were in love with him. Before I say one word, you shall answer your own question: Which was it? Nay, madam, you shall answer me another: If it has come to this dreadful end, whose fault is it?'

She stared at me like one dazzled. 'Good God!' she said once, in a kind of bursting exclamation; and then a second time in a whisper to herself: 'Great God!—In the name of mercy, Mackellar, what is wrong?' she cried. 'I am made up; I can hear all.'

'You are not fit to hear,' said I. 'Whatever it was, you shall say first it was your fault.'

'O!' she cried, with a gesture of wringing her hands, 'this man will drive me mad! Can you not put *me* out of your thoughts?'

'I think not once of you,' I cried. 'I think of none but my dear unhappy master.'

'Ah!' she cried, with her hand to her heart, 'is Henry dead?'

'Lower your voice,' said I. 'The other.'

I saw her sway like something stricken by the wind; and I know not whether in cowardice or misery, turned aside and looked upon the floor. 'These are dreadful tidings,' said I at length, when her silence began to put me in some fear; 'and you and I behove to be the more bold if the house is to be saved.' Still she answered nothing. 'There is Miss Katharine, besides,' I added: 'unless we bring this matter through, her inheritance is like to be of shame.'

I do not know if it was the thought of her child or the naked word shame that gave her deliverance; at least I had no sooner spoken than a sound passed her lips, the like of it I never heard; it was as though she had lain buried under a hill and sought to move that burthen. And the next moment she had found a sort of voice.

'It was a fight,' she whispered. 'It was not——?' and she paused upon the word.

'It was a fair fight on my dear master's part,' said I. 'As for the other, he was slain in the very act of a foul stroke.'

'Not now!' she cried.

'Madam,' said I, 'hatred of that man glows in my bosom like a burning fire; ay, even now he is dead. God knows, I would have stopped the fighting, had I dared. It is my shame I did not. But when I saw him fall, if I could have spared one thought from pitying of my master, it had been to exult in that deliverance.'

I do not know if she marked; but her next words were, 'My lord?'

'That shall be my part,' said I.

'You will not speak to him as you have to me?' she asked.

'Madam,' said I, 'have you not someone else to think of? Leave my lord to me.'

'Some one else?' she repeated.

'Your husband,' said I. She looked at me with a countenance illegible. 'Are you going to turn your back on him?' I asked.

Still she looked at me; then her hand went to her heart again. 'No,' said she.

'God bless you for that word!' I said. 'Go to him now, where he sits in the hall; speak to him—it matters not what you say; give him your hand; say, "I know all";—if God gives you grace enough, say, "forgive me."'

'God strengthen you, and make you merciful,' said she. 'I will go to my husband.'

'Let me light you there,' said I, taking up the candle.

'I will find my way in the dark,' she said, with a shudder, and I think the shudder was at me.

So we separated—she downstairs to where a little light glimmered in the hall door, I along the passage to my lord's room. It seems hard to say why, but I could not burst in on the old man as I could on the young woman; with whatever reluctance, I must knock. But his old slumbers were light, or perhaps he slept not; and at the first summons I was bidden enter.

He, too, sat up in bed; very aged and bloodless he looked; and whereas he had a certain largeness of appearance when dressed for daylight, he now seemed frail and little, and his face (the wig being laid aside) not bigger than a child's. This daunted me; nor less, the haggard surmise of misfortune in his eye. Yet his voice was even peaceful as he inquired my errand. I set my candle down upon a chair, leaned on the bed-foot, and looked at him.

'Lord Durrisdeer,' said I, 'It is very well known to you that I am a partisan in your family.'

'I hope we are none of us partisans,' said he. 'That you love my son sincerely, I have always been glad to recognise.'

'O! my lord, we are past the hour of these civilities,' I replied. 'If we are to save anything out of the fire, we must look the fact in its bare countenance. A partisan I am; partisans we have all been; it is as a partisan that I am here in the middle of the night to plead before you. Hear me; before I go, I will tell you why.'

'I would always hear you, Mr Mackellar,' said he, 'and that at any hour, whether of the day or night, for I would be always sure you had a reason. You spoke once before to very proper purpose; I have not forgotten that.'

'I am here to plead the cause of my master,' I said. 'I need not tell you how he acts. You know how he is placed. You know with what generosity he has always met your other—met your wishes,' I corrected myself, stumbling at that name of son. 'You know—you must know—what he has suffered—what he has suffered about his wife.'

'Mr Mackellar!' cried my lord, rising in bed like a bearded lion.

'You said you would hear me,' I continued. 'What you do not know, what you should know, one of the things I am here to speak of, is the persecution he must bear in private. Your back is not turned before one whom I dare not name to you falls upon him with the most unfeeling taunts; twits him—pardon me, my lord—twits him with your partiality, calls him Jacob, calls him clown, pursues him with ungenerous raillery, not to be borne by man.

And let but one of you appear, instantly he changes; and my master must smile and courtesy to the man who has been feeding him with insults; I know, for I have shared in some of it, and I tell you the life is insupportable. All these months it has endured; it began with the man's landing; it was by the name of Jacob that my master was greeted the first night.'

My lord made a movement as if to throw aside the clothes and rise. 'If there be any truth in this——' said he.

'Do I look like a man lying?' I interrupted, checking him with my hand.

'You should have told me at first,' he said.

'Ah, my lord! indeed I should, and you may well hate the face of this unfaithful servant!' I cried.

'I will take order,' said he, 'at once,' and again made the movement to rise.

Again I checked him. 'I have not done,' said I. 'Would God I had! All this my dear, unfortunate patron has endured without help or countenance. Your own best word, my lord, was only gratitude. O, but he was your son too! He had no other father. He was hated in the country, God knows how unjustly. He had a loveless marriage. He stood on all hands without affection or support—dear, generous, ill-fated, noble heart!'

'Your tears do you much honour and me much shame,' says my lord, with a palsied trembling. 'But you do me some injustice. Henry has been ever dear to me, very dear. James (I do not deny it, Mr Mackellar), James is perhaps dearer; you have not seen my James in quite a favourable light; he has suffered under his misfortunes; and we can only remember how great and how unmerited these were. And even now his is the more affectionate nature. But I will not speak of him. All that you say of Henry is most true; I do not wonder, I know him to be very magnanimous; you will say I trade upon the knowledge? It is possible; there are dangerous virtues: virtues that tempt the encroacher. Mr Mackellar, I will make it up to him; I will take order with all this. I have been weak; and, what is worse, I have been dull.'

'I must not hear you blame yourself, my lord, with that

which I have yet to tell upon my conscience,' I replied. 'You have not been weak; you have been abused by a devilish dissembler. You saw yourself how he had deceived you in the matter of his danger; he has deceived you throughout in every step of his career. I wish to pluck him from your heart; I wish to force your eyes upon your other son; ah, you have a son there!'

'No, no,' said he, 'two sons—I have two sons.'

I made some gesture of despair that struck him; he looked at me with a changed face. 'There is much worse behind?' he asked, his voice dying as it rose upon the question.

'Much worse,' I answered. 'This night he said these words to Mr Henry: "I have never known a woman who did not prefer me to you, and I think who did not continue to prefer me."'

'I will hear nothing against my daughter,' he cried; and from his readiness to stop me in this direction, I conclude his eyes were not so dull as I had fancied, and he had looked not without anxiety upon the siege of Mrs Henry.

'I think not of blaming her,' cried I. 'It is not that. These words were said in my hearing to Mr Henry; and if you find them not yet plain enough, these others but a little after: "Your wife, who is in love with me."'

'They have quarrelled?' he said.

I nodded.

'I must fly to them,' he said, beginning once again to leave his bed.

'No, no!' I cried, holding forth my hands.

'You do not know,' said he. 'These are dangerous words.'

'Will nothing make you understand, my lord?' said I.

His eyes besought me for the truth.

I flung myself on my knees by the bedside. 'O, my lord,' cried I, 'think on him you have left; think of this poor sinner whom you begot, whom your wife bore to you, whom we have none of us strengthened as we could; think of him, not of yourself; he is the other sufferer—think of him! That is the door for sorrow—Christ's door, God's door: O! it stands open. Think of him, even as he thought of you. *Who is to tell the old man?*"—these were his words.

It was for that I came; that is why I am here pleading at your feet.'

'Let me get up,' he cried, thrusting me aside, and was on his feet before myself. His voice shook like a sail in the wind, yet he spoke with a good loudness; his face was like the snow, but his eyes were steady and dry. 'Here is too much speech,' said he. 'Where was it?'

'In the shrubbery,' said I.

'And Mr Henry?' he asked. And when I had told him he knotted his old face in thought.

'And Mr James?' says he.

'I have left him lying,' said I, 'beside the candles.'

'Candles?' he cried. And with that he ran to the window, opened it, and looked abroad. 'It might be spied from the road.'

'Where none goes by at such an hour,' I objected.

'It makes no matter,' he said. 'One might.—Hark!' cries he. 'What is that?'

It was the sound of men very guardedly rowing in the bay; and I told him so.

'The free-traders,' said my lord. 'Run at once, Mackellar; put these candles out. I will dress in the meanwhile; and when you return we can debate on what is wisest.'

I groped my way downstairs, and out at the door. From quite a far way off a sheen was visible, making points of brightness in the shrubbery; in so black a night it might have been remarked for miles; and I blamed myself bitterly for my incaution. How much more sharply when I reached the place! One of the candlesticks was overthrown, and that taper quenched. The other burned steadily by itself, and made a broad space of light upon the frosted ground. All within that circle seemed, by the force of contrast and the overhanging blackness, brighter than by day. And there was the bloodstain in the midst; and a little farther off Mr Henry's sword, the pommel of which was of silver; but of the body, not a trace. My heart thumped upon my ribs, the hair stirred upon my scalp, as I stood there staring—so strange was the sight, so dire the fears it wakened. I looked right and left; the ground was so hard, it told no story. I stood and listened till my ears ached, but the night was hollow about me like an empty church; not even a ripple stirred upon the shore; it seemed you might have heard a pin drop in the county.

I put the candle out, and the blackness fell about me groping dark; it was like a crowd surrounding me; and I went back to the house of Durrisdeer, with my chin upon my shoulder, startling, as I went, with craven suppositions. In the door a figure moved to meet me, and I had near screamed with terror ere I recognised Mrs Henry.

'Have you told him?' says she.

'It was he who sent me,' said I. 'It is gone.—But why are you here?'

'It is gone!' she repeated. 'What is gone?'

'The body,' said I. 'Why are you not with your husband?'

'Gone?' said she. 'You cannot have looked. Come back.'

'There is no light now,' said I. 'I dare not.'

'I can see in the dark. I have been standing here so long—so long,' said she. 'Come, give me your hand.'

We returned to the shrubbery hand in hand, and to the fatal place.

'Take care of the blood,' said I.

'Blood?' she cried, and started violently back.

'I suppose it will be,' said I. 'I am like a blind man.'

'No,' said she, 'nothing! Have you not dreamed?'

'Ah, would to God we had!' cried I.

She spied the sword, picked it up, and seeing the blood, let it fall again with her hands thrown wide. 'Ah!' she cried, and then, with an instant courage, handled it the second time. 'I will take it back and clean it properly,' says she, and again looked about her on all sides. 'It cannot be that he was dead?' she added.

'There was no flutter of his heart,' said I, and then remembering: 'Why are you not with your husband?'

'It is no use,' said she; 'he will not speak to me.'

'Not speak to you?' I repeated. 'Oh! you have not tried.'

'You have a right to doubt me,' she replied, with a gentle dignity.

At this, for the first time, I was seized with sorrow for her. 'God knows, madam,' I cried, 'God knows I am not so hard as I appear; on this dreadful night who can veneer his words? But I am a friend to all who are not Henry Durie's enemies.'

'It is hard, then, you should hesitate about his wife,' said she.

I saw all at once, like the rending of a veil, how nobly she had borne this unnatural calamity, and how generously my reproaches.

'We must go back and tell this to my lord,' said I.

'Him I cannot face,' she cried.

'You will find him the least moved of all of us,' said I.

'And yet I cannot face him,' said she.

'Well,' said I, 'you can return to Mr Henry; I will see my lord.'

As we walked back, I bearing the candlesticks, she the sword—a strange burthen for that woman—she had another thought. 'Should we tell Henry?' she asked.

'Let my lord decide,' said I.

My lord was nearly dressed when I came to his chamber. He heard me with a frown. 'The free-traders,' said he. 'But whether dead or alive?'

'I thought him—' said I, and paused, ashamed of the word.

'I know; but you may very well have been in error. Why should they remove him if not living?' he asked. 'O! here is a great door of hope. It must be given out that he departed—as he came—without any note of preparation. We must save all scandal.'

I saw he had fallen, like the rest of us, to think mainly of the house. Now that all the living members of the family were plunged in irremediable sorrow, it was strange how we turned to that conjoint abstraction of the family itself, and sought to bolster up the airy nothing of its reputation: not the Duries only, but the hired steward himself.

'Are we to tell Mr Henry?' I asked him.

'I will see,' said he. 'I am going first to visit him; then I go forth with you to view the shrubbery and consider.'

We went downstairs into the hall. Mr Henry sat by the table with his head upon his hand, like a man of stone. His wife stood a little back from him, her hand at her mouth;

it was plain she could not move him. My old lord walked very steadily to where his son was sitting; he had a steady countenance, too, but methought a little cold. When he was come quite up, he held out both his hands and said, 'My son!'

With a broken, strangled cry, Mr Henry leaped up and fell on his father's neck, crying and weeping, the most pitiful sight that ever a man witnessed. 'O! father,' he cried, 'you know I loved him; you know I loved him in the beginning; I could have died for him—you know that! I would have given my life for him and you. O! say you know that. O! say you can forgive me. O, father, father, what have I done—what have I done? And we used to be bairns together!' and wept and sobbed, and fondled the old man, and clutched him about the neck, with a passion of a child in terror.

And then he caught sight of his wife (you would have thought for the first time), where she stood weeping to hear him, and in a moment had fallen at her knees. 'And O my lass,' he cried, 'you must forgive me, too! Not your husband—I have only been the ruin of your life. But you knew me when I was a lad; there was no harm in Henry Durie then; he meant aye to be a friend to you. It's him—it's the old bairn that played with you—O, can ye never, never forgive him?'

Throughout all this my lord was like a cold, kind spectator with his wits about him. At the first cry, which was indeed enough to call the house about us, he had said to me over his shoulder, 'Close the door.' And now he nodded to himself.

'We may leave him to his wife now,' says he. 'Bring a light, Mr Mackellar.'

Upon my going forth again with my lord, I was aware of a strange phenomenon; for though it was quite dark, and the night not yet old, methought I smelt the morning. At the same time there went a tossing through the branches of the evergreens, so that they sounded like a quiet sea, and the air puffed at times against our faces, and the flame of the candle shook. We made the more speed, I believe, being surrounded by this bustle; visited the scene of the duel, where my lord looked upon the blood with stoicism; and passing farther on toward the landing place, came at last upon some evidences of the truth. For, first of all, where was a pool across the path, the ice had been trodden in, plainly by more than one man's weight; next, and but a little farther, a young tree was broken, and down by the landing place, where the traders' boats were usually beached, another stain of blood marked where the body must have been infallibly set down to rest the bearers.

The stain we set ourselves to wash away with the sea-water, carrying it in my lord's hat; and as we were thus engaged there came up a sudden moaning gust and left us instantly benighted.

'It will come to snow,' says my lord; 'and the best thing that we could hope. Let us go back now; we can do nothing in the dark.'

As we went houseward, the wind being again subsided, we were aware of a strong pattering noise about us in the night; and when we issued from the shelter of the trees, we found it raining smartly.

Throughout the whole of this, my lord's clearness of mind, no less than his activity of body, had not ceased to minister to my amazement. He set the crown upon it in the council we held on our return. The free-traders had certainly secured the Master, though whether dead or alive we were still left to our conjectures; the rain would, long before day, wipe out all marks of the transaction; by this we must profit. The Master had unexpectedly come after the fall of night; it must now be given out he had as suddenly departed before the break of day; and, to make all this plausible, it now only remained for me to mount into the man's chamber, and pack and conceal his baggage. True, we still lay at the discretion of the traders; but that was the incurable weakness of our guilt.

I heard him, as I said, with wonder, and hastened to obey. Mr and Mrs Henry were gone from the hall; my lord, for warmth's sake, hurried to his bed; there was still no sign of stir among the servants, and as I went up the tower stair, and entered the dead man's room, a horror of solitude weighed upon my mind. To my extreme surprise, it was all in the disorder of departure. Of his three portmanteaus, two were already locked; a third lay open and near full. At once there flashed upon me some suspicion of the truth. The man had been going, after all; he had but waited upon Crail, as Crail waited upon the wind; early in the night the seamen had perceived the weather changing; the boat had come to give notice of the change and call the passenger aboard, and the boat's crew had stumbled on him lying in his blood. Nay, and there was more behind. This pre-arranged departure shed some light upon his inconceivable insult of the night before; It was a parting shot, hatred being no longer checked by policy. And, for another thing, the nature of that insult, and the conduct of Mrs Henry, pointed to one conclusion, which I have never verified, and can now never verify until the great assize—the conclusion that he had at last forgotten himself, had gone too far in his advances, and had been rebuffed. It can never be verified, as I say; but as I thought of it that morning among his baggage, the thought was sweet to me like honey.

Into the open portmanteau I dipped a little ere I closed it. The most beautiful lace and linen, many suits of those fine plain clothes in which he loved to appear; a book or two, and those of the best, Caesar's 'Commentaries,' a volume of Mr Hobbes, the 'Henriade' of M de Voltaire, a book upon the Indies, one on the mathematics, far beyond where I have studied: these were what I observed with very mingled feelings. But in the open portmanteau, no papers of any description. This set me musing. It was possible the man was dead; but, since the traders had carried him away, not likely. It was possible he might still die of his wound; but it was also possible he might not. And in this latter case I was determined to have the means of some defence.

One after another I carried his portmanteaus to a loft in the top of the house which we kept locked; went to my own room for my keys, and, returning to the loft, had the gratification to find two that fitted pretty well. In one of the portmanteaus there was a shagreen letter case, which I cut open with my knife; and thenceforth (so far as any credit went) the man was at my mercy. Here was a vast deal of gallant correspondence, chiefly of his Paris days; and, what was more to the purpose, here were the copies of his own reports to the English Secretary, and the originals of the Secretary's answers: a most damning series: such as to publish would be to wreck the Master's honour and to set a price upon his life. I chuckled to myself as I ran through the documents; I rubbed my hands, I sang aloud in my glee. Day found me at the pleasing task; nor did I then remit my diligence, except in so far as I went to the window—looked out for a moment, to see the frost quite gone, the world turned black again, and the rain and the wind driving in the day—and to assure myself that the lugger was gone from its anchorage, and the Master (whether dead or alive) now tumbling on the Irish Sea.

It is proper I should add in this place the very little I have subsequently angled out upon the doings of that night. It took me a long while to gather it; for we dared not openly ask, and the free-traders regarded me with enmity, if not with scorn. It was near six months before we even knew for certain that the man survived; and it was years before I learned from one of Crail's men, turned publican on his ill-gotten gain, some particulars which smack to me of truth. It seems the traders found the Master struggled on one elbow, and now staring round him, and now gazing at the candle, or at his hand, which was all bloodied, like a man stupid. Upon their coming, he would seem to have found his mind, bade them carry him aboard, and hold their tongues; and on the captain asking how he had come in such a pickle, replied with a burst of passionate swearing and incontinently fainted. They held some debate, but they were momently looking for a wind, they were highly paid to smuggle him to France, and did not care to delay. Besides which, he was well enough liked by these abominable wretches: they supposed him under capital sentence, knew not in what mischief he might have got his wound, and judged it a piece of good nature to remove him out of the way of danger. So he was taken aboard, recovered on the passage over, and was set ashore a convalescent at the Havre de Grace. What is truly notable: he said not a word to any one of the duel, and not a trader knows to this day in what quarrel, or by the hand of what adversary, he fell. With any other man I should have set this down to natural decency; with him, to pride. He could not bear to avow, perhaps even to himself, that he had been vanquished by one whom he had so much insulted and whom he so cruelly despised.

CHAPTER SIX

Summary of Events during the Master's Second Absence

OF THE HEAVY sickness which declared itself next morning I can think with equanimity, as of the last unmingled trouble that befell my master; and even that was perhaps a mercy in disguise; for what pains of the body could equal the miseries of his mind? Mrs Henry and I had the watching by the bed. My old lord called from time to time to take the news, but would not usually pass the door. Once, I remember, when hope was nigh gone, he stepped to the bedside, looked a while in his son's face, and turned away with a singular gesture of the head and hand thrown up, that remains upon my mind as something tragic; such grief and such a scorn of sublunary things were there expressed. But the most of the time Mrs Henry and I had the room to ourselves, taking turns by night, and bearing each other company by day, for it was dreary watching. Mr Henry, his shaven head bound in a napkin, tossed to and fro without remission, beating the bed with his hands. His tongue never lay; his voice ran continuously like a river, so that my heart was weary with the sound of it. It was notable, and to me inexpressibly mortifying, that he spoke all the while on matters of no import: comings and goings, horses—which he was ever calling to have saddled, thinking perhaps (the poor soul!) that he might ride away from his discomfort—matters of the garden, the salmon nets, and (what I particularly raged to hear) continually of his affairs, ciphering figures and holding disputation with the tenantry. Never a word of his father or his wife, nor of the Master, save only for a day or two, when his mind dwelled entirely in the past, and he supposed himself a boy again and upon some innocent child's play with his brother. What made this the more affecting: it appeared the Master had then run some peril of his life, for there was a cry—'O! Jamie will be drowned—O, save Jamie!' which he came over and over with a great deal of passion.

This, I say, was affecting, both to Mrs Henry and myself; but the balance of my master's wanderings did him little justice. It seemed he had set out to justify his brother's calumnies; as though he was bent to prove himself a man of a dry nature, immersed in money-getting. Had I been there alone, I would not have troubled my thumb; but all the while, as I listened, I was estimating the effect on the man's wife, and telling myself that he fell lower every day. I was the one person on the surface of the globe that comprehended him, and I was bound there should be yet another. Whether he was to die there and his virtues perish: or whether he should save his days and come back to that inheritance of sorrows, his right memory: I was bound he should be heartily lamented in the one case, and unaffectedly welcomed in the other, by the person he loved the most, his wife.

Finding no occasion of free speech, I bethought me at last of a kind of documentary disclosure; and for some nights, when I was off duty, and should have been asleep, I gave my time to the preparation of that which I may call my budget. But this I found to be the easiest portion of my task, and that which remained—namely, the presentation to my lady—almost more than I had fortitude to overtake. Several days I went about with my papers under my arm, spying for some juncture of talk to serve as introduction. I will not deny but that some offered; only when they did my tongue clove to the roof of my mouth; and I think I might have been carrying about my packet till this day, had not a fortunate accident delivered me from all my hesitations. This was at night, when I was once more leaving the room, the thing not yet done, and myself in despair at my own cowardice.

'What do you carry about with you, Mr Mackellar?' she asked. 'These last days, I see you always coming in and out with the same armful.'

I returned upon my steps without a word, laid the papers before her on the table, and left her to her reading. Of what that was, I am now to give you some idea; and the best will be to reproduce a letter of my own which came first in the budget, and of which (according to an excellent habitude) I have preserved the scroll. It will show, too, the moderation of my part in these affairs, a thing which some have called recklessly in question.

Durrisdeer, 1757.

HONOURED MADAM,

I trust I would not step out of my place without occasion; but I see how much evil has flowed in the past to all of your noble house from that unhappy and secretive fault of reticency, and the papers on which I venture to call your attention are family papers, and all highly worthy your acquaintance.

I append a schedule with some necessary observations,

And am,
Honoured Madam,
Your ladyship's obliged, obedient servant,

EPHRAIM MACKELLAR.

Schedule of Papers.

A.   Scroll of ten letters from Ephraim Mackellar to the Hon. James Durie, Esq., by courtesy Master of Ballantrae, during the latter's residence in Paris: under dates . . . (*follow the dates*) . . . *Nota:* to be read in connection with B and C.

B.   Seven original letters from the said Mr of Ballantrae to the said E. Mackellar, under dates . . . (*follow the dates*).

C.   Three original letters from the said Mr of Ballantrae to the Hon. Henry Durie, Esq., under dates . . . (*follow the dates*) . . . *Nota:* given me by Mr Henry to answer: copies of my answers A4, A5, and A9 of these productions. The purport of Mr Henry's communications, of which I can find no scroll, may be gathered from those of his unnatural brother.

D.   A correspondence, original and scroll, extending over a period of three years till January of the current year, between the said Mr of Ballantrae and

—— ——, Under Secretary of State; twenty-seven in all. *Nota:* found among the Master's papers.

Weary as I was with watching and distress of mind, it was impossible for me to sleep. All night long I walked in my chamber, revolving what should be the issue, and sometimes repenting the temerity of my immixture in affairs so private; and with the first peep of the morning I was at the sickroom door. Mrs Henry had thrown open the shutters, and even the window, for the temperature was mild. She looked steadfastly before her; where was nothing to see, or only the blue of the morning creeping among woods. Upon the stir of my entrance she did not so much as turn about her face: a circumstance from which I augured very ill.

'Madam,' I began; and then again, 'Madam'; but could make no more of it. Nor yet did Mrs Henry come to my assistance with a word. In this pass I began gathering up the papers where they lay scattered on the table; and the first thing that struck me, their bulk appeared to have diminished. Once I ran them through, and twice; but the correspondence with the Secretary of State, on which I had reckoned so much against the future, was nowhere to be found. I looked in the chimney; amid the smouldering embers, black ashes of paper fluttered in the draught; and at that my timidity vanished.

'Good God, madam,' cried I, in a voice not fitting for a sickroom, 'Good God, madam, what have you done with my papers?'

'I have burned them,' said Mrs Henry, turning about. 'It is enough, it is too much, that you and I have seen them.'

'This is a fine night's work that you have done!' cried I. 'And all to save the reputation of a man that ate bread by the shedding of his comrades' blood, as I do by the shedding of ink.'

'To save the reputation of that family in which you are a servant, Mr Mackellar,' she returned, 'and for which you have already done so much.'

'It is a family I will not serve much longer,' I cried, 'for I am driven desperate. You have stricken the sword out of my hands; you have left us all defenceless. I had always these letters I could shake over his head; and now—what is to do? We are so falsely situate we dare not show the man the door; the country would fly on fire against us; and I had this one hold upon him—and now it is gone—now he may come back tomorrow, and we must all sit down with him to dinner, go for a stroll with him on the terrace, or take a hand at cards, of all things, to divert his leisure! No, madam! God forgive you, if He can find it in His heart; for I cannot find it in mine.'

'I wonder to find you so simple, Mr Mackellar,' said Mrs Henry. 'What does this man value reputation? But he knows how high we prize it; he knows we would rather die than make these letters public; and do you suppose he would not trade upon the knowledge? What you call your sword, Mr Mackellar, and which had been one indeed against a man of any remnant of propriety, would have been but a sword of paper against him. He would smile in your face at such a threat. He stands upon his degradation, he makes that his strength; it is in vain to struggle with such characters.' She cried out this last a little desperately, and then with more quiet: 'No, Mr Mackellar; I have thought upon this matter all night, and there is no way out of it. Papers or no papers, the door of this house stands open for him; he is the rightful heir, forsooth! If we sought to exclude him, all would redound against poor Henry, and I should see him stoned again upon the streets. Ah! if Henry dies, it is a different matter! They have broke the entail for their own good purposes; the estate goes to my daughter; and I shall see who sets foot upon it. But if Henry lives, my poor Mr Mackellar, and that man returns, we must suffer: only this time it will be together.'

On the whole I was well pleased with Mrs Henry's attitude of mind; nor could I even deny there was some cogency in that which she advanced about the papers.

'Let us say no more about it,' said I. 'I can only be sorry I trusted a lady with the originals, which was an unbusinesslike proceeding at the best. As for what I said of leaving the service of the family, it was spoken with the tongue only; and you may set your mind at rest. I belong to Durrisdeer, Mrs Henry, as if I had been born there.'

I must do her the justice to say she seemed perfectly relieved; so that we began this morning, as we were to continue for so many years, on a proper ground of mutual indulgence and respect.

The same day, which was certainly prededicate to joy, we observed the first signal of recovery in Mr Henry; and about three of the following afternoon he found his mind again, recognising me by name with the strongest evidences of affection. Mrs Henry was also in the room, at the bedfoot; but it did not appear that he observed her. And indeed (the fever being gone) he was so weak that he made but the one effort and sank again into a lethargy. The course of his restoration was now slow, but equal; every day his appetite improved; every week we were able to remark an increase both of strength and flesh; and before the end of the month he was out of bed and had even begun to be carried in his chair upon the terrace.

It was perhaps at this time that Mrs Henry and I were the most uneasy in mind. Apprehension for his days was at an end; and a worse fear succeeded. Every day we drew consciously nearer to a day of reckoning; and the days passed on, and still there was nothing. Mr Henry bettered in strength, he held long talks with us on a great diversity of subjects, his father came and sat with him and went again; and still there was no reference to the late tragedy or to the former troubles which had brought it on. Did he remember, and conceal his dreadful knowledge? or was the whole blotted from his mind? This was the problem that kept us watching and trembling all day when we were in his company, and held us awake at night when we were in our lonely beds. We knew not even which alternative to hope for, both appearing so unnatural, and pointing so directly to an unsound brain. Once this fear offered, I observed his conduct with sedulous particularity. Something of the child he exhibited: a cheerfulness quite foreign to his previous character, an interest readily aroused, and then very tenacious, in small matters which he had heretofore despised. When he was stricken down, I was his only confidant, and I may say his only friend, and he was on terms of division with his wife; upon his recovery, all was changed, the past forgotten, the wife first and even single in his thoughts. He turned to her with all his emotions, like a child to its mother, and seemed secure of sympathy; called her in all his needs with something of that querulous familiarity that marks a certainty of indulgence; and I must say, in justice to the woman, he was never disappointed. To her, indeed, this changed behaviour was inexpressibly affecting; and I think she felt it secretly as a reproach; so that I have seen her, in early days, escape out of the room that she might indulge herself in weeping. But to me the change appeared not natural; and viewing it along with all the rest, I began to wonder, with many head-shakings, whether his reason were perfectly erect.

As this doubt stretched over many years, endured indeed until my master's death, and clouded all our subsequent relations, I may well consider of it more at large. When he was able to resume some charge of his affairs, I had many opportunities to try him with precision. There was no lack of understanding, nor yet of authority; but the old continuous interest had quite departed; he grew readily fatigued, and fell to yawning; and he carried into money relations, where it is certainly out of place, a facility that bordered upon slackness. True, since we had no longer the exactions of the Master to contend against, there was the less occasion to raise strictness into principle or do battle for a farthing. True, again, there was nothing excessive in these relaxations, or I would have been no party to them. But the whole thing marked a change, very slight yet very perceptible; and though no man could say my master had gone at all out of his mind, no man could deny that he had drifted from his character. It was the same to the end, with his manner and appearance. Some of the heat of the fever lingered in his veins: his movements a little hurried, his speech notably more voluble, yet neither truly amiss. His whole mind stood open to happy impressions, welcoming these and making much of them; but the smallest suggestion of trouble or sorrow he received with visible impatience, and dismissed again with immediate relief. It was to this temper that he owed the felicity of his later days; and yet here it was, if anywhere, that you could call the man insane. A great part of this life consists in contemplating what we cannot cure; but Mr Henry, if he could not dismiss solicitude by an effort of the mind, must instantly and at whatever cost annihilate the cause of it; so that he played alternately the ostrich and the bull. It is to this strenuous cowardice of pain that I have to set down all the unfortunate and excessive steps of his subsequent career. Certainly this was the reason of his beating M'Manus, the groom, a thing so much out of all his former practice, and which awakened so much comment at the time. It is to this, again, that I must lay the total loss of near upon two hundred pounds, more than the half of which I could have saved if his impatience would have suffered me. But he preferred loss or any desperate extreme to a continuance of mental suffering.

All this has led me far from our immediate trouble: whether he remembered or had forgotten his late dreadful act; and if he remembered, in what light he viewed it. The truth burst upon us suddenly, and was indeed one of the chief surprises of my life. He had been several times abroad, and was now beginning to walk a little with an arm, when it chanced I should be left alone with him upon the terrace. He turned to me with a singular furtive smile, such as schoolboys use when in fault; and says he, in a private whisper, and without the least preface: 'Where have you buried him?'

I could not make one sound in answer.

'Where have you buried him?' he repeated. 'I want to see his grave.'

I conceived I had best take the bull by the horns. 'Mr Henry,' said I, 'I have news to give that will rejoice you exceedingly. In all human likelihood, your hands are clear of blood. I reason from certain indices; and by these it should appear your brother was not dead, but was carried in a swound on board the lugger. But now he may be perfectly recovered.'

What there was in his countenance I could not read. 'James?' he asked.

'Your brother James,' I answered. 'I would not raise a hope that may be found deceptive, but in my heart I think it very probable he is alive.'

'Ah!' says Mr Henry; and suddenly rising from his seat with more alacrity than he had yet discovered, set one finger on my breast, and cried at me in a kind of screaming whisper, 'Mackellar'—these were his words—'nothing can kill that man. He is not mortal. He is bound upon my back to all eternity—to all God's eternity!' says he, and, sitting down again, fell upon a stubborn silence.

A day or two after, with the same secret smile, and first looking about as if to be sure we were alone, 'Mackellar,' said he, 'when you have any intelligence, be sure and let me know. We must keep an eye upon him, or he will take us when we least expect.'

'He will not show face here again,' said I.

'O yes, he will,' said Mr Henry. 'Wherever I am, there will he be.' And again he looked all about him.

'You must not dwell upon this thought, Mr Henry,' said I.

'No,' said he, 'that is a very good advice. We will never think of it, except when you have news. And we do not know yet,' he added; 'he may be dead.'

The manner of his saying this convinced me thoroughly of what I had scarce ventured to suspect: that, so far from suffering any penitence for the attempt, he did but lament his failure. This was a discovery I kept to myself, fearing it might do him a prejudice with his wife. But I might have saved myself the trouble; she had divined it for herself, and found the sentiment quite natural. Indeed, I could not but say that there were three of us, all of the same mind; nor could any news have reached Durrisdeer more generally welcome than tidings of the Master's death.

This brings me to speak of the exception, my old lord. As soon as my anxiety for my own master began to be relaxed, I was aware of a change in the old gentleman, his father, that seemed to threaten mortal consequences. His face was pale and swollen; as he sat in the chimney-side with his Latin, he would drop off sleeping and the book roll in the ashes; some days he would drag his foot, others stumble in speaking. The amenity of his behaviour appeared more extreme; full of excuses for the least trouble, very thoughtful for all; to myself, of a most flattering civility. One day, that he had sent for his lawyer, and remained a long while private, he met me as he was crossing the hall with painful footsteps, and took me kindly by the hand. 'Mr Mackellar,' said he, 'I have had many occasions to set a proper value on your services; and today, when I re-cast my will, I have taken the freedom to name you for one of my executors. I believe you bear love enough to our house to render me this service.' At that very time he passed the greater portion of his days in slumber, from which it was often difficult to rouse him; seemed to have lost all count of years, and had several times (particularly on waking) called for his wife and for an old servant whose very gravestone was now green with moss. If I had been put to my oath, I must have declared he was incapable of testing; and yet there was never a will drawn more sensible in every trait, or showing a more excellent judgement both of persons and affairs.

His dissolution, though it took not very long, proceeded by infinitesimal gradations. His faculties decayed together steadily; the power of his limbs was almost gone, he was extremely deaf, his speech had sunk into mere mumblings; and yet to the end he managed to discover something of his former courtesy and kindness, pressing the hand of any that helped him, presenting me with one of his Latin books, in which he had laboriously traced my name, and in a thousand ways reminding us of the greatness of that loss which it might almost be said we had already suffered. To the end, the power of articulation returned to him in flashes; it seemed he had only forgotten the art of speech as a child forgets his lesson, and at times he would call some part of it to mind. On the last night of his life he suddenly broke silence with these words from Virgil: '*Gnatique patrisque, alma, precor, miserere,*' perfectly uttered, and with a fitting accent. At the sudden clear sound of it we started from our several occupations; but it was in vain we turned to him; he sat there silent, and, to all appearance, fatuous. A little later he was had to bed with more difficulty than ever before; and some time in the night, without any mortal violence, his spirit fled.

At a far later period I chanced to speak of these particulars with a doctor of medicine, a man of so high a reputation that I scruple to adduce his name. By his view of it, father and son both suffered from the same affection: the father from the strain of his unnatural sorrows—the son, perhaps in the excitation of the fever; each had ruptured a vessel in the brain, and there was probably (my doctor added) some predisposition in the family to accidents of that description. The father sank, the son recovered all the externals of a healthy man; but it is like there was some destruction in those delicate tissues where the soul resides and does her earthly business; her heavenly, I would fain hope, cannot be thus obstructed by material accidents. And yet, upon a more mature opinion, it matters not one jot; for He who shall pass judgment on the records of our life is the same that formed us in frailty.

The death of my old lord was the occasion of a fresh surprise to us who watched the behaviour of his successor. To any considering mind, the two sons had between them slain their father, and he who took the sword might be even said to have slain him with his hand; but no such thought appeared to trouble my new lord. He was becomingly grave; I could scarce say sorrowful, or only with a pleasant sorrow; talking of the dead with a regretful cheerfulness, relating old examples of his character, smiling at them with a good conscience; and when the day of the funeral came round, doing the honours with exact propriety. I could perceive, besides, that he found a solid gratification in his accession to the title; the which he was punctilious in exacting.

And now there came upon the scene a new character, and one that played his part, too, in the story; I mean the present lord, Alexander, whose birth (17th July 1757) filled the cup of my poor master's happiness. There was nothing then left him to wish for; nor yet leisure to wish for it. Indeed, there never was a parent so fond and doting as he showed himself. He was continually uneasy in his son's absence. Was the child abroad? the father would be watching the clouds in case it rained. Was it night? he would rise out of his bed to observe its slumbers. His conversation grew even wearyful to strangers, since he talked of little but his son. In matters relating to the estate, all was designed with a particular eye to Alexander; and it would be:—'Let us put it in hand at once, that the wood may be grown against Alexander's majority'; or, 'This will fall in again handsomely for Alexander's marriage.' Every day this absorption of the man's nature became more observable, with many touching and some very blameworthy particulars. Soon the child could walk abroad with him, at first on the terrace, hand in hand, and afterward at large about the policies; and this grew to be my lord's chief occupation. The sound of their two voices (audible a great way off, for they spoke loud) became familiar in the neighbourhood; and for my part I found it more agreeable than the sound of birds. It was pretty to see the pair returning full of briers, and the father as flushed and sometimes as bemuddied as the child, for they were equal sharers in all sorts of boyish entertainment, digging in the beach, damming of streams, and what not; and I have seen them gaze through a fence at cattle with the same childish contemplation.

The mention of these rambles brings me to a strange scene of which I was a witness. There was one walk I never followed myself without emotion, so often had I gone there upon miserable errands, so much had there befallen against the house of Durrisdeer. But the path lay handy from all points beyond the Muckle Ross; and I was driven, although much against my will, to take my use of it perhaps once in the two months. It befell when Mr Alexander was of the age of six or seven, I had some business on the far side in the morning, and entered the shrubbery, on my homeward way, about nine of a bright forenoon. It was that time of year when the woods are all in their spring colours, the thorns all in flower, and the birds in the high season of their singing. In contrast to this merriment, the shrubbery was only the more sad, and I the more oppressed by its associations. In this situation of spirit it struck me disagreeably to hear voices a little way in front, and to recognise the tones of my lord and Mr Alexander. I pushed ahead, and came presently into their view. They stood together in the open space where the duel was, my lord with his hand on his son's shoulder, and speaking with some gravity. At least, as he raised his head upon my coming, I thought I could perceive his countenance to lighten.

'Ah!' says he, 'here comes the good Mackellar. I have just been telling Sandie the story of this place, and how there was a man whom the devil tried to kill, and how near he came to kill the devil instead.'

I had thought it strange enough he should bring the child into that scene; that he should actually be discoursing of his act, passed measure. But the worst was yet to come: for he added, turning to his son—'You can ask Mackellar; he was here and saw it.'

'Did you really see the devil?' asked the child.

'I have not heard the tale,' I replied; 'and I am in a press of business.' So far I said, sourly, fencing with the embarrassment of the position; and suddenly the bitterness of the past, and the terror of that scene by candlelight, rushed in upon my mind. I bethought me that, for a difference of a second's quickness in parade, the child before me might have never seen the day; and the emotion that always fluttered round my heart in that dark shrubbery burst forth in words. 'But so much is true,' I cried, 'that I have met the devil in these woods, and seen him foiled here. Blessed be God that we escaped with life—blessed be God that one stone yet stands upon another in the walls of Durrisdeer! And, O! Mr Alexander, if ever you come by this spot, though it was a hundred years hence, and you came with the gayest and the highest in the land, I would step aside and remember a bit prayer.'

My lord bowed his head gravely. 'Ah!' says he, 'Mackellar is always in the right. Come, Alexander, take your bonnet off.' And with that he uncovered, and held out his hand. 'O Lord,' said he, 'I thank Thee and my son thanks Thee, for Thy manifold great mercies. Let us have peace for a little; defend us from the evil man. Smite him, O Lord, upon the lying mouth!' The last broke out of him like a cry; and at that, whether remembered anger choked his utterance, or whether he perceived this was a singular sort of prayer, at least he suddenly came to a full stop; and, after a moment, set back his hat upon his head.

'I think you have forgot a word, my lord,' said I. '"Forgive us our trespasses, as we forgive them that trespass against us. For Thine is the kingdom, and the power, and the glory, for ever and ever. Amen.'''

'Ah! that is easy saying,' said my lord. 'That is very easy saying, Mackellar. But for me to forgive!—I think I would cut a very silly figure if I had the affectation to pretend it.'

'The bairn, my lord!' said I, with some severity, for I thought his expressions little fitted for the ears of children.

'Why, very true,' said he. 'This is dull work for a bairn. Let's go nesting.'

I forget if it was the same day, but it was soon after, my lord, finding me alone, opened himself a little more on the same head.

'Mackellar,' he said, 'I am now a very happy man.'

'I think so indeed, my lord,' said I, 'and the sight of it gives me a light heart.'

'There is an obligation in happiness—do you not think so?' says he musingly.

'I think so indeed,' says I, 'and one in sorrow too. If we are not here to try to do the best, in my humble opinion the sooner we are away the better for all parties.'

'Any, but if you were in my shoes, would you forgive him?' asks my lord.

The suddenness of the attack a little gravelled me, 'It is a duty laid upon us strictly,' said I.

'Hut!' said he. 'These are expressions! Do you forgive the man yourself?'

'Well—no!' said I. 'God forgive me, I do not.'

'Shake hands upon that!' cries my lord, with a kind of joviality.

'It is an ill sentiment to shake hands upon,' said I, 'for Christian people. I think I will give you mine on some more evangelical occasion.'

This I said, smiling a little; but as for my lord, he went from the room laughing aloud.

For my lord's slavery to the child I can find no expression adequate. He lost himself in that continual thought: business, friends, and wife being all alike forgotten, or only remembered with a painful effort, like that of one struggling with a posset. It was most notable in the matter of his wife.

Since I had known Durrisdeer, she had been the burthen of his thought and the loadstone of his eyes; and now she was quite cast out. I have seen him come to the door of a room, look round, and pass my lady over as though she were a dog before the fire. It would be Alexander he was seeking, and my lady knew it well. I have heard him speak to her so ruggedly that I nearly found it in my heart to intervene: the cause would still be the same, that she had in some way thwarted Alexander. Without doubt this was in the nature of a judgment on my lady; without doubt she had the tables turned upon her, as only Providence can do it; she who had been cold so many years to every mark of tenderness, it was her part now to be neglected.

An odd situation resulted: that we had once more two parties in the house, and that now I was of my lady's. Not that ever I lost the love I bore my master. But, for one thing, he had the less use for my society. For another, I could not but compare the case of Mr Alexander with that of Miss Katharine; for whom my lord had never found the least attention. And for a third, I was wounded by the change he discovered to his wife, which struck me in the nature of an infidelity. I could not but admire, besides, the constancy and kindness she displayed. Perhaps her sentiment to my lord, as it had been founded from the first in pity, was that rather of a mother than a wife; perhaps it pleased her—if I may say so—to behold her two children so happy in each other; the more as one had suffered so unjustly in the past. But, for all that, and though I could never trace in her one spark of jealousy, she must fall back for society on poor neglected Miss Katharine; and I, on my part, came to pass my spare hours more and more with the mother and daughter. It would be easy to make too much of this division, for it was a pleasant family, as families go; still the thing existed; whether my lord knew it or not, I am in doubt. I do not think he did; he was bound up so entirely in his son; but the rest of us knew it, and in a manner suffered from the knowledge.

What troubled us most, however, was the great and growing danger to the child. My lord was his father over again; it was to be feared the son would prove a second

Master. Time has proved these fears to have been quite exaggerate. Certainly there is no more worthy gentleman today in Scotland than the seventh Lord Durrisdeer. Of my own exodus from his employment it does not become me to speak, above all in a memorandum written only to justify his father . . .

[EDITOR'S NOTE.—*Five pages of Mr Mackellar's MS are here omitted. I have gathered from their perusal an impression that Mr Mackellar, in his old age, was rather an exacting servant. Against the seventh Lord Durrisdeer (with whom, at any rate, we have no concern) nothing material is alleged.*—R.L.S.]

. . . But our fear at the time was lest he should turn out, in the person of his son, a second edition of his brother. My lady had tried to interject some wholesome discipline; she had been glad to give that up, and now looked on with secret dismay; sometimes she even spoke of it by hints; and sometimes, when there was brought to her knowledge some monstrous instance of my lord's indulgence, she would betray herself in a gesture or perhaps an exclamation. As for myself, I was haunted by the thought both day and night: not so much for the child's sake as for the father's. The man had gone to sleep, he was dreaming a dream, and any rough awakening must infallibly prove mortal. That he should survive the child's death was inconceivable; and the fear of its dishonour made me cover my face.

It was this continual preoccupation that screwed me up at last to a remonstrance: a matter worthy to be narrated in detail. My lord and I sat one day at the same table upon some tedious business of detail; I have said that he had lost his former interest in such occupations; he was plainly itching to be gone, and he looked fretful, weary, and methought older than I had ever previously observed. I suppose it was the haggard face that put me suddenly upon my enterprise.

'My lord,' said I, with my head down, and feigning to continue my occupation—'or, rather, let me call you again by the name of Mr Henry, for I fear your anger, and want you to think upon old times——'

'My good Mackellar!' said he; and that in tones so kindly that I had near forsook my purpose. But I called to mind that I was speaking for his good, and stuck to my colours.

'Has it never come in upon your mind what you are doing?' I asked.

'What I am doing?' he repeated; 'I was never good at guessing riddles.'

'What you are doing with your son?' said I.

'Well,' said he, with some defiance in his tone, 'and what am I doing with my son?'

'Your father was a very good man,' says I, straying from the direct path. 'But do you think he was a wise father?'

There was a pause before he spoke, and then: 'I say nothing against him,' he replied. 'I had the most cause perhaps; but I say nothing.'

'Why, there it is,' said I. 'You had the cause at least. And yet your father was a good man; I never knew a better, save on the one point, nor yet a wiser. Where he stumbled, it is highly possible another man should fall. He had the two sons—'

My lord rapped suddenly and violently on the table.

'What is this?' cried he. 'Speak out!'

'I will, then,' said I, my voice almost strangled with the thumping of my heart. 'If you continue to indulge Mr Alexander, you are following in your father's footsteps. Beware, my lord, lest (when he grows up) your son should follow in the Master's.'

I had never meant to put the thing so crudely; but in the extreme of fear there comes a brutal kind of courage, the most brutal indeed of all; and I burnt my ships with that plain word. I never had the answer. When I lifted my head my lord had risen to his feet, and the next moment he fell heavily on the floor. The fit or seizure endured not very long; he came to himself vacantly, put his hand to his head, which I was then supporting, and says he, in a broken voice: 'I have been ill,' and a little after: 'Help me.' I got him to his feet, and he stood pretty well, though he kept hold of the table. 'I have been ill, Mackellar,' he said again. 'Something broke, Mackellar—or was going to break, and then all swam away. I think I was very angry. Never you mind, Mackellar;

never you mind, my man. I wouldnae hurt a hair upon your head. Too much has come and gone. It's a certain thing between us two. But I think, Mackellar, I will go to Mrs Henry—I think I will go to Mrs Henry,' said he, and got pretty steadily from the room, leaving me overcome with penitence.

Presently the door flew open, and my lady swept in with flashing eyes. 'What is all this?' she cried. 'What have you done to my husband? Will nothing teach you your position in this house? Will you never cease from making and meddling?'

'My lady,' said I, 'since I have been in this house I have had plenty of hard words. For a while they were my daily diet, and I swallowed them all. As for today, you may call me what you please; you will never find the name hard enough for such a blunder. And yet I meant it for the best.'

I told her all with ingenuity, even as it is written here; and when she had heard me out, she pondered, and I could see her animosity fall. 'Yes,' she said, 'you meant well indeed. I have had the same thought myself, or the same temptation rather, which makes me pardon you. But, dear God, can you not understand that he can bear no more? He can bear no more!' she cried. 'The cord is stretched to snapping. What matters the future if he have one or two good days?'

'Amen,' said I. 'I will meddle no more. I am pleased enough that you should recognise the kindness of my meaning.'

'Yes,' said my lady; 'but when it came to the point, I have to suppose your courage failed you; for what you said was said cruelly.' She paused, looking at me; then suddenly smiled a little, and said a singular thing: 'Do you know what you are, Mr Mackellar? You are an old maid.'

No more incident of any note occurred in the family until the return of that ill-starred man, the Master. But I have to place here a second extract from the memoirs of Chevalier Burke, interesting in itself, and highly necessary for my purpose. It is our only sight of the Master on his Indian travels; and the first word in these pages of Secundra Dass. One fact, it is to observe, appears here very clearly, which if we had known some twenty years ago, how many calamities and sorrows had been spared!—that Secundra Dass spoke English.

CHAPTER SEVEN

Adventure of Chevalier Burke in India
EXTRACTED FROM HIS MEMOIRS

. . . HERE WAS I, therefore, on the streets of that city, the name of which I cannot call to mind, while even then I was so ill acquainted with its situation that I knew not whether to go south or north. The alert being sudden, I had run forth without shoes or stockings; my hat had been struck from my head in the mellay; my kit was in the hands of the English; I had no companion but the cipaye, no weapon but my sword, and the devil a coin in my pocket. In short, I was for all the world like one of those calendars with whom Mr Galland has made us acquainted in his elegant tales. These gentlemen, you will remember, were forever falling in with extraordinary incidents; and I was myself upon the brink of one so astonishing that I protest I cannot explain it to this day.

The cipaye was a very honest man; he had served many years with the French colours, and would have let himself be cut to pieces for any of the brave countrymen of Mr Lally. It is the same fellow (his name has quite escaped me) of whom I have narrated already a surprising instance of generosity of mind—when he found Mr de Fessac and myself upon the ramparts, entirely overcome with liquor, and covered us with straw while the commandant was passing by. I consulted him, therefore, with perfect freedom. It was a fine question what to do; but we decided at last to escalade a garden wall, where we could certainly sleep in the shadow of the trees, and might perhaps find an occasion to get hold of a pair of slippers and a turban. In that part of the city we had only the difficulty of the choice, for it was a quarter consisting entirely of walled gardens, and the lanes which divided them were at that hour of the night deserted. I gave the cipaye a back, and we had soon dropped into a large enclosure full of trees. The place was soaking with the dew, which, in that country, is exceedingly unwholesome, above all to whites; yet my fatigue was so extreme that I was already half asleep, when the cipaye recalled me to my senses. In the far end of the enclosure a bright light had suddenly shone out, and continued to burn steadily among the leaves. It was a circumstance highly unusual in such a place and hour; and, in our situation, it behoved us to proceed with some timidity. The cipaye was sent to reconnoitre, and pretty soon returned with the intelligence that we had fallen extremely amiss, for the house belonged to a white man, who was in all likelihood English.

'Faith,' says I, 'if there is a white man to be seen, I will have a look at him; for, the Lord be praised! there are more sorts than the one!'

The cipaye led me forward accordingly to a place from which I had a clear view upon the house. It was surrounded with a wide verandah; a lamp, very well trimmed, stood upon the floor of it, and on either side of the lamp there sat a man, cross-legged, after the Oriental manner. Both, besides, were bundled up in muslin like two natives; and yet one of them was not only a white man, but a man very well known to me and the reader, being indeed that very Master of Ballantrae of whose gallantry and genius I have had to speak so often. Word had reached me that he was come to the Indies, though we had never met and I heard little of his occupations. But, sure, I had no sooner recognised him, and found myself in the arms of so old a comrade, than I supposed my tribulations were quite done. I stepped plainly forth into the light of the moon, which shone exceeding strong, and hailing Ballantrae by name, made him in a few words master of my grievous situation. He turned, started the least thing in the world, looked me fair in the face while I was speaking, and when I had done addressed himself to his companion in the barbarous native dialect. The second person, who was of an extraordinary delicate appearance, with legs like walking canes and fingers like the stalk of a tobacco pipe,[1] now rose to his feet.

'The Sahib,' says he, 'understands no English language.

1. *Note by Mr Mackellar.*—Plainly Secundra Dass.—E. McK.

I understand it myself, and I see you make some small mistake—O! which may happen very often. But the Sahib would be glad to know how you come in a garden?'

'Ballantrae!' I cried, 'have you the damned impudence to deny me to my face?'

Ballantrae never moved a muscle, staring at me like an image in a pagoda.

'The Sahib understands no English language,' says the native, as glib as before. 'He be glad to know how you come in a garden?'

'O! the divil fetch him,' says I. 'He would be glad to know how I come in a garden, would he? Well, now, my dear man, just have the civility to tell the Sahib, with my kind love, that we are two soldiers here whom he never met and never heard of, but the cipaye is a broth of a boy, and I am a broth of a boy myself; and if we don't get a full meal of meat, and a turban, and slippers, and the value of a gold mohur in small change as a matter of convenience, bedad, my friend, I could lay my finger on a garden where there is going to be trouble.'

They carried their comedy so far as to converse a while in Hindustanee; and then says the Hindu, with the same smile, but sighing as if he were tired of the repetition, 'The Sahib would be glad to know how you come in a garden?'

'Is that the way of it?' says I, and laying my hand on my sword hilt I bade the cipaye draw.

Ballantrae's Hindu, still smiling, pulled out a pistol from his bosom, and though Ballantrae himself never moved a muscle I knew him well enough to be sure he was prepared.

'The Sahib thinks you better go away,' says the Hindu.

Well, to be plain, it was what I was thinking myself; for the report of a pistol would have been, under Providence, the means of hanging the pair of us.

'Tell the Sahib I consider him no gentleman,' says I, and turned away with a gesture of contempt.

I was not gone three steps when the voice of the Hindu called me back. 'The Sahib would be glad to know if you are a damn low Irishman,' says he; and at the words Ballantrae smiled and bowed very low.

'What is that?' says I.

'The Sahib say you ask your friend Mackellar,' says the Hindu. 'The Sahib he cry quits.'

'Tell the Sahib I will give him a cure for the Scots fiddle when next we meet,' cried I.

The pair were still smiling as I left.

There is little doubt some flaws may be picked in my own behaviour; and when a man, however gallant, appeals to posterity with an account of his exploits, he must almost certainly expect to share the fate of Cæsar and Alexander, and to meet with some detractors. But there is one thing that can never be laid at the door of Francis Burke: he never turned his back on a friend . . .

(Here follows a passage which the Chevalier Burke has been at the pains to delete before sending me his manuscript. Doubtless it was some very natural complaint of what he supposed to be an indiscretion on my part; though, indeed, I can call none to mind. Perhaps Mr Henry was less guarded; or it is just possible the Master found the means to examine my correspondence, and himself read the letter from Troyes: in revenge for which this cruel jest was perpetrated on Mr Burke in his extreme necessity. The Master, for all his wickedness, was not without some natural affection; I believe he was sincerely attached to Mr Burke in the beginning; but the thought of treachery dried up the springs of his very shallow friendship, and his detestable nature appeared naked.—E.McK.)

CHAPTER EIGHT

The Enemy in the House

IT IS A STRANGE thing that I should be at a stick for a date—the date, besides, of an incident that changed the very nature of my life, and sent us all into foreign lands. But the truth is, I was stricken out of all my habitudes, and find my journals very ill redd-up, the day not indicated sometimes for a week or two together, and the whole fashion of the thing like that of a man near desperate. It was late in March at least, or early in April, 1764. I had slept heavily, and wakened with a premonition of some evil to befall. So strong was this upon my spirit that I hurried downstairs in my shirt and breeches, and my hand (I remember) shook upon the rail. It was a cold, sunny morning, with a thick white frost; the blackbirds sang exceeding sweet and loud about the house of Durrisdeer, and there was a noise of the sea in all the chambers. As I came by the doors of the hall, another sound arrested me—of voices talking. I drew nearer, and stood like a man dreaming. Here was certainly a human voice, and that in my own master's house, and yet I knew it not; certainly human speech, and that in my native land; and yet, listen as I pleased, I could not catch one syllable. An old tale started up in my mind of a fairy wife (or perhaps only a wandering stranger), that came to the place of my fathers some generations back, and stayed the matter of a week, talking often in a tongue that signified nothing to the hearers; and went again, as she had come, under cloud of night, leaving not so much as a name behind her. A little fear I had, but more curiosity; and I opened the hall door, and entered.

The supper things still lay upon the table; the shutters were still closed, although day peeped in the divisions; and the great room was lighted only with a single taper and the shining of the fire. Close in the chimney sat two men. The one that was wrapped in a cloak and wore boots, I knew at once: it was the bird of ill omen back again. Of the other, who was set close to the red embers, and made up into a bundle like a mummy, I could but see that he was an alien, of a darker hue than any man of Europe, very fraily built, with a singular tall forehead, and a secret eye. Several packets and a small valise were on the floor; and to judge by the smallness of this luggage, and by the condition of the Master's boots, grossly patched by some unscrupulous country cobbler, evil had not prospered.

He rose upon my entrance; our eyes crossed; and I know not why it should have been, but my courage rose like a lark on a May morning.

'Ha!' said I, 'is this you?'—and I was pleased with the unconcern of my own voice.

'It is even myself, worthy Mackellar,' says the Master.

'This time you have brought the black dog visibly upon your back,' I continued.

'Referring to Secundra Dass?' asked the Master. 'Let me present you. He is a native gentleman of India.'

'Hum!' said I. 'I am no great lover either of you or your friends, Mr Bally. But I will let a little daylight in, and have a look at you.' And so saying, I undid the shutters of the eastern window.

By the light of the morning I could perceive the man was changed. Later, when we were all together, I was more struck to see how lightly time had dealt with him; but the first glance was otherwise.

'You are getting an old man,' said I.

A shade came upon his face. 'If you could see yourself,' said he, 'you would perhaps not dwell upon the topic.'

'Hut!' I returned, 'old age is nothing to me. I think I have been always old; and I am now, I thank God, better known and more respected. It is not every one that can say that, Mr Bally! The lines in *your* brow are calamities; your life begins to close in upon you like a prison; death will soon be rapping at the door; and I see not from what source you are to draw your consolations.'

Here the Master addressed himself to Secundra Dass in Hindustanee, from which I gathered (I freely confess, with

a high degree of pleasure) that my remarks annoyed him.
All this while, you may be sure, my mind had been busy
upon other matters, even while I rallied my enemy; and
chiefly as to how I should communicate secretly and quickly
with my lord. To this, in the breathing space now given
me, I turned all the forces of my mind; when, suddenly
shifting my eyes, I was aware of the man himself standing
in the doorway, and, to all appearance, quite composed. He
had no sooner met my looks than he stepped across the
threshold. The Master heard him coming, and advanced
upon the other side; about four feet apart, these brothers
came to a full pause, and stood exchanging steady looks,
and then my lord smiled, bowed a little forward, and turned
briskly away.

'Mackellar,' says he, 'we must see to breakfast for these
travellers.'

It was plain the Master was a trifle disconcerted; but
he assumed the more impudence of speech and manner.
'I am as hungry as a hawk,' says he. 'Let it be something
good, Henry.'

My lord turned to him with the same hard smile. 'Lord
Durrisdeer,' says he.

'O! never in the family,' returned the Master.

'Every one in this house renders me my proper title,' says
my lord. 'If it please you to make an exception, I will leave
you to consider what appearance it will bear to strangers,
and whether it may not be translated as an effect of impotent
jealousy.'

I could have clapped my hands together with delight:
the more so as my lord left no time for any answer, but,
bidding me with a sign to follow him, went straight out of
the hall.

'Come quick,' says he; 'we have to sweep vermin from the
house.' And he sped through the passages, with so swift a
step that I could scarce keep up with him, straight to the
door of John Paul, the which he opened without summons
and walked in. John was, to all appearance, sound asleep,
but my lord made no pretence of waking him.

'John Paul,' said he, speaking as quietly as ever I heard
him, 'you served my father long, or I would pack you

from the house like a dog. If in half an hour's time I find you gone, you shall continue to receive your wages in Edinburgh. If you linger here or in St Bride's—old man, old servant, and altogether—I shall find some very astonishing way to make you smart for your disloyalty. Up and begone. The door you let them in by will serve for your departure. I do not choose my son shall see your face again.'

'I am rejoiced to find you bear the thing so quietly,' said I, when we were forth again by ourselves.

'Quietly!' cries he, and put my hand suddenly against his heart, which struck upon his bosom like a sledge.

At this revelation I was filled with wonder and fear. There was no constitution could bear so violent a strain—his least of all, that was unhinged already; and I decided in my mind that we must bring this monstrous situation to an end.

'It would be well, I think, if I took word to my lady,' said I. Indeed, he should have gone himself, but I counted—not in vain—on his indifference.

'Ay,' says he, 'do. I will hurry breakfast: we must all appear at the table, even Alexander; it must appear we are untroubled.'

I ran to my lady's room, and with no preparatory cruelty disclosed my news.

'My mind was long ago made up,' said she. 'We must make our packets secretly today, and leave secretly to-night. Thank Heaven, we have another house! The first ship that sails shall bear us to New York.'

'And what of him?' I asked.

'We leave him Durrisdeer,' she cried. 'Let him work his pleasure upon that.'

'Not so, by your leave,' said I. 'There shall be a dog at his heels that can hold fast. Bed he shall have, and board, and a horse to ride upon, if he behave himself; but the keys—if you think well of it, my lady—shall be left in the hands of one Mackellar. There will be good care taken; trust him for that.'

'Mr Mackellar,' she cried, 'I thank you for that thought. All shall be left in your hands. If we must go into a savage country, I bequeath it to you to take our vengeance. Send

Macconochie to St Bride's, to arrange privately for horses and to call the lawyer. My lord must leave procuration.'

At that moment my lord came to the door, and we opened our plan to him.

'I will never hear of it,' he cried; 'he would think I feared him. I will stay in my own house, please God, until I die. There lives not the man can beard me out of it. Once and for all, here I am, and here I stay, in spite of all the devils in hell.' I can give no idea of the vehemency of his words and utterance; but we both stood aghast, and I in particular, who had been a witness of his former self-restraint.

My lady looked at me with an appeal that went to my heart and recalled me to my wits. I made her a private sign to go, and when my lord and I were alone, went up to him where he was racing to and fro in one end of the room like a half-lunatic, and set my hand firmly on his shoulder.

'My lord,' says I, 'I am going to be the plain dealer once more; if for the last time, so much the better, for I am grown weary of the part.'

'Nothing will change me,' he answered. 'God forbid I should refuse to hear you; but nothing will change me.' This he said firmly, with no signal of the former violence, which already raised my hopes.

'Very well,' said I. 'I can afford to waste my breath.' I pointed to a chair, and he sat down and looked at me. 'I can remember a time when my lady very much neglected you,' said I.

'I never spoke of it while it lasted,' returned my lord, with a high flush of colour; 'and it is all changed now.'

'Do you know how much?' I said. 'Do you know how much it is all changed? The tables are turned, my lord! It is my lady that now courts you for a word, a look—ay, and courts you in vain. Do you know with whom she passes her days while you are out gallivanting in the policies? My lord, she is glad to pass them with a certain dry old grieve of the name of Ephraim Mackellar; and I think you may be able to remember what that means, for I am the more in a mistake or you were once driven to the same company yourself.'

'Mackellar!' cries my lord, getting to his feet. 'O my God, Mackellar!'

'It is neither the name of Mackellar nor the name of God that can change the truth,' said I; 'and I am telling you the fact. Now for you, that suffered so much, to deal out the same suffering to another, is that the part of any Christian? But you are so swallowed up in your new friend that the old are all forgotten. They are all clean vanished from your memory. And yet they stood by you at the darkest; my lady not the least. And does my lady ever cross your mind? Does it ever cross your mind what she went through that night?—or what manner of a wife she has been to you thenceforward?—or in what kind of a position she finds herself today? Never. It is your pride to stay and face him out, and she must stay along with you. O! my lord's pride—that's the great affair! And yet she is the woman, and you are a great hulking man! She is the woman that you swore to protect; and, more betoken, the own mother of that son of yours!'

'You are speaking very bitterly, Mackellar,' said he; 'but, the Lord knows, I fear you are speaking very true. I have not proved worthy of my happiness. Bring my lady back.'

My lady was waiting near at hand to learn the issue. When I brought her in, my lord took a hand of each of us, and laid them both upon his bosom. 'I have had two friends in my life,' said he. 'All the comfort ever I had, it came from one or other. When you two are in a mind, I think I would be an ungrateful dog—' He shut his mouth very hard, and looked on us with swimming eyes. 'Do what ye like with me,' says he, 'only don't think—' He stopped again. 'Do what you please with me: God knows I love and honour you.' And dropping our two hands, he turned his back and went and gazed out of the window. But my lady ran after, calling his name, and threw herself upon his neck in a passion of weeping.

I went out and shut the door behind me, and stood and thanked God from the bottom of my heart.

At the breakfast board, according to my lord's design, we were all met. The Master had by that time plucked off his patched boots and made a toilet suitable to the hour; Secundra Dass was no longer bundled up in wrappers, but wore a decent plain black suit, which misbecame him strangely; and the pair were at the great window, looking forth, when the family entered. They turned; and the black man (as they had already named him in the house) bowed almost to his knees, but the Master was for running forward like one of the family. My lady stopped him, curtsying low from the far end of the hall, and keeping her children at her back. My lord was a little in front: so there were the three cousins of Durrisdeer face to face. The hand of time was very legible on all; I seemed to read in their changed faces a *memento mori;* and what affected me still more, it was the wicked man that bore his years the handsomest. My lady was quite transfigured into the matron, a becoming woman for the head of a great tableful of children and dependants. My lord was grown slack in his limbs; he stooped; he walked with a running motion, as though he had learned again from Mr Alexander; his face was drawn; it seemed a trifle longer than of old; and it wore at times a smile very singularly mingled, and which (in my eyes) appeared both bitter and pathetic. But the Master still bore himself erect, although perhaps with effort; his brow barred about the centre with imperious lines, his mouth set as for command. He had all the gravity and something of the splendour of Satan in the 'Paradise Lost.' I could not help but see the man with admiration, and was only surprised that I saw him with so little fear.

But indeed (as long as we were at the table) it seemed as if his authority were quite vanished and his teeth all drawn. We had known him a magician that controlled the elements; and here he was, transformed into an ordinary gentleman, chatting like his neighbours at the breakfast board. For now the father was dead, and my lord and lady reconciled, in what ear was he to pour his calumnies? It came upon me in a kind of vision how hugely I had overrated the man's subtlety. He had his malice still; he was false as ever; and, the occasion being gone that made his strength, he sat there impotent; he was still the viper, but now spent his venom on a file. Two more thoughts occurred to me while yet we sat at breakfast: the first, that he was abashed—I had almost said, distressed—to find his wickedness quite unavailing; the second, that perhaps my lord was in the right, and we did amiss to fly from our dismasted enemy. But my poor master's leaping heart came in my mind, and I remembered it was for his life we played the coward.

When the meal was over, the Master followed me to my room, and, taking a chair (which I had never offered him), asked me what was to be done with him.

'Why, Mr Bally,' said I, 'the house will still be open to you for a time.'

'For a time?' says he. 'I do not know if I quite take your meaning.'

'It is plain enough,' said I. 'We keep you for our reputation; as soon as you shall have publicly disgraced yourself by some of your misconduct, we shall pack you forth again.'

'You are become an impudent rogue,' said the Master, bending his brows at me dangerously.

'I learned in a good school,' I returned. 'And you must have perceived yourself that with my old lord's death your power is quite departed. I do not fear you now, Mr Bally; I think even—God forgive me—that I take a certain pleasure in your company.'

He broke out in a burst of laughter, which I clearly saw to be assumed.

'I have come with empty pockets,' says he, after a pause.

'I do not think there will be any money going,' I replied. 'I would advise you not to build on that.'

'I shall have something to say on the point,' he returned.

'Indeed?' said I. 'I have not a guess what it will be, then.'

'O! you affect confidence,' said the Master. 'I have still one strong position—that you people fear a scandal, and I enjoy it.'

'Pardon me, Mr Bally,' says I. 'We do not in the least fear a scandal against you.'

He laughed again. 'You have been studying repartee,' he said. 'But speech is very easy, and sometimes very deceptive.

I warn you fairly: you will find me vitriol in the house. You would do wiser to pay money down and see my back.' And with that he waved his hand to me and left the room.

A little after, my lord came with the lawyer, Mr Carlyle; a bottle of old wine was brought, and we all had a glass before we fell to business. The necessary deeds were then prepared and executed, and the Scots estates made over in trust to Mr Carlyle and myself.

'There is one point, Mr Carlyle,' said my lord, when these affairs had been adjusted, 'on which I wish that you would do us justice. This sudden departure coinciding with my brother's return will be certainly commented on. I wish you would discourage any conjunction of the two.'

'I will make a point of it, my lord,' said Mr Carlyle. 'The Mas—Mr Bally does not, then, accompany you?'

'It is a point I must approach,' said my lord. 'Mr Bally remains at Durrisdeer, under the care of Mr Mackellar; and I do not mean that he shall even know our destination.'

'Common report, however—' began the lawyer.

'Ah! but, Mr Carlyle, this is to be a secret quite among ourselves,' interrupted my lord. 'None but you and Mackellar are to be made acquainted with my movements.'

'And Mr Bally stays here? Quite so,' said Mr Carlyle. 'The powers you leave—' Then he broke off again. 'Mr Mackellar, we have a rather heavy weight upon us.'

'No doubt, sir,' said I.

'No doubt,' said he. 'Mr Bally will have no voice?'

'He will have no voice,' said my lord; 'and, I hope, no influence. Mr Bally is not a good adviser.'

'I see,' said the lawyer.—'By the way, has Mr Bally means?'

'I understand him to have nothing,' replied my lord. 'I give him table, fire, and candle in this house.'

'And in the matter of an allowance? If I am to share the responsibility, you will see how highly desirable it is that I should understand your views,' said the lawyer. 'On the question of an allowance?'

'There will be no allowance,' said my lord. 'I wish Mr Bally to live very private. We have not always been gratified with his behaviour.'

'And in the matter of money,' I added, 'he has shown himself an infamous bad husband. Glance your eye upon that docket, Mr Carlyle, where I have brought together the different sums the man has drawn from the estate in the last fifteen or twenty years. The total is pretty.'

Mr Carlyle made the motion of whistling. 'I had no guess of this,' said he. 'Excuse me once more, my lord, if I appear to push you; but it is really desirable I should penetrate your intentions. Mr Mackellar might die, when I should find myself alone upon this trust. Would it not be rather your lordship's preference that Mr Bally should—ahem—should leave the country?'

My lord looked at Mr Carlyle. 'Why do you ask that?' said he.

'I gather, my lord, that Mr Bally is not a comfort to his family,' says the lawyer, with a smile.

My lord's face became suddenly knotted. 'I wish he was in hell!' cried he, and filled himself a glass of wine, but with a hand so tottering that he spilled the half into his bosom. This was the second time that, in the midst of the most regular and wise behaviour, his animosity had spurted out. It startled Mr Carlyle, who observed my lord thenceforth with covert curiosity; and to me it restored the certainty that we were acting for the best in view of my lord's health and reason.

Except for this explosion the interview was very successfully conducted. No doubt Mr Carlyle would talk, as lawyers do, little by little. We could thus feel we had laid the foundations of a better feeling in the country, and the man's own misconduct would certainly complete what we had begun. Indeed, before his departure, the lawyer showed us there had already gone abroad some glimmerings of the truth.

'I should perhaps explain to you, my lord,' said he, pausing, with his hat in his hand, 'that I have not been altogether surprised with your lordship's dispositions in the case of Mr Bally. Something of this nature oozed out when he was last in Durrisdeer. There was some talk of a woman at St Bride's, to whom you had behaved extremely handsome, and Mr Bally with no small degree of cruelty. There was the

entail, again, which was much controverted. In short, there
was no want of talk, back and forward; and some of our
wiseacres took up a strong opinion. I remained in suspense,
as became one of my cloth; but Mr Mackellar's docket here
has finally opened my eyes.—I do not think, Mr Mackellar,
that you and I will give him that much rope.'

The rest of that important day passed prosperously through.
It was our policy to keep the enemy in view, and I took my
turn to be his watchman with the rest. I think his spirits
rose as he perceived us to be so attentive, and I know that
mine insensibly declined. What chiefly daunted me was the
man's singular dexterity to worm himself into our troubles.
You may have felt (after a horse accident) the hand of a bone-
setter artfully divide and interrogate the muscles, and settle
strongly on the injured place? It was so with the Master's
tongue, that was so cunning to question; and his eyes, that
were so quick to observe. I seemed to have said nothing, and
yet to have let all out. Before I knew where I was the man
was condoling with me on my lord's neglect of my lady and
myself, and his hurtful indulgence to his son. On this last
point I perceived him (with panic fear) to return repeatedly.
The boy had displayed a certain shrinking from his uncle;
it was strong in my mind his father had been fool enough
to indoctrinate the same, which was no wise beginning: and
when I looked upon the man before me, still so handsome,
so apt a speaker, with so great a variety of fortunes to relate,
I saw he was the very personage to captivate a boyish fancy.
John Paul had left only that morning; it was not to be
supposed he had been altogether dumb upon his favourite
subject: so that here would be Mr Alexander in the part of
Dido, with a curiosity inflamed to hear; and there would be
the Master, like a diabolical Aeneas, full of matter the most
pleasing in the world to any youthful ear, such as battles,
sea disasters, flights, the forests of the West, and (since his
later voyage) the ancient cities of the Indies. How cunningly
these baits might be employed, and what an empire might
be so founded, little by little, in the mind of any boy, stood
obviously clear to me. There was no inhibition, so long as
the man was in the house, that would be strong enough to

hold these two apart; for if it be hard to charm serpents, it is no very difficult thing to cast a glamour on a little chip of manhood not very long in breeches. I recalled an ancient sailorman who dwelt in a lone house beyond the Figgate Whins (I believe, he called it after Portobello), and how the boys would troop out of Leith on a Saturday, and sit and listen to his swearing tales, as thick as crows about a carrion: a thing I often remarked as I went by, a young student, on my own more meditative holiday diversion. Many of these boys went, no doubt, in the face of an express command; many feared, and even hated, the old brute of whom they made their hero; and I have seen them flee from him when he was tipsy, and stone him when he was drunk. And yet there they came each Saturday! How much more easily would a boy like Mr Alexander fall under the influence of a high-looking, high-spoken gentleman adventurer, who should conceive the fancy to entrap him; and the influence gained, how easy to employ it for the child's perversion!

I doubt if our enemy had named Mr Alexander three times before I perceived which way his mind was aiming— all this train of thought and memory passed in one pulsation through my own—and you may say I started back as though an open hole had gaped across a pathway. Mr Alexander: there was the weak point, there was the Eve in our perishable paradise; and the serpent was already hissing on the trail.

I promise you, I went the more heartily about the preparations; my last scruple gone, the danger of delay written before me in huge characters. From that moment forth I seem not to have sat down or breathed. Now I would be at my post with the Master and his Indian; now in the garret buckling a valise; now sending forth Macconochie by the side postern and the wood-path to bear it to the trysting place; and, again, snatching some words of counsel with my lady. This was the *verso* of our life in Durrisdeer that day; but on the *recto* all appeared quite settled, as of a family at home in its paternal seat; and what perturbation may have been observable, the Master would set down to the blow of his unlooked-for coming, and the fear he was accustomed to inspire.

Supper went creditably off, cold salutations passed, and the company trooped to their respective chambers. I attended the Master to the last. We had put him next door to his Indian, in the north wing; because that was the most distant and could be severed from the body of the house with doors. I saw he was a kind friend or a good master (whichever it was) to his Secundra Dass—seeing to his comfort; mending the fire with his own hand, for the Indian complained of cold; inquiring as to the rice on which the stranger made his diet; talking with him pleasantly in the Hindustanee, while I stood by, my candle in my hand, and affected to be overcome with slumber. At length the Master observed my signals of distress. 'I perceive,' says he, 'that you have all your ancient habits: early to bed and early to rise. Yawn yourself away!'

Once in my own room, I made the customary motions of undressing, so that I might time myself; and when the cycle was complete, set my tinderbox ready, and blew out my taper. The matter of an hour afterward I made a light again, put on my shoes of list that I had worn by my lord's sickbed, and set forth into the house to call the voyagers. All were dressed and waiting—my lord, my lady, Miss Katharine, Mr Alexander, my lady's woman Christie; and I observed the effect of secrecy even upon quite innocent persons, that one after another showed in the chink of the door a face as white as paper. We slipped out of the side postern into a night of darkness, scarce broken by a star or two; so that at first we groped and stumbled and fell among the bushes. A few hundred yards up the woodpath Macconochie was waiting us with a great lantern; so the rest of the way we went easy enough, but still in a kind of guilty silence. A little beyond the abbey the path debouched on the main road; and some quarter of a mile farther, at the place called Eagles, where the moors begin, we saw the lights of the two carriages stand shining by the wayside. Scarce a word or two was uttered at our parting, and these regarded business: a silent grasping of hands, a turning of faces aside, and the thing was over; the horses broke into a trot, the lamplight sped like Will-o'-the-Wisp upon the broken moorland, it dipped beyond Stony Brae; and there were Macconochie and I alone with our lantern on the road.

There was one thing more to wait for, and that was the reappearance of the coach upon Cartmore. It seems they must have pulled up upon the summit, looked back for a last time, and seen our lantern not yet moved away from the place of separation. For a lamp was taken from a carriage, and waved three times up and down by way of a farewell. And then they were gone indeed, having looked their last on the kind roof of Durrisdeer, their faces toward a barbarous country. I never knew before the greatness of that vault of night in which we two poor serving-men—the one old, and the old elderly—stood for the first time deserted; I had never felt before my own dependency upon the countenance of others. The sense of isolation burned in my bowels like a fire. It seemed that we who remained at home were the true exiles, and that Durrisdeer and Solwayside, and all that made my country native, its air good to me, and its language welcome, had gone forth and was far over the sea with my old masters.

The remainder of that night I paced to and fro on the smooth highway, reflecting on the future and the past. My thoughts, which at first dwelled tenderly on those who were just gone, took a more manly temper as I considered what remained for me to do. Day came upon the inland mountain-tops, and the fowls began to cry, and the smoke of home-steads to arise in the brown bosom of the moors, before I turned my face homeward, and went down the path to where the roof of Durrisdeer shone in the morning by the sea.

At the customary hour I had the Master called, and awaited his coming in the hall with a quiet mind. He looked about him at the empty room and the three covers set.

'We are a small party,' said he. 'How comes that?'

'This is the party to which we must grow accustomed,' I replied.

He looked at me with a sudden sharpness. 'What is all this?' said he.

'You and I and your friend Mr Dass are now all the company,' I replied. 'My lord, my lady, and the children are gone upon a voyage.'

'Upon my word!' said he. 'Can this be possible? I have

indeed fluttered your Volscians in Corioli! But this is no reason why our breakfast should go cold. Sit down, Mr Mackellar, if you please'—taking, as he spoke, the head of the table, which I had designed to occupy myself—'and as we eat, you can give me the details of this evasion.'

I could see he was more affected than his language carried, and I determined to equal him in coolness. 'I was about to ask you to take the head of the table,' said I; 'for though I am now thrust into the position of your host, I could never forget that you were, after all, a member of the family.'

For a while he played the part of entertainer, giving directions to Macconochie, who received them with an evil grace, and attending specially upon Secundra. 'And where has my good family withdrawn to?' he asked carelessly.

'Ah! Mr Bally, that is another point,' said I. 'I have no orders to communicate their destination.'

'To me,' he corrected.

'To any one,' said I.

'It is the less pointed,' said the Master; '*c'est de bon ton*: my brother improves as he continues. And I, dear Mr Mackellar?'

'You will have bed and board, Mr Bally,' said I. 'I am permitted to give you the run of the cellar, which is pretty reasonably stocked. You have only to keep well with me, which is no very difficult matter, and you shall want neither for wine nor a saddle-horse.'

He made an excuse to send Macconochie from the room.

'And for money?' he inquired. 'Have I to keep well with my good friend Mackellar for my pocket-money also? This is a pleasing return to the principles of boyhood.'

'There was no allowance made,' said I; 'but I will take it on myself to see you are supplied in moderation.'

'In moderation?' he repeated. 'And you will take it on yourself?' He drew himself up, and looked about the hall at the dark rows of portraits. 'In the name of my ancestors, I thank you,' says he; and then, with a return to irony, 'But there must certainly be an allowance for Secundra Dass?' he said. 'It is not possible they have omitted that?'

'I will make a note of it, and ask instructions when I write,' said I.

And he, with a sudden change of manner, and leaning forward with an elbow on the table—'Do you think this entirely wise?'

'I execute my orders, Mr Bally,' said I.

'Profoundly modest,' said the Master; 'perhaps not equally ingenuous. You told me yesterday my power was fallen with my father's death. How comes it, then, that a peer of the realm flees under cloud of night out of a house in which his fathers have stood several sieges? that he conceals his address, which must be a matter of concern to his Gracious Majesty and to the whole republic? and that he should leave me in possession, and under the paternal charge of his invaluable Mackellar? This smacks to me of a very considerable and genuine apprehension.'

I sought to interrupt him with some not very truthful denegation; but he waved me down, and pursued his speech.

'I say, it smacks of it,' he said; 'but I will go beyond that, for I think the apprehension grounded. I came to this house with some reluctancy. In view of the manner of my last departure, nothing but necessity could have induced me to return. Money, however, is that which I must have. You will not give with a good grace; well, I have the power to force it from you. Inside of a week, without leaving Durrisdeer, I will find out where these fools are fled to. I will follow; and when I have run my quarry down, I will drive a wedge into that family that shall once more burst it into shivers. I shall see then whether my Lord Durrisdeer' (said with indescribable scorn and rage) 'will choose to buy my absence; and you will all see whether, by that time, I decide for profit or revenge.'

I was amazed to hear the man so open. The truth is, he was consumed with anger at my lord's successful flight, felt himself to figure as a dupe, and was in no humour to weigh language.

'Do you consider *this* entirely wise?' said I, copying his words.

'These twenty years I have lived by my poor wisdom,' he answered with a smile that seemed almost foolish in its vanity.

'And come out a beggar in the end,' said I, 'if beggar be a strong enough word for it.'

'I would have you to observe, Mr Mackellar,' cried he, with a sudden imperious heat, in which I could not but admire him, 'that I am scrupulously civil; copy me in that, and we shall be the better friends.'

Throughout this dialogue I had been incommoded by the observation of Secundra Dass. Not one of us, since the first word, had made a feint of eating: our eyes were in each other's faces—you might say, in each other's bosoms; and those of the Indian troubled me with a certain changing brightness, as of comprehension. But I brushed the fancy aside, telling myself once more he understood no English; only, from the gravity of both voices, and the occasional scorn and anger in the Master's, smelled out there was something of import in the wind.

For the matter of three weeks we continued to live together in the house of Durrisdeer: the beginning of that most singular chapter of my life—what I must call my intimacy with the Master. At first he was somewhat changeable in his behaviour: now civil, now returning to his old manner of flouting me to my face; and in both I met him half-way. Thanks be to Providence, I had now no measure to keep with the man; and I was never afraid of black brows, only of naked swords. So that I found a certain entertainment in these bouts of incivility, and was not always ill inspired in my rejoinders. At last (it was at supper) I had a droll expression that entirely vanquished him. He laughed again; and again; and 'Who would have guessed,' he cried, 'that this old wife had any wit under his petticoats?'

'It is no wit, Mr Bally,' said I: 'a dry Scots humour, and something of the driest.' And, indeed, I never had the least pretension to be thought a wit.

From that hour he was never rude with me, but all passed between us in a manner of pleasantry. One of our chief times of daffing was when he required a horse, another bottle, or some money. He would approach me then after the manner of a schoolboy, and I would carry it on by way of being his father: on both sides, with an infinity of mirth. I could not but perceive that he thought more of me, which tickled that poor part of mankind, the vanity. He dropped, besides (I must suppose unconsciously), into a manner that was not only familiar, but even friendly; and this, on the part of one who had so long detested me, I found the more insidious. He went little abroad; sometimes even refusing invitations. 'No,' he would say, 'what do I care for these thick-headed bonnet-lairds? I will stay at home, Mackellar; and we shall share a bottle quietly, and have one of our good talks.' And, indeed, mealtime at Durrisdeer must have been a delight to any one, by reason of the brilliancy of the discourse. He would often express wonder at his former indifference to my society. 'But, you see,' he would add, 'we were upon opposite sides. And so we are today; but let us never speak of that. I would think much less of you if you were not staunch to your employer.' You are to consider he seemed to me quite impotent for any evil; and how it is a most engaging form of flattery when (after many years) tardy justice is done to a man's character and parts. But I have no thought to excuse myself. I was to blame; I let him cajole me, and, in short, I think the watchdog was gone sound asleep, when he was suddenly aroused.

I should say the Indian was continually travelling to and fro in the house. He never spoke, save in his own dialect and with the Master; walked without sound; and was always turning up where you would least expect him, fallen into a deep abstraction, from which he would start (upon your coming) to mock you with one of his grovelling obeisances. He seemed so quiet, so frail, and so wrapped in his own fancies, that I came to pass him over without much regard, or even to pity him for a harmless exile from his country. And yet without doubt the creature was still eavesdropping; and without doubt it was through his stealth and my security that our secret reached the Master.

It was one very wild night, after supper, and when we had been making more than usually merry, that the blow fell on me.

'This is all very fine,' says the Master, 'but we should do better to be buckling our valise.'

'Why so?' I cried. 'Are you leaving?'

'We are all leaving tomorrow in the morning,' said he. 'For the port of Glascow first, thence for the province of New York.'

I suppose I must have groaned aloud.

'Yes,' he continued, 'I boasted; I said a week, and it has taken me near twenty days. But never mind; I shall make it up; I will go the faster.'

'Have you the money for this voyage?' I asked.

'Dear and ingenuous personage, I have,' said he. 'Blame me, if you choose, for my duplicity; but while I have been wringing shillings from my daddy, I had a stock of my own put by against a rainy day. You will pay for your own passage, if you choose to accompany us on our flank march; I have enough for Secundra and myself, but not more—enough to be dangerous, not enough to be generous. There is, however, an outside seat upon the chaise which I will let you have upon a moderate commutation; so that the whole menagerie can go together—the house-dog, the monkey, and the tiger.'

'I go with you,' said I.

'I count upon it,' said the Master. 'You have seen me foiled; I mean you shall see me victorious. To gain that I will risk wetting you like a sop in this wild weather.'

'And at least,' I added, 'you know very well you could not throw me off.'

'Not easily,' said he. 'You put your finger on the point with your usual excellent good sense. I never fight with the inevitable.'

'I suppose it is useless to appeal to you?' said I.

'Believe me, perfectly,' said he.

'And yet, if you would give me time, I could write—' I began.

'And what would be my Lord Durrisdeer's answer?' asks he.

'Ay,' said I, 'that is the rub.'

'And, at any rate, how much more expeditious that I should go myself!' says he. 'But all this is quite a waste of breath. At seven to-morrow the chaise will be at the door. For I start from the door, Mackellar; I do not skulk through woods and take my chaise upon the wayside—shall we say, at Eagles?'

My mind was now thoroughly made up. 'Can you spare me quarter of an hour at St Bride's?' said I. 'I have a little necessary business with Carlyle.'

'An hour, if you prefer,' said he. 'I do not seek to deny that the money for your seat is an object to me; and you could always get the first to Glascow with saddle-horses.'

'Well,' said I, 'I never thought to leave old Scotland.'

'It will brisken you up,' says he.

'This will be an ill journey for someone,' I said. 'I think, sir, for you. Something speaks in my bosom; and so much it says plain—that this is an ill-omened journey.'

'If you take to prophecy,' says he, 'listen to that.'

There came up a violent squall off the open Solway, and the rain was dashed on the great windows.

'Do ye ken what that bodes, warlock?' said he, in a broad accent; 'that there'll be a man Mackellar unco sick at sea.'

When I got to my chamber, I sat there under a painful excitation, hearkening to the turmoil of the gale, which struck full upon that gable of the house. What with the pressure on my spirits, the eldritch cries of the wind among the turret tops, and the perpetual trepidation of the masoned house, sleep fled my eyelids utterly. I sat by my taper, looking on the black panes of the window, where the storm appeared continually on the point of bursting in its entrance; and upon that empty field I beheld a perspective of consequences that made the hair to rise upon my scalp. The child corrupted, the home broken up, my master dead, or worse than dead, my mistress plunged in desolation—all these I saw before me painted brightly on the darkness; and the outcry of the wind appeared to mock at my inaction.

CHAPTER NINE

Mr Mackellar's Journey with the Master

THE CHAISE CAME to the door in a strong drenching mist. We took our leave in silence: the house of Durrisdeer standing with drooping gutters and windows closed, like a place dedicate to melancholy. I observed the Master kept his head out, looking back on these splashed walls and glimmering roofs, till they were suddenly swallowed in the mist; and I must suppose some natural sadness fell upon the man at this departure; or was it some prevision of the end? At least, upon our mounting the long brae from Durrisdeer, as we walked side by side in the wet, he began first to whistle and then to sing the saddest of our country tunes, which sets folk weeping in a tavern, 'Wandering Willie.' The set of words he used with it I have not heard elsewhere, and could never come by any copy; but some of them which were the most appropriate to our departure linger in my memory. One verse began—

Home was home then, my dear, full of kindly faces;
Home was home then, my dear, happy for the child.

And ended somewhat thus—

Now, when day dawns on the brow of the moorland,
  Lone stands the house, and the chimney-stone is cold,
Lone let it stand, now the folks are all departed,
    The kind hearts, the true hearts, that loved
      the place of old.

I could never be a judge of the merit of these verses; they were so hallowed by the melancholy of the air, and were sung (or rather 'soothed') to me by a master singer at a time so fitting. He looked in my face when he had done, and saw that my eyes watered.

'Ah! Mackellar,' said he, 'do you think I have never a regret?'

'I do not think you could be so bad a man,' said I, 'if you had not all the machinery to be a good one.'

'No, not all,' says he: 'not all. You are there in error. The malady of not wanting, my evangelist.' But methought he sighed as he mounted again into the chaise.

All day long we journeyed in the same miserable weather: the mist besetting us closely, the heavens incessantly weeping on my head. The road lay over moorish hills, where was no sound but the crying of moor-fowl in the wet heather and the pouring of the swollen burns. Sometimes I would doze off in slumber, when I would find myself plunged at once in some foul and ominous nightmare, from the which I would awake strangling. Sometimes, if the way was steep and the wheels turning slowly, I would overhear the voices from within, talking in that tropical tongue which was to me as inarticulate as the piping of the fowls. Sometimes, at a longer ascent, the Master would set foot to ground and walk by my side, mostly without speech. And all the time, sleeping or waking, I beheld the same black perspective of approaching ruin; and the same pictures rose in my view, only they were now painted upon hillside mist. One, I remember, stood before me with the colours of a true illusion. It showed me my lord seated at a table in a small room; his head, which was at first buried in his hands, he slowly raised, and turned upon me a countenance from which hope had fled. I saw it first on the black window panes, my last night in Durrisdeer; it haunted and returned upon me half the voyage through; and yet it was no effect of lunacy, for I have come to a ripe old age with no decay of my intelligence; nor yet (as I was then tempted to suppose) a heaven sent warning of the future, for all manner of calamities befell, not that calamity—and I saw many pitiful sights, but never that one.

It was decided we should travel on all night; and it was singular, once the dusk had fallen, my spirits somewhat rose. The bright lamps, shining forth into the mist and on the smoking horses and the hodding postboy, gave me perhaps an outlook intrinsically more cheerful than what day had shown; or perhaps my mind had become wearied of its melancholy. At least I spent some waking hours,

not without satisfaction in my thoughts, although wet and
weary in my body; and fell at last into a natural slumber
without dreams. Yet I must have been at work even in the
deepest of my sleep; and at work with at least a measure of
intelligence. For I started broad awake, in the very act of
crying out to myself

Home was home then, my dear, happy for the child,

stricken to find in it an appropriateness, which I had not
yesterday observed, to the Master's detestable purpose in
the present journey.

We were then close upon the city of Glasgow, where we
were soon breakfasting together at an inn, and where (as the
devil would have it) we found a ship in the very article of
sailing. We took our places in the cabin; and, two days after,
carried our effects on board. Her name was the *Nonesuch*, a
very ancient ship, and very happily named. By all accounts
this should be her last voyage; people shook their heads
upon the quays, and I had several warnings offered me
by strangers in the street to the effect that she was rotten
as a cheese, too deeply loaden, and must infallibly founder
if we met a gale. From this it fell out we were the only
passengers; the Captain, M'Murtrie, was a silent, absorbed
man, with the Glascow or Gaelic accent; the mates ignorant
rough seafarers, come in through the hawsehole; and the
Master and I were cast upon each other's company.

The *Nonesuch* carried a fair wind out of the Clyde, and for
near upon a week we enjoyed bright weather and a sense of
progress. I found myself (to my wonder) a born seaman, in
so far at least as I was never sick; yet I was far from tasting
the usual serenity of my health. Whether it was the motion
of the ship on the billows, the confinement, the salted food,
or all of these together, I suffered from a blackness of spirit
and a painful strain upon my temper. The nature of my
errand on that ship perhaps contributed; I think it did
no more; the malady (whatever it was) sprang from my
environment; and if the ship were not to blame, then it
was the Master. Hatred and fear are ill bedfellows; but (to
my shame be it spoken) I have tasted those in other places,
lain down and got up with them, and eaten and drunk

with them, and yet never before, nor after, have I been so
poisoned through and through, in soul and body, as I was
on board the *Nonesuch*. I freely confess my enemy set me a
fair example of forbearance; in our worst days displayed the
most patient geniality, holding me in conversation as long
as I would suffer, and when I had rebuffed his civility,
stretching himself on deck to read. The book he had on
board with him was Mr Richardson's famous *Clarissa*,
and among other small attentions he would read me passages
aloud; nor could any elocutionist have given with greater
potency the pathetic portions of that work. I would retort
upon him with passages out of the Bible, which was all
my library—and very fresh to me, my religious duties
(I grieve to say it) being always and even to this day
extremely neglected. He tasted the merits of the work
like the connoisseur he was; and would sometimes take
it from my hand, turn the leaves over like a man that
knew his way, and give me, with his fine declamation, a
Roland for my Oliver. But it was singular how little he
applied his reading to himself; it passed high above his
head like summer thunder; Lovelace and Clarissa, the tales
of David's generosity, the psalms of his penitence, the
solemn questions of the Book of Job, the touching poetry
of Isaiah—they were to him a source of entertainment
only, like the scraping of a fiddle in a change house.
This outer sensibility and inner toughness set me against
him; it seemed of a piece with that impudent grossness
which I knew to underlie the veneer of his fine manners;
and sometimes my gorge rose against him as though he
were deformed—and sometimes I would draw away as
though from something partly spectral. I had moments
when I thought of him as of a man of pasteboard—as
though, if one should strike smartly through the buckram
of his countenance, there would be found a mere vacuity
within. This horror (not merely fanciful, I think) vastly
increased my detestation of his neighbourhood; I began
to feel something shiver within me on his drawing near;
I had at times a longing to cry out; there were days when
I thought I could have struck him. This frame of mind
was doubtless helped by shame, because I had dropped

during our last days at Durrisdeer into a certain toleration of the man; and if any one had then told me I should drop into it again, I must have laughed in his face. It is possible he remained unconscious of this extreme fever of my resentment; yet I think he was too quick; and rather that he had fallen, in a long life of idleness, into a positive need of company, which obliged him to confront and tolerate my unconcealed aversion. Certain, at least, that he loved the note of his own tongue, as, indeed, he entirely loved all the parts and properties of himself; a sort of imbecility which almost necessarily attends on wickedness. I have seen him driven, when I proved recalcitrant, to long discourses with the skipper; and this, although the man plainly testified his weariness, fiddling miserably with both hand and foot, and replying only with a grunt.

After the first week out we fell in with foul winds and heavy weather. The sea was high. The *Nonesuch* being an old-fashioned ship, and badly loaden, rolled beyond belief; so that the skipper trembled for his masts, and I for my life. We made no progress on our course. An unbearable ill-humour settled on the ship: men, mates, and master, girding at one another all day long. A saucy word on the one hand, and a blow on the other, made a daily incident. There were times when the whole crew refused their duty; and we of the afterguard were twice got under arms—being the first time that ever I bore weapons—in the fear of mutiny.

In the midst of our evil season sprang up a hurricane of wind; so that all supposed she must go down. I was shut in the cabin from noon of one day till sundown of the next. The Master was somewhere lashed on deck; Secundra had eaten of some drug and lay insensible; so you may say I passed these hours in an unbroken solitude. At first I was terrified beyond motion, and almost beyond thought, my mind appearing to be frozen. Presently there stole in on me a ray of comfort. If the *Nonesuch* foundered, she would carry down with her into the deeps of that unsounded sea the creature whom we all so feared and hated; there would be no more Master of Ballantrae, the fish would sport among his ribs; his schemes all brought to nothing, his harmless enemies at peace. At first, I have said, it was but a ray

of comfort; but it had soon grown to be broad sunshine.
The thought of the man's death, of his deletion from this
world, which he embittered for so many, took possession
of my mind. I hugged it; I found it sweet in my belly. I
conceived the ship's last plunge, the sea bursting upon all
sides into the cabin, the brief mortal conflict there, all by
myself, in that closed place; I numbered the horrors, I had
almost said with satisfaction; I felt I could bear all and more,
if the *Nonesuch* carried down with her, overtook by the same
ruin, the enemy of my poor master's house. Towards noon
of the second day the screaming of the wind abated; the
ship lay not so perilously over, and it began to be clear to
me that we were past the height of the tempest. As I hope
for mercy, I was singly disappointed. In the selfishness of
that vile, absorbing passion of hatred, I forgot the case of
our innocent shipmates, and thought but of myself and my
enemy. For myself, I was already old; I had never been
young, I was not formed for the world's pleasures, I had few
affections; it mattered not the toss of a silver tester whether
I was drowned there and then in the Atlantic, or dribbled
out a few more years, to die, perhaps no less terribly, in a
deserted sickbed. Down I went upon my knees—holding
on by the locker, or else I had been instantly dashed across
the tossing cabin—and, lifting up my voice in the midst of
that clamour of the abating hurricane, impiously prayed for
my own death. 'O God!' I cried, 'I would be liker a man if
I rose and struck this creature down; but Thou madest me
a coward from my mother's womb. O Lord, Thou madest
me so, Thou knowest my weakness, Thou knowest that any
face of death will set me shaking in my shoes. But, lo! here
is Thy servant ready, his mortal weakness laid aside. Let
me give my life for this creature's; take the two of them,
Lord! take the two, and have mercy on the innocent!' In
some such words as these, only yet more irreverent and
with more sacred adjurations, I continued to pour forth my
spirit. God heard me not, I must suppose in mercy; and I
was still absorbed in my agony of supplication when some
one, removing the tarpaulin cover, let the light of the sunset
pour into the cabin. I stumbled to my feet ashamed, and was
seized with surprise to find myself totter and ache like one

that had been stretched upon the rack. Secundra Dass, who had slept off the effects of his drug, stood in a corner not far off, gazing at me with wild eyes; and from the open skylight the captain thanked me for my supplications.

'It's you that saved the ship, Mr Mackellar,' says he. 'There is no craft of seamanship that could have kept her floating: well may we say, "Except the Lord the city keep, the watchmen watch in vain"!'

I was abashed by the captain's error; abashed, also, by the surprise and fear with which the Indian regarded me at first, and the obsequious civilities with which he soon began to cumber me. I know now that he must have overheard and comprehended the peculiar nature of my prayers. It is certain, of course, that he at once disclosed the matter to his patron; and looking back with greater knowledge, I can now understand what so much puzzled me at the moment, those singular and (so to speak) approving smiles with which the Master honoured me. Similarly, I can understand a word that I remember to have fallen from him in conversation that same night; when, holding up his hand and smiling, 'Ah! Mackellar,' said he, 'not every man is so great a coward as he thinks he is—nor yet so good a Christian.' He did not guess how true he spoke! For the fact is, the thoughts which had come to me in the violence of the storm retained their hold upon my spirit; and the words that rose to my lips unbidden in the instancy of prayer continued to sound in my ears: with what shameful consequences it is fitting I should honestly relate; for I could not support a part of such disloyalty as to describe the sins of others and conceal my own.

The wind fell, but the sea hove ever the higher. All night the *Nonesuch* rolled outrageously; the next day dawned, and the next, and brought no change. To cross the cabin was scarce possible; old experienced seamen were cast down upon the deck, and one cruelly mauled in the concussion; every board and block in the old ship cried out aloud; and the great bell by the anchor-bitts continually and dolefully rang. One of these days the Master and I sat alone together at the break of the poop. I should say the *Nonesuch* carried a high, raised poop. About the top of it ran considerable bulwarks, which made the ship unweatherly: and these, as they approached the front on each side, ran down in a fine, old-fashioned, carven scroll to join the bulwarks of the waist. From this disposition, which seems designed rather for ornament than use, it followed there was a discontinuance of protection: and that, besides, at the very margin of the elevated part where (in certain movements of the ship) it might be the most needful. It was here we were sitting: our feet hanging down, the Master betwixt me and the side, and I holding on with both hands to the grating of the cabin skylight; for it struck me it was a dangerous position, the more so as I had continually before my eyes a measure of our evolutions in the person of the Master, which stood out in the break of the bulwarks against the sun. Now his head would be in the zenith and his shadow fall quite beyond the *Nonesuch* on the farther side; and now he would swing down till he was underneath my feet, and the line of the sea leaped high above him like the ceiling of a room. I looked on upon this with a growing fascination, as birds are said to look on snakes. My mind, besides, was troubled with an astonishing diversity of noises; for now that we had all sails spread in the vain hope to bring her to the sea, the ship sounded like a factory with their reverberations. We spoke first of the mutiny with which we had been threatened; this led us on to the topic of assassination; and that offered a temptation to the Master more strong than he was able to resist. He must tell me a tale, and show me at the same time how clever he was, and how wicked. It was a thing he did always with affectation and display; generally with a good effect. But this tale, told in a high key in the midst of so great a tumult, and by a narrator who was one moment looking down at me from the skies and the next peering up from under the soles of my feet—this particular tale, I say, took hold upon me in a degree quite singular.

'My friend the count,' it was thus that he began his story, 'had for an enemy a certain German baron, a stranger in Rome. It matters not what was the ground of the count's enmity; but as he had a firm design to be revenged, and that with safety to himself, he kept it secret even from the baron. Indeed, that is the first principle of vengeance; and hatred betrayed is hatred impotent. The count was a man of a curious, searching mind; he had something of the artist; if anything fell for him to do, it must always be done with an exact perfection, not only as to the result, but in the very means and instruments, or he thought the thing miscarried. It chanced he was one day riding in the outer suburbs, when he came to a disused byroad branching off into the moor which lies about Rome. On the one hand was an ancient Roman tomb; on the other a deserted house in a garden of evergreen trees. This road brought him presently into a field of ruins, in the midst of which, in the side of a hill, he saw an open door, and, not far off, a single stunted pine no greater than a currant bush. The place was desert and very secret; a voice spoke in the count's bosom that there was something here to his advantage. He tied his horse to the pine tree, took his flint and steel in his hand to make a light, and entered into the hill. The doorway opened on a passage of old Roman masonry, which shortly after branched in two. The count took the turning to the right, and followed it, groping forward in the dark, till he was brought up by a kind of fence, about elbow-high, which extended quite across the passage. Sounding forward with his foot, he found an edge of polished stone, and then vacancy. All his curiosity was now awakened, and, getting some rotten sticks that lay about the floor, he made a fire. In front of him was a profound well; doubtless some neighbouring peasant had once used it for his water, and it was he that had set up the fence. A long while the count stood leaning on the rail and looking down into the pit. It was of Roman foundation, and, like all that nation set their hands to, built as for eternity; the sides were still straight, and the joints smooth; to a man who should fall in, no escape was possible. "Now," the count was thinking, "a strong impulsion brought me to this place. What for? what have I gained? why should I be sent to gaze into this well?" when the rail of the fence gave suddenly under his weight, and he came within an ace of falling headlong in. Leaping back to save himself, he trod out the last flicker of his fire, which gave him thenceforward no more light, only an incommoding smoke. "Was I sent here to my death?" says he, and shook from head to foot.

And then a thought flashed in his mind. He crept forth on hands and knees to the brink of the pit, and felt above him in the air. The rail had been fast to a pair of uprights; it had only broken from the one, and still depended from the other. The count set it back again as he had found it, so that the place meant death to the first comer, and groped out of the catacomb like a sick man. The next day, riding in the Corso with the baron, he purposely betrayed a strong preoccupation. The other (as he had designed) inquired into the cause; and he, after some fencing, admitted that his spirits had been dashed by an unusual dream. This was calculated to draw on the baron—a superstitious man, who affected the scorn of superstition. Some rallying followed, and then the count, as if suddenly carried away, called on his friend to beware, for it was of him that he had dreamed. You know enough of human nature, my excellent Mackellar, to be certain of one thing: I mean that the baron did not rest till he had heard the dream. The count, sure that he would never desist, kept him in play till his curiosity was highly inflamed, and then suffered himself, with seeming reluctance, to be overborne. "I warn you," says he, "evil will come of it; something tells me so. But since there is to be no peace either for you or me except on this condition, the blame be on your own head! This was the dream:—I beheld you riding, I know not where, yet I think it must have been near Rome, for on your one hand was an ancient tomb, and on the other a garden of evergreen trees. Methought I cried and cried upon you to come back in a very agony of terror; whether you heard me I know not, but you went doggedly on. The road brought you to a desert place among ruins, where was a door in a hillside, and hard by the door a misbegotten pine. Here you dismounted (I still crying on you to beware), tied your horse to the pine tree, and entered resolutely in by the door. Within, it was dark; but in my dream I could still see you, and still besought you to hold back. You felt your way along the right-hand wall, took a branching passage to the right, and came to a little chamber, where was a well with a railing. At this—I know not why—my alarm for you increased a thousandfold, so that I seemed to scream myself hoarse with warnings, crying it was still time, and bidding you begone at once from that vestibule. Such was the word I used in my dream, and it seemed then to have a clear significancy; but today, and awake, I profess I know not what it means. To all my outcry you rendered not the least attention, leaning the while upon the rail and looking down intently in the water. And then there was made to you a communication; I do not think I even gathered what it was, but the fear of it plucked me clean out of my slumber, and I awoke shaking and sobbing. And now," continues the count, "I thank you from my heart for your insistency. This dream lay on me like a load; and now I have told it in plain words and in the broad daylight, it seems no great matter."—"I do not know," says the baron. "It is in some points strange. A communication, did you say! O! it is an odd dream. It will make a story to amuse our friends."—"I am not so sure," says the count. "I am sensible of some reluctancy. Let us rather forget it."—"By all means," says the baron. And (in fact) the dream was not again referred to. Some days after, the count proposed a ride in the fields, which the baron (since they were daily growing faster friends) very readily accepted. On the way back to Rome, the count led them insensibly by a particular route. Presently he reined in his horse, clapped his hand before his eyes, and cried out aloud. Then he showed his face again (which was now quite white, for he was a consummate actor), and stared upon the baron. "What ails you?" cries the baron. "What is wrong with you?"—"Nothing," cries the count. "It is nothing. A seizure, I know not what. Let us hurry back to Rome." But in the meanwhile the baron had looked about him; and there, on the left-hand side of the way as they went back to Rome, he saw a dusty byroad with a tomb upon the one hand and a garden of evergreen trees upon the other.—"Yes," says he, with a changed voice. "Let us by all means hurry back to Rome. I fear you are not well in health."—"O, for God's sake!" cried the count, shuddering; "back to Rome and let me get to bed." They made their return with scarce a word; and the count, who should by rights have gone into society, took to his bed and gave out he had a touch of country fever. The next day the baron's horse was found tied to the pine, but himself was never heard of from that hour.—And now, was that a murder?' says the Master, breaking sharply off.

'Are you sure he was a count?' I asked.

'I am not certain of the title,' said he, 'but he was a gentleman of family: and the Lord deliver you, Mackellar, from an enemy so subtle!'

These last words he spoke down at me, smiling from high above; the next, he was under my feet. I continued to follow his evolutions with a childish fixity: they made me giddy and vacant, and I spoke as in a dream.

'He hated the baron with a great hatred?' I asked.

'His belly moved when the man came near him,' said the Master.

'I have felt that same,' said I.

'Verily!' cries the Master. 'Here is news indeed! I wonder—do I flatter myself? or am I the cause of these ventral perturbations?'

He was quite capable of choosing out a graceful posture, even with no one to behold him but myself, and all the more if there were any element of peril. He sat now with one knee flung across the other, his arms on his bosom, fitting the swing of the ship with an exquisite balance, such as a featherweight might overthrow. All at once I had the vision of my lord at the table, with his head upon his hands; only now, when he showed me his countenance, it was heavy with reproach. The words of my own prayer—*I were liker a man if I struck this creature down*—shot at the same time into my memory. I called my energies together, and (the ship then heeling downward toward my enemy) thrust at him swiftly with my foot. It was written I should have the guilt of this attempt without the profit. Whether from my own uncertainty or his incredible quickness, he escaped the thrust, leaping to his feet and catching hold at the same moment of a stay.

I do not know how long a time passed by: I lying where I was upon the deck, overcome with terror and remorse and shame: he standing with the stay in his hand, backed against the bulwarks, and regarding me with an expression singularly mingled. At last he spoke.

'Mackellar,' said he, 'I make no reproaches, but I offer

you a bargain. On your side, I do not suppose you desire to have this exploit made public; on mine, I own to you freely I do not care to draw my breath in a perpetual terror of assassination by the man I sit at meat with. Promise me—but no,' says he, breaking off, 'you are not yet in the quiet possession of your mind; you might think I had extorted the promise from your weakness; and I would leave no door open for casuistry to come in—that dishonesty of the conscientious. Take time to meditate.'

With that he made off up the sliding deck like a squirrel, and plunged into the cabin. About half an hour later he returned—I still lying as he had left me.

'Now,' says he, 'will you give me your troth as a Christian, and a faithful servant of my brother's, that I shall have no more to fear from your attempts?'

'I give it you,' said I.

'I shall require your hand upon it,' says he.

'You have the right to make conditions,' I replied, and we shook hands.

He sat down at once in the same place and the old perilous attitude.

'Hold on!' cried I, covering my eyes. 'I cannot bear to see you in that posture. The least irregularity of the sea might plunge you overboard.'

'You are highly inconsistent,' he replied, smiling, but doing as I asked. 'For all that, Mackellar, I would have you to know you have risen forty feet in my esteem. You think I cannot set a price upon fidelity? But why do you suppose I carry that Secundra Dass about the world with me? Because he would die or do murder for me tomorrow; and I love him for it. Well, you may think it odd, but I like you the better since this afternoon. I thought you were magnetised with the Ten Commandments; but no—God damn my soul!'—he cries, 'the old wife has blood in his body after all! Which does not change the fact,' he continued, smiling again, 'that you have done well to give your promise; for I doubt if you would ever shine in your new trade.'

'I suppose,' said I, 'I should ask your pardon and God's for my attempt. At any rate, I have passed my word, which I will keep faithfully. But when I think of those you persecute—' I paused.

'Life is a singular thing,' said he, 'and mankind a very singular people. You suppose yourself to love my brother. I assure you, it is merely custom. Interrogate your memory; and when first you came to Durrisdeer, you will find you considered him a dull, ordinary youth. He is as dull and ordinary now, though not so young. Had you instead fallen in with me, you would to-day be as strong upon my side.'

'I would never say you were ordinary, Mr Bally,' I returned; 'but here you prove yourself dull. You have just shown your reliance on my word—in other terms, that is, my conscience—the same which starts instinctively back from you, like the eye from a strong light.'

'Ah!' says he, 'but I mean otherwise. I mean had I met you in my youth. You are to consider I was not always as I am today; nor (had I met in with a friend of your description) should I have ever been so.'

'Hut, Mr Bally,' says I, 'you would have made a mock of me; you would never have spent ten civil words on such a Square-toes.'

But he was now fairly started on his new course of justification, with which he wearied me throughout the remainder of the passage. No doubt in the past he had taken pleasure to paint himself unnecessarily black, and made a vaunt of his wickedness, bearing it for a coat of arms. Nor was he so illogical as to abate one item of his old confessions. 'But now that I know you are a human being,' he would say, 'I can take the trouble to explain myself. For I assure you I am human too, and have my virtues like my neighbours.' I say, he wearied me, for I had only the one word to say in answer: twenty times I must have said it: 'Give up your present purpose and return with me to Durrisdeer: then I will believe you.'

Thereupon he would shake his head at me. 'Ah! Mackellar, you might live a thousand years and never understand my nature,' he would say. 'This battle is now committed, the hour of reflection quite past, the hour for mercy not yet come. It began between us when we span a coin in the hall of Durrisdeer, now twenty years ago; we have had our ups and downs, but never either of us dreamed of giving in; and as for me, when my glove is cast, life and honour go with it.'

'A fig for your honour!' I would say. 'And by your leave, these war-like similitudes are something too high-sounding for the matter in hand. You want some dirty money; there is the bottom of your contention; and as for your means, what are they? to stir up sorrow in a family that never harmed you, to debauch (if you can) your own nephew, and to wring the heart of your born brother! A footpad that kills an old granny in a woollen mutch with a dirty bludgeon, and that for a shilling piece and a paper of snuff—there is all the warrior that you are.'

When I would attack him thus (or somewhat thus) he would smile, and sigh like a man misunderstood. Once, I remember, he defended himself more at large, and had some curious sophistries, worth repeating, for a light upon his character.

'You are very like a civilian to think war consists in drums and banners,' said he. 'War (as the ancients said very wisely) is *ultima ratio*. When we take our advantage unrelentingly, then we make war. Ah! Mackellar, you are a devil of a soldier in the steward's room at Durrisdeer, or the tenants do you sad injustice!'

'I think little of what war is or is not,' I replied. 'But you weary me with claiming my respect. Your brother is a good man, and you are a bad one—neither more nor less.'

'Had I been Alexander—' he began.

'It is so we all dupe ourselves,' I cried. 'Had I been St Paul, it would have been all one; I would have made the same hash of that career that you now see me making of my own.'

'I tell you,' he cried, bearing down my interruption, 'had I been the least petty chieftain in the Highlands, had I been the least king of naked negroes in the African desert, my people would have adored me. A bad man, am I? Ah! but I was born for a good tyrant! Ask Secundra Dass; he will tell you I treat him like a son. Cast in your lot with me tomorrow, become my slave, my chattel, a thing I can command as I command the powers of my own limbs and spirit—you will see no more that dark side that I turn upon the world in anger. I must have all or none. But where all is given I give it back with usury. I have a kingly nature: there is my loss!'

'It has been hitherto rather the loss of others,' I remarked, 'which seems a little on the hither side of royalty.'

'Tilly-vally!' cried he. 'Even now, I tell you, I would spare that family in which you take so great an interest: yes, even now—tomorrow I would leave them to their petty welfare, and disappear in that forest of cutthroats and thimble-riggers that we call the world. I would do it tomorrow!' says he. 'Only—only—'

'Only what?' I asked.

'Only they must beg it on their bended knees. I think in public, too,' he added, smiling. 'Indeed, Mackellar, I doubt if there be a hall big enough to serve my purpose for that act of reparation.'

'Vanity, vanity!' I moralised. 'To think that this great force for evil should be swayed by the same sentiment that sets a lassie mincing to her glass!'

'O! there are double words for everything: the word that swells, the word that belittles; you cannot fight me with a word!' said he. 'You said the other day that I relied on your conscience: were I in your humour of detraction, I might say I built upon your vanity. It is your pretension to be *un homme de parole;* 'tis mine not to accept defeat. Call it vanity, call it virtue, call it greatness of soul—what signifies the expression? But recognise in each of us a common strain: that we both live for an idea.'

It will be gathered from so much familiar talk, and so much patience on both sides, that we now lived together upon excellent terms. Such was again the fact, and this time more seriously than before. Apart from disputations such as that which I have tried to reproduce, not only consideration reigned, but, I am tempted to say, even kindness. When I fell sick (as I did shortly after our great storm), he sat by my berth to entertain me with his conversation, and treated me with excellent remedies, which I accepted with security. Himself commented on the circumstance. 'You see,' says he, 'you begin to know me better. A very little while ago, upon this lonely ship, where no one but myself has any smattering of science, you would have made sure I had designs upon your life. And, observe, it is since I found you had designs upon my own that I have shown you most respect. You will tell me if this speaks of a small mind.' I found little to reply. In so far as regarded myself, I believed him to mean well; I am, perhaps, the more a dupe of his dissimulation, but I believed (and I still believe) that he regarded me with genuine kindness. Singular and sad fact! so soon as this change began, my animosity abated, and these haunting visions of my master passed utterly away. So that, perhaps, there was truth in the man's last vaunting word to me, uttered on the twenty-second day of July, when our long voyage was at last brought almost to an end, and we lay becalmed at the sea end of the vast harbour of New York, in a gasping heat, which was presently exchangéd for a surprising waterfall of rain. I stood on the poop, regarding the green shores near at hand, and now and then the light smoke of the little town, our destination. And as I was even then devising how to steal a march on my familiar enemy, I was conscious of a shade of embarrassment when he approached me with his hand extended.

'I am now to bid you farewell,' said he, 'and that for ever. For now you go among my enemies, where all your former prejudices will revive. I never yet failed to charm a person when I wanted; even you, my good friend—to call you so for once—even you have now a very different portrait of me in your memory, and one that you will never quite forget. The voyage has not lasted long enough, or I should have wrote the impression deeper. But now all is at an end, and we are again at war. Judge by this little interlude how dangerous I am; and tell those fools'—pointing with his finger to the town—' to think twice and thrice before they set me at defiance.'

CHAPTER TEN

Passages at New York

I HAVE MENTIONED I was resolved to steal a march upon the Master; and this, with the complicity of Captain M'Murtrie, was mighty easily effected: a boat being partly loaded on the one side of our ship, and the Master placed on board of it, the while a skiff put off from the other, carrying me alone. I had no more trouble in finding a direction to my lord's house, whither I went at top speed, and which I found to be on the outskirts of the place, a very suitable mansion, in a fine garden, with an extraordinary large barn, byre, and stable, all in one. It was here my lord was walking when I arrived; indeed, it had become his chief place of frequentation, and his mind was now filled with farming. I burst in upon him breathless, and gave him my news: which was indeed no news at all, several ships having outsailed the *Nonesuch* in the interval.

'We have been expecting you long,' said my lord; 'and indeed, of late days, ceased to expect you any more. I am glad to take your hand again, Mackellar. I thought you had been at the bottom of the sea.'

'Ah! my lord, would God I had!' cried I. 'Things would have been better for yourself.'

'Not in the least,' says he grimly. 'I could not ask better. There is a long score to pay, and now—at last—I can begin to pay it.'

I cried out against his security.

'O!' says he, 'this is not Durrisdeer, and I have taken my precautions. His reputation awaits him; I have prepared a welcome for my brother. Indeed, fortune has served me; for I found here a merchant of Albany who knew him after the 'Forty-five, and had mighty convenient suspicions of a murder: someone of the name of Chew it was, another Albanian. No one here will be surprised if I deny him my door; he will not be suffered to address my children, nor even to salute my wife: as for myself, I make so much exception for a brother that he may speak to me. I should lose my pleasure else,' says my lord, rubbing his palms.

Presently he bethought himself, and set men off running, with billets, to summon the magnates of the province. I cannot recall what pretext he employed; at least, it was successful; and when our ancient enemy appeared upon the scene, he found my lord pacing in front of his house under some trees of shade, with the Governor upon one hand and various notables upon the other. My lady, who was seated in the verandah, rose with a very pinched expression and carried her children into the house.

The Master, well dressed, and with an elegant walking sword, bowed to the company in a handsome manner, and nodded to my lord with familiarity. My lord did not accept the salutation, but looked upon his brother with bended brows.

'Well, sir,' says he at last, 'what ill wind brings you hither of all places, where (to our common disgrace) your reputation has preceded you?'

'Your lordship is pleased to be civil,' cries the Master, with a fine start.

'I am pleased to be very plain,' returned my lord; 'because it is needful you should clearly understand your situation. At home, where you were so little known, it was still possible to keep appearances; that would be quite vain in this province; and I have to tell you that I am quite resolved to wash my hands of you. You have already ruined me almost to the door, as you ruined my father before me;—whose heart you also broke. Your crimes escape the law; but my friend the Governor has promised protection to my family. Have a care, sir!' cries my lord, shaking his cane at him: 'if you are observed to utter two words to any of my innocent household, the law shall be stretched to make you smart for it.'

'Ah!' says the Master, very slowly. 'And so this is the advantage of a foreign land! These gentlemen are unacquainted with our story, I perceive. They do not know that I am the true Lord Durrisdeer; they do not know you are my younger brother, sitting in my place under a sworn family compact; they do not know (or they would not be seen with you in familiar correspondence) that every acre is mine before God Almighty—and every doit of the money you withhold from me, you do it as a thief, a perjurer, and a disloyal brother!'

'General Clinton,' I cried, 'do not listen to his lies. I am the steward of the estate, and there is not one word of truth in it. The man is a forfeited rebel turned into a hired spy: there is his story in two words.'

It was thus (in the heat of the moment) I let slip his infamy.

'Fellow,' said the Governor, turning his face sternly on the Master, 'I know more of you than you think for. We have some broken ends of your adventures in the provinces, which you will do very well not to drive me to investigate. There is the disappearance of Mr Jacob Chew with all his merchandise; there is the matter of where you came ashore from with so much money and jewels, when you were picked up by a Bermudan out of Albany. Believe me, if I let these matters lie, it is in commiseration for your family, and out of respect for my valued friend, Lord Durrisdeer.'

There was a murmur of applause from the provincials.

'I should have remembered how a title would shine out in such a hole as this,' says the Master, white as a sheet: 'no matter how unjustly come by. It remains for me, then, to die at my lord's door, where my dead body will form a very cheerful ornament.'

'Away with your affectations!' cries my lord. 'You know very well I have no such meaning; only to protect myself from calumny, and my home from your intrusion. I offer you a choice. Either I shall pay your passage home on the first ship, when you may perhaps be able to resume your occupations under Government, although God knows I would rather see you on the highway! Or, if that likes you not, stay here and welcome! I have inquired the least sum on which body and soul can be decently kept together in New York; so much you shall have, paid weekly; and if you cannot labour with your hands to better it, high time you should betake yourself to learn. The condition is—that you speak with no member of my family except myself,' he added.

I do not think I have ever seen any man so pale as was the Master; but he was erect and his mouth firm.

'I have been met here with some very unmerited insults,' said he, 'from which I have certainly no idea to take refuge by flight. Give me your pittance; I take it without shame, for it is mine already—like the shirt upon your back; and I choose to stay until these gentlemen shall understand me better. Already they must spy the cloven hoof, since with all your pretended eagerness for the family honour, you take a pleasure to degrade it in my person.'

'This is all very fine,' says my lord; 'but to us who know you of old, you must be sure it signifies nothing. You take that alternative out of which you think that you can make the most. Take it, if you can, in silence; it will serve you better in the long-run, you may believe me, than this ostentation of ingratitude.'

'O, gratitude, my lord!' cries the Master, with a mounting intonation, and his forefinger very conspicuously lifted up. 'Be at rest: it will not fail you. It now remains that I should salute these gentlemen whom we have wearied with our family affairs.'

And he bowed to each in succession, settled his walking-sword, and took himself off, leaving every one amazed at his behaviour, and me not less so at my lord's.

We were now to enter on a changed phase of this family division. The Master was by no manner of means so helpless as my lord supposed, having at his hand, and entirely devoted to his service, an excellent artist in all sorts of goldsmith work. With my lord's allowance, which was not so scanty as he had described it, the pair could support life; and all the earnings of Secundra Dass might be laid upon one side for any future purpose. That this was done, I have no doubt. It was in all likelihood the Master's design to gather a sufficiency, and then proceed in quest of that treasure which he had buried long before among the mountains; to which, if he had confined himself, he would have been more happily inspired. But unfortunately for himself and all of us, he took counsel of his anger. The public disgrace of his arrival—which I sometimes wonder he could manage to survive—rankled in his bones; he was in that humour when a man—in the words of the old adage—will cut off his nose to spite his face; and he must make himself a public spectacle in the hopes that some of the disgrace might spatter on my lord.

He chose, in a poor quarter of the town, a lonely, small house of boards, overhung with some acacias. It was furnished in front with a sort of hutch opening, like that of a dog's kennel, but about as high as a table from the ground, in which the poor man that built it had formerly displayed some wares; and it was this which took the Master's fancy and possibly suggested his proceedings. It appears, on board the pirate ship he had acquired some quickness with the needle—enough, at least, to play the part of tailor in the public eye; which was all that was required by the nature of his vengeance. A placard was hung above the hutch, bearing these words in something of the following disposition:

JAMES DURIE,
FORMERLY MASTER OF BALLANTRAE.
CLOTHES NEATLY CLOUTED.

SECUNDRA DASS,
DECAYED GENTLEMAN OF INDIA.
FINE GOLDSMITH WORK.

Underneath this, when he had a job, my gentleman sat withinside tailor-wise and busily stitching. I say, when he had a job; but such customers as came were rather for Secundra, and the Master's sewing would be more in the manner of Penelope's. He could never have designed to gain even butter to his bread by such a means of livelihood: enough for him that there was the name of Durie dragged in the dirt on the placard, and the sometime heir of that proud family set up cross-legged in public for a reproach upon his brother's meanness. And in so far his device succeeded that there was murmuring in the town and a party formed highly inimical to my lord. My lord's favour with the Governor laid him more open on the other side; my lady (who was never so well received in the colony) met with painful innuendoes; in a party of women, where it would be the topic most natural to introduce, she was almost debarred from the naming of needlework; and I have seen her return with a flushed countenance, and vow that she would go abroad no more.

In the meanwhile my lord dwelled in his decent mansion, immersed in farming; a popular man with his intimates, and careless or unconscious of the rest. He laid on flesh; had a bright, busy face; even the heat seemed to prosper with him; and my lady—in despite of her own annoyances—daily blessed Heaven her father should have left her such a paradise. She had looked on from a window upon the Master's humiliation; and from that hour appeared to feel at ease. I was not so sure myself; as time went on, there seemed to me a something not quite wholesome in my lord's condition. Happy he was, beyond a doubt, but the grounds of this felicity were secret; even in the bosom of his family he brooded with manifest delight upon some private thought; and I conceived at last the suspicion (quite unworthy of us both) that he kept a mistress somewhere in the town. Yet he went little abroad, and his day was very fully occupied; indeed, there was but a single period, and that pretty early in the morning, while Mr Alexander was at his lesson book, of which I was not certain of the disposition. It should be borne in mind, in the defence of that which I now did, that I was always in some fear my lord was not quite justly in his reason; and with our enemy sitting so still in the same town with us, I did well to be upon my guard. Accordingly I made a pretext, had the hour changed at which I taught Mr Alexander the foundation of ciphering and the mathematic, and set myself instead to dog my master's footsteps.

Every morning, fair or foul, he took his gold-headed cane, set his hat on the back of his head—a recent habitude, which I thought to indicate a burning brow—and betook himself to make a certain circuit. At the first his way was among pleasant trees and beside a graveyard, where he would sit a while, if the day were fine, in meditation. Presently the path turned down to the waterside, and came back along the harbour front and past the Master's booth. As he approached this second part of his circuit, my Lord Durrisdeer began to pace more leisurely, like a man delighted with the air and scene; and before the booth, half-way between that and the water's edge, would pause a little, leaning on his staff. It was the hour when the Master sate within upon his board and plied his needle. So these two brothers would gaze upon each other with hard faces; and then my lord move on again, smiling to himself.

It was but twice that I must stoop to that ungrateful necessity of playing spy. I was then certain of my lord's purpose in his rambles and of the secret source of his delight. Here was his mistress: it was hatred and not love that gave him healthful colours. Some moralists might have been relieved by the discovery; I confess that I was dismayed. I found this situation of two brethren not only odious in itself, but big with possibilities of further evil; and I made it my practice, in so far as many occupations would allow, to go by a shorter path and be secretly present at their meeting. Coming down one day a little late, after I had been near a week prevented, I was struck with surprise to find a new development. I should say there was a bench against the Master's house, where customers might sit to parley with the shopman; and here I found my lord seated, nursing his cane and looking pleasantly forth upon the bay. Not three feet from him sat the Master, stitching. Neither spoke; nor (in this new situation) did my lord so much as cast a glance upon his enemy. He tasted his neighbourhood, I must suppose, less indirectly in the bare proximity of person; and, without doubt, drank deep of hateful pleasures.

He had no sooner come away than I openly joined him.

'My lord, my lord,' said I, 'this is no manner of behaviour.'

'I grow fat upon it,' he replied: and not merely the words, which were strange enough, but the whole character of his expression, shocked me.

'I warn you, my lord, against this indulgency of evil feeling,' said I. 'I know not to which it is more perilous, the soul or the reason; but you go the way to murder both.'

'You cannot understand,' said he. 'You had never such mountains of bitterness upon your heart.'

'And if it were no more,' I added, 'you will surely goad the man to some extremity.'

'To the contrary; I am breaking his spirit,' says my lord.

Every morning for hard upon a week my lord took his same place upon the bench. It was a pleasant place, under the green acacias, with a sight upon the bay and shipping, and a sound (from some way off) of mariners singing at their employ. Here the two sat without speech or any external movement, beyond that of the needle, or the Master biting off a thread, for he still clung to his pretence of industry; and here I made a point to join them, wondering at myself and my companions. If any of my lord's friends went by, he would hail them cheerfully, and cry out he was there to give some good advice to his brother, who was now (to his delight) grown quite industrious. And even this the Master accepted with a steady countenance; what was in his mind, God knows, or perhaps Satan only.

All of a sudden, on a still day of what they call the Indian Summer, when the woods were changed into gold and pink and scarlet, the Master laid down his needle and burst into a fit of merriment. I think he must have been preparing it a long while in silence, for the note in itself was pretty naturally pitched; but breaking suddenly from so extreme a silence, and in circumstances so averse from mirth, it sounded ominously on my ear.

'Henry,' said he, 'I have for once made a false step, and for once you have had the wit to profit by it. The farce of the cobbler ends today; and I confess to you (with my compliments) that you have had the best of it. Blood will out; and you have certainly a choice idea of how to make yourself unpleasant.'

Never a word said my lord; it was just as though the Master had not broken silence.

'Come,' resumed the Master, 'do not be sulky; it will spoil your attitude. You can now afford (believe me) to be a little gracious; for I have not merely a defeat to accept. I had meant to continue this performance till I had gathered enough money for a certain purpose; I confess ingenuously I have not the courage. You naturally desire my absence from this town; I have come round by another way to the same idea. And I have a proposition to make; or, if your lordship prefers, a favour to ask.'

'Ask it,' says my lord.

'You may have heard that I had once in this country a considerable treasure,' returned the Master; 'it matters not whether or no—such is the fact; and I was obliged to bury it in a spot of which I have sufficient indications. To the recovery of this has my ambition now come down; and, as it is my own, you will not grudge it me.'

'Go and get it,' says my lord. 'I make no opposition.'

'Yes,' said the Master; 'but to do so I must find men and carriage. The way is long and rough, and the country infested with wild Indians. Advance me only so much as shall be needful: either as a lump sum, in lieu of my allowance; or, if you prefer it, as a loan, which I shall repay on my return. And then, if you so decide, you may have seen the last of me.'

My lord stared him steadily in the eyes; there was a hard smile upon his face, but he uttered nothing.

'Henry,' said the Master, with a formidable quietness, and drawing at the same time somewhat back—'Henry, I had the honour to address you.'

'Let us be stepping homeward,' says my lord to me, who was plucking at his sleeve; and with that he rose, stretched himself, settled his hat, and, still without a syllable of response, began to walk steadily along the shore.

I hesitated a while between the two brothers, so serious a climax did we seem to have reached. But the Master had resumed his occupation, his eyes lowered, his hand seemingly as deft as ever; and I decided to pursue my lord.

'Are you mad?' I cried, so soon as I had overtook him. 'Would you cast away so fair an opportunity?'

'Is it possible you should still believe in him?' inquired my lord, almost with a sneer.

'I wish him forth of this town!' I cried. 'I wish him anywhere and anyhow but as he is.'

'I have said my say,' returned my lord, 'and you have said yours. There let it rest.'

But I was bent on dislodging the Master. That sight of him patiently returning to his needlework was more than my imagination could digest. There was never a man made, and the Master the least of any, that could accept so long a series of insults. The air smelt blood to me. And I vowed there should be no neglect of mine if, through any chink of possibility, crime could be yet turned aside. That same day, therefore, I came to my lord in his business room, where he sat upon some trivial occupation.

'My lord,' said I, 'I have found a suitable investment for my small economies. But these are unhappily in Scotland; it will take some time to lift them, and the affair presses. Could your lordship see his way to advance me the amount against my note?'

He read me a while with keen eyes. 'I have never inquired into the state of your affairs, Mackellar,' says he. 'Beyond the amount of your caution, you may not be worth a farthing, for what I know.'

'I have been a long while in your service, and never told a lie, nor yet asked a favour for myself,' said I, 'until today.'

'A favour for the Master,' he returned quietly. 'Do you take me for a fool, Mackellar? Understand it once and for all, I treat this beast in my own way; fear nor favour shall not move me; and before I am hoodwinked, it will require a trickster less transparent than yourself. I ask service, loyal service; not that you should make and mar behind my back, and steal my own money to defeat me.'

'My lord,' said I, 'these are very unpardonable expressions.'

'Think once more, Mackellar,' he replied; 'and you will see they fit the fact. It is your own subterfuge that is unpardonable. Deny (if you can) that you designed this money to evade my orders with, and I will ask your pardon freely. If you cannot, you must have the resolution to hear your conduct go by its own name.'

'If you think I had any design but to save you—' I began.

'O! my old friend,' said he, 'you know very well what I

think! Here is my hand to you with all my heart; but of money, not one rap.'

Defeated upon this side, I went straight to my room, wrote a letter, ran with it to the harbour, for I knew a ship was on the point of sailing; and came to the Master's door a little before dusk. Entering without the form of any knock, I found him sitting with his Indian at a simple meal of maize porridge with some milk. The house within was clean and poor; only a few books upon a shelf distinguished it, and (in one corner) Secundra's little bench.

'Mr Bally,' said I, 'I have near five hundred pounds laid by in Scotland, the economies of a hard life. A letter goes by yon ship to have it lifted. Have so much patience till the return ship comes in, and it is all yours, upon the same condition you offered to my lord this morning.'

He rose from the table, came forward, took me by the shoulders, and looked me in the face, smiling.

'And yet you are very fond of money!' said he. 'And yet you love money beyond all things else, except my brother!'

'I fear old age and poverty,' said I, 'which is another matter.'

'I will never quarrel for a name. Call it so,' he replied.— 'Ah! Mackellar, Mackellar, if this were done from any love to me, how gladly would I close upon your offer!'

'And yet,' I eagerly answered—'I say it to my shame, but I cannot see you in this poor place without compunction. It is not my single thought, nor my first; and yet it's there! I would gladly see you delivered. I do not offer it in love, and far from that; but, as God judges me—and I wonder at it too!—quite without enmity.'

'Ah!' says he, still holding my shoulders, and now gently shaking me, 'you think of me more than you suppose. "And I wonder at it too,"' he added, repeating my expression and, I suppose, something of my voice. 'You are an honest man, and for that cause I spare you.'

'Spare me?' I cried.

'Spare you,' he repeated, letting me go and turning away. And then, fronting me once more: 'You little know what I would do with it, Mackellar! Did you think I had swallowed my defeat indeed? Listen: my life has been a series of unmerited cast-backs. That fool, Prince Charlie, mismanaged a most promising affair: there fell my first fortune. In Paris I had my foot once more high up on the ladder: that time it was an accident; a letter came to the wrong hand, and I was bare again. A third time I found my opportunity; I built up a place for myself in India with an infinite patience; and then Clive came, my rajah was swallowed up, and I escaped out of the convulsion, like another Aeneas, with Secundra Dass upon my back. Three times I have had my hand upon the highest station: and I am not yet three-and-forty. I know the world as few men know it when they come to die—Court and camp, the East and the West; I know where to go, I see a thousand openings. I am now at the height of my resources, sound of health, of inordinate ambition. Well, all this I resign; I care not if I die, and the world never hear of me; I care only for one thing, and that I will have. Mind yourself; lest, when the roof falls, you, too, should be crushed under the ruins.'

As I came out of his house, all hope of intervention quite destroyed, I was aware of a stir on the harbourside, and, raising my eyes, there was a great ship newly come to anchor. It seems strange I could have looked upon her with so much indifference, for she brought death to the brothers of Durrisdeer. After all the desperate episodes of this contention, the insults, the opposing interests, the fraternal duel in the shrubbery, it was reserved for some poor devil in Grub Street, scribbling for his dinner, and not caring what he scribbled, to cast a spell across four thousand miles of the salt sea, and send forth both these brothers into savage and wintry deserts, there to die. But such a thought was distant from my mind; and while all the provincials were fluttered about me by the unusual animation of their port, I passed throughout their midst on my return homeward, quite absorbed in the recollection of my visit and the Master's speech.

The same night there was brought to us from the ship a little packet of pamphlets. The next day my lord was under engagement to go with the Governor upon some party of pleasure; the time was nearly due, and I left him for a moment alone in his room and skimming through the pamphlets. When I returned, his head had fallen upon the table, his arms lying abroad amongst the crumpled papers.

'My lord, my lord!' I cried as I ran forward, for I supposed he was in some fit.

He sprang up like a figure upon wires, his countenance deformed with fury, so that in a strange place I should scarce have known him. His hand at the same time flew above his head, as though to strike me down. 'Leave me alone!' he screeched, and I fled, as fast as my shaking legs would bear me, for my lady. She, too, lost no time; but when we returned, he had the door locked within, and only cried to us from the other side to leave him be. We looked in each other's faces, very white—each supposing the blow had come at last.

'I will write to the Governor to excuse him,' says she. 'We must keep our strong friends.' But when she took up the pen it flew out of her fingers. 'I cannot write,' said she. 'Can you?'

'I will make a shift, my lady,' said I.

She looked over me as I wrote. 'That will do,' she said, when I had done. 'Thank God, Mackellar, I have you to lean upon! But what can it be now? What, what can it be?'

In my own mind I believed there was no explanation possible, and none required; it was my fear that the man's madness had now simply burst forth its way, like the long-smothered flames of a volcano; but to this (in mere mercy to my lady) I durst not give expression.

'It is more to the purpose to consider our own behaviour,' said I. 'Must we leave him there alone?'

'I do not dare disturb him,' she replied. 'Nature may know best; it may be Nature that cries to be alone; and we grope in the dark. O yes, I would leave him as he is.'

'I will, then, despatch this letter, my lady, and return here, if you please, to sit with you,' said I.

'Pray do,' cries my lady.

All afternoon we sat together, mostly in silence, watching my lord's door. My own mind was busy with the scene that had just passed, and its singular resemblance to my vision. I must say a word upon this, for the story has gone abroad with great exaggeration, and I have even seen it printed, and my own name referred to for particulars. So much was the same: here was my lord in a room, with his head upon the table, and when he raised his face, it wore such an expression as distressed me to the soul. But the room was different, my lord's attitude at the table not at all the same, and his face, when he disclosed it, expressed a painful degree of fury instead of that haunting despair which had always (except once, already referred to) characterised it in the vision. There is the whole truth at last before the public; and if the differences be great, the coincidence was yet enough to fill me with uneasiness. All afternoon, as I say, I sat and pondered upon this quite to myself; for my lady had trouble of her own, and it was my last thought to vex her with fancies. About the midst of our time of waiting, she conceived an ingenious scheme, had Mr Alexander fetched, and bid him knock at his father's door. My lord sent the boy about his business, but without the least violence, whether of manner of expression; so that I began to entertain a hope the fit was over.

At last, as the night fell and I was lighting a lamp that stood there trimmed, the door opened and my lord stood within upon the threshold. The light was not so strong that we could read his countenance; when he spoke, methought his voice a little altered, but yet perfectly steady.

'Mackellar,' said he, 'carry this note to its destination with your own hand. It is highly private. Find the person alone when you deliver it.'

'Henry,' says my lady, 'you are not ill?'

'No, no,' says he querulously, 'I am occupied. Not at all; I am only occupied. It is a singular thing a man must be supposed to be ill when he has any business! Send me supper to this room, and a basket of wine: I expect the visit of a friend. Otherwise I am not to be disturbed.'

And with that he once more shut himself in.

The note was addressed to one Captain Harris, at a tavern on the port side. I knew Harris (by reputation) for a dangerous adventurer, highly suspected of piracy in the past, and now following the rude business of an Indian trader. What my lord should have to say to him, or he to my lord, it passed my imagination to conceive: or yet how my lord had heard of him, unless by a disgraceful trial from which the man was recently escaped. Altogether I went upon the errand with reluctance, and from the little I saw of the captain, returned from it with sorrow. I found him in a foul-smelling chamber, sitting by a guttering candle and an empty bottle; he had the remains of a military carriage, or rather perhaps it was an affectation, for his manners were low.

'Tell my lord, with my service, that I will wait upon his lordship in the inside of half an hour,' says he when he had read the note; and then had the servility, pointing to his empty bottle, to propose that I should buy him liquor.

Although I returned with my best speed, the captain followed close upon my heels, and he stayed late into the night. The cock was crowing a second time when I saw (from my chamber window) my lord lighting him to the gate, both men very much affected with their potations, and sometimes leaning one upon the other to confabulate. Yet the next morning my lord was abroad again early with a hundred pounds of money in his pocket. I never supposed that he returned with it; and yet I was quite sure it did not find its way to the Master, for I lingered all morning within view of the booth. That was the last time my Lord Durrisdeer passed his own enclosure till we left New York; he walked in his barn, or sat and talked with his family, all much as usual; but the town saw nothing of him, and his daily visits to the Master seemed forgotten. Nor yet did Harris reappear; or not until the end.

I was now much oppressed with a sense of the mysteries in which we had begun to move. It was plain, if only from his change of habitude, my lord had something on his mind of a grave nature; but what it was, whence it sprang, or why he should now keep the house and garden, I could make no guess at. It was clear, even to probation, the pamphlets had some share in this revolution; I read all I could find, and they were all extremely insignificant, and of the usual kind of party scurrility; even to a high politician, I could spy out no particular matter of offence, and my lord was a man rather indifferent on public questions. The truth is, the pamphlet

which was the spring of this affair lay all the time on my
lord's bosom. There it was that I found it at last, after he was
dead, in the midst of the north wilderness: in such a place, in
such dismal circumstances, I was to read for the first time
these idle, lying words of a Whig pamphleteer declaiming
against indulgency to Jacobites:—'Another notorious Rebel,
the M——r of B——e, is to have his Title restored,' the
passage ran. 'This Business has been long in hand, since
he rendered some very disgraceful Services in Scotland and
France. His Brother, L——d D——r, is known to be no
better than himself in Inclination; and the supposed Heir,
who is now to be set aside, was bred up in the most
detestable Principles. In the old Phrase, it is *six of the
one* and *half a dozen of the other;* but the Favour of such
a Reposition is too extreme to be passed over.' A man
in his right wits could not have cared two straws for
a tale so manifestly false; that Government should ever
entertain the notion was inconceivable to any reasoning
creature, unless possibly the fool that penned it; and my
lord, though never brilliant, was ever remarkable for sense.
That he should credit such a rodomontade, and carry the
pamphlet on his bosom and the words in his heart, is the
clear proof of the man's lunacy. Doubtless the mere mention
of Mr Alexander, and the threat directly held out against
the child's succession, precipitated that which had so long
impended. Or else my master had been truly mad for a long
time, and we were too dull or too much used to him, and
did not perceive the extent of his infirmity.

About a week after the day of the pamphlets I was
late upon the harbourside, and took a turn towards the
Master's, as I often did. The door opened, a flood of
light came forth upon the road, and I beheld a man taking
his departure with friendly salutations. I cannot say how
singularly I was shaken to recognise the adventurer Harris.
I could not but conclude it was the hand of my lord that
had brought him there; and prolonged my walk in very
serious and apprehensive thought. It was late when I came
home, and there was my lord making up his portmanteau
for a voyage.

'Why do you come so late?' he cried. 'We leave tomorrow

for Albany, you and I together; and it is high time you were about your preparations.'

'For Albany, my lord?' I cried. 'And for what earthly purpose?'

'Change of scene,' said he.

And my lady, who appeared to have been weeping, gave me the signal to obey without more parley. She told me a little later (when we found occasion to exchange some words) that he had suddenly announced his intention after a visit from Captain Harris, and her best endeavours, whether to dissuade him from the journey, or to elicit some explanation of its purpose, had alike proved unavailing.

CHAPTER ELEVEN

The Journey in the Wilderness

WE MADE A prosperous voyage up that fine river of the Hudson, the weather grateful, the hills singularly beautified with the colours of the autumn. At Albany we had our residence at an inn, where I was not so blind and my lord not so cunning but what I could see he had some design to hold me prisoner. The work he found for me to do was not so pressing that we should transact it apart from necessary papers in the chamber of an inn; nor was it of such importance that I should be set upon as many as four or five scrolls of the same document. I submitted in appearance; but I took private measures on my own side, and had the news of the town communicated to me daily by the politeness of our host. In this way I received at last a piece of intelligence for which, I may say, I had been waiting. Captain Harris (I was told) with 'Mr Mountain, the trader,' had gone by up the river in a boat. I would have feared the landlord's eye, so strong the sense of some complicity upon my master's part oppressed me. But I made out to say I had some knowledge of the captain, although none of Mr Mountain, and to inquire who else was of the party. My informant knew not; Mr Mountain had come ashore upon some needful purchases; had gone round the town buying, drinking, and prating; and it seemed the party went upon some likely venture, for he had spoken much of great things he would do when he returned. No more was known, for none of the rest had come ashore, and it seemed they were pressed for time to reach a certain spot before the snow should fall.

And sure enough, the next day there fell a sprinkle even in Albany; but it passed as it came, and was but a reminder of what lay before us. I thought of it lightly then, knowing so little as I did of that inclement province: the retrospect is different; and I wonder at times if some of the horror of these events which I must now rehearse flowed not from the foul skies and savage winds to which we were exposed, and the agony of cold that we must suffer.

The boat having passed by, I thought at first we should have left the town. But no such matter. My lord continued his stay in Albany, where he had no ostensible affairs, and kept me by him, far from my due employment, and making a pretence of occupation. It is upon this passage I expect, and perhaps deserve, censure. I was not so dull but what I had my own thoughts. I could not see the Master entrust himself into the hands of Harris, and not suspect some underhand contrivance. Harris bore a villainous reputation, and he had been tampered with in private by my lord; Mountain, the trader, proved, upon inquiry, to be another of the same kidney; the errand they were all gone upon being the recovery of ill-gotten treasures, offered in itself a very strong incentive to foul play; and the character of the country where they journeyed promised impunity to deeds of blood. Well: it is true I had all these thoughts and fears, and guesses of the Master's fate. But you are to consider I was the same man that sought to dash him from the bulwarks of a ship in the mid-sea; the same that, a little before, very impiously but sincerely offered God a bargain, seeking to hire God to be my bravo. It is true again that I had a good deal melted towards our enemy. But this I always thought of as a weakness of the flesh, and even culpable; my mind remaining steady and quite bent against him. True, yet again, that it was one thing to assume on my own shoulders the guilt and danger of a criminal attempt, and another to stand by and see my lord imperil and besmirch himself.

But this was the very ground of my inaction. For (should I anyway stir in the business) I might fail indeed to save the Master, but I could not miss to make a byword of my lord.

Thus it was that I did nothing; and upon the same reasons, I am still strong to justify my course. My lord had carried with him several introductions to chief people of the town and neighbourhood; others he had before encountered in New York: with this consequence, that he went much abroad, and I am sorry to say was altogether too convivial in his habits. I was often in bed, but never asleep, when he returned; and there was scarce a night when he did not betray the influence of liquor. By day he would still lay upon me endless tasks, which he showed considerable ingenuity to fish up and renew, in the manner of Penelope's web. I never refused, as I say, for I was hired to do his bidding; but I took no pains to keep my penetration under a bushel, and would sometimes smile in his face.

'I think I must be the devil and you Michael Scott,' I said to him one day. 'I have bridged Tweed and split the Eildons; and now you set me to the rope of sand.'

He looked at me with shining eyes, and looked away again, his jaw chewing, but without words.

'Well, well, my lord,' said I, 'your will is my pleasure. I will do this thing for the fourth time; but I would beg of you to invent another task against tomorrow, for by my troth, I am weary of this one.'

'You do not know what you are saying,' returned my lord, putting on his hat and turning his back to me. 'It is a strange thing you should take a pleasure to annoy me. A friend—but that is a different affair. It is a strange thing. I am a man that has had ill fortune all my life through. I am still surrounded by contrivances. I am always treading in plots,' he burst out. 'The whole world is banded against me.'

'I would not talk wicked nonsense if I were you,' said I; 'but I will tell you what I *would* do—I would put my head in cold water, for you had more last night than you could carry.'

'Do ye think that?' said he, with a manner of interest highly awakened. 'Would that be good for me? It's a thing I never tried.'

'I mind the days when you had no call to try, and I wish, my lord, that they were back again,' said I. 'But the plain truth is, if you continue to exceed, you will do yourself a mischief.'

'I don't appear to carry drink the way I used to,' said my lord. 'I get overtaken, Mackellar. But I will be more upon my guard.'

'That is what I would ask of you,' I replied. 'You are to bear in mind that you are Mr Alexander's father: give the bairn a chance to carry his name with some responsibility.'

'Ay, ay,' said he. 'Ye're a very sensible man, Mackellar, and have been long in my employ. But I think, if you have nothing more to say to me I will be stepping. If you have nothing more to say?' he added, with that burning, childish eagerness that was now so common with the man.

'No, my lord, I have nothing more,' said I, drily enough.

'Then I think I will be stepping,' says my lord, and stood and looked at me, fidgeting with his hat, which he had taken off again. 'I suppose you will have no errands? No? I am to meet Sir William Johnson, but I will be more upon my guard.' He was silent for a time, and then, smiling: 'Do you call to mind a place, Mackellar—it's a little below Eagles—where the burn runs very deep under a wood of rowans? I mind being there when I was a lad—dear, it comes over me like an old song!—I was after the fishing, and I made a bonny cast. Eh, but I was happy. I wonder, Mackellar, why I am never happy now?'

'My lord,' said I, 'if you would drink with more moderation you would have the better chance. It is an old byword that the bottle is a false consoler.'

'No doubt,' said he, 'no doubt. Well, I think I will be going.'

'Good morning, my lord,' said I.

'Good morning, good morning,' said he, and so got himself at last from the apartment.

I give that for a fair specimen of my lord in the morning; and I must have described my patron very ill if the reader does not perceive a notable falling off. To behold the man thus fallen: to know him accepted among his companions for a poor, muddled toper, welcome (if he were welcome at all) for the bare consideration of his title; and to recall the virtues he had once displayed against such odds of fortune; was not this a thing at once to rage and to be humbled at?

In his cups, he was more excessive. I will give but the one scene, close upon the end, which is strongly marked upon my memory to this day, and at the time affected me almost with horror.

I was in bed, lying there awake, when I heard him stumbling on the stair and singing. My lord had no gift of music, his brother had all the graces of the family, so that when I say singing, you are to understand a manner of high, carolling utterance, which was truly neither speech nor song. Something not unlike is to be heard upon the lips of children, ere they learn shame; from those of a man grown elderly it had a strange effect. He opened the door with noisy precaution; peered in, shading his candle; conceived me to slumber; entered, set his light upon the table, and took off his hat. I saw him very plain; a high, feverish exultation appeared to boil in his veins, and he stood and smiled and smirked upon the candle. Presently he lifted up his arm, snapped his fingers, and fell to undress. As he did so, having once more forgot my presence, he took back to his singing; and now I could hear the words, which were these from the old song of the 'Twa Corbies' endlessly repeated:

> And over his banes when they are bare
> The wind sall blaw for evermair!

I have said there was no music in the man. His strains had no logical succession except in so far as they inclined a little to the minor mode; but they exercised a rude potency upon the feelings, and followed the words, and signified the feelings of the singer with barbaric fitness. He took it first in the time and manner of a rant; presently this ill-favoured gleefulness abated, he began to dwell upon the notes more feelingly, and sank at last into a degree of maudlin pathos that was to me scarce bearable. By equal steps, the original briskness of his acts declined; and when he was stripped to his breeches, he sat on the bedside and fell to whimpering. I know nothing less respectable than the tears of drunkenness, and turned my back impatiently on this poor sight.

But he had started himself (I am to suppose) on that slippery descent of self-pity; on the which, to a man unstrung by old sorrows and recent potations, there is no arrest except exhaustion. His tears continued to flow, and the man to sit there, three parts naked, in the cold air of the chamber. I twitted myself alternately with inhumanity and sentimental weakness, now half rising in my bed to interfere, now reading myself lessons of indifference and courting slumber, until, upon a sudden, the *quantum mutabus ab illo* shot into my mind; and calling to remembrance his old wisdom, constancy, and patience, I was overborne with a pity almost approaching the passionate, not for my master alone, but for the sons of man.

At this I leaped from my place, went over to his side and laid a hand on his bare shoulder, which was cold as stone. He uncovered his face and showed it me all swollen and begrutten like a child's; and at the sight my impatience partially revived.

'Think shame to yourself,' said I. 'This is bairnly conduct. I might have been snivelling myself, if I had cared to swill my belly with wine. But I went to my bed sober like a man. Come: get into yours, and have done with this pitiable exhibition.'

'O, Mackellar,' said he, 'my heart is wae!'

'Wae?' cried I. 'For a good cause, I think. What words were these you sang as you came in? Show pity to others, we then can talk of pity to yourself. You can be the one thing or the other, but I will be no party to half-way houses. If you're a striker, strike, and if you're a bleater, bleat!'

'Ay!' cries he, with a burst, 'that's it—strike! that's talking! Man, I've stood it all too long. But when they laid a hand upon the child, when the child's threatened'—his momentary vigour whimpering off—'my child, my Alexander!'—and he was at his tears again.

I took him by the shoulders and shook him. 'Alexander!' said I. 'Do you even think of him? Not you! Look yourself in the face like a brave man, and you'll find you're but a self-deceiver. The wife, the friend, the child, they're all equally forgot, and you sunk in a mere bog of selfishness.'

'Mackellar,' said he, with a wonderful return to his old manner and appearance, 'you may say what you will of me, but one thing I never was—I was never selfish.'

'I will open your eyes in your despite,' said I. 'How long have we been here? and how often have you written to your family? I think this is the first time you were ever separate: have you written at all? Do they know if you are dead or living?'

I had caught him here too openly; it braced his better nature; there was no more weeping, he thanked me very penitently, got to bed, and was soon fast asleep; and the first thing he did the next morning was to sit down and begin a letter to my lady: a very tender letter it was too, though it was never finished. Indeed, all communication with New York was transacted by myself; and it will be judged I had a thankless task of it. What to tell my lady, and in what words, and how far to be false and how far cruel, was a thing that kept me often from my slumber.

All this while, no doubt, my lord waited with growing impatiency for news of his accomplices. Harris, it is to be thought, had promised a high degree of expedition; the time was already overpast when word was to be looked for; and suspense was a very evil counsellor to a man of an impaired intelligence. My lord's mind throughout this interval dwelled almost wholly in the Wilderness, following that party with whose deeds he had so much concern. He continually conjured up their camps and progresses, the fashion of the country, the perpetration in a thousand different manners of the same horrid fact, and that consequent spectacle of the Master's bones lying scattered in the wind. These private, guilty considerations I would continually observe to peep forth in the man's talk, like rabbits from a hill. And it is the less wonder if the scene of his meditations began to draw him bodily.

It is well known what pretext he took. Sir William Johnson had a diplomatic errand in these parts; and my lord and I (from curiosity, as was given out) went in his company. Sir William was well attended and liberally supplied. Hunters brought us venison, fish was taken for us daily in the streams, and brandy ran like water. We proceeded by day and encamped by night in the military style; sentinels were set and changed; every man had his named duty; and Sir William was the spring of all. There was much in this that might at times have entertained me; but, for our misfortune, the weather was extremely harsh, the days were in the beginning open, but the nights frosty from the first. A painful keen wind blew most of the time, so that we sat in the boat with blue fingers, and at night, as we scorched our faces at the fire, the clothes upon our back appeared to be of paper. A dreadful solitude surrounded our steps; the land was quite dispeopled, there was no smoke of fires, and save for a single boat of merchants on the second day, we met no travellers. The season was indeed late, but this desertion of the waterways impressed Sir William himself; and I have heard him more than once express a sense of intimidation. 'I have come too late, I fear; they must have dug up the hatchet'; he said; and the future proved how justly he had reasoned.

I could never depict the blackness of my soul upon this journey. I have none of those minds that are in love with the unusual: to see the winter coming and to lie in the field so far from any house, oppressed me like a nightmare; it seemed, indeed, a kind of awful braving of God's power; and this thought, which I daresay only writes me down a coward, was greatly exaggerated by my private knowledge of the errand we were come upon. I was besides encumbered by my duties to Sir William, whom it fell upon me to entertain; for my lord was quite sunk into a state bordering on *pervigilium*, watching the woods with a rapt eye, sleeping scarce at all, and speaking sometimes not twenty words in a whole day. That which he said was still coherent; but it turned almost invariably upon the party for whom he kept his crazy look-out. He would tell Sir William often, and always as if it were a new communication, that he had 'a brother somewhere in the woods,' and beg that the sentinels should be directed 'to inquire for him.' 'I am anxious for news of my brother,' he would say. And sometimes, when we were under way, he would fancy he spied a canoe far off upon the water or a camp on the shore, and exhibit painful agitation. It was impossible but Sir William should be struck with these singularities; and at last he led me aside, and hinted his uneasiness. I touched my head and shook it; quite rejoiced to prepare a little testimony against possible disclosures.

'But in that case,' cries Sir William, 'is it wise to let him go at large?'

'Those that know him best,' said I, 'are persuaded that he should be humoured.'

'Well, well,' replied Sir William, 'it is none of my affairs. But if I had understood, you would never have been here.'

Our advance into this savage country had thus uneventfully proceeded for about a week, when we encamped for a night at a place where the river ran among considerable mountains clothed in wood. The fires were lighted on a level space at the water's edge; and we supped and lay down to sleep in the customary fashion. It chanced the night fell murderously cold; the stringency of the frost seized and bit me through my coverings, so that pain kept me wakeful; and I was afoot again before the peep of day, crouching by the fires or trotting to and fro at the stream's edge, to combat the aching of my limbs. At last dawn began to break upon hoar woods and mountains, the sleepers rolled in their robes, and the boisterous river dashing among spears of ice. I stood looking about me, swaddled in my stiff coat of a bull's fur, and the breath smoking from my scorched nostrils, when, upon a sudden, a singular, eager cry rang from the borders of the wood. The sentries answered it, the sleepers sprang to their feet; one pointed, the rest followed his direction with their eyes, and there, upon the edge of the forest, and betwixt two trees, we beheld the figure of a man reaching forth his hands like one in ecstasy. The next moment he ran forward, fell on his knees at the side of the camp, and burst in tears.

This was John Mountain, the trader, escaped from the most horrid perils; and his first word, when he got speech, was to ask if we had seen Secundra Dass.

'Seen what?' cries Sir William.

'No,' said I, 'we have seen nothing of him. Why?'

'Nothing?' says Mountain. 'Then I was right after all.' With that he struck his palm upon his brow. 'But what takes him back?' he cried. 'What takes the man back among dead bodies? There is some damned mystery here.'

This was a word which highly aroused our curiosity, but I shall be more perspicacious if I narrate these incidents in their true order. Here follows a narrative which I have compiled out of three sources, not very consistent in all points:

First, a written statement by Mountain, in which everything criminal is cleverly smuggled out of view;

Second, two conversations with Secundra Dass; and *Third*, many conversations with Mountain himself, in which he was pleased to be entirely plain; for the truth is he regarded me as an accomplice.

NARRATIVE OF THE TRADER, MOUNTAIN

The crew that went up the river under the joint command of Captain Harris and the Master numbered in all nine persons, of whom (if I except Secundra Dass) there was not one that had not merited the gallows. From Harris downward the voyagers were notorious in that colony for desperate, bloody-minded miscreants; some were reputed pirates, the most hawkers of rum; all ranters and drinkers; all fit associates, embarking together without remorse, upon this treacherous and murderous design. I could not hear there was much discipline or any set captain in the gang; but Harris and four others, Mountain himself, two Scotsmen—Pinkerton and Hastie—and a man of the name of Hicks, a drunken shoemaker, put their heads together and agreed upon the course. In a material sense, they were well provided; and the Master in particular brought with him a tent where he might enjoy some privacy and shelter.

Even this small indulgence told against him in the minds of his companions. But indeed he was in a position so entirely false (and even ridiculous) that all his habit of command and arts of pleasing were here thrown away. In the eyes of all, except Secundra Dass, he figured as a common gull and designated victim; going unconsciously to death; yet he could not but suppose himself the contriver and the leader of the expedition; he could scarce help but so conduct himself; and at the least hint of authority or condescension, his deceivers would be laughing in their sleeves. I was so used to see and to conceive him in a high, authoritative attitude, that when I had conceived his position on this journey, I was pained and could have blushed. How soon he may have entertained a first surmise, we cannot know; but it was long, and the party had advanced into the Wilderness beyond the reach of any help, ere he was fully awakened to the truth.

It fell thus. Harris and some others had drawn apart into the woods for consultation, when they were startled by a rustling in the brush. They were all accustomed to the arts of Indian warfare, and Mountain had not only lived and hunted, but fought and earned some reputation, with the savages. He could move in the woods without noise, and follow a trail like a hound; and upon the emergence of this alert, he was deputed by the rest to plunge into the thicket for intelligence. He was soon convinced there was a man in his close neighbourhood, moving with precaution but without art among the leaves and branches; and coming shortly to a place of advantage, he was able to observe Secundra Dass crawling briskly off with many backward glances. At this he knew not whether to laugh or cry; and his accomplices, when he had returned and reported, were in much the same dubiety. There was now no danger of an Indian onslaught; but on the other hand, since Secundra Dass was at the pains to spy upon them, it was highly probable he knew English, and if he knew English it was certain the whole of their design was in the Master's knowledge. There was one singularity in the position. If Secundra Dass knew and concealed his knowledge of English, Harris was a proficient in several of the tongues of India, and as his career in that part of the world had been a great deal worse than profligate, he had not thought proper to remark upon the circumstance. Each side had thus a spyhole on the counsels of the other. The plotters, so soon as this advantage was explained, returned to camp; Harris, hearing the Hindustanee was once more closeted with his master, crept to the side of the tent; and the rest, sitting about the fire with their tobacco, awaited his report with impatience. When he came at last, his face was very black. He had overheard enough to confirm the worst of his suspicions. Secundra Dass was a good English scholar; he had been some days creeping and listening, the Master was now fully informed of the conspiracy, and the pair proposed on the morrow to fall out of line at a carrying place and plunge at a venture in the woods: preferring the full risk of famine, savage beasts, and savage men to their position in the midst of traitors.

What, then, was to be done? Some were for killing the Master on the spot; but Harris assured them that would be a crime without profit, since the secret of the treasure must die along with him that buried it. Others were for desisting at once from the whole enterprise and making for New York; but the appetising name of treasure, and the thought of the long way they had already travelled, dissuaded the majority. I imagine they were dull fellows for the most part. Harris, indeed, had some acquirements, Mountain was no fool, Hastie was an educated man; but even these had manifestly failed in life, and the rest were the dregs of colonial rascality. The conclusion they reached, at least, was more the offspring of greed and hope than reason. It was to temporise, to be wary and watch the Master, to be silent and supply no further aliment to his suspicions, and to depend entirely (as well as I make out) on the chance that their victim was as greedy, hopeful, and irrational as themselves, and might, after all, betray his life and treasure.

Twice in the course of the next day Secundra and the Master must have appeared to themselves to have escaped; and twice they were circumvented. The Master, save that the second time he grew a little pale, displayed no sign of disappointment, apologised for the stupidity with which he had fallen aside, thanked his recapturers as for a service, and rejoined the caravan with all his usual gallantry and cheerfulness of mien and bearing. But it is certain he had smelled a rat; for from thenceforth he and Secundra spoke only in each other's ear, and Harris listened and shivered by the tent in vain. The same night it was announced they were to leave the boats and proceed by foot, a circumstance which (as it put an end to the confusion of the portages) greatly lessened the chances of escape.

And now there began between the two sides a silent contest, for life on the one hand, for riches on the other. They were now near that quarter of the desert in which the Master himself must begin to play the part of guide;

and using this for a pretext of persecution, Harris and his men sat with him every night about the fire, and laboured to entrap him into some admission. If he let slip his secret, he knew well it was the warrant for his death; on the other hand, he durst not refuse their questions, and must appear to help them to the best of his capacity, or he practically published his mistrust. And yet Mountain assures me the man's brow was never ruffled. He sat in the midst of these jackals, his life depending by a thread, like some easy, witty householder at home by his own fire; an answer he had for everything—as often as not, a jesting answer; avoided threats, evaded insults; talked, laughed, and listened with an open countenance; and, in short, conducted himself in such a manner as must have disarmed suspicion, and went near to stagger knowledge. Indeed, Mountain confessed to me they would soon have disbelieved the captain's story, and supposed their designated victim still quite innocent of their designs; but for the fact that he continued (however ingeniously) to give the slip to questions, and the yet stronger confirmation of his repeated efforts to escape. The last of these, which brought things to a head, I am now to relate. And first I should say that by this time the temper of Harris's companions was utterly worn out; civility was scarce pretended; and, for one very significant circumstance, the Master and Secundra had been (on some pretext) deprived of weapons. On their side, however, the threatened pair kept up the parade of friendship handsomely; Secundra was all bows, the Master all smiles; and on the last night of the truce he had even gone so far as to sing for the diversion of the company. It was observed that he had also eaten with unusual heartiness, and drank deep, doubtless from design.

At least, about three in the morning, he came out of the tent into the open air, audibly mourning and complaining, with all the manner of a sufferer from surfeit. For some while, Secundra publicly attended on his patron, who at last became more easy, and fell asleep on the frosty ground behind the tent, the Indian returning within. Some time after, the sentry was changed; had the Master pointed out to him, where he lay in what is called a robe of buffalo:

and thenceforth kept an eye upon him (he declared) without remission. With the first of the dawn, a draught of wind came suddenly and blew open one side of the corner of the robe; and with the same puff the Master's hat whirled in the air and fell some yards away. The sentry thinking it remarkable the sleeper should not awaken, thereupon drew near; and the next moment, with a great shout, informed the camp their prisoner was escaped. He had left behind his Indian, who (in the first vivacity of the surprise) came near to pay the forfeit of his life, and was, in fact, inhumanly mishandled; but Secundra, in the midst of threats and cruelties, stuck to it with extraordinary loyalty, that he was quite ignorant of his master's plans, which might indeed be true, and of the manner of his escape, which was demonstrably false. Nothing was therefore left to the conspirators but to rely entirely on the skill of Mountain. The night had been frosty, the ground quite hard; and the sun was no sooner up than a strong thaw set in. It was Mountain's boast that few men could have followed that trail, and still fewer (even of the native Indians) found it. The Master had thus a long start before his pursuers had the scent, and he must have travelled with surprising energy for a pedestrian so unused, since it was near noon before Mountain had a view of him. At this conjuncture the trader was alone, all his companions following, at his own request, several hundred yards in the rear; he knew the Master was unarmed; his heart was besides heated with the exercise and lust of hunting; and seeing the quarry so close, so defenceless, and seeming so fatigued, he vaingloriously determined to effect the capture with his single hand. A step or two farther brought him to one margin of a little clearing; on the other, with his arms folded and his back to a huge stone, the Master sat. It is possible Mountain may have made a rustle, it is certain, at least, the Master raised his head and gazed directly at that quarter of the thicket where his hunter lay; 'I could not be sure he saw me,' Mountain said; 'he just looked my way like a man with his mind made up, and all the courage ran out of me like rum out of a bottle.' And presently, when the Master looked away again, and appeared to resume those meditations in which he had sat immersed before the trader's coming, Mountain slunk stealthily back and returned to seek the help of his companions.

And now began the chapter of surprises, for the scout had scarce informed the others of his discovery, and they were yet preparing their weapons for a rush upon the fugitive, when the man himself appeared in their midst, walking openly and quietly, with his hands behind his back.

'Ah, men!' says he, on his beholding them. 'Here is a fortunate encounter. Let us get back to camp.'

Mountain had not mentioned his own weakness or the Master's disconcerting gaze upon the thicket, so that (with all the rest) his return appeared spontaneous. For all that, a hubbub arose; oaths flew, fists were shaken, and guns pointed.

'Let us get back to camp,' said the Master. 'I have an explanation to make, but it must be laid before you all. And in the meanwhile I would put up these weapons, one of which might very easily go off and blow away your hopes of treasure. I would not kill,' says he, smiling, 'the goose with the golden eggs.'

The charm of his superiority once more triumphed; and the party, in no particular order, set off on their return. By the way, he found occasion to get a word or two apart with Mountain.

'You are a clever fellow and a bold,' says he, 'but I am not so sure that you are doing yourself justice. I would have you to consider whether you would not do better, ay, and safer, to serve me instead of serving so commonplace a rascal as Mr Harris. Consider of it,' he concluded, dealing the man a gentle tap upon the shoulder, 'and don't be in haste. Dead or alive, you will find me an ill man to quarrel with.'

When they were come back to the camp, where Harris and Pinkerton stood guard over Secundra, these two ran upon the Master like viragoes, and were amazed out of measure when they were bidden by their comrades to 'stand back and hear what the gentleman had to say.' The Master had not flinched before their onslaught; nor, at this proof of the ground he had gained, did he betray the least sufficiency.

'Do not let us be in haste,' says he. 'Meat first and public speaking after.'

With that they made a hasty meal: and as soon as it was done, the Master, leaning on one elbow, began his speech. He spoke long, addressing himself to each except Harris, finding for each (with the same exception) some particular flattery. He called them 'bold, honest blades,' declared he had never seen a more jovial company, work better done, or pains more merrily supported. 'Well then,' says he, 'some one asks me, "Why the devil I ran away?" But that is scarce worth answer, for I think you all know pretty well. But you know only pretty well: that is a point I shall arrive at presently, and be you ready to remark it when it comes. There is a traitor here: a double traitor: I will give you his name before I am done; and let that suffice for now. But here comes some other gentleman and asks me, "Why, in the devil, I came back?" Well, before I answer that question, I have one to put to you. It was this cur here, this Harris, that speaks Hindustanee?' cries he, rising on one knee and pointing fair at the man's face, with a gesture indescribably menacing; and when he had been answered in the affirmative, 'Ah!' says he, 'then are all my suspicions verified, and I did rightly to come back. Now, men, hear the truth for the first time.' Thereupon he launched forth in a long story, told with extraordinary skill, how he had all along suspected Harris, how he had found the confirmation of his fears, and how Harris must have misrepresented what passed between Secundra and himself. At this point he made a bold stroke with excellent effect. 'I suppose,' says he, 'you think you are going shares with Harris, I suppose you think you will see to that yourselves; you would naturally not think so flat a rogue could cozen you. But have a care! These half-idiots have a sort of cunning, as the skunk has its stench; and it may be news to you that Harris has taken care of himself already. Yes, for him the treasure is all money in the bargain. You must find it or go starve. But he has been paid beforehand; my brother paid him to destroy me; look at him, if you doubt—look at him, grinning and gulping, a detected thief!' Thence, having made this happy impression, he explained how he had escaped, and thought better of it, and at last concluded to come back, lay the truth before the company, and take his chance with them once more: persuaded as he was, they would instantly depose Harris and elect some other leader. 'There is the whole truth,' said he: 'and, with one exception, I put myself entirely in your hands. What is the exception? There he sits,' he cried, pointing once more to Harris; 'a man that has to die! Weapons and conditions are all one to me; put me face to face with him, and if you give me nothing but a stick, in five minutes I will show you a sop of broken carrion, fit for dogs to roll in.'

It was dark night when he made an end; they had listened in almost perfect silence; but the firelight scarce permitted any one to judge, from the look of his neighbours, with what result of persuasion or conviction. Indeed, the Master had set himself in the brightest place, and kept his face there, to be the centre of men's eyes: doubtless on a profound calculation. Silence followed for a while, and presently the whole party became involved in disputation: the Master lying on his back, with his hands knit under his head and one knee flung across the other, like a person unconcerned in the result. And here, I daresay, his bravado carried him too far and prejudiced his case. At least, after a cast or two back and forward, opinion settled finally against him. It's possible he hoped to repeat the business of the pirate ship, and be himself, perhaps, on hard enough conditions, elected leader; and things went so far that way that Mountain actually threw out the proposition. But the rock he split upon was Hastie. This fellow was not well liked, being sour and slow, with an ugly, glowering disposition, but he had studied some time for the Church at Edinburgh College, before ill conduct had destroyed his prospects; and he now remembered and applied what he had learned. Indeed, he had not proceeded very far, when the Master rolled carelessly upon one side, which was done (in Mountain's opinion) to conceal the beginnings of despair upon his countenance. Hastie dismissed the most of what they had heard as nothing to the matter: what they wanted was the treasure. All that was said of Harris might be true, and they would have to see to that in time. But what had that to do with the treasure? They had heard a vast of words; but the truth was just this, that Mr Durie was damnably frightened and had several times run off. Here he was—whether caught or come back was all one to Hastie: the point was to make an end of the business. As for the talk of deposing and electing captains, he hoped they were all free men and could attend their own affairs. That was dust flung in their eyes, and so was the proposal to fight Harris. 'He shall fight no one in this camp; I can tell him that,' said Hastie. 'We had trouble enough to get his arms away from him, and we should look pretty fools to give them back again. But if it's excitement the gentleman is after, I can supply him with more than perhaps he cares about. For I have no intention to spend the remainder of my life in these mountains; already I have been too long; and I propose that he should immediately tell us where that treasure is, or else immediately be shot. And there,' says he, producing his weapon, 'there is the pistol that I mean to use.'

'Come, I call you a man,' cries the Master, sitting up and looking at the speaker with an air of admiration.

'I didn't ask you to call me anything,' returned Hastie; 'which is it to be?'

'That's an idle question,' said the Master. 'Needs must when the devil drives. The truth is we are within easy walk of the place, and I will show it you tomorrow.'

With that, as if all were quite settled, and settled exactly to his mind, he walked off to his tent, whither Secundra had preceded him.

I cannot think of these last turns and wriggles of my old enemy, except with admiration; scarce even pity is mingled with the sentiment, so strongly the man supported, so boldly resisted his misfortunes. Even at that hour, when he perceived himself quite lost, when he saw he had but effected an exchange of enemies, and overthrown Harris to set Hastie up, no sign of weakness appeared in his behaviour, and he withdrew to his tent, already determined (I must suppose) upon affronting the incredible hazard of his last expedient, with the same easy, assured, genteel expression and demeanour as he might have left a theatre withal to join a supper of the wits. But doubtless within, if we could see there, his soul trembled.

Early in the night word went about the camp that he was sick; and the first thing the next morning he called Hastie to his side, and inquired most anxiously if he had any skill in medicine. As a matter of fact, this was a vanity of that fallen divinity student's, to which he had cunningly addressed himself. Hastie examined him; and being flattered, ignorant, and highly suspicious, knew not in the least whether the man was sick or malingering. In this state he went forth again to his companions; and (as the thing which would give himself most consequence either way) announced that the patient was in a fair way to die.

'For all that,' he added, with an oath, 'and if he bursts by the wayside, he must bring us this morning to the treasure.'

But there were several in the camp (Mountain among the number) whom this brutality revolted. They would have seen the Master pistolled, or pistolled him themselves, without the smallest sentiment of pity; but they seemed to have been touched by his gallant fight and unequivocal defeat the night before; perhaps, too, they were even already beginning to oppose themselves to their new leader: at least, they now declared that (if the man was sick) he should have a day's rest in spite of Hastie's teeth.

The next morning he was manifestly worse, and Hastie himself began to display something of humane concern, so easily does even the pretence of doctoring awaken sympathy. The third the Master called Mountain and Hastie to the tent, announced himself to be dying, gave them full particulars as to the position of the cache, and begged them to set out incontinently on the quest, so that they might see if he deceived them, and (if they were at first unsuccessful) he should be able to correct their error.

But here arose a difficulty on which he doubtless counted. None of these men would trust another, none would consent to stay behind. On the other hand, although the Master seemed extremely low, spoke scarce above a whisper, and lay much of the time insensible, it was still possible it was a fraudulent sickness; and if all went treasure hunting, it might prove they had gone upon a wild goose chase, and return to find their prisoner flown. They concluded, there-fore, to hang idling round the camp, alleging sympathy to their reason; and certainly, so mingled are our dispositions, several were sincerely (if not very deeply) affected by the natural peril of the man whom they callously designed to murder. In the afternoon, Hastie was called to the bedside to pray: the which (incredible as it must appear) he did with unction; about eight at night the wailing of Secundra announced that all was over; and before ten, the Indian, with a link stuck in the ground, was toiling at the grave. Sunrise of next day beheld the Master's burial, all hands attending with great decency of demeanour; and the body was laid in the earth, wrapped in a fur robe, with only the face uncovered, which last was of a waxy whiteness, and had the nostrils plugged according to some Oriental habit of Secundra's. No sooner was the grave filled than the lamentations of the Indian once more struck concern to every heart; and it appears this gang of murderers, so far from resenting his outcries, although both distressful and (in such a country) perilous to their own safety, roughly but kindly endeavoured to console him.

But if human nature is even in the worst of men occa-sionally kind, it is still, and before all things, greedy; and they soon turned from the mourner to their own concerns. The cache of the treasure being hard by, although yet unidentified, it was concluded not to break camp; and the day passed, on the part of the voyagers, in unavailing exploration of the woods, Secundra the while lying on his master's grave. That night they placed no sentinel, but lay altogether about the fire, in the customary woodman fash-ion, the heads outward, like the spokes of a wheel. Morning found them in the same disposition; only Pinkerton, who lay on Mountain's right, between him and Hastie, had (in the hours of darkness) been secretly butchered, and there lay, still wrapped as to his body in his mantle, but offering above that ungodly and horrific spectacle of the scalped head. The gang were that morning as pale as a company of phantoms, for the pertinacity of Indian war (or, to speak more correctly, Indian murder) was well known to all. But they laid the chief blame on their unsentinelled posture; and, fired with the neighbourhood of the treasure, determined to continue where they were. Pinkerton was buried hard by the Master; the survivors again passed the day in exploration, and returned in a mingled humour of anxiety and hope, being partly certain they were now close on the discovery of what they sought, and on the other hand (with the return of darkness) infected with the fear of Indians. Mountain was the first sentry; he declares he neither slept nor yet sat down, but kept his watch with a perpetual and straining vigilance, and it was even with unconcern that (when he saw by the stars his time was up) he drew near the fire to awaken his successor. This man (it was Hicks the shoemaker) slept on the lee side of the circle, something farther off in consequence than those to windward, and in a place darkened by the blowing smoke. Mountain stooped and took him by the shoulder; his hand was at once smeared by some adhesive wetness; and (the wind at the moment veering) the firelight shone upon the sleeper, and showed him, like Pinkerton, dead and scalped.

It was clear they had fallen in the hands of one of those matchless Indian braves, that will sometimes follow a party for days, and in spite of indefatigable travel, and unsleeping watch, continue to keep up with their advance, and steal a scalp at every resting place. Upon this discovery, the treasure seekers, already reduced to a poor half-dozen, fell into mere dismay, seized a few necessaries, and, deserting the remainder of their goods, fled outright into the forest. Their fire they left still burning, and their dead comrade unburied. All day they ceased not to flee, eating by the way, from hand to mouth; and since they feared to sleep, continued to advance at random even in the hours of darkness. But the limit of man's endurance is soon reached; when they rested at last it was to sleep profoundly; and when they woke, it was to find that the enemy was still upon their heels, and death and mutilation had once more lessened and deformed their company.

By this they had become light-headed, they had quite missed their path in the Wilderness, their stores were already running low. With the further horrors it is superfluous that I should swell this narrative, already too prolonged. Suffice it to say that when at length a night passed by innocuous, and they might breathe again in the hope that the murderer had at last desisted from pursuit, Mountain and Secundra were alone. The trader is firmly persuaded their unseen enemy was some warrior of his own acquaintance, and that he himself was spared by favour. The mercy extended to Secundra he explains on the ground that the East Indian was thought to be insane; partly from the fact that, through all the horrors of the flight, and while others were casting away their very food and weapons, Secundra continued to stagger forward with a mattock on his shoulder, and partly because, in the last days, and with a great degree of heat and fluency, he perpetually spoke with himself in his own language. But he was sane enough when it came to English.

'You think he will be gone quite away?' he asked, upon their blest awakening in safety.

'I pray God so, I believe so, I dare to believe so,' Mountain had replied almost with incoherence, as he described the scene to me.

And indeed he was so much distempered that until he met us, the next morning, he could scarce be certain whether he had dreamed, or whether it was a fact, that Secundra had thereupon turned directly about and returned without a word upon their footprints, setting his face for these wintry and hungry solitudes along a path whose every stage was mile-stoned with a mutilated corpse.

CHAPTER TWELVE

The Journey in
the Wilderness (continued)

MOUNTAIN'S STORY, AS it was laid before Sir William Johnson and my lord, was shorn, of course, of all the earlier particulars, and the expedition described to have proceeded uneventfully, until the Master sickened. But the latter part was very forcibly related, the speaker visibly thrilling to his recollections; and our then situation, on the fringe of the same desert, and the private interests of each, gave him an audience prepared to share in his emotions. For Mountain's intelligence not only changed the world for my Lord Durrisdeer, but materially affected the designs of Sir William Johnson.

These I find I must lay more at length before the reader. Word had reached Albany of dubious import; it had been rumoured some hostility was to be put in act; and the Indian diplomatist had, thereupon, sped into the Wilderness, even at the approach of winter, to nip that mischief in the bud. Here, on the borders, he learned that he was come too late; and a difficult choice was thus presented to a man (upon the whole) not any more bold than prudent. His standing with the painted braves may be compared to that of my Lord President Culloden among the chiefs of our own Highlanders at the 'Forty-five; that is as much as to say, he was, to these men, reason's only speaking-trumpet, and counsels of peace and moderation, if they were to prevail at all, must prevail singly through his influence. If, then, he should return, the province must lie open to all the abominable tragedies of Indian war—the houses blaze, the wayfarer be cut off, and the men of the woods collect their usual disgusting spoil of human scalps. On the other side, to go farther forth, to risk so small a party deeper in the desert, to carry words of peace among warlike savages already rejoicing to return to war: here was an extremity from which it was easy to perceive his mind revolted.

'I have come too late,' he said more than once, and would fall into a deep consideration, his head bowed in his hands, his foot patting the ground.

At length he raised his face and looked upon us, that is to say, upon my lord, Mountain, and myself, sitting close round a small fire, which had been made for privacy in one corner of the camp.

'My lord, to be quite frank with you, I find myself in two minds,' said he. 'I think it very needful I should go on, but not at all proper I should any longer enjoy the pleasure of your company. We are here still upon the waterside; and I think the risk to southward no great matter. Will not yourself and Mr Mackellar take a single boat's crew and return to Albany?'

My lord, I should say, had listened to Mountain's narrative, regarding him throughout with a painful intensity of gaze; and, since the tale concluded, had sat as in a dream. There was something very daunting in his look; something to my eyes not rightly human; the face, lean, and dark, and aged, the mouth painful, the teeth disclosed in a perpetual rictus; the eyeball swimming clear of the lids upon a field of bloodshot white. I could not behold him myself without a jarring irritation, such as, I believe, is too frequently the uppermost feeling on the sickness of those dear to us. Others, I could not but remark, were scarce able to support his neighbourhood—Sir William eviting to be near him, Mountain dodging his eye, and, when he met it, blenching and halting in his story. At this appeal, however, my lord appeared to recover his command upon himself.

'To Albany?' said he, with a good voice.

'Not short of it, at least,' replied Sir William. 'There is no safety nearer hand.'

'I would be very sweir to return,' says my lord. 'I am not afraid—of Indians,' he added, with a jerk.

'I wish that I could say so much,' returned Sir William, smiling; 'although, if any man durst say it, it should be myself. But you are to keep in view my responsibility, and that as the voyage has now become highly dangerous, and your business—if you ever had any,' says he,—'brought quite to a conclusion by the distressing family intelligence you have received, I should be hardly justified if I even suffered you to proceed, and run the risk of some obloquy if anything regrettable should follow.'

My lord turned to Mountain. 'What did he pretend he died of?' he asked.

'I don't think I understand your honour,' said the trader, pausing, like a man very much affected, in the dressing of some cruel frostbites.

For a moment my lord seemed at a full stop; and then, with some irritation, 'I ask you what he died of. Surely that's a plain question,' said he.

'O! I don't know,' said Mountain. 'Hastie even never knew. He seemed to sicken natural, and just pass away.'

'There it is, you see!' concluded my lord, turning to Sir William.

'Your lordship is too deep for me,' replied Sir William.

'Why,' says my lord, 'this is a matter of succession; my son's title may be called in doubt; and the man being supposed to be dead of nobody can tell what, a great deal of suspicion would be naturally roused.'

'But, God damn me, the man's buried!' cried Sir William.

'I will never believe that,' returned my lord, painfully trembling. 'I'll never believe it!' he cried again, and jumped to his feet. 'Did he *look* dead?' he asked of Mountain.

'Look dead?' repeated the trader. 'He looked white. Why, what would he be at? I tell you, I put the sods upon him.'

My lord caught Sir William by the coat with a hooked hand. 'This man has the name of my brother,' says he, 'but it's well understood that he was never canny.'

'Canny?' says Sir William. 'What is that?'

'He's not of this world,' whispered my lord, 'neither him nor the black deil that serves him. I have struck my sword throughout his vitals,' he cried; 'I have felt the hilt dirl on his breastbone, and the hot blood spirt in my very face, time and again, time and again!' he repeated, with a gesture indescribable. 'But he was never dead for that,' said he, and sighed aloud. 'Why should I think he was dead now? No, not till I see him rotting,' says he.

Sir William looked across at me with a long face. Mountain forgot his wounds, staring and gaping.

'My lord,' said I, 'I wish you would collect your spirits.' But my throat was so dry, and my own wits so scattered, I could add no more.

'No,' says my lord, 'it's not to be supposed that he would understand me. Mackellar does, for he kens all, and has seen him buried before now. This is a very good servant to me, Sir William, this man Mackellar; he buried him with his own hands—he and my father—by the light of two siller candlesticks. The other man is a familiar spirit; he brought him from Coromandel. I would have told ye this long syne, Sir William, only it was in the family.' These last remarks he made with a kind of melancholy composure, and his time of aberration seemed to pass away. 'You can ask yourself what it all means,' he proceeded. 'My brother falls sick, and dies, and is buried, or so they say; and all seems very plain. But why did the familiar go back? I think ye must see for yourself it's a point that wants some clearing.'

'I will be at your service, my lord, in half a minute,' said Sir William, rising.—'Mr Mackellar, two words with you'; and he led me without the camp, the frost crunching in our steps, the trees standing at our elbow, hoar with frost, even as on that night in the long shrubbery. 'Of course, this is midsummer madness,' said Sir William, as soon as we were gotten out of hearing.

'Why, certainly,' said I. 'The man is mad. I think that manifest.'

'Shall I seize and bind him?' asked Sir William. 'I will upon your authority. If these are all ravings, that should certainly be done.'

I looked down upon the ground, back at the camp, with its bright fires and the folk watching us, and about me on the woods and mountains; there was just the one way that I could not look, and that was in Sir William's face.

'Sir William,' said I at last, 'I think my lord not sane, and have long thought him so. But there are degrees in madness; and whether he should be brought under restraint—Sir William, I am no fit judge,' I concluded.

'I will be the judge,' said he. 'I ask for facts. Was there, in all that jargon, any word of truth or sanity? Do you hesitate?' he asked. 'Am I to understand you have buried this gentleman before?'

'Not buried,' said I; and then, taking up courage at last, 'Sir William,' said I, 'unless I were to tell you a long story, which much concerns a noble family (and myself not in the least), it would be impossible to make this matter clear to you. Say the word, and I will do it, right or wrong. And, at any rate, I will say so much, that my lord is not so crazy as he seems. This is a strange matter, into the tail of which you are unhappily drifted.'

'I desire none of your secrets,' replied Sir William; 'but I will be plain, at the risk of incivility, and confess that I take little pleasure in my present company.'

'I would be the last to blame you,' said I, 'for that.'

'I have not asked either for your censure or your praise, sir,' returned Sir William. 'I desire simply to be quit of you; and to that effect, I put a boat and complement of men at your disposal.'

'This is fairly offered,' said I, after reflection. 'But you must suffer me to say a word upon the other side. We have a natural curiosity to learn the truth of this affair; I have some of it myself; my lord (it is very plain) has but too much. The matter of the Indian's return is enigmatical.'

'I think so myself,' Sir William interrupted, 'and I propose (since I go in that direction) to probe it to the bottom. Whether or not the man has gone like a dog to die upon his master's grave, his life, at least, is in great danger, and I propose, if I can, to save it.—There is nothing against his character?'

'Nothing, Sir William,' I replied.

'And the other?' he said. 'I have heard my lord, of course; but, from the circumstances of his servant's loyalty, I must suppose he had some noble qualities.'

'You must not ask me that!' I cried. 'Hell may have noble flames. I have known him a score of years, and always hated, and always admired, and always slavishly feared him.'

'I appear to intrude again upon your secrets,' said Sir William, 'believe me, inadvertently. Enough that I will see the grave, and (if possible) rescue the Indian. Upon these terms, can you persuade your master to return to Albany?'

'Sir William,' said I, 'I will tell you how it is. You do not see my lord to advantage; it will seem even strange to you that I should love him; but I do, and I am not alone. If he goes back to Albany, it must be by force, and it will be the death warrant of his reason, and perhaps his life. That is my sincere belief; but I am in your hands, and ready to obey, if you will assume so much responsibility as to command.'

'I will have no shred of responsibility; it is my single endeavour to avoid the same,' cried Sir William. 'You insist upon following this journey up; and be it so! I wash my hands of the whole matter.'

With which word he turned upon his heel and gave the order to break camp; and my lord, who had been hovering near by, came instantly to my side.

'Which is it to be?' said he.

'You are to have your way,' I answered. 'You shall see the grave.'

The situation of the Master's grave was, between guides, easily described; it lay, indeed, beside a chief landmark of the Wilderness, a certain range of peaks, conspicuous by their design and altitude, and the source of many brawling tributaries to that inland sea, Lake Champlain. It was therefore possible to strike for it direct, instead of following back the blood-stained trail of the fugitives, and to cover, in some sixteen hours of march, a distance which their perturbed wanderings had extended over more than sixty. Our boats we left under a guard upon the river; it was, indeed, probable we should return to find them frozen fast; and the small equipment with which we set forth upon the expedition included not only an infinity of furs to protect us from the cold, but an arsenal of snow shoes to render travel possible, when the inevitable snow should fall. Considerable alarm was manifested at our departure; the march was conducted with soldierly precaution, the camp at night sedulously chosen and patrolled; and it was a consideration of this sort that arrested us, the second day, within not many hundred yards of our destination—the night being already imminent, the spot in which we stood well qualified to be a strong camp for a party of our numbers;

and Sir William, therefore, on a sudden thought, arresting our advance.

Before us was the high range of mountains toward which we had been all day deviously drawing near. From the first light of the dawn, their silver peaks had been the goal of our advance across a tumbled lowland forest, thrid with rough streams, and strewn with monstrous boulders; the peaks (as I say) silver, for already at the higher altitudes the snow fell nightly; but the woods and the low ground only breathed upon with frost. All day heaven had been charged with ugly vapours, in the which the sun swam and glimmered like a shilling piece; all day the wind blew on our left cheek barbarous cold, but very pure to breathe. With the end of the afternoon, however, the wind fell; the clouds, being no longer reinforced, were scattered or drunk up; the sun set behind us with some wintry splendour, and the white brow of the mountains shared its dying glow.

It was dark ere we had supper; we ate in silence, and the meal was scarce despatched before my lord slunk from the fireside to the margin of the camp; whither I made haste to follow him. The camp was on high ground, overlooking a frozen lake, perhaps a mile in its longest measurement; all about us the forest lay in heights and hollows; above rose the white mountains; and higher yet, the moon rode in a fair sky. There was no breath of air; nowhere a twig creaked; and the sounds of our own camp were hushed and swallowed up in the surrounding stillness. Now that the sun and the wind were both gone down, it appeared almost warm, like a night of July: a singular illusion of the sense, when earth, air, and water were strained to bursting with the extremity of frost.

My lord (or what I still continued to call by his loved name) stood with his elbow in one hand, and his chin sunk in the other, gazing before him on the surface of the wood. My eyes followed his, and rested almost pleasantly upon the frosted contexture of the pines, rising in moonlit hillocks, or sinking in the shadow of small glens. Hard by, I told myself, was the grave of our enemy, now gone where the wicked cease from troubling, the earth heaped for ever on his once so active limbs. I could not but think of him as somehow fortunate to be thus done with man's anxiety and weariness, the daily expense of spirit, and that daily river of circumstance to be swum through, at any hazard, under the penalty of shame or death. I could not but think how good was the end of that long travel; and with that, my mind swung at a tangent to my lord. For was not my lord dead also? a maimed soldier, looking vainly for discharge, lingering derided in the line of battle? A kind man, I remembered him; wise, with a decent pride, a son perhaps too dutiful, a husband only too loving, one that could suffer and be silent, one whose hand I loved to press. Of a sudden, pity caught in my windpipe with a sob; I could have wept aloud to remember and behold him; and standing thus by his elbow, under the broad moon, I prayed fervently either that he should be released, or I strengthened to persist in my affection.

'O God,' said I, 'this was the best man to me and to himself, and now I shrink from him. He did no wrong, or not till he was broke with sorrows; these are but his honourable wounds that we begin to shrink from. O cover them up, O take him away, before we hate him!'

I was still so engaged in my own bosom, when a sound broke suddenly upon the night. It was neither very loud nor very near; yet, bursting as it did from so profound and so prolonged a silence, it startled the camp like an alarm of trumpets. Ere I had taken breath, Sir William was beside me, the main part of the voyagers clustered at his back, intently giving ear. Methought, as I glanced at them across my shoulder, there was a whiteness, other than moonlight, on their cheeks; and the rays of the moon reflected with a sparkle on the eyes of some, and the shadows lying black under the brows of others (according as they raised or bowed the head to listen) gave to the group a strange air of animation and anxiety. My lord was to the front, couching a little forth, his hand raised as for silence: a man turned to stone. And still the sounds continued, breathlessly renewed with a precipitate rhythm.

Suddenly Mountain spoke in a loud, broken whisper, as of a man relieved. 'I have it now,' he said; and, as we all turned to hear him, 'the Indian must have known the cache,' he added. 'That is he—he is digging out the treasure.'

'Why, to be sure!' exclaimed Sir William. 'We were geese not to have supposed so much.'

'The only thing is,' Mountain resumed, 'the sound is very close to our old camp. And, again, I do not see how he is there before us, unless the man had wings!'

'Greed and fear are wings,' remarked Sir William. 'But this rogue has given us an alert, and I have a notion to return the compliment.—What say you, gentlemen, shall we have a moonlight hunt?'

It was so agreed; dispositions were made to surround Secundra at his task; some of Sir William's Indians hastened in advance; and a strong guard being left at our headquarters, we set forth along the uneven bottom of the forest; frost crackling, ice sometimes loudly splitting under foot; and overhead the blackness of pinewoods and the broken brightness of the moon. Our way led down into a hollow of the land; and as we descended, the sounds diminished and had almost died away. Upon the other slope it was more open, only dotted with a few pines, and several vast and scattered rocks that made inky shadows in the moonlight. Here the sounds began to reach us more distinctly; we could now perceive the ring of iron, and more exactly estimate the furious degree of haste with which the digger plied his instrument. As we neared the top of the ascent, a bird or two winged aloft and hovered darkly in the moonlight; and the next moment we were gazing through a fringe of trees upon a singular picture.

A narrow plateau, overlooked by the white mountains, and encompassed nearer hand by woods, lay bare to the strong radiance of the moon. Rough goods, such as make the wealth of foresters, were sprinkled here and there upon the ground in meaningless disarray. About the midst, a tent stood, silvered with frost: the door open, gaping on the black interior. At the one end of this small stage lay what seemed the tattered remnants of a man. Without doubt we had arrived upon the scene of Harris's encampment; there were the goods scattered in the panic of flight; it was in yon tent the Master breathed his last; and the frozen carrion that lay before us was the body of the drunken shoemaker. It was always moving to come upon the theatre of any tragic incident; to come upon it after so many days, and to find it (in the seclusion of a desert) still unchanged, must have impressed the mind of the most careless. And yet it was not that which struck us into pillars of stone; but the sight (which yet we had been half-expecting) of Secundra ankle-deep in the grave of his late master. He had cast the main part of his raiment by, yet his frail arms and shoulders glistered in the moonlight with a copious sweat; his face was contracted with anxiety and expectation; his blows resounded on the grave, as thick as sobs; and behind him, strangely deformed and ink-black upon the frosty ground, the creature's shadow repeated and parodied his swift gesticulations. Some nightbirds arose from the boughs upon our coming, and then settled back; but Secundra, absorbed in his toil, heard or heeded not at all.

I heard Mountain whisper to Sir William, 'Good God! it's the grave! He's digging him up!' It was what we had all guessed, and yet to hear it put in language thrilled me. Sir William violently started.

'You damned sacrilegious hound!' he cried. 'What's this?'

Secundra leaped in the air, a little breathless cry escaped him, the tool flew from his grasp, and he stood one instant staring at the speaker. The next, swift as an arrow, he sped for the woods upon the farther side; and the next again, throwing up his hands with a violent gesture of resolution, he had begun already to retrace his steps.

'Well, then, you come, you help—' he was saying. But by now my lord had stepped beside Sir William; the moon shone fair upon his face, and the words were still upon Secundra's lips, when he beheld and recognised his master's enemy. 'Him!' he screamed, clasping his hands, and shrinking on himself.

'Come, come!' said Sir William. 'There is none here to do you harm, if you be innocent; and if you be guilty, your escape is quite cut off. Speak, what do you here among the graves of the dead and the remains of the unburied?'

'You no murderer?' inquired Secundra. 'You true man? You see me safe?'

'I will see you safe, if you be innocent,' returned Sir William. 'I have said the thing, and I see not wherefore you should doubt it.'

'These all murderers,' cried Secundra, 'that is why! He

kill—murderer,' pointing to Mountain; 'these two hire-
murderers,' pointing to my lord and myself—'all gallows-
murderers! Ah! I see you all swing in a rope. Now I go
save the Sahib; he see you swing in a rope. The Sahib,' he
continued, pointing to the grave, 'he not dead. He bury, he
not dead.'

My lord uttered a little noise, moved nearer to the grave,
and stood and stared in it.

'Buried and not dead?' exclaimed Sir William. 'What kind
of rant is this?'

'See, Sahib,' said Secundra. 'The Sahib and I alone with
murderers; try all way to escape, no way good. Then try this
way: good way in warm climate, good way in India; here,
in this damn cold place, who can tell? I tell you pretty good
hurry: you help, you light a fire, help rub.'

'What is the creature talking of?' cried Sir William. 'My
head goes round.'

'I tell you I bury him alive,' said Secundra. 'I teach him
swallow his tongue. Now dig him up pretty good hurry, and
he not much worse. You light a fire.'

Sir William turned to the nearest of his men. 'Light a fire,'
said he. 'My lot seems to be cast with the insane.'

'You good man,' returned Secundra. 'Now I go dig the
Sahib up.'

He returned as he spoke to the grave, and resumed his
former toil. My lord stood rooted, and I at my lord's side,
fearing I knew not what.

The frost was not yet very deep, and presently the Indian
threw aside his tool, and began to scoop the dirt by handfuls.
Then he disengaged a corner of a buffalo robe; and then I saw
hair catch among his fingers: yet a moment more, and the
moon shone on something white. A while Secundra crouched
upon his knees, scraping with delicate fingers, breathing with
puffed lips; and when he moved aside, I beheld the face of
the Master wholly disengaged. It was deadly white, the eyes
closed, the ears and nostrils plugged, the cheeks fallen, the
nose sharp as if in death; but for all he had lain so many
days under the sod, corruption had not approached him,
and (what strangely affected all of us) his lips and chin were
mantled with a swarthy beard.

'My God!' cried Mountain, 'he was as smooth as a baby when we laid him there!'

'They say hair grows upon the dead,' observed Sir William; but his voice was thick and weak.

Secundra paid no heed to our remarks, digging swift as a terrier in the loose earth. Every moment the form of the Master, swathed in his buffalo robe, grew more distinct in the bottom of that shallow trough; the moon shining strong, and the shadows of the standers-by, as they drew forward and back, falling and fitting over his emergent countenance. The sight held us with a horror not before experienced. I dared not look my lord in the face; but for as long as it lasted, I never observed him to draw breath; and a little in the background one of the men (I know not whom) burst into a kind of sobbing.

'Now,' said Secundra, 'you help me lift him out.'

Of the flight of time I have no idea; it may have been three hours, and it may have been five, that the Indian laboured to reanimate his master's body. One thing only I know, that it was still night, and the moon was not yet set, although it had sunk low, and now barred the plateau with long shadows, when Secundra uttered a small cry of satisfaction: and, leaning swiftly forth, I thought I could myself perceive a change upon that icy countenance of the unburied. The next moment I beheld his eyelids flutter; the next they rose entirely, and the week-old corpse looked me for a moment in the face.

So much display of life I can myself swear to. I have heard from others that he visibly strove to speak, that his teeth showed in his beard, and that his brow was contorted as with an agony of pain and effort. And this may have been; I know not, I was otherwise engaged. For at that first disclosure of the dead man's eyes my Lord Durrisdeer fell to the ground, and when I raised him up he was a corpse.

Day came, and still Secundra could not be persuaded to desist from his unavailing efforts. Sir William, leaving a small party under my command, proceeded on his embassy with the first light; and still the Indian rubbed the limbs and breathed in the mouth of the dead body. You would think such labours might have vitalised a stone; but, except for that one moment (which was my lord's death), the black spirit of the Master held aloof from its discarded clay; and by about the hour of noon, even the faithful servant was at length convinced. He took it with unshaken quietude.

'Too cold,' said he, 'good way in India, no good here.' And, asking for some food, which he ravenously devoured as soon as it was set before him, he drew near to the fire and took his place at my elbow. In the same spot, as soon as he had eaten, he stretched himself out, and fell into a childlike slumber, from which I must arouse him, some hours afterwards, to take his part as one of the mourners at the double funeral. It was the same throughout; he seemed to have outlived at once, and with the same effort, his grief for his master and his terror of myself and Mountain.

One of the men left with me was skilled in stone cutting; and before Sir William returned to pick us up, I had chiselled on a boulder this inscription, with a copy of which I may fitly bring my narrative to a close:

J. D.
HEIR TO A SCOTTISH TITLE,
A MASTER OF THE ARTS AND GRACES,
ADMIRED IN EUROPE, ASIA, AMERICA,
IN WAR AND PEACE,
IN THE TENTS OF SAVAGE HUNTERS AND THE
CITADELS OF KINGS, AFTER SO MUCH
ACQUIRED, ACCOMPLISHED, AND
ENDURED, LIES HERE FORGOTTEN.

H. D.
HIS BROTHER,
AFTER A LIFE OF UNMERITED DISTRESS,
BRAVELY SUPPORTED,
DIED ALMOST IN THE SAME HOUR,
AND SLEEPS IN THE SAME GRAVE
WITH HIS FRATERNAL ENEMY.

THE PIETY OF HIS WIFE AND ONE OLD
SERVANT RAISED THIS STONE
TO BOTH.

WEIR OF HERMISTON

An Unfinished Romance

──

Introduced by Roderick Watson

TO MY WIFE

I saw rain falling and the rainbow drawn
On Lammermuir. Hearkening I heard again
In my precipitous city beaten bells
Winnow the keen sea wind. And here afar,
Intent on my own race and place, I wrote.
　　Take thou the writing: thine it is. For who
Burnished the sword, blew on the drowsy coal,
Held still the target higher, chary of praise
And prodigal of counsel – who but thou?
So now, in the end, if this the least be good,
If any deed be done, if any fire
Burn in the imperfect page, the praise be thine.

Contents

Introduction

'He wrote hard all that morning of the last day' – Stevenson's stepson remembered – 'his half-finished book, *Hermiston*, he judged the best he had ever written, and a sense of successful effort made him buoyant and happy as nothing else could.'

Stevenson never did finish *Weir of Hermiston*, and the manuscript's last words might indeed apply to the cerebral stroke that cut him down at the age of 45 on the evening of 3 December 1894 – 'It seemed unprovoked, a wilful convulsion of brute nature . . .'

We can only speculate on how the novel would have developed, but Stevenson's notes and letters give us a general sense of what was going to happen. – Frank Innes will seduce young Christina, and Archie Weir will kill him for it, only to be imprisoned for trial at the command of his own father, the Lord Justice-Clerk. In this way the book's early confrontations between father and son, between generous feeling and the strictures of the law, will take place all over again, but this time in mortal and mutually tragic terms. Of course it is legally impossible for a judge to try his own son, but their imagined confrontation would be none the less powerful for taking place privately, or perhaps in the condemned cell, prior to the trial. Here, too, young Archie would finally grow up, confronting his own capacity for reckless violence and making a commitment to Christina, despite the fact that she is carrying Frank Innes's child. And old Adam Weir, Archie's father, with his delight in the law as a justified sword of terror, would have that delight turned against the sinews of his own heart in the cruelest possible way.

These intimate and painful scenes would mark the undoubted climax of the book's various difficult confrontations between action and judgement and love and duty, but their resolution seems to have been planned to be a violent one. Stevenson imagined the four black Elliot brothers riding out once again, as they did to avenge their own father's death so many years before. But they are respectable middle-aged citizens now, and perhaps the old days of rough border justice are gone forever? And who can tell if they should even be *allowed* to succeed in breaking Archie out of jail? Where would it leave his father, for example, and could such a tale ever reach a 'happy ending'?

One thing is clear, and it is that *Weir of Hermiston* is not the simple adventure story it might have been had its author planned it ten years earlier. Like *The Master of Ballantrae* before it, Stevenson's last novel sets out, in part, to deconstruct the very terms of its own fascination with romance. Thus the undoubtedly tragic love affair between Archie Weir and Christina Elliot is reported to us with a narrative distance which sees the couple, not without an air of amused affection, as 'a pair of children at the old game of falling in love.' Yet even as Stevenson's ironic prose captures the comedy of Christina's silliness and Archie's moonstruck gaze, it also reflects on the fact that these foolish illusions will bring death in their wake. And it reflects, too, on what the novelist can and cannot convey about what goes on in the human heart. The effect is both liberating and disturbing, very far indeed from the sympathetic engagement with the idea of 'love' which might be expected in more conventional romance fiction:

> Had a doctor of medicine come into that loft, he would have diagnosed a healthy, well-developed, eminently vivacious lass lying on her face in a fit of the sulks; not one who has just contracted, or was just contracting, a mortal sickness of the mind which should yet carry her towards death and despair. Had it been a doctor of psychology, he might have been pardoned for divining in the girl a passion of childish vanity, self-love *in excelsis,* and no more. It is to be understood that I have been painting chaos and describing the inarticulate.

Christina's inner life is described as if she were lying in 'mutable and blinding wreaths of haze'. Sulking on her bed, she is caught up in constructing 'the first chapter of her love-story', and Stevenson sees her as being moved, not so much by her 'destiny' as by her own half-baked ideas of it, in love with herself and growing solemn with 'that idea of Fate – a pagan Fate, uncontrolled by any Christian diety, obscure lawless, and august,' before she slips into 'a gray frock and a pink kerchief'. The same self-regarding and self-deluding portentousness characterised Mrs Weir's philosophy of life by which she raised her son Archie, based as it was on 'a kind of ecstasy of tenderness' with easy tears for martyred Covenanters, and the curiously seductive idea of persecuted babes and innocents. (Young Archie was brought up to lisp about whether he was 'justifieed' or not.)

The ironic spirit in which all this is narrated is not out of keeping with the Lord Justice-Clerk himself, whose response to such matters of romance and sentiment was to cry 'Signor Feedle-eerie! Oh, for God's sake, no more of the Signor!' And certainly the character of Adam Weir dominates the novel with his crude speech and his refusal to call a spade anything other than a spade. The coarse and incisive aspects of Hermiston's judicial character were taken from Robert MacQueen, Lord Braxfield, the 'hanging judge' from Edinburgh in the second half of the eighteenth century, but Stevenson gives a considered and considering air to Hermiston which seems to have been lacking in his real-life counterpart. There is a certain existential honesty about Weir, too, in that he refuses to cloak the harsh truth of his calling by any show of moral pomp: 'Heedious! I never gave twa thoughts to heediousness, I have no call to be bonny. I'm a man that gets through with my day's business, and let that suffice.'

Adam Weir's broad Scots voice speaks for all those elements in the national culture which take pride in the proposition (somewhere between materialism and Calvinism) that 'facts are chiels that winna ding'. His response to his wife's early death is not without its own rough gentleness, but then again, there's no doubt that he terrorised the 'puir bitch' when she was alive. Stevenson regarded the creation of Adam Weir as 'a thing of beauty and a joy forever, and so far as he has gone, *far* my best character.' (Letter to Charles Baxter.)

If these words suggest a certain ambivalent regard for the old monster, then that is entirely appropriate, for Stevenson uses him (just as he uses the romance plot between Archie and Christina) to examine some of the darker facets of the 'Scottish myth'. Tales of violence on lonely and legendary moors, with the sufferings of the Covenanters at places like 'the Weaver's Stane' and the bloody exploits of the 'four brothers of Cauldstaneslap', were the heartfelt stuff of Stevenson's childhood, learned at the lap of his first nurse, Cummie. But now those stories are being told with an ironical distance, for *Weir of Hermiston* imitates the earnestly garrulous tones of a folk-teller when it recounts the exploits of 'Hob', 'Gib', 'Clem' and 'Dand', whose very names make them sound like minor devils from one of James Hogg's supernatural tales. Yet these brothers have grown up to become a respectable farmer, a radical (if religiose) weaver, a wealthy Glasgow inventor-businessman and a sub-Burnsian shepherd-poet, representing between them nothing less than the archetypal cornerstones of eighteenth century Scottish identity. Their legend may have begun in bloody violence, but it has been followed by respectability and indeed a measure of complacency. How will these crouse figures fare if they take once more to the sword? Or are the old legends dead and gone forever? It seems clear that this was a question that Stevenson was asking himself in *Weir of Hermiston*, a question with clear relevance, indeed, to much of his earlier output as a writer.

In just the same way, Lord Justice-Clerk Hermiston must stand for the whole history of a Scottish Protestant engagement with patriarchal authority in which the Father, the State and then God stand before us like 'an Alp', each to be obeyed or disobeyed as we will, but always with terror: 'God was love: the name of my lord (to all who knew him) was fear.' The dilemma of Archie's divided feelings goes deep to the roots of how the Scottish Protestant ethic sees Being itself, in the guise of the Old Testament Father through which Adam Weir ('adamantine' indeed) speaks for the irreducible terror of the Law, with a capacity for judgement so strong that it can look at 'brute nature' without flinching – an inheritance which his more imaginative and sensitive son lacks and dreads but cannot deny:

> 'This is my father,' he said. 'I draw my life from him; the flesh upon my bones is his, the bread I am fed with is the wages of these horrors.'

Archie quotes from *Macbeth* when he learns that his father does, after all, seem to care for him:

'I did not know the old man had so much blood in him.' He had never dreamed this sire of his, this aboriginal antique, this adamantine Adam, had even so much of a heart to be moved in the least degree for another . . .

But of course the line refers to the death of Duncan and the murder of a king. The moment could not be more psychologically revealing, and it's not long before it is made explicit: 'I do not love my father; I wonder sometimes if I do not hate him. There's my shame; perhaps my sin . . .' What hope can there be for someone who resists necessity, who would rebel – Satan-like – against the demands of Law itself, and what hope for a rebel as weak and petulant as Archie sometimes seems to be? On the other hand, must the revolt of feeling and imagination always be constructed as weak and somehow 'feminine' – the 'dwaibly' inheritance from a dwaibly mother?

These are the deep symbolic undercurrents which make *Weir of Hermiston* more than a melodrama about the conflict between young love and old authority. Adam Weir brings us (and his creator) face to face with Scottish culture's love-hate relationship with the Calvinist ethic (conceived of as brutally practical and masculine), as opposed to an imaginative life which is presumed to operate in the maternal sphere. Can these terms ever be reconciled? Should they even be supported, for surely their very proposition is part of the adamantine value system that belongs to Hermiston and his like? (This same equation would be worked-through again in 1901, with George Douglas Brown's novel *The House with the Green Shutters*). Seen in this more critical light, even the self-consciously 'legendary' attributes of the Elliott brothers serve only to evoke a whole history of complacement delight in murderous violence and sentimental verse.

These two elements – Law and Legend – are exposed for what they are and brought together – and into conflict – by the tender love affair between Christina and Archie, but that story, too, is coloured by an ironic distance in the telling, a distance which sees their first clumsy feelings for each other as a deadly game, 'artfully' played by Fate 'with this poor pair of children'. Here is romance, not to mention romantic fiction, and all the historical and metaphysical matter of Scotland too, brilliantly laid bare with the precision of a dark fable about 'brute nature', and the way we try to clothe it, promote it, or evade it with mythologies of 'love', 'history', 'action' and 'justice'.

'I expect,' wrote Stevenson to Charles Baxter, '*The Justice-Clerk* to be my masterpiece.' *The Justice Clerk* (soon to be called *Weir of Hermiston*) was indeed an oustanding conception. But 'brute nature' had the last word.

Roderick Watson

Introductory

In the wild end of a moorland parish, far out of the sight of any house, there stands a cairn among the heather, and a little by east of it, in the going down of the braeside, a monument with verses half defaced. It was here that Claverhouse shot with his own hand the Praying Weaver of Balweary, and the chisel of Old Mortality has clinked on that lonely gravestone. Public and domestic history have thus marked with a bloody finger this hollow among the hills; and since the Cameronian gave his life there, two hundred years ago, in a glorious folly, and without comprehension or regret, the silence of the moss has been broken once again by the report of firearms and the cry of the dying.

The Deil's Hags was the old name. But the place is now called Francie's Cairn. For a while it was told that Francie walked. Aggie Hogg met him in the gloaming by the cairnside, and he spoke to her, with chattering teeth, so that his words were lost. He pursued Rob Todd (if any one could have believed Robbie) for the space of half a mile with pitiful entreaties. But the age is one of incredulity; these superstitious decorations speedily fell off; and the facts of the story itself, like the bones of a giant buried there and half dug up, survived, naked and imperfect, in the memory of the scattered neighbours. To this day, of winter nights, when the sleet is on the window and the cattle are quiet in the byre, there will be told again, amid the silence of the young and the additions and corrections of the old, the tale of the Justice-Clerk and of his son, young Hermiston, that vanished from men's knowledge; of the two Kirsties and the Four Black Brothers of the Cauldstaneslap; and of Frank Innes, 'the young fool advocate,' that came into these moorland parts to find his destiny.

CHAPTER ONE

Life and Death of Mrs Weir

The Lord Justice-Clerk was a stranger in that part of the country; but his lady wife was known there from a child, as her race had been before her. The old 'riding Rutherfords of Hermiston,' of whom she was the last descendant, had been famous men of yore, ill neighbours, ill subjects, and ill husbands to their wives though not their properties. Tales of them were rife for twenty miles about; and their name was even printed in the page of our Scots histories, not always to their credit. One bit the dust at Flodden; one was hanged at his peel door by James the Fifth; another fell dead in a carouse with Tom Dalyell; while a fourth (and that was Jean's own father) died presiding at a Hell-Fire Club, of which he was the founder. There were many heads shaken in Crossmichael at that judgment; the more so as the man had a villainous reputation among high and low, and both with the godly and the worldly. At that very hour of his demise, he had ten going pleas before the Session, eight of them oppressive. And the same doom extended even to his agents; his grieve, that had been his right hand in many a left-hand business, being cast from his horse one night and drowned in a peat-hag on the Kye-skairs; and his very doer (although lawyers have long spoons) surviving him not long, and dying on a sudden in a bloody flux.

In all these generations, while a male Rutherford was in a saddle with his lads, or brawling in a change-house, there would be always a white-faced wife immured at home in the old peel or the later mansion-house. It seemed this succession of martyrs bided long, but took their vengeance in the end, and that was in the person of the last descendant, Jean. She bore the name of the Rutherfords, but she was the daughter of their trembling wives. At the first she was not wholly without charm. Neighbours recalled in her, as a child, a strain of elfin wilfulness, gentle little mutinies, sad little gaieties, even a morning gleam of

I

beauty that was not to be fulfilled. She withered in the growing, and (whether it was the sins of her sires or the sorrows of her mothers) came to her maturity depressed, and, as it were, defaced; no blood of life in her, no grasp or gaiety; pious, anxious, tender, tearful, and incompetent.

It was a wonder to many that she had married – seeming so wholly of the stuff that makes old maids. But chance cast her in the path of Adam Weir, then the new Lord-Advocate, a recognised, risen man, the conqueror of many obstacles, and thus late in the day beginning to think upon a wife. He was one who looked rather to obedience than beauty, yet it would seem he was struck with her at the first look. 'Wha's she?' he said, turning to his host; and, when he had been told, 'Ay,' says he, 'she looks menseful. She minds me – '; and then, after a pause (which some have been daring enough to set down to sentimental recollections), 'Is she releegious?' he asked, and was shortly after, at his own request, presented. The acquaintance, which it seems profane to call a courtship, was pursued with Mr Weir's accustomed industry, and was long a legend, or rather a source of legends, in the Parliament House. He was described coming, rosy with much port, into the drawing-room, walking direct up to the lady, and assailing her with pleasantries, to which the embarrassed fair one responded, in what seemed a kind of agony, 'Eh, Mr Weir!' or 'O, Mr Weir!' or 'Keep me, Mr Weir!' On the very eve of their engagement, it was related that one had drawn near to the tender couple, and had overheard the lady cry out, with the tones of one who talked for the sake of talking, 'Keep me, Mr Weir, and what became of him?' and the profound accents of the suitor reply, 'Haangit, mem, haangit.' The motives upon either side were much debated. Mr Weir must have supposed his bride to be somehow suitable; perhaps he belonged to that class of men who think a weak head the ornament of women – an opinion invariably punished in this life. Her descent and her estate were beyond question. Her wayfaring ancestors and her litigious father had done well by Jean. There was ready money and there were broad acres, ready to fall wholly to the husband, to lend dignity to his descendants, and to himself a title, when he should be called upon the Bench. On the side of Jean, there was perhaps some fascination of curiosity as to this unknown male animal that approached her with the roughness of a ploughman and the *aplomb* of an advocate. Being so trenchantly opposed to all she knew, loved, or understood, he may well have seemed to her the extreme, if scarcely the ideal, of his sex. And besides, he was an ill man to refuse. A little over forty at the period of his marriage, he looked already older, and to the force of manhood added the senatorial dignity of years; it was, perhaps, with an unreverend awe, but he was awful. The Bench, the Bar, and the most experienced and reluctant witness, bowed to his authority – and why not Jeannie Rutherford?

The heresy about foolish women is always punished, I have said, and Lord Hermiston began to pay the penalty at once. His house in George Square was wretchedly ill-guided; nothing answerable to the expense of maintenance but the cellar, which was his own private care. When things went wrong at dinner, as they continually did, my lord would look up the table at his wife: 'I think these broth would be better to sweem in than to sup.' Or else to the butler: 'Here, M'Killop, awa' wi' this Raadical gigot – tak' it to the French, man, and bring me some puddocks! It seems rather a sore kind of a business that I should be all day in Court haanging Raadicals, and get nawthing to my denner.' Of course this was but a manner of speaking, and he had never hanged a man for being a radical in his life; the law, of which he was the faithful minister, directing otherwise. And of course these growls were in the nature of pleasantry, but it was of a recondite sort; and uttered as they were in his resounding voice, and commented on by that expression which they called in the Parliament House 'Hermiston's hanging face' – they struck mere dismay into the wife. She sat before him speechless and fluttering; at each dish, as at a fresh ordeal, her eye hovered toward my lord's countenance and fell again; if he but ate in silence, unspeakable relief was her portion; if there were complaint, the world was darkened. She would seek out the cook, who was always her *sister in the Lord*. 'O, my dear, this is the most dreidful thing that my lord can never be contented in his own house!' she would begin; and weep and pray with the cook; and then the cook would pray with Mrs Weir; and the next day's meal would never be a penny the better – and the next cook (when she came) would be worse, if anything, but just as pious. It was often wondered that Lord Hermiston bore it as he did; indeed, he was a stoical old voluptuary, contented with sound wine and plenty of it. But there were moments when he overflowed. Perhaps half a dozen times in the history of his married life – 'Here! tak' it awa,' and bring me a piece bread and kebbuck!' he had exclaimed, with an appalling explosion of his voice and rare gestures. None thought to dispute or to make excuses; the service was arrested; Mrs Weir sat at the head of the table whimpering without disguise; and his lordship opposite munched his bread and cheese in ostentatious disregard. Once only, Mrs Weir had ventured to appeal. He was passing her chair on his way into the study.

'O, Edom!' she wailed, in a voice tragic with tears, and reaching out to him both hands, in one of which she held a sopping pocket-handkerchief.

He paused and looked upon her with a face of wrath, into which there stole, as he looked, a twinkle of humour.

'Noansense!' he said. 'You and your noansense! What do I want with a Christian faim'ly? I want Christian broth! Get me a lass that can plain-boil a potato, if she was a whüre off the streets.' And with these words, which echoed in her tender ears like blasphemy, he had passed on to his study and shut the door behind him.

Such was the housewifery in George Square. It was better at Hermiston, where Kirstie Elliott, the sister of a neighbouring bonnet-laird, and an eighteenth cousin of the lady's, bore the charge of all, and kept a trim house and a good country table. Kirstie was a woman in a thousand, clean, capable, notable; once a moorland Helen, and still comely as a blood horse and healthy as the hill wind. High in flesh and voice and colour, she ran the house with her whole intemperate soul, in a bustle, not without buffets. Scarce more pious than decency in those days required, she was the cause of many an anxious thought and many a tearful prayer to Mrs Weir. Housekeeper and mistress renewed the parts of Martha and Mary; and though with a pricking conscience, Mary reposed on Martha's strength as on a rock. Even Lord Hermiston held Kirstie in a particular regard. There were few with whom he unbent so gladly, few whom he favoured with so many pleasantries. 'Kirstie and me maun have our joke,' he would declare, in high good-humour, as he buttered Kirstie's scones, and she waited at table. A man who

had no need either of love or of popularity, a keen reader of men
and of events, there was perhaps only one truth for which he was
quite unprepared: he would have been quite unprepared to learn
that Kirstie hated him. He thought maid and master were well
matched; hard, handy, healthy, broad Scots folk, without a hair
of nonsense to the pair of them. And the fact was that she made
a goddess and an only child of the effete and tearful lady; and
even as she waited at table her hands would sometimes itch for
my lord's ears.

Thus, at least, when the family were at Hermiston, not only
my lord, but Mrs Weir too, enjoyed a holiday. Free from the
dreadful looking-for of the miscarried dinner, she would mind
her seam, read her piety books, and take her walk (which was
my lord's orders), sometimes by herself, sometimes with Archie,
the only child of that scarce natural union. The child was her
next bond to life. Her frosted sentiment bloomed again, she
breathed deep of life, she let loose her heart, in that society.
The miracle of her motherhood was ever new to her. The
sight of the little man at her skirt intoxicated her with the
sense of power, and froze her with the consciousness of her
responsibility. She looked forward, and, seeing him in fancy
grow up and play his diverse part on the world's theatre, caught
in her breath and lifted up her courage with a lively effort. It was
only with the child that she forgot herself and was at moments
natural; yet it was only with the child that she had conceived
and managed to pursue a scheme of conduct. Archie was to
be a great man and a good; a minister if possible, a saint for
certain. She tried to engage his mind upon her favourite books,
Rutherford's *Letters*, Scougal's *Grace Abounding*, and the like.
It was a common practice of hers (and strange to remember now)
that she would carry the child to the Deil's Hags, sit with him
on the Praying Weaver's stone, and talk of the Covenanters till
their tears ran down. Her view of history was wholly artless, a
design in snow and ink; upon the one side, tender innocents
with psalms upon their lips; upon the other, the persecutors,
booted, bloodyminded, flushed with wine: a suffering Christ,
a raging Beelzebub. *Persecutor* was a word that knocked upon
the woman's heart; it was her highest thought of wickedness, and
the mark of it was on her house. Her great-great-grandfather
had drawn the sword against the Lord's anointed on the field of

Rullion Green, and breathed his last (tradition said) in the arms of the detestable Dalyell. Nor could she blind herself to this, that had they lived in those old days, Hermiston himself would have been numbered alongside of Bloody MacKenzie and the politic Lauderdale and Rothes, in the band of God's immediate enemies. The sense of this moved her to the more fervour; she had a voice for that name of *persecutor* that thrilled in the child's marrow; and when one day the mob hooted and hissed them all in my lord's travelling carriage, and cried, 'Down with the persecutor! down with Hanging Hermiston!' and mamma covered her eyes and wept, and papa let down the glass and looked out upon the rabble with his droll formidable face, bitter and smiling, as they said he sometimes looked when he gave sentence, Archie was for the moment too much amazed to be alarmed, but he had scarce got his mother by herself before his shrill voice was raised demanding an explanation: why had they called papa a persecutor?

'Keep me, my precious!' she exclaimed. 'Keep me, my dear! this is poleetical. Ye must never ask me anything poleetical, Erchie. Your faither is a great man, my dear, and it's no for me or you to be judging him. It would be telling us all, if we behaved ourselves in our several stations the way your faither does in his high office; and let me hear no more of any such disrespectful and undutiful questions! No that you meant to be undutiful, my lamb; your mother kens that – she kens it well, dearie!' And so slid off to safer topics, and left on the mind of the child an obscure but ineradicable sense of something wrong.

Mrs Weir's philosophy of life was summed in one expression – tenderness. In her view of the universe, which was all lighted up with a glow out of the doors of hell, good people must walk there in a kind of ecstasy of tenderness. The beasts and plants had no souls; they were here but for a day, and let their day pass gently! And as for the immortal men, on what black, downward path were many of them wending, and to what a horror of an immortality! 'Are not two sparrows,' 'Whosoever shall smite thee,' 'God Sendeth His rain,' 'Judge not, that ye be not judged' – these texts made her body of divinity; she put them on in the morning with her clothes and lay down to sleep with them at night; they haunted her like a favourite air, they clung about her like a favourite perfume. Their minister was a marrowy expounder of the law, and my lord sat under him with relish; but Mrs Weir respected him from far off; heard him (like the cannon of a beleaguered city) usefully booming outside on the dogmatic ramparts; and meanwhile, within and out of shot, dwelt in her private garden which she watered with grateful tears. It seems strange to say of this colourless and ineffectual woman, but she was a true enthusiast, and might have made the sunshine and the glory of a cloister. Perhaps none but Archie knew she could be eloquent; perhaps none but he had seen her – her colour raised, her hands clasped or quivering – glow with gentle ardour. There is a corner of the policy of Hermiston, where you come suddenly in view of the summit of Black Fell, sometimes like the mere grass top of a hill, sometimes (and this is her own expression) like a precious jewel in the heavens. On such days, upon the sudden view of it, her hand would tighten on the child's fingers, her voice rise like a song. '*I to the hills!*' she would repeat. 'And O, Erchie, are nae these like the hills of Naphtali?' and her tears would flow.

Upon an impressionable child the effect of this continual and pretty accompaniment to life was deep. The woman's quietism and piety passed on to his different nature undiminished; but whereas in her it was a native sentiment, in him it was only an implanted dogma. Nature and the child's pugnacity at times revolted. A cad from the Potterrow once struck him in the mouth; he struck back, the pair fought it out in the back stable lane towards the Meadows, and Archie returned with a considerable decline in the number of his front teeth, and unregenerately boasting of the losses of the foe. It was a sore day for Mrs Weir; she wept and prayed over the infant backslider until my lord was due from Court, and she must resume that air of tremulous composure with which she always greeted him. The judge was that day in an observant mood, and remarked upon the absent teeth.

'I am afraid Erchie will have been fechting with some of they blagyard lads,' said Mrs Weir.

My lord's voice rang out as it did seldom in the privacy of his own house. 'I'll have nonn of that, sir!' he cried. 'Do you hear me? – nonn of that! No son of mine shall be speldering in the glaur with any dirty raibble.'

The anxious mother was grateful for so much support; she

had even feared the contrary. And that night when she put the child to bed – 'Now, my dear, ye see!' she said, 'I told you what your faither would think of it, if he heard ye had fallen into this dreidful sin; and let you and me pray to God that ye may be keepit from the like temptation or stren'thened to resist it!'

The womanly falsity of this was thrown away. Ice and iron cannot be welded; and the points of view of the Justice-Clerk and Mrs Weir were not less unassimilable. The character and position of his father had long been a stumbling-block to Archie, and with every year of his age the difficulty grew more instant. The man was mostly silent; when he spoke at all, it was to speak of the things of the world, always in a worldly spirit, often in language that the child had been schooled to think coarse, and sometimes with words that he knew to be sins in themselves. Tenderness was the first duty, and my lord was invariably harsh. God was love, the name of my lord (to all who knew him) was fear. In the world, as schematised for Archie by his mother, the place was marked for such a creature. There were some whom it was good to pity and well (though very likely useless) to pray for; they were named reprobates, goats, God's enemies, brands for the burning; and Archie tallied every mark of identification, and drew the inevitable private inference that the Lord Justice-Clerk was the chief of sinners.

The mother's honesty was scarce complete. There was one influence she feared for the child and still secretly combated; that was my lord's; and half unconsciously, half in a wilful blindness, she continued to undermine her husband with his son. As long as Archie remained silent, she did so ruthlessly, with a single eye to heaven and the child's salvation; but the day came when Archie spoke. It was 1801, and Archie was seven, and beyond his years for curiosity and logic, when he brought the case up openly. If judging were sinful and forbidden, how came papa to be a judge? to have that sin for a trade? to bear the name of it for a distinction?

'I can't see it,' said the little Rabbi, and wagged his head.

Mrs Weir abounded in commonplace replies.

'No, I canna see it,' reiterated Archie. 'And I'll tell you what, mamma, I don't think you and me's justifeed in staying with him.'

The woman awoke to remorse; she saw herself disloyal to

her man, her sovereign and bread-winner, in whom (with what she had of worldliness) she took a certain subdued pride. She expatiated in reply on my lord's honour and greatness; his useful services in this world of sorrow and wrong, and the place in which he stood, far above where babes and innocents could hope to see or criticise. But she had builded too well – Archie had his answers pat: Were not babes and innocents the type of the kingdom of heaven? Were not honour and greatness the badges of the world? And at any rate, how about the mob that had once seethed about the carriage?

'It's all very fine,' he concluded, 'but in my opinion, papa has no right to be it. And it seems that's not the worst yet of it. It seems he's called "the Hanging Judge" – it seems he's crooool. I'll tell you what it is, mamma, there's a tex' borne in upon me: It were better for that man if a milestone were bound upon his back and him flung into the deepestmost pairts of the sea.'

'O, my lamb, ye must never say the like of that!' she cried. 'Ye're to honour faither and mother, dear, that your days may be long in the land. It's Atheists that cry out against him – French Atheists, Erchie! Ye would never surely even yourself down to be saying the same thing as French Atheists? It would break my heart to think that of you. And O, Erchie, here arena *you* setting up to *judge*? And have ye no forgot God's plain command – the First with Promise, dear? Mind you upon the beam and the mote!'

Having thus carried the war into the enemy's camp, the terrified lady breathed again. And no doubt it is easy thus to circumvent a child with catchwords, but it may be questioned how far it is effectual. An instinct in his breast detects the quibble, and a voice condemns it. He will instantly submit, privately hold the same opinion. For even in this simple and antique relation of the mother and the child, hypocrisies are multiplied.

When the Court rose that year and the family returned to Hermiston, it was a common remark in all the country that the lady was sore failed. She seemed to loose and seize again her touch with life, now sitting inert in a sort of durable bewilderment, anon waking to feverish and weak activity. She dawdled about the lasses at their work, looking stupidly on; she fell to rummaging in old cabinets and presses, and desisted when half through; she would begin remarks with an air of animation and drop them without a struggle. Her common appearance was of one who has forgotten something and is trying to remember; and when she overhauled, one after another, the worthless and touching mementoes of her youth, she might have been seeking the clue to that lost thought. During this period, she gave many gifts to the neighbours and house lasses, giving them with a manner of regret that embarrassed the recipients.

The last night of all she was busy on some female work, and toiled upon it with so manifest and painful a devotion that my lord (who was not often curious) inquired as to its nature.

She blushed to the eyes. 'O, Edom, it's for you!' she said. 'It's slippers. I – I hae never made ye any.'

'Ye daft auld wife!' returned his lordship. 'A bonny figure I would be, palmering about in bauchles!'

The next day, at the hour of her walk, Kirstie interfered. Kirstie took this decay of her mistress very hard; bore her a grudge, quarrelled with railed upon her, the anxiety of a genuine love wearing the disguise of temper. This day of all days she insisted disrespectfully, with rustic fury, that Mrs Weir should stay at home. But, 'No, no,' she said, 'it's my lord's orders,' and set forth us usual. Archie was visible in the acre bog, engaged upon some childish enterprise, the instrument of which was mire; and she stood and looked at him a while like one about to call; then thought otherwise, sighed, and shook her head, and proceeded on her rounds alone. The house lasses were at the burnside washing, and saw her pass with her loose, weary, dowdy gait.

'She's a terrible feckless wife, the mistress!' said the one.

'Tut,' said the other, 'the wumman's seeck.'

'Weel, I canna see nae differ in her,' returned the first. 'A füshionless quean, a feckless carline.'

The poor creature thus discussed rambled a while in the grounds without a purpose. Tides in her mind ebbed and flowed, and carried her to and fro like seaweed. She tried a path, paused, returned, and tried another; questing, forgetting her quest; the spirit of choice extinct in her bosom, or devoid of sequency. On a sudden, it appeared as though she had remembered, or had formed a resolution, wheeled about, returned with hurried steps, and appeared in the dining-room, where Kirstie was at the cleaning, like one charged with an important errand.

'Kirstie?' she began, and paused; and then with conviction, 'Mr Weir isna speeritually minded, but he has been a good man to me.'

It was perhaps the first time since her husband's elevation that she had forgotten the handle to his name, of which the tender, inconsistent woman was not a little proud. And when Kirstie looked up at the speaker's face, she was aware of a change.

'Godsake, what's the maitter wi' ye, mem?' cried the house-keeper, starting from the rug.

'I do not ken,' answered her mistress, shaking her head. 'But he is not speeritually minded, my dear.'

'Here, sit down with ye! Godsake, what ails the wife?' cried Kirstie, and helped and forced her into the lord's own chair by the cheek of the hearth.

'Keep me, what's this?' she gasped. 'Kirstie, what's this? I'm frich'ened.'

They were her last words.

It was the lowering nightfall when my lord returned. He had the sunset in his back, all clouds and glory; and before him, by the wayside, spied Kirstie Elliott waiting. She was dissolved in tears, and addressed him in the high, false note of barbarous mourning, such as still lingers modified among Scots heather.

'The Lord peety ye, Hermiston! the Lord prepare ye!' she keened out. 'Weary upon me, that I should have to tell it!'

He reined in his horse and looked upon her with the hanging face.

'Has the French landit?' cried he.

'Man, man,' she said, 'is that a' ye can think of? The Lord prepare ye: the Lord comfort and support ye!'

'Is onybody deid?' says his lordship. 'It's no Erchie?'

'Bethankit, no!' exclaimed the woman startled into a more natural tone. 'Na, na, it's no sae bad as that. It's the mistress, my lord; she just fair flittit before my e'en. She just gi'ed a sab and was by wi' it. Eh, my bonny Miss Jeannie, that I mind sae weel!' And forth again upon that pouring tide of lamentation in which women of her class excel and overabound.

Lord Hermiston sat in the saddle beholding her. Then he seemed to recover command upon himself.

'Weel, it's something of the suddenest,' said he. 'But she was a dwaibly body from the first.'

And he rode home at a precipitate amble with Kirstie at his horse's heels.

Dressed as she was for her last walk, they had laid the dead lady on her bed. She was never interesting in life; in death she was not impressive; and as her husband stood before her, with his hands crossed behind his powerful back, that which he looked upon was the very image of the insignificant.

'Her and me were never cut out for one another,' he remarked at last. 'It was a daft-like marriage.' And then, with a most unusual gentleness of tone, 'Puir bitch,' said he, 'puir bitch!' Then suddenly: 'Where's Erchie?'

Kirstie had decoyed him to her room and given him 'a jeely-piece.'

'Ye have some kind of gumption, too,' observed the judge, and considered his housekeeper grimly. 'When all's said,' he added, 'I micht have done waur – I micht have been marriet upon a skirling Jezebel like you!'

'There's naebody thinking of you, Hermiston!' cried the offended woman. 'We think of her that's out of her sorrows. And could *she* have done waur? Tell me that, Hermiston – tell me that before her clay-cauld corp!'

'Weel, there's some of them gey an' ill to please,' observed his lordship.

CHAPTER TWO

Father and Son

My Lord Justice-Clerk was known to many; the man Adam Weir perhaps to none. He had nothing to explain or to conceal; he sufficed wholly and silently to himself; and that part of our nature which goes out (too often with false coin) to acquire glory or love, seemed in him to be omitted. He did not try to be loved, he did not care to be; it is probable the very thought of it was a stranger to his mind. He was an admired lawyer, a highly unpopular judge; and he looked down upon those who were his inferiors in either distinction, who were lawyers of less grasp or judges not so much detested. In all the rest of his days and doings, not one trace of vanity appeared; and he went on through life with a mechanical movement, as of the unconscious, that was almost august.

He saw little of his son. In the childish maladies with which the boy was troubled, he would make daily inquiries and daily pay him a visit, entering the sick-room with a facetious and appalling countenance, letting off a few perfunctory jests, and going again swiftly, to the patient's relief. Once, a court holiday falling opportunely, my lord had his carriage, and drove the child himself to Hermiston, the customary place of convalescence. It is conceivable he had been more than usually anxious, for that journey always remained in Archie's memory as a thing apart, his father having related to him from beginning to end, and with much detail, three authentic murder cases. Archie went the usual round of other Edinburgh boys, the high school and the college; and Hermiston looked on, or rather looked away, with scarce an affectation of interest in his progress. Daily, indeed, upon a signal after dinner, he was brought in, given nuts and a glass of port, regarded sardonically, sarcastically questioned. 'Well, sir, and what have you donn with you book to-day?' my lord might begin, and set him posers in law Latin. To a child just stumbling into Corderius, Papinian and Paul proved quite

invincible. But papa had memory of no other. He was not harsh
to the little scholar, having a vast fund of patience learned upon
the bench, and was at no pains whether to conceal or to express
his disappointment. 'Well, ye have a long jaunt before ye yet!'
he might observe, yawning, and fall back on his own thoughts
(as like as not) until the time came for separation, and my lord
would take the decanter and the glass, and be off to the back
chambers looking on the Meadows, where he toiled on his
cases till the hours were small. There was no 'fuller man' on
the bench; his memory was marvellous, though wholly legal;
if he had to 'advise' extempore, none did it better; yet there
was none who more earnestly prepared. As he thus watched in
the night, or sat at table and forgot the presence of his son, no
doubt but he tasted deeply of recondite pleasures. To be wholly
devoted to some intellectual exercise is to have succeeded in life;
and perhaps only in law and the higher mathematics may this
devotion be maintained, suffice to itself without reaction, and
find continual rewards without excitement. This atmosphere of
his father's sterling industry was the best of Archie's education.
Assuredly it did not attract him; assuredly it rather rebutted
and depressed. Yet it was still present, unobserved like the
ticking of a clock, an arid ideal, a tasteless stimulant in the
boy's life.

But Hermiston was not all of one piece. He was, besides, a
mighty toper; he could sit at wine until the day dawned, and
pass directly from the table to the bench with a steady hand and
a clear head. Beyond the third bottle, he showed the plebeian
in a larger print; the low, gross accent, the low, foul mirth,
grew broader and commoner; he became less formidable, and
infinitely more disgusting. Now, the boy had inherited from
Jean Rutherford a shivering delicacy, unequally mated with
potential violence. In the playing-fields, and amongst his own
companions, he repaid a coarse expression with a blow; at his
father's table (when the time came for him to join these revels)
he turned pale and sickened in silence. Of all the guests whom
he there encountered, he had toleration for only one: David
Keith Carnegie, Lord Glenalmond. Lord Glenalmond was tall
and emaciated, with long features and long delicate hands. He
was often compared with the statue of Forbes of Culloden in
the Parliament House; and his blue eye, at more than sixty,

preserved some of the fire of youth. His exquisite disparity with any of his fellow-guests, his appearance as of an artist and an aristocrat stranded in rude company, riveted the boy's attention; and as curiosity and interest are the things in the world that are the most immediately and certainly rewarded, Lord Glenalmond was attracted by the boy.

'And so this is your son, Hermiston?' he asked, laying his hand on Archie's shoulder. 'He's getting a big lad.'

'Hout!' said the gracious father, 'just his mother over again – daurna say boo to a goose!'

But the stranger retained the boy, talked to him, drew him out, found in him a taste for letters, and a fine, ardent, modest, youthful soul; and encouraged him to be a visitor on Sunday evenings in his bare, cold, lonely dining-room, where he sat and read in the isolation of a bachelor grown old in refinement. The beautiful gentleness and grace of the old judge, and the delicacy of his person, thoughts, and language, spoke to Archie's heart in its own tongue. He conceived the ambition to be such another; and, when the day came for him to choose a profession, it was in emulation of Lord Glenalmond, not of Lord Hermiston, that he chose the Bar. Hermiston looked on at this friendship with some secret pride, but openly with the intolerance of scorn. He scarce lost an opportunity to put them down with a rough jape; and, to say truth, it was not difficult, for they were neither of them quick. He had a word of contempt for the whole crowd of poets, painters, fiddlers, and their admirers, the bastard race of amateurs, which was continually on his lips. 'Signor Feedle-eerie!' he would say. 'O, for Goad's sake, no more of the Signor!'

'You and my father are great friends, are you not?' asked Archie once.

'There is no man that I more respect, Archie,' replied Lord Glenalmond. 'He is two things of price. He is a great lawyer, and he is upright as the day.'

'You and he are so different,' said the boy, his eyes dwelling on those of his old friend, like a lover's on his mistress's.

'Indeed so,' replied the judge; 'very different. And so I fear are you and he. Yet I would like it very ill if my young friend were to misjudge his father. He has all the Roman virtues: Cato and Brutus were such; I think a son's heart might well be proud of such an ancestry of one.'

'And I would sooner he were a plaided herd,' cried Archie, with sudden bitterness.

'And that is neither very wise, nor I believe entirely true,' returned Glenalmond. 'Before you are done you will find some of these expressions rise on you like a remorse. They are merely literary and decorative; they do not aptly express your thought, nor is your thought clearly apprehended, and no doubt your father (if he were here) would say, "Signor Feedle-eerie!"'

With the infinitely delicate sense of youth, Archie avoided the subject from that hour. It was perhaps a pity. Had he but talked – talked freely – let himself gush out in words (the way youth loves to do and should), there might have been no tale to write upon the Weirs of Hermiston. But the shadow of a threat of ridicule sufficed; in the slight tartness of these words he read a prohibition; and it is likely that Glenalmond meant it so.

Besides the veteran, the boy was without confidant or friend. Serious and eager, he came through school and college, and moved among a crowd of the indifferent, in the seclusion of his shyness. He grew up handsome, with an open, speaking countenance, with graceful, youthful ways; he was clever, he took prizes, he shone in the Speculative Society. It should seem he must become the centre of a crowd of friends; but something that was in part the delicacy of his mother, in part the austerity of his father, held him aloof from all. It is a fact, and a strange one, that among his contemporaries Hermiston's son was thought to be a chip of the old block. 'You're a friend of Archie Weir's?' said one to Frank Innes; and Innes replied, with his usual flippancy and more than his usual insight: 'I know Weir, but I never met Archie.' No one had met Archie, a malady most incident to only sons. He flew his private signal, and none heeded it; it seemed he was abroad in a world from which the very hope of intimacy was banished; and he looked round about him on the concourse of his fellow-students, and forward to the trivial days and acquaintances that were to come, without hope or interest.

As time went on, the tough and rough old sinner felt himself drawn to the son of his loins and sole continuator of his new family, with softnesses of sentiment that he could hardly credit and was wholly impotent to express. With a face, voice, and manner trained through forty years to terrify and repel, Rhadamanthus may be great, but he will scarce be engaging. It is a fact that he tried to propitiate Archie, but a fact that cannot be too lightly taken; the attempt was so unconspicuously made, the failure so stoically supported. Sympathy is not due to these steadfast iron natures. If he failed to gain his son's friendship, or even his son's toleration, on he went up the great, bare staircase of his duty, uncheered and undepressed. There might have been more pleasure in his relations with Archie, so much he may have recognised at moments; but pleasure was a by-product of the singular chemistry of life, which only fools expected.

An idea of Archie's attitude, since we are all grown up and have forgotten the days of our youth, it is more difficult to convey. He made no attempt whatsoever to understand the man with whom he dined and breakfasted. Parsimony of pain, glut of pleasure, these are the two alternating ends of youth; and Archie was of the parsimonious. The wind blew cold out of a certain quarter – he turned his back upon it; stayed as little as was possible in his father's presence; and when there, averted his eyes as much as was decent from his father's face. The lamp shone for many hundred days upon these two at table – my lord, ruddy, gloomy, and unreverent; Archie with a potential brightness that was always dimmed and veiled in that society; and there were not, perhaps, in Christendom two men more radically strangers. The father, with a grand simplicity, either spoke of what interested himself, or maintained an unaffected silence. The son turned in his head for some topic that should be quite safe, that would spare him fresh evidences either of my lord's inherent grossness or of the innocence of his inhumanity; treading gingerly the ways of intercourse, like a lady gathering up her skirts in a by-path. If he made a mistake, and my lord began to abound in matter of offence, Archie drew himself up, his brow grew dark, his share of the talk expired; but my lord would faithfully and cheerfully continue to pour out the worst of himself before his silent and offended son.

'Well, it's a poor hert that never rejoices!' he would say, at the conclusion of such a nightmare interview. 'But I must get to my plew-stilts.' And he would seclude himself as usual in the back room, and Archie go forth into the night and the city quivering with animosity and scorn.

CHAPTER THREE

In the Matter of
the Hanging of Duncan Jopp

It chanced in the year 1813 that Archie strayed one day into
the Judiciary Court. The macer made room for the son of the
presiding judge. In the dock, the centre of men's eyes, there
stood a whey-coloured, misbegotten caitiff, Duncan Jopp, on
trial for his life. His story, as it was raked out before him in that
public scene, was one of disgrace and vice and cowardice, the
very nakedness of crime; and the creature heard and it seemed
at times as though he understood – as if at times he forgot the
horror of the place he stood in, and remembered the shame of
what had brought him there. He kept his head bowed and his
hands clutched upon the rail; his hair dropped in his eyes and at
times he flung it back; and now he glanced about the audience
in a sudden fellness of terror, and now looked in the face of his
judge and gulped. There was pinned about his throat a piece of
dingy flannel; and that it was perhaps that turned the scale in
Archie's mind between disgust and pity. The creature stood in
a vanishing point; yet a little while, and he was still a man, and
had eyes and apprehension; yet a little longer, and with a last
sordid piece of pageantry, he would cease to be. And here, in
the meantime, with a trait of human nature that caught at the
beholder's breath, he was tending a sore throat.

Over against him, my Lord Hermiston occupied the bench
in the red robes of criminal jurisdiction, his face framed in
the white wig. Honest all through, he did not affect the virtue
of impartiality; this was no case for refinement; there was a
man to be hanged, he would have said, and he was hanging
him. Nor was it possible to see his lordship, and acquit him
of gusto in the task. It was plain he gloried in the exercise of
his trained faculties, in the clear sight which pierced at once
into the joint of fact, in the rude, unvarnished gibes with which
he demolished every figment of defence. He took his ease and

jested, unbending in that solemn place with some of the freedom of the tavern; and the rag of man with the flannel round his neck was hunted gallowsward with jeers.

Duncan had a mistress, scarce less forlorn and greatly older than himself, who came up, whimpering and curtseying, to add the weight of her betrayal. My lord gave her the oath in his most roaring voice, and added an intolerant warning.

'Mind what ye say now, Janet,' said he. 'I have an e'e upon ye, I'm ill to jest with.'

Presently, after she was tremblingly embarked on her story, 'And what made ye do this, ye auld runt?' the Court interposed. 'Do ye mean to tell me ye was the panel's mistress?'

'If you please, ma loard,' whined the female.

'Godsake! ye made a bonny couple,' observed his lordship; and there was something so formidable and ferocious in his scorn that not even the galleries thought to laugh.

The summing up contained some jewels.

'These two peetiable creatures seem to have made up thegither, it's not for us to explain why.' – 'The panel, who (whatever else he may be) appears to be equally ill set-out in mind and boady.' – 'Neither the panel nor yet the old wife appears to have had so much common sense as even to tell a lie when it was necessary.' And in the course of sentencing, my lord had this *obiter dictum*: 'I have been the means, under God, of haanging a great number, but never just such a disjaskit rascal as yourself.' The words were strong in themselves; the light and heat and detonation of their delivery, and the savage pleasure of the speaker in his task, made them tingle in the ears.

When all was over, Archie came forth again into a changed world. Had there been the least redeeming greatness in the crime, any obscurity, any dubiety, perhaps he might have understood. But the culprit stood, with his sore throat, in the sweat of his mortal agony, without defence or excuse: a thing to cover up with blushes: a being so much sunk beneath the zones of sympathy that pity might seem harmless. And the judge had pursued him with a monstrous, relishing gaiety, horrible to be conceived, a trait for nightmares. It is one thing to spear a tiger, another to crush a toad; there are aesthetics even of the slaughter-house; and the loathsomeness of Duncan Jopp enveloped and infected the image of his judge.

Archie passed by his friends in the High Street with incoherent words and gestures. He saw Holyrood in a dream, remembrance of its romance awoke in him and faded; he had a vision of the old radiant stories, of Queen Mary and Prince Charlie, of the hooded stag, of the splendour and crime, the velvet and bright iron of the past; and dismissed them with a cry of pain. He lay and moaned in the Hunter's Bog, and the heavens were dark above him and the grass of the field an offence. 'This is my father,' he said. 'I draw my life from him; the flesh upon my bones is his, the bread I am fed with is the wages of these horrors.' He recalled his mother, and ground his forehead in the earth. He thought of flight, and where was he to flee to? of other lives, but was there any life worth living in this den of savage and jeering animals?

The interval before the execution was like a violent dream. He met his father; he would not look at him, he could not speak to him. It seemed there was no living creature but must have been swift to recognise that imminent animosity; but the hide of the Justice-Clerk remained impenetrable. Had my lord been talkative, the truce could never have subsisted; but he was by fortune in one of his humours of sour silence; and under the very guns of his broadside, Archie nursed the enthusiasm of rebellion. It seemed to him, from the top of his nineteen years' experience, as if he were marked at birth to be the perpetrator of some signal action, to set back fallen Mercy, to overthrow the usurping devil that sat, horned and hoofed, on her throne. Seductive Jacobin figments, which he had often refuted at the Speculative, swam up in his mind and startled him as with voices: and he seemed to himself to walk accompanied by an almost tangible presence of new beliefs and duties.

On the named morning he was at the place of execution. He saw the fleering rabble, the flinching wretch produced. He looked on for a while at a certain parody of devotion, which seemed to strip the wretch of his last claim to manhood. Then followed the brutal instant of extinction, and the paltry dangling of the remains like a broken jumping-jack. He had been prepared for something terrible, not for this tragic meanness. He stood a moment silent, and then – 'I denounce this God-defying murder,' he shouted; and his father, if he must have disclaimed the sentiment, might have owned the stentorian voice with which it was uttered.

Frank Innes dragged him from the spot. The two handsome lads followed the same course of study and recreation, and felt a certain mutual attraction, founded mainly on good looks. It had never gone deep; Frank was by nature a thin, jeering creature, not truly susceptible whether of feeling or inspiring friendship; and the relation between the pair was altogether on the outside, a thing of common knowledge and the pleasantries that spring from a common acquaintance. The more credit to Frank that he was appalled by Archie's outburst, and at least conceived the design of keeping him in sight, and, if possible, in hand, for the day. But Archie, who had just defied – was it God or Satan? – would not listen to the word of a college companion.

'I will not go with you,' he said. 'I do not desire your company, sir; I would be alone.'

'Here, Weir, man, don't be absurd,' said Innes, keeping a tight hold upon his sleeve. 'I will not let you go until I know what you mean to do with yourself; it's no use brandishing that staff.' For indeed at that moment Archie had made a sudden – perhaps a warlike – movement. 'This has been the most insane affair; you know it has. You know very well that I'm playing the good Samaritan. All I wish is to keep you quiet.'

'If quietness is what you wish, Mr Innes,' said Archie, 'and you will promise to leave me entirely to myself, I will tell you so much, that I am going to walk in the country and admire the beauties of nature.'

'Honour bright?' asked Frank.

'I am not in the habit of lying, Mr Innes,' retorted Archie. 'I have the honour of wishing you good-day.'

'You won't forget the Spec.?' asked Innes.

'The Spec.?' said Archie. 'O no, I won't forget the Spec.'

And the one young man carried his tortured spirit forth of the city and all the day long, by one road and another, in an endless pilgrimage of misery; while the other hastened smilingly to spread the news of Weir's access of insanity, and to drum up for that night a full attendance at the Speculative, where further eccentric developments might certainly be looked for. I doubt if Innes had the least belief in his prediction; I think it flowed rather from a wish to make the story as good and the scandal as great as possible; not from any ill-will to Archie – from the mere pleasure of beholding interested faces. But for all that his words were prophetic. Archie did not forget the Spec.; he put in an appearance there at the due time, and, before the evening was over, had dealt a memorable shock to his companions. It chanced he was the president of the night. He sat in the same room where the Society still meets – only the portraits were not there: the men who afterwards sat for them were then but beginning their career. The same lustre of many tapers shed its light over the meeting; the same chair, perhaps, supported him that so many of us have sat in since. At times he seemed to forget the business of the evening, but even in these periods he sat with a great air of energy and determination. At times he meddled bitterly, and launched with defiance those fines which are the precious and rarely used artillery of the president. He little thought, as he did so, how he resembled his father, but his friends remarked upon it, chuckling. So far, in his high place above his fellow-students, he seemed set beyond the possibility of any scandal; but his mind was made up – he was determined to fulfil the sphere of his offence. He signed to Innes (whom he had just fined, and who just impeached his ruling) to succeed him in the chair, stepped down from the platform, and took his place by the chimney-piece, the shine of many wax tapers from above illuminating his pale face, the glow of the great red fire relieving from behind his slim figure. He had to propose, as an amendment to the next subject in the case-book, 'Whether capital punishment be consistent with God's will or man's policy?'

A breath of embarrassment, of something like alarm, passed round the room, so daring did these words appear upon the lips of Hermiston's only son. But the amendment was not seconded; the previous question was promptly moved and unanimously voted, and the momentary scandal smuggled by. Innes triumphed in the fulfilment of his prophecy. He and Archie were now become the heroes of the night; but whereas every one crowded about Innes, when the meeting broke up, but one of all his companions came to speak to Archie.

'Weir, man! That was an extraordinary raid of yours!' observed this courageous member, taking him confidentially by the arm as they went out.

'I don't think it a raid,' said Archie grimly. 'More like a war. I saw that poor brute hanged this morning, and my gorge rises at it yet.'

'Hut-tut,' returned his companion, and, dropping his arm like something hot, he sought the less tense society of others.

Archie found himself alone. The last of the faithful – or was it only the boldest of the curious? – had fled. He watched the black huddle of his fellow-students draw off down and up the street, in whispering or boisterous gangs. And the isolation of the moment weighed upon him like an omen and an emblem of his destiny in life. Bred up in unbroken fear himself, among trembling servants, and in a house which (at the least ruffle in the master's voice) shuddered into silence, he saw himself on the brink of the red valley of war, and measured the danger and length of it with awe. He made a détour in the glimmer and shadow of the streets, came into the back stable lane, and watched for a long while the light burn steady in the Judge's room. The longer he gazed upon that illuminated window-blind, the more blank became the picture of the man who sat behind it, endlessly turning over sheets of process, pausing to sip a glass of port, or rising and passing heavily about his book-lined walls to verify some reference. He could not combine the brutal judge and the industrious, dispassionate student; the connecting link escaped him; from such a dual nature, it was impossible he should predict behaviour; and he asked himself if he had done well to plunge into a business of which the end could not be foreseen? and presently after, with a sickening decline of confidence, if he had done loyally to strike his father? For he had struck him – defied him twice over and before a cloud of witnesses – struck him a public buffet before crowds. Who had called him to judge his father in these precarious and high questions? The office was usurped. It might have become a stranger; in a son – there was no blinking it – in a son, it was disloyal. And now, between these two natures so antipathetic, so hateful to each other, there was depending an unpardonable affront: and the providence of God alone might foresee the manner in which it would be resented by Lord Hermiston.

These misgivings tortured him all night and arose with him in the winter's morning; they followed him from class to class, they made him shrinkingly sensitive to every shade of manner in his companions, they sounded in his ears through the current voice of the professor; and he brought them home with him at night unabated and indeed increased. The cause of this increase lay in a chance encounter with the celebrated Dr Gregory. Archie stood looking vaguely in the lighted window of a book shop, trying to nerve himself for the approaching ordeal. My lord and he had met and parted in the morning as they had now done for long, with scarcely the ordinary civilities of life; and it was plain to the son that nothing had yet reached the father's ears. Indeed, when he recalled the awful countenance of my lord, a timid hope sprang up in him that perhaps there would be found no one bold enough to carry tales. If this were so, he asked himself, would he begin again? and he found no answer. It was at this moment that a hand was laid upon his arm, and a voice said in his ear, 'My dear Mr Archie, you had better come and see me.'

He started, turned round, and found himself face to face with Dr Gregory. 'And why should I come to see you?' he asked, with the defiance of the miserable.

'Because you are looking exceeding ill,' said the doctor, 'and you very evidently want looking after, my young friend. Good folk are scarce, you know; and it is not every one that would be quite so much missed as yourself. It is not every one that Hermiston would miss.'

And with a nod and a smile, the doctor passed on.

A moment after, Archie was in pursuit, and had in turn, but more roughly, seized him by the arm.

'What do you mean? what did you mean by saying that? What makes you think that Hermis – my father would have missed me?'

The doctor turned about and looked him all over with a clinical eye. A far more stupid man than Dr Gregory might have guessed the truth; but ninety-nine out of a hundred, even if they had been equally inclined to kindness, would have blundered by some touch of charitable exaggeration. The doctor was better inspired. He knew the father well; in that white face of intelligence and suffering, he divined something of the son; and he told, without apology or adornment, the plain truth.

'When you had the measles, Mr Archibald, you had them gey and ill; and I thought you were going to slip between my fingers,' he said. 'Well, your father was anxious. How did I know it? says you. Simply because I am a trained observer. The sign that I saw him make, ten thousand would have missed; and perhaps – *perhaps*, I say, because he's a hard man to judge of – but perhaps he never made another. A strange thing to consider! It was this. One day I came to him: "Hermiston," said I, "there's a change." He never said a word, just glowered at me (if ye'll pardon the phrase) like a wild beast. "A change for the better," said I. And I distinctly heard him take his breath.'

The doctor left no opportunity for anticlimax; nodding his cocked hat (a piece of antiquity to which he clung) and repeating 'Distinctly' with raised eyebrows, he took his departure, and left Archie speechless in the street.

The anecdote might be called infinitely little, and yet its meaning for Archie was immense. 'I did not know the old man had so much blood in him.' He had never dreamed this sire of his, this aboriginal antique, this adamantine Adam, had even so much of a heart as to be moved in the least degree for another – and that other himself, who had insulted him! With the generosity of youth, Archie was instantly under arms upon the other side: had instantly created a new image of Lord Hermiston, that of a man who was all iron without and all sensibility within. The mind of the vile jester, the tongue that had pursued Duncan Jopp with unmanly insults, the unbeloved countenance that he had known and feared for so long, were all forgotten; and he hastened home, impatient to confess his misdeeds, impatient to throw himself on the mercy of this imaginary character.

He was not to be long without a rude awakening. It was in the gloaming when he drew near the doorstep of the lighted house, and was aware of the figure of his father approaching from the opposite side. Little daylight lingered; but on the door being opened, the strong yellow shine of the lamp gushed out upon the landing and shone full on Archie, as he stood, in the old-fashioned observance of respect, to yield precedence. The Judge came without haste, stepping stately and firm; his chin raised, his face (as he entered the lamplight) strongly illumined, his mouth set hard. There was never a wink of change in his expression; without looking to the right or left, he mounted the stair, passed close to Archie, and entered the house. Instinctively, the boy, upon his first coming, had made a movement to meet him; instinctively, he recoiled against the railing, as the old man swept by him in a pomp of indignation. Words were needless; he knew all – perhaps more than all – and the hour of judgment was at hand.

It is possible that, in this sudden revulsion of hope, and before these symptoms of impending danger, Archie might have fled. But not even that was left to him. My lord, after hanging up his cloak and hat, turned round in the lighted entry, and made him an imperative and silent gesture with his thumb, and with the strange instinct of obedience, Archie followed him into the house.

All dinner-time there reigned over the Judge's table a palpable silence, and as soon as the solids were despatched he rose to his feet.

'M'Killup, tak' the wine into my room,' said he; and then to his son: 'Archie, you and me has to have a talk.'

It was at this sickening moment that Archie's courage, for the first and last time, entirely deserted him. 'I have an appointment,' said he.

'It'll have to be broken, then,' said Hermiston, and led the way into his study.

The lamp was shaded, the fire trimmed to a nicety, the table covered deep with orderly documents, the backs of law books made a frame upon all sides that was only broken by the window and the doors.

For a moment Hermiston warmed his hands at the fire, presenting his back to Archie; then suddenly disclosed on him the terrors of the Hanging Face.

'What's this I hear of ye?' he asked.

There was no answer possible to Archie.

'I'll have to tell ye, then,' pursued Hermiston. 'It seems ye've been skirling against the father that begot ye, and one of his Maijesty's Judges in this land; and that in the public street, and while an order of the Court was being executit. Forbye which, it would appear that ye've been airing your opeenions in a Coallege Debatin' Society'; he paused a moment: and then, with extraordinary bitterness, added: 'Ye damned eediot.'

'I had meant to tell you,' stammered Archie. 'I see you are well informed.'

'Muckle obleeged to ye,' said his lordship, and took his usual seat. 'And so you disapprove of Caapital Punishment?' he added.

'I am sorry, sir, I do,' said Archie.

'I am sorry, too,' said his lordship. 'And now, if you please, we shall approach this business with a little more parteecularity. I hear that at the hanging of Duncan Jopp – and, man! ye had a fine client there – in the middle of all the riff-raff of the ceety, ye thought fit to cry out, "This is a damned murder, and my gorge rises at the man that haangit him." '

'No, sir, these were not my words,' cried Archie.

'What were yer word, then?' asked the Judge.

'I believe I said, "I denounce it as a murder!" ' said the son. 'I beg your pardon – a God-defying murder. I have no wish to conceal the truth,' he added, and looked his father for a moment in the face.

'God, it would only need that of it next!' cried Hermiston. 'There was nothing about your gorge rising, then?'

'That was afterwards, my lord, as I was leaving the Speculative. I said I had been to see the miserable creature hanged, and my gorge rose at it.'

'Did ye, though?' said Hermiston. 'And I suppose ye knew who haangit him?'

'I was present at the trial, I ought to tell you that, I ought to explain. I ask your pardon beforehand for any expression that may seem undutiful. The position in which I stand is wretched,' said the unhappy hero, now fairly face to face with the business he had chosen. 'I have been reading some of your cases. I was present while Jopp was tried. It was a hideous business. Father, it was a hideous thing! Grant he was vile, why should you hunt him with a vileness equal to his own? It was done with glee – that is the word – you did it with glee; and I looked on, God help me! with horror.'

'You're a young gentleman that doesna approve of Caapital Punishment,' said Hermiston. 'Weel, I'm an auld man that does. I was glad to get Jopp haangit, and what for would I pretend I wasna? You're all for honesty, it seems; you couldn't even steik your mouth on the public street. What for should I steik mines upon the bench, the King's officer, bearing the sword, a dreid to evil-doers, as I was from the beginning, and as I will be to

the end! Mair than enough of it! Heedious! I never gave twa
thoughts to heediousness, I have no call to be bonny. I'm a man
that gets through with my day's business, and let that suffice.'

The ring of sarcasm had died out of his voice as he went on;
the plain words became invested with some of the dignity of the
Justice-seat.

'It would be telling you if you could say as much,' the speaker
resumed. 'But ye cannot. Ye've been reading some of my cases,
ye say. But it was not for the law in them, it was to spy out
your faither's nakedness, a fine employment in a son. You're
splairging; you're running at lairge in life like a wild nowt. It's
impossible you should think any longer of coming to the Bar.
You're not fit for it; no splairger is. And another thing: son
of mines or no son of mines, you have flung fylement in public
on one of the Senators of the Coallege of Justice, and I would
make it my business to see that ye were never admitted there
yourself. There is a kind of a decency to be observit. Then
comes the next of it – what am I to do with ye next? Ye'll
have to find some kind of a trade, for I'll never support ye
in idleset. What do ye fancy ye'll be fit for? The pulpit? Na,
they could never get diveenity into that bloackhead. Him that
the law of man whammles is no likely to do muckle better by
the law of God. What would ye make of hell? Wouldna your
gorge rise at that? Na, there's no room for splairgers under the
fower quarters of John Calvin. What else is there? Speak up.
Have ye got nothing of your own?'

'Father, let me go to the Peninsula,' said Archie. 'That's all
I'm fit for – to fight.'

'All? quo' he!' returned the Judge. 'And it would be enough
too, if I thought it. But I'll never trust ye so near the French,
you that's so Frenchifeed.'

'You do me injustice there, sir,' said Archie. 'I am loyal;
I will not boast; but any interest I may have ever felt in the
French – '

'Have ye been so loyal to me?' interrupted his father.

There came no reply.

'I think not,' continued Hermiston. 'And I would send no man
to be a servant to the King, God bless him! that has proved such
a shauchling son to his own faither. You can splairge here on
Edinburgh street, and where's the hairm? It doesna play buff

on me! And if there were twenty thousand eediots like yourself, sorrow a Duncan Jopp would hang the fewer. But there's no splairging possible in a camp; and if you were to go to it, you would find out for yourself whether Lord Well'n'ton approves of caapital punishment or not. You a sodger!' he cried, with a sudden burst of scorn. 'Ye auld wife, the sodgers would bray at ye like cuddies!'

As at the drawing of a curtain, Archie was aware of some illogicality in his position, and stood abashed. He had a strong impression, besides, of the essential valour of the old gentleman before him, how conveyed it would be hard to say.

'Well, have ye no other proposeetion?' said my lord again.

'You have taken this so calmly, sir, that I cannot but stand ashamed,' began Archie.

'I'm nearer voamiting, though, than you would fancy,' said my lord.

The blood rose to Archie's brow.

'I beg your pardon, I should have said that you had accepted my affront. . . . I admit it was an affront; I did not think to apologise, but I do, I ask your pardon; it will not be so again, I pass you my word of honour. . . . I should have said that I admired your magnanimity with – this – offender,' Archie concluded with a gulp.

'I have no other son, ye see,' said Hermiston. 'A bonny one I have gotten! But I must just do the best I can wi' him, and what am I to do? If ye had been younger, I would have wheepit ye for this rideeculous exhibeetion. The way it is, I have just to grin and bear. But one thing is to be clearly understood. As a faither, I must grin and bear it; but if I had been the Lord Advocate instead of the Lord Justice-Clerk, son or no son, Mr Erchibald Weir would have been in a jyle the night.'

Archie was now dominated. Lord Hermiston was coarse and cruel; and yet the son was aware of a bloomless nobility, an ungracious abnegation of the man's self in the man's office. At every word, this sense of the greatness of Lord Hermiston's spirit struck more home; and along with it that of his own impotence, who had struck – and perhaps basely struck – at his own father, and not reached so far as to have even nettled him.

'I place myself in your hands without reserve,' he said.

'That's the first sensible word I've had of ye the night,' said Hermiston. 'I can tell ye, that would have been the end of it, the one way or the other; but it's better ye should come there yourself, than what I would have had to hirstle ye. Weel, by my way of it – and my way is the best – there's just the one thing it's possible that ye might be with decency, and that's a laird. Ye'll be out of hairm's way at the least of it. If ye have to rowt, ye can rowt amang the kye; and the maist feck of the caapital punishment ye're like to come across'll be guddling trouts. Now, I'm for no idle lairdies; every man has to work, if it's only at peddling ballants; to work, or to be wheeped, or to be haangit. If I set ye down at Hermiston, I'll have to see you work that place the way it has never been workit yet; ye must ken about the sheep like a herd; ye must be my grieve there, and I'll see that I gain by ye. Is that understood?'

'I will do my best,' said Archie.

'Well, then, I'll send Kirstie word the morn, and ye can go yourself the day after,' said Hermiston. 'And just try to be less of an eediot!' he concluded, with a freezing smile, and turned immediately to the papers on his desk.

CHAPTER FOUR

Opinions of the Bench

Late the same night, after a disordered walk, Archie was admitted into Lord Glenalmond's dining-room, where he sat, with a book upon his knee, beside three frugal coals of fire. In his robes upon the bench, Glenalmond had a certain air of burliness: plucked of these, it was a may-pole of a man that rose unsteadily from his chair to give his visitor welcome. Archie had suffered much in the last days, he had suffered again that evening; his face was white and drawn, his eyes wild and dark. But Lord Glenalmond greeted him without the least mark of surprise or curiosity.

'Come in, come in,' said he. 'Come in and take a seat. Carstairs' (to his servant) 'make up the fire, and then you can bring a bit of supper,' and again to Archie, with a very trivial accent: 'I was half expecting you,' he added.

'No supper,' said Archie. 'It is impossible that I should eat.'

'Not impossible,' said the tall old man, laying his hand upon his shoulder, 'and, if you will believe me, necessary.'

'You know what brings me?' said Archie, as soon as the servant had left the room.

'I have a guess, I have a guess,' replied Glenalmond. 'We will talk of it presently – when Carstairs has come and gone, and you have had a piece of my good Cheddar cheese and a pull at the porter tankard: not before.'

'It is impossible I should eat,' repeated Archie.

'Tut, tut!' said Lord Glenalmond. 'You have eaten nothing to-day, and I venture to add, nothing yesterday. There is no case that may not be made worse: this may be a very disagreeable business, but if you were to fall sick and die, it would be still more so, and for all concerned – for all concerned.'

'I see you must know all,' said Archie. 'Where did you hear it?'

'In the mart of scandal, in the Parliament House,' said

32

Glenalmond. 'It runs riot below among the bar and the public, but it sifts up to us upon the bench, and rumour has some of her voices even in the divisions.'

Carstairs returned at this moment, and rapidly laid out a little supper; during which Lord Glenalmond spoke at large and a little vaguely on indifferent subjects, so that it might be rather said of him that he made a cheerful noise, than that he contributed to human conversation; and Archie sat upon the other side, not heeding him, brooding over his wrongs and errors.

But so soon as the servant was gone, he broke forth again at once. 'Who told my father? Who dared to tell him? Could it have been you?'

'No, it was not me,' said the Judge; 'although – to be quite frank with you, and after I had seen and warned you – it might have been me. I believe it was Glenkindie.'

'That shrimp!' cried Archie.

'As you say, that shrimp,' returned my lord; 'although really it is scarce a fitting mode of expression for one of the senators of the College of Justice. We were hearing the parties in a long, crucial case, before the fifteen; Creech was moving at some length for an infeftment; when I saw Glenkindie lean forward to Hermiston with his hand over his mouth and make him a secret communication. No one could have guessed its nature from your father; from Glenkindie, yes, his malice sparked out of him a little grossly. But your father, no. A man of granite. The next moment he pounced upon Creech. "Mr Creech," says he, "I'll take a look of that sasine," and for thirty minutes after,' said Glenalmond, with a smile, 'Messrs. Creech and Co. were fighting a pretty uphill battle, which resulted, I need hardly add, in their total rout. The case was dismissed. No, I doubt if ever I heard Hermiston better inspired. He was literally rejoicing *in apicibus juris*.'

Archie was able to endure no longer. He thrust his plate away and interrupted the deliberate and insignificant stream of talk. 'Here,' he said, 'I have made a fool of myself, if I have not made something worse. Do you judge between us – judge between a father and a son. I can speak to you; it is not like . . . I will tell you what I feel and what I mean to do; and you shall be the judge,' he repeated.

'I decline jurisdiction,' said Glenalmond, with extreme seri-
ousness. 'But, my dear boy, if it will do you any good to talk,
and if it will interest you at all to hear what I may choose to
say when I have heard you, I am quite at your command. Let
an old man say it, for once, and not need to blush: I love you
like a son.'

There came a sudden sharp sound in Archie's throat. 'Ay,'
he cried, 'and there it is! Love! Like a son! And how do you
think I love my father?'

'Quietly, quietly,' says my lord.

'I will be very quiet,' replied Archie. 'And I will be baldly
frank. I do not love my father; I wonder sometimes if I do not
hate him. There's my shame; perhaps my sin; at least, and in the
sight of God, not my fault. How was I to love him? He has never
spoken to me, never smiled upon me; I do not think he ever
touched me. You know the way he talks? You do not talk so,
yet you can sit and hear him without shuddering, and I cannot.
My soul is sick when he begins with it; I could smite him in the
mouth. And all that's nothing. I was at the trial of this Jopp.
You were not there, but you must have heard him often; the
man's notorious for it, for being – look at my position! he's my
father and this is how I have to speak of him – notorious for
being a brute and cruel and a coward. Lord Glenalmond, I give
you my word, when I came out of that Court, I longed to die –
the shame of it was beyond my strength: but I – I – ' he rose
from his seat and began to pace the room in a disorder. 'Well,
who am I? A boy, who have never been tried, have never done
anything except this twopenny impotent folly with my father.
But I tell you, my lord, and I know myself, I am at least that
kind of a man – or that kind of a boy, if you prefer it – that I
could die in torments rather than that any one should suffer as
that scoundrel suffered. Well, and what have I done? I see it
now. I have made a fool of myself, as I said in the beginning;
and I have gone back, and asked my father's pardon, and placed
myself wholly in his hands – and he has sent me to Hermiston,'
with a wretched smile, 'for life, I suppose – and what can I say?
he strikes me as having done quite right, and let me off better
than I had deserved.'

'My poor, dear boy!' observed Glenalmond. 'My poor dear
and, if you will allow me to say so, very foolish boy! You are

only discovering where you are; to one of your temperament, or of mine, a painful discovery. The world was not made for us; it was made for ten hundred millions of men, all different from each other and from us; there's no royal road there, we just have to sclamber and tumble. Don't think that I am at all disposed to be surprised; don't suppose that I ever think of blaming you; indeed I rather admire! But there fall to be offered one or two observations on the case which occur to me and which (if you will listen to them dispassionately) may be the means of inducing you to view the matter more calmly. First of all, I cannot acquit you of a good deal of what is called intolerance. You seem to have been very much offended because your father talks a little sculduddery after dinner, which it is perfectly licit for him to do, and which (although I am not very fond of it myself) appears to be entirely an affair of taste. Your father, I scarcely like to remind you, since it is so trite a commonplace, is older than yourself. At least, he is *major* and *sui juris*, and may please himself in the matter of his conversation. And, do you know, I wonder if he might not have as good an answer against you and me? We say we sometimes find him *coarse*, but I suspect he might retort that he finds us always dull. Perhaps a relevant exception.'

He beamed on Archie, but no smile could be elicited.

'And now,' proceeded the Judge, 'for "Archibald on Capital Punishment." This is a very plausible academic opinion; of course I do not and I cannot hold it; but that's not to say that many able and excellent persons have not done so in the past. Possibly, in the past also, I may have a little dipped myself in the same heresy. My third client, or possibly my fourth, was the means of a return in my opinions. I never saw the man I more believed in; I would have put my hand in the fire, I would have gone to the cross for him; and when it came to trial he was gradually pictured before me, by undeniable probation, in the light of so gross, so cold-blooded, and so black-hearted a villain, that I had a mind to have cast my brief upon the table. I was then boiling against the man with even a more tropical temperature than I had been boiling for him. But I said to myself: "No, you have taken up his case; and because you have changed your mind it must not be suffered to let drop. All that rich tide of eloquence that you prepared last night with so much enthusiasm is out of place, and yet you must not desert him, you must say something." So I said something, and I got him off. It made my reputation. But an experience of that kind is formative. A man must not bring his passions to the bar – or to the bench,' he added.

The story had slightly rekindled Archie's interest. 'I could never deny,' he began – 'I mean I can conceive that some men would be better dead. But who are we to know all the springs of God's unfortunate creatures? Who are we to trust ourselves where it seems that God Himself must think twice before He treads, and to do it with delight? Yes, with delight. *Tigris ut aspera*.'

'Perhaps not a pleasant spectacle,' said Glenalmond. 'And yet, do you know, I think somehow a great one.'

'I've had a long talk with him to-night,' said Archie.

'I was supposing so,' said Glenalmond.

'And he struck me – I cannot deny that he struck me as something very big,' pursued the son. 'Yes, he is big. He never spoke about himself; only about me. I suppose I admired him. The dreadful part – '

'Suppose we did not talk about that,' interrupted Glenalmond. 'You know it very well, it cannot in any way help that you should brood upon it, and I sometimes wonder whether you and I – who are a pair of sentimentalists – are quite good judges of plain men.'

'How do you mean?' asked Archie.

'*Fair* judges, I mean,' replied Glenalmond. 'Can we be just to them? Do we not ask too much? There was a word of yours just now that impressed me a little when you asked me who we were to know all the springs of God's unfortunate creatures. You applied that, as I understood, to capital cases only. But does it – I ask myself – does it not apply all through? Is it any less difficult to judge of a good man or of a half-good man, than of the worst criminal at the bar? And may not each have relevant excuses?'

'Ah, but we do not talk of punishing the good,' cried Archie.

'No, we do not talk of it,' said Glenalmond. 'But I think we do it. Your father, for instance.'

'You think I have punished him?' cried Archie.

Lord Glenalmond bowed his head.

'I think I have,' said Archie. 'And the worst is, I think he feels it! How much, who can tell, with such a being? But I think he does.'

'And I am sure of it,' said Glenalmond

'Has he spoken to you, then?' cried Archie.

'O no,' replied the judge.

'I tell you honestly,' said Archie, 'I want to make it up to him. I will go, I have already pledged myself to go to Hermiston. That was to him. And now I pledge myself to you, in the sight of God, that I will close my mouth on capital punishment and all other subjects where our views may clash, for – how long shall I say? when shall I have sense enough? – ten years. Is that well?'

'It is well,' said my lord.

'As far as it goes,' said Archie. 'It is enough as regards myself, it is to lay down enough of my conceit. But as regards him, whom I have publicly insulted? What am I to do to him? How do you pay attentions to a – an Alp like that?'

'Only in one way,' replied Glenalmond. 'Only by obedience, punctual, prompt, and scrupulous.'

'And I promise that he shall have it,' answered Archie. 'I offer you my hand in pledge of it.'

'And I take your hand as a solemnity,' replied the judge. 'God bless you, my dear, and enable you to keep your promise. God guide you in the true way, and spare your days, and preserve to you your honest heart.' At that, he kissed the young man upon the forehead in a gracious, distant, antiquated way; and instantly launched, with a marked change of voice, into another subject. 'And now, let us replenish the tankard; and I believe, if you will try my Cheddar again, you would find you had a better appetite. The Court has spoken, and the case is dismissed.'

'No, there is one thing I must say,' cried Archie. 'I must say it in justice to himself. I know – I believe faithfully, slavishly, after our talk – he will never ask me anything unjust. I am proud to feel it, that we have that much in common, I am proud to say it to you.'

The Judge, with shining eyes, raised his tankard. 'And I think perhaps that we might permit ourselves a toast,' said he. 'I should like to propose the health of a man very different from me and very much my superior – a man from whom I have often differed, who has often (in the trivial expression) rubbed me the wrong way, but whom I have never ceased to respect and, I may add, to be not a little afraid of. Shall I give you his name?'

'The Lord Justice-Clerk, Lord Hermiston,' said Archie, almost with gaiety; and the pair drank the toast deeply.

It was not precisely easy to re-establish, after these emotional passages, the natural flow of conversation. But the Judge eked out what was wanting with kind looks, produced his snuff-box (which was very rarely seen) to fill in a pause, and at last, despairing of any further social success, was upon the point of getting down a book to read a favourite passage, when there came a rather startling summons at the front door, and Carstairs ushered in my Lord Glenkindie, hot from a midnight supper. I am not aware that Glenkindie was ever a beautiful object, being short, and gross-bodied, and with an expression of sensuality comparable to a bear's. At that moment, coming in hissing from many potations, with a flushed countenance and blurred eyes, he was strikingly contrasted with the tall, pale, kingly figure of Glenalmond. A rush of confused thought came over Archie – of shame that this was one of his father's elect friends; of pride, that at the least of it Hermiston could carry his liquor; and last of all, of rage, that he should have here under his eyes the man that had betrayed him. And then that too passed away; and he sat quiet, biding his opportunity.

The tipsy senator plunged at once into an explanation with Glenalmond. There was a point reserved yesterday, he had been able to make neither head nor tail of it, and seeing lights in the house, he had just dropped in for a glass of porter – and at this point he became aware of the third person. Archie saw the cod's mouth and the blunt lips of Glenkindie gape at him for a moment, and the recognition twinkle in his eyes.

'Who's this?' said he. 'What? is this possibly you, Don Quickshot? And how are ye? And how's your father? And what's all this we hear of you? It seems you're a most extra-ordinary leveller, by all tales. No king, no parliaments, and your gorge rises at the macers, worthy men! Hoot, toot! Dear, dear me! Your father's son too! Most rideeculous!'

Archie was on his feet, flushing a little at the reappearance of his unhappy figure of speech, but perfectly self-possessed. 'My lord – and you, Lord Glenalmond, my dear friend,' he began, 'this is a happy chance for me, that I can make my confession and offer my apologies to two of you at once.'

'Ah, but I don't know about that. Confession? It'll be judeecial, my young friend,' cried the jocular Glenkindie. 'And I'm afraid to listen to ye. Think if ye were to make me a coanvert!'

'If you would allow me, my lord,' returned Archie, 'what I have to say is very serious to me; and be pleased to be humorous after I am gone!'

'Remember, I'll hear nothing against the macers!' put in the incorrigible Glenkindie.

But Archie continued as though he had not spoken. 'I have played, both yesterday and today, a part for which I can only offer the excuse of youth. I was so unwise as to go to an execution; it seems I made a scene at the gallows; not content with which, I spoke the same night in a college society against capital punishment. This is the extent of what I have done, and in case you hear more alleged against me, I protest my innocence. I have expressed my regret already to my father, who is so good as to pass my conduct over – in a degree, and upon the condition that I am to leave my law studies.' . . .

CHAPTER FIVE

Winter on the Moors

I   AT HERMISTON

The road to Hermiston runs for a great part of the way up the valley of a stream, a favourite with anglers and with midges, full of falls and pools, and shaded by willows and natural woods of birch. Here and there, but at great distances, a byway branches off, and a gaunt farmhouse may be descried above in a fold of the hill; but the more part of the time, the road would be quite empty of passage and the hills of habitation. Hermiston parish is one of the least populous in Scotland; and, by the time you came that length, you would scarce be surprised at the inimitable smallness of the kirk, a dwarfish, ancient place seated for fifty, and standing in a green by the burn-side among two-score gravestones. The manse close by, although no more than a cottage, is surrounded by the brightness of a flower-garden and the straw roofs of bees; and the whole colony, kirk and manse, garden and graveyard, finds harbourage in a grove of rowans, and is all the year round in a great silence broken only by the drone of the bees, the tinkle of the burn, and the bell on Sundays. A mile beyond the kirk the road leaves the valley by a precipitous ascent, and brings you a little after to the place of Hermiston, where it comes to an end in the back-yard before the coach-house. All beyond and about is the great field of the hills; the plover, the curlew, and the lark cry there; the wind blows as it blows in a ship's rigging, hard and cold and pure; and the hill-tops huddle one behind another like a herd of cattle into the sunset.

The house was sixty years old, unsightly, comfortable; a farmyard and a kitchen-garden on the left, with a fruit wall where little hard green pears came to their maturity about the end of October.

The policy (as who should say the park) was of some extent, but very ill reclaimed; heather and moorfowl had crossed the boundary wall and spread and roosted within; and it would have tasked a landscape gardener to say where policy ended and unpolicied nature began. My lord had been led by the influence of Mr Sheriff Scott into a considerable design of planting; many acres were accordingly set out with fir, and the little feathery besoms gave a false scale and lent a strange air of a toy-shop to the moors. A great, rooty sweetness of bogs was in the air, and at all seasons an infinite melancholy piping of hill birds. Standing so high and with so little shelter, it was a cold, exposed house, splashed by showers, drenched by continuous rains that made the gutters to spout, beaten upon and buffeted by all the winds of heaven; and the prospect would be often black with tempest, and often white with the snows of winter. But the house was wind and weather proof, the hearths were kept bright, and the rooms pleasant with live fires of peat; and Archie might sit of an evening and hear the squalls bugle on the moorland, and watch the fire prosper in the earthy fuel, and the smoke winding up the chimney, and drink deep of the pleasures of shelter.

Solitary as the place was, Archie did not want neighbours. Every night, if he chose, he might go down to the manse and share a 'brewst' of toddy with the minister – a hare-brained ancient gentleman, long and light and still active, though his knees were loosened with age, and his voice broke continually in childish trebles – and his lady wife, a heavy, comely dame, without a word to say for herself beyond good-even and good-day. Harum-scarum, clodpole young lairds of the neighbourhood paid him the compliment of a visit. Young Hay of Romanes rode down to call, on his crop-eared pony; young Pringle of Drumanno came up on his bony grey. Hay remained on the hospitable field, and must be carried to bed; Pringle got somehow to his saddle about 3 A.M., and (as Archie stood with the lamp on the upper doorstep) lurched, uttered a senseless view-holloa, and vanished out of the small circle of illumination like a wraith. Yet a minute or two longer the clatter of his break-neck flight was audible, then it was cut off by the intervening steepness of the hill; and again, a great while after, the renewed beating of phantom horse-hoofs, far in the valley of the Hermiston, showed that the horse at least, if not his rider, was still on the homeward way.

There was a Tuesday club at the 'Crosskeys' in Crossmichael, where the young bloods of the country-side congregated and drank deep on a percentage of the expense, so that he was left gainer who should have drunk the most. Archie had no great mind to this diversion, but he took it like a duty laid upon him, went with a decent regularity, did his manfullest with the liquor, held up his head in the local jests, and got home again and was able to put up his horse, to the admiration of Kirstie and the lass that helped her. He dined at Driffel, supped at Windielaws. He went to the new year's ball at Huntsfield and was made welcome, and thereafter rode to hounds with my Lord Muirfell, upon whose name, as that of a legitimate Lord of Parliament, in a work so full of Lords of Session, my pen should pause reverently. Yet the same fate attended him here as in Edinburgh. The habit of solitude tends to perpetuate itself, and an austerity of which he was quite unconscious, and a pride which seemed arrogance, and perhaps was chiefly shyness, discouraged and offended his new companions. Hay did not return more than twice, Pringle never at all, and there came a time when Archie even desisted from the Tuesday Club, and became in all things – what he had had the name of almost from the first – the Recluse of Hermiston. High-nosed Miss Pringle of Drumanno and high-stepping Miss Marshall of the Mains were understood to have had a difference of opinion about him the day after the ball – he was none the wiser, he could not suppose himself to be remarked by these entrancing ladies. At the ball itself my Lord Muirfell's daughter, the Lady Flora, spoke to him twice, and the second time with a touch of appeal, so that her colour rose and her voice trembled a little in his ear, like a passing grace in music. He stepped back with a heart on fire, coldly and not ungracefully excused himself, and a little after watched her dancing with young Drumanno of the empty laugh, and was harrowed at the sight, and raged to himself that this was a world in which it was given to Drumanno to please, and to himself only to stand aside and envy. He seemed excluded, as of right, from the favour of such society – seemed to extinguish mirth wherever he came, and was quick to feel the wound, and desist, and retire into solitude. If he had but understood the figure he presented, and the impression he made on these bright eyes and tender hearts; if he had but guessed that the Recluse of Hermiston, young, graceful, well spoken, but always cold, stirred the maidens of the county with the charm of Byronism when Byronism was new, it may be questioned whether his destiny might not even yet have been modified. It may be questioned, and I think it should be doubted. It was in his horoscope to be parsimonious of pain to himself, or of the chance of pain, even to the avoidance of any opportunity of pleasure; to have a Roman sense of duty, an instinctive aristocracy of manners and taste; to be the son of Adam Weir and Jean Rutherford.

II KIRSTIE

Kirstie was now over fifty, and might have sat to a sculptor. Long of limb, and still light of foot, deep-breasted, robust-loined, her golden hair not yet mingled with any trace of silver, the years had but caressed and embellished her. By the lines of a rich and vigorous maternity, she seemed destined to be the bride of heroes and the mother of their children; and behold, by the iniquity of fate, she had passed through her youth alone, and drew near to the confines of age, a childless woman. The tender ambitions that she had received at birth had been, by time and disappointment, diverted into a certain barren zeal of industry and fury of interference. She carried her thwarted ardours into housework, she washed floors with her empty heart. If she could not win the love of one with love, she must dominate all by her temper. Hasty, wordy, and wrathful, she had a drawn quarrel with most of her neighbours, and with the others not much more than armed neutrality. The grieve's wife had been 'sneisty'; the sister of the gardener who kept house for him had shown herself 'upsitten'; and she wrote to Lord Hermiston about once a year demanding the discharge of the offenders, and justifying the demand by much wealth of detail. For it must not be supposed that the quarrel rested with the wife and did not take in the husband also – or with the gardener's sister, and did not speedily include the gardener himself. As the upshot of all this petty quarrelling and intemperate speech, she was practically excluded (like a lightkeeper on his tower) from the comforts of human association; except with her own indoor drudge, who, being but a lassie and entirely at her mercy, must submit to the

shifty weather of 'the mistress's' moods without complaint, and
be willing to take buffets or caresses according to the temper
of the hour. To Kirstie, thus situate and in the Indian summer
of her heart, which was slow to submit to age, the gods sent
this equivocal good thing of Archie's presence. She had known
him in the cradle and paddled him when he misbehaved; and
yet, as she had not so much as set eyes on him since he
was eleven and had his last serious illness, the tall, slender,
refined, and rather melancholy young gentleman of twenty
came upon her with the shock of a new acquaintance. He
was 'Young Hermiston,' 'the laird himsel' ': he had an air
of distinctive superiority, a cold straight glance of his black
eyes, that abashed the woman's tantrums in the beginning, and
therefore the possibility of any quarrel was excluded. He was
new, and therefore immediately aroused her curiosity; he was
reticent, and kept it awake. And lastly he was dark and she
fair, and he was male and she female, the everlasting fountains
of interest.

Her feeling partook of the loyalty of a clanswoman, the
hero-worship of a maiden aunt, and the idolatry due to a god.
No matter what he had asked of her, ridiculous or tragic, she
would have done it and joyed to do it. Her passion, for it
was nothing less, entirely filled her. It was a rich physical
pleasure to make his bed or light his lamp for him when he
was absent, to pull off his wet boots or wait on him at dinner
when he returned. A young man who should have so doted on
the idea, moral and physical, of any woman, might be properly
described as being in love, head and heels, and would have
behaved himself accordingly. But Kirstie – though her heart
leaped at his coming footsteps – though, when he patted her
shoulder, her face brightened for the day – had not a hope or
thought beyond the present moment and its perpetuation to the
end of time. Till the end of time she would have had nothing
altered, but still continue delightedly to serve her idol, and be
repaid (say twice in the month) with a clap on the shoulder

I have said her heart leaped – it is the accepted phrase. But
rather, when she was alone in any chamber of the house, and
heard his foot passing on the corridors, something in her bosom
rose slowly until her breath was suspended, and as slowly fell
again with a deep sigh, when the steps had passed and she was

disappointed of her eyes' desire. This perpetual hunger and thirst of his presence kept her all day on the alert. When he went forth at morning, she would stand and follow him with admiring looks. As it grew late and drew to the time of his return, she would steal forth to a corner of the policy wall and be seen standing there sometimes by the hour together, gazing with shaded eyes, waiting the exquisite and barren pleasure of his view a mile off on the mountains. When at night she had trimmed and gathered the fire, turned down his bed, and laid out his night-gear – when there was no more to be done for the king's pleasure, but to remember him fervently in her usually very tepid prayers, and go to bed brooding upon his perfections, his future career, and what she should give him the next day for dinner – there still remained before her one more opportunity; she was still to take in the tray and say good-night. Sometimes Archie would glance up from his book with a preoccupied nod and a perfunctory salutation which was in truth a dismissal; sometimes – and by degrees more often – the volume would be laid aside, he would meet her coming with a look of relief; and the conversation would be engaged, last out the supper, and be prolonged till the small hours by the waning fire. It was no wonder that Archie was fond of company after his solitary days; and Kirstie, upon her side, exerted all the arts of her vigorous nature to ensnare his attention. She would keep back some piece of news during dinner to be fired off with the entrance of the supper tray, and form as it were the *lever de rideau* of the evening's entertainment. Once he had heard her tongue wag, she made sure of the result. From one subject to another she moved by insidious transitions, fearing the least silence, fearing almost to give him time for an answer lest it should slip into a hint of separation. Like so many people of her class, she was a brave narrator; her place was on the hearth-rug and she made it a rostrum, mimeing her stories as she told them, fitting them with vital detail, spinning them out with endless 'quo' he's' and 'quo' she's,' her voice sinking into a whisper over the supernatural or the horrific; until she would suddenly spring up in affected surprise, and pointing to the clock, 'Mercy, Mr Archie!' she would say, 'whatten a time o' night is this of it! God forgive me for a daft wife!' So it befell, by good management, that she was not only the first to begin these nocturnal conversations, but invariably the first to break them off; so she managed to retire and not to be dismissed.

III   A BORDER FAMILY

Such an unequal intimacy has never been uncommon in Scotland, where the clan spirit survives; where the servant tends to spend her life in the same service, a helpmeet at first, then a tyrant, and at last a pensioner; where, besides, she is not necessarily destitute of the pride of birth, but is, perhaps, like Kirstie, a connection of her master's, and at least knows the legend of her own family, and may count kinship with some illustrious dead. For that is the mark of the Scot of all classes: that he stands in an attitude towards the past unthinkable to Englishmen, and remembers and cherishes the memory of his forebears, good or bad; and there burns alive in him a sense of identity with the dead even to the twentieth generation. No more characteristic instance could be found than in the family of Kirstie Elliott. They were all, and Kirstie the first of all, ready and eager to pour forth the particulars of their genealogy, embellished with every detail that memory had handed down or fancy fabricated; and, behold! from every ramification of that tree dangled a halter. The Elliotts themselves have had a chequered history; but these Elliotts deduced, besides, from three of the most unfortunate of the border clans – the Nicksons, the Ellwalds, and the Crozers. One ancestor after another might be seen appearing a moment out of the rain and the hill mist upon his furtive business, speeding home, perhaps, with a paltry booty of lame horses and lean kine, or squealing and dealing death in some moorland feud of the ferrets and the wild cats. One after another closed his obscure adventures in mid-air, triced up to the arm of the royal gibbet or the Baron's dule-tree. For the rusty blunderbuss of Scots criminal justice, which usually hurt nobody but jurymen, became a weapon of precision for the Nicksons, the Ellwalds, and the Crozers. The exhilaration of their exploits seemed to haunt the memories of their descendants alone, and the shame to be forgotten. Pride glowed in their bosoms to publish their relationship to 'Andrew Ellwald of the Laverockstanes, called "Unchancy Dand," who

was justifeed wi' seeven mair of the same name at Jeddart in
the days of King James the Sax.' In all this tissue of crime
and misfortune, the Elliotts of Cauldstaneslap had one boast
which must appear legitimate: the males were gallows-birds,
born outlaws, petty thieves, and deadly brawlers; but, according
to the same tradition, the females were all chaste and faithful.
The power of ancestry on the character is not limited to the
inheritance of cells. If I buy ancestors by the gross from the
benevolence of Lyon King of Arms, my grandson (if he is
Scottish) will feel a quickening emulation of their deeds.
The men of the Elliotts were proud, lawless, violent as of
right, cherishing and prolonging a tradition. In like manner
with the women. And the women, essentially passionate and
reckless, who crouched on the rug, in the shine of the peat fire,
telling these tales, had cherished through life a wild integrity
of virtue.

Her father Gilbert had been deeply pious, a savage discipli-
narian in the antique style, and withal a notorious smuggler. 'I
mind when I was a bairn getting mony a skelp and being shoo'd
to bed like pou'try,' she would say. 'That would be when the
lads and their bit kegs were on the road. We've had the riffraff
of two-three counties in our kitchen, mony's the time, betwix'
the twelve and the three; and their lanterns would be standing
in the forecourt, ay, a score o' them at once. But there was
nae ungodly talk permitted at Cauldstaneslap; my faither was
a consistent man in walk and conversation; just let slip an aith,
and there was the door to ye! He had that zeal for the Lord,
it was a fair wonder to hear him pray, but the faimily has aye
had a gift that way.' This father was twice married, once to a
dark woman of the old Ellwald stock, by whom he had Gilbert,
presently of Cauldstaneslap; and, secondly, to the mother of
Kirstie. 'He was an auld man when he married her, a fell auld
man wi' a muckle voice – you could hear him rowting from the
top o' the Kye-skairs,' she said; 'but for her, it appears she was
a perfit wonder. It was gentle blood she had, Mr Archie, for
it was your ain. The country-side gaed gyte about her and her
gowden hair. Mines is no to be mentioned wi' it, and there's
few weemen has mair hair than what I have, or yet a bonnier
colour. Often would I tell my dear Miss Jeannie – that was your
mother, dear, she was cruel ta'en up about her hair, it was unco

tender, ye see – "Houts, Miss Jeannie," I would say, "just fling your washes and your French dentifrishes in the back o' the fire, for that's the place for them; and awa' down to a burn side, and wash yersel' in cauld hill water, and dry your bonny hair in the caller wind o' the muirs, the way that my mother aye washed hers, and that I have aye made it a practice to have wishen mines – just you do what I tell ye, my dear, and ye'll give me news of it! Ye'll have hair, and routh of hair, a pigtail as thick's my arm," I said, "and the bonniest colour like the clear gowden guineas, so as the lads in kirk'll no can keep their eyes off it!" Weel, it lasted out her time, puir thing! I cuttit a lock of it upon her corp that was lying there sae cauld. I'll show it ye some of thir days if ye're good. But, as I was sayin', my mither – '

On the death of the father there remained golden-haired Kirstie, who took service with her distant kinsfolk, the Ruther-fords, and black-a-vised Gilbert, twenty years older, who farmed the Cauldstaneslap, married, and begot four sons between 1773 and 1784, and a daughter, like a postscript, in '97, the year of Camperdown and Cape St Vincent. It seemed it was a tradition in the family to wind up with a belated girl. In 1804, at the age of sixty, Gilbert met an end that might be called heroic. He was due home from market any time from eight at night till five in the morning, and in any condition from the quarrelsome to the speechless, for he maintained to that age the goodly customs of the Scots farmer. It was known on this occasion that he had a good bit of money to bring home; the word had gone round loosely. The laird had shown his guineas, and if anybody had but noticed it, there was an ill-looking vagabond crew, the scum of Edinburgh, that drew out of the market long ere it was dusk and took the hill-road by Hermiston, where it was not to be believed that they had lawful business. One of the country-side, one Dickieson, they took with them to be their guide, and dear he paid for it! Of a sudden, in the ford of the Broken Dykes, this vermin clan fell on the laird, six to one, and him three parts asleep, having drunk hard. But it is ill to catch an Elliott. For a while, in the night and the black water that was deep as to his saddle-girths, he wrought with his staff like a smith at his stithy, and great was the sound of oaths and blows. With that the ambuscade was burst, and he rode for home with a pistol-ball in him, three knife wounds, the loss of his front teeth, a broken rib and bridle, and a dying horse. That was a race with death that the laird rode! In the mirk night, with his broken bridle and his head swimming, he dug his spurs to the rowels in the horse's side, and the horse, that was even worse off than himself, the poor creature! screamed out loud like a person as he went, so that the hills echoed with it, and the folks at Cauldstaneslap got to their feet about the table and looked at each other with white faces. The horse fell dead at the yard gate, the laird won the length of the house and fell there on the threshold. To the son that raised him he gave the bag of money. 'Hae,' said he. All the way up the thieves had seemed to him to be at his heels, but now the hallucination left him – he saw them again in the place of the ambuscade – and the thirst of vengeance seized on his dying mind. Raising himself and pointing with an imperious finger into the black night from which he had come, he uttered the single command, 'Brocken Dykes,' and fainted. He had never been loved, but he had been feared in honour. At that sight, at that word, gasped out at them from a toothless and bleeding mouth, the old Elliott spirit awoke with a shout in the four sons. 'Wanting the hat,' continues my author, Kirstie, whom I but haltingly follow, for she told this tale like one inspired, 'wanting guns, for there wasna twa grains o' pouder in the house, wi' nae mair weepons than their sticks into their hands, the fower o' them took the road. Only Hob, and that was the eldest, hunkered at the doorsill where the blood had rin, fyled his hand wi' it, and haddit it up to Heeven in the way o' the auld Border aith. "Hell shall have her ain again this nicht!" he raired, and rode forth upon his errand.' It was three miles to Broken Dykes, down hill, and a sore road. Kirstie has seen men from Edinburgh dismounting there in plain day to lead their horses. But the four brothers rode it as if Auld Hornie were behind and Heaven in front. Come to the ford, and there was Dickieson. By all tales, he was not dead, but breathed and reared upon his elbow, and cried out to them for help. It was at a graceless face that he asked mercy. As soon as Hob saw, by the glint of the lantern, the eyes shining and the whiteness of the teeth in the man's face, 'Damn you!' says he; 'ye hae your teeth, hae ye?' and rode his horse to and fro upon that human remnant. Beyond that, Dandie must dismount with the lantern to be their guide; he was the youngest son, scarce twenty at the time. 'A' nicht long they gaed in the wet heath and jennipers, and whaur they gaed they neither knew nor cared, but just followed the bluid-stains and the footprints o' their faither's murderers. And a' nicht Dandie had his nose to the grund like a tyke, and the ithers followed and spak' naething, neither black nor white. There was nae noise to be heard, but just the sough of the swalled burns, and Hob, the dour yin, risping his teeth as he gaed.' With the first glint of the morning they saw they were on the drove road, and at that the four stopped and had a dram to their breakfasts, for they knew that Dand must have guided them right, and the rogues could be but little ahead, hot foot for Edinburgh by the way of the Pentland Hills. By eight o'clock they had word of them – a shepherd had seen four men 'uncoly mishandled' go by in the last hour. 'That's yin a piece,' says Clem, and swung his cudgel. 'Five o' them!' says Hob. 'God's death, but the faither was a man! And him drunk!' And then there befell them what my author termed 'a sair misbegowk,' for they were overtaken by a posse of mounted neighbours come to aid in the pursuit. Four sour faces looked on the reinforcement. 'The Deil's broughten you!' said Clem, and they rode thenceforward in the rear of the party with hanging heads. Before ten they had found and secured the rogues, and by three of the afternoon, as they rode up the Vennel with their prisoners, they were aware of a concourse of people bearing in their midst something that dripped. 'For the boady of the saxt,' pursued Kirstie, 'wi' his head smashed like a hazelnit, had been a' that nicht in the chairge o' Hermiston Water, and it dunting it on the stanes, and grunding it on the shallows, and flinging the deid thing heels-ower-hurdie at the Fa's o' Spango; and in the first o' the day, Tweed had got a hold o' him and carried him off like a wind, for it was uncoly swalled, and raced wi' him, bobbing under brae-sides, and was long playing with the creature in the drumlie lynns under the castle, and at the hinder end of all cuist him up on the starling of Crossmichael brig. Sae there they were a' thegither at last (for Dickieson had been brought in on a cart long syne), and folk could see what mainner o' man my brither had been that had held his head again sax and saved the siller, and him drunk!' Thus died of honourable injuries and in the savour of fame Gilbert Elliott of the Cauldstaneslap; but his sons had scarce less glory out of the business. Their savage haste, the skill with which Dand had found and followed the trail, the barbarity to the wounded Dickieson (which was like an open secret in the county), and the doom which it was currently supposed they had intended for the others, struck and stirred popular imagination. Some century earlier the last of the minstrels might have fashioned the last of the ballads out of that Homeric fight and chase; but the spirit was dead, or had been reincarnated already in Mr Sheriff Scott, and the degenerate moorsmen must be content to tell the tale in prose, and to make of the 'Four Black Brothers' a unit after the fashion of the 'Twelve Apostles' or the 'Three Musketeers.'

Robert, Gilbert, Clement, and Andrew – in the proper Border diminutives, Hob, Gib, Clem, and Dand Elliott – these ballad heroes, had much in common; in particular, their high sense of the family and the family honour; but they went diverse ways, and prospered and failed in different businesses. According to Kirstie, 'they had a' bees in their bonnets but Hob.' Hob the laird was, indeed, essentially a decent man. An elder of the Kirk, nobody had heard an oath upon his lips, save, perhaps, thrice or so at the sheep-washing, since the chase of his father's murderers. The figure he had shown on that eventful night disappeared as if swallowed by a trap. He who had ecstatically dipped his hand in the red blood, he who had ridden down Dickieson, became, from that moment on, a stiff and rather graceless model of the rustic proprieties; cannily profiting by the high war prices, and yearly stowing away a little nest-egg in the bank against calamity; approved of and sometimes consulted by the greater lairds for the massive and placid sense of what he said, when he could be induced to say anything; and particularly valued by the minister, Mr Torrance, as a right-hand man in the parish, and a model to parents. The transfiguration had been for the moment only; some Barbarossa, some old Adam of our ancestors, sleeps in all of us till the fit circumstance shall call it into action; and, for as sober as he now seemed, Hob had given once for all the measure of the devil that haunted him. He was married, and, by reason of the effulgence of that legendary night, was adored by his wife. He had a mob of little lusty, barefoot children who marched in a caravan the long miles to school, the stages of whose pilgrimage were marked by acts of spoliation and mischief, and who were qualified in the country-side as 'fair pests.' But in the house, if 'faither was in,' they were quiet as mice. In short, Hob moved through life in a great peace – the reward of any one who shall have killed his man, with any formidable and figurative circumstance, in the midst of a country gagged and swaddled with civilisation.

It was a current remark that the Elliotts were 'guid and bad, like sanguishes'; and certainly there was a curious distinction, the men of business coming alternately with the dreamers. The second brother, Gib, was a weaver by trade, had gone out early into the world to Edinburgh, and come home again with his wings singed. There was an exaltation in his nature which had led him to embrace with enthusiasm the principles of the French Revolution, and had ended by bringing him under the hawse of my Lord Hermiston in that furious onslaught of his upon the Liberals, which sent Muir and Palmer into exile and dashed the party into chaff. It was whispered that my lord, in his great scorn for the movement, and prevailed upon a little by a sense of neighbourliness, had given Gib a hint. Meeting him one day in the Potterrow, my lord had stopped in front of him: 'Gib, ye eediot,' he had said, 'what's this I hear of you? Poalitics, poalitics, poalitics, weaver's poalitics, is the way of it, I hear. If ye arena a'thegither dozened with eediocy, ye'll gang your ways back to Cauldstaneslap, and ca' your loom, and ca' your loom, man!' And Gilbert had taken him at the word and returned, with an expedition almost to be called flight, to the house of his father. The clearest of his inheritance was that family gift of prayer of which Kirstie had boasted; and the baffled politician now turned his attention to religious matters – or, as others said, to heresy and schism. Every Sunday morning he was in Crossmichael, where he had gathered together, one by one, a sect of about a dozen persons, who called themselves 'God's Remnant of the True Faithful,' or, for short, 'God's Remnant.' To the profane, they were known as 'Gib's Deils.' Bailie Sweedie, a noted humorist in the town, vowed that the proceedings always opened to the tune of 'The Deil Fly Away with the Exciseman,' and that the sacrament was dispensed in the form of hot whisky-toddy; both wicked hits at the evangelist, who had been suspected of smuggling in his youth, and had been overtaken (as the phrase went) on the streets of Crossmichael one Fair day. It was known that every Sunday they prayed for a blessing on the arms of Bonaparte. For this, 'God's Remnant,' as they were 'skailing' from the cottage that did duty for a temple, had been repeatedly stoned by the bairns, and Gib himself hooted by a squadron of Border volunteers in which his own brother, Dand, rode in a uniform and with a drawn sword. The 'Remnant' were believed, besides, to be 'antinomian in principle,' which might otherwise have been a serious charge, but the way public opinion then blew it was quite swallowed up and forgotten in the scandal about Bonaparte. For the rest, Gilbert had set up his loom in an outhouse at Cauldstaneslap, where he laboured assiduously six days of the week. His brothers, appalled by his political opinions, and willing to avoid dissension in the household, spoke but little to him; he less to them, remaining absorbed in the study of the Bible and almost constant prayer. The gaunt weaver was dry-nurse at Cauldstaneslap, and the bairns loved him dearly. Except when he was carrying an infant in his arms, he was rarely seen to smile – as, indeed, there were few smilers in that family. When his sister-in-law rallied him, and proposed that he should get a wife and bairns of his own, since he was so fond of them, 'I have no clearness of mind upon that point,' he would reply. If nobody called him in to dinner, he stayed out. Mrs Hob, a hard, unsympathetic woman, once tried the experiment. He went without food all day, but at dusk, as the light began to fail him, he came into the house of his own accord, looking puzzled. 'I've had a great gale of prayer upon my speerit,' said he. 'I canna mind sae muckle's what I had for denner.' The creed of God's Remnant was justified in the life of its founder. 'And yet I dinna ken,' said Kirstie. 'He's maybe no more stockfish than his neeghbours! He rode wi' the rest o' them, and had a good stamach to the work, by a' that I hear! God's Remnant! The deil's clavers! There wasna muckle Christianity in the way Hob guided Johnny Dickieson, at the least of it; but Guid kens! Is he a Christian even? He might be a Mahommedan or a Deevil or a Fireworshipper, for what I ken.'

The third brother had his name on a door-plate, no less, in the city of Glasgow, 'Mr Clement Elliott,' as long as your arm. In his case, that spirit of innovation which had shown itself timidly in the case of Hob by the admission of new manures, and which had run to waste with Gilbert in subversive politics and heretical religions, bore useful fruit in many ingenious mechanical improvements. In boyhood, from his addiction to strange devices of sticks and string, he had been counted the most eccentric of the family. But that was all by now; and he was a partner of his firm, and looked to die a bailie. He too had married, and was rearing a plentiful family in the smoke and din of Glasgow; he was wealthy, and could have bought out his brother, the cock-laird, six times over, it was whispered; and when he slipped away to Cauldstaneslap for a well-earned holiday, which he did as often as he was able, he astonished the neighbours with his broadcloth, his beaver hat, and the ample plies of his neckcloth. Though an eminently solid man at bottom, after the pattern of Hob, he had contracted a certain Glasgow briskness and *aplomb* which set him off. All the other Elliotts were as lean as a rake, but Clement was laying on fat, and he panted sorely when he must get into his boots. Dand said, chuckling: 'Ay, Clem has the elements of a corporation.' 'A provost and corporation,' returned Clem. And his readiness was much admired.

The fourth brother, Dand, was a shepherd to his trade, and by starts, when he could bring his mind to it, excelled in the business. Nobody could train a dog like Dandie; nobody, through the peril of great storms in the winter time, could do more gallantly. But if his dexterity were exquisite, his diligence was but fitful; and he served his brother for bed and board, and a trifle of pocket-money when he asked for it. He loved money well enough, knew very well how to spend it, and could make a shrewd bargain when he liked. But he preferred a vague knowledge that he was well to windward to any counted coins in the pocket; he felt himself richer so. Hob would expostulate: 'I'm an amature herd.' Dand would reply, 'I'll keep your sheep to you when I'm so minded, but I'll keep my liberty too. Thir's no man can coandescend on what I'm worth.' Clem would expound to him the miraculous result of compound interest, and recommend investments. 'Ay, man?' Dand would say; 'and do you think, if I took Hob's siller, that I wouldna drink it or wear it on the lassies? And, anyway, my kingdom is no of this world. Either I'm a poet or else I'm nothing.' Clem would remind him of old age. 'I'll die young,

like Robbie Burns,' he would say stoutly. No question but he
had a certain accomplishment in minor verse. His 'Hermiston
Burn,' with its pretty refrain –

'I love to gang thinking whaur ye gang linking,
Hermiston burn, in the howe;'

his 'Auld, auld Elliotts, clay-cauld Elliots, dour, bauld Elliotts
of auld,' and his really fascinating piece about the Praying
Weaver's Stone, had gained him in the neighbourhood the
reputation, still possible in Scotland, of a local bard; and,
though not printed himself, he was recognised by others who
were and who had become famous. Walter Scott owed to Dandie
the text of the 'Raid of Wearie' in the *Minstrelsy*; and made him
welcome at his house, and appreciated his talents, such as they
were, with all his usual generosity. The Ettrick Shepherd was
his sworn crony; they would meet, drink to excess, roar out
their lyrics in each other's faces, and quarrel and make it up
again till bedtime. And besides these recognitions, almost to
be called official, Dandie was made welcome for the sake of
his gift through the farmhouses of several contiguous dales,
and was thus exposed to manifold temptations which he rather
sought than fled. He had figured on the stool of repentance,
for once fulfilling to the letter the tradition of his hero and
model. His humorous verses to Mr Torrance on that occasion –
'Kenspeckle here my lane I stand' – unfortunately too indelicate
for further citation, ran through the country like a fiery cross;
they were recited, quoted, paraphrased, and laughed over
as far away as Dumfries on the one hand and Dunbar on
the other.

These four brothers were united by a close bond, the bond
of that mutual admiration – or rather mutual hero-worship –
which is so strong among the members of secluded families
who have much ability and little culture. Even the extremes
admired each other. Hob, who had as much poetry as the tongs,
professed to find pleasure in Dand's verses; Clem, who had no
more religion than Claverhouse, nourished a heartfelt, at least
an open-mouthed, admiration of Gib's prayers; and Dandie
followed with relish the rise of Clem's fortunes. Indulgence
followed hard on the heels of admiration. The laird, Clem,
and Dand, who were Tories and patriots of the hottest quality,

excused to themselves, with a certain bashfulness, the radical and revolutionary heresies of Gib. By another division of the family, the laird, Clem, and Gib, who were men exactly virtuous, swallowed the dose of Dand's irregularities as a kind of clog or drawback in the mysterious providence of God affixed to bards, and distinctly probative of poetical genius. To appreciate the simplicity of their mutual admiration it was necessary to hear Clem, arrived upon one of his visits, and dealing in a spirit of continuous irony with the affairs and personalities of that great city of Glasgow where he lived and transacted business. The various personages, ministers of the church, municipal officers, mercantile big-wigs, whom he had occasion to introduce, were all alike denigrated, all served but as reflectors to cast back a flattering side-light on the house of Cauldstaneslap. The Provost, for whom Clem by exception entertained a measure of respect, he would liken to Hob. 'He minds me o' the laird there,' he would say. 'He has some of Hob's grand, whunstane sense, and the same way with him of steiking his mouth when he's no very pleased.' And Hob, all unconscious, would draw down his upper lip and produce, as if for comparison, the formidable grimace referred to. The unsatisfactory incumbent of St Enoch's Kirk was thus briefly dismissed: 'If he had but twa fingers o' Gib's, he would waken them up.' And Gib, honest man! would look down and secretly smile. Clem was a spy whom they had sent out into the world of men. He had come back with the good news that there was nobody to compare with the Four Black Brothers, no position that they would not adorn, no official that it would not be well they should replace, no interest of mankind, secular or spiritual, which would not immediately bloom under their supervision. The excuse of their folly is in two words: scarce the breadth of a hair divided them from the peasantry. The measure of their sense is this: that these symposia of rustic vanity were kept entirely within the family, like some secret ancestral practice. To the world their serious faces were never deformed by the suspicion of any simper of self-contentment. Yet it was known. 'They hae a guid pride o' themsel's!' was the word in the country-side.

Lastly, in a Border story, there should be added their 'to-names.' Hob was The Laird. 'Roy ne puis, prince ne daigne'; he was the laird of Cauldstaneslap – say fifty acres – *ipsissimus*.

Clement was Mr Elliott, as upon his door-plate, the earlier Dafty having beeen discarded as no longer applicable, and indeed only a reminder of misjudgment and the imbecility of the public; and the youngest, in honour of his perpetual wanderings, was known by the sobriquet of Randy Dand.

It will be understood that not all this information was communicated by the aunt, who had too much of the family failing herself to appreciate it thoroughly in others. But as time went on, Archie began to observe an omission in the family chronicle.

'Is there not a girl too?' he asked.

'Ay: Kirstie. She was named for me, or my grandmother at least – it's the same thing,' returned the aunt, and went on again about Dand, whom she secretly preferred by reason of his gallantries.

'But what is your niece like?' said Archie at the next opportunity.

'Her? As black's your hat! But I dinna suppose she would maybe be what you would ca' *ill-looked* a'thegither. Na, she's a kind of a handsome jaud – a kind o' gipsy,' said the aunt, who had two sets of scales for men and women – or perhaps it would be more fair to say that she had three, and the third and the most loaded was for girls.

'How comes it that I never see her in church?' said Archie.

''Deed, and I believe she's in Glesgie with Clem and his wife. A heap good she's like to get of it! I dinna say for men folk, but where weemen folk are born, there let them bide. Glory to God, I was never far'er from here than Crossmichael.'

In the meanwhile it began to strike Archie as strange, that while she thus sang the praises of her kinsfolk, and manifestly relished their virtues and (I may say) their vices like a thing creditable to herself, there should appear not the least sign of cordiality between the house of Hermiston and that of Cauldstaneslap. Going to church of a Sunday, as the lady housekeeper stepped with her skirts kilted, three tucks of her white petticoat showing below, and her best India shawl upon her back (if the day were fine) in a pattern of radiant dyes, she would sometimes overtake her relatives preceding her more leisurely in the same direction. Gib of course was absent: by skreigh of day he had been gone to Crossmichael and his fellow-heretics; but the rest of the family would be seen marching in open order: Hob and Dand, stiff-necked, straight-backed six-footers, with severe dark faces, and their plaids about their shoulders; the convoy of children scattering (in a state of high polish) on the wayside, and every now and again collected by the shrill summons of the mother; and the mother herself, by a suggestive circumstance which might have afforded matter of thought to a more experienced observer than Archie, wrapped in a shawl nearly identical with Kirstie's, but a thought more gaudy and conspicuously newer. At the sight, Kirstie grew more tall – Kirstie showed her classical profile, nose in air and nostril spread, the pure blood came in her cheek evenly in a delicate living pink.

'A braw day to ye, Mistress Elliott,' said she, and hostility and gentility were nicely mingled in her tones. 'A fine day, mem,' the laird's wife would reply with a miraculous curtsey, spreading the while her plumage – setting off, in other words, and with arts unknown to the mere man, the pattern of her India shawl. Behind her, the whole Cauldstaneslap contingent marched in closer order, and with an indescribable air of being in the presence of the foe; and while Dandie saluted his aunt with a certain familiarity as of one who was well in court, Hob marched on in awful immobility. There appeared upon the face of this attitude in the family the consequences of some dreadful feud. Presumably the two women had been principals in the original encounter, and the laird had probably been drawn into the quarrel by the ears, too late to be included in the present skin-deep reconciliation.

'Kirstie,' said Archie one day, 'what is this you have against your family?'

'I dinna complean,' said Kirstie, with a flush. 'I say naething.'

'I see you do not – not even good-day to your own nephew,' said he.

'I hae naething to be ashamed of,' said she. 'I can say the Lord's prayer with a good grace. If Hob was ill, or in preeson or poverty, I would see to him blithely. But for curtchying and complimenting and colloguing, thank ye kindly!'

Archie had a bit of a smile: he leaned back in his chair. 'I think you and Mrs Robert are not very good friends,' says he slyly, 'when you have your India shawls on?'

She looked upon him in silence, with a sparkling eye but an indecipherable expression; and that was all that Archie was ever destined to learn of the battle of the India shawls.

'Do none of them ever come here to see you?' he inquired.

'Mr Archie,' said she, 'I hope that I ken my place better. It would be a queer thing, I think, if I was to clamjamfry up your faither's house – that I should say it! – wi' a dirty, black-a-vised clan, no ane o' them it was worth while to mar soap upon but just mysel'! Na, they're all damnifeed wi' the black Ellwalds. I have nae patience wi' black folk.' Then, with a sudden consciousness of the case of Archie, 'No that it maitters for men sae muckle,' she made haste to add, 'but there's naebody can deny that it's unwomanly. Long hair is the ornament o' woman ony way; we've good warrandise for that – it's in the Bible – and wha can doubt that the Apostle had some gowden-haired lassie in his mind – Apostle and all, for what was he but just a man like yersel'?'

CHAPTER SIX

A Leaf from
Christina's Psalm-Book

Archie was sedulous at church. Sunday after Sunday he sat down and stood up with that small company, heard the voice of Mr Torrance leaping like an ill-played clarionet from key to key, and had an opportunity to study his moth-eaten gown and the black thread mittens that he joined together in prayer, and lifted up with a reverent solemnity in the act of benediction. Hermiston pew was a little square box, dwarfish in proportion with the kirk itself, and enclosing a table not much bigger than a footstool. There sat Archie, an apparent prince, the only undeniable gentleman and the only great heritor in the parish, taking his ease in the only pew, for no other in the kirk had doors. Thence he might command an undisturbed view of that congregation of solid plaided men, strapping wives and daughters, oppressed children, and uneasy sheep-dogs. It was strange how Archie missed the look of race; except the dogs, with their refined foxy faces and inimitably curling tails, there was no one present with the least claim to gentility. The Cauldstaneslap party was scarcely an exception; Dandie perhaps, as he amused himself making verses through the interminable burden of the service, stood out a little by the glow in his eye and a certain superior animation of face and alertness of body; but even Dandie slouched like a rustic. The rest of the congregation, like so many sheep, oppressed him with a sense of hob-nailed routine, day following day – of physical labour in the open air, oatmeal porridge, peas bannock, the somnolent fireside in the evening, and the night-long nasal slumbers in a box-bed. Yet he knew many of them to be shrewd and humorous, men of character, notable women, making a bustle in the world and radiating an influence from their low-browed doors. He knew besides they were like other men; below the crust of custom, rapture found a way; he had heard them beat the timbrel before Bacchus – had heard them shout and carouse over their whisky-toddy; and not the most Dutch-bottomed and severe faces among them all, not even the solemn elders themselves, but were capable of singular gambols at the voice of love. Men drawing near to an end of life's adventurous journey – maids thrilling with fear and curiosity on the threshold of entrance – women who had borne and perhaps buried children, who could remember the clinging of the small dead hands and the patter of the little feet now silent – he marvelled that among all those faces there should be no face of expectation, none that was mobile, none into which the rhythm and poetry of life had entered. 'O for a live face,' he thought; and at times he had a memory of Lady Flora; and at times he would study the living gallery before him with despair, and would see himself go on to waste his days in that joyless, pastoral place, and death come to him, and his grave be dug under the rowans, and the Spirit of the Earth laugh out in a thunder-peal at the huge fiasco.

On this particular Sunday, there was no doubt but that the spring had come at last. It was warm, with a latent shiver in the air that made the warmth only the more welcome. The shallows of the stream glittered and tinkled among bunches of primrose. Vagrant scents of the earth arrested Archie by the way with moments of ethereal intoxication. The grey, Quakerish dale was still only awakened in places and patches from the sobriety of its winter colouring; and he wondered at its beauty; an essential beauty of the old earth it seemed to him, not resident in particulars but breathing to him from the whole. He surprised himself by a sudden impulse to write poetry – he did so sometimes, loose, galloping octosyllabics in the vein of Scott – and when he had taken his place on a boulder, near some fairy falls and shaded by a whip of a tree that was already radiant with new leaves, it still more surprised him that he should find nothing to write. His heart perhaps bent in time to some vast indwelling rhythm of the universe. By the time he came to a corner of the valley and could see the kirk, he had so lingered by the way that the first psalm was finishing. The nasal psalmody, full of turns and trills and graceless graces, seemed the essential voice of the kirk itself upraised in thanksgiving. 'Everything's alive,' he said; and again cries it aloud, 'thank God, everything's alive!' He lingered yet a while in the kirk-yard. A tuft of primroses was blooming hard by the leg of an old, black table tombstone, and he stopped to contemplate the random apologue. They stood forth on the cold earth with a trenchancy of contrast; and he was struck with a sense of incompleteness in the day, the season, and the beauty that surrounded him – the chill there was in the warmth, the gross black clods about the opening primroses, the damp earthy smell that was everywhere intermingled with the scents. The voice of the aged Torrance within rose in an ecstasy. And he wondered if Torrance also felt in his old bones the joyous influence of the spring morning; Torrance, or the shadow of what once was Torrance, that must come so soon to lie outside here in the sun and rain with all his rheumatisms, while a new minister stood in his room and thundered from his own familiar pulpit? The pity of it, and something of the chill of the grave, shook him for a moment as he made haste to enter.

He went up the aisle reverently, and took his place in the pew with lowered eyes, for he feared he had already offended the kind old gentleman in the pulpit, and was sedulous to offend no further. He could not follow the prayer, not even the heads of it. Brightness of azure, clouds of fragrance, a tinkle of falling water and singing birds, rose like exhalations from some deeper, aboriginal memory, that was not his, but belonged to the flesh on his bones. His body remembered; and it seemed to him that his body was in no way gross, but ethereal and perishable like a strain of music; and he felt for it an exquisite tenderness as for a child, an innocent, full of beautiful instincts and destined to an early death. And he felt for old Torrance – of the many supplications, of the few days – a pity that was near to tears. The prayer ended. Right over him was a tablet in the wall, the only ornament in the roughly masoned chapel – for it was no more; the tablet commemorated, I was about to say the virtues, but rather the existence of a former Rutherford of Hermiston; and Archie, under the trophy of his long descent and local greatness, leaned back in the pew and contemplated vacancy with the shadow of a smile between playful and sad, that became him strangely. Dandie's sister, sitting by the side of Clem in her new Glasgow finery, chose that moment to observe the young laird. Aware of the stir of his entrance, the little formalist had kept her eyes fastened and her face prettily composed during the prayer. It was not hypocrisy, there was no one further from a hypocrite. The girl had been taught to behave: to look up, to look down, to look unconscious, to look seriously impressed in church, and in every conjuncture to look her best. That was the game of female life, and she played it frankly. Archie was the one person in church who was of interest, who was somebody new, reputed eccentric, known to be young, and a laird, and still unseen by Christina. Small wonder that, as she stood there in her attitude of pretty decency, her mind should run upon him! If he spared a glance in her direction, he should know she was a well-behaved young lady who had been to Glasgow. In reason he must admire her clothes, and it was possible that he should think her pretty. At that her heart beat the least thing in the world; and she proceeded, by way of a corrective, to call up and dismiss a series of fancied pictures of the young man who should now, by rights, be looking at her. She settled on the plainest of them, – a pink short young man with a dish face and no figure, at whose admiration she could afford to smile; but for all that, the consciousness of his gaze (which was really fixed on Torrance and his mittens) kept her in something of a flutter till the word Amen. Even then, she was far too well-bred to gratify her curiosity with any impatience. She resumed her seat languidly – this was a Glasgow touch – she composed her dress, rearranged her nosegay of primroses, looked first in front, then behind upon the other side, and at last allowed her eyes to move, without hurry, in the direction of the Hermiston pew. For a moment, they were riveted. Next she had plucked her gaze home again like a tame bird who should have meditated flight. Possibilities crowded on her; she hung over the future and grew dizzy; the image of this young man, slim, graceful, dark, with the inscrutable half-smile, attracted and repelled her like a chasm. 'I wonder, will I have met my fate?' she thought, and her heart swelled.

Torrance was got some way into this first exposition, positing a deep layer of texts as he went along, laying the foundations of his discourse, which was to deal with a nice point in divinity, before Archie suffered his eyes to wander. They fell first of all on Clem, looking insupportably prosperous, and patronising Torrance with the favour of a modified attention, as of one who was used to better things in Glasgow. Though he had never before set eyes on him, Archie had no difficulty in identifying him, and no hesitation in pronouncing him vulgar, the worst of the family. Clem was leaning lazily forward when Archie first saw him. Presently he leaned nonchalantly back; and that deadly instrument, the maiden, was suddenly unmasked in profile. Though not quite in the front of the fashion (had anybody cared!), certain artful Glasgow mantua-makers, and her own inherent taste, had arrayed her to great advantage. Her accoutrement was, indeed, a cause of heart-burning, and almost of scandal, in that infinitesimal kirk company. Mrs Hob had said her say at Cauldstaneslap. 'Daft-like!' she had pronounced it. 'A jaiket that'll no meet! Whaur's the sense of a jaiket that'll no button upon you, if it should come to be weet? What do ye ca thir things? Demmy brokens, d'ye say? They'll be brokens wi' a vengeance or ye can win back! Weel, I have naething to do wi' it – it's no good taste.' Clem, whose purse had thus metamorphosed his sister, and who was not insensible to the advertisement, had come to the rescue with a 'Hoot, woman! What do you ken of good taste that has never been to the ceety?' And Hob, looking on the girl with pleased smiles, as she timidly displayed her finery in the midst of the dark kitchen, had thus ended the dispute: 'The cutty looks weel,' he had said, 'and it's no very like rain. Wear them the day, hizzie; but it's no a thing to make a practice o'.' In the breasts of her rivals, coming to the kirk very conscious of white under-linen, and their faces splendid with much soap, the sight of the toilet had raised a storm of varying emotion, from the mere unenvious admiration that was expressed in a long-drawn 'Eh!' to the angrier feeling that found vent in an emphatic 'Set her up!' Her frock was of straw-coloured jaconet muslin, cut low at the bosom and short at the ankle, so as to display her *demi-broquins* of Regency violet, crossing with many straps upon a yellow cobweb stocking. According to the pretty fashion in which our grandmothers did not hesitate to appear, and our great-aunts went forth armed for the pursuit and capture of our great-uncles, the dress was drawn up so as to mould the contour of both breasts, and in the nook between, a cairngorm brooch maintained it. Here, too, surely in a very enviable position, trembled the nosegay of primroses. She wore on her shoulders – or rather, on her back and not her shoulders, which it scarcely passed – a French coat of sarsenet,

tied in front with Margate braces, and of the same colour with
her violet shoes. About her face clustered a disorder of dark
ringlets, a little garland of yellow French roses surmounted her
brow, and the whole was crowned by a village hat of chipped
straw. Amongst all the rosy and all the weathered faces that
surrounded her in church, she glowed like an open flower –
girl and raiment, and the cairngorm that caught the daylight
and returned it in a fiery flash, and the threads of bronze and
gold that played in her hair.

Archie was attracted by the bright thing like a child. He
looked at her again and yet again, and their looks crossed.
The lip was lifted from her little teeth. He saw the red blood
work vividly under her tawny skin. Her eye, which was great
as a stag's, struck and held his gaze. He knew who she must be
– Kirstie, she of the harsh diminutive, his housekeeper's niece,
the sister of the rustic prophet, Gib – and he found in her the
answer to his wishes.

Christina felt the shock of their encountering glances, and
seemed to rise, clothed in smiles, into a region of the vague
and bright. But the gratification was not more exquisite than
it was brief. She looked away abruptly, and immediately began
to blame herself for that abruptness. She knew what she should
have done, too late – turned slowly with her nose in the air. And
meantime his look was not removed, but continued to play upon
her like a battery of cannon constantly aimed, and now seemed
to isolate her alone with him, and now seemed to uplift her,
as on a pillory, before the congregation. For Archie continued
to drink her in with his eyes, even as a wayfarer comes to a
well-head on a mountain, and stoops his face, and drinks with
thirst unassuageable. In the cleft of her little breasts the fiery eye
of the topaz and the pale florets of primrose fascinated him. He
saw the breasts heave, and the flowers shake with the heaving,
and marvelled what should so much discompose the girl. And
Christina was conscious of his gaze – saw it, perhaps, with the
dainty plaything of an ear that peeped among her ringlets; she
was conscious of changing colour, conscious of her unsteady
breath. Like a creature tracked, run down, surrounded, she
sought in a dozen ways to give herself a countenance. She used
her handkerchief – it was a really fine one – then she desisted
in a panic: 'He would only think I was too warm.' She took

to reading in the metrical psalms, and then remembered it was sermon-time. Last she put a 'sugar-bool' in her mouth, and the next moment repented of the step. It was such a homely-like thing! Mr Archie would never be eating sweeties in kirk; and, with a palpable effort, she swallowed it whole, and her colour flamed high. At this signal of distress Archie awoke to a sense of his ill-behaviour. What had he been doing? He had been exquisitely rude in church to the niece of his housekeeper; he had stared like a lackey and a libertine at a beautiful and modest girl. It was possible, it was even likely, he would be presented to her after service in the kirkyard, and then how was he to look? And there was no excuse. He had marked the tokens of her shame, of her increasing indignation, and he was such a fool that he had not understood them. Shame bowed him down, and he looked resolutely at Mr Torrance; who little supposed, good worthy man, as he continued to expound justification by faith, what was his true business: to play the part of derivative to a pair of children at the old game of falling in love.

Christina was greatly relieved at first. It seemed to her that she was clothed again. She looked back on what had passed. All would have been right if she had not blushed, a silly fool! There was nothing to blush at, if she *had* taken a sugar-bool. Mrs MacTaggart, the elder's wife in St Enoch's, took them often. And if he had looked at her, what was more natural than that a young gentleman should look at the best-dressed girl in church? And at the same time, she knew far otherwise, she knew there was nothing casual or ordinary in the look, and valued herself on its memory like a decoration. Well, it was a blessing he had found something else to look at! And presently she began to have other thoughts. It was necessary, she fancied, that she should put herself right by a repetition of the incident, better managed. If the wish was father to the thought, she did not know or she would not recognise it. It was simply as a manoeuvre of propriety, as something called for to lessen the significance of what had gone before, that she should a second time meet his eyes, and this time without blushing. And at the memory of the blush, she blushed again, and became one general blush burning from head to foot. Was ever anything so indelicate, so forward, done by a girl before? And here she was, making an exhibition of herself before the congregation about nothing!

She stole a glance upon her neighbours, and behold! they were steadily indifferent, and Clem had gone to sleep. And still the one idea was becoming more and more potent with her, that in common prudence she must look again before the service ended. Something of the same sort was going forward in the mind of Archie, as he struggled with the load of penitence. So it chanced that, in the flutter of the moment when the last psalm was given out, and Torrance was reading the verse, and the leaves of every psalm-book in church were rustling under busy fingers, two stealthy glances were sent out like antennae among the pews and on the indifferent and absorbed occupants, and drew timidly nearer to the straight line between Archie and Christina. They met, they lingered together for the least fraction of time, and that was enough. A charge as of electricity passed through Christina, and behold! the leaf of her psalm-book was torn across.

Archie was outside by the gate of the graveyard, conversing with Hob and the minister and shaking hands all round with the scattering congregation, when Clem and Christina were brought up to be presented. The laird took off his hat and bowed to her with grace and respect. Christina made her Glasgow curtsey to the laird, and went on again up the road for Hermiston and Cauldstaneslap, walking fast, breathing hurriedly with a heightened colour, and in this strange frame of mind, that when she was alone she seemed in high happiness, and when any one addressed her she resented it like a contradiction. A part of the way she had the company of some neighbour girls and a loutish young man; never had they seemed so insipid, never had she made herself so disagreeable. But these struck aside to their various destinations or were out-walked and left behind; and when she had driven off with sharp words the proffered convoy of some of her nephews and nieces, she was free to go on alone up Hermiston brae, walking on air, dwelling intoxicated among clouds of happiness. Near to the summit she heard steps behind her, a man's steps, light and very rapid. She knew the foot at once and walked the faster. 'If it's me he's wanting, he can run for it,' she thought, smiling.

Archie overtook her like a man whose mind was made up.

'Miss Kirstie,' he began.

'Miss Christina, if you please, Mr Weir,' she interrupted. 'I canna bear the contraction.'

'You forget it has a friendly sound for me. Your aunt is an old friend of mine, and a very good one. I hope we shall see much of you at Hermiston?'

'My aunt and my sister-in-law doesna agree very well. Not that I have much ado with it. But still when I'm stopping in the house, if I was to be visiting my aunt, it would not look considerate-like.'

'I am sorry,' said Archie.

'I thank you kindly, Mr Weir,' she said. 'I whiles think myself it's a great peety.'

'Ah, I am sure your voice would always be for peace!' he cried.

'I wouldna be too sure of that,' she said. 'I have my days like other folk, I suppose.'

'Do you know, in our old kirk, among our good old grey dames, you made an effect like sunshine.'

'Ah, but that would be my Glasgow clothes!'

'I did not think I was so much under the influence of pretty frocks.'

She smiled with a half look at him. 'There's more than you!' she said. 'But you see I'm only Cinderella. I'll have to put all these things by in my trunk; next Sunday I'll be as grey as the rest. They're Glasgow clothes, you see, and it would never do to make a practice of it. It would seem terrible conspicuous.'

By that they were come to the place where their ways severed. The old grey moors were all about them; in the midst a few sheep wandered; and they could see on the one hand the straggling caravan scaling the braes in front of them for Cauldstaneslap, and on the other, the contingent from Hermiston bending off and beginning to disappear by detachments into the policy gate. It was in these circumstances that they turned to say farewell, and deliberately exchanged a glance as they shook hands. All passed as it should, genteelly; and in Christina's mind, as she mounted the first steep ascent for Cauldstaneslap, a gratifying sense of triumph prevailed over the recollection of minor lapses and mistakes. She had kilted her gown, as she did usually at that rugged pass; but when she spied Archie still standing and gazing after her, the skirts came down again as if by enchantment. Here was a piece of nicety for that upland parish, where the matrons marched with their coats kilted in the rain, and the lasses walked barefoot to kirk through the dust of summer, and went bravely down by the burn-side, and sat on stones to make a public toilet before entering! It was perhaps an air wafted from Glasgow; or perhaps it marked a stage of that dizziness of gratified vanity, in which the instinctive act passed unperceived. He was looking after! She unloaded her bosom of a prodigious sigh that was all pleasure, and betook herself to run. When she had overtaken the stragglers of her family, she caught up the niece whom she had so recently repulsed, and kissed and slapped her, and drove her away again, and ran after her with pretty cries and laughter. Perhaps she thought the laird might still be looking! But it chanced the little scene came under the view of eyes less favourable; for she overtook Mrs Hob marching with Clem and Dand.

'You're shürely fey, lass!' quoth Dandie.

'Think shame to yersel', miss!' said the strident Mrs Hob. 'Is this the gait to guide yersel' on the way hame frae kirk? You're shürely no sponsible the day! And anyway I would mind my guid claes.'

'Hoot!' said Christina, and went on before them head in air, treading the rough track with the tread of a wild doe.'

She was in love with herself, her destiny, the air of the hills, the benediction of the sun. All the way home, she continued under the intoxication of these sky-scraping spirits. At table she could talk freely of young Hermiston; gave her opinion of him off-hand and with a loud voice, that he was a handsome young gentleman, real well mannered and sensible-like, but it was a pity he looked doleful. Only – the moment after – a memory of his eyes in church embarrassed her. But for this inconsiderable check, all through meal-time she had a good appetite, and she kept them laughing at table, until Gib (who had returned before them from Crossmichael and his separative worship) reproved the whole of them for their levity.

Singing 'in to herself' as she went, her mind still in the turmoil of a glad confusion, she rose and tripped upstairs to a little loft, lighted by four panes in the gable, where she slept with one of her nieces. The niece, who followed her, presuming on 'Auntie's' high spirits, was flounced out of the apartment with small ceremony, and retired, smarting and half tearful, to bury her woes in the byre among the hay. Still humming, Christina divested herself of her finery, and put her treasures one by one in her great green trunk. The last of these was the psalm-book; it was a fine piece, the gift of Mistress Clem, in a distinct old-faced type, on paper that had begun to grow foxy in the warehouse – not by service – and she was used to wrap it in a handkerchief every Sunday after its period of service was over, and bury it end-wise at the head of her trunk. As she now took it in hand the book fell open where the leaf was torn, and she stood and gazed upon that evidence of her bygone discomposure. There returned again the vision of the two brown eyes staring at her, intent and bright, out of that dark corner of the kirk. The whole appearance and attitude, the smile, the suggested gesture of young Hermiston came before her in a flash at the sight of the torn page. 'I was surely fey!' she said, echoing the words of Dandie, and at the suggested doom her high spirits deserted her. She flung herself prone upon the bed, and lay there, holding the psalm-book in her hands for hours, for the more part in a mere stupor of unconsenting pleasure and unreasoning fear. The fear was superstitious; there came up again and again in her memory Dandie's ill-omened words, and a hundred grisly and black tales out of the immediate neighbourhood read her a commentary on their force. The pleasure was never realised. You might say the joints of her body thought and remembered, and were gladdened, but her essential self, in the immediate theatre of consciousness, talked feverishly of something else, like a nervous person at a fire. The image that she most complacently dwelt on was that of Miss Christina in her character of the Fair Lass of Cauldstaneslap, carrying all before her in the straw-coloured frock, the violet mantle, and the yellow cobweb stockings. Archie's image, on the other hand, when it presented itself was never welcomed – far less welcomed with any ardour, and it was exposed at times to merciless criticism. In the long vague dialogues she held in her mind, often with imaginary, often with unrealised interlocutors, Archie, if he were referred to at all, came in for savage handling. He was described as 'looking like a stirk,' 'staring like a caulf,' 'a face like a ghaist's.' 'Do you call that manners?' she said; or, 'I soon put him in his place.' ' "*Miss Christina if you please, Mr*

Weir!" says I, and just flyped up my skirt tails.' With gabble
like this she would entertain herself long whiles together, and
then her eye would perhaps fall on the torn leaf, and the eyes
of Archie would appear again from the darkness of the wall,
and the voluble words deserted her, and she would lie still and
stupid, and think upon nothing with devotion, and be sometimes
raised by a quiet sigh. Had a doctor of medicine come into
the loft, he would have diagnosed a healthy, well-developed,
eminently vivacious lass lying on her face in a fit of the sulks; not
one who had just contracted, or was just contracting, a mortal
sickness of the mind which should yet carry her towards death
and despair. Had it been a doctor of psychology, he might have
been pardoned for divining in the girl a passion of childish
vanity, self-love *in excelsis*, and no more. It is to be understood
that I have been painting chaos and describing the inarticulate.
Every lineament that appears is too precise, almost every word
used too strong. Take a finger-post in the mountains on a day
of rolling mists; I have but copied the names that appear upon
the pointers, the names of definite and famous cities far distant,
and now perhaps basking in sunshine; but Christina remained all
these hours, as it were, at the foot of the post itself, not moving,
and enveloped in mutable and blinding wreaths of haze.

The day was growing late and the sunbeams long and level,
when she sat suddenly up, and wrapped in its handkerchief
and put by that psalm-book which had already played a part
so decisive in the first chapter of her love-story. In the absence
of the mesmerist's eye, we are told nowadays that the head of a
bright nail may fill his place, if it be steadfastly regarded. So that
torn page had riveted her attention on what might else have been
but little, and perhaps soon forgotten; while the ominous words
of Dandie – heard, not heeded, and still remembered – had lent
to her thoughts, or rather to her mood, a cast of solemnity, and
that idea of Fate – a pagan Fate, uncontrolled by any Christian
deity, obscure, lawless, and august – moving indissuadably in
the affairs of Christian men. Thus even that phenomenon of
love at first sight, which is so rare and seems so simple and
violent, like a disruption of life's tissue, may be decomposed
into a sequence of accidents happily concurring.

She put on a grey frock and a pink kerchief, looked at herself
a moment with approval in the small square of glass that served

her for a toilet mirror, and went softly downstairs through the sleeping house that resounded with the sound of afternoon snoring. Just outside the door, Dandie was sitting with a book in his hand, not reading, only honouring the Sabbath by a sacred vacancy of mind. She came near him and stood still.

'I'm for off up the muirs, Dandie,' she said.

There was something unusually soft in her tones that made him look up. She was pale, her eyes dark and bright; no trace remained of the levity of the morning.

'Ay, lass? Ye'll have ye're ups and downs like me, I'm thinkin',' he observed.

'What for do ye say that?' she asked.

'O, for naething,' says Dand. 'Only I think ye're mair like me than the lave of them. Ye've mair of the poetic temper, tho' Guid kens little enough of the poetic taalent. It's an ill gift at the best. Look at yoursel'. At denner you were all sunshine and flowers and laughter, and now you're like the star of evening on a lake.'

She drank in this hackneyed compliment like wine, and it glowed in her veins.

'But I'm saying, Dand' – she came nearer him – 'I'm for the muirs. I must have a braith of air. If Clem was to be speiring for me, try and quaiet him, will ye no?'

'What way?' said Dandie. 'I ken but the ae way, and that's leein'. I'll say ye had a sair heed, if ye like.'

'But I havena,' she objected.

'I daursay no',' he returned. 'I said I would say ye had; and if ye like to nay-say me when ye come back, it'll no mateerially maitter, for my chara'ter's clean gane a'ready past reca'.'

'O, Dand, are ye a leear?' she asked, lingering.

'Folks say sae,' replied the bard.

'Wha says sae?' she pursued.

'Them that should ken the best,' he responded. 'The lassies, for ane.'

'But, Dand, you would never lee to me?' she asked.

'I'll leave that for your pairt of it, ye girzie,' said he. 'Ye'll lee to me fast eneuch, when ye hae gotten a jo. I'm tellin' ye and it's true; when you have a jo, Miss Kirstie, it'll be for guid and ill. I ken: I was made that way mysel', but the deil was in my luck! Here, gang awa wi' ye to your muirs, and let me be; I'm in an hour of inspiraution, ye upsetting tawpie!'

But she clung to her brother's neighbourhood, she knew not why.

'Will ye no gie's a kiss, Dand?' she said. 'I aye likit ye fine.'

He kissed her and considered her a moment; he found something strange in her. But he was a libertine through and through, nourished equal contempt and suspicion of all womankind, and paid his way among them habitually with idle compliments.

'Gae wa' wi' ye!' said he. 'Ye're a dentie baby, and be content wi' that!'

That was Dandie's way; a kiss and a comfit to Jenny – a bawbee and my blessing to Jill – and good-night to the whole clan of ye, my dears! When anything approached the serious, it became a matter for men, he both thought and said. Women, when they did not absorb, were only children to be shoo'd away. Merely in his character of connoisseur, however, Dandie glanced carelessly after his sister as she crossed the meadow. 'The brat's no that bad!' he thought with surprise, for though he had just been paying her compliments, he had not really looked at her. 'Hey! what's yon?' For the grey dress was cut with short sleeves and skirts, and displayed her trim strong legs clad in pink stockings of the same shade as the kerchief she wore round her shoulders, and that shimmered as she went. This was not her way in undress; he knew her ways and the ways of the whole sex in the country-side, no one better; when they did not go barefoot, they wore stout 'rig and furrow' woollen hose of an invisible blue mostly, when they were not black outright; and Dandie, at sight of this daintiness, put two and two together. It was a silk handkerchief, then they would be silken hose; they matched – then the whole outfit was a present of Clem's, a costly present, and not something to be worn through bog and briar, or on a late afternoon of Sunday. He whistled. 'My denty May, either your heid's fair turned, or there's some ongoings!' he observed, and dismissed the subject.

She went slowly at first, but ever straighter and faster for the Cauldstaneslap, a pass among the hills to which the farm owed its name. The Slap opened like a doorway between two rounded hillocks; and through this ran the short cut to

Hermiston. Immediately on the other side it went down through the Deil's Hags, a considerable marshy hollow of the hill tops, full of springs, and crouching junipers, and pools where the black peat-water slumbered. There was no view from here. A man might have sat upon the Praying Weaver's stone a half century, and seen none but the Cauldstaneslap children twice in the twenty-four hours on their way to the school and back again, an occasional shepherd, the irruption of a clan of sheep, or the birds who haunted about the springs, drinking and shrilly piping. So, when she had once passed the Slap, Kirstie was received into seclusion. She looked back a last time at the farm. It still lay deserted except for the figure of Dandie, who was now seen to be scribbling in his lap, the hour of expected inspiration having come to him at last. Thence she passed rapidly through the morass, and came to the farther end of it, where a sluggish burn discharges, and the path for Hermiston accompanies it on the beginning of its downward path. From this corner a wide view was opened to her of the whole stretch of braes upon the other side, still sallow and in places rusty with the winter, with the path marked boldly, here and there by the burn-side a tuft of birches, and – two miles off as the crow flies – from its enclosures and young plantations, the windows of Hermiston glittering in the western sun.

Here she sat down and waited, and looked for a long time at these far-away bright panes of glass. It amused her to have so extended a view, she thought. It amused her to see the house of Hermiston – to see 'folk'; and there was an indistinguishable human unit, perhaps the gardener, visibly sauntering on the gravel paths.

By the time the sun was down and all the easterly braes lay plunged in clear shadow, she was aware of another figure coming up the path at a most unequal rate of approach, now half running, now pausing and seeming to hesitate. She watched him at first with a total suspension of thought. She held her thought as a person holds his breathing. Then she consented to recognise him. 'He'll no be coming here, he canna be; it's no possible.' And there began to grow upon her a subdued choking suspense. He *was* coming; his hesitations had quite ceased, his step grew firm and swift; no doubt remained; and the question loomed up before her instant: what was she to do? It was all very well to say that her brother was a laird himself; it was all very well to speak of casual intermarriages and to count cousinship, like Auntie Kirstie. The difference in their social station was trenchant; propriety, prudence, all that she had ever learned, all that she knew, bade her flee. But on the other hand the cup of life now offered to her was too enchanting. For one moment, she saw the question clearly, and definitely made her choice. She stood up and showed herself an instant in the gap relieved upon the sky line; and the next, fled trembling and sat down glowing with excitement on the Weaver's stone. She shut her eyes, seeking, praying for composure. Her hand shook in her lap, and her mind was full of incongruous and futile speeches. What was there to make a work about? She could take care of herself, she supposed! There was no harm in seeing the laird. It was the best thing that could happen. She would mark a proper distance to him once and for all. Gradually the wheels of her nature ceased to go round so madly, and she sat in passive expectation, a quiet, solitary figure in the midst of the grey moss. I have said she was no hypocrite, but here I am at fault. She never admitted to herself that she had come up the hill to look for Archie. And perhaps after all she did not know, perhaps came as a stone falls. For the steps of love in the young, and especially in girls, are instinctive and unconscious.

In the meantime Archie was drawing rapidly near, and he at least was consciously seeking her neighbourhood. The afternoon had turned to ashes in his mouth; the memory of the girl had kept him from reading and drawn him as with cords; and at last, as the cool of the evening began to come on, he had taken his hat and set forth, with a smothered ejaculation, by the moor path to Cauldstaneslap. He had no hope to find her; he took the off chance without expectation of result and to relieve his uneasiness. The greater was his surprise, as he surmounted the slope and came into the hollow of the Deil's Hags, to see there, like an answer to his wishes, the little womanly figure in the grey dress and the pink kerchief sitting little, and low, and lost, and acutely solitary, in these desolate surroundings and on the weatherbeaten stone of the dead weaver. Those things that still smacked of winter were all rusty about her, and those things that already relished of the spring had put forth the tender and lively colours of the season. Even in the unchanging face of the deathstone, changes were to be remarked; and in the channeled lettering, the moss began to renew itself in jewels of green. By an afterthought that was a stroke of art, she had turned up over her head the back of the kerchief; so that it now framed becomingly her vivacious and yet pensive face. Her feet were gathered under her on the one side, and she leaned on her bare arm, which showed out strong and round, tapered to a slim wrist, and shimmered in the fading light.

Young Hermiston was struck with a certain chill. He was reminded that he now dealt in serious matters of life and death. This was a grown woman he was approaching, endowed with her mysterious potencies and attractions, the treasury of the continued race, and he was neither better nor worse than the average of his sex and age. He had a certain delicacy which had preserved him hitherto unspotted, and which (had either of them guessed it) made him a more dangerous companion when his heart should be really stirred. His throat was dry as he came near; but the appealing sweetness of her smile stood between them like a guardian angel.

For she turned to him and smiled, though without rising. There was a shade in this cavalier greeting that neither of them perceived; neither he, who simply thought it gracious and charming as herself; nor yet she, who did not observe (quick as she was) the difference between rising to meet the laird, and remaining seated to receive the expected admirer.

'Are ye stepping west, Hermiston?' said she, giving him his territorial name after the fashion of the country-side.

'I was,' said he, a little hoarsely, 'but I think I will be about the end of my stroll now. Are you like me, Miss Christina? The house would not hold me. I came here seeking air.'

He took his seat at the other end of the tombstone and studied her, wondering what was she. There was infinite import in the question alike for her and him.

'Ay,' she said. 'I couldna bear the roof either. It's a habit of mine to come up here about the gloaming when it's quaiet and caller.'

'It was a habit of my mother's also,' he said gravely. The recollection half startled him as he expressed it. He looked around. 'I have scarce been here since. It's peaceful,' he said, with a long breath.

'It's no like Glasgow,' she replied. 'A weary place, yon Glasgow! But what a day have I had for my hame-coming, and what a bonny evening!'

'Indeed, it was a wonderful day,' said Archie. 'I think I will remember it years and years until I come to die. On days like this – I do not know if you feel as I do – but everything appears so brief, and fragile, and exquisite, that I am afraid to touch life. We are here for so short a time; and all the old people before us – Rutherfords of Hermiston, Elliotts of the Cauldstaneslap – that were here but a while since riding about and keeping up a great noise in this quiet corner – making love too, and marrying – why, where are they now? It's deadly commonplace, but, after all, the commonplaces are the great poetic truths.'

He was sounding her, semi-consciously, to see if she could understand him; to learn if she were only an animal the colour of flowers, or had a soul in her to keep her sweet. She, on her part, her means well in hand, watched, womanlike, for any opportunity to shine, to abound in his humour, whatever that might be. The dramatic artist, that lies dormant or only half awake in most human beings, had in her sprung to his feet in a divine fury, and chance had served her well. She looked upon him with a subdued twilight look that became the hour of the day and the train of thought; earnestness shone through her like stars in the purple west; and from the great but controlled upheaval of her whole nature there passed into her voice, and rang in her lightest words, a thrill of emotion.

'Have you mind of Dand's song?' she answered. 'I think he'll have been trying to say what you have been thinking.'

'No, I never heard it,' he said. 'Repeat it to me, can you?'

'It's nothing wanting the tune,' said Kirstie.

'Then sing it me,' said he.

'On the Lord's Day? That would never do, Mr Weir!'

'I am afraid I am not so strict a keeper of the Sabbath, and there is no one in this place to hear us, unless the poor old ancient under the stone.'

'No that I'm thinking that really,' she said. 'By my way of thinking, it's just as serious as a psalm. Will I sooth it to ye, then?'

'If you please,' said he, and, drawing near to her on the tombstone, prepared to listen.

She sat up as if to sing. 'I'll only can sooth it to ye,' she explained. 'I wouldna like to sing out loud on the Sabbath. I think the birds would carry news of it to Gilbert,' and she smiled. 'It's about the Elliotts,' she continued, 'and I think there's few bonnier bits in the book-poets, though Dand has never got printed yet.'

And she began, in the low, clear tones of her half voice, now sinking almost to a whisper, now rising to a particular note which was her best, and which Archie learned to wait for with growing emotion: –

> 'O they rade in the rain, in the days that are gane,
> In the rain and the wind and the lave,
> They shoutit in the ha' and they routit on the hill,
> But they're a' quaitit noo in the grave.
> Auld, auld Elliotts, clay-cauld Elliotts, dour, bauld
> Elliotts of auld!'

All the time she sang she looked steadfastly before her, her knees straight, her hands upon her knee, her head cast back and up. The expression was admirable throughout, for had she not learned it from the lips and under the criticism of the author? When it was done, she turned upon Archie a face softly bright, and eyes gently suffused and shining in the twilight, and his heart rose and went out to her with boundless pity and sympathy. His question was answered. She was a human being tuned to a sense of the tragedy of life; there were pathos and music and a great heart in the girl.

He arose instinctively, she also; for she saw she had gained a point, and scored the impression deeper, and she had wit enough left to flee upon a victory. They were but commonplaces that remained to be exchanged, but the low, moved voices in which they passed made them sacred in the memory. In the falling greyness of the evening he watched her figure winding through the morass, saw it turn a last time and wave a hand, and then pass through the Slap; and it seemed to him as if something went along with her out of the deepest of his heart. And something surely had come, and come to dwell there. He had retained from childhood a picture, now half obliterated by the passage of time and the multitude of fresh impressions, of his mother telling him, with the fluttered earnestness of her voice, and often with dropping tears, the tale of the 'Praying Weaver,' on the very scene of his brief tragedy and long repose. And now there was a companion piece; and he beheld, and he should behold for ever, Christina perched on the same tomb, in the grey colours of the evening, gracious, dainty, perfect as a flower, and she also singing –

'Of old, unhappy far off things, And battles long ago,'

of their common ancestors now dead, of their rude wars composed, their weapons buried with them, and of these strange changelings, their descendants, who lingered a little in their places, and would soon be gone also, and perhaps sung of by others at the gloaming hour. By one of the unconscious arts of tenderness the two women were enshrined together in his memory. Tears, in that hour of sensibility, came into his eyes indifferently at the thought of either; and the girl, from being something merely bright and shapely, was caught up into the zone of things serious as life and death and his dead mother. So that in all ways and on either side, Fate played his game artfully with this poor pair of children. The generations were prepared, the pangs were made ready, before the curtain rose on the dark drama.

In the same moment of time that she disappeared from Archie, there opened before Kirstie's eyes the cup-like hollow in which the farm lay. She saw, some five hundred feet below her, the house making itself bright with candles, and this was a broad hint to her to hurry. For they were only kindled on a Sabbath night with a view to that family worship which rounded in the incomparable tedium of the day and brought on the relaxation of supper. Already she knew that Robert must be within-sides at the head of the table, 'waling the portions'; for it was Robert in his quality of family priest and judge, not the gifted Gilbert, who officiated. She made good time accordingly down the steep ascent, and came up to the door panting as the three younger brothers, all roused at last from slumber, stood together in the cool and the dark of the evening with a fry of nephews and nieces about them, chatting and awaiting the expected signal. She stood back; she had no mind to direct attention to her late arrival or to her labouring breath.

'Kirstie, ye have shaved it this time, my lass?' said Clem. 'Whaur were ye?'

'O, just taking a dander by mysel',' said Kirstie.

And the talk continued on the subject of the American War, without further reference to that truant who stood by them in the covert of the dusk, thrilling with happiness and the sense of guilt.

The signal was given, and the brothers began to go in one after another, amid the jostle and throng of Hob's children.

Only Dandie, waiting till the last, caught Kirstie by the arm. 'When did ye begin to dander in pink hosen, Mistress Elliott?' he whispered slyly.

She looked down; she was one blush. 'I maun have forgotten to change them,' said she; and went into prayers in her turn with a troubled mind, between anxiety as to whether Dand should have observed her yellow stockings at church, and should thus detect her in a palpable falsehood, and shame that she had already made good his prophecy. She remembered the words of it, how it was to be when she had gotten a jo, and that that would be for good and evil. 'Will I have gotten my jo now?' she thought with a secret rapture.

And all through prayers, where it was her principal business to conceal the pink stockings from the eyes of the indifferent Mrs Hob – and all through supper, as she made a feint of eating and sat at the table radiant and constrained – and again when she had left them and come into her chamber, and was alone with her sleeping niece, and could at last lay aside the armour of society – the same words sounded within her, the same profound note of happiness, of a world all changed and renewed, of a day that had been passed in Paradise, and of a night that was to be heaven opened. All night she seemed to be conveyed smoothly upon a shallow stream of sleep and waking, and through the bowers of Beulah; all night she cherished to her heart that exquisite hope; and if, towards morning, she forgot it a while in a more profound unconsciousness, it was to catch again the rainbow thought with her first moment of awaking.

CHAPTER SEVEN

Enter Mephistopheles

Two days later a gig from Crossmichael deposited Frank Innes at the doors of Hermiston. Once in a way, during the past winter, Archie, in some acute phase of boredom, had written him a letter. It had contained something in the nature of an invitation, or a reference to an invitation – precisely what, neither of them now remembered. When Innes had received it, there had been nothing further from his mind than to bury himself in the moors with Archie; but not even the most acute political heads are guided through the steps of life with unerring directness. That would require a gift of prophecy which has been denied to man. For instance, who could have imagined that, not a month after he had received the letter, and turned it into mockery, and put off answering it, and in the end lost it, misfortunes of a gloomy cast should begin to thicken over Frank's career? His case may be briefly stated. His father, a small Morayshire laird with a large family, became recalcitrant and cut off the supplies; he had fitted himself out with the beginnings of quite a good law library, which, upon some sudden losses on the turf, he had been obliged to sell before they were paid for; and his bookseller, hearing some rumour of the event, took out a warrant for his arrest. Innes had early word of it, and was able to take precautions. In this immediate welter of his affairs, with an unpleasant charge hanging over him, he had judged it the part of prudence to be off instantly, had written a fervid letter to his father at Inverauld, and put himself in the coach for Crossmichael. Any port in a storm! He was manfully turning his back on the Parliament House and its gay babble, on porter and oysters, the racecourse and the ring; and manfully prepared, until these clouds should have blown by, to share a living grave with Archie Weir at Hermiston.

To do him justice, he was no less surprised to be going than

Archie was to see him come; and he carried off his wonder with an infinitely better grace.

'Well, here I am!' said he, as he alighted. 'Pylades has come to Orestes at last. By the way, did you get my answer? No? How very provoking! Well, here I am to answer for myself, and that's better still.'

'I am very glad to see you, of course,' said Archie. 'I make you heartily welcome, of course. But you surely have not come to stay, with the Courts still sitting; is that not most unwise?'

'Damn the Courts!' says Frank. 'What are the Courts to friendship and a little fishing?'

And so it was agreed that he was to stay, with no term to the visit but the term which he had privily set to it himself – the day, namely, when his father should have come down with the dust, and he should be able to pacify the bookseller. On such vague conditions there began for these two young men (who were not even friends) a life of great familiarity and, as the days drew on, less and less intimacy. They were together at meal times, together o' nights when the hour had come for whisky-toddy; but it might have been noticed (had there been any one to pay heed) that they were rarely so much together by day. Archie had Hermiston to attend to, multifarious activities in the hills, in which he did not require, and had even refused, Frank's escort. He would be off sometimes in the morning and leave only a note on the breakfast table to announce the fact; and sometimes, with no notice at all, he would not return for dinner until the hour was long past. Innes groaned under these desertions; it required all his philosophy to sit down to a solitary breakfast with composure, and all his unaffected good-nature to be able to greet Archie with friendliness on the more rare occasions when he came home late for dinner.

'I wonder what on earth he finds to do, Mrs Elliott?' said he one morning, after he had just read the hasty billet and sat down to table.

'I suppose it will be business, sir,' replied the housekeeper dryly, measuring his distance off to him by an indicated curtsy.

'But I can't imagine what business!' he reiterated.

'I suppose it will be *his* business,' retorted the austere Kirstie.

He turned to her with that happy brightness that made the

charm of his disposition, and broke into a peal of healthy and natural laughter.

'Well played, Mrs Elliott!' he cried; and the housekeeper's face relaxed into the shadow of an iron smile. 'Well played indeed!' said he. 'But you must not be making a stranger of me like that. Why, Archie and I were at the High School together, and we've been to college together, and we were going to the Bar together, when – you know! Dear, dear me! what a pity that was! A life spoiled, a fine young fellow as good as buried here in the wilderness with rustics; and all for what? A frolic, silly, if you like, but no more. God, how good your scones are, Mrs Elliott!'

'They're no mines, it was the lassie made them,' said Kirstie; 'and, saving your presence, there's little sense in taking the Lord's name in vain about idle vivers that you fill your kyte wi'.'

'I daresay you're perfectly right, ma'am,' quoth the imperturbable Frank. 'But as I was saying, this is a pitiable business, this about poor Archie; and you and I might do worse than put our heads together, like a couple of sensible people, and bring it to an end. Let me tell you, ma'am, that Archie is really quite a promising young man, and in my opinion he would do well at the Bar. As for his father, no one can deny his ability, and I don't fancy any one would care to deny that he has the deil's own temper – '

'If you'll excuse me, Mr Innes, I think the lass is crying on me,' said Kirstie, and flounced from the room.

'The damned, cross-grained, old broomstick!' ejaculated Innes.

In the meantime, Kirstie had escaped into the kitchen, and before her vassal gave vent to her feelings.

'Here, ettercap! Ye'll have to wait on yon Innes! I canna haud myself in. "Puir Erchie!" I'd "puir Erchie" him, if I had my way! And Hermiston with the deil's ain temper! God, let him take Hermiston's scones out of his mouth first. There's no a hair on ayther o' the Weirs that hasna mair spunk and dirdum to it than what he has in his hale dwaibly body! Settin' up his snash to me! Let him gang to the black toon where he's mebbe wantit – birling in a curricle – wi' pimatum on his heid – making a mess o' himsel' wi' nesty hizzies – a fair disgrace!' It was impossible to hear without admiration Kirstie's graduated disgust, as she brought forth, one after another, these somewhat baseless charges. Then she remembered her immediate purpose, and turned again on her fascinated auditor. 'Do ye no hear me, tawpie? Do ye no hear what I'm tellin' ye? Will I have to shoo ye in to him? If I come to attend to ye, mistress!' And the maid fled the kitchen, which had become practically dangerous, to attend on Innes' wants in the front parlour.

Tantaene irae? Has the reader perceived the reason? Since Frank's coming there were no more hours of gossip over the supper tray! All his blandishments were in vain; he had started handicapped on the race for Mrs Elliott's favour.

But it was a strange thing how misfortune dogged him in his efforts to be genial. I must guard the reader against accepting Kirstie's epithets as evidence; she was more concerned for their vigour than for their accuracy. Dwaibly, for instance; nothing could be more calumnious. Frank was the very picture of good looks, good humour, and manly youth. He had bright eyes with a sparkle and a dance to them, curly hair, a charming smile, brilliant teeth, an admirable carriage of the head, the look of a gentleman, the address of one accustomed to please at first sight and to improve the impression. And with all these advantages, he failed with every one about Hermiston; with the silent shepherd, with the obsequious grieve, with the groom who was also the ploughman, with the gardener and the gardener's sister – a pious, down-hearted woman with a shawl over her ears – he failed equally and flatly. They did not like him, and they showed it. The little maid, indeed, was an exception; she admired him devoutly, probably dreamed of him in her private hours; but she was accustomed to play the part of silent auditor to Kirstie's tirades and silent recipient of Kirstie's buffets, and she had learned not only to be a very capable girl of her years, but a very secret and prudent one besides. Frank was thus conscious that he had one ally and sympathiser in the midst of that general union of disfavour that surrounded, watched, and waited on him in the house of Hermiston; but he had little comfort or society from that alliance, and the demure little maid (twelve on her last birthday) preserved her own counsel, and tripped on his service, brisk, dumbly responsive, but inexorably unconversational. For the others, they were beyond hope and beyond endurance. Never had a young Apollo been cast among such rustic barbarians. But perhaps the cause of his ill-success lay in one trait which was habitual and unconscious with him, yet diagnostic of the man. It was his practice to approach any one person at the expense of some one else. He offered you an alliance against the some one else; he flattered you by slighting him; you were drawn into a small intrigue against him before you knew how. Wonderful are the virtues of this process generally; but Frank's mistake was in the choice of the some one else. He was not politic in that; he listened to the voice of irritation. Archie had offended him at first by what he had felt to be rather a dry reception, had offended him since by his frequent absences. He was besides the one figure continually present in Frank's eye; and it was to his immediate dependants that Frank could offer the snare of his sympathy. Now the truth is that the Weirs, father and son, were surrounded by a posse of strenuous loyalists. Of my lord they were vastly proud. It was a distinction in itself to be one of the vassals of the 'Hanging Judge,' and his gross, formidable joviality was far from unpopular in the neighbourhood of his home. For Archie they had, one and all, a sensitive affection and respect which recoiled from a word of belittlement.

Nor was Frank more successful when he went farther afield. To the Four Black Brothers, for instance, he was antipathetic in the highest degree. Hob thought him too light, Gib too profane. Clem, who saw him but for a day or two before he went to Glasgow, wanted to know what the fule's business was, and whether he meant to stay here all session time! 'Yon's a drone,' he pronounced. As for Dand, it will be enough to describe their first meeting, when Frank had been whipping a river and the rustic celebrity chanced to come along the path.

'I'm told you're quite a poet,' Frank had said.

'Wha tell't ye that, mannie?' had been the unconciliating answer.

'O, everybody!' says Frank.

'God! Here's fame!' said the sardonic poet, and he had passed on his way.

Come to think of it, we have here perhaps a truer explanation of Frank's failures. Had he met Mr Sheriff Scott he could have turned a neater compliment, because Mr Scott would have been a friend worth making. Dand, on the other hand, he did not value sixpence, and he showed it even while he tried to flatter. Condescension is an excellent thing, but it is strange how one-sided the pleasure of it is! He who goes fishing among the Scots peasantry with condescension for a bait will have an empty basket by evening.

In proof of this theory Frank made a great success of it at the Crossmichael Club, to which Archie took him immediately on his arrival; his own last appearance on that scene of gaiety. Frank was made welcome there at once, continued to go regularly, and had attended a meeting (as the members ever after loved to tell) on the evening before his death. Young Hay and young Pringle appeared again. There was another supper at Windielaws, another dinner at Driffel; and it resulted in Frank being taken to the bosom of the county people as unreservedly as he had been repudiated by the country folk. He occupied Hermiston after the manner of an invader in a conquered capital. He was perpetually issuing from it, as from a base, to toddy parties, fishing parties, and dinner parties, to which Archie was not invited, or to which Archie would not go. It was now that the name of The Recluse became general for the young man. Some say that Innes invented it; Innes, at least, spread it abroad.

'How's all with your Recluse today?' people would ask.

'O, reclusing away!' Innes would declare, with his bright air of saying something witty; and immediately interrupt the general laughter which he had provoked much more by his air than his words, 'Mind you, it's all very well laughing, but I'm not very well pleased. Poor Archie is a good fellow, an excellent fellow, a fellow I always liked. I think it small of him to take his little disgrace so hard and shut himself up. "Grant that it is a ridiculous story, painfully ridiculous," I keep telling him. "Be a man! Live it down, man!" But not he. Of course it's just solitude, and shame, and all that. But I confess I'm beginning to fear the result. It would be all the pities in the world if a really promising fellow like Weir was to end ill. I'm seriously tempted to write to Lord Hermiston, and put it plainly to him.'

'I would if I were you,' some of his auditors would say, shaking the head, sitting bewildered and confused at this new view of the matter, so deftly indicated by a single word. 'A capital idea!'

they would add, and wonder at the *aplomb* and position of this young man, who talked as a matter of course of writing to Hermiston and correcting him upon his private affairs.

And Frank would proceed, sweetly confidential: 'I'll give you an idea, now. He's actually sore about the way that I'm received and he's left out in the county – actually jealous and sore. I've rallied him and I've reasoned with him, told him that every one was most kindly inclined towards him, told him even that *I* was received merely because I was his guest. But it's no use. He will neither accept the invitations he gets, nor stop brooding about the ones where he's left out. What I'm afraid of is that the wound's ulcerating. He had always one of those dark, secret, angry natures – a little underhand and plenty of bile – you know the sort. He must have inherited it from the Weirs, whom I suspect to have been a worthy family of weavers somewhere; what's the cant phrase? – sedentary occupation. It's precisely the kind of character to go wrong in a false position like what his father's made for him, or he's making for himself, whichever you like to call it. And for my part, I think it a disgrace,' Frank would say generously.

Presently the sorrow and anxiety of this disinterested friend took shape. He began in private, in conversations of two, to talk vaguely of bad habits and low habits. 'I must say I'm afraid he's going wrong altogether,' he would say. 'I'll tell you plainly, and between ourselves, I scarcely like to stay there any longer; only, man, I'm positively afraid to leave him alone. You'll see, I shall be blamed for it later on. I'm staying at a great sacrifice. I'm hindering my chances at the Bar, and I can't blind my eyes to it. And what I'm afraid of is that I'm going to get kicked for it all round before all's done. You see, nobody believes in friendship nowadays.'

'Well, Innes,' his interlocutor would reply, 'it's very good of you, I must say that. If there's any blame going, you'll always be sure of *my* good word, for one thing.'

'Well,' Frank would continue, 'candidly, I don't say it's pleasant. He has a very rough way with him; his father's son, you know. I don't say he's rude – of course, I couldn't be expected to stand that – but he steers very near the wind. No, it's not pleasant; but I tell ye, man, in conscience I don't think it would be fair to leave him. Mind you, I don't say there's anything actually wrong. What I say is that I don't like the looks of it, man!' and he would press the arm of his momentary confidant.

In the early stages I am persuaded there was no malice. He talked but for the pleasure of airing himself. He was essentially glib, as becomes the young advocate, and essentially careless of the truth, which is the mark of the young ass; and so he talked at random. There was no particular bias, but that one which is indigenous and universal, to flatter himself and to please and interest the present friend. And by thus milling air out of his mouth, he had presently built up a presentation of Archie which was known and talked of in all corners of the county. Wherever there was a residential house and a walled garden, wherever there was a dwarfish castle and a park, wherever a quadruple cottage by the ruins of a peel-tower showed an old family going down, and wherever a handsome villa with a carriage approach and a shrubbery marked the coming up of a new one – probably on the wheels of machinery – Archie began to be regarded in the light of a dark, perhaps a vicious mystery, and the future developments of his career to be looked for with uneasiness and confidential whispering. He had done something disgraceful, my dear. What, was not precisely known, and that good kind young man, Mr Innes, did his best to make light of it. But there it was. And Mr Innes was very anxious about him now; he was really uneasy, my dear; he was positively wrecking his own prospects because he dared not leave him alone. How wholly we all lie at the mercy of a single prater, not needfully with any malign purpose! And if a man but talks of himself in the right spirit, refers to his virtuous actions by the way, and never applies to them the name of virtue, how easily his evidence is accepted in the court of public opinion!

All this while, however, there was a more poisonous ferment at work between the two lads, which came late indeed to the surface, but had modified and magnified their dissensions from the first. To an idle, shallow, easy-going customer like Frank, the smell of a mystery was attractive. It gave his mind something to play with, like a new toy to a child; and it took him on the weak side, for like many young men coming to the Bar, and before they have been tried and found wanting, he flattered himself he was a fellow of unusual quickness and penetration.

They knew nothing of Sherlock Holmes in those days, but there was a good deal said of Talleyrand. And if you could have caught Frank off his guard, he would have confessed with a smirk that, if he resembled any one, it was the Marquis de Talleyrand-Périgord. It was on the occasion of Archie's first absence that this interest took root. It was vastly deepened when Kirstie resented his curiosity at breakfast, and that same afternoon there occurred another scene which clinched the business. He was fishing Swingleburn, Archie accompanying him, when the latter looked at his watch.

'Well, good-bye,' said he. 'I have something to do. See you at dinner.'

'Don't be in such a hurry,' cries Frank. 'Hold on till I get my rod up. I'll go with you; I'm sick of flogging this ditch.'

And he began to reel up his line.

Archie stood speechless. He took a long while to recover his wits under this direct attack; but by the time he was ready with his answer, and the angle was almost packed up, he had become completely Weir, and the hanging face gloomed on his young shoulders. He spoke with a laboured composure, a laboured kindness even; but a child could see that his mind was made up.

'I beg your pardon, Innes; I don't want to be disagreeable, but let us understand one another from the beginning. When I want your company, I'll let you know.'

'O!' cries Frank, 'you don't want my company, don't you?'

'Apparently not just now,' replied Archie. 'I even indicated to you when I did, if you'll remember – and that was at dinner. If we two fellows are to live together pleasantly – and I see no reason why we should not – it can only be by respecting each other's privacy. If we begin intruding – '

'O, come! I'll take this at no man's hands. Is this the way you treat a guest and an old friend?' cried Innes.

'Just go home and think over what I said by yourself,' continued Archie, 'whether it's reasonable, or whether it's really offensive or not; and let's meet at dinner as though nothing had happened. I'll put it this way, if you like – that I know my own character, that I'm looking forward (with great pleasure, I assure you) to a long visit from you, and that I'm taking precautions at the first. I see the thing that we – that

I, if you like – might fall out upon, and I step in and *obsto principiis*. I wager you five pounds you'll end by seeing that I mean friendliness, and I assure you, Francie, I do,' he added, relenting.

Bursting with anger, but incapable of speech, Innes shouldered his rod, made a gesture of farewell, and strode off down the burn-side. Archie watched him go without moving. He was sorry, but quite unashamed. He hated to be inhospitable, but in one thing he was his father's son. He had a strong sense that his house was his own and no man else's; and to lie at a guest's mercy was what he refused. He hated to seem harsh. But that was Frank's look-out. If Frank had been commonly discreet, he would have been decently courteous. And there was another consideration. The secret he was protecting was not his own merely; it was hers: it belonged to that inexpressible she who was fast taking possession of his soul, and whom he would soon have defended at the cost of burning cities. By the time he had watched Frank as far as the Swingleburnfoot, appearing and disappearing in the tarnished heather, still stalking at a fierce gait but already dwindled in the distance into less than the smallness of Lilliput, he could afford to smile at the occurrence. Either Frank would go, and that would be a relief – or he would continue to stay, and his host must continue to endure him. And Archie was now free – by devious paths, behind hillocks and in the hollow of burns – to make for the trysting-place where Kirstie, cried about by the curlew and the plover, waited and burned for his coming by the Covenanter's stone.

Innes went off down-hill in a passion of resentment, easy to be understood, but which yielded progressively to the needs of his situation. He cursed Archie for a cold-hearted, unfriendly, rude dog: and himself still more passionately for a fool in having come to Hermiston when he might have sought refuge in almost any other house in Scotland. But the step once taken, was practically irretrievable. He had no more ready money to go anywhere else; he would have to borrow from Archie the next club-night; and ill as he thought of his host's manners, he was sure of his practical generosity. Frank's resemblance to Talleyrand strikes me as imaginary; but at least not Talleyrand himself could have more obediently taken his lesson from the facts. He met Archie at dinner without resentment, almost with cordiality. You must take your friends as you find them, he would have said. Archie couldn't help being his father's son, or his grandfather's, the hypothetical weaver's, grandson. The son of a hunks, he was still a hunks at heart, incapable of true generosity and consideration; but he had other qualities with which Frank could divert himself in the meanwhile, and to enjoy which it was necessary that Frank should keep his temper.

So excellently was it controlled that he awoke next morning with his head full of a different, though a cognate subject. What was Archie's little game? Why did he shun Frank's company? What was he keeping secret? Was he keeping tryst with somebody, and was it a woman? It would be a good joke and a fair revenge to discover. To that task he set himself with a great deal of patience, which might have surprised his friends, for he had been always credited not with patience so much as brilliancy; and little by little, from one point to another, he at last succeeded in piecing out the situation. First he remarked that, although Archie set out in all the directions of the compass, he always came home again from some point between the south and west. From the study of a map, and in consideration of the great expanse of untenanted moorland running in that direction towards the sources of the Clyde, he laid his finger on Cauldstaneslap and two other neighbouring farms, Kingsmuirs and Polintarf. But it was difficult to advance farther. With his rod for a pretext, he vainly visited each of them in turn; nothing was to be seen suspicious about this trinity of moorland settlements. He would have tried to follow Archie, had it been the least possible, but the nature of the land precluded the idea. He did the next best, ensconced himself in a quiet corner, and pursued his movements with a telescope. It was equally in vain, and he soon wearied of his futile vigilance, left the telescope at home, and had almost given the matter up in despair, when, on the twenty-seventh day of his visit, he was suddenly confronted with the person whom he sought. The first Sunday Kirstie had managed to stay away from kirk on some pretext of indisposition, which was more truly modesty; the pleasure of beholding Archie seemed too sacred, too vivid for that public place. On the two following, Frank had himself been absent on some of his excursions among the neighbouring families. It was not until the fourth, accordingly, that Frank had

occasion to set eyes on the enchantress. With the first look, all
hesitation was over. She came with the Cauldstaneslap party;
then she lived at Cauldstaneslap. Here was Archie's secret, here
was the woman, and more than that – though I have need here
of every manageable attenuation of language – with the first
look, he had already entered himself as rival. It was a good
deal in pique, it was a little in revenge, it was much in genuine
admiration; the devil may decide the proportions! I cannot, and
it is very likely that Frank could not.

'Mighty attractive milkmaid,' he observed, on the way home.

'Who?' said Archie.

'O, the girl you're looking at – aren't you? Forward there on
the road. She came attended by the rustic bard; presumably,
therefore, belongs to his exalted family. The single objection
for the four black brothers are awkward customers. If anything
were to go wrong, Gib would gibber, and Clem would prove
inclement; and Dand fly in danders, and Hob blow up in
gobbets. It would be a Helliott of a business!'

'Very humorous, I am sure,' said Archie.

'Well, I am trying to be so,' said Frank. 'It's none too easy
in this place, and with your solemn society, my dear fellow.
But confess that the milkmaid has found favour in your eyes,
or resign all claim to be a man of taste.'

'It is no matter,' returned Archie.

But the other continued to look at him, steadily and
quizzically, and his colour slowly rose and deepened under
the glance, until not impudence itself could have denied that
he was blushing. And at this Archie lost some of his control.
He changed his stick from one hand to the other, and – 'O, for
God's sake, don't be an ass!' he cried.

'Ass? That's the retort delicate without doubt,' says Frank.
'Beware of the homespun brothers, dear. If they come into the
dance, you'll see who's an ass. Think now, if they only applied
(say) a quarter as much talent as I have applied to the question
of what Mr Archie does with his evening hours, and why he is
so unaffectedly nasty when the subject's touched on – '

'You are touching on it now,' interrupted Archie, with
a wince.

'Thank you. That was all I wanted, an articulate confession,'
said Frank.

'I beg to remind you – ' began Archie.

But he was interrupted in turn. 'My dear fellow, don't. It's quite needless. The subject's dead and buried.'

And Frank began to talk hastily on other matters, an art in which he was an adept, for it was his gift to be fluent on anything or nothing. But although Archie had the grace or the timidity to suffer him to rattle on, he was by no means done with the subject. When he came home to dinner, he was greeted with a sly demand, how things were looking 'Cauldstaneslap ways.' Frank took his first glass of port out after dinner to the toast of Kirstie, and later in the evening he returned to the charge again.

'I say, Weir, you'll excuse me for returning again to this affair. I've been thinking it over, and I wish to beg you very seriously to be more careful. It's not a safe business. Not safe, my boy,' said he.

'What?' said Archie.

'Well, it's your own fault if I must put a name on the thing; but really, as a friend, I cannot stand by and see you rushing head down into these dangers. My dear boy,' said he, holding up a warning cigar, 'consider! What is to be the end of it?'

'The end of what?' – Archie, helpless with irritation, persisted in this dangerous and ungracious guard.

'Well, the end of the milkmaid; or, to speak more by the card, the end of Miss Christina Elliott of the Cauldstaneslap.'

'I assure you,' Archie broke out, 'this is all a figment of your imagination. There is nothing to be said against that young lady; you have no right to introduce her name into the conversation.'

'I'll make a note of it,' said Frank. 'She shall henceforth be nameless, nameless, nameless, Gregarach! I make a note besides of your valuable testimony to her character. I only want to look at this thing as a man of the world. Admitted she's an angel – but, my good fellow, is she a lady?'

This was torture to Archie. 'I beg your pardon,' he said, struggling to be composed, 'but because you have wormed yourself into my confidence – '

'O, come!' cried Frank. 'Your confidence? It was rosy but unconsenting. Your confidence, indeed? Now, look! This is what I must say, Weir, for it concerns your safety and good character, and therefore my honour as your friend. You say I wormed myself into your confidence. Wormed is good. But what have I done? I have put two and two together, just as the parish will be doing to-morrow, and the whole of Tweeddale in two weeks, and the black brothers – well, I won't put a date on that; it will be a dark and stormy morning! Your secret, in other words, is poor Poll's. And I want to ask of you as a friend whether you like the prospect? There are two horns to your dilemma, and I must say for myself I should look mighty ruefully on either. Do you see yourself explaining to the four Black Brothers? or do you see yourself presenting the milkmaid to papa as the future lady of Hermiston? Do you? I tell you plainly, I don't!'

Archie rose. 'I will hear no more of this,' he said, in a trembling voice.

But Frank again held up his cigar. 'Tell me one thing first. Tell me if this is not a friend's part that I am playing?'

'I believe you think it so,' replied Archie. 'I can go as far as that. I can do so much justice to your motives. But I will hear no more of it. I am going to bed.'

'That's right, Weir,' said Frank heartily. 'Go to bed and think over it; and I say, man, don't forget your prayers! I don't often do the moral – don't go in for that sort of thing – but when I do there's one thing sure, that I mean it.'

So Archie marched off to bed, and Frank sat alone by the table for another hour or so, smiling to himself richly. There was nothing vindictive in his nature; but, if revenge came in his way, it might as well be good, and the thought of Archie's pillow reflections that night was indescribably sweet to him. He felt a pleasant sense of power. He looked down on Archie as on a very little boy whose strings he pulled – as on a horse whom he had backed and bridled by sheer power of intelligence, and whom he might ride to glory or the grave at pleasure. Which was it to be? He lingered long, relishing the details of schemes that he was too idle to pursue. Poor cork upon a torrent, he tasted that night the sweets of omnipotence, and brooded like a deity over the strands of that intrigue which was to shatter him before the summer waned.

CHAPTER EIGHT

A Nocturnal Visit

Kirstie had many causes of distress. More and more as we grow old – and yet more and more as we grow old and are women, frozen by the fear of age – we come to rely on the voice as the single outlet of the soul. Only thus, in the curtailment of our means, can we relieve the straitened cry of the passion within us; only thus, in the bitter and sensitive shyness of advancing years, can we maintain relations with those vivacious figures of the young that still show before us and tend daily to become no more than the moving wall-paper of life. Talk is the last link, the last relation. But with the end of the conversation, when the voice stops and the bright face of the listener is turned away, solitude falls again on the bruised heart. Kirstie had lost her 'Cannie hour at e'en'; she could no more wander with Archie, a ghost if you will, but a happy ghost, in fields Elysian. And to her it was as if the whole world had fallen silent; to him, but an unremarkable change of amusements. And she raged to know it. The effervescency of her passionate and irritable nature rose within her at times to bursting point.

This is the price paid by age for unseasonable ardours of feeling. It must have been so for Kirstie at any time when the occasion chanced; but it so fell out that she was deprived of this delight in the hour when she had most need of it, when she had most to say, most to ask, and when she trembled to recognise her sovereignty not merely in abeyance but annulled. For, with the clairvoyance of a genuine love, she had pierced the mystery that had so long embarrassed Frank. She was conscious, even before it was carried out, even on that Sunday night when it began, of an invasion of her rights; and a voice told her the invader's name. Since then, by arts, by accident, by small things observed, and by the general drift of Archie's humour, she had passed beyond all possibility of doubt. With a sense of justice that Lord Hermiston might have envied, she had that day in church considered and admitted the attractions of the young Kirstie; and with the profound humanity and sentimentality of her nature, she had recognised the coming of fate. Not thus would she have chosen. She had seen, in imagination, Archie wedded to some tall, powerful, and rosy heroine of the golden locks, made in her own image, for whom she would have strewed the bride-bed with delight; and now she could have wept to see the ambition falsified. But the gods had pronounced, and her doom was otherwise.

She lay tossing in bed that night, besieged with feverish thoughts. There were dangerous matters pending, a battle was toward, over the fate of which she hung in jealousy, sympathy, fear, and alternate loyalty and disloyalty to either side. Now she was reincarnated in her niece, and now in Archie. Now she saw, through the girl's eyes, the youth on his knees to her, heard his persuasive instances with a deadly weakness, and received his overmastering caresses. Anon, with a revulsion, her temper raged to see such utmost favours of fortune and love squandered on a brat of a girl, one of her own house, using her own name – a deadly ingredient – and that 'didna ken her ain mind an' was as black's your hat.' Now she trembled lest her deity should plead in vain, loving the idea of success for him like a triumph of nature; anon, with returning loyalty of her own family and sex, she trembled for Kirstie and the credit of the Elliotts. And again she had a vision of herself, the day over for her old-world tales and local gossip, bidding farewell to her last link with life and brightness and love; and behind and beyond, she saw but the blank butt-end where she must crawl to die. Had she then come to the lees? she, so great, so beautiful, with a heart as fresh as a girl's and strong as womanhood? It could not be, and yet it was so; and for a moment her bed was horrible to her as the sides of the grave. And she looked forward over a waste of hours, and saw herself go on to rage, and tremble, and be softened, and rage again, until the day came and the labours of the day must be renewed.

Suddenly she heard feet on the stairs – his feet, and soon after the sound of a window sash flung open. She sat up with her heart beating. He had gone to his room alone, and he had not gone to bed. She might again have one of her night cracks; and at the entrancing prospect, a change came over her

mind; with the approach of this hope of pleasure, all the baser
metal became immediately obliterated from her thoughts. She
rose, all woman, and all the best of woman, tender, pitiful,
hating the wrong, loyal to her own sex – and all the weakest
of that dear miscellany, nourishing, cherishing next her soft
heart, voicelessly flattering, hopes that she would have died
sooner than have acknowledged. She tore off her nightcap,
and her hair fell about her shoulders in profusion. Undying
coquetry awoke. By the faint light of her nocturnal rush, she
stood before the looking-glass, carried her shapely arms above
her head, and gathered up the treasures of her tresses. She was
never backward to admire herself; that kind of modesty was a
stranger to her nature; and she paused, struck with a pleased
wonder at the sight. 'Ye daft auld wife!' she said, answering
a thought that was not; and she blushed with the innocent
consciousness of a child. Hastily she did up the massive and
shining coils, hastily donned a wrapper, and with the rushlight
in her hand, stole into the hall. Below stairs she heard the
clock ticking the deliberate seconds, and Frank jingling with
the decanters in the dining-room. Aversion rose in her, bitter
and momentary. 'Nesty, tippling puggy!' she thought; and the
next moment she had knocked guardedly at Archie's door and
was bidden enter.

Archie had been looking out into the ancient blackness,
pierced here and there with a rayless star; taking the sweet
air of the moors and the night into his bosom deeply; seeking,
perhaps finding, peace after the manner of the unhappy. He
turned round as she came in, and showed her a pale face against
the window-frame.

'Is that you Kirstie?' he asked. 'Come in!'

'It's unco late, my dear,' said Kirstie, affecting unwillingness.

'No, no,' he answered, 'not at all. Come in, if you want a
crack. I am not sleepy, God knows!'

She advanced, took a chair by the toilet table and the candle,
and set the rushlight at her foot. Something – it might be in
the comparative disorder of her dress, it might be the emotion
that now welled in her bosom – had touched her with a wand
of transformation, and she seemed young with the youth of
goddesses.

'Mr Erchie,' she began, 'what's this that's come to ye?'

'I am not aware of anything that has come,' said Archie, and blushed, and repented bitterly that he had let her in.

'O, my dear, that'll no dae!' said Kirstie. 'It's ill to blend the eyes of love. O, Mr Erchie, tak a thocht ere it's ower late. Ye shouldna be impatient o' the braws o' life, they'll a' come in their saison, like the sun and the rain. Ye're young yet; ye've mony cantie years afore ye. See and dinna wreck yersel' at the outset like sae mony ithers! Hae patience – they telled me aye that was the owercome o' life – hae patience, there's a braw day coming yet. Gude kens it never cam to me; and here I am, wi' nayther man nor bairn to ca' my ain, wearying a' folks wi' my ill tongue, and you just the first, Mr Erchie!'

'I have a difficulty in knowing what you mean,' said Archie.

'Weel, and I'll tell ye,' she said. 'It's just this, that I'm feared. I'm feared for ye, my dear. Remember, your faither is a hard man, reaping where he hasna sowed and gaithering where he hasna strawed. It's easy speakin', but mind! Ye'll have to look in the gurly face o'm, where it's ill to look, and vain to look for mercy. Ye mind me o' a bonny ship pitten oot into the black and gowsty seas – ye're a' safe still, sittin' quait and crackin' wi' Kirstie in your lown chalmer; but whaur will ye be the morn, and in whatten horror o' the fearsome tempest, cryin' on the hills to cover ye?'

'Why, Kirstie, you're very enigmatical tonight – and very eloquent,' Archie put in.

'And, my dear Mr Erchie,' she continued, with a change of voice, 'ye mauna think that I canna sympathise wi' ye. Ye mauna think that I havena been young mysel'. Lang syne, when I was a bit lassie, no twenty yet – ' She paused and sighed. 'Clean and caller, wi' a fit like the hinney bee,' she continued. 'I was aye big and buirdly, ye maun understand; a bonny figure o' a woman, though I say it that suldna – built to rear bairns – braw bairns they suld hae been, and grand I would hae likit it! But I was young, dear, wi' the bonny glint o' youth in my e'en, and little I dreamed I'd ever be tellin' ye this, an auld, lanely, rudas wife! Weel, Mr Erchie, there was a lad cam' courtin' me, as was but naetural. Mony had come before, and I would nane o' them. But this yin had a tongue to wile the birds frae the lift and the bees frae the foxglove bells. Deary me, but it's lang syne!

Folk have dee'd sinsyne and been buried, and are forgotten, and bairns been born and got merrit and got bairns o' their ain. Sinsyne woods have been plantit, and have grawn up and are bonny trees, and the joes sit in their shadow, and sinsyne auld estates have changed hands, and there have been wars and rumours of wars on the face of the earth. And here I'm still – like an auld droopit craw – lookin' on and craikin'! But, Mr Erchie, do ye no think that I have mind o' it a' still? I was dwalling then in my faither's house; and it's a curious thing that we were whiles trysted in the Deil's Hags. And do ye no think that I have mind of the bonny simmer days, the lang miles o' the bluid-red heather, the cryin' o' the whaups, and the lad and the lassie that was trysted? Do ye no think that I mind how the hilly sweetness ran about my hairt? Ay, Mr Erchie, I ken the way o' it – fine do I ken the way – how the grace o' God takes them, like Paul of Tarsus, when they think it least, and drives the pair o' them into a land which is like a dream, and the world and the folks in 't are nae mair than clouds to the puir lassie, and heeven nae mair than windle-straes, if she can but pleesure him! Until Tam dee'd – that was my story,' she broke off to say, 'he dee'd, and I wasna at the buryin'. But while he was here, I could take care o' mysel'. And can yon puir lassie?'

Kirstie, her eyes shining with unshed tears, stretched out her hand towards him appealingly; the bright and the dull gold of her hair flashed and smouldered in the coils behind her comely head, like the rays of an eternal youth; the pure colour had risen in her face; and Archie was abashed alike by her beauty and her story. He came towards her slowly from the window, took up her hand in his and kissed it.

'Kirstie,' he said hoarsely, 'you have misjudged me sorely. I have always thought of her, I wouldna harm her for the universe, my woman!'

'Eh, lad, and that's easy sayin',' cried Kirstie, 'but it's nane sae easy doin'! Man, do ye no comprehend that it's God's wull we should be blendit and glamoured, and have nae command over our ain members at a time like that? My bairn,' she cried, still holding his hand, 'think o' the puir lass! have pity upon her, Erchie! and O, be wise for twa! Think o' the risk she rins! I have seen ye, and what's to prevent ithers! I saw ye once in the Hags, in my ain howf, and I was wae to see ye there – in pairt for the omen, for I think there's a weird on the place – and in pairt for pure nakit envy and bitterness o' hairt. It's strange ye should forgather there tae! God! but yon puir, thrawn, auld Covenanter's seen a heap o' human natur since he lookit his last on the musket barrels, if he never saw nane afore,' she added, with a kind of wonder in her eyes.

'I swear by my honour I have done her no wrong,' said Archie. 'I swear by my honour and the redemption of my soul that there shall none be done her. I have heard of this before. I have been foolish, Kirstie, not unkind and, above all, not base.'

'There's my bairn!' said Kirstie, rising. 'I'll can trust ye noo, I'll can gang to my bed wi' an easy hairt.' And then she saw in a flash how barren had been her triumph. Archie had promised to spare the girl, and he would keep it; but who had promised to spare Archie? What was to be the end of it? Over a maze of difficulties she glanced, and saw, at the end of every passage, the flinty countenance of Hermiston. And a kind of horror fell upon her at what she had done. She wore a tragic mask. 'Erchie, the Lord peety you, dear, and peety me! I have buildit on this foundation' – laying her hand heavily on his shoulder – 'and buildit hie, and pit my hairt in the buildin' of it. If the hale hypothec were to fa', I think, laddie, I would dee! Excuse a daft wife that loves ye, and that kenned your mither. And for His name's sake keep yersel' frae inordinate desires; haud your heart in baith your hands, carry it canny and laigh; dinna send it up like a bairn's kite into the collieshangie o' the wunds! Mind, Maister Erchie dear, that this life's a' disappointment, and a mouthfu' o' mools is the appointed end.'

'Ay, but Kirstie, my woman, you're asking me ower much at last,' said Archie, profoundly moved, and lapsing into the broad Scots. 'Ye're asking what nae man can grant ye, what only the Lord of heaven can grant ye if He see fit. Ay! And can even He? I can promise ye what I shall do, and you can depend on that. But how I shall feel – my woman, that is long past thinking of!'

They were both standing by now opposite each other. The face of Archie wore the wretched semblance of a smile; hers was convulsed for a moment.

'Promise me ae thing,' she cried, in a sharp voice. 'Promise me ye'll never do naething without telling me.'

'No, Kirstie, I canna promise ye that,' he replied. 'I have promised enough, God kens!'

'May the blessing of God lift and rest upon ye, dear!' she said.

'God bless ye, my old friend,' said he.

CHAPTER NINE

At the Weaver's Stone

It was late in the afternoon when Archie drew near by the hill path to the Praying Weaver's stone. The Hags were in shadow. But still, through the gate of the Slap, the sun shot a last arrow, which sped far and straight across the surface of the moss, here and there touching and shining on a tussock, and lighted at length on the gravestone and the small figure awaiting him there. The emptiness and solitude of the great moors seemed to be concentred there, and Kirstie pointed out by that figure of sunshine for the only inhabitant. His first sight of her was thus excruciatingly sad, like a glimpse of a world from which all light, comfort, and society were on the point of vanishing. And the next moment, when she had turned her face to him and the quick smile had enlightened it, the whole face of nature smiled upon him in her smile of welcome. Archie's slow pace was quickened; his legs hasted to her though his heart was hanging back. The girl, upon her side, drew herself together slowly and stood up, expectant; she was all languor, her face was gone white; her arms ached for him, her soul was on tip-toes. But he deceived her, pausing a few steps away, not less white than herself, and holding up his hand with a gesture of denial.

'No, Christina, not to-day,' he said. 'To-day I have to talk to you seriously. Sit ye down, please, there where you were. Please!' he repeated.

The revulsion of feeling in Christina's heart was violent. To have longed and waited these weary hours for him, rehearsing her endearments – to have seen him at last come – to have been ready there, breathless, wholly passive, his to do what he would with – and suddenly to have found herself confronted with a grey-faced, harsh schoolmaster – it was too rude a shock. She could have wept, but pride withheld her . She sat down on the stone, from which she had arisen, part with the instinct of obedience, part as though she had been thrust there. What was this? Why was she rejected? Had she ceased to please? She stood here offering her wares, and he would none of them! And yet they were all his! His to take and keep, not his to refuse though! In her quick petulant nature, a moment ago on fire with hope, thwarted love and wounded vanity wrought. The schoolmaster that there is in all men, to the despair of all girls and most women, was now completely in possession of Archie. He had passed a night of sermons, a day of reflection; he had come wound up to do his duty; and the set mouth, which in him only betrayed the effort of his will, to her seemed the expression of an averted heart. It was the same with his constrained voice and embarrassed utterance; and if so – if it was all over – the pang of the thought took away from her the power of thinking.

He stood before her some way off. 'Kirstie, there's been too much of this. We've seen too much of each other.' She looked up quickly and her eyes contracted. 'There's no good ever comes of these secret meetings. They're not frank, not honest truly, and I ought to have seen it. People have begun to talk; and it's not right of me. Do you see?'

'I see somebody will have been talking to ye,' she said sullenly.

'They have, more than one of them,' replied Archie.

'And whae were they?' she cried. 'And what kind o' love do ye ca' that, that's ready to gang round like a whirligig at folk talking? Do ye think they havena talked to me?'

'Have they indeed?' said Archie, with a quick breath. 'That is what I feared. Who were they? Who has dared – ?'

Archie was on the point of losing his temper.

As a matter of fact, not any one had talked to Christina on the matter; and she strenuously repeated her own first question in a panic of self-defence.

'Ah, well! what does it matter?' he said. 'They were good folk that wished well to us, and the great affair is that there are people talking. My dear girl, we have to be wise. We must not wreck our lives at the outset. They may be long and happy yet, and we must see to it, Kirstie, like God's rational creatures and not like fool children. There is one thing we must see to before all. You're worth waiting for, Kirstie! worth waiting for a generation; it would be enough reward.' – And here he remembered the schoolmaster again, and very unwisely took

to following wisdom. 'The first thing that we must see to, is
that there shall be no scandal about for my father's sake. That
would ruin all; do ye no see that?'

Kirstie was a little pleased, there had been some show of
warmth of sentiment in what Archie had said last. But the
dull irritation still persisted in her bosom; with the aboriginal instinct, having suffered herself, she wished to make
Archie suffer.

And besides, there had come out the word she had always
feared to hear from his lips, the name of his father. It is not
to be supposed that, during so many days with a love avowed
between them, some reference had not been made to their
conjoint future. It had in fact been often touched upon, and
from the first had been the sore point. Kirstie had wilfully closed
the eye of thought; she would not argue even with herself;
gallant, desperate little heart, she had accepted the command
of that supreme attraction like the call of fate and marched
blindfold on her doom. But Archie, with his masculine sense of
responsibility, must reason; he must dwell on some future good,
when the present good was all in all to Kirstie; he must talk – and
talk lamely, as necessity drove him – of what was to be. Again
and again he had touched on marriage; again and again been
driven back into indistinctness by a memory of Lord Hermiston.
And Kirstie had been swift to understand and quick to choke
down and smother the understanding; swift to leap up in flame
at a mention of that hope, which spoke volumes to her vanity
and her love, that she might one day be Mrs Weir of Hermiston;
swift, also, to recognise in his stumbling or throttled utterance
the death-knell of these expectations, and constant, poor girl! in
her large-minded madness, to go on and to reck nothing of the
future. But these unfinished references, these blinks in which
his heart spoke, and his memory and reason rose up to silence
it before the words were well uttered, gave her unqualifiable
agony. She was raised up and dashed down again bleeding. The
recurrence of the subject forced her, for however short a time,
to open her eyes on what she did not wish to see; and it had
invariably ended in another disappointment. So now again, at
the mere wind of its coming, at the mere mention of his father's
name – who might seem indeed to have accompanied them in
their whole moorland courtship, an awful figure in a wig with

an ironical and bitter smile, present to guilty consciousness –
she fled from it head down.

'Ye havena told me yet,' she said, 'who was it spoke?

'Your aunt for one,' said Archie.

'Auntie Kirstie?' she cried. 'And what do I care for my Auntie
Kirstie?'

'She cares a great deal for her niece,' replied Archie, in kind
reproof.

'Troth, and it's the first I've heard of it,' retorted the girl.

'The question here is not who it is, but what they say, what
they have noticed,' pursued the lucid schoolmaster. 'That is
what we have to think of in self-defence.'

'Auntie Kirstie, indeed! A bitter, thrawn auld maid that's
fomented trouble in the country before I was born, and will
be doing it still, I daur say, when I'm deid! It's in her nature;
it's as natural for her as it's for a sheep to eat.'

'Pardon me, Kirstie, she was not the only one,' interposed
Archie. 'I had two warnings, two sermons, last night, both most
kind and considerate. Had you been there, I promise you you
would have grat, my dear! And they opened my eyes. I saw we
were going a wrong way.'

'Who was the other one?' Kirstie demanded.

By this time Archie was in the condition of a hunted beast.
He had come, braced and resolute; he was to trace out a line of
conduct for the pair of them in a few cold, convincing sentences;
he had now been there some time, and he was still staggering
round the outworks and undergoing what he felt to be a savage
cross-examination.

'Mr Frank!' she cried. 'What nex', I would like to ken?'

'He spoke most kindly and truly.'

'What like did he say?'

'I am not going to tell you; you have nothing to do with that,'
cried Archie, startled to find he had admitted so much.

'O, I have naething to do with it!' she repeated, springing
to her feet. 'A'body at Hermiston's free to pass their opinions
upon me, but I have naething to do wi' it! Was this at prayers
like? Did ye ca' the grieve into the consultation? Little wonder
if a'body's talking, when ye make a'body ye're confidants! But
as you say, Mr Weir, – most kindly, most considerately, most
truly, I'm sure – I have naething to do with it. And I think I'll

better be going. I'll be wishing you good evening, Mr Weir.'
And she made him a stately curtsey, shaking as she did so from
head to foot, with the barren ecstasy of temper.

Poor Archie stood dumbfounded. She had moved some steps
away from him before he recovered the gift of articulate
speech.

'Kirstie!' he cried. 'O, Kirstie woman!'

There was in his voice a ring of appeal, a clang of mere
astonishment that showed the schoolmaster was vanquished.

She turned round on him. 'What do ye Kirstie me for?' she
retorted. 'What have ye to do wi' me? Gang to your ain freends
and deave them!'

He could only repeat the appealing 'Kirstie!'

'Kirstie, indeed!' cried the girl, her eyes blazing in her white
face. 'My name is Miss Christina Elliott, I would have ye to
ken, and I daur ye to ca' me out of it. If I canna get love,
I'll have respect, Mr Weir. I'm come of decent people, and
I'll have respect. What have I done that ye should lightly me?
What have I done? What have I done? O, what have I done?'
and her voice rose upon the third repetition. 'I thocht – I thocht
– I thocht I was sae happy!' and the first sob broke from her
like the paroxysm of some mortal sickness.

Archie ran to her. He took the poor child in his arms, and she
nestled to his breast as to a mother's, and clasped him in hands
that were strong like vices. He felt her whole body shaken by the
throes of distress, and had pity upon her beyond speech. Pity,
and at the same time a bewildered fear of this explosive engine
in his arms, whose works he did not understand, and yet had
been tampering with. There arose from before him the curtains
of boyhood, and he saw for the first time the ambiguous face
of woman as she is. In vain he looked back over the interview;
he saw not where he had offended. It seemed unprovoked, a
wilful convulsion of brute nature. . . .

Glossary

Antinomian, a Christian sect who feel that believers need not follow the moral law if they have been visited by grace

Auld Hornie, the Devil

ayther, either

ballant, ballad

bauchled, bungled

bauchles, old shoes

bauld, bold

begowk, make a fool of

birling, whirling, ringing

black-a-vised, dark complexioned, grim looking

blate, bashful

bonnet-laird, small farm-holder

bool, a ball, a marble, a sugar sweet

boss, hollow

bouman, tenant who rents cattle and grazing and shares the profits

brae, rising ground, a slope

braws, fine things

to play buff on, to fool, to deceive

butt end, the outer room of a cottage

ca', to drive; to call

caller, fresh

canny, careful, shrewd

cantie, cheerful, pleasant

carline, old woman

clamjamfry, crowd, rabble

clavers, idle chatter

clouted brogues, patched shoes

clour, blow

coble, small boat

cock-laird, small land-owner

collieshangie, commotion, turmoil

colloguing, chatting together

crack, lively conversation

Cruachan!, rallying cry of the Campbells

cuddy, donkey

cuist, cast

cutty, mischievious girl

D. of A., Duke of Argyll

dander, stroll

danders, cinders

daurna, dare not

deave, deafen

demmy brokens; demi-broquins, fashionably high laced pumps

denty, dainty

dirdum, blame, uproar, excitement

disjaskit, worn-out

doer, agent

dour, sullen, hard

drumlie, muddy, dark

dule-tree, gallows

dunt, stroke, blow, knock

dwaibly, shaky, infirm

ettercap, spider, spiteful person

fashious, troublesome

feck, quantity, a number

feckless, feeble, incompetent

fell, strong, very

fey, strange, unlike oneself, fated

fit, foot

flit, to depart

flyped, turned inside-out

Folk of Peace, Fairies

forbye, in addition to

fushionless, spiritless, weak

fyled, dirtied, defiled

gang, to go

gey an', very

gigot, leg of mutton

girzie, (diminutive of Grizel) a maidservant

glaur, mud, filth

gleg, brisk

gliff, look, glance

gloaming, twilight

glower, scowl

grat, wept

grieve, foreman

guddling, catching fish with the hands

gurley, stormy, troubled

gyte, mad, distracted

haar, sea fog

haddit, held

heels-owre-hurdie, head over heels

hinney, honey

hirstle, drive, bustle

hizzie, wench

howe, hollow

howf, haunt, hang-out, shelter

hunkered, crouched

hypothec, (Scots law) security on business; *the hale h.*, the whole affair

infefment, (Scots law) investing a new owner with rights and possessions

jeely-piece, bread and jam

jo; joes, sweetheart(s)

jouk, duck

kebbuck, cheese

ken, to know

kenspeckle, well-known, familiar, conspicuous

kep, catch

kye, cattle

kyte, belly

laigh, low

laird, gentleman landowner

landward, country

Lang Dykes, (Edinburgh) now Princes Street

lave, the rest, remainder

lightly, insult

linking, walking arm in arm

lippen, to trust

loof, palm of hand

lown, still, sheltered, calm

lynn, pool at a waterfall

Lyon King of Arms, chief of Scottish heraldic law

macer, officer of the court

maun, must

menseful, sensible, polite

misbegowk, disappointment

mools, mould, earth

muckle, much, big, great

my lane, by myself

new-harled, newly roughcast

nowt, black cattle

Old Mortality, Robert Paterson (1715–1801), who travelled the country cleaning and looking after monuments to the Covenanters. See also Scott's novel of that name

palmering, wandering aimlessly

panel, (Scots law) the accused

peel, fortified tower

pirliecue, a closing flourish, a second sermon

pitmirk, dark as the pit
play, village fair
poke, bag
policy, enclosed grounds
puddock, frog
puggy, monkey
quean, girl, young woman
questions, (my questions) my Catechism
raxing, reaching
rig and furrow, (as in ploughing, ribbed
risping, grating
routh, plenty, abundance
rowpit, sold up at auction
rowt, rant, roaring
rudas, coarse-featured, rough-mannered
runt, stump, dried up or short person
sanguishes, sandwiches
sasine, (Scots law), act or deed of legal possesion of property
sculduddery, gross speech or behaviour
session, (Scots law) the Court of Session (supreme court)
shauchling, shuffling
sinsyne, since then
skailing, dispersing, pouring out
skelp, slap
skirling, shrieking
skreigh-o'-day, crack of dawn
slockens, moistens
snash, impudence, abuse
sneisty, supercilious
sooth, sing under the breath
sough, noise, sound, whisper, report
soutar, shoemaker
Spec., (The Speculative Society) an Edinburgh University debating society of the time
speir, to ask
speldering, sprawling
spunk and dirdum, spirit and vigour
steik, to shut
sweir, unwilling
syne, since
Tamson's mear, Tamson's mare (to go on foot)
tautit, ragged
tawpie, careless foolish girl
tenty, careful
thir, these
thrawn, stubborn, perverse
tod, fox
tow, rope
trokings, dealings
twine, part
unchancy, unlucky
unco, strange, extraordinary
uncoly, strangely
upsitten, inactive, indifferent
vivers, victuals
wae, sad, unhappy
waling, choosing
warrandise, guarantee, an undertaking
waur, worse
wean, child
weird, fate
whammles, upsets
whaup, curlew
Whig, (Whigamore) cant name for those loyal to King George
whilliewhas, flatteries
win, reach
windlestrae, dry grass
wuddy, the gallows rope
wyte, blame

Robert Louis Stevenson

Pictures of the Mind

Many highly talented and famous artists have lent striking imaginative interpretation to Robert Louis Stevenson's most powerful writing. This elegant book celebrates the diverse range of art inspired by this much loved author and is the perfect testimony to his ability to entertain.

"a lovely book...glorious illustrations"   *The Herald*
"a wonderful tribute to Stevenson'   *The Independent*
128pp (120 colour plates)   086241 492 X   £14.99 P

The Strange Case of Dr Jekyll and Mr Hyde

Stevenson's chilling study of the conflict between good and evil is an all-time classic, superbly brought to life by Robert Trotter in this best-selling audio version.
"One of the best voices currently recording in Scotland"
Gramophone Magazine

2 Cassettes (2hr) 1 85968 082 8   £7.99

Travels with a Donkey in the Cevennes

In September 1878, Robert Louis Stevenson set out from Le Monastier to tramp through through the wild region of the Cevennes - his only companion was a donkey.
"A beguiling mix of vivacity, warmth and humour" *Good Book Guide*
2 Cassettes (2hr 24min) 1 85968 065 8   £7.99

The Body Snatcher and other stories

The Body Snatcher - By night sinister figures deliver shrouded burdens to Dr Knox's assistants, Fettes and MacFarlane, and although some of the bodies are suspiciously 'fresh', few questions are asked.
Thrawn Janet and *The Tale of Tod Lapraik* - Two terifying tales in Scots
2 cassettes (1 hr 39min)   1 85968 067 4   £7.99

All Canongate titles including those listed above are available direct from Canongate Books, 14 High Street, Edinburgh, Scotland, EH1 1TE. Tel 0131 557 5111
Postage and packing free on all orders within the UK.
Our current catalogue will also be sent on request

CANONGATE CLASSICS